Here is a novel as robust, as braggart, as witty and capricious as the Elizabethan world it portrays. Its hero, Robert Greene, was one of that brilliant group—Peele, Marlowe, Lodge, Nash, Shakespeare—whose lives were as colorful and many-sided as their works. We follow Greene from his boyhood in a Puritan home at Norwich to his formative years at Cambridge, thence to his adventures and vicissitudes in Italy, and so back to London, where he made a precarious livelihood by his pen and his wits, and died, worn out by the intensity of his living, at the age of thirty-four. In him are all the contradictions of his time: magnificence of life and squalor, soaring idealism and creeping meanness, patriotism and lawlessness. He consorted with thieves and ruffled it at court; he blasphemed and repented; blackmailed yet was a generous giver; he was one of the literary notables of the reign and he left to posterity one of the bitterest passages ever penned against Shakespeare.

Throughout the book, the men and women of Shakespeare's London come and go, with their loves, hatreds, friendships, and enmities, with their triumphs and downfalls. There are scenes in town and country; at the court of the aging Queen, the theatre, the tavern, the university. Religion and politics, the stage, persecution, and the plague—here is every aspect of Elizabethan England.

GARLAND OF BAYS

GARLAND OF BAYS

THE MACMILLAN COMPANY
NEW YORK · BOSTON · CHICAGO · DALLAS
ATLANTA · SAN FRANCISCO

GARLAND OF BAYS

by

GWYN JONES

NEW YORK

THE MACMILLAN COMPANY

1938

PRINTED IN THE UNITED STATES OF AMERICA
BY THE POLYGRAPHIC COMPANY OF AMERICA, N.Y.

To

MY WIFE

CONTENTS

PART I

TOMBLAND IN NORWICH

CHAPTER I

GREENE'S EARLIEST MEMORY, like Adam's, was of a garden. And very warm, very comfortable, very pleasant it was. When you turned round, looking for you didn't know what, the clear mild light fell full on your face, and you could half shut your eyes and feel the mellow brightness of it bathing their insides and giving a pale yellow fringe to the belt of green where you still saw the grass glistening with polished blades like tiny curved swords. There would come the faintest breeze to touch your face, softer and gentler even than Fawn's tongue, but not wet, without the hurried gasp of breath behind it that came from the dog, drawn lightly from forehead to chin, with a calm caress to hair and throat; then gone, and the air settling again to its own genial embrace, sun-irradiated and restful. Things around were only half seen, shapes of things half realised: patches of colour from the flowers, flaming red far away by the wall, creeping blue and yellow near at hand, vague masses of purple and gold and orange-tawny, fronds dripping with pink and paler green than the lawn, nothing with a name to it more than leaf or flower. The garden seemed huge and limitless, a world itself, with a wall impassable as the wall of paradise; no other noise than the heavy zooming of honey-burdened bees and the indistinct crickling of a rake-hell grasshopper rubbing his legs and scratching his head as he made up his mind where to jump next.

He remembered too that it ended in tears. Tears of loneliness and desolation, come swiftly from perfect rightness around him. The sun was still as gracious, the bees droning as friendly, the dog still sprawled with black, soft companionship, but the afternoon had changed to dread. He grew aware of his smallness in this world ringed with stone; still centre, but no monarch. The tall red flowers

were menacing as spears, what crawling things in the
low borders who could say? The marigolds jeered at him,
the fruit trees as the next breeze took them were astir
with threats. When he turned, frightened, to face the sun,
he stared straight into its blaze, was dazzled, and then
found before his eyes large patches of woolly blackness
writhing like animals. He rubbed his eyes, they squelched
flashes through gloom, felt wet; he rubbed harder to cure
them, and as he rubbed he was crying. Now indeed he was
all alone; when the dog came to see what was the matter
he felt him an enemy and hit him across the face, so that
two of his fingers were grazed on the needle-teeth. When
he saw a tiny drain of blood to the scratch he bawled with
fear and dismay, not least overcome by a sense of his helplessness. Then he felt a midget rage and tore at his cushion,
all the while bellowing and striking vainly at the interested
dog. How it went afterwards he did not know. Perhaps his mother came, or his father. Perhaps he fell
asleep.

From the earliest time he could remember his mother
used to tell him stories. Many of them frightened him,
but never more than deliciously so while he was still on her
lap. At times, indeed, he gurgled with frightened joy, and
by his quivering attention drove her to renewed ransacking
of her store of legends. Thus she told of the two-headed
horseman of Rising and the redoubtable ghost of Sir Robert
Vanting of Vanting Castle, all hooked teeth and nothingness, whose digestion puzzled the boy considerably. It was
no small pleasure to hear of the Great Dog of Banham,
very fond of babies, and there were vampires galore,
practised bloodsuckers, themselves fat and blub-lipped,
who lived only for hours of darkness when they could climb
out of the hollow grave and away to find some well-nurtured
lad of Robin's size and, fastening lovingly on his throat,
suck him dry. This gave them a reservoir of blood, so
that when they were at last tracked down and a pick-axe
driven into their breasts, the blood spouted up in a great

scarlet column, enough to drench a cemetery. Oftentimes they had recently fed, and then there would be spewed-up gore coagulate at the mouth-corners. There were witches too—oldish women, skinny, with long fingers and longer nails and hooked noses from which Robin imagined there must always hang a quaky water-drop. These could turn the butter sour, spoil the cows' milk, ruin the harvest, or kill you by means of a waxen dummy into which they stuck pins, and then if the dummy was you you would feel the pain just where the pin went in, or they might melt the dummy away before a good fire and you perished as though the devil had you by the knees. Hearing this, he felt certain that old Granny Jennings, who lived three doors down, must be a witch, and took care never to meet her eye when she spoke to him.

But downstairs he was never really afraid. It was well-known that so long as you kept with the grown-ups nothing could harm you. Dragons might consume armies of knights, spectres deprive heroes of speech, but so long as you had hold of a parent's hand you made a magic circle of your own into which dragons and spectres most obligingly would never intrude. It was afterwards, at night, in bed in the dark, that he gripped at his sister Alice till he woke her and made her frightened too, so that they clung tightly to each other and listened with agony for the headless horror climbing the stairs. Luckily they had a charm. No bogy had power if cold iron stood between you. So young Robert Greene begged a thin-worn horseshoe from the smithy near the Guildhall, and this never left their bedroom. To his mother he said it was for good luck, but his sister and he knew you needed more than good luck to keep away a fiend with a tail that could light him in the dark. Alice had less imagination than he, she was never afraid to go upstairs in the dark despite the tales she heard, and he found her the greatest help. He liked to go upstairs clinging to the tail of her dress—to keep her from feeling nervous, he would tell his mother—and he was even gladder to have her to hold on to when he woke up in the middle of the night and knew that something nasty was not far away. It was a bad day for young Greene when he heard talk that he and Alice were to have separate beds.

There were stories besides, less gruesome, less shocking too, but none the less enthralling. He and Alice were sometimes taken across to the Cathedral, into the nave, where their mother and father would point not at the lovely vaulting there but at the three hundred and more sculptured bosses illustrating the course of scriptural history, and with their help get into the children's heads the story of Eden, of Joseph, of David the man after God's own heart, of warriors and saints, apostles and disciples, of their gentle helper Jesus. They heard of the splendours of heaven, transcending human understanding, of palaces of jasponyx and mansions of porphyry, pavements of pearl and ramparts of crystal, thrones cut from diamonds and footstools from sapphires, of infinite space ablaze with an infinity of gems, and all this dim in the presence of the Godhead. They heard of hell too: grim, arched with iron and bolted with brass, filled with red-edged smoke blasted from the restless floor incessantly, where pitch boiled beneath the feet of the damned; a great lurid cavern filled with the roar of flames and echoing with the shrieks of those in deadly torment—that is, of those who practised wickedness in this life, and papists. The boy attended earnestly to all this, and drew for himself mental pictures of the two estates. Sometimes, as his mother spoke of heaven, he imagined he saw Christ rising with a glory of virgins through the nacreous air, that blessed company of maidens whose prayers God himself heard standing. Or as his father, earnest in faith, told him of hell, he saw its grisly monarch with three-pronged fork hooking out those who here abjured grace, and glaring round under scaly eyebrows for new subjects. At such moments he longed for martyrdom, like young Hugh of Lincoln or St. William of Norwich, papists though they were, or like those brave men who went to the stake under Bloody Mary of execrable memory. Only the martyrs were safe, he felt—and those who thought as his father did. He began at this time to stand in great awe of his father, who spoke of hell as though he had been there and returned unscathed, perhaps after wringing Beelzebub's nose; who was wise enough to know the passports to heaven and be an important guildsman, and who could beat him till his mother ran from the room crying louder than he. God, in his imagination, tended to look like his father smiling; Satan, like his father whip in hand, menacing, implacable, and suffering even while he inflicted punishment.

When Robert Greene was six years old he no longer thought the garden behind the house the vast illimitable world of his infant days. For one thing Mousehold Heath was big enough to dwarf it, for another his quick fancy had supplied him with conceptions of places beside which even Mousehold Heath shrank to a pinhead. Nor did he spend more time in the garden than he had to. Robert Greene the elder was jealous of his flowers and fruit trees and not slow to correct. He beat his children the more readily because he felt that every stripe was an incantation against the devil and a propitiation of the stern God he chose to worship. He beat them ultimately that they might go to heaven. To damage a flower bed was to disobey an earthly father, for them God's regent on earth; children who would do this might be expected to disobey a heavenly father, and it was kind to give them the dogwhip to save them from hell fire. He felt sincerely that he was a kinder father than those who thrashed their children regularly, from an unsatisfactory conclusion that it would do them good. Without a fault found he would have burned off his hand before raising it against them, and would have laid down his life to save theirs. By his lights he loved them passionately, and when his third child Tobias died at the age of three months he sorrowed for a son gone from earth far more than he rejoiced in a son received into heaven, and weeks must pass before he bent contrite knees and asked forgiveness for what was weakness if not sin.

That his wife should complain—he was prepared to condone in woman so human a failing, but not in himself.

So unyielding were his opinions in general that it was a blessing for his family that the deep-set caution which made his business prosper held him back from too thorough a prosecution of them. For instance, he was a young man of twenty when the brothers Kett raised their peasant army to fight against the enclosure of the common land around Norwich. It was a cause near his heart, but he was not to be found under the flag of the Wymondham tanner even when he captured the city and defeated the first army sent against him. This meant that fifteen years later he could take his son to see the cage on the top of Norwich Castle from which a few shreds of cloth still fluttered as a warning to other tanners to know their place, or point out to him that other cage on the steeple of Wymondham Church where Robert's brother, William Kett, was starved to death because he too thought God gave the land to the people. Again, during the reign of the late Queen there were martyrs enough at the Lollard's Pit, beyond the Bishop's Bridge. The year of his marriage was stained by a deathroll of eight, the month, July, by the burning in one fire of Simon Millar of Lynn and Elizabeth Cooper, a friend of his mother's, of the parish of St. Andrew. He himself followed whitefaced the procession across the bridge and watched frail flesh vindicate the faith he held but did not loudly profess. Having succeeded to the saddler's business, having taken a wife and prepared himself for the responsibility of fatherhood, he did not covet the martyrdom that would cost him all he had in this world. Back from the burnings, to which he was invariably drawn, he prayed mightily, cursing with a steadfast heart the Royal Whore of Babylon, begging that the paw of the Seven-Headed Beast might soon be lifted from the nation, appealing to God to reveal himself with majesty and thunder. Later he repented that he had not borne firmer witness, and with the accession of a protestant ruler promised himself that henceforth he would be unflinching. Certainly he kept his children from the devil's work. So they came to feel about him much as they did about the celestial and infernal deities. They feared him, stood in awe of him, and loved him as much as it was possible to love anyone so superior to their own wretched clay—so deft a whip-wielder too. He was, at the death of Tobias, of whom Robert soon remembered nothing at all, thirty-three years old, sternly handsome, mature of manner, his passions well under control. His business was thriving in a way that discredited Job's lamentation that the evil prosper and the righteous are ground into the dust. You could ask in Norwich for Robert Greene, saddler, and everyone knew of whom you were speaking. Young Robert came to find, to his amazement, that there were at least half-a-dozen in the town bearing his name, but was consoled to know that his father was *the* Robert Greene. He felt too that he had the most wonderful father in the world. It was a sign of near-divinity that his father, like Jehovah, had created a garden in which he took his ease during the cool of the evening.

His mother was three years younger than her husband, and it was from her he inherited his red hair. Alice was dark like her father. It did not take him long to discover that in all things he was his mother's white boy and that she could deny him little. His earliest memories of her were that she was nursing him after he had fallen and hurt himself, that he had been crying and she was making everything all right again, and several times that she was upstairs with a taper sitting by the bedside, bringing him something to eat after he had been thrashed and sent supperless to bed. In everything she was kind and protective, prepared to hide his wrong-doing from her husband, make excuses for him, attempt to cover up his minor offences. He remembered how on more than one occasion she smuggled him off to bed that his father's temper might be improved by the morning. And he associated her with lovely smells from the kitchen, sweet-scented herbs, the rich odours of jam-making, and with the taste of candied peel and preserved

ginger which he wheedled out of her as shamelessly as a
spaniel. Constantly she administered with her story-telling
to his taste for the marvellous; from her he learned to
read a little, to tell the time, to write a beautiful hand,
and to recognise the different messages of the church bells
that seemed never to be silent in Norwich. With her he
visited Grancher Beetham at Wroxham, an old man for
whom he had affection untouched with fright, a narrator
with a memory reaching back past the burnings of '31 and
the birth of the good Queen, who could even remember
how when he was a lad not much older than his grandson
then was they had lit bonfires and roasted an ox at the side
of Wroxham Broad because the good Queen's father had
succeeded to the throne of England. There was a Pope
Julius in those days and then a Pope Leo and then, let's see,
what was his name? Adrian, that's right. Did the young
rascal know his history, eh? Bring a boy up to know his
history, Jane, then he can't go wrong, said Grancher
Beetham; and the old man, as glad of a listener as Robert
Greene of an entertainer, would talk at great length about
Cardinal Wolsey and Thomas Cromwell and the sweating
sickness of he couldn't remember the year but Anne Boleyn,
the good Queen's mother, had to be sent away from the
King because of contagion, and oftenest of all he talked
about the battle at Flodden in which his elder brother lost
his life. Ah Flodden, Flodden! And if his hearer looked
especially attentive he would recite to him immediately
after his account of the battle the ballad about some other
battle at Chevy Chase, which he seemed to confuse with it.
Grancher Beetham had a very poor opinion of the Scots
and explained to his uncomprehending grandson that there
would yet be difficulties because of them, above all because
of a Mary who was a Scot. Robert, however, confused her
with that Bloody Mary he knew was dead, and could not
share the old man's alarm. It was with his mother too that
he visited Granny Jennings who lived three doors down,
feeling disturbed when she smiled at him, torn between
first thoughts which warned him to have nothing to do

with her and reflection which made it clear that if they stayed friends she was not likely to make a waxen image of him and stick pins in it. He must have hidden these feelings well, for when she died not long after his sixth birthday he found she had left money to make a ring whereby he might remember her.

Yet because his mother was closer to him, kinder in small things, than his father, he did not admire her equally. Love her, yes—but then other boys and girls had mothers who were kind to them, but had anyone else in the world so godlike a father? His mother's words soon died from his ear, those of his father, though he disobeyed them oftentimes, seemed graven there.

Certain events stood out in exaggerated relief from the flat pattern of existence. One of the best remembered was the episode of the beetle.

It was the beginning of the cold weather and there had been a fire in the living room, a fire of coal. It might have been the middle of October, when the curtains were drawn and the light inside was yellow. There were two men visitors, one whose name he did not know, the other the George Crashfield who kept the two mastiffs of which he was slightly afraid, and the conversation was being carried on in a serious, deep-toned way that delighted him though he understood little of it. He could not remember afterwards whether Alice was there or not. But the bass voices seemed to set cords trembling far inside him, their resonance thrummed through the pit of his stomach, he was actually aware of a physical tremor passing from Crashfield's body to his by way of the chair on which Crashfield was sitting and against which he was deliberately holding his foot. The tremor was particularly strong when the speaker used words like *mood*, *room*, *rumour*, and brought him so exquisite a pleasure that he dreaded lest soon he be sent to bed. It was already past his usual time. Once again he heard the name of Mary who was Queen of Scotland and was as much puzzled as when Grancher

Beetham talked of her. His attention was challenged when
he heard her described as a scarlet woman, and he thought
how much he would like to see such a rarity, glowing like
the red-hot pokers against the high wall of the garden.
He hoped, if she was part of a fair, that it would visit
Norwich, when he would be satisfied to receive a beating
if he might steal off and see her. Though if she were Bloody
Mary—and Bloody Mary must be a scarlet woman—and
if Mary was dead—it was all very puzzling. It was when
Crashfield and his father began to speak strongly against
the bull-baiting at Norwich market, where not a bull
could be slaughtered till it had given fair sport to the
onlookers, that they first saw the beetle.

He was a small beetle from the garden, his dull black
wings folded foppishly to his sides, very spick and span and
walking briskly across the space between the men's feet.
Robert saw him first, realised that he must have found the
garden cold, and was pleased to think how comfortable
he must now feel with the warmth of the fire falling on him.
"Beetle," said Crashfield, and then the boy saw his father
bend forward, pick up the beetle, and without a word
fling him away. He leaned forward, gaping, for his father's
aim sent the beetle straight into hell. For one moment his
brisk and tiny feet scuttled desperately across a piece of
coal, and then, as the boy heard the gush of blood through
his eardrums, the beetle checked, changed direction, and
rushed frantically to where he fell into the white-hot heart
of the fire. "Gone!" said Crashfield, his voice throbbing
into Robert Greene, and they went on to talk of seasonable
matters, the early frosts, crops, the art of cheesemaking,
things like that. But the boy took with him to bed
the vision of the tiny creature finicking with his
hot feet before annihilation. Probably a papist beetle,
fortunate in his mortality. His father was now even
more godlike, with power to hurl over a black cliff to a
red hell.

He remembered well the accident which left Alice with
a two-inch white scar on her forehead. They had been

playing together on the patch of grass in the garden, and
finally the game turned to horses. At first Robert was content
to drive her around the ring with a long switch, but he
longed for other mastery, and insisted that he ride on her
back. She agreed to try. With the aid of a step he mounted,
clutched her tight, and spurred her to a gallop. Laughter
jolted out of him, he shouted encouragement. "Come on,
Alice, come on! Gee up, there!" He beat her sides impar-
tially. "No, don't hit me!" "Gee up! Gee up, mare!"
"Oh, I've got to stop!" "Gee up. Gee up. Come on, horse!"
But her strength was gone, she stumbled and fell, with her
rider a-sprawl on top of her. His fists braked in a bed of
flowers, and he was restored to seriousness even before he
heard his sister screaming blue murder. Her forehead had
come up against the border of ornamental tiles and was
badly cut. When she put her hands up and brought them
away bloody she screamed more than ever, throwing him
into a state very near panic. He was afraid for her and for
himself. He was afraid of a beating and the curse of Cain,
and could do nothing better as the door was flung open and
his mother dashed out than cry as loudly as the victim.
As his mother ran in with Alice, he held on to her skirt, and
cried again as she dashed his hand away before she could
fetch rags and salve. He watched the operation, frightened
by his own wickedness, and yet fascinated to see the slow
blood crawl from the new-wiped wound. Amidst it all he
thought of the broken flowers and trembled. "Horses!"
exclaimed his mother, after tearful explanations; "Horses
indeed! You little bully you! Don't you realise your own
strength?" He mumbled. "You wait till your father
comes in!"

He did, very worried. His mother, he knew, would never
lay a finger on him except in the heat of the moment,
but his father—he waited till he came in. Whatever
the elder Robert Greene might think of the wounding,
he would think but one way of the flowers destroyed
by those braking fists. So he thought. But his mother
repented, and he had no beating after all, because she

assured her husband she had punished him enough already. But the memory of his sick, dog-like fright was not easily lost.

Another of these events was his first acquaintance with the drama. At this time he must have been eight years old, for before the summer was over he had started school. Possibly it was this which decided his father to take him to see *The Nice Wanton*, of whose moral bent he was assured. Greene remembered that the performance took place in the Big Field, where a stage had been erected on trestles, and that like many other small boys he stood throughout its duration between his father's knees, feeling very proud of his position and safe as though guarded by cohorts of angels. "I want you, Robin," his father told him, "to be very attentive to all you see. There are a kind of plays that are lewd and a shame before heaven, but this is none such. When you have seen it I want you to be able to say: I am a Barnabas!" Barnabas turned out to be the only dutiful child of Xantippe, for Ishmael and Dalila flung away their school books and fought much with each other and their new friend Iniquity. The part he remembered best was where Ishmael and Iniquity, after trial by Daniel for felony and murder, were led out to the gallows, whither he would like to have accompanied them, for he had not yet seen a hanging. "Barnabas," whispered his father, repeating the lesson of the Prologue; "the name means 'son of comfort.'" And before they left the field there was an address to all parents present that they should not spare the rod and spoil the child—comfortless admonitions they seemed to Greene, who doubted whether a parent breathing stood in need of them. Last came the prayer for the Queen's Royal Majesty and the welfare of the realm, and then he remembered the company breaking up and straggling homewards through the fields. As they walked towards Tombland his father asked him which part of the play he had liked best. "Where Iniquity and Dalila had a fight," he considered, "or when they led them out to hang them." He was afraid to ask his father to take him to the hanging itself if ever they saw the play again, but ventured the question whether Daniel had gone out too to see that execution kept at the heel of judgment. His father laughed grimly. "Iniquity is not yet out of the world, my son. But now he lives at Rome."

CHAPTER II

By the time his son was twelve years old Robert
Greene the elder admitted that the example of Barnabas,
son of comfort, had been largely wasted on him, and that
his preoccupation with the part of Iniquity might prove
prophetic. He took counsel of God, of his wife, of other
fathers who feared for their sons, and of William Hall,
Headmaster of Norwich Grammar School. But the schoolmaster's advice and comfort were of a kind he could
not accept. He was made to understand, though, that
young Robert was more proficient in his studies than
his poor showings at the end of each year suggested.
His difficulty, Hall thought, was his lack of concentration
upon the work given him in class, not lack of intelligence
or willingness to work. "He will work harder than most
if he can settle what he shall work at." He gave
instances of what he meant. While other boys were being
grounded in accidence and the three concordances Robert
Greene must have his thumb in Sturmius, translating
odd sentences of *De Amicitia* before he knew the gender
of the title word, and then, when the class was at work
on Sturmius, nothing would do but for him to be poking
his nose into parts of the school Terence, only for Terence
to lose his charm once he grew the object of study.
Greene speculated whether the boy might be kept on a
tighter rein.

"If the bit hurts his jaws enough, he'll be glad to take
direction."

"Not he. Besides we are aiming here at a love of learning,
not a dread of its methods." And the disapproving Greene
was forced to listen while Hall expounded to him the ideals
and methods of the lamented Roger Ascham, then three
years dead, the great benefits of whose conversation Hall
had received, besides his book *The Schoolmaster*, printed not

more than twelve months ago. "Here at Norwich," he ended, "we imagine that what has been good enough for our Sovereign Queen is good enough for us too." This was a clinching argument, but Greene was not to be convinced. They flogged sense into boys at Eton and St. Paul's, and they were of greater reputation than Norwich Grammar School. Moreover—"It has been held a good saying that he who spares the rod hates the child, Master Hall." "But wisdom neither began nor ended with Solomon, Master Greene—and we must admit that all was not wisdom in a man who took wives by the hundred." Hall, a bachelor, chuckled, but his visitor was not amused and pressed for more information.

"His character then, Master Hall?" What could Ascham's methods do for that?

In some ways not an easy boy—that was the gist of Hall's disquisition. Yes, it was true he had been caught pilfering. Venial, much of it, of course. Strawberries from the Bishop's garden—Greene and Berry and Wotton Secundus had been flogged for that. Plums too—Greene and Wotton Secundus and Tertius caught with their booty, and a flogging for two of them and a light penalty for Tertius, too young to know what he was doing. A piece of oak groining stolen from the shop of Master Carter—Greene convicted and flogged for that. A Tully stolen from the boy Barnet—an unhappy feature of this case was that the boy Barnet was repeatedly beaten by his father for his carelessness in losing it. A sling stolen from the boy Slater—a flogging for Greene and one for Slater too, since boys were not permitted to bring slings into school. Hall waved his hand, nothing more than the usual temporary confusion of *meum* and *tuum*, no doubt Greene senior had printed his lesson on the young rascal's back: Ha-ha-ha! A pleasant boy too, in general free from insolence, given to scraping mud off his shoes to the school-room floor rather from absent-mindedness than any wish to commit a nuisance, always eager to lift his cap to the master, happy to run an errand, and if not too proud to benefit by the labours of his fellows, not ungrateful enough to refuse a touch to their copies of verses—"as I know from the recurrence of certain incompatibilities of gender peculiar to this one scholar."

But Hall's good humour was no comfort to Greene's father. Pilfering led to felony, and felony to the gallows. Idleness was a challenge to Satan, it led to sin, which imperilled the immortal soul, which in turn might well lead to eternal damnation. No parent worthy the name could view such prospects and not take action. Solemnly he decided to thrash his son twice as hard for future offences, and meantime to bring before his eyes the horrors of the pit into which he was in danger of falling. He found material for his sermon in the expressed views of his sect, and slowly elaborated his discourse. He delivered it on Christmas Day.

Dinner was over. A thanksgiving followed, Alice and young Robert standing throughout its duration with less gratitude for what was safely over than anticipation of the merriment they were hoping to share at the Wottons'.

"Robert."

"Father?"

"I want you to come with me upstairs."

This was the normal prelude to a ceremonial thrashing and shook him badly. He looked bewildered at his mother, feeling strongly that he was clean of fault, yet aware he found it easier than his parents to forget wrong-doing. "Go on, Robin," she encouraged him; "your father only wants to talk to you." "Jane!" her husband warned sternly; then: "Robert, come upstairs with me." "Yes, father." As they started to climb he was relieved to see that his father did not step aside for the whip, and therefore mounted without qualms, his eyes level with the backs of his father's knees. It was not only the angle of vision. His father was not quite so olympian in his eyes now as five or six years ago. They went into his half of the bedroom which had been partitioned off for him and Alice. "Sit down, Robert." "Yes, father."

"You know what day it is?"

"Christmas Day."

"Why is it called Christmas Day?"

"Because it is the birthday of our Lord Jesus Christ."

"And why should our Lord Jesus Christ have a birthday on earth?"

"Because he came down to save us."

"Save us from what?"

"From sin and the devil."

"I am glad," his father commended drily, "that you know so much. Perhaps you also know what happens to those who will not let Jesus save them?"

Robert thought. "Yes, father."

"You do?"

"They go to hell, father."

"Quite right. They do, and rightly so. Rightly so, isn't it, Robert?" Robert's doubtful nod he accepted as agreement that the heavenly disposition was a proper one. "Now, let us have a candle lighted here." Robert heard his father's steps creaking downstairs, and was dumbfounded that he should be lighting a candle while it was still far from dark. Still, he kept silence.

"Now, Robert—you know where hell is?"

He looked around vaguely. Precise geographical bearings could hardly be expected. "Down there. Down under," he suggested.

"You are quite right. And a very long way down it is, too. As far below this earth as heaven is above it. No one ever comes back when once he has gone to hell, you know that?"

"Yes, father."

"Now do you know anything about hell?"

He genuinely believed he did. "I know all you have told me about it."

"But have you ever thought about it?"

"A bit."

"A bit? Not more than that?" said his father, thus doing

him an injustice; "Then perhaps that is why." Feeling that
some question was expected of him, Robert thought confusedly for a moment before repeating the last word.
"Why?" he said. "Why what, father?" "Why you seem so
eager to go there!" was the reply.

He was beginning to feel frightened. "Go—go
where?"

"To burn in hell—as you most certainly shall!"

"But—but I don't want to!"

"Then why are you so wicked?"

How could he explain that he did what he did for the fun
it gave him or because he wanted something so badly—
certainly not because he wanted to go to hell? Nobody
wanted to go there, surely. Nor could he see that he was
wicked enough to deserve hell.

"I want to tell you of hell," his father now began, lowering
his voice for greater effect. "I want to tell you of the place
where you are in grave danger of finding yourself. I should
fail in my duty if I neglected to do this." He paused, relishing
his catalogue of horrors, marshalling their order. "We know
what hell is like as though we had looked into it with our
own eyes, for not only did Christ, the Son of God, descend
within it and lead out again the patriarchs who awaited
him there, but also visions have been granted to many
holy men who have written them down as a warning to us,
that we may repent in time of those things that are loathsome to God. You say hell is underneath us. It is so, indeed.
If a man fell for a year he would not reach it, and yet, such
is God's power, you can be transported there in a night.
It is a huge place, hell—its bounds go out to chaos, but its
roots may not be discovered even by its malignant Prince.
You must imagine it filled with a million smokes and vapours,
each worse than the last, and yet the best of them unendurable to the wretches dwelling there. Such is their virulence
that when they breathe they feel the insides of their nostrils
cut away by redhot knives, and their lungs are as though
plucked with glowing pincers, and their eyelids seem filled
with quicklime and the hair shrivelled on their heads.

And of this there is no end. Then there is no light in hell, but all is darkness so intense that men must grope about in it, and all they can ever hope to see are the ugly shapes of those that torment them. These are the fiends, who have great hooks and mallets, with which they tear and strike the unhappy damned and throw them one to the other like pilchclouts, and all the time they curse and revile their victims, for they too suffer, and the damned curse and revile their tormentors and themselves, and the vaults of hell are filled with screeches and yellings, with lamentation and uproar, with screams of agony and remorse that can now avail them nothing. I want you to see that scene, my son. Look—here is a great black devil now! Behold his hook! See how he thrusts it through the bowels of this miserable creature and pitchforks him to his companion yonder. And he receives him with a dreadful blow of his mallet, enough to kill twenty men in this life, and yet with it all he is whole and must endure this endlessly. And at the same time notice his face and limbs! See how the maggots crawl down from his nose, and the mouth is stuffed with frogs and adders, and newts eat into the wax of the ears, and the breastbone is hollowed out by nests of creeping things, and his members continually devoured by ants and pismires. And yet nothing is eaten away, but is always there to be eaten again. Wouldn't it be dreadful if we recognised *your* face there, Robert?

"Look at this candle, Robert? You notice the flame? You know what would happen if you put your finger in it?" Yes, Robert knew that. "And you know that there is flame in hell—but not flame like this! For that is a thousand times hotter and more fierce, and rages so that with a lick it consumes the thickest bars of iron, and yet the damned must bear it. And there is boiling lead and pitch in hell, so hot that it has been boiling since hell was first created, and growing hotter each moment, and this laps up to the necks of the damned, and the fiends may be seen with spoons and ladles, holding it to the lips of the immoderate

on earth, and so it splashes about their mouths and back
into their throats and they cannot even cry out with anguish
as the drench goes down and purges them of all their
bowels, and this not once, nor twice, but for all eternity.
And the pilferers there—they have their nails dragged out
so delicately, and the flesh is torn in small strips from their
fingers and toes, and foul birds rend their scalps and chew
their hearts as here on earth they were rent and devoured
by the foul sin of covetousness. If here they stole fruit, there
brazen fruit shall be brought them on a molten dish, and
eat it they must, though if they had the world to give, give
it they would for respite. If money, there they must pick
up from the blazing floor whitehot coins that sizzle as the
flesh touches them, and as they stoop they are roared at
and buffeted by their infernal hosts, who hook them into
the liquid fire and there stir them about like rags in a pan.
Robert, my son! Robert! Is this to be your fate? Shall you
be tormented so throughout a million ages and then know
that a million million await you? Ay, you can cry now!
Better such tears than those of iron. For the worst thing the
damned must endure, besides which these other miseries
are comforts, is that they must suffer for ever, that there is
no term set to their wretchedness. Theirs is not the fierce
agony of the stake, but an infinity of woe, and therefore
they cry out and reproach themselves as you do now, they
wail and gnash their teeth, they howl for the forgiveness
that can never reach them, and as they strike and wound
themselves the fiends' task is so much the easier." He put
his hand on the head of his weeping son. "Remember—
there is still time for you to escape this fate. But let there
be no delay, for who can tell when the call shall come and
a man's soul be required of him? By the grace of God and
your father's correction we need not despair of improve-
ment."

His son found no incongruity in this last sentence. His
father's eloquence had made him a deity again. His imagination was always ahead of his mentor's words, making him
see horrors greater than any his father was describing, so

it was no wonder he broke down and cried. All that night he felt on the brink of the pit, its reek was in his nostrils the indubitable stench of boiling pitch; and he assured himself he was the wickedest creature in Norwich. His delight in bull-baiting and dog-fighting, his visit to the travelling players unknown to his father, gambling for the pence he wheedled out of his mother, his readiness to take what belonged to his neighbour, these seemed more than tally enough to condemn him. All he could hope for was that a life of remorse and prayer might blot out in God's sight the matchless depravity of his first twelve years. He would never again read those portions of Ovid and the satirists, he would be diligent, a very Barnabas. He would give up friends like Berry and Wotton Secundus in School, and acquaintances outside it like Charlie Boys and the farm lads at Bratton and the groom at the Red Lion. He did not think about proselytising. He was too concerned to save himself. These others might pursue their present courses and roast at the end of them. Let them be beetles, so long as he was saved. Christmas Day should mark a new life for Robert Greene.

His father was delighted with the change that soon showed itself. Walter Hall noticed it too. Greene was now docile as, under his master's eye, he followed closely the reasons why Livy would not have used this word and would have abhorred that construction. In Walter Hall's opinion it was too good to last. But Robert Greene senior had no such misgivings for a time. He believed wholeheartedly in the power of sudden conversion, and had complete faith in the power of the Word. To keep him in mind of salvation he made his son copy out in his beautiful handwriting St. Augustine's sentence about the thief hanging on the cross: *There was one thief saved and no more, therefore presume not, and there was one saved: and therefore despair not.* With this task before him, young Robert Greene startled his schoolmaster by asking for Augustine's own Latin words. He would copy those out too, and hang them alongside the others where his eyes might alight on them first thing every morning. And his father told him he should be grateful to his mother who had taught him to make such shapely letters, whereby he might keep himself mindful of great truths.

CHAPTER III

But it happened with Robert Greene as with most of those constrained rather by fear than a love of virtue. In six months' time there were veils over the vision of hell, and he no longer read St. Augustine's words about presumption and despair. Before the end of the year Walter Hall had forgotten that Greene for a while had prepared his Livy with an industry worthy of that phoenix of pupils, John Whitney, whose untimely death moved his friend and tutor, Roger Ascham, to self-confessed misorderly metre, "wrung out of him," he admitted "more by chance than either by skill or use." But Hall had too many things to do to spare time for fourteeners on Greene. He was one of ninety boys, each a problem to this unusual schoolmaster. It was something to know he possessed fair copies of so much. God must look after the rest.

"Robertus Greene."

"Yes, dominus?"

"Take good care you go not to the devil."

"Yes, dominus."

Robert spent at least a week each summer with his grandfather at Wroxham. Had his father known how leniently Grancher Beetham treated him, he would never have allowed him this holiday. Now that Robert was old enough to appreciate such details, the old man enlarged his account of Flodden, attributing deeds to his brother that brought about the victory there, and then padding out his own lack of service with tales of the hidings he used to deal out to his contemporaries at home. It seemed as though he and brother John would have been too much for the whole Scottish army. John had slain a dozen or more, so William, had he been there, presumably would have dealt with the rest of the thirty thousand. There

had been a corn merchant's son in Wroxham who wanted
to marry William's sweetheart, oh it would be thirty, forty,
nigh on fifty years ago, but William had met him one day,
delivered a challenge, and defeated him in the grandest
stand-up fight in the annals of the village. In his day, too,
Grancher Beetham had been a noted football player.
When he rushed down the street his opponents were scattered like chaff, blood flowed from their noses, their ribs
bent like wires at the touch of his elbows, their shins ached
for weeks from his onslaught. Naturally enough, the girls
for miles around fell in love with handsome William.
"Ay, I could have had my pick, Robert," he assured his
grandson. "I was a fine young fellow in those days. I'd
be much your height and weight when I was fourteen or
fifteen, or a bit stockier perhaps. Ay, indeed, you are the
living image of me then." It was cheering to hear this after
too much reproof and blame at his own home. "The living
image!" his grandfather confirmed, holding him at arm's
length. "We've all got the same coloured hair on our
side—me and your mother and you. What about Tobias
—did he have red hair?" But Greene did not remember his
brother now. "Perhaps he took after the Greenes. You
never know. But for hair, I always say you can't beat our
colour. It frames the face. You ought to grow a beard when
you get older, that's what you ought to do. My word,
you'll be like me—you'll be a proper mischief-maker among
the girls when you get older!" Greene blushed a little. "As
I said, I had my choice. When I married your granny it
wasn't because I could not have had anybody else, oh no.
It was because I loved her and she loved me, and we didn't
allow any corn merchant's sons to come between. Ah,
she was a proud woman, your granny, the day we came
back from church together!" Among other things, the old
man explained to him that red-haired folk were expected
to have hot tempers. "Some say a lot of us are mad, but
don't you pay any attention to that. We've got our wits
about us, we redheads. We are too sharp for most, that's
the truth of it. If my brother John had lived, I don't doubt

he'd be the sharpest man in Norfolk today. I really believe John was sharper than me."

Grancher Beetham belonged to an age when folk married very young. "You courting yet, Robert?"

"No, good gracious no, Grancher. I'm only just gone fourteen!"

"Ah well, you'll meet some nice girl one of these days, I'm sure, and then it'll be whoopsie-doopsie and off to church with you. Your sister Alice courting?"

Robert tried without brutality to explain that he didn't care what his sister was doing. "She helps mother."

"That's right. I've got good grandchildren. And your mother can do with some help, with a lump of a boy like you about. Like me at your age—none too tidy, eh?"

There were the usual warnings about the Scottish Mary, whom Greene no longer confused with Mary who married Philip the Spaniard. Riccio, Darnley, Bothwell—what a woman! What a monster! And now this year the Ridolfi plot, and not a couple of months ago the Duke of Norfolk beheaded for her sake. There would be no rest in England till her head was off her shoulders. As Peter Wentworth declared in the House of Commons, this was the most notorious whore in all the world. Who could say with assurance that even then, as they were speaking together, some devil's work was not brewing in which this Empress of Babylon would be found to have part? "When the head is off, Robert," said Grancher Beetham, and tapped his nose, "that's a snake past harming you."

The old man liked a lad of spirit. "I never was one for a lot of mumping and moping, Robert. What is life for if we can't enjoy it, eh? Don't you ever become a snuffler down your nose, young fellow. And don't stuff your head too much over books." He gave his usual piece of advice, inconsistently now. "So long as you know the history of your country, that's enough to see you right." It followed from this that there was no daily task to be performed at Wroxham as at home. He went fishing on the broads, had the use of a boat and a horse, swam almost every day, beat about the woods and fields with local boys of his own age, and spent all the money he could lay his hands on at the Wroxham fair. Grancher Beetham saw to it that the woman who kept house for him, a tidy body, repaired damage to his clothes, and the old man had some very good ointment for bruises and abrasions. It was sufficiently a panacea to soothe his own rheumatism and his house-keeper's ear-ache. Greene found it useful on many occasions.

One of these was after his fight with a yokel from the farm behind the Three Beeches. He had been swimming at the pool there with three other boys when the farmer and his lumpish helper appeared. "Who be you?" asked the farmer, and all four gave their names. "Where be from?" Greene was from Tombland, in Norwich, a fact which should have impressed his questioner. "Oh, you be a Nor-wich b——, be you? Hear that, Bill boy? This un's a Nor-wich b——." "Norwich b——s be no good," said Bill boy. "I 'ouldn't pee on they." "No, that ee 'ouldn't, Bill boy."

Then Bill boy changed his mind. "No, you don't!" cried Greene.

"Ay I do!"

"You don't then!"

"Don't shove I now!"

"Keep off then!"

"I said don't shove I!"

"And I said keep off!"

"Then take that, ee Norwich b——!"

"Fair play," cried the farmer. "Let young un get his breeches on!" So Greene donned his shirt and breeches in a low state of spirits, and without confidence prepared for battle. He was discouraged to feel that even his fellow swimmers were against him. It was now Wroxham versus Norwich, and they would not be sorry to see him get the worse of it. They fought, and he had more than he wanted from Bill boy before the farmer grew tired of the sport and after a brisk cut of his cane across the buttocks of the boy nearest him went off with his man, promising that his dog would tear the guts out of the next Norwich b—— who dared bathe behind the Three Beeches. Greene's comrades were now ashamed of themselves, they knew they should have cheered their own man on to victory, and kept a sheepish silence while he used his shirt to clean from his face the tears, blood, and running from the nose which covered it. "Fine lot of b——s you are!" he half sobbed, using the word closest his mind. "Gang of mingy Wroxham b——s! Get that b—— in Norwich, that's what—find someone'd murder him. No fear—you don't come home with me. Lot of mingy Wroxham b——s!" They recognised where justice lay, swallowed his insults, and for a time shamefacedly followed him at a distance of ten to twenty yards, but soon he rounded on them with the most frightful profanity, using language that would have turned his mother's face milkwhite and sent his father hotfoot for the whip, calling them objects which the distinction of the sexes guaranteed they were not, hurling at them the most degrading epithets that sprang to mind, and so injuring their self-esteem that they too resorted to these wordy weapons and followed him with curses and jeers. Home he went to Grancher Beetham's, thoroughly ashamed of his blubbered, puffy face, enraged to think that he was near tears again, and muttering his favourite name for all dwellers in Wroxham.

The old man was outside his cottage. "Jesus save us!" he cried. "What have you been doing with yourself?"

"Fight," said Greene. "I've had a fight."

"God in heaven preserve us! As though I can't see it. Come here!" William tried to be angry, but he was remembering the trimming he once gave the corn merchant's son. "Did you win?" he asked, the bathing over and the best ointment in Norfolk plastered on his grandson's face.

"I believe so," Greene lied, in better spirits now.

"Not that we can have a lot of fighting going on, mind."

"No."

"Let's see now—who did you say he was?"

Before Greene went to bed, which he was glad to do early, William had shown him how to tuck a man's head under your arm and fist him till he roared for mercy.

Sometimes Alice came with him to Wroxham, and though he scorned all girls he was still able to enjoy himself when hampered by her company. She could not climb trees, throw off her clothes and swim, or run fast enough to test him; her aim with a stone was bad; she had scruples about the treatment of animals, fish, and birds. In fact, she was not a boy; but she flattered him with the knowledge of his own superiority—that valuable female gift to thick-skinned man. Her cries of alarm when he perilously changed places in the boat, her white suffering face when he hung far out over a dipping limb, her implorations when he announced some foolhardy project, were dear to his masculinity. He promised to show her nests, to find her a baby rabbit, and sometimes kept his word, and at all times it was his right to decide where they would go and what they would do when they got there. More than once he quarrelled with his Wroxham companions because they spoke contemptuously of a girl accompanying them on one of their jaunts.

It was during the winter following his Wroxham fisticuffs that he got drunk for the first time. Unfairly, he was inclined to blame his father for this, but all his father did was to send him on an errand to the Boltons' house about some harness which young Adam Bolton should have received that day, and insist that he should see Adam in person and take pains not to offend so good a customer. He certainly did not foresee that Adam would offer his son wine, and his son accept it. Greene the puritan despised this Adam as a vessel empty of grace, but Greene the saddler was as willing as the next man to take his money, so this particular evening Robert was knocking at the door of the Boltons' fine house on the Market Square and asking for the young master. Master Adam was at home, and Greene was shown into his presence.

"Come in, Master Robert Greene, and close the door."

"Yes, sir. Thank you, sir. My father says——" He rattled off the message. "And since it was for a gentleman of your quality and the design so quaint, he thought with your permission not to hurry the finishing strokes, and so you might be pleased to wait another forty-eight hours for the finest worked harness in the city."

Adam Bolton pushed his chin forward and upwards as he thought this over, at the same time protruding his lips as he had once seen a royal messenger do. Finally he was pleased to state that he was pleased to agree to the elder Greene's suggestions. He was five years older than Greene, but most impressive at first sight and sound. "Do you drink wine, boy?"

"Yes, if you please," Greene lied calmly. So a large glassful was poured out for him and pushed across the table. "Thank you. Your very good health, Master Bolton," he said, and took off half of it to show he was a hardened drinker. But the other was so unimpressed that he at once put down a glassful himself, without saying more than "Ah!" and smacking his lips appreciatively.

"Robert Greene, Robert Greene's son, eh?" he asked. His caller was still standing. "Help your father, eh?"

"I am still at the Grammar School, Master Bolton."

"Hm—a scholar!" Robert was surprised to see him scratch at his growing beard. "I see." Once more he thrust out his chin and protruded his lips. "You'll know some Latin, I'll be bound?" Greene admitted this, willingly, whereupon, as though his mind was made up, Bolton hooked a chair forward with his foot. "Come and sit down, Robert." So he came, bringing his half glass of wine with him. "Grammar School, eh? Tell me—was the name of the woman, the queen, the whatever-it-was the strong man Herchilles worked for called Omphalos?"

"Omphale, sir."

"You sure? Sure it wasn't Omphalos?"

"Omphalos is the Greek word for navel, sir."

At that Bolton laughed in a manner that suggested he had emptied a number of glasses before Greene called. "Good God, Robert, it's a good thing you called here to-night. Queen Omphalos—Queen Navel, eh? What'you think of that, Robert?"

"Her Umbilical Majesty, sir," Greene suggested.

"Good!" the other praised. "I must remember that. Have another glass of wine. Haven't you finished that one yet?" This was soon attended to. "I can see you haven't been wasting your time at school, Robert. Of course," he admitted, "I've been to school in my time; but I was too much of a devil to learn, I'm afraid. Eton, Robert—that's where I was for a time, but I didn't really take to it. I didn't study as I ought, Robert. When you leaving the Grammar School?" Next year, he thought. "Can't teach you any more, I'll be bound. What you doing after that?" Greene couldn't be sure. He was hoping his father would let him go to the University, but hope and conviction were two different things. "That's right. You go to the University," Bolton advised, as though the disposition of events were in his own hands. "I never wanted to go myself. I was never much for books, you know—just a wag, Robert. Like boy, like man—just a mad wag! The Old Adam they used to call me. But a lad like you—it will be the making of you. You've got a gift for learning, anyone can see that, and when you come down it'll be with a fine position as secretary to some great man in London." He drank wine with enviable ease. "Ever been to London?" Greene was ashamed to have to admit that he had not, but during the next twenty minutes he had the benefit of the next best thing—his companion's account of the great city, the chances there for a promising youngster or a wag like himself, and, not least, some of his own exploits within and immediately outside its boundaries. Crude though most of this was, it was sufficient to fill the homestaying youth with envy and wonder. One day he must see all this for himself; he too must set the Thames on fire. He asked questions, and the twenty minutes became forty, during which he sipped away his wine and felt older and wiser. The Old Adam drank more busily, and eventually exposed the mystery of Queen Omphalos. He was writing a letter to a lady he had met once in London and who he knew was now staying for a couple of months in the neighbourhood. He explained to his new confidant that he could put all to the hazard and call on her, but he preferred a more sophisticated method of approach—the London, the Court method. He had met her at a reception, though he wasn't sure which one; he hoped she had not forgotten him because he had squeezed her hand very lovingly and she had not resented it; she was a widow with the whole town at her mercy but somehow he fancied she would not have forgotten Adam Bolton, that Norwich wag who squeezed her hand so gallantly and sighed as he did so. They had another glass of wine, and he spoke with confidence of his prospects. She must find local company very dull; she was living in seclusion which was contrary to her nature; unless Adam was mistaken she had no natural bent towards the abstinences of widowhood; once she knew he was at hand he did not doubt his welcome. "Blood stock, Robert! Just like a horse. *You know*."

The boy nodded. He knew—or at least would not be churlish enough to admit he didn't. Adam, thoroughly confidential now, fetched a stick from a corner and thrust it at him. "See those initials, Robert?" They were cleverly entwined. "B.C. Now they don't mean B.C.—anno B.C., that is—they're her initials, see. Beatrice Constant —lovely name, isn't it, Robert? I'm going to carve 'to me' after them. See the idea—B Constant to me?" Greene suggested a verse to be carved spirally round the stick. "What verse?" "Lemme think." He thought to such good purpose that in less than a minute he recited aloud:

Now that I pledge my Heart to Thee,
Nor from Love's Wounding Arrow flee—
B Constant, Sweet, to me!

"It's genius!" Adam acclaimed. If he had to give his opinion, young Greene was a better poet than—than, let me see now—Virgil, that's right. Better than fifty Virgils. Better than the Headmaster of Eton, too. Better than the ballad-pedlar who visited the town a fortnight before. Then they returned to Herchilles, and Greene soon discovered that his host's peculiar pronunciation of this name arose from a confusion of Alcmene's son by Jove with him begotten by Peleus on Thetis—an unforeseen result of divine promiscuity. How to express the thing gracefully, that was Adam's trouble. At last he came out with it flatly: "How would you write this letter, Robert?" Almost servilely he supplied writing materials, and sat with wine and meditation for fifteen minutes till he could restrain himself no longer.

"What you got there, Robert?" he coaxed.

"I haven't finished."

"Never mind—let's hear what you got." So Greene read it out without a hiccough.

To The
  Most Worshipful Lady,
    Mistress Beatrice Constant:
Lady:

It is reported by a witty writer of another age that no labour of Hercules so distressed him as his task at the spinning wheel of Omphale. Pardon then, if before a greater sovereignty I break more words than he did gossameres, and with better cause of dismay; for as his brave heart and mighty thews were bound to female service, so I now am dedicate to Your Dear Majesty. Let it not displease you I am thus bold to write, for has not Alcander well expressed it in his pithy *Dialogues:*

He who would take a kingdom must set his head to pledge. Believing you now, as it were, in the Occident of the World, your humblest servitor would—

"That's as far as I've got," he broke off.

"Genius!" cried Adam again. He pressed more wine on the genius, assured him he had never heard language to equal it, vowed that letters written hitherto compared with this masterpiece were so much material for the privy, but discovered when he tried to urge him to the effort necessary for its completion that he had a very tipsy genius on his hands. Fuddled himself, he could think of nothing better than to give him a glass of peppermint, to disguise the smell of the wine, and then: "Goo' bye," they said.

"*Salve atque vale!*" cried Greene. "*Atque!*" echoed his host.

One thing that night saved Robert from a flogging that might have marked him for life. When he reached home very ill, having been sick a couple of times on the way, his father was not in. His mother and Alice lifted him over the door-sill, which he seemed powerless to surmount, and half-dragged, half-carried him upstairs, where he was stripped and placed in bed with a couple of flannel-wrapped hot bricks to his feet. Whether these were good for intoxication his mother did not know, but she felt happier heating them than doing nothing. Downstairs mother and daughter speculated tearfully what this unparalleled outbreak of Robert's might be and thanked heaven that they had the management of him, while he, humped on his side, slept without visions and for a time without qualms. But while it was still dark Alice from the other side of the partition heard him rid his stomach of more of its uneasy burden, and tapped quietly to see if she could help. "Go to sleep," he said miserably. "Leave me alone!" Before he fell asleep the second time he had vowed fervently never to touch wine again.

But he did. Two or three times with the Old Adam during the next couple of months. The letter was completed and delivered, but Adam did not tell him until after the return of Mistress Constant to London whether he had been favoured. Then he chuckled and dropped hints that worried Greene, who believed neverthless that there was no truth in them. By this time he suspected that Bolton was not all he pretended to be. He had assessed his wit and understanding, and did not think highly of them. Yet he was jealous of him, not unaccountably.

In the end his father heard of the acquaintance, and decided it must be not allowed. Who knew into what courses that young fool might lead his son? He gave orders, but they were disobeyed, and there could be only one consequence of this. Rebelliously the boy took a beating from his father. He was getting too old for the whip now. He was sulky and for a time would not cry out, which the elder Greene interpreted as insolent defiance and so laid on heavier. "A stiff-necked generation of vipers!" he panted, the lash swishing round his son, "I'll break your pride for you!" He did too, that time again, and desisted only when his son at last screamed for mercy. His wife was crying when he came downstairs. "Silence, woman! Would you rather your son writhe now or in hell for ever?" He did not catch what she sobbed out in answer, but: "Silence I said! I'll be master in my own house!" He hung up the whip, his duty done, another shrewd blow dealt at the devil. He'd teach the young scoundrel! And that night he prayed for him. But Jane managed to smuggle some food upstairs to Robert, though she dared not stay with him while he ate it. "Don't let your father know you've had this."

He was always on excellent terms with his mother and sister. Even the shock of his coming home drunk could not alienate him from Jane for more than a day or two. To her he tried to explain how it had happened, defended himself cleverly, swore it should never happen again, and it ended with forgiveness and orders to Alice that she should never mention the occurrence to anyone. During a short illness of his mother's, he found out how much he loved her and went tearfully into hiding, begging God not to let her die and he'd be better and never do anything she didn't like any more; but no sooner was she downstairs and active again than he felt ashamed of his weakness. Instead of candy, he was now cadging pence which she gave him from her housekeeping store, always with warnings that she could not afford it and that he had had money from her only so many days ago.

"Never mind, mother," he used to persuade her. "I've spent all that."

"Then you shouldn't have! What did you spend it on?"

"You wouldn't ask a thing like that, mother!" he protested.

"Oh yes I would! You don't get another farthing out of me till I know where that other went." An argument started, and then as she mixed the dough or basted the meat or whatever her task might be, he would be close on her heels, getting in the way, saying: "Come on, mother—I'll go if you give me something to spend." "I won't, and that's the end of it!" "Then I'll stay here." She used threats, which he knew she did not mean. "Oh no you won't, mother." "I will! I'll smack your head!" "Come on, mother—where d'you keep the money?" "I'll tell your father about you!" "Oh—him!" He pulled a face. "Come on, mother—you've got it in that purse." "Go away, will you!" "Look—let me get it for you." "Put that purse down!" But usually she yielded. "I don't know what your father would say if he knew you were getting all this money." "Oh—him!" He pushed out his lips as he had seen Adam Bolton do, and puffed his contempt.

His mother was not really much concerned about what he did with the money he got from her. Let the boy have a bit of pleasure, so long as it did no one any harm. What neither she nor her husband suspected was that he had

safely hidden behind some old books in his room the sum
of almost six shillings—his winnings at dice. It had taken
him more than a year to put this together, for the luck of
the throw in any one month might mean a considerable
setback. Charlie Boyes, Wotton Secundus, George and Cecil
Haysham from Bratton, and Nat Goodly from the Red
Lion were his usual mates; though he and Wotton Secundus
had in teaching boys at the Grammar School a side-line
more profitable than their main business. These beginners
were certain to lose, for Wotton had somehow come to
possess a false dice which he and Greene had cunning enough
to use sparingly. Bound to get nabbed otherwise—they
were agreed upon that—and they never introduced it into
the legitimate senior ring. The choice of players showed that
one man's money was as good as another's, for Greene and
Wotton were the sons of respectable and comfortably-off
tradesmen of the city, the Haysham boys were sons of a
gentleman farmer and socially their superiors, while Goodly
was a groom at his inn. He was older than the rest of them,
getting on for twenty, and as he was the poorest off for
prospects Providence had arranged that he should be the
biggest winner at their gatherings. Very properly, the Haysham boys lost most—on one occasion between them they
lost fifteen pence, which frightened even the winners. They
had various meeting places, throughout the summer months,
and regretted that the winter gave them only the chance of
an infrequent gamble in the stable of the Red Lion. Nat
knew that it would be as much as his job was worth to be
discovered thus corrupting the sons of gentlemen, and had
to be certain that there was no danger of surprisal before
he issued his invitations. And when this was possible, the
gamesters revelled in a gamblers' paradise: lying on bundles
of hay and casting on to a flat board, with the smells
of feed and beasts all around them, the whole adventure
spiced with that extra wickedness which accompanies sin
indoors. Greene and Wotton would make their way there
on foot, but the two Haysham boys rode over on ponies
which Nat would attend to with more care than he

paid to most travellers' animals. For this he had no pay,
nor would he take a tip. While gambling with these
lads he acquired status, and would do nothing to imperil
it. He was a healthy-looking bumpkin, a good fellow
enough.

CHAPTER IV

I T WAS HIS acquaintance on the one hand with the Old Adam, on the other with this groom, which led to one of the most important decisions of his life soon after his sixteenth birthday. Nat, he understood, was courting. For his own part he had so far been little concerned with the other sex. He felt for them contempt because they were not men; sometimes he had to acknowledge a distinct antagonism, at other times an unconfessable and tiresome shyness. Now, however, Nat was courting, and the circumstance suggested to Greene a gratifying use of the literary ability hailed by Adam Bolton. It was obvious that no man worthy the name of lover should neglect to set his passion on paper. If he were in love himself, surely he would spend his lifetime telling the world and the lady, and he saw no reason why Nat should not feel the same way. Anyhow, he would mention it to him. Somewhere at the back of his mind there may have been the idea of profit; undoubtedly he was experiencing a new sensibility; but in the the main his motives were pure.

"I suppose you love Susan a lot, Nat?"

"Well ay, I suppose I do."

"That's right. It isn't only the great folk who can love, is it?"

"No, I suppose it ain't."

"No." Greene appeared to think profoundly. "There must be a lot of other fellows in love with a girl like Susan —are there?"

"If there be, I ain't afraid'vum."

"Of course you are not." A phrase of Grancher Beetham's seemed to fit in here. "I bet a fellow like you, Nat— he could have his pick, I shouldn't be surprised."

Nat shrugged. "Suppose I could, too," he agreed. "Happen though I don't want no pick."

"No. I suppose you write her a lot of love-letters, eh?"

"Letters!" Nat was amazed. "What for? What 'ud a decent girl be doing with they things?"

"Well, if a king falls in love with a queen he always writes her letters, as you know. Or if it was an earl and a countess, or a princess or anything like that—they always send each other letters."

"Well, I ain't no king and she ain't no queen."

"Still, you ought to send her something, Nat."

"So I do, Robert. I sent her a favour—I give her one anyway—and a fortnight ago I give her a pair of blue garters which she haven't wore yet."

But Greene was shaking his head. "You don't think a king would give favours that way, do you? He'd send them with a long letter, with some poetry in it. That's the right way to do it, Nat."

"But I ain't a king. I'm a groom."

"Never mind. Who knows what you may be one day, Nat? You might own an inn like this."

Nat didn't really think so, but he admitted he might.

"So you may as well do things the right way, eh Nat?"

"P'raps I might."

"Then why don't you write Susan letters?"

Nat grinned. "One good reason I can think on is I can't write, Robert."

"Still, you would like to?"

"Can't say I mind much whether I do or whether I don't."

"Then don't you worry," Greene assured him. "I'll write a letter for you."

"Ay, but man alive——"

"What's the matter now, Nat?"

"Well, Robert, she don't read neither."

The tempter waved his hand. "I'll read it to her."

He did, too. Once the matter was decided, it was odd how eager Nat grew to press it to a conclusion. He wished to collaborate in composing the letter, but this Greene would not allow. At the end of a description drawn in equal parts

from the *Amores* and Aeneas Silvius he refused to insert:
"And I hope you did like the blue garters I give you for
your pretty legs." He could not be shaken. "No, Nat, it
wouldn't be right. You leave it all to me." Nat's ignorance
weighed on him like lead, so he had to give way—"Though
she don't look exactly what you got there, Robert." So
one fine evening away went Robert Greene to deliver the
letter to Susan, chambermaid at the Red Lion. "A letter
for me!" She couldn't believe it, and turned the mysterious
thing over and over in her red hands. "And I am to read
it to you," he volunteered. But there was a difficulty, for
there was nowhere private where this could be done. Evidently kings and queens had special advantages. "Well,
we shall have to go somewhere," Greene pointed out, so
she arranged to see him outside the kitchen door at a
slack hour; and it was there that eventually he rather recited
than read to her his own composition. On the whole its
reception pleased him. She giggled a lot, and once slapped
his hand, but was both impressed and delighted—indeed,
enchanted by the concluding couplet:

> *Since I to my Love true will be,*
> *Let then my Love be true to Me!*

She was two years older than Greene, two years younger
than Nat, pleasant-faced, plump, happy by nature. "And
Nat wrote that to me?" "He did, Susan. And now you
must write back to him." He made clear just how this
could be done, refused to give her time to think, and went
home with his commission. He had to explain to her that
the letter was her own property, and suggested that it
be worn nearest the heart by day and kept under the
pillow by night.

Altogether he wrote for this simple pair six letters, all
florid in expression and full of classical allusions and noble
sentiments. Nat, true, attained no consistency; he was sometimes a Sicilian shepherd, sometimes a Latin poet, sometimes
an emperor; and Susan, with allowance for her sex,

underwent corresponding changes; yet they accepted these
oddities for the romance it brought them. Pen, ink, and paper
Greene obtained from school, so he was well satisfied with
a seat in the stable during a magnificent bear-baiting in the
Red Lion yard and with a set of dice Nat gave him, one of
them guaranteed to show the five every time, which greatly
added to his and Wotton's effectiveness as initiators of new
boys. Susan's payment was of a deadlier kind, though she
knew nothing of it. His addresses to her charms and virtues
lit fires in him. With a kind of loyalty to Nat he told himself that it had nothing to do with her, that he wouldn't
care though Susan had never been born, that he didn't care
for real girls anyway. It was the girls he found in books
that interested him. He didn't care, he didn't care—it
wasn't Susan—any more than he cared whether Adam
Bolton had ever met Mistress Constant. Yet it was now he
began the metamorphosis into sweethearts of his own of
the Corinna and Briseis of his reading, of Lucretia, Lesbia,
Canidia, of the deep-browed Faustine, of Aphrodite Pan-
demos herself, and all those who at the blue midnight spread
their hair for breathless lovers. Soon these glorious mistresses
coiled white limbs inside his brain, tangled with their throats
and milky flanks his sleeping hours, offered him their lips
in dreams and drowsings. Compared with these the local
girls were dull and coarse-grained, poor subjects of an
English Art of Love. Yet before long he was mixing them
all up together, daughters and wives with goddesses and
the supple ladies of antiquity. Faces were strangely imposed
on bodies of his fancy. He began to feel angry with boys
who had attractive sisters and jealous of men with handsome wives. His father, that battler against nature, would
have broken his arm on him had he known one-quarter
the thoughts that occupied him at this time. And always he
had the stimulus supplied by learned, oft-times dessicated,
commentators upon the lewder classics. High domes sprouting a scabrous mildew.

But all this would have led to no immediate crisis had not
Susan become too proud of her letters to keep them for her

own eyes. She would have liked more of them, and sharing
was a form of multiplication. Also, they raised her to the
level of a true inamorata with a lovesick swain, and she
was willing for favoured individuals to know her rank. She
found it a great happiness to have them read aloud to her
until she had memorised them, and it is certain that several
guests at the Red Lion did her the service. From that to the
name of the composer was a short step, and Greene, unawares, was winning a fame both limited and diffuse as
these gentlefolk intruded a well-bred nose into the comical
idyll and then went their ways. That was all about it for
Susan and Nat, who had not sense enough to know when
they were being sneered at, and perhaps preferred the
sneers and pence of their superiors to their indifference; but
it had marked consequences for Robert Greene.

Expectedly, among those who came to know of Susan's
love letters and therefore of the gifted Robert Greene, was
her mistress, the owner of the Red Lion. This was the widow
of the famous John Petherill who kept it altogether fifty-
two winters. No one was surprised that so managing a man
saw two wives into the grave and yet had strength to
marry a third on his sixtieth birthday; and still less could
there be surprise that it was now his turn to go first. His
third wife was Lucy Greatrex, already, at the age of twenty,
the widow of that Geoffrey Greatrex who lost his life by
drowning during the Wensum floods which preceded the
Plague. This Lucy was now in her 'thirties, four years a
widow, admired more by those who spent guineas at the
Red Lion than the dribblers of pence. Perhaps her two-fold
experience had made her wary, for though she had customers who hoped to pick up an inn and a fine woman at
a stroke, and though rumour credited her with kindness
to men of substance—Sir John Goring was one of them—
she had not married again. Greene had hardly set eyes on
her, for when he visited the Red Lion to throw dice with
Wotton, Nat, and the Hayshams, to see and be seen were
equally no part of their business. He was much surprised
when Susan told him one afternoon in early November

that Mistress Petherill had said next time he went there she would have an errand for him.

"Maybe she wants 'ee to write a letter for her, Master Robert."

"Maybe," he said, irritated to know that Susan had been talking. And yet, as he waited downstairs for news of him to ascend to the mistress his irritation vanished, and he began to experience not only the artist's pride in his craft and any tribute to it, but also the hope that Susan might be right and he was about to find employment.

"You told her then?" he asked Susan, when she came for him.

"I showed her," she admitted.

"Well, they were your letters," he granted, running his hand over the heads of birds, beasts, and monsters which ornamented the handrail. All at once it was clear to him that his gambling had been discovered and he was to be warned to stay away. Should he turn back now, at once? And then she would tell his father. No, he must go on with it. "Here you be," said Susan; "you better knock and go in when she says."

Greene lowered his voice. "Is she—is she——" He gave it up, mumbling.

"Not so bad as some," said Susan.

He went inside, ready to plead that his father should be told nothing, and stood cap in hand by the door. "If you please, ma'am," he began. Mistress Petherill was standing near the fireplace, the table and lamp were between them, the grey window behind her to the left. The flames were bright enough to throw shapeless, fluttering lines and masses past her to the ceiling, for the lamp was dim and the corners past the window muddled with shadows. "If you please, ma'am," he said, bright and nervous.

"So you are Robert Greene, are you?" He liked her voice, soft, deep, firm.

"Yes, ma'am."

"Then I want to see you."

"Oh!"

"You had better shut the door behind you."

"Yes." He did this, wondering whether he ought to await exposure or confess and beg for mercy. "I—er——"

"Come over here."

He went around the table to stand in front of her, dismayed that she looked such a lady, trying to think out a second good lie in case the first failed. She was shorter than he, but he felt his insignificance did not justify the physical advantage. The warmth of the fire came full on his right side, and he looked away from her at the flames. He was worried by her silence, coughed, and changed his cap from one hand to the other. "Well, young man," she challenged. "What have you to say for yourself?"

"I don't know," he admitted.

"You don't know!" It whipped into his mind that she was more amused than angry. "Where do you get such notions? Setting such ideas in Susan's head! Making Nat and her look so ridiculous."

"I meant no harm, if you please."

"What an excuse!"

"They liked it," he said. "I did not know Susan would show her letters. They were not for anyone else to see."

"Which suggests you do not know much about young women. So perhaps you are not such a bad young man as you appear. Does your father know about this?"

"Heaven forbid, Mistress Petherill!"

"I know your father well." *Liar*, he thought. "Perhaps I ought to tell him."

"Heaven forbid!" he repeated, with a comically desperate emphasis that made her smile. He smiled too, but she cut it from his face with a new severity: "Well, don't forget that your impudence won't save you again. Now you go away from here and let me have no more of you or your letters, you understand?"

He understood. He turned near the door. "I'm very glad you are not going to tell my father, Mistress Petherill." He called up all his assurance, but felt as hot as fire. "I knew you were too gracious a lady."

Surprised but pleased, she waved him away, and he went downstairs elated. He saw neither Susan nor Nat, and took a roundabout way home. It was dark, but he knew every step of the way, and enlivened the time with recollections of his own dexterity at the interview. He thought a great deal about Mistress Petherill throughout the evening and for an hour or so after he had gone to bed. He recalled her voice, her appearance; he began to thread lines of verse; and suddenly, he did not know when it started, he was feeling for her the sensuous and magnificent adoration of a boy in calf-love with a woman twice his age. No lustful image disturbed the nobility of this new passion; he felt ashamed of his study-furnished fancies for months back; this, he hoped, would prove the passion of all time. Why, Cupid must have borrowed Vulcan's hammer and struck him full swing betwixt his startled eyes.

Instantaneous recognition of a deity.

In the morning things seemed different again, but the morning soon changed to afternoon, and that to potent darkness. He found an excuse to see Nat almost every day now, and if he could help it did not leave the Red Lion without a glimpse of Mistress Petherill. Once he pushed boldly into the tap-room, saying that he had a message for a person of his own invention, but Mistress Petherill was not there, he grew nervous with the men around him, backed out at last and met her at the door. "You here, Master Greene?" He could not even cough out that he had a message, grew red as a cockscomb, and hurried off feeling the biggest fool in the county of Norfolk. For five minutes he almost hated her. But the next day he was back again, watching, waiting, hoping, despairing. And brooding over her in absence he thought of Neaera (his special name for her) with an exquisiteness of worship and idealisation which soon transported him to a jellied heaven of delight. Standing in the darkness outside the inn, he rejoiced that there was no corporeal basis to their relationship; for he imagined a sufficiency of happiness in the unattainable presence of the

loved one, in being permitted to touch her fingers, she seated
and exalted, he on his knees and preferably in pain; or, their
postures much the same, he would wish to read her protestations of undying love, prolonged descriptions of her eyes
like glassy streams, her hair like clouds at sunset, her teeth
like pearls of India, her lips like cherries, her throat a pillar
of ivory, her bosom a nest of cupids, her waist a circumference of bliss, her all a golden Atlantis. He longed to perform
some notable deed, resounding to her glory: to rescue her
from fire at peril of his life; to burst in upon a dozen stalwart
ruffians who had threatened her with shame, and, she
crouched behind him in a corner, kill three or four of the
boldest and keep the rest at bay till rescuers arrived; to
save her from the claws of a bear escaped during an entertainment in the Red Lion Yard, maybe losing an arm,
maybe losing two, but amply repaid with a kiss before he
swooned: in short, to do something gloriously idiotic,
which there was not the slightest chance of his ever doing.
Walking to school he sighed for knight-errantry; over
his book he dreamed of monsters ravaging Broadland;
on his way home he visualized prodigies of valour. The
Twelve Labours were nothing to those he performed for
Mistress Petherill.

These adventures could be carried through nowhere
more successfully than in his brain, but he gave proof at
this time that he had the making of a poet by the several
songs he composed to his lady and the image-laden flow
of prose he damned up in letters so far undelivered to her.
The crabbed proprieties of realistic description appealed to
him no more than to the writer of the Song of Solomon.
If within ten lines Mistress Petherill was an ocean of joy,
a world of delight, a heaven of bliss, a microcosm of unutter-
able perfections, and equally a jewel, a casket, a doe, a
flower, or a goddess—so be it, let her be all these things,
and a vision of felicity, a mirror of glory, and a crystal
fountain as well. He allowed himself only one form of
conscious deception in these letters. He was much given to
the authority of the ancients—as Ovid so wittily said, as

we may believe with the wise Tully, witness Isocrates his Orations, and the like—and when he did not find the reference pat, he would both invent one and find an author for it, such as the Alcander of the first letter for Adam Bolton, and the Menocrates, Dianerges, Culius, and the wise Forbrantine whose names were now to be found in his own letters to Neaera. The one to give him most pleasure was the Grand Master of Pandonus, whose very likeness he knew, so often did he refer to his unwritten works for guidance. It was hard not to believe implicitly in these scholars, so unjustly omitted from learning's pantheon.

In early January Mistress Petherill received her first letter, signed *Boretrus*. She recognised the handwriting and the sentiments, and handed the sheet to Sir John Goring, down from London for a change of air and ladies. He was amused, reading it in bed, one arm around her. He was equally amused with the second, which arrived two days later, and the third and the fourth. He was amused to think of young Greene walking over from his father's house to push these effusions under the Red Lion door. He was still more amused at the idea of a reply. And he said that he admired the boy. And envied him his phrases. "'To the Mistress of my Soul, these greetings: Of Happiness in Love there is no End. An endless Throng of the Elect of Cupid have echoed the words of the wise Forbrantine that though men may sail to Seas beyond the Moon, yet, etc. etc.,'— he'll make a poet, Lucy, my girl. 'More fatal than the Musket Ball or the Grim Carronado those flashing beams from Your Celestial Orbs'—and the verses too:

> *When my Neaera's beauty's seen,*
> *Her dewy hair and crystal e'en,*
> *Her lilied cheeks and ivory brow,*
> *Her breast where roses bud in snow,*
> *The brief circumference of her waist,*
> *Within whose round all sweets are placed——*

Derivative, but far from contemptible, Lucy, and based on the most accurate observation, my sweet. The boy will go far." He laughed at a jest Mistress Petherill could not understand. "This Culius of his, and the Grand Master, they give me an idea. I might spend a year or two writing the works of Ovid's brother under the rose, by far the better poet of the two, but whose memory and writings have unfortunately not been preserved." He referred more than once to the wisdom of a reply. He enjoyed his caresses more for Robert Greene and felt kindly towards him. The brief circumference more than spanned by his comfortable arm, the lilied cheek near his, he found time to reflect how literature enriches life and art gives a flavour to experience. He told Lucy some of this, without expecting her to understand more than a quarter of his words.

And so as the days went by there was no reply for Robert Greene. But worship and study sustained him. One day when he had been drawn to the inn Mistress Petherill gave him a charming smile and that was solace for a month. Nor was new ambition a slackener of the hours. Suddenly he had discovered how much he wanted to go to the University and distinguish himself in the world's eyes and Neaera's. Besides, it seemed to him the door he must push open if he was to find room in a bigger world than Norwich. While saddlers and chandlers and louts in general stayed at home, the scholar would find employment at law, at court, with the army, in diplomatic service, or in the households of great men. Candle or beacon-light—the choice was there. If he stayed in his father's business—well, that was all: he stayed in his father's business. At the gayest become a stupid mock-gallant like Adam Bolton. But if he found a place in London and then came swaggering home, dressed in red and yellow, money spilling from his pockets— Neaera must notice him then. Not just another acorn in an oak wood. He thought too that the University and then London would take him away from home, and at home he was coming to dislike his father and all his ways. The impressive being of his childhood was now a petty-souled tradesman, reconciling God and Mammon after his own sanctimonious fashion, a tyrant wherever he could be, yet servile towards those he professed to despise, an ignoramus and a hypocrite. That he might have to enter the business and spend the next twenty or thirty years under his father's eye scared and repelled him, but nothing could help him short of running away—a ridiculous course he would never adopt—apart from the chance offered him by the University. And that he feared would be denied him. Yet his father could afford to pay for him. Why shouldn't he then? What did he intend to do with the money—make a golden idol of it? Unjustly he vowed all the puritans were the same; he reckoned their strictness the instinct of the miser, their self-denial fright or meanness, their denial of others the true measure of their lack of charity with the world. Narrow-headed, tight-brained canters! Who knew whether if he were given the chance he might not become famous throughout the nation? His talent considered—— They need not fear he wouldn't work hard. Here at the Grammar School, admittedly, drudging with *hic*, *haec*, *hoc* and the irrelevancies of the gerund—but that was over, and now he could read Horace with the best of the class and string together a dozen hexameters while the others were counting syllables on their fingers. Walter Hall had said he would distinguish himself at the University, provided he worked, and he was prepared to make the solemnest promises to do that. "If he doesn't send me——" he would tell himself; "if he doesn't——" But the exact threat to meet the case always eluded him. All he could do was knuckle under.

Unless he won a scholarship. Then he could get to the University and cost his father nothing. How could there be objection? So he worked.

It was about the end of February that Sir John Goring announced that the two scholarships offered each year by his family would this year be awarded partly on the recommendation of the headmaster, Walter Hall, partly to the composers of the two most accomplished poems on the merits and achievements of his father, the late Sir John, second in power locally to the Norfolk family, and illustrious father of a noble son. Walter Hall went out to Carbrank, Sir John's seat, where he was graciously if briefly received, offered wine and a damaged folio, and heard with gladness that Sir John—"And I still have as good an ear for quantity as any man in this county"—would entrust no one else with the reading of the work submitted. Hall was impressed by the might of brain behind the friendly eyes, and went back to Norwich to tell everyone Sir John was the greatest Latin scholar in England. He extolled the generosity of his patron, and swore that while such men lived England's glory would increase. Urged as much by the gift of the folio as by his official position, he set to work on a pious tribute to the School's benefactor, and at the same time those boys who wished for Sir John's patronage began to study the facts which had been obligingly communicated to Hall, and then applied themselves wholeheartedly to checking spondees and dactyls on their fingertips. Greene was of their number. He worked with an industry shocking to his mother, who honestly expected him to collapse under it, and incredible to his father, who began to think that, after all, if his son was successful in this, and Sir John would pay for him, he would not put a stop to it. He saw to it that Robert had quiet and opportunity for his task. Had he known enough Latin, he might have heard the voice of God commanding him to give a hand with the ode. *Dux*, he said one day aloud, *dux illustris;* but thought it too poor a contribution to the catalogue of the former Sir John's titles. Besides, his man Vose, cutting out leather behind him, had lifted his head, wondering where the ducks were.

Had he but known it, there was no need for help or doubt. Sir John received the candidates' verses one morning after his return from the Red Lion. He sat down with his feet raised to ease his back, picked out a line here and there, yawned, thought there had been a great and wasted expenditure of energy, and threw all save two copies on the back of the fire. That of Robert Greene and the next longest were those saved from the burning. Seeing Greene's beautiful and familiar handwriting, Sir John remembered that all great men have their whims—indeed, that sometimes there is no other way to recognise a great man. Besides, Lucy had a kind heart and wanted him to do something for the lad. Fair was fair: they had had their sport, and the least they could do was to recompense their entertainer. And later, up in London, among his cronies—So you had him whipped out of the county? they would ask; and then he would roar with laughter: Great God in heaven, gentlemen, I know a trick worth two of that. I had my laugh out, and then I sent the lad—ha-ha-ha!—I sent him—ha-ha-ha! —why, gentlemen, I sent him to the University! He would be famous for life after a jest like that. It would be superb, worthy of a king. He grew facetious, there before the fire, one hand holding the manuscript ode, the other smoothing his right leg. He hoped the boy would turn out a credit to him. From the general tone of Boretrus's correspondence he expected much. He had no fear so promising a youngster would long be seduced from the glory of life by the arid attractions of the quadrivium or be weaned from the full breasts of experience by the thin drink of moderation. Yes, one of the exhibitions was Robert Greene's. This reminded him that he had better at least glance at the ode. It was quite a long one, and in extolling the father's merits had not neglected the son's. This pleased the judge, not because he was grateful for a schoolboy's praise, but because it confirmed his opinion of Greene's perception. After a week or two he followed Lucy's advice and told Walter Hall his choice, with which that good man cordially though respectfully agreed, begging leave to congratulate Sir John on his keen ear. The award was announced at a gathering of the school, and the two odes were read aloud with excellent intonation and patience by their composers. Sir John regretted he could not be there, but affairs of state prevented him. All there assembled, except the parents of some of the unsuccessful candidates, were convinced those affairs could not be in better hands, and rousing cheers were

given for the man who in October would send the victors
to Cambridge.

Naturally, Greene's parents were delighted. His mother's
faith in him was now justified before the whole city, and his
father saw clearly those benefits of a University education
he had been doubtful of before. People were saying you
couldn't get a strawberry from a nettle. Clever father, clever
son.

There was but one blot on Greene's fair copybook of joy.
Now that he was to leave Norwich for many years, what of
Mistress Petherill? How support an absence from Neaera?
To his disappointment he found the problem solve itself.
He began to fall out of love. The process was jarred and
then quickened when Nat told him one day, with homely
detail, how Sir John spent nights with the mistress. With
Nat he grinned, but could think of no pleasantry of his own,
and hurried off to the fields for an emotional purge. There
he longed for cataclysms, the bursting of stars, inundations
from the grey seas, the sickening lapse of the firmament's
foundations. He swore himself to a celibate's life, and cursed
the sex morbidly from Juvenal. But no god answered from
heaven, and eventually it seemed best to go home. Once
more a sudden boiling of jealousy made him groan. He
felt he should have—the things he should have done skipped
through his mind like goblins, thumb to nose, mocking him
with his own voice. Yet no one of them told him to reject
Sir John's charity. Still, he knew he would do something
terrible.

But what? These terrible things, the more you thought of
them, the more terrible they sounded—and the less
attractive. To stab himself on the doorstep of the Red Lion
would be a fine gesture, but would Neaera appreciate it?
He could never know. To drown himself—no better. To
waylay Sir John, to challenge him—good at night but poor
over breakfast. He grew cynical. Was any woman worth it?
As the Latin poet put it—— Ha-ha-ha! He thought his
laughter mordant. No doubt people could see the difference
in him.

He could not deceive himself for long. Congratulations over, he became as insignificant as ever. And had there not been two scholarships? Walking, he told himself it was only in his hidden heart he was unique. But, Neaera, if only you had been different!

He prepared for Cambridge. The first step to fame and fortune.

PART II
LUSTY JUVENTUS

"MEARES," SAID ROBERT GREENE, "it took me two years at Cambridge to find out where all the September spiders go. You know how you see them, big and little, scuttling across walls and floors, and hanging their threads wherever you must put your face; And then, all at once—where are they?"

"Where then, Robert?"

"They come to Cambridge, most of them, to take degrees. I thought as I watched them to-day—here we are, masters, fellows, tutors, professors, and small fry like you and me, all in our black gowns—we are a race of spiders, I tell you."

"Some because they live on bottles then."

"Carry the comparison as far as you like. Here at St. John's we even make up our own beds, and I'm sure all spiders do that. I should say too that our meat diet is equally sumptuous. Or which would you say get the better of it, the spiders who eat the flies or we who eat what the flies leave us?"

Meares would not debate the question. "I prefer Pliny's bees. We are here sucking sweetness from learning's flowers——"

"The Fellows?" Greene laughed.

"Figuratively, Robert, only. But I am glad term is starting again." He sighed and looked far from glad.

"Glad to see ahead monastic hours, cold in winter, and foul food? And endless chapel?" Greene looked out of the window on to the cobbled court. "You were lucky to get away, Meares. Did you bring back any new books?"

"Ariosto, as I promised. It is in my bundle here. I'll unpack and then you can have it. Where are we putting the new commoner?"

"You know who he is?"

CHAPTER V

"MEARES," SAID ROBERT GREENE, "it took me two years at Cambridge to find out where all the September spiders go. You know how you see them, big and little, scuttling across walls and floors, and hanging their threads wherever you must put your face? And then, all at once—where are they?"

"Where then, Robert?"

"They come to Cambridge, most of them, to take degrees. I thought as I watched them to-day—here we are, masters, fellows, tutors, professors, and small fry like you and me, all in our black gowns—we are a race of spiders, I tell you."

"Some because they live on bottles then."

"Carry the comparison as far as you like. Here at St. John's we even make up our own beds, and I'm sure all spiders do that. I should say too that our meat diet is equally sumptuous. Or which would you say get the better of it: the spiders who eat the flies or we who eat what the flies leave us?"

Meares would not debate the question. "I prefer Pliny's bees. We are here sucking sweetness from learning's flowers——"

"The Fellows?" Greene laughed.

"Figuratively, Robert, only. But I am glad term is starting again." He sighed and looked far from glad.

"Glad to see ahead monastic hours, cold in winter, and foul food? And endless chapel?" Greene looked out of the window on to the cobbled court. "You were lucky to get away, Meares. Did you bring back any new books?"

"Ariosto, as I promised. It is in my bundle here. I'll unpack and then you can have it. Where are we putting the new commoner?"

"You know who he is?"

"Not even his name. Some poor blubberer fresh from school, just as we were. These new men are the devil himself for a week or two."

Greene looked at the corner right of the door. "He can go there. Just where the draught rushes in from the stairs. He may need cooling down. I am glad you brought the Ariosto, George. You take anything of mine you want, won't you? I shall be Italianate by the end of next summer."

"You'll have to travel, Robert. I'd travel myself if I had someone to pay for me. Someone might be fool enough one day. You know, Robert—you are getting fatter."

"I believe you are right." He felt his own limbs, poked a finger into his belly, and beat a fist on his chest. "Jesus! If we all put on weight we shall never get into this rat-hole of ours."

It was a spartan room, with a stone floor, and containing four narrow wooden bedsteads which took up most of the space. There was a wooden shelf clamped into the wall above each bed, and on two of these Greene and Meares were rummaging their belongings. Meares was a short, dapper-looking man of Greene's own age and, like him, at the beginning of his third year of residence.

"You haven't seen Coppinger?" he asked.

"He was as lucky as you. It's more than a month since he left for London. No, I haven't seen him."

"He will keep his old place, I suppose, now that I have taken Rainsford's?"

"He won't have much choice, will he?"

"You know, Robert—he is the senior here. He should have first choice. I wonder if he will mind?"

"No, Coppinger won't mind. If it was any comfort to us, I really think he would sleep like a bat from the ceiling. Help me fix this, will you, please?"

They went on talking as they did this, exchanging what little news they had, wondering whether the new Master would be a change for better or worse, discussing without undue modesty their chances of a degree at the end of the year, and, later, puzzling where their room-mates could be.

Meares came from Bristol, and the wet weather had meant a trying journey to London, and one not much better thence to Cambridge. He gave a comical description of this, and Greene, not to be outdone, invented ancient journeys of his own from Norwich to Dereham, to Swaffham, even to King's Lynn. "But now I live in luxury," he commented, pressing the unyielding board he was to sleep on, "and I have no worries." They grimaced their dismay.

It was four o'clock before Coppinger arrived, to greet them warmly.

"Edmund! You got here then?"

"By the grace of God, Robert."

"And the help of a horse!"

"And the help of a horse," Coppinger agreed smiling. He explained that he had been to pay his respects to the new Master. "I tell you, both of you, this man is worth ten of the other." They had started, he did not know how, to discuss recent events in London, especially the religious issues of the time, and less fortunate students had a long wait outside the Master's door. "This man is sound. No persecutor like Still. I look forward to the benefits of his rule."

This was good news. John Still had been too active a Master for most, not only in his determination to root puritanism out of the College, but also in his interference with the lives of those under him. He had consequently offended not only the graver sort, like Coppinger, but that large number, too, like Greene and Meares, who wanted some relaxation of the iron discipline of their University life.

"You think, Edmund, this Richard Howland will be more tolerant? That we shall find life easier under him?"

Coppinger was pulling at the straps of his bag. "I think men of my belief will. Oh, here you are—the Lucian, Robert!" Greene's thanks embarrassed him. "Why so, Robert? You would do as much for me."

Then Meares thought it time to say something of their new arrangements. "By the way, Edmund, now that

Rainsford has gone—— We thought you might like to keep your old bed, so I have changed over. You are senior here—would you like it any other way?"

"I am satisfied, George. I like this old bed of mine." Meares winked at Greene. "That reminds me," Coppinger went on; "the new man? Has he arrived yet?" They talked till the bell summoned them to Hall for the evening meal.

Here for a time there was a rush of greetings, for though there was a rule that no student should leave his College during the vacations, it was a rule not difficult to circumvent. Even John Still had not insisted upon quiet the first day of term. It looked odd without Camborne opposite; the freshmen were a poor lot; the food was as bad as ever; yes, that was Howland at the head of the table—gossip always new and always the same. Around the Master the fellows and doctors were making a great flourish of Latin, cowing the freshmen with their presence and learning. Hadman's thin, high-pitched voice was heard as usual above all others, making some side-splitting joke about a point of Greek syntax, and Gray hurled the names of obscure authorities at Bremer, who caught them, pawed them over, and flung them back again. Personalities were pointed out to the ignorant: Clayton, who had this year been made a fellow and would yet be made Master—best keep in with Clayton if you were here for some years; Moulton, whose *Dialogus Contra* Somebody-or-Other had already been twenty years in preparation; Criddle, the least-liked instructor in logic; Harrison, who for three years had been on diplomatic missions in Tartary, and then retired to the seclusion of a College, disgusted, it was said, with the ways of monarchs; Faber, more human in students' eyes, baselessly reputed to be the father of the new baby at the Dolphin; and the eccentric Bellowes who one day put on his gown but forgot his breeches and in that array marched solemnly to Schools. At table Coppinger did not sit with his room-mates, but with the graduates higher up the table. Greene saw him in earnest conversation with Eggerton, one of the strongestfaithed puritans in the College. Hell fire or Howland? he wondered; the succession or episcopacy? Poor Coppinger! God help the bishops if he got his way. There was something about Coppinger's face that reminded him of his earliest recollections of his own father: sternly gentle, handsome, impressive. A squarish, strong face. Greene watched him gesture over his meat, then turn to attend to Criddle who had touched his elbow, listening with his beautiful smile expressing his full agreement, then back he turned to Eggerton, the smile vanishing and the same gesture once more.

Supper over, they listened to a long grace by the new Master. Rather less imperious than Still, Greene found. Still used to thank the Almighty as one deity another, his benedictions were less the expression of his hopeful faith than commands, he advised God what was best for Him. O Lord! Still would begin; we beg thee in thy goodness and mercy —and then he showed him precisely what he should do for the world, for England, for Cambridge, and most especially for St. John's College. Greene missed from the present grace and prayer not only these advices, but also Still's famous passage beginning: And root out of our hearts, O Lord, that stubborn sin of spiritual presumption, whereby men of weak and shallow intellect, none other than bladders of vanity, would scan the measures enacted on your glorious behalf by Her Majesty's most excellent Bishops. . . . This grace must be oil to Coppinger and his sect. He wondered what Hadman and Clayton were thinking of it.

They went back to their own room. "What was the meat like where you were sitting, Edmund?"

"I saw nothing wrong with it."

"Did you taste nothing wrong with it?"

"You are too fidgety with your food, Robert."

"I told him he was getting fat," said Meares.

"You liked the grace to-night, Edmund?"

Coppinger nodded. "For the first time in three years I fully enjoyed the thank-offering. I came here before Still, and it makes me happy to be here now he has gone." He bent forward and picked at the toe of his shoe. "I hope to outlast all his kind."

"Well, you have the years on your side."

Coppinger stood up abruptly. "I have God on my side." His features took on beauty from some inner source. His companions thought he would add to what he had said, but instead he looked at each of them in turn and unexpectedly smiled. Greene saw a vision of Coppinger at the stake, the fire to his knees, his face with that same rapt look on it. He shivered and turned away to the window. "You thank heaven——" he started to say. "I do, Robert. Every hour!" Greene shrugged his shoulders: That you live under this reign, not the last, was what he had in mind. He felt the cold of the evening biting under the window frame and shook himself as he went back to kneel on his bed and grope for the books his friends had brought him. "I'm grateful for these. In return I shall later offer you a share of a meat pasty I bought at the Mitre this morning." He began to turn over pages of the Italian poet. "If you know Latin, this language is child's play. I'll be reading it in a week better than I do Greek now. Why don't you start too, Edmund, and add to your graces?" Sitting or sprawling on their beds, they began to argue about the tongues indispensable to the man soon to enter the world. Italian, cried Greene, hot with a new love; Spanish, reckoned Meares, in readiness for the great struggle that must come; Latin, Greek, and Hebrew, Coppinger maintained, so that a man need not be hoodwinked by knaves or misled by fools. They were about this when there came a knock at their door.

"Number Four," said Coppinger. "Come in!" he called, sorry to relinquish what he knew a winning argument. Then the door was pushed open and they saw the new-comer.

He was a slender young man of Greene's height, with a clear, pale face and waving dark brown hair accentuating the height and narrowness of his forehead. His eyes were dark and soft like a woman's, his lips full and seemingly too red. He was dressed in dark clothes as they, but they felt rather than noticed the difference of quality that marked them from their own homely severe stuffs. A young exquisite, thought Coppinger with exasperation. Half a woman, thought Meares. Startlingly beautiful, they all thought. He stood with confidence and grace, looking at them from the doorway. "My name is Sidley, gentlemen. I am told I share this room with you." His voice was musical, deeper than one expected, his words deliberately enunciated. He made a friendly gesture towards them with his right hand, thin and white and ringed.

"Will you bring your things inside?" said Coppinger. "My name is Edmund Coppinger." He gave the names of the other two. "Let me help you." As he passed Sidley to get to the door his strongly-shaped head and broad shoulders looked clumsy, his attitude awkward.

"Thank you," said Sidley. "Do I make myself a nuisance?"

"You are entitled to make yourself one-fourth of the nuisance of this room," Greene assured him, getting from the bed and offering his hand.

Coppinger put his head around the door. "Is all this yours?"

"It is. Is it too much?"

"As much as the rest of us have between us," Coppinger told him curtly. Greene and Meares were surprised at his tone. "Let's have a look at it, anyway," Meares said good-naturedly. "You can see, Master Sidley, we are not too well-blest for room here. Name of God!" Greene heard him exclaim, as he looked outside. "There is enough for a voyage!"

Greene went to view the cause of the trouble. He could smell the slightest trace of perfume from Sidley, standing in front of him. He was surprised at the delicacy and pallor of his face. "Don't worry, gentlemen," Sidley was assuring them. "We can throw away all that cannot find place." He had the easy manner of an equal. "There is some of it can be quickly disposed of if you are willing to help." He laughed at Meares. "We'll call the term a voyage."

All four helping or looking as though they were willing to help, the different pieces of baggage were brought inside the room, and the three settled themselves again as though to resume their argument, while the new arrival considered what to do with the space at his disposal. "Have you seen the Master?" Coppinger reminded him. Yes, he had. Thoughtfully, he loosened the straps of the largest bag, and then to their amazement began to produce bottles of wine, green, white, and black. Greene watched Coppinger struggling between his knowledge that he had no right to be observing what was taking place and his longing to deliver warning and reproof. At last—"You don't know, Sidley, perhaps, that we are not allowed to bring wine into our rooms?"

Sidley ran his fingers down the long thin neck of the bottle he had last put down. "Yes, I did know."

"But you bring it here?"

"As you see."

Coppinger was somewhat set back by this. "Have you come here then, intending to break the rules?"

Sidley laughed, more to himself than aloud. "I hope to break all those I don't like."

This silenced Coppinger, and now the three gave over any pretence at discussion and frankly watched Sidley, who now that he had his wine on the floor in front of him was rummaging again. "You see," he explained, as they noticed that one portmanteau contained nothing but a fine coat of black and white fur; "I like to be as comfortable as I can. I was told how cold it gets here in winter without a fire, so I thought I might need this around my shoulders or on top of the bed."

"You'll find the bed rather hard, won't you?" Coppinger asked him, as though concerned.

"I shall manage. I have used hard beds before."

"You have? Where?"

Sidley seemed amused by this rudeness. "At sea," he replied.

"You have been a sailor?" Greene asked, to prevent too blunt a comment from Coppinger.

"I have sailed," Sidley admitted. He looked around him. "A miserable light here, isn't it?" His eye avoided Coppinger, but travelled from Greene to Meares and back again. "Good enough to drink by, though. Do we get nothing better?"

"Not unless we pay for it."

Sidley started to bring out books. "May I see those?" Greene asked him.

"Of course you may. Consider them as though yours. I should be pleased if you would stack them on the shelf there for me when you've done." He seemed to shovel them up at him where he crouched on the bed near him: Guevara, a Machiavelli in French, the *Decamerone*, Thomas Holy's version of *The Courtier*, Montemayor and Sanazzaro, Alain Chartier's *Delectable Demands and Pleasant Questions*, Golding's *Metamorphoses*, a Ronsard in three volumes, Aretine, Marco Polo and Mandeville, and lastly a Longus. "You must let me read these, Sidley. There are many here I know nothing of." "I admit to being short of text-books," Sidley laughed at him; "I shall be a borrower too."

Coppinger picked up a couple of volumes, and put them down again. "I am going to talk to Eggerton," he announced, "I may read in his room for a time. I see nothing here I want to read." He went out heavily.

"I fancy friend Coppinger approves neither of my goods nor of me," Sidley suggested. "I should be sorry to make an enemy so soon."

Greene tried to tell him that Coppinger was the best of men, strict in many ways, but generous-hearted and willing to help anyone with word or deed. "A puritan, is he?" Sidley interrupted. He flicked dust from his knees. "Well, who can reconcile the different devils in men? Religion with one, drink and women with another. I think if you two would put ust a few of these smaller things anywhere you have room, there'll be no need to throw away anything except a couple of empty bottles in an hour or so." Both Greene and Meares had yielded to the insolent charm of his manner, and now they obliged

him. "We get something more to eat to-night?" They
explained that supper was at five, and that apart from chapel
in twenty minutes or so their night was at an end. "Then
hell take my father's soul," Sidley swore—an oath that
startled his listeners—"if I haven't brought in all drink and
no food!" The promise of a share in Greene's pasty brought
forth an extravagance of thanks. "Full hearts, full heads,
full bellies," said Greene, but Sidley shook his head. "Bellies
first, with your permission, Master Greene. Bellies first!"

After chapel there was still no sign of Coppinger's return.
"Anyhow, we need not wait for him," Greene ruled. "Now
that he and Eggerton are together after more than a
month, they'll argue till bedtime. Shall I do the cutting
up? We must leave him his quarter, though." Sidley ate
like a hungry man, but a courteous one, and pressed wine
on his companions, and enlivened the informal meal
with droll stories of things that had happened to him or
that he knew of from friends. Soon he had Greene and
Meares laughing as loudly as they dared. He had established
the superiority of the man with experience over those who
find life in books, and they let him capture the talk. Occasionally they did remember that they had two years' standing
and this was a freshman who should be diffident if not
respectful, but a glance at the magnificent coat flung at
the top of the bed as though it were a fivepenny blanket,
or the gurgle of wine as Sidley gestured away denial and
went on filling their glasses was more than enough to
convince them that the ordinary rules could not be applied
here. Thinking of their talk of spiders—— No, Greene
decided, this was a gorgeous butterfly settled down among
them. As the wine came to affect him more he imagined
Sidley's pallor increased, the darkness of his eyes grew
deeper, his lips appeared red as blood, his face became
luminous in the drab room. His beautiful mouth was giving
utterance to sentiments more unholy each minute, but when
he laughed Greene found himself laughing with him. He
was dazzled by the brilliance of the newcomer's personality;
he had never met so fascinating a man. And yet he could

be no older than himself. He saw that Meares was allowing him undoubted priority, and had no wish to do otherwise himself. Life as he had known it, for the past few years especially, suddenly seemed dull and worthless. The spider and the butterfly indeed. To be brilliant and graceful like this man before him was the purpose of living. No need to write or paint, compose or carve—Sidley, he felt, had only to live. He was the flower of life. And all the time good temper promoted by Sidley's wine kept him from envy. He knew only admiration. And he went on drinking.

Coppinger returned late from Eggerton's room. Eggerton shared with Criddle who, as doctor and tutor, could stay up as late as he liked. Criddle had been drawn into their talk, and it was long after the proper hour when they said good-night. Coming back across the court to his own stairway Coppinger was aware of a strange restlessness within himself. He felt something evil near him, and stopped once to look around the blackened buildings. So powerfully affected was he that before starting to walk again he muttered a short prayer. "I believe in Thee, O my God," he said urgently. "I do not ask that Thou shouldst spare me mine adversaries. Only I ask for the strength that Thou alone canst give. Give me Thy strength this night that I may know and conquer what assails me." Clasping his hands tightly together he went on and entered his room. He found Greene and Meares dead drunk across their beds and Sidley sitting back on his against the wall, his black and white coat around him. The room was foul with wine and vomit. Sidley's wide, ringed eyes always on him, he crossed to the window and flung it open, and then caught Meares by the shoulders and pulled him as straight as he could. Then he went to take hold of Greene, but a great terror caught at him and he knew that he was shivering with it. He looked from his shaking hands towards the motionless Sidley. The high, narrow forehead, the glowing transparency of his face, made whiter by the livid mouth and blotches of his eyes, the unearthly elongation of his features in the uncertain light—"I know you," he heard himself challenge; "I know you. You are Belial!"

Sidley's teeth glittered through his red mouth. "And you are Michael!"

"Then I defy thee!" cried Coppinger, but the darkness rose up against him and he fell fainting to the ground.

CHAPTER VI

Within a week of the commencement of term Meares was dead—drowned in the river, no one knew how. He had gone out in the early evening without permission, he had not returned, but his room-mates, fearful they might betray him, made no report of his absence till they found him absent from disputations next day. Then the search was begun through University and town, and Meares' body was discovered before nightfall. He had gone out without money on his person, he had no worries, and it was decided he had fallen into the river accidentally. There was no one to take his place in their room, so now they were three together. Coppinger, with the approval of the other two, wrote a noble letter to the father, dwelling on Meares' many virtues, and trusting that those bereaved would find comfort in God. "Not that they will," said Sidley. Coppinger struck the table with his clenched fist. "They will," he declared loudly.—"So they are godly people," he qualified, staring at the interrupter. Somehow, none of the three seemed to mourn after Meares. Sidley, for one, had known him so short a time, and Greene, who had known him longer, now had Sidley. Coppinger should have felt it more, but he too—— No, his thoughts were not often with Meares. Too often they also were with Sidley.

For Greene found himself vanquished by the personality of his new friend. The impressions of the first night, with all their vividness, had become fixed. His life had so far contained nothing even remotely like Sidley. He was wicked—Greene came to think he was desperately wicked—but he invested wickedness with a brightness and sparkle which made it exceedingly attractive. Partly this was because he was handsome as the devil, with a beauty of face and manner that challenged grossness and conquered it. His shape and movements were refined and dainty and yet clean of effeminacy; there was an elegance in the way he held his hands when idle. Partly it was because he was socially much Greene's superior, and wealthy with it. His father, Sir Ralph Sidley, owned several estates, the most important of them Braiding Hall, in Lincolnshire. "You see, Greene, we Sidleys have always taken all we could get, and being devoid of gratitude we have been able to keep it," he explained. He was a relative of Lord Charters', he had been to Court, he had been stroked on the head by the Queen and had dared pay a compliment that had been well received. These things disguise sin. Yet he was no puffed-up son of a fine family, afraid to sully his hand by offering it to the sons of tradesmen at College with him. Greene found out before Christmas that the Master had offered him better quarters with one of the doctors, who would also be pleased to help him with his studies; but this made no appeal to Sidley, who scorned doctors and allied himself with the wilder spirits whatever their status, men like Portington and Callimet and Grebe, like Greene too. A College, he told Greene, was like a ship; the members were like gentlemen-venturers, each equal till the end of the voyage, when most would draw better prize-money than he.

In Greene's eyes his experience was extraordinary. His brief statement that he had been a sailor he could expand considerably. As a small boy he had been with his father to Constantinople, and the year before he entered College he had sailed with Captain Henry Brace to the West Coast of Africa for negroes. Black women, he told Greene, were better than white in many ways. When he explained the ways Greene was chilled, but while he was thinking out a counter from his stay-at-home brain Sidley would snap his fingers and be describing the Golden Trade, and sometimes pull out of his bag a huge folded map of the world, decorated with sea serpents and whales, with lion-headed eagles and black men with spears, and, pointing to the left hind foot of an elephant whose tusks covered half a continent, say: "There we were, Greene. Just there;" and then Greene would forget the reply he had thought of and lie on his stomach over the map, following Sidley's finger as it slowly brought him back to England. Here they put in for water, here they took fifty strong blacks, here they landed for fresh meat, the mate died at this point, here he changed ship to Captain Jonathan Hamer's *Firefly* and sailed for Portsmouth: a thrilling chronicle. He had seen men flogged to death and guns fired in earnest. He had sent a challenge to a duel, but admitted it had never taken place. He had done so many of the things all young men wish to do, and some things besides. And now he was at the University to improve his knowledge of books, so that he would not loll his head when men around him talked of learned things. He had no model among the great figures of the age, but realised that when Walsingham, Raleigh, Cecil, Sidney, the Queen herself were proud to study, he would be a fool if he did otherwise.

To Coppinger he was evil incarnate. Neither had referred to the happenings of the first night of term but neither had forgotten. To Sidley every moment of Coppinger's return was still vivid: his opening the window and trying to settle the drunkards more comfortably, his hardly credible denunciation of him, Sidley, as Belial, his own unpremeditated answer, and Coppinger's collapse. Divinity, apparently, was stronger than strong drink. He had exerted all his strength to drag Coppinger to his bed, and then lay down himself, having extinguished the light. To Coppinger the event was less clear. Had he dreamed it all? Yet his conviction stayed with him. He found in Sidley an incarnation of the Antichrist, one who could never be brought to grace. He had come to the University as though to blight it. He was more frightening than the papists or episcopalians, for they were assailable with the weapons of argument and conversion, but this was like a fallen angel, forever exempt from mercy. Coppinger did not believe that he could ever change Sidley. He must fight against him, though, and soon he came to believe that the battleground was the soul of Robert Greene. Week after week, almost daily, he saw signs of change in Greene as he gave way more and more to Sidley's influence. He was already the Greene who had come up two years before, the Greene he had caused alter for the better. In thinking this he did not flatter himself. There was about Coppinger's daily life the beauty of an ideal pursued if not fully realised, and over a period of time he had made a powerful impression on the younger man. At first Greene had thought him a puritan like his father, therefore a hypocrite, therefore to be despised. To Greene, heady with success, his purity of life seemed merely stupid, the austere limits of his conversation prescribed by a sickly prudence, his willingness to help his fellows half sycophancy, half a means to ingratiation. But these views had to be modified and then abandoned. He came to see that the light by which Coppinger steered his course was no muddy, smoke-shot flare, but a clear beam irradiating every action, every thought of his. He offered help because he was generous, he was careful of speech because he chose never to be offensive, his life was well-regulated because he knew such a life pleased his maker. He was a man who had to subjugate no small intellectual pride, and never, even indirectly, did he show a hint of spiritual arrogance. What satisfaction he knew came from awareness of his own shortcomings. Greene would always remember the happiness of first using Coppinger's Christian name and knowing that he was accepted in full friendship. He came to discover that Coppinger was very human, that he was tried as sorely as any man, that the serenity he had attained so early was not unbroken. He admired him greatly, and loved him not a little.

Of this Coppinger was aware. Greene had become soberer in his conversation, less the roaring boy. He was maturer.

But now he feared a violent swing backwards. Greene's countenancing bawdy talk distressed him more than anything else. For women Coppinger felt neither the unnatural dislike of a man like Hadman nor the bleak indifference of Criddle, College products both, but rather he honoured them and felt that their accepted weakness, so severely censured by men, demanded tenderness and protection more than indiscriminate abuse. One day he might marry like his father before him, and refused to listen to those who preached that man's poor choice is ever to take to bed a Dalila, a Jezebel, or an Aholibah. For him there could be no happiness without reverence, no duration of love without a pure regard. He was repelled by a loose phrase, disgusted beyond measure by the language Sidley freely employed, and pained that Greene should continue to listen to him. He found small comfort in the circumstance that Greene's tongue so far was not used for a similar dissemination of filth. No man can touch pitch and remain undefiled. From listening to abetting, from abetting to imitation were short strides. He was fiercely indignant that money and leisure should produce a man of Sidley's stamp and then loose him in the College to corrupt young scholars. The books he had brought too? What were they but a collection of snares? The best of them were idle and uninstructive, the worst were sewers into which base men had spewed their foulness. An end in sweet strong flame was too good for them. It would smelt out their dross, while vile annihilation was their need. And the drinking? He was tempted to inform the Master of the wine brought into College by Sidley. This was a misdemeanour which opened the door to graver faults. "A liquorous mouth," he quoted unavailingly, "hath oft a lecherous tail." Strong wine was a mocker; and the drunkard mocked humanity out of his mouth. He was afraid for Greene.

He was not surprised to find Sidley little better than an atheist. He had seen him play with his rings during prayers in Chapel, and yawn without disguise in the middle of the

Fellow's homily. Of God's own word he knew no more than a facile memory and the frequent repetition of the services enabled him to catch without effort. The second day of term he had given a taste of his quality when roused at five o'clock. "Do we get up at this hour?" he asked. "It is too early, Coppinger. Why, I am afraid to show myself outside lest I come across God himself walking in the garden." Sometimes he intoned absurdities through his nose, as an insult to Coppinger's sect, and with an assumption of knowing what he talked about promised that Whitgift would yet eradicate the stupidity and false pride which set men against the Queen's own religion. Coppinger was infuriated by the lightness with which this young rake dismissed as wrong-headed and ridiculous questions over which he had racked his brain for years for a true answer.

"A Church is like a State, Coppinger. It can tolerate no insubordination. You are loyal or you are an enemy, and enemies must be destroyed. Eh, Greene, have I put it well?"

"Then under papist rule you would be a papist, would you?" It was Greene who put the question.

"My sovereign's faith is good enough for me," Sidley admitted.

"You have no conviction of right and wrong," Coppinger challenged him.

"I have. I think it wrong to go against my sovereign."

"Even though your sovereign does wrong?"

"My sovereign can do no wrong!"

"Then under Mary you would have persecuted the martyrs?"

"Under Mary I should have lighted a candle at your funeral pyre, Coppinger."

"Sidley, for God's sake don't say things you don't mean!" Greene interrupted with dismay.

"My good Robertus, of course I mean them. Have you ever known a man more eager for martyrdom than

Coppinger here? Is there an ounce of humility in him? Isn't his single heart a better guide than a bench of bishops? Doesn't he know more about Christ's own Church than Christ did? Does he admit the guidance of others? Not he! He must be the guide, he and his kind." He beat impatiently on his knee. "And a damned joyless kind they are!"

Sidley had a contempt for the martyrs, unredeemed even by admiration for their courage. To Coppinger the Protestant martyrs were an example and an inspiration. There seemed not a subject on which they could agree, and Greene was surprised that neither made a move to other quarters. But Coppinger would not go and leave him to Sidley, and Sidley, accepting the challenge, was satisfied to stay. Thus Greene felt the pull from both of them, and suffered between the irreconcilable alternatives of their examples. That Coppinger was really in the right—he could not doubt it; but increasingly he fell under Sidley's control. Coppinger saw the new manner settling on him like a garment, and to his mind not fitting him well. Not only were they roommates, but they were otherwise too much in company. When the nature of the lectures or examinations permitted they would be seated next to each other; frequently they walked together to and from Schools to the lectures of the University professors; and Sidley more than once went along to the public disputations to hear Greene take part in preparation for his degree. That he underwent little improvement at these was clear from his sharp comments afterwards. One day he startled Greene by declaring he did not expect to take a degree now that he knew the procedure. Learning made fools of men, he could see that ever more clearly; he was of the mind of those Goths who would not permit the burning of a library because the books would keep the men of the land dull and nerveless. All the Colleges were concerned with was a perpetuation of their own fatuities. The *Dialectics* of Ramus indeed! God curse Ramus for a hard-bound old fool! With sudden accessions of rage he ground his teeth to think that tutors who had never

set foot over their College doors should presume to instruct
and afterwards examine the man who had travelled past
Hercules' Pillars, seen the glowing colours of the inland
sea, and ventured his neck among the ebon men of Africa.
Within a couple of months he had established in Greene
the habit of calling at one of the inns, the Mitre, the Rose,
or the Dolphin, before they returned to College from the
afternoon disputations. "The best tutors in the University,
Robertus," he assured him, pulling out a cork. Drinking
here, they were often joined by Portington, who came from
outside Norwich, or the scandalous Callimet and Grebe,
or Pughe of Christ's, who would always maintain when
drunk that the Welsh were the oldest families in these
islands and therefore in the world, and that the English
were the merest over-night mushrooms with no growth
to guarantee their long lasting. Sidley explained his late
return one night: "I have been returning a sinner to
Christ's bosom. Where he now snoreth mightily." Coppinger
walked from the room, whereupon Sidley grinned at
Greene, who knew the brief misery of conflicting
loyalties.

"Why do what you can to annoy Coppinger, Sidley?"
he asked him once outright.

"I am not concerned with annoying Coppinger, Robertus.
I do what I do because it pleases me to do it. That is reason
enough. Coppinger can be delighted or aggrieved. Why
should I care?"

"But you do annoy him."

"Then more fool he to let me!" He frowned. "Breath
of Jesus, I am tired of this scholar's life already. I think
I'll go to America, Robertus."

"To-night?"

"Laugh if you like! What about running away together,
eh Robertus?"

They started to laugh, but Sidley looked more than half
in earnest. "I'll not come back next year. Coppinger shall
rule here undivided, and you can see how you like
that."

One day during the second half of term he told Greene of Coppinger's extraordinary conduct on the night of his arrival. "He shivered, Robertus, as though hell blew cold not hot, and fixed me with his eye. Over your precious body he confronted me—me, Belial!" He resorted to powerfully acted pantomime, glaring at his listener. "'And you are Michael,' I retorted from the bed here." He leapt like a cat on his bed, and crouched. "'Then I defy thee!' and down he goes like a stunned man." He grinned, but his face altered as he watched Greene. "Dost thou defy me too? Are all the fools in Cambridge here? Laugh, man, or I'll strike you! Laugh!" he almost screamed. "Laugh, damn you, laugh!" His expression was that of a fiend for a moment, and then he leaned back twisting his lips to a smile. Greene had felt horror as the story came to its climax, and he must have shown this. "Poor Edmund," he muttered. "Sidley, you frighten me at times."

"It will be good for your soul," Sidley jeered. "Otherwise what is hell for?"

"More than to frighten us, Sidley, I do believe."

"To make fools of us," Sidley retorted. "So that we'll go on our knees and whine the few years we get given us, and grow old men before we've been young ones." He wiped sweat from his forehead. "We'll have some wine, Robertus."

He expounded to Greene at times a fragmentary philosophy. It was simple and selfish, nor could Greene with all his admiration be blind to its immorality. If Sidley wanted and was able to do a thing, he did it. The consequences to himself he was willing to risk, the consequences to others were not for him to worry about. He was himself—the sun and moon shone for him, the sea was made for his pleasure, the fruits of the earth for his convenience. With what had gone before him he was unconcerned, unless in some way it touched his interests; and he was contemptuous of what might come after. "Once we are dead, Robertus, what does it matter? Let the world get better or worse, we shall not be here to know."

"But reputation, Sidley—to leave a sweet name behind?"

"You'll know nothing of it, Robertus. Why worry yourself? St. Francis and Heliogabalus—is one at this moment better off than the other?"

"I should say the saint is."

"And the other is in hell, eh?"

"Had I lived a life like his, I should expect hell certainly."

Sidley laughed. "Don't be afraid of hell, Robertus. There are some very good fellows there by all accounts. I look forward to meeting them."

When Greene retorted that such opinions must lead to a wasted life and eventual misery, he could retort that so far his life had been preferable to Greene's. "I have done those things, Robertus, that you are still reading about. Which is the better course? While you have been home-staying, I have been overseas, sailing each bloodshot day towards the night of Africa; I have looked on marvellous life and death, on strange beasts; I have eaten foods of excelling richness and revolting foulness, I have drunk wine to float me to Elysium and water in which maggots crawled; I have set foot on three continents. Which is the better?" He would not allow Greene to answer. "Wake up to a new world, Robertus. The old one is dying under us. Why, the new century is in sight! Men look forward now, not back. It isn't what Ramus says—that abominable hell-destined dialectician! Pay no attention to him and his like—rest on the strength of your own mind and thrust forward from there. Ambition, Robertus! Ambition! You must become more than a country priest or piddling pedagogue. I tell you, Robertus, before I would end my days after such a fashion, I'd crawl on my hands and knees to London and beg crusts in the kennel." Over different hours he elaborated these matters, and Greene knew his counters weak.

A few days before the end of term, stung by Sidley's taking it for granted he had never done anything out of the ordinary, he told him that he too had had a paramour. This was after Sidley, sitting back in his favourite corner, had read to him the beauty of Olympia, from Ariosto's Eleventh Canto, waving his hand to illustrate his lines. "Another of the world's riches you and Coppinger miss, Robertus." But this he would not accept. He spoke of Neaera, allowed himself consummation. Actually Sidley thought him a liar, but even so used the episode for instruction, commending him for his spirit, pointing out the dear joys of naughtiness, quoting Machiavelli, urging him to greater exploits. He proceeded to make Greene wriggle with the coarseness of his chaff, yet, for the first time able to pretend himself an equal in experience, Greene found no little pleasure in it.

So the first term wore to an end, a period of stress and change for Greene, but one not without its gains. His usual studies were followed with less than usual diligence, but he went a long way towards proficiency in Italian reading and began to accumulate knowledge of a kind never specifically included in a College course. He was beginning to see for himself that art and letters had not died with the first century, and that as there were brave men before Agamemnon so there were great poets after Juvenal. So far he drew no conclusions from this, however. He was content to read Sidley's books and Meares' Ariosto, which seemed now to have become his own. In the Schools his nimble wits and quick invention were enough to save him from disaster.

Yet already the graver sort throughout the College had reason for alarm that the new Master, while no bigot, for which they were thankful, was also no disciplinarian. The College was rowdier, there were interruptions to the studies and gossip of the doctors, undergraduates spoke English openly before their seniors. Portington was fined for keeping a dog in his room, and Criddle was terrified one night when he got into bed with a capful of mice. The sensitive lamented that it was learning's end. Eggerton said to Coppinger a few days before term ended: "Was it not, after all, better under Still?"

CHAPTER VII

DURING THE SECOND term Greene became better
acquainted with Harrison, the former envoy to Cathay
and present Fellow. This was more than it seemed, for to
be admitted to even part friendship with Harrison was
something of a triumph. He was a far from jovial man,
and the only member of the College, apart from the Master,
to have a room to himself. Sidley was near the mark when
he described him as a rook—he had the right-shaped
head and the right-coloured habit, he had the right kind
of eye. When he wished he had the right kind of voice
too. He was a dry man. He appeared to wait on what
you had to say—that he might tear at it. But he had the
smells of Tartary in the sleeves of his gown, and it
was an honour for Greene to meet him on other than
lecturing terms.

It happened when Sidley broke a bottle under unusual
circumstances at the Mitre. It was after a dreary lecture
of Criddle's that Greene, Portington and Pughe returned
there to meet Sidley and wash divinity out of their throats.
They found the inn crowded, not only with University
men. Sidley was seated with Callimet and greeted them with
banter for their industry. Near him, to the right of the
green-glassed window, was a group of five men, loud-
voiced and confident drinkers, whom Greene imagined to
be followers of one of the lesser lords at Court, from the
badges sewn in their caps and scraps of their talk. "Drawer!"
cried Sidley. "Your office here!" The strangers ordered
beer at the same time, and when it came, their leader, a
thick-set, fair-headed man, stood up and shouted: "A
health to the Queen!" Everyone in the parlour stood too
and did honour to the toast, and a cheer followed it.
"Drawer!" shouted Fairhead; "drink for everyone for a
toast to Sir John Hart!" Greene asked Sidley who Sir

John Hart might be. "Some foolish gentleman with foolish followers," was the reply he got. "Do as I do." He called out to the drawer at the strangers' table: "Your dearest and best wine here to drink Sir John Hart's health."

At this Fairhead stood up again. "And who are you to give orders in the matter?"

Sidley answered coolly: "An admirer of Sir John's."

"I am glad to hear it. Drawer—beer for this gentleman."

"Wine, and the best of it. With a touch of spice. You know my way, drawer."

The drawer hesitated between the orders. Fairhead grew very red when Sidley added: "And wine for every gentleman here to drink Sir John's good health. The best wine in the house."

At this Fairhead came round the table. The chatter had ceased. All eyes were on the two of them. With a jerk of his arm Fairhead brought his companions to their feet. "Harry," he ordered one of them, "your mug of beer!" Harry fetched it. "Now," he said, setting it down on the table in front of Sidley, "we will see you drink a health all on your own."

Sidley was as white as death. "You will?"

Fairhead tapped his sword. "We will."

Sidley bent forward towards the pot, but instead of taking it up his fingers closed on the neck of a half-emptied bottle. "Give me the use of a sword and we can settle the quarrel now."

"You drink your beer. We'll talk about swords later."

Smash! Sidley had swung the bottle against the edge of the table, and now drew back with the neck-half a dagger in his hand. From the side Greene watched his foot hook under the table. He stood up himself, as did Pughe, though with no idea of what to do. "Come a foot nearer," snarled Sidley, "and by God I'll drive this through your eyes!"

Fairhead was screwing his face up as though to laugh, but Greene saw his thin-slitted eyes calculating the throw of the table rather than any danger from the bottle. "Well, here's a young hot-head, God bless my soul." He changed front. "All right, my lad, I'm not the one to hurt a brave youngster. You shall have your wine. Drawer—the best wine for this young gentleman!" He turned to wink at his companions. "I'll drink the beer myself." He picked up the pot. "Your health, my handsome sir!" Then with the quickness of sight he threw the pot into Sidley's face and dived over the table at his right arm. Sidley cried out as he twisted it down and back, and the bottle clanked to the floor near Greene's foot. In a moment Greene's hands were at Fairhead's throat, when he found a sword-point pricking his ribs.

It was then Harrison made his voice heard. Greene saw him coming towards them from the doorway. "Master Sidley! Master Greene! All you gentlemen of the University!" Fairhead was loosening his grip. "And you, John Hunter——"

Fairhead drew off from Sidley. "You, sir!"

"Draw off your men."

The fair-headed Hunter gave an order, and then: "I am glad to see your Excellency," he said. "Just a little fun here, nothing more. I didn't know your Excellency was at the University."

Apologetically, he tried to dust down Sidley's clothes, but Sidley struck his hand. "No malice, young gentleman."

Harrison had sent for the landlord, who had been out of danger in the cellar. He now had the room cleared of all save Sidley's and Hunter's parties. "What happened here?"

"A minute or two's sport, that is all, your Excellency. You know me too well——"

"I do. Master Sidley—your account of it?"

"There is no harm done, sir."

"Thanks to me. Your account of it?"

"It was nothing, your Excellency. Just a word or two from young spitfire here——"

"Did I ask you, Hunter?"

"I have a clear mind, your Excellency. You could not do better than ask me.'

Soon Harrison had heard enough. "You know, Hunter, to what penalty you are liable for brawling in this town?"

"Not brawling, your Excellency! Just drinking a health to my master. Why, I'd have followed it with a health to you! I don't forget the old times."

Said Harrison drily: "Sometimes the old times forget you. I advise you never to rely on them." He spoke to Pughe. "I shall see that news of you goes to your College. You other four gentlemen return to College where I will see you this evening. If there are any good-byes," he hinted, "they must be said now, for Sir John's men will be out-side the town in half-an-hour and I doubt they will ever return."

Hunter opened his eyes. There was to be no punishment then? "No offence, young sir," he suggested to Sidley. "I'll stand you friend next time."

"I do not need your friendship, fellow!"

"As you please." He laughed. "Then we shall never split another bottle together."

But Sidley did not laugh with him and the students left the inn. They parted company with Pughe, and talked excitedly all the way back, and if anything Greene admired Sidley still more for his courage.

After supper they were summoned by Harrison to the Master's room, to hear what had been decided for them. Less than any of them Sidley had reason for confidence, for it was his second visit to Howland in disgrace, but there was no reference to past exploits, just a brief summary by Howland of what Harrison had reported to him, an invi-tation to speak in their own defence which none of them accepted, a short reproof, and the announcement of sentence. The Master had decided there was no need of a flogging—Sidley started like a horse—and they would be confined to the College for the rest of the term. The Master made it clear that he expected a better standard of conduct in return for leniency. They might go. Go they did, back to Greene's room where they found Coppinger anxious to know what had happened. He was distressed to see with what bravado Greene now carried off the whole thing, as though he had added to his manhood by a clash with the authorities. He expected Portington and Callimet to talk like fools and Sidley like a knave, but he was sorry to find Greene as foolish and vicious. Sidley, to annoy him, declared the only thing that troubled him was how they could get plenty to drink into College, and Callimet grew young-man-bawdy about the girl who would have to manage without him. Portington thought she would find someone to console her, and Sidley, watching Coppinger, went on to make generalisations about the faithlessness and lasciviousness of the sex. "Eh, Robertus?" he concluded.

"Think before you answer, Robert," Coppinger interrupted.

"Well, Edmund, there is no denying the evidence of experience."

"One man's experience is a tiny drop in a very great ocean, Robert. We ought not to forget that only the weak, the vicious, and the liars talk so glibly about their experience, as you call it. The rest of us have some regard for our mothers, our sisters, and some men their wives. I ask you to think before you answer, that is all, Robert."

Greene felt, as so often with Coppinger, that brief pull of what he felt to be right against what Sidley and his kind would applaud him for believing. "But you puritans are the worst of all, Edmund—the hottest poker from hell could not burn more against women."

"Some of us, yes. But not the best of us."

"The best of you," said Sidley, "like women as well as other men, eh?" Callimet and Portington joined in his laugh. "Are you one of the best?"

Coppinger coloured. "I sometimes think, Sidley, there is a greater devil in you than you know of." He turned his

back on them, as though to rummage on his shelf. Sidley
pulled down the corners of his mouth, assuming a ridiculous
mock-serious expression, at which two of his companions
guffawed. "The gospel according to St. Edmund," he
gibed.

Greene was relieved of his embarrassment by a summons
to the culprits to attend on Harrison. He was the last
from the room. "I'll see you later, Edmund," he said.
"You must not mind Sidley. He does not mean one half of
what he says."

"That half will see him to hell." He picked up a book.
"Come back without the others. I shall be reading."

"If I can." He smiled at him and went out, closing the
door behind him. He shook his head in the corridor,
hurrying after the others. He was almost irritated that
Edmund should be right and Sidley fascinating. And like
the others he was wondering what Harrison would have to
say to them.

He received them with less austerity than they were
expecting, and made no attempt to read a moral into the
happenings of the afternoon. For a while Greene took no
part in the conversation; he listened while Sidley, more
especially, and Harrison discovered they had acquaintance
in common. He was not without envy as names with titles
were tossed into the air like balls. "Ah yes," said Harrison,
"this Sir John Hart—a north-countryman lately gone to
Court, so he must needs have his followers to scuffle and
dispute the wall with the followers of other knights lately
gone to Court. Perhaps later, gentlemen, you will find
your own amusement in such persons—if you have not to
bear their wrongs."

"You knew this Hunter, sir?" Portington suggested
respectfully.

"Some years ago, yes." Greene was interested to see
this cold, reserved man prepared to talk. He wondered.
Had the meeting with Hunter brought back the old life?
Made him restive? "He was with me on my voyage to
Cathay."

"Cathay, sir!" It was a flattering echo from Sidley and Callimet—discreetly questioning, quick with interest.

Harrison waved his hand. "No other place." They thought he would speak of it, but he went on: "This John Hunter. You should have made friends with him, Master Sidley. He is not beneath your notice."

"He did his best to make me look a young fool."

"At my age you come to think there are less becoming combinations than youth and folly. He told me all about it once again when you had gone. He was too clever for you—admit it."

"He took an advantage. I thought him honest if stupid."

"He is neither, Master Sidley. He is a very cunning, greedy soldier of fortune, with a pretty use of brute force and stratagem. He would be a good dog at your heels when you yourself go up to London." He began to question the young men what they would do in the future. Portington and Callimet knew. Their lives were shaped for them. "And you, Master Greene?"

"I must get to London."

"You have friends there?"

Greene shook his head. "I must hope for employment."

"With a great man?"

"If I am fortunate."

Harrison studied Greene for a moment before replying. "Then let me say nothing to discourage you."

"I have no choice, sir."

"Hm. Your father—what is he?"

"A saddler." Greene felt ashamed to admit it, though Portington and Sidley knew as much already.

"A useful trade. I advise you to learn it, Master Greene. Leather is a durable thing, and it's a poor pair of shoes contains none of it."

Uncertain whether this was a compliment or an insult, Greene said slowly that he did not wish to spend his life in Norwich.

"Why not? You think it better to be the hanger-on of

some rich clown in London than your own master in Norwich?" Harrison watched him sharply before addressing the four of them. "This is the new vice of the age: that young men must get to London. Those with land come up with fifty acres on their backs, and a field for each shoe; those without land gape for gold and sustenance. Of rich and poor one man's head is as empty as his neighbour's belly. And fate bangs both like drums." He smiled sourly. "You had better believe me."

"But a useful life there?" said Sidley.

"There is no such thing."

"But why not, sir?"

"Because men go to Court to flatter and cozen. They go that they may advance themselves, that they may stand on other men's heads, and live more like a lady's glove than a bright sword."

"And if they stay in Colleges?" asked Callimet.

"They are less to blame. Unless they are such whose whoremaster is a page of syntax, whose tyrant a sentence of Buchanan. Or those who lead the apes of ignorance to the hell of pedantry."

"Such apes——"

"As yourselves," Harrison concluded roughly.

"What I have always said," Sidley agreed. "Three parts of learning is folly."

"Are you acquainted with so much of it you can hazard a guess?"

"I judge by what I know, sir."

"Hmph!" said Harrison. He turned to Greene. "Your room-mate is Edmund Coppinger, is he not?"

"And Ralph Sidley."

"Then I see you between two fires. You must be well toasted!"

Greene laughingly admitted that he was.

"And which is the hotter?"

"I think Sidley nearer the devil, sir."

"And therefore you frequent him. You see, gentlemen, the way of this world?" He said words that might have been Greene's own an hour earlier. "Attractive wickedness will always carry it over dull virtue. If only we could make virtue bright and wickedness as dull as it is stupid, we should have paradise on earth."

Soon after this they left him, Greene returning to his own room, the other three to Callimet's. Greene was glad Sidley was not returning with him. He had not treated Edmund as he should, and would be glad of a talk with him. He found him still reading.

"Well, Edmund."

"Well, Robert." He set his work aside. "You have come off safely from the rook?"

"Well enough. I don't want you to think I was against you in the talk we had here earlier. I wish to heaven Sidley would mind his business more where you are concerned."

Coppinger smiled. "Don't think I take him at more than his true worth. Will you refuse a piece of advice, Robert?"

"I should welcome it, Edmund."

"You must think of me as a fabulously young grandfather, always offering advice which you invariably ignore. The Master was generous, don't you think?"

"It might have been worse."

"You might have been flogged, Robert. You have seen floggings in hall. Can you imagine yourself in the position?"

"Hardly."

"Robert, you will be."

"I think not."

"Criddle has been here this evening. He has been telling me. Howland is both merciful and slack, but you will not go free of a beating next time. Nor will Sidley."

"Sidley will never allow himself to be flogged!"

"Better men than he have been—in this same hall. Don't deceive yourself, Robert. You think I want to break you of his company. Well, I do, but at the moment I am thinking of your pride and self-esteem. A flogging for a man your age is not quickly forgotten by others or the recipient." He almost pleaded with Greene. "Stop drinking so heavily, Robert. That is the root of your evil."

"I am not a boy, Edmund!"

"There are better proofs of manliness than getting drunk. Sidley is talking of getting wine into the College although you are gated——"

"Well?"

"I won't have it in this room."

"But, Edmund——"

"Think what you like. I will not have it in this room. It may be better if you tell Sidley so, but I mean it and shall not hesitate to tell him so myself. If you must drink, then drink elsewhere."

"But if he persists in bringing it in?"

"I shall tell the Master."

"You would not do a thing like that?"

"I hope you won't put me to the proof." He frowned. "You know my views. You know that the room is as much mine as anybody's. You know the College rules. I will not be an abettor."

"I didn't think we'd be talking like this, Edmund."

"It is best we should. What would happen if Criddle or Eggerton called here for me one night?"

Greene shrugged his shoulders. "Here is Sidley. You had better tell him."

"Tell me what? That you disapprove of me, Coppinger?"

"That if you bring wine into this room again, I shall report it to the Master."

"And get Robertus and me into trouble?"

"You will get yourselves into trouble."

Sidley turned away to his bed, whistling. "Well?" Greene asked.

"Well what, Robertus?"

"What do you say to that, Sidley?"

Sidley stretched himself. "That the wine will be here on Thursday. That is all."

They began to undress in silence.

But Sidley did not get to Thursday of the week without further trouble. He was talking with half-a-dozen others when Criddle passed on his way to see Eggerton. The tutor was past them ten yards when a very well-managed hog-like grunt came from the group behind him. He thought to turn, but controlled himself, until two more grunts and some laughter convinced him he was the victim of clowning. Turn or go on? His vanity if not his courage came to help him. He turned and walked back to the group.

"Who made that ridiculous noise?"

Sidley eyed him contemptuously. "I cleared my throat," he admitted insolently.

"Follow me to the Master, please."

"And why?"

"Because I tell you to!"

"But why do you tell me to?"

Criddle opened his arms as he turned to the others. "You will remember this, please. Master Sidley, will you follow me?"

"You don't take me to the Master for clearing my throat, do you?"

"I take you to the Master for impertinence."

Sidley appeared to humour a madman. "Then I shall be delighted to come." He too opened his arms in mockery of Criddle's gesture. "You will remember this, please." Portington and Callimet made no attempt to hide their grins. "You too, Masters Portington and Callimet, will follow me." Criddle looked around him, enraged. "You will all follow me to the Master!" "Certainly we will." The procession went on its way, commented on gleefully by all who saw it.

The Master was not too sympathetic. He realised the absurdity of marching seven men before him, whose offence it was so impossible to prove. Listening to the confederates' account of what had happened he felt irritation and helplessness. He lacked the ruthlessness which would have met the situation with punishment just or unjust but at any rate salutary. He was obliged to dismiss the seven with a severe lecture on the evils of wasting their time in idle gossip and of so conducting themselves that they laid themselves open to such reproaches as Criddle's. And then he had to placate Criddle and reason with him because there had been no flogging. Sidley, Portington and Callimet, however, he kept in mind. If they came before him again, he would make an example of them before the whole College.

Sidley did not carry out his threat to obtain wine by Thursday. Maybe his second visit to the Master taught him the wisdom of caution. More likely, he found it no such easy matter now that Portington and Callimet, who with Greene would be most willing to oblige him, were prisoners like himself. He had to be content with College fare, and did not pretend to like it. But when he must, he oftentimes told Greene, he could live hard with the next man. Coppinger even, he sneered.

"You think he would tell the Master?"

"I know he would."

"To disgrace me, yes; but you, a friend?"

"His principles——"

"To hell with them!"

"But he believes——"

"There was never a rogue yet who couldn't justify his roguery. A damned convenient set of principles I call it which allow a man to have his own way. He is like the rest of the canters."

They paid other visits to Harrison, and on one occasion Coppinger was invited. But he and his host were none too friendly. Coppinger's independence of opinion this one night made him appear awkward and too assertive; his manner contrasted badly with Sidley's, who could flatter

Harrison's past without derogation of his present lack of
state. When the younger man spoke of his own travels to
Constantinople and West Africa, it was always in a way
to assure listeners that these were trifles compared with the
elder's mighty journeyings; yellow held it over black; the
Grand Turk was a zany to Prester John; the Great Alexander nowhere showed his greatness more than by going
East not South.

"You saw Prester John?" asked Coppinger.

Harrison looked down his long nose. "Sir John de
Mandeville wrote of him two hundred and fifty years ago.
He could hardly expect such long life."

"You saw his kingdom?"

"I saw many marvels, but not that."

"But you think there is such a kingdom?"

Before Harrison could answer, Sidley interrupted: "I
have spoken with sailors who saw his court, sir. Honest
men, too." Harrison laughed. "Then you convince Master
Coppinger at your leisure."

Without offence Sidley announced that Coppinger would
never be convinced.

In one way Greene's being confined to College was an
advantage. He turned to his set studies for want of better
to do and worked hard in readiness for his examination in
the summer. Grammar and rhetoric lay behind him, logic
around him; his bracing foes were Boethius and Aristotle.
He was attending lectures in philosophy with Moulton,
in logic with Criddle—these last a trial. As a rhyming exercise and an aid to memory he was turning key passages
from the *Topica* into hexameters, and Criddle's accidental
discovery of this convinced him he had a more than usually
promising disciple. Greene made afresh the comforting
discovery that there is no subject so dull industry cannot
make it endurable, and that learning, however crabbed
and angular, cannot be entirely without charm. He told
Coppinger these thoughts, and Coppinger agreed with
them; he told them to Sidley who listened with
pretended dismay and then rebutted them. He read till

the rims of his eyes were sore and Sidley called him a spider.

So, uneventfully, the term came to an end, and the four offenders received again the common privileges of under-graduates. They celebrated their freedom by making straight for the Mitre, where Sidley greeted acquaintances with masterful hilarity. Pughe was there, likewise free of durance, and for delight cursing frequently in his own language. Before the afternoon was out he had taught Sidley a dozen obscenities in Welsh and Sidley had made trial of them on the unblushing maidservants amidst howls of laughter. It ended with Pughe and Sidley going upstairs at the Mitre and Callimet going off to find the trades-man's daughter he hoped had not forgotten him; but Greene and Portington kept each other company back to College.

Coppinger was reading in their room, so Portington soon went off and left the room-mates together. Greene was slightly tipsy, but Coppinger made no remark about it.

"You were glad to get outside the gates again?"

"Need a man ask!"

"We lose the good of life in monk's or felon's cell, Robert. You left Sidley drinking?"

"With Mistress Joan, and Pughe with Mistress Jane."

Coppinger put one book on top of another. "You did not want to stay?"

"Not particularly."

"Your deeds are not so bad as your words, Robert."

"Perhaps not. Can I ask you a question?"

"I think you may."

"Have you ever been in love, Edmund?"

Coppinger coloured a little. "And why should you want to know that?"

"Not altogether an idle curiosity."

"No, I have not then."

"You know what Criddle thinks of women?"

"I think he is wrong."

"You know what Sidley professes to think of them?"

"I despise him from the bottom of my heart. He is in danger of confusing his own mother and sister with the degraded creatures he degrades still further. Would you take him to your own home, Robert?"

"He's not a leper. I don't think I need be afraid to."

"I should not take him into mine. You have not been in love either, Robert?"

"Desperately." He laughed at Coppinger's gesture. "With a woman twice my age, for many months together." He went on to talk about Mistress Petherill, and was perturbed to find the sweetness of calf-love still in his mind. He liked to think himself too old for idealism, too experienced. For his own amusement he jested at himself. "To have touched her hand, Edmund, would have been reward enough for a thousand toils and troubles. And she the mistress of old Goring all the time! Does it make you laugh?"

Coppinger shook his head. "You had more from her than Goring did, can't you see that? Goring had what Sidley has paid for this afternoon. You had the opening of a world."

"I think I should be willing to change places."

"I think you would not. Unless I am much mistaken, Robert, neither you nor I would." He changed the subject. "You think your mother will have no difficulty in bringing this other Greene into the world?"

"We are going to be a most damnably sorted family, Edmund, I can see that. Alice in '56, myself in '58, young Tobias in '61, God rest his soul. And now after fifteen years a sister Anne last year and a sister or brother to come this June. Alice and I shall look like this new generation's parents. I want to go home this summer to see them."

"You should be able to. Howland is easy-going enough to give you leave. A strange thing—I have heard you talking of your family for three years now till I feel I know them."

"They would be delighted to see you in Norwich. Why don't you come?"

Coppinger laughed, shaking his head. "But some time I hope to, never fear." He stood up. "I promised to see Eggerton. By the way, those verses of yours from Guazzo—they are good."

Greene was eager. "You liked them?"

"You have a talent for hexameters. Even Criddle thinks so."

"And he is the worst judge you could meet on a long journey. Well, you go to Eggerton and I'll look out of the window!"

He was still there with his verses when Sidley returned. He assured Greene he was tired and had reason to be. The reason he elaborated till Greene felt jealous and uncomfortable and in a way angry. He stretched himself on his bed, face to the wall, and for once Greene found him graceless and slack. He went on looking out of the window, thinking of the eternal struggle between light and dark, good and bad, the strong and never quite equal pull of irreconcilables. Life and love! Erotic images fought in his mind with a thrilling idealism, the sharp pricks of sensation with the wonder and glory and beauty of love. With his feet clogged in mud, yet he stretched out his hands with the platonists. He longed for a perfect mistress, the phoenix of her sex, the pearl of the echoing world. Before her he would kneel for ever, and pass from knowledge of her physical perfection to an apprehension of universal, of heavenly, beauty; advance to the contemplation of it and finally to complete union. Beside these panoramas of sun-cloud glory, carnality was muddy. He wanted to snatch at pen and paper and write for eternity a poem of true values. For a moment again he gave himself to abnegation and wonder, and then the devil sent up new battalions. This Mistress Joan now—he shook his head. As Sidley had said—— He saw Sidley asleep and shook his head over him too. There must be some delight in lust he had not yet found. And yet it was not lust he wanted, but worship. Mistress Petherill not Mistress Joan—before either a palpable divinity. He wished he were a prince of men, a king, that he might find this treasure. Sacrifice, he said, was the way of love. Not greedy possession. That was for others, not him.

One week went by like another until June. On the tenth of that month George Crashfield of Norwich called on Greene to tell him his mother had been brought to bed of a boy, who was to be called Tobias after the boy who died. He was a fine boy too, well-mannered before, during, and after his arrival. In addition Crashfield brought messages from every member of the family except one-year-old Anne, and hopes that Greene would proceed bachelor of arts that month. Greene could see Crashfield found absurd this rapid and late increase of family, but thanked him courteously and sent back news he hoped to be with them for part of the summer. Then he hurried back to College to tell the news to those who ought to hear it.

He met Coppinger at the gates and told him humorously that he had a young brother. Coppinger congratulated him on that and the safety of his mother, and they went indoors together, to where Sidley was aslant on his bed reading Machiavelli. Greene was wondering what his reception would be, but he met the situation magnificently, with well-chosen sentiments and no hint of a joke. Then he turned to Coppinger with a courtesy he did not often show him. "You may disagree, Coppinger, but I think the occasion ought not to pass without its ceremony. I should like us to drink to the safe arrival of Tobias Greene." "And so should I!" said Greene enthusiastically; "Come on, Edmund, you'll drink too!" Coppinger was smiling. "I shall be happy to. We can get some beer from Hall for this, I know." "Beer? It does not fit the occasion." Sidley rummaged under his bed. "I have here one bottle and no more of the choicest rhenish in this city. Will you drink?" "Do, Edmund!" Greene begged.

He nodded.

"Then what about fetching Portington? He is from Norwich. He would like to join in, I'm sure."

Sidley took the mission on himself. "I am glad you agreed

to this, Edmund," Greene said warmly once he had gone. "I know it is the only bottle."

Portington arrived, generous with good wishes and eager for a drink. "On this occasion, Greene, the heart of every Norwich man beats high with hope that the new Greene will be still more promising than his brother. Don't spill it, Sidley, there's a good fellow!" He took his glass.

"Well, Greene, it is your toast."

"The boy and his mother!"

They emptied the glasses. "I can only hope, Greene— speaking as one son of Norwich to another—that there may be more ceremonies of this nature, and that I may be always invited to assist at them."

"Then you should start a family of your own, Portington." The son of Norwich winked.

Sidley suggested that they go out to celebrate, but Greene made excuses. So Portington and Sidley went off, leaving the other two to their reading. Twice Greene broke the silence: to ask Coppinger when he should ask the Master for permission to visit his home, and to express doubt over his chance of success at his forthcoming disputations. The first time Coppinger told him to act at once, the second time he asserted he could not fail. "Could Criddle be severe with the man who versifies Boethius?"

Fifteen minutes before supper he left to see Criddle, telling Greene he would be with him till bed time. It was lucky he left then, for five minutes later Sidley came in with four bottles of wine under his gown and hid them in his bed. He had been drinking, though not immoderately, and heard with satisfaction that Coppinger would not be back after supper. "We'll drink another glass to that brother of yours," he promised. "We'll ask Portington and Callimet in for the evening."

"You are not afraid of what Edmund may do?"

Sidley looked at Greene as though he had not rightly heard him. "Afraid of Coppinger? You choose your words poorly, Robertus."

"I meant rather, afraid of the consequences of what he may do?"

"In the first place he won't know. In the second, not even Coppinger and his principles could object to a proper observance of what must be a unique experience for Tobias Greene. I can only say you are not treating him at all well, Robertus. Let's go and have what they call supper here."

Coppinger enjoyed his evening. The Pelagian heresy, though a little mouldy to more finicky tastes, was a substantial joint for supper; and with Eggerton in particular he took a good cut off John Cassian. When the argument slackened, Hadman by a daring flight of fancy derived the name Pelagius from the Welsh Morgan; and Harrison, having established that *stink* and *stench*, *blink* and *blench* were the same words, drily suggested an analogy of *wink* with *wench*. The hit spread to the lower table and was greeted as a philological gem by those who argued from cause to effect. Bremer proved to his own satisfaction that the quince was so called because it was the fifth fruit to be tasted by Adam, and this brought them back to original sin and Pelagius. Then, after a grace which did not curse the puritans, he went off to Criddle's rooms, and Eggerton too, and they argued freely but without heat over the precise meaning of Aristotle's *perepetaia*, the numbers and orders of angels, Grindal's chances of survival, Gabriel Harvey's views on English versification, and whether beauty is in the beheld or the beholder. No one of them changed an opinion, but all were satisfied. The time passed quickly to near ten o'clock. It was then Criddle reminded Coppinger he had promised to return that day to the College librarian the folio Martianus Capella he himself needed, and put an end to Coppinger's apologies by offering to come and get it from his room. Coppinger would have preferred some other arrangement, but there seemed no real reason for demurring, and after good nights from Eggerton they went on their errand. That was the end of Coppinger's enjoyment for some time.

He opened the door of his room after one quiet knock, and the smell of wine hung on his face like September cobwebs. He heard Criddle's sharp sniff, wanted to draw back but could not, and Criddle was looking over his shoulder and pushing at his back to miss nothing. Sidley and Greene were very comfortable indeed. Each was lying on his bed with wine to hand, and from the half sentence Coppinger heard were conversing with the ingratiating wisdom of the decently drunk. Sidley indeed seemed not at all perturbed by their intrusion. He kept his position, looking at them with equal affability and dullness; but Greene was wider awake to what Criddle's presence must mean. "Ha!" said Criddle—a gasping, satisfied, can-I-believe-my-eyes "Ha!" "'S Coppinger," said Sidley. "Come in, Coppinger. We are in need of wisdom!"

"Ha!" said Criddle again.

"Criddle!" said Sidley. "Criddle, Criddle, Give him wine and make him piddle." He ran his fingers round his pointed jaws. "Poetry, Robertus. You try some."

But nothing urged Greene to poetic composition. He had struggled to his feet, was standing awkwardly, and had neither verse nor immediately intelligible prose at command.

"Wine," said Criddle, advancing into the room and picking up the bottle nearest Greene. "You see, Coppinger?"

Coppinger saw more than the wine. He saw the bewildered fright of Greene, the goosish affability of Sidley, the ridiculousness of Criddle, now with right on his side and his enemy on the hip. He heard him say: "You are a witness, Coppinger. We must fetch the Master."

"No," cried Greene. "No, no. Don't fetch the Master!"

"Master?" echoed Sidley. "Master, Master, fetch him faster!" He chuckled at his versatility in rhyme.

"You stay here, Coppinger."

Criddle hurried off, for justice without charity. "Get a grip on yourself, for God's sake, Sidley!" begged Coppinger. The drunkard waved his hand. "You fool! You poor, pitiable fool! Can't you see the plight you are in?"

"Plight?" said Sidley; "Worse my plight is, better the fight is. Family motto, eh Robertus?" He uttered a series of staccato hiccoughs.

Coppinger turned impatiently to Greene. "Robert——" There seemed nothing useful he could say, and he sat down by the door with his head resting between his hands. "You are too late," was all he said as Greene, sick-looking but almost sobered, thrust two bottles into hiding behind the books.

"What will happen, Edmund?"

Footsteps were coming hurriedly towards the door. There was no need to answer. Coppinger got to his feet as the Master entered, followed by Criddle, indecently hasty with superfluous explanations, Clayton and Gray. Greene hung his head with shame and fright, but Sidley remained un-abashed. He would have drunk from the neck of his bottle had not the outraged Criddle snatched it from him. This roused him slightly and he told Criddle he was a rude fellow who deserved whipping.

"That will do, sir!" said Howland.

"You heard him?" This was Criddle appealing to Clayton and Gray. "Has there ever been——"

Howland cut him short. "You know who I am?"

"No," said Sidley. "Who?"

Greene attempted to excuse himself. "Reverend Master— a brother was born to me two days ago. We were drinking his health. We heard to-day."

"You too are drunk, sir!"

Greene swallowed. He felt too ill to be bothered with the need for clear thinking and waited miserably on the event. Howland saw that the bottles and glasses were collected, and prepared to withdraw with the tutors, leaving the room and its inmates in charge of Coppinger. "I am heartily sorry, Master Coppinger, you have been put off with such room-mates. We shall look for an improve-ment." A thought came to Howland. "This is not the first time, perhaps? Hm. You need not answer, Master

Coppinger.'' Criddle started at that. That Coppinger should shelter such rascals! "Good night, Master Coppinger.''

When the room was cleared, Greene threw himself on his bed. Disputations a month ahead, his bachelor's degree, his hopes of a triumphal visit home—and this. And sick as a dog into the bargain! If a man could only conquer circumstance by forgetting it! He groaned aloud. Coppinger was attempting some rough comfort when there was another tap at the door. It was Criddle. He summoned Coppinger outside. "Flogging," he whispered gleefully; "flogging in Hall at three on Saturday. I am glad Howland is roused at last. Clayton counselled it, and I was happy to support him." He looked reprovingly at Coppinger. "You should not shelter iniquity, you know. A sterner morality, Coppinger—it's the need of the age. I thought you would be glad to hear." Coppinger gave him a heavy good night and shut the door in his face.

At five o'clock he was waked by Sidley pulling at his arm. Sitting up, he saw Greene half dressed already. Sidley's face looked longer and paler, and he brought out a powerful oath when he saw that the sleeper was sensible at last. "Christ's blood, Coppinger, you are the Seven Sleepers in one! Wake up, man!" He looked away to Greene and then back. "What is to happen?"

"You are to be flogged the day after to-morrow."

Sidley reached for his clothes. "You say?"

"On Saturday at three. In Hall."

They watched Sidley dress. He was just throwing on his clothes. "How do you know?"

Coppinger explained. Greene cried out sharply with dismay. "I am sorry, Robert. I am sorry for you too, Sidley, now it has come to this."

"I am much obliged to you," Sidley sneered. "You brought them here, you blasted hypocrite!"

"In a way I did."

"Edmund!"

"Criddle came back with me for a book he wanted. It was not my fault you had been drinking."

"For Christ's sake don't make a sermon of it," said Sidley violently.

"You don't believe me then?"

"Does it matter?"

"You believe me, Robert?"

Greene gulped and nodded. "What are you going to do, Sidley?"

"I am going away."

"You are in my charge, Sidley, you and Greene."

"Consider yourself discharged of office. I'm going. What about you, Greene?"

"In God's name, Edmund—Coppinger—what can we do?"

"Don't ask him, you fool! He'll advise you to stay and be beaten. Are you coming with me?"

"But where, Sidley? In God's name where?"

"Anywhere. What does it matter?" He was throwing things into a bundle. "The world's end, before I'll be treated like a child here. Are you coming?"

"I can't! How can I? I've got nowhere to go."

"Then stay and be flogged and be damned to you!"

He had fastened the corners of his bundle. "Don't forget, Sidley. You are in my charge. You are staying here." Coppinger was nearest the door of the three.

"Am I?" Greene saw delicate sprays of blood climb from neck to cheek and then shrink down. "You keep away, Coppinger!" He saw Coppinger take a step forward. "I warn you, Coppinger!"

"Edmund—let him go!"

"It is not my choice. Put down your bundle, Sidley."

Then Greene saw the dagger in Sidley's hand. "Edmund!"

"Touch me, Coppinger, and as you believe in God I'll drive this through your heart!" It was the same tone and gesture as against Hunter at the Mitre.

As on his first night of residence Coppinger saw Belial—the high white forehead, red mouth, and monstrous eyes,

Staring, he felt the room whirl around and from him, a dissolution of stone and wood and iron, and silence pressed its thumbs over his gushing ears. A great cold hand bristled the hair at the back of his head, and he began to shake. "Go," he cried. "Go, and take damnation with you!"

He closed his eyes and when he opened them again Sidley had gone. Greene found it fitting that he should fall on his knees and pray as in agony. "Sidley," he muttered, "I'll come——" Watching Coppinger's face: "Michael!" he thought. And then sat down aching, sick, at the thought of the flogging.

CHAPTER VIII

Not even third terms of a College year last for
ever, and so Greene found it. The dragging terror and
rebelliousness of the days until his flogging, the humiliating
ceremony itself—the victim drawn up on the shoulders of
a porter, buttocks bared, the birch swung with detachment
and dexterity, the interested silence of the spectators, the
knowledge that to most of them his pain and ignominy
were sport and pleasure—these slid into the past; as did
his shame and tears and hate and fury afterwards. Criddle
he wanted to murder, and thought it impossible he could
again sit calmly in front of him; but no murder was done.
He hated even Coppinger for an hour, till even his birch-
scalded bottom could not justify such wrong-headedness.
And he found two salves: one applied by Coppinger's
gentle fingers, the other the praises of Portington and
Callimet, who came to see him that Saturday evening
and called him a hero that he had not betrayed them.
This was what his self-respect needed—an antidote to
absurdity. He saw that he *had* been a hero, a scapegoat
at the same time. Sidley had run away, afraid to take
his medicine, the other two left their lashes for his one
bare backside—he was a martyr, and worth the lot of
them put together.

In the weeks that followed there was no news of Sidley.
Coppinger told him that the Master had written to Sir
Ralph in Northamptonshire, but could say nothing of an
answer. They speculated, Greene eagerly, Coppinger with
distaste, whether he had gone home or to London; and,
remembering past conversations, Greene even thought it
possible he might have taken passage in some ship bound
for the Americas. One night, when they had been discussing likely matters for Greene's examinations the next
week, Greene told Coppinger how he had heard from

Sidley the tale of their strange encounter, Belial and
Michael. Coppinger was much upset, as though still
affected by the memory. "You saw his face the morning
he went? There is a devil in Sidley if in any man." "He
says there is a devil in every man." "Fit doctrine,"
Coppinger said angrily, "for a consort of the Gadarene
swine!"

"You will admit he cast you for the archangel's part in
his Morality?"

Coppinger looked Greene in the eyes. "Did he cast you
equally well as the battleground between us?"

It was something to think over, certainly.

In intervals between studies, though. Resolutely he shut
distraction from his ears, though not from his thoughts
entirely. He dined now off *Summa* and slept with Porphyry,
and Coppinger helped him as much as he could. For one
thing, he saw Criddle and told him something of their
room-triangle, reminded him how impressed he had been
by Greene's versifying, gave it as an unshakable opinion
that Greene would be eternally benefited by fair treatment
now and during disputations. The tutor, whose grudge
was altogether against Sidley, came to agree, and they
rejoiced together that that corrupter of young men would
do no more harm at St. John's.

Greene did well in his examinations. The interest taken
in his case did him no harm, and though Criddle, Clayton,
and Bremer were somewhat inclined to pooh-pooh his
ignorance of weighty matters mastered by themselves, they
found this more to their praise than his discredit. Bremer,
a lover of obscure authorities, was the ideal examiner of a
would-be bachelor. He spent much of the time when Greene
should be revealing his ignorance in offering him references
to volumes the young man had never heard of; and the
astute candidate never forgot to thank him and promise
to consult these treasuries. In July he became Baccalaureus
in Artibus.

Better still, despite his earlier disgrace, he received permission to spend the summer at home. It was a strong argument

that there were two members of his family he had never seen, and the change would improve his health, affected by the fierce studies of the preceding months. He could go at the end of July. The first thing he did when he left the Master was go seek out Portington who might be going to Norwich or at least be sending messages there, and ask him never to refer to the flogging, to which Portington agreed with promises extravagant even in a matter of life and death. Callimet rhythmically threatened to beat to butcher's meat anyone he heard speak of it.

A few days later he and Coppinger were sorting out their possessions and wondering what should be done with those of Sidley. "These books——"

"Let's leave them here, Edmund. Some message must come from him before long. He may leave them to the College library."

Coppinger hoped not and said so. "And this coat?"

It was the coat of black and white fur which held vivid memories for both of them. "I don't know." Greene picked it up. "The moths will see to this for us, I expect. If he leaves it here, it may be useful in the winter." He felt through the pouch-pockets inside. "Nothing."

"Robert!" It was Coppinger holding Meares's Ariosto. "Do you ever think of George Meares now?"

Greene admitted he never did. "And yet he shared this room with us not ten months ago. Short memories, Edmund, in the world and out of it. Will Sidley last as long?"

"Only if you wish him to. I don't like the end of the College year—do you?"

"This one I like beyond words. You'll not change your mind and come with me to Norwich?"

Coppinger put the Ariosto with Greene's books. "Not this year. Sometime, never fear. I must get to London. I have work to do there. I shall look forward to seeing you in the winter."

"If you find anyone there who wants a secretary from

the University," Greene suggested, grinning, "don't forget what a promising lad I am, will you?"

"You will have other ambitions in a twelvemonth. Soldier, sailor, tinker, tailor, rich man——"

"Poor man, beggar man, or thief!"

"You should avoid that last unenviable trio. Are you packing to-night?"

Their farewell was an affectionate one. Since Sidley's flight, Greene was finding himself content to come under Coppinger's influence in a way reminiscent of the year before. On his last night in College he refused an invitation to a session at the Rose with Portington, Callimet, and two ladies besides the shapely Joan, that they might be together. They spoke for a happy meeting in October before Greene set off for Norwich by post-horse, and Greene turned to wave where the corner of the street would cut him from sight. He was unused to the saddle now and broke the journey at the Bull at Thetford, reaching Norwich in the mid-afternoon next day. Riding over the cobbles, with all the old landmarks thrusting themselves upon him, he was warmly happy, and experienced a stomachy home-sickness more and more as he came into Tombland and saw his father's shop. It looked smaller, that was all. He saw Alice come out of doors and start off in the other direction. "Alice! Alice!" She turned, recognising his voice, and came running towards him as he kicked his foot out of the far stirrup and dismounted.

"It's Robin! You!"

"Me, Alice! I'm a Bachelor of Arts."

The horse was thankful to stand, his back his own, while they embraced. With a shock he felt against him the round-ness of her bosom—he had thought of her as a child still.

Gurley the workman stuck his head out of the window. "It's Master Robert!" And out came Robert Greene, the elder. Former enmities, coldnesses, misunderstandings, these were forgotten. They were father and son. "Father!" He kissed his son. "Robert, my boy!" The horse stood patient. "Gurley, see to the horse. Come and see your mother!"

Young Robert called out to neighbours as they walked to the door, Alice a-flutter behind them,

"He's a Bachelor of Arts, father!"

"You are, Robert?" He looked as modest as he could, which was not very modest. "Yes, father—Baccalaureus in Artibus!"

"My good boy! My good, good boy!"

His mother cried to see him. "Good heavens, mother, don't cry! I'm a Bachelor of Arts!" The title delighted him here by its uniqueness, whereas at Cambridge baccalaureates were like beech leaves in April—plentiful and bright green. "Do you hear that, Jane? You hear what your boy is?" But she welcomed the son, not the bachelor; there would have been no less warmth without the distinction. He saw that she was looking much older these two years. "You haven't seen Tobias, Robin. Nor Anne." No, he hadn't. He put his arm around her. "Shall we?" They were sleeping, and he begged her not to wake them up to show to him. Anne was dark like her father, Tobias had wisps of red hair. "You like them, Robin?"

Alice laid the table at once, and while they ate—he keenly, they hardly at all—he talked and they listened. Whatever Alice's errand had been, it was left undone; Greene the elder seemed content for the shop and its workmen to look after themselves; and had not Tobias waked himself and Anne by his demands to be fed, Jane would have been the last to move. As it was she came back suckling Tobias, in order to miss nothing. As he entertained them, Greene's dull life at Cambridge took on rainbow hues. Professors, fellows, tutors and scholars became more remarkable every minute. Where Clayton called for admiration, Harrison was a subject of rhapsody; in retrospect Criddle was amusing and Howland monumental. He spoke with pride of Coppinger, a Master of Arts ("*Magister*, mother, not *Baccalaureus*"), with sorrow of Meares, with discretion of Portington and Callimet; he shook his head over the Cymric Pughe. Before he knew it he was talking of Sidley, a pale Sidley true, but wonderful. The son of a knight, a courtier himself, one who had kissed Her Majesty's hand and sailed to Africa, and was as handsome as the unveiled face of virtue. He spoke of his familiarity with this paragon until his father's face grew thoughtful, and then he broke off into a full account of how cleverly he had let Bremer ramble on whilst posing him, and how triumph had crowned a year of industry and good behaviour. To please his father he mentioned twice that St. John's was the most puritan College in either University, and insisted on the blessings they enjoyed in the way of daily prayer. He concluded with the wish that they would one day be honoured with the company of Coppinger—"A man after your own heart, father."

In the evening he went into the garden with his father. Like the shop it seemed smaller, but it was brilliant with flowers and associations. They talked gravely together about the past and future and about the flowers, and the elder Greene expressed his considerable satisfaction with his son's achievements.

"You will have to settle what you intend to be, of course."

He waited.

"It is hard to make up one's mind, father."

"You want to be a saddler after me?"

"With your permission, no."

The coming of Tobias had made a difference. "There's your brother now—no doubt he will take to it more kindly." He went on to talk of the goodness of God who thus arranged for the continuance of his trade. "When you went to Cambridge I felt you were lost to saddlery, Robert, and it was a grief to me. Not that I let it interfere between you and your way of life." He suggested by a gesture and the expression of his face that the Almighty had looked after his own. "You will try schoolmastering?"

Greene knelt and drew a blade of grass from between two stones. "I think not, father."

"You will stay on at the University, maybe?"

"I hope to proceed Master of Arts. After that——"

"A Tutor, or a Fellow?"

He shredded the grass between his teeth. "It is too far ahead, father. The disposition is in God's hands more than mine."

The sentiment pleased his father, as he knew it would. "But you must have some inclination? The University life is a noble one, surely?"

"A dull one, father, for a young man."

"We are not altogether choosers, remember. These friends of yours you have been telling us about——" He took his son by the arm. "They can do something for you?"

"They may. They may not."

"You told us a lot about this man Sidley. It seems to me——"

It was one thing to think as much yourself, quite another to have your father speculating. "He has left the University, father. If he can do anything for me, he will; but who can say we shall meet again?"

Baby Anne wailed from the house. "A cross child," his father told him. "Unlike Tobias. The boy is a model. But his sister is not as strong as we should like. Your mother looks well?"

Greene did not care to say what he knew to be the truth. Her children were draining her. "Quite well. And very happy."

"Your sister Alice?"

He laughed. "I thought she might be married by this time." The enormity of the lie striking him, he amplified it. "With children herself."

His father frowned. "She will take no one. She is a fool. She could have married Crashfield's son but would not. She could have married more than once. I reproach myself for giving her her head and fear she will be a judgment on me." He spoke more harshly. "It is no regulation of God for women to be unwed at almost twenty. They are monsters."

"But, father——"

"I know what you would say. The less we speak of
Majesty the better, I think. You yourself know nothing of
the anxieties of parenthood. She is a reproach to me.
There is a curse on the woman who has no children in
honest wedlock."

Greene went back indoors, thinking for the first time in
two years of the sort of life his sister had at home. He felt
the old irritation at his father's righteousness, was disposed
to take her side, but now it had been drawn to his attention,
none the less wondered at her spinsterhood. Nineteen—
and girls three and four years younger made wives and
mothers, like Wotton's sister, and Mistress Grant down the
road, and Mistress Petherill of the Red Lion, twice a widow
and how many times a mistress at thirty-two. But he told
himself: What young men were there in Norwich to take
a girl's eye? The old proverb was a true one: Home-staying
youths have ever homely wits; and Alice was quick and
bright and tender; too good for these thick-wits and pudding-
heads. Young Crashfield indeed! What was he to deserve
her? He wagged his head with indignation, but yet must
conclude his father was not without his rights and it was
time she married.

He was much about the house his first days home, sitting
in the kitchen with his mother, in the garden with his
father, in the workshop with Gurley and Vose. They were
glad to have him talk, and though he told few deliberate
lies, he certainly never missed a good effect for the sake of
an exaggeration here and an omission there. Gurley told
Vose the young master was a mighty clever young fellow,
and Vose, threading silver wire through leather, maintained he was cleverer than that. The old man kept saying
to Greene: "You picked up a wealth o' learning at College,
I'll be bound." After long debate whether he knew more
than Walter Hall, they asked him to settle it for them, and
it was more than Greene could do frankly to award the
prize to his former schoolmaster. He explained that Hall
had read more. "Of course, he is much older than I am."

"Ay, that's right. You picked up a wealth o' learning at College, I'll be bound."

One by one he visited the neighbours, elated to find himself equal to all, superior to most. They called him "Master Greene's clever son," or "Young Master Greene from Cambridge," and many of the locals who used to call him Robin now dropped the familiar name and treated him with unexpected deference. His opinion counted with his elders. Finally he went down to Wroxham to spend a week with Grancher William Beetham, and Alice went with him. Old William, most venerable now, and an institution of the town, was pitifully pleased to see him. "Ay, Robert, ay—I always said you would wear the cap and gown. You are a fine handsome lad, Robert—just the lad I was at your age." He had a little rag in his hand with which he was continually wiping his eyes, and it was hard to know whether he was tearful or not. "The image of me, Robert! It might be myself I see in front of me. When my hair was red——" He wiped his eyes. "I'm getting an old man, Robert. I shan't be here long." But he cheered up within a minute. "Remember Bill boy, Robert? The one you thrashed in Milkin's field? He's a big fighter about here now. Cudgel-playing, Robert—but you'd beat him again." He laughed thinly. "Ay, you'd beat him like a bag of beans, Robert." "But I don't fight now, Grancher." William chuckled. "Tell that to your father! Not fight, eh? A lad like you—the living image of me—right, left, right, the old curled swing, and in through his guard, fetch her up, swing left, right, feint and swing, down you come, and crack goes his head! Not fight, eh?"— "Not so often, anyhow, Grancher." "No, no, we don't want to be bullies," William agreed. "Let me feel your muscle, Robert. Ah, you want to harden that. It's the books, Robert, the books. Now when I was a lad about here——"

He was as fond of Alice as of her brother. "Eh, you are the one to make the lads turn their heads. My hair was that colour to a pin-prick, Robert. Sit on my knee, my lovely. Ay, ay, ay, I mind the time once the lasses didn't sit there without tickling. Eh, eh, my handsome sweeting!" He dabbed up with his bit of damp rag. "The days go by, the years go by—I'm an old man, my dears. I won't be here long. I'll think when you go back: Shall I ever see my handsome ones again?" His grand-daughter kissed him, and he brightened like a sparrow. "The boat is still here, Robert. You must take her out in it. If I was ten years younger I'd be with you. And the pony—you can borrow him from the Reeve Fairway with Grancher Beetham's compliments. Can you ride a horse, Alice my dovelet?"

It was a happy week. The weather was hot and dry, and they watched men and women take the second hay harvest from the wide meadows. One day they helped, but Alice went giddy in the sunshine. They took food to one or other of the flat islands in the river, and she watched him fish and was glad when he caught little or nothing. They were now great talkers together, and he found his old hostility to his father passed over to her. That their mother should have a second child within a year of the first hurt them both, and she blamed their father bitterly for this. Finally, she spoke of his plans for marrying her off, and he knew fear in her voice. She laughed at young George Crashfield, who had since married someone else, and she surprised her brother by telling him that there had been hints she should take Dornett the butcher. "Good God, Alice, he wouldn't force you to do a thing like that!" She didn't know what to say. "You know, Alice, what you want is service with a lady. Isn't there anyone——?" He thought of Lady Goring, but remembered Sir John's reputation with women. Not without a thought for Mistress Petherill, he decided he'd strangle the old pig first. The Howards? Hm, not these days. Roman Catholics too! What a house for a puritan's daughter! "We ought to be able to think of somewhere, Alice. Next year when I get back to Cambridge—— There was Sidley, too." Sidley had a mother and sister, he knew. But how get in touch

with him again? With his rod lying idle at his side, he began
to tell Alice about Sidley, though with a proper caution
still. "You are like me in a way, Alice. You want something better than Norwich can show. I made a mistake,
perhaps. I could have left Cambridge with Sidley and
been anything by now, and once I knew how you felt
about things at home, we might have arranged—— Yes,"
he scratched his head; "Don't worry, Alice, if I get into
a big household next year, I won't forget you. As for
Dornett—I'd stick the fat pig through the gizzard first!"

Timidly at first, she asked him his plans, and he unfolded
vast canvases of ambition. First and foremost to leave
Cambridge and get to London, to take service with a
nobleman, to win favour at Court, to know Leicester and
Sidney and Grindal, the puritan faction. These were
stirring times. The capital was a hotbed of intrigue and
plotting, Bernadino de Mendoza over since the beginning
of the year, a change of fortune rumoured for Don John
in the Netherlands, new overtures for an Alençon wooing,
Walsingham against, Burghley and Sussex hotly for, talk
of all kinds about Mary Queen of Scots, still in Shrews-
bury's care. Stirrings, too, among the poets. Gabriel Harvey
had been incautious about a poem of Master Edmund
Spenser's soon to come before the world; after Skelton,
Wyatt and Howard, there had arisen Edwardes, Gascoigne
and Sackville; there were rhymesters in the Universities.
The future was a huge question and promise; but a man
must be in the midst of things. No droning life away in
monastic seclusion, no cutting out leather for lesser men,
no pedagogy in a tiny country school. "I can do great
things," he vowed. "Fame is a mirror of burnished bronze,
and all the thinning centuries shall see my face in it. I
mean it, Alice! Robert Greene—I'll make the name live
longer than I do!" Serious till then, he began to laugh.
"You think me a fool, I expect."

"No, Robin, I don't. I think no one a fool with ideas
beyond his shop and his belly. I sometimes wish I had been
born a man too—to share in the world more."

"I could never imagine you a man, Alice. You be satisfied you are what you are."

She smiled to find his ambitions all for himself.

At the end of the week they returned home. Old William felt something going out of his bosom with them. "You'll come again?" Yes, they would come again. "Ay, but when? When? You stayed away a long time, Robert—too long by far." He explained that he could not leave the University. "Well, learning's learning. I was never one to say no to it. You've always heard me say to know your history, Robert. Where's my rag, Alice?" He took it. "My eyes are bad. I don't see all I'd like to. But we mustn't complain. I might be worse. I'm a wonderful old man for my age." He began to laugh when they agreed with him. "Ay, I'm a limber old man enough. Tell your mother she don't need more babies, Alice. She's getting too old for it, tell her. You courting, Robert?" "I'm still at the University, Grancher." "Don't court there, do they? It wouldn't have done for me when I was your age, that's all I know. Your grannie and me—I remember—gracious! You courting, Alice?" He wiped his eyes and saw no blushes. "God bless us, what's come over the people? Haven't the young 'uns eyes in their heads? All I can say is, if there had been a bonny fresh wench like you round Wroxham way when I was a colt, I'd a-given her a ring or many a green gown, that's all. Ay, ay, ay, young people aren't what they were. It's this Popery." Greene began to explain, but it was useless. "You must go? Will I ever see you again?" He dragged his feet to the doorway to see them off. "Good-bye. God bless my handsome ones! You are my living image, Robert. Good-bye."

At home it was exactly the same as when they left. The sight of his father working so hard suggested to him he should borrow or exchange books with Walter Hall, and much too late for graciousness he visited the school. Hall was unchanged, and possibly unchangeable; the same to-day as when Greene first dipped into accidence and muddled his concordances. He found him kindly, eager for gossip from the University, regretful that men of his time were no more, perturbed by a change of text for the first term's work in rhetoric. Progress—yes; but idle change— deplorable! "But life is all change, Robertus. Even here we have our changes. I shall need a new assistant next year. You would not care——?" Greene was fecund of excuse. "No," said Hall, "I did not think you would. You won't stay in Norwich, I know. It might be better if you did. You attended Harvey's lectures, you say?"

It was mid-August before he paid a visit to the Red Lion. Many times he thought to go but did not. He was no longer a boy, true, but Mistress Petherill had not to think back far to when he was. He was afraid he might feel a fool, still more afraid he might appear such. The honeyed phrases of his letters to her seeped through forgetfulness to memory; he laughed admiringly at his coinage of philo- sophers; not without pride he began to jot down the old love verses and from a distance of more than three years appraised them favourably. Comparing them with his latest productions, he noted his increased mastery of form and surer handling of imagery. But the Red Lion? After all, he was a man now.

Arrived at the inn yard, he turned away to the stables, hoping to see Nat. A new boy was rubbing down a fine chestnut horse. Yes, Nat was still working there. He shouted into the loft, and Nat came down, shy and clumsy.

"Master Greene!"

"No, still Robert Greene, Nat. Shake hands, man, and don't look stupid."

It was a bashful ceremony for Nat. "Hm. You've growed, Master Robert, in College."

They went up to the loft and lay on the straw, and Nat picked his teeth with a blade of it just like old times.

"You wed, Nat?"

"Ay, I'm wed."

"To Susan?"

"Well ay—who else, Robert?" Ay, they had a boy.
"Shouldn't be surprised, Robert, if he gets a playmate one
o' these months."

"You won't waste the field for want of a ploughing, I
can see, Nat."

"That's how it goes, Robert." Mistress had raised his
pay when he married. "Ay, I be happy enough. 'Tisn'
altogether what you got makes you happy, Robert. You
not wed yet?"

"You are as bad as my grandfather, Nat. No, I'm not
wed, nor expecting to get wed. How's the Mistress?"

"Naught wrong with her."

"Still a bit—frisky?"

"It's none of my business, Robert. I keep myself to
myself out here in the stables. If they crowned the
Shah of Pershy indoors, I'd just eat another apple out
here."

Greene commended his wisdom. "Well, I'm going inside.
I should like to come and see you and Susan and young
Nat one day."

"You come, Robert. It's like old days back again seeing
you. I an't set eyes on the Hayshams these four year.
You've done me good, Robert."

Jauntily, he walked across the yard and so to the parlour.
There were five or six drinkers there of the type he remembered from his first visit. The same drawer was attending
to their shouted orders. He asked for ale, and sat at a small
table on his own to drink it, a mouthful at a time, for he
might have long to wait for Neaera's appearance. He
measured the clock round with pints, and was gulping his
way through the third when the hostess entered with a
pleasant good evening for the company. By Jupiter, she
was a lovely woman! Of form more than feature, and that
was good enough. Why, he had almost—— She recognised him, and he stood up and bowed, whereupon she
dropped a curtsy. He felt his mouth go dry, himself a
little heady, like the flash of sun on diamonds it came into
his mind to follow her out into the passage, to speak

fluently, poetically, passionately, to touch her gown, to
beg——

She had gone, and with assumed indifference but his
heart beating a hammer-stroke on his suddenly brittle ribs,
he looked into the brown face of his beer and broke it
with his mouth.

CHAPTER IX

W<small>ITHIN THE WEEK</small> he had paid three more visits to the Red Lion. On the first of these he did not see Mistress Petherill, on the second he bowed to her, on the third they had less than a minute's talk together in the busy parlour. It was progress of a kind, but hardly brisk enough. Nor could he quite make up his mind whether his conduct should be modest and thus insinuating, or confident, even flaunting, the unmistakable dash and competence of the man who in his time has put down money and played tickle-my-lady. What drove him to persist was that he would feel ten times the man if he could tell all likely to be impressed that he had a mistress. He went over to Bratton, too, but the Haysham boys had left home, one for a week, the other they feared for ever. Wotton Secundus was at Oxford, so only Nat remained of the old gambling school. He visited Susan, big with her second child, but did not enjoy himself, despite her deference, and decided never to go there again. It was with Nat in the loft, eating apples on the straw, with the thuds and bumps of shoving horses below them, he was completely content. He was sufficiently a desperado in retrospect, sufficiently a seducer in anticipation, and the present was hay scented and unhurried.

Three days from the end of the month there was a change —as startling as it was delightful. Early in the evening he reached the inn yard and saw Nat before turning into the parlour for a sight of the hostess. There were the usual drinkers, so he took his pint to his small table and laid the dust of his walk. He had not been there ten minutes when Sidley entered. His heart beat as much as for Mistress Petherill. "Sidley!" The drinkers were not afraid to be curious. "If it's not Robertus!" They threw their arms round each other, and clapped each other's back. "Why,

Sidley——" "Come up to my room. I'm staying here."
He gave a magnificent order for wine as he led Greene
out.

"But, Sidley! What are you doing here?"

"You look as pleased as a bridegroom. Yes—go on
in!"

His manservant was there, and he sent him out
for the evening. "Sit down, Robertus. Baccalaureus, I
suppose?"

"Could I fail?"

"No. How about the buttocks?"

Greene laughed. "You can't expect an answer.
Where have you been? What have you been doing?
How have you managed? Why are you here in Norwich?
What——?"

"Give me a chance to answer, man! You are thicker
with questions than a lost dog with fleas. Take your time,
Robertus!"

They talked for two hours. Greene's tale was soon done,
but Sidley had been home where his father said little and
his mother commended him for not being flogged; he had
been to London for a month, and he was now returning
to his family. He had come through Cambridge, inquired
after Greene, and thought to fetch a circuit into Lincolnshire by way of Norwich.

"I thought you might be in America, Sidley."

"There were less likely guesses. I'll go there yet."

"Did the University——"

"It can do nothing, Robertus. If they press for my
return next year, on my soul it will be America and nothing
else!" He tilted the bottle. "You are not drinking."

"I dare not get drunk, Sidley; that is the truth."

Sidley laughed at him. "You should keep your father
more under control, Robertus."

"I want you to come over to visit us. You will?"

"To-morrow, in a plum-coloured habit, a black hat on
my head, a prayer book in each hand, escorted by dumb
mutes."

"You won't find us——"

"I shall find you after my heart, Robertus. That stern man, your father; that gentlewoman, your mother; that sweet child your sister Alice, the youthful Anne, and now fat-foot Tobias—you see how I remember them?"

"You have had time to forget such unimportant——"

Sidley scowled. "For Christ's sake, Robertus, don't learn the lesson of humility. I hate such fine behaviour." He lifted his eyebrows to clear the scowl. "Am I humble?"

"No, we can grant you that."

"Then model yourself, Robertus; model yourself on perfection. Here, you can safely drink one more glass. Come on, man, it won't drown you! My God, you are a different creature back at home." Greene thought him near to sneering, and must have shown this in his face. "I come all the way to Norwich to see you, and be damned if you are grateful enough to drink my health. I thought better of you, Robertus; I did, indeed. By the way——" He dropped his eyelid. "This Mistress Petherill of yours——"

Greene laughed self-consciously. He hoped his lies would not find him out.

"She's a pretty woman. She's a fine woman. You did well to get her in bed. I shall have to work if I am to be so fortunate, especially now I find you mousing. You must not think it unfriendly if I look out for myself in a matter of this kind. More wine, Robertus?"

Greene was disturbed by such talk, but covered his confusion by firmly refusing more drink. "You get me tipsy, Sidley, and you may find to-morrow a long way off." He explained it was time for him to go, and they made provisional arrangements for his call. "I'll come over in the morning and tell you. Sidley, Sidley, I am glad to see you!"

Sidley brought him a hundred yards or more from the inn. "My first visit to Norwich, Robertus. A charming city. A man might well hang up his hat here."

"That is because you see it for the first time and can get out when you like. No, no, I want something better, Sidley."

"You may find something bigger." He laughed at Greene without offending him. "And now I'll go back to my business."

"Business, Sidley?"

"With my hostess. Your former mistress. I shall to-night progress as far as her waist."

"You are absurdly confident," Greene answered jealously.

"She has had opportunities. She knows each step in the dance. And I'm too good a customer for her to want me to go. Her waist, Robertus, at least." He crooked his arm and winked, enjoying Greene's expression, before they said good night.

At home the news came like a bomb from a mortar. A knight's son to visit them to-morrow! And a knight's son who might be of use to Robert—he was careful to tell them that. Was the house fit to receive him? In vain Greene begged them not to worry, that this knight's son was the only one of his kind and loved all simple things, that he prized friendship and not splendour. What did he like to eat? He assured them Sidley had lost no weight on College fare. Had he ever eaten off ware? Yes, he had filled himself off wood and been glad to. Was he delicate in his drinking? No, if necessary a jug of water from the spring—— But they were determined to be flustered, and Greene could say nothing of much use till his father supported him with: "Woman, you fuss yourself! Like Adam before him, he is but a man." They went to bed, excited, with a plan to rise with the day, borrow the maidservant from next door, and set to. Greene the elder, calm enough to outward view, communed sympathetically with his son by pitying glances over the womenfolk's heads.

In the morning his mother and Alice, their own maidservant and the borrowed one, bustled mightily; Gurley was taken from the workshop to do menial and, for a craftsman, undignified jobs, and Robert Greene ran errands for all. He should have foreseen this—that he as a man could ask another man into a barn to dine, but that women still have their mysteries. There seemed to be more scrubbing and scouring, polishing and swilling, than the worth of it. He knew that his mother was upset because the cutlery was horn-handled. "Will he be staying at our house?" He swore he would not, but could not explain that drink and Mistress Petherill made him so certain. "But we must ask him!" In what room could he go? Why had they not a proper guest-chamber? Share a room with Robert? That dark little atticky place? Impossible. Jane would have given up her own and her husband's room, but knew Robert senior would not hear of it. Alice would have to move. There was no help for it. There was an airing of the best sheets, the best counterpane, the best bed-curtains, lest he decide and they be caught unawares. Greene took a head-wagging enjoyment as he ran at everyone's beck and call.

At ten o'clock the work was done, and Gurley, not Robert, was sent to the Red Lion with the master of the house's compliments and a formal invitation to Master Ralph Sidley to honour the Greene household by dining with it at twelve o'clock. He brought back formal acceptance and still more compliments. Jane and Alice were about their dressing by this time, Greene was with his father in the workshop.

"This Ralph Sidley, Robert——"

"Father?"

"He is not one of those of whom the Book says they shall go down to the mouth of hell? I should be sorry to entertain such at my table, and you know it."

Greene defended his friend. A gentleman, a scholar of St. John's College, a this-that-and-the-other. "A man of Sir Philip Sidney's stamp, father."

"Hm," said his father magisterially. "Sir Philip is well enough, I hear."

Jane gave Tobias his feed before her bodice was laced and she was ready. Alice, however, kept out of the way until Sidley's arrival was announced by Gurley from his window a little before twelve. He had come the short distance on horseback and his man was riding behind him. His suit was dark and he was carrying his hat in his left hand as he came down the street, and magnificence shone through and from him. At the door, where Greene, his father and mother were awaiting him, he dismounted, handed his reins to the man, who went off without a word, and came towards them with the gravity of an ambassador. As he made his greetings, Greene was amazed that even Sidley could be so perfect. A sober splendour shone from his white forehead, the first faint lines set there and around his eyes by debauchery appeared the imprint of midnight studies, it was a joy to watch his lips move, to hear his quiet, rich voice. Listening, Greene knew he had struck the happiest mean between extravagance and bareness, between the high conduct of a great man and the humility of a good. He wondered when last his mother's hand had been kissed. If Alice's ever.

As though a stranger, he saw that his sister was beautiful. Her dress was quiet of style and colour, but she had tied a ribbon over her hair, and he saw his father's eyes travel to and from that ribbon a number of times during dinner. It drew her hair back from her ears. Her features seemed clearer cut. He wished he could look into a mirror to see just how handsome he was himself.

The dinner was all it should be. Meat, game and poultry, fish, eels; jellies, candies, sauces, tarts and pies; beer in plenty, wine in moderation; preserves and spices, sugared fruits—he wondered what his father was thinking of it, and decided he was pleased. He had taken to Sidley, there could be no doubt of that. He was listening with care to an account of Walsingham's appearance or to Sidley's views on the abuses of travel, occasionally delivering a short sermon with which his guest said he fully agreed. In order to be on safe ground, Sidley gave them all a fantastic and

entirely imaginative account of the religion of the blacks
of the West Coast of Africa, drew terrifying descriptions
of jungle gods he may or may not have seen, touched
lightly on cannibalism, measured temples, shuddered at
witch doctors, and finally extolled the piety of English
sea captains in transporting these otherwise damned
souls to Christian servitude in America. At one and
the same time he was theological to Greene's father,
edifying to his mother, adventurous and charming to
Alice, and a puzzle to Greene. He drank only two
glassfuls of wine, saying he was content with little when
it was good. He promised to taste the home-made wines
of Jane and Alice later, in the garden. He praised
everything.

After dinner the men of the house took him through
the saddlery. He watched old Vose at work and sighed
regretfully. "I can't get work done like this at home,"
he admitted. "The strength and delicacy—you have the
fingers for this, my friend." He turned diffidently to the
master. "I have a broken strap or two at the inn.
Perhaps——" It was settled that Gurley should call for
the portmanteaux to-morrow.

Then they sat in the garden with Alice and her mother.
The charm of gardens, he said, was intimacy. In their way
acres with cows were good, he jestingly referred to the
spaciousness of Braiding, an eternity of flat fields, to the
river-divided meadows at Leesome Hall, and the orchards.
"You must see us one day, Robertus, when you leave the
University a Master and a man of mark. My lady mother"—
he bent his head as with involuntary worship—"she will
be glad to meet my friend." The home-made wines were
brought forth—elderberry, cowslip, parsnip, blackberry—
blood-sullen in the sunlight, and the corks were loosed with
juicy *thops*. Thin slices of cake were served, and frantic
birds twittered for their share. Sidley took his glass,
passed it under nostrils which Greene could have sworn
dilated at the smell, and with an unfussed elaborateness
sipped to the health of Mistress Jane Greene and her

daughter. All smiles, they acknowledged his favour, and sipping too, wished him happiness. "I have it," he replied, and spread his arms to include them, the causes of it. "We are plain folk, but happy," said the elder Greene. "The quiet mind is richer than a crown," said Sidley.

He brought his winey lips to the edge of his glass. "I spoke a pentameter, Robertus," he smiled. "You failed to cap it."

"I will one day."

"Your son will be a poet—you know that, Mistress Greene?"

Said the father: "I have naught against poets so they be godly. All others are an abomination before the Lord."

"You think so?"

The elder Robert could not accept the courteous question without answering it. "Lewd balladmongers, stirrers up of vain desires, pothouse scribblers and crowders with their bawdry—what can a sound man think of them, Master Sidley?"

"But not all are such. The Queen herself—God bless her Majesty!—can turn her couplet with the next. There is no muddy well on Helicon, Master Greene, but a crystal-bright spring, fit dwelling-place of angels and the muses." He saw the subject dangerous and skirted from it. He threw crumbs to the sparrows, and watched them rise, flutter, drop again with angry wings. "These birds, unlike Adam, have not lost their garden, nor, I think (he smiled at Alice) their angel."

Greene watched his sister flush and laugh. Laughing too, for the first time he thought of her as interesting Sidley. He wondered what that agile-minded deceiver was thinking as he sat there demurely with his half-emptied glass of parsnip wine and dainty remnant of cake. If—— He must speak with Sidley, carefully, tactfully. Not that he thought—— He took up the bottle. "Let me fill your glass, Sidley." The other offered it affably. "You are teaching me bad habits, Robertus. But with wine so delicious, from hands so benevolent, I cannot refuse. Sir"—to his host—"your continued prosperity!"

It became time to feed the young children, and the elder Greene knew he must see to his men. Mother and father made to excuse themselves, but begged their guest to stay at his ease. "You like the Red Lion inn, Master Sidley?"

He found it comfortable enough.

"If you would be willing to stay a time under our roof," said Greene the elder; "it would be an honour to us, young sir."

Sidley was on his feet, with a ceremonious bow as to majesty. He did not know words of thanks enough, but he knew the inconveniences of a guest in a house where there were nursing babies, he had a certain amount of business at the Red Lion (Greene jerked his chin as though memory of Mistress Petherill had landed on it like a fist), in short, if they would excuse him—he got so far as Greene had expected, and then with a complete change of front appeared to break down beneath a burden of kind wishes, and said if they would permit him he would be delighted to come to them the next day.

This settled, father and mother withdrew to discuss whether they would have preferred him to dispense with their offer after all, and the three young people were left to a rather freer conversation. Sidley declared it a slight to Mistress Alice to leave any of her wines untried, and the elderberry was straightway tapped. He now set himself to please her, and regarded her brother as little more than a peg for used topics of conversation. Soon she was asking him about London, the Court, the dresses the ladies wore there. He was no haphazard describer, vague about colours and stuffs. He had the eye of a painter, words were his pigments; velvets, taffetas, stiff brocades, silks and satins, he knew them; he patted his neck for ruffs, billowed out monstrous farthingales, ran his fingers across pearl-

embroidered bodices, looped up petticoats; cut and slashed
and puffed and gashed; plucked at sleeves and smoothed out
waistbands; the French, the Spanish, the Venetian heel;
ribbons, roses, fans and snippets; he was a tailor talking.
He knew ten colours between red and purple, five where
green became blue, cream and ivory he vowed as distinct
as black and white. He heeded Greene only to say: "As
Robertus knows, As Robertus will tell you," and similar
tags. "But, Sidley——" He waved the interruption aside.
"I'll tell you of a dress of my lady Strange's——" No, he
would have no more cake, but just one more glass of the
elderberry wine. His tongue took on a new celerity, he
became wittier, his gestures carved the air. Then, to
Greene's relief, he seemed to realise he was losing control
of himself and declined more wine. A drink of water
instead—— When Alice was gone to the house to fetch
it he laughed at Greene's worried face. "No danger,
Robertus, I have finished. I shan't get tipsy and disgrace
you."

He seemed quite sober when at last he must go, and
was taken into the house to see Anne and Tobias. Unlike
Greene, who for the life of him could not feign interest in
very young children, he kissed Anne and counted Tobias's
toes, and swore the boy had so high a forehead already
that he must prove a prodigy. His long, white fingers went
to his own forehead as he said it. His leave-taking set a
new standard of manners for the house. He kissed the
hands of Jane and Alice (Greene, furtively watching, could
not see that he lingered over one more than the other), and
vowed to his host that there were matters arising out of
that day's talk he must give the benefit of a maturer consideration. He would be with them for dinner the following
day.

Greene walked back with him to the Red Lion. If Sidley
was aware of the interest he created amongst those who
saw him, he showed no signs of it, but it was a source of
satisfaction to Greene.

"Well, Sidley?"

"Yours is the most charming family in the world, Robertus. I mark this day with a red letter."

"You like us enough to leave the Red Lion?"

"Hm, hm."

"And wine-bibbing?"

"Hm, hm."

"And an orderly progression from Mistress Petherill's waist to——"

"You should feel relieved, Robertus."

"And why? What did you think of my father, Sidley?"

"I struck a spark from him once, I believe. Was I the hammer or the anvil? One thing is certain—He'll not let you be a melodious saddler. Leather or letters, Robertus—you cannot have both."

"I'll do without leather."

"A dependable material, but I should not care to live on it. You'll choose wisely. Your father was exactly what you said he would be."

"And my mother?"

"I fell in love with her!"

"And with my sister too?"

Sidley stopped short, opened his mouth, shut it and walked on again. "You are as blear-eyed as all brothers. You have never really looked at her, have you?"

"To-day, yes."

"And what did you think of her?"

"She seemed to me, Sidley, to be a woman all at once, and a beautiful one."

"It took you years, in fact, to see what I saw in five seconds. From what you had to say about her I had looked on her as a child."

"It might be better——" Greene began.

They were crossing a field. Sidley stopped abruptly. "I know what you want to say, fond brother. I think it best left unsaid."

"So long as we understand each other, Sidley."

He saw Sidley's face stiffen and elongate with the arching of his eyebrows and the deepening of its jaw-lines. "You poor, incredible fool, Greene!"

But he stood his ground. "Not entirely, Sidley. Think back a year."

Sidley's anger gave way to vexation. "Indeed to the living God, Robertus, I don't know whether to knock you down or pack my bags for Lincolnshire. Anyhow, let's walk or we shall look a comic pair. You think no more of me than that?"

Greene tried to explain. He stumbled amidst ill-chosen words, and was interrupted. "Very well, very well. You want me not to come?"

But he replied with exasperation that he did want him to come.

"After all, Robertus, you did ask me, didn't you?"

"Look here, Sidley, let us forget we said anything about it, shall we? If you could only understand——"

Sidley linked his arm in his companion's. "I understand, Robertus, I understand you fully. Well—Alice is a sister to me too. Does that satisfy you?"

It did, and they talked of other matters till Greene left him at the entrance to the inn yard.

The next day he shifted himself to Tombland, leaving his man and some of his possessions at the Red Lion. He wore a different habit, somewhat gayer, but wore it with gravity. After dinner Greene took him to see what was noteworthy in the town. "God help us, Robertus, you've got more churches than people! Surely the preachers must take in each other's washing!" And later—"I am not of a meditative turn, as you know, but I find it most fitting, this cheek-by-jowl arrangement of places to drink and places to worship. The followers of Apollo's younger brother combined the two, I have no doubt, and so showed their superiority over later ages." They broke their journey to drink at a number of these places, and Sidley insisted on paying each time. Eventually they made their way to Mousehold Heath, gazed and admired, and returned home with a far from true account of their sight-seeing. The evening sped quickly, and after half an hour down-stairs when the rest of the family had retired, Greene saw Sidley to his room and then went off to his own.

Sidley threw his window wide open to look out into the empty street. He saw two dark streaks whip across from the other side and lose themselves in the shadows thrown by the Greenes' house. Rats, to gnaw at security, greedy to destroy. So thinking, he rubbed the back of his neck, and shaped his lips to a silent whistle. He knew he was in Alice's room. He opened the presses into which his own clothes had been laid. There was nothing whatever of hers in them, yet he felt femininity potent everywhere. He did not feel much like sleep, so he went to the window again. In a night or two the harvest moon would be full for cats and lovers. With a brief peevishness he wished himself back at the Red Lion. A night like this—he'd be through Mistress Petherill's door or window by this time. Rout or conquest, it would be settled one way or the other—and he did not envisage rout. A handsome woman, not to be wooed with sighs and poetry, but an arm round the waist, a forced kiss, a hand inside the corsage. That was the way to prosper. He laughed quietly at Greene, a too-sad diplomatist, letting I-would-ma'am wait upon I-dare-not, a nervous kitten near a jug of cream. He laughed again at these thoughts in a puritan household. And yet Greene, pater-familias, takes to new breeding like the gamest cock in spring, and his son all he knew of him, and now the puritan miss aflame for London, fine clothes, the world poured out like a basket. Well, she should come to no harm for him. Let her work out her own destiny, or her father for her. He cared not.

He undressed and got between the lavendered sheets. He was a fool to be wasting his time here. A couple of days for grace-sake and he'd be off to Lincolnshire. But he had not intended Robertus to become such another sobersides as

Coppinger. There was mettle in him. He was far from contemptible, Sidley thought.

Two days later Greene told him that under colour of a visit to Grandfather Beetham they might visit the Wroxham September fair. Even though his father suspected what they were at, he could not well object. This suited Sidley, and he added his persuasions to those of Greene at table. Midway through his plea he caught Alice's eyes upon him, and made her one in the project. "There is an inn, Robertus? Then let Alice stay with your grandfather and we can try the inn. You approve, sir?" Her father did not like it, but her mother spoke up for her, and he would have been a churl to refuse.

"But why Alice?" Greene asked him later, with a hint of his old mistrust.

"Because you are a selfish limb of the devil, Robertus, that is why. D'you ever do anything for her pleasure? Not you!" He grinned. "It's not a woman's world, this. A little fun must suffice them a long time. Be gracious!" Greene looked at him doubtfully, and Sidley, knowing every thought in his head, burst out laughing in his face. "You are in danger of becoming not only a fool, Robertus, but a solemn fool."

"You wanted to go, Alice?" he asked his sister. "Then I am glad we asked." She was amused by his *We*, but too happy to quarrel with it.

They set off early on the first morning of the two days' fair, and were at Wroxham as soon as old William could have wished. He was out in his garden getting the sun. "Ay, it's a fine time o' year. Ay, I'm well, I thank you kindly, young gentleman. I can't see you as well as I should like to. Where's my chicken? Where's my sweeting? Where's her grancher's handsome apple-blossom? Eh, eh?" He would see them off and on for two days. He knew days now short as heart-beats—happy ones like things remembered. Ay, he was just the man for a fair when he was young; there was no one better at a fair than William Beetham, unless it would be his brother John. He explained to Sidley how brother John had won the battle of Flodden, dabbing at his eyes, and finally breaking into surprisingly strong laughter. He sped them on their way. "Go on, you young ones. Be happy while you can. I was never one to mope, thank God. I remember in '41 it would be—or '40—or was it '41——" They left him there under his tree, talking to himself, and started for the fairground. It was in the meadows this side of Wroxham Broad, and they could hear the murmur of it swell to babble and then uproar as they drew near. The men had their purses tied with leather thongs and thrust inside their doublets, Alice having entrusted all her money to her brother. At Grancher Beetham's she had tied a ribbon in her hair, and now swung her hat in one hand and held Robin's arm with the other. The fair was laid out in long streets of booths, sheds, tents and stalls, three of them, double-rowed, running the whole length of the pitch. Near where they entered was the horse fair, where sweating, swearing men ran horses around inside the small rings of possible buyers, or forced them up on their back legs, striking out like demons. The hairs clotted on their haunches, they blew spume from their frothy jaws, neighed with shrilling nostrils, caught the excitement of the crowd. Sidley, recognisably a man with money, had the touts round him like flies before he advanced twenty yards, but he went on untroubled except that he struck with good will at any hand laid on his arm or shoulder. He was asked, prayed, begged, cursed at to watch the fine fillies, the dashing geldings, the big-boned stallions; a dozen dealers had the very nag he'd been looking for all his life. A ruffian pushed his hand into his neighbour's face to get nearer the prey, the neighbour hooked his legs from under him, there were fists flying loose for everybody who cared to stop one before they were past the horse fair and at the beginning of the cloth market. "Small beer to Bartholomew's," laughed Sidley, pushing in between Alice and an arguer retreating backwards. He gave him his elbow over the kidneys, which brought him whirling round with an oath, but what he saw of Sidley did not invite him to stay and he ran off whooping. All who had wares to sell were bawling them: What d'ye lack? What is't you buy? where are the lucky lads? Hoy-oy there, the lasses? What d'you lack, my fine gentlemen? Ribbons for your ladies, come buy, come buy! Favours for a pretty wench, come buy, come buy! Who'll have garters? Who'll have garters? Perfect yellow for honour and joy! Who'll treat the lucky maids? Who'll buy them favours?

The further they went the more confused were the cries. Hawkers ran around them, thrusting their wares right into their hands, and from the side booths a hundred voices yelled attractions.

"Buy fine gingerbreads! Buy gilt gingerbread! Who'll buy this food of angels?"

"Who'll take pears? Who'll take rattles?"

"Who buys fiddles? Italian fiddles? The sweetest music this side heaven!"

"Eggs and butter! Cheese for gentles! And the veriest popinjay of all this world, who talks and sings like a Christian child. Come buy him for your sweetheart!"

"Jellied eels! Jellied eels! They do not bind you, jellied eels!"

Greene had one arm for Alice, one he kept tightly across his doublet over his purse. Sidley took pushes to save her. "You are enjoying it?" As she had never enjoyed anything before. They looked around for somewhere to eat. On their way to Pie Corner, they were offered salves for corns, diamonds and mousetraps, drums and ballads, ale and purses; and Sidley bought Alice a neckerchief, a bunch of ribbons, and a singing bird in a cage. Her brother bought her glass-headed pins, a puzzle of twisted nails, and a sweetmeat baby. Jostled and breathless, at last they found seats under an awning, and had roast pig and cold clear beer. There was little less din here than otherwhere. The crowd was falling over its centipede feet, and Pig Market was famous for both porkers and purses. A beggar with

sores kicked a beggar without legs, a tall dismal man sang
a ballad of fresh love.

As they ate and drank, they discussed what to do for
the rest of the day. So far they had not spared a moment
for the monsters and performers. Alice must see as much
as she could. And the puppet plays—what of them? The
Miracle of the Creation? And the hourly beating of the
Vice? How stretch out the day for all its wonders? Visit
which first when all were clamorous? They set off, hardening their ears to all that offended them. Skirting the third
street, they saw two thieves thrown into the Broad and
there pelted with refuse. "Will they drown them?" Alice
gasped. "Good riddance if they do," was all the sympathy
they got from Sidley. Now came an apparently unending
pilgrimage to strange shrines: the talking dog, the boy
with a cow's face, the hare that beat the tabor, the three
kings of the East, the hairy woman, the fire-eaters, the
tightrope dancers, the smallest horse in the known world,
the Guinea sea-serpent, the Dutch hermaphrodite, the
contortionists who folded their arms behind their shoulders
and their legs behind their backs (or said they did), the
man who bent iron bars and tossed aside with a finger the
stone Greene and Sidley heaved at in vain. These and
others, till they were forgetting what they had seen and
what not. They spent half an hour with the Italian dolls,
where Greene had his empty pocket turned inside out,
and then looked for food again. As it grew late, drunkenness increased immeasurably, there were squabbles and
brawls, the wardens and the watch were not to be found
where danger waited, screams of delight and terror made
Alice shrink, and Sidley too gave her an arm for safety.
He enjoyed the grip of her fingers and several times covered
her hand with his own disengaged one (they had lost the
singing bird and its cage), giving it a protective squeeze,
but openly for Greene to see. Strumpets were plying their
wares, some baring their bosoms to catch connies, the
courtesy men prowled for fools, solicitous, helpful, one
hand brushing down the unwary, the other lifting the

purse; twice they saw men with blood streaming down
their faces, and once a battle of viragoes cheered on by a
ring of men. Greene's legs were aching, and he felt Alice
heavy on his arm. "Shall we go?" She nodded. Then she
sighed. The great day was over.

Greene and Sidley slept after all on the floor of Grancher
Beetham's kitchen. Every inn was full to the stables. Sidley
did not overlook that Greene spread himself where it would
be impossible to open the kitchen door without disturbing
him. The morning and early afternoon they spent at the
fair again, but a change in the weather to steady rain
after noon made it easier for them to leave in good
time, take a decent farewell of old William, and reach
Norwich before Jane could feel alarmed. The cherries
safely eaten, they were not afraid to confess; yes, they
had been at the fair and had bought presents for the
whole household, maid-servant and all. Downstairs after
a change of clothing, they changed the house with their
cheerfulness and excitement, and Jane was sorry to hear
that their guest must return to Lincolnshire in three days'
time.

Those days went quickly. On Sidley's last night there, he
and Greene again stayed downstairs to talk after the house
was still. Greene said he would be glad to get back to
Cambridge now the other was leaving them. "You know,
Sidley, I should have been an ass to run away with
you. I should be ignominiously instead of comfortably
here, returning just the same in October. Yet you did
wisely."

"I think so too. The scholar's life is not for me."

"Think me a fool—your flogging would have seemed
worse to me than my own."

"In retrospect only. When the birch came down like a
shower of burning oil, you had no thought in the world
save for your skinned bottom."

"Not only in retrospect." He sighed the late hour sigh.
"I wish I saw the future clearer."

"You'd be the court magician then. Her Sovereign Majesty is not a little given to such flummery. It will unroll in its own good time, say I."

"What is your future to be, Sidley?"

"Succession to my father, to whom I wish long life."

"But now, immediately."

He scraped his chair back. "London for the winter. Next spring I start the Grand Tour. My father commands it, and I wish it. Coppinger will deplore my contact with the New Circe when you tell him."

"I must try not to be envious. So you are leaving home?" He reflected a short while. "I wish——"

"Don't be afraid, man!"

"About Alice my sister. I wish she could enjoy a fuller life than here. She doesn't like it, Sidley." His tongue loosened, and he told his companion much of what he and Alice had talked over that week at Wroxham. "Dornett!" he cried, and slapped his thighs hard and stared angrily at the fire.

"But your father will not force her into marriage?"

Greene thought he might. He made the outlook blacker than it was. "What I hoped, Sidley, was that you might know of some household that would receive her—some good, safe household." He expressed the idea over and over again in different words.

"It might be done. What would your father say to it?"

"I don't see how he could refuse."

"I do! I certainly think he would. You mean a nobleman's household, of course. Not just——"

"Where she could take fitting service—yes." He began praising Alice.

"Then what if I promise to do what I can in London while I am there this winter?"

"Don't you think it might be better if it were not in London?"

Sidley laughed as loudly as the hour would let him. "Damn my soul, Robertus, there's as sour a puritan in

you as in Coppinger! Send her to France, to a nunnery!
You and your sister are to have a wider life than at Norwich,
but be hanged if she shall go with you to Court! Yes,
you are Coppinger's boy now with a vengeance."

But they discussed the idea seriously before they went
to bed.

CHAPTER X

Not a fortnight after his gift-littered departure, and before Greene had returned to Cambridge, Sidley was with them again. This time with compliments, still more gifts, and an invitation from Lady Sidley, backed with letters and seals, that Mistress Alice Greene might be allowed to enter her personal service. Mistress Jane Greene and for that matter Master Robert Greene were pressingly invited to accompany their daughter to Braiding and satisfy themselves that her office would be seemly and such as they would themselves choose. Sidley gave the personal explanation that his mother looked forward with joy to increasing her household with a maiden so charming now that she must lose her son for three years.

"You are leaving home for three years, Master Sidley?"

"I make the Grand Tour, sir. I follow in the footsteps of many worthy men."

"And many unworthy, Master Sidley."

"Theirs is a path I shall not enter on," said Sidley smoothly. "I leave in the spring, but the winter I must spend at Court." His tone suggested that come what might he must fit himself for his part in the national councils.

Alice was tremulous to go. Her brother, now it had come to the push, was wondering whether he had been a meddler for the worse; Jane was torn between grief at losing her and delight at such a step forward in the world; her father felt one moment that no daughter of his should be entering a distant household with its thousand temptations, the next that she was off his hands and her feet set in a good way. And in their different fashions all were glad that Master Ralph would not be at home—a circumstance he relished. The decision was never really in doubt; the practical arrangements were what had to be settled. Jane, it was clear, could not go to Braiding—Tobias was too much in need of her, and would be for months. Nor could the elder Robert make up his mind to the journey. It was a busy time of the year for him, and apart from that he was uncomfortable at the thought of meeting these Sidleys. It was easy for him to set his mind at rest with his son's recommendations of Master Ralph, the fact that he had entered the strongly-puritan St. John's, the good impression he had made during his visit, the formal letter from his mother—these were eloquent of honour and sobriety. Besides, Braiding was only a couple of days' easy journey—a day to a man in a hurry—they could see Alice almost at will. And she was old enough to look out for herself. He knew her training. At the first hint of anything wrong she would come home. It was a good opening for the girl. He would suggest Robert go with his friend to see her settled in. Since taking his degree Robert was a sound man, and was proving a credit to his father.

Jane's doubts were not so easily dispersed, but were of a different nature. They arose from a counting of petticoats and nightgowns, of dimity slips and stockings and shoes. She checked off yards on her fingers, moving her lips without sound, called in her husband to calculate prices, and persuaded him without difficulty to lay out money on many necessities and one or two luxuries. "I had more easily visit the Indies," he remarked drily. But Jane dismissed this masculine prejudice with the contempt it deserved. "You would like the Lady Sidley to look over your daughter's clothes and find them few and poor and darned like a she-tinker's cast-offs?" "Have it your own way, woman!" Fal-lals, fol-de-lols—the women were all alike. They'd never mend.

Greene asked Sidley when he was expected back. In two days. They decided that Greene and his sister should follow ten days later, which would give him just time to reach the University for the beginning of term. Sidley was willing for anything. "You must not keep Criddle waiting, must you, Robertus?" He spent the two days in Tombland, though he would have preferred the Red Lion and Mistress

Petherill. As it was, he insisted that Greene and he visit
the inn for some hours one evening, and he caused his
companion much initial embarrassment by asking for the
hostess and treating her with considerable familiarity,
promising her never again two such admirers—"My good
friend Robertus Greene, Bachelor of Arts, of long standing;
my unworthy self, dear lady, later to arrive at the starting
post but that much hotter-footed for the course." She kept
him literally at a distance, laughed easily at his protestations, and admitted she had long known Master Greene
a young man of parts. "And what parts!" echoed Sidley,
looking from one to the other. With suitably extravagant
gesture, he spoke of the new Helen of Norwich, fairer than
her of Troy, and compared with whom Corinna was a
gummy hag, Lais a weedy trollop; but the good lady
went on laughing at him, and when he moved towards
her, put a hand to her ear, called out "Coming!" and
hastened from the room. Greene was chagrined by his own
tightness of tongue and because he had been wordy too
often where he should be bold. "I can see the end of you
already," he scolded. "Some husband's sword a foot inside
your navel."

He rode with Sidley a third of the way to King's Lynn.
"We'll see you then?" cried Sidley at parting. Greene
wanted to say a number of things, but somehow they were
unsaid when he turned his horse and headed into a storm
of rain. He was wet and depressed before he reached home.
A triviality bothered him as much as his uncertainty of
what was best for his sister. He could not forget how pain-
stakingly he had acquired Italian, and yet it was Sidley
not he who should behold the sea-enchanted Venice, Rome
the grand, and Florence from the hill of Fiesole. The heavenly
disposition of men's estates carried less authority the more
one thought of it. So affected was he that five miles from
Norwich he shut his ears to the implorations of a beggar
woman and her child trudging the now muddy roadside.
Her appeals became curses when he was well past her, and
for a few minutes he was righteous and justified, but a

growing conviction of pettiness upset him still further, and he was more surly than usual the rest of the day.

Faster for Jane than for Alice the interval passed to the departure. It was to be Greene's leave-taking too. Crashfield, making one of his quarterly journeys to Cambridge, had agreed to shift some of his baggage there, the rest he would take with him to Braiding for a few days. Then he would go by way of Peterborough and Huntingdon to the University, possibly, he thought, accompanied by the London-bound Sidley. Jane was almost out of her mind with the anxiety of these two of her children leaving home and the other two hourly dependent on her. Sewing hard for Alice, she felt she was neglecting Robert; washing for Robert, she knew she and not the maid should be changing Anne's napkins; Tobias had a wicked appetite. She needed three pairs of hands and a longer day to use them in. "You'll not know yourself when we are gone, mother!" But she expected no comfort from their absence.

They were to have their father's escort as far as King's Lynn, where they would spend the night and be met on the morrow by servants from Braiding. They had a dry day but a cold one for the time of year. Greene the elder looked a tradesman from heaven as he sat his good horse, well-clothed, handsome and resolute, without a sword but carrying a long, heavy stick, and as his son knew, with pistols under his cloak. Nothing but Alice's face was visible as he helped her to the saddle, so hooded and cloaked was she. Greene himself was all scholar. The farewells outside the house were brief, for Jane's husband would not have it otherwise. Tears were bad things to show in public, and he mistrusted his wife on these occasions. So they just waved to her where she stood before Gurley and Vose and the maid, Anne in her arms clawing out to the horses. "Godspeed!" cried all who saw them go. "God be wi' ye, young master and mistress!" Jane waved, heavy-hearted, hampered by the child, and then they were clattering off. Greene was at once the old traveller and began discussing the weather and the roads with his father, pulling at a strap

here and a knot there, finding an excuse for a laugh, and
feeling a half-contemptuous brotherly pity for Alice's
swimmy eyes and mouth moving as though with a swallow.
"Are you cold?" he asked, but she shook her head. "You
have enough here to keep you warm," said her father,
humorously eyeing the packhorse.

Some way out of town they were overtaken by a stranger,
riding a substantial cob, with a small valise behind him. He
gave them greetings in the name of the Lord, with a strong
nasal intonation, and their father returned them with such
Christian additions that he slackened pace a little and
they fell into conversation. He was a wayside preacher
bound for a conventicle this side King's Lynn, where
the godly were numerous and not unblest, and had certain
messages for men he did not name. He knew Robert
Greene of Norwich as a man to trust and worship with—
his name had been mentioned only the night before by the
good man with whom he had stayed in Norwich. Who
was he? Greene and Alice took the lead, and the two puritans
muttered along behind them.

He asked her for the tenth time if she was glad to be
going, and for the tenth time she answered yes. Strange,
they said, how quickly all this had come about after their
talk together at Wroxham. Then it was he who was to enter
a nobleman's house: now it was she. Whirligig with a
vengeance. Occasionally as the other riders came near,
Greene spoke of his life at Cambridge. "Cambridge?"
called out the preacher; "You are at Cambridge?" His
father explained. "St. John's College? You know Master
Eggerton?" Yes, he knew Eggerton. "And Master
Criddle?" He knew Criddle. "And Master Edmund
Coppinger?" He was Master Coppinger's closest friend.
"I am glad to hear it!" He turned to Greene's father, to
say that Master Coppinger was one of the most promising
of the younger men. "Your son is in good company."
They now rode together for a while, and Greene and the
preacher did most of the talking. "Then tell them you met
Philip Stoneaway of Ashford. They will know me, and

think none the worse of you for it." They dropped back once more, and brother and sister returned to speculation about the Sidley home.

They broke their journey to eat at Dereham, where Stoneaway shared their table and ate very well indeed. He was a good talker too, when he could be won from doctrine. Greene heard with interest of the rumoured defeat and ill health of Don John in the Netherlands. "He has burned himself out like a farthing candle," said Stoneaway. "Women and warfare, love and hate, have combined to destroy him. The Enterprise of England threatens us so much the less. Nor are matters gone past hope for the Hollanders." He feared nothing from Her Majesty's interest in Alençon; she would make a poor fool of him before she finished. Had she not made a fool of him already? She made these foreigners jump on a string: the hell-spawned Philip, Eric of Sweden, and the Archduke Charles, jumpers all. Alençon? There'd be (his voice sank to the lowest whisper) rebellion first.

On then to King's Lynn at a steady five miles an hour. Some distance this side the town Stoneaway took his leave of them, showing an unexpected jollity in wishing Alice well. "A sound man," said their father; "an improving man, Master Stoneaway." Greene could see that the preacher's account of Coppinger and maybe others had done him good in his father's eyes. They were at the Howard Arms by seven o'clock, Alice not a little tired and her excitement dulled. They were at their food in their own room when there was a knock at the door and a serving man came in to tell them that a gentleman from Braiding asked the honour of waiting on them. Alice's hands went to her hair, thinking it Sidley come; her father said he might come in. It was not Sidley, but a stumpy young man in rather fine clothes, carrying a black velvet cap worked with silver wire, who bowed to them from the doorway and again when he was near the table. He had a wholesome rather than a handsome face. He gave his name as Copson, his office as understeward at Braiding, and said it would be his pleasure and duty to escort brother and sister there the next day. He hoped they were comfortable, and that their treatment at the inn was all they could wish. He had taken the liberty of saying a word to the host. At Greene's offer to join them he bowed again, regretted that he had other business to see to, and begged that he might be excused. Otherwise, they would be delayed in the morning, and reach Braiding uncomfortably late.

"A very pleasant young fellow," Greene suggested when he had gone.

Alice knew he had been interested in her. "I thought him reliable."

Her father saw nothing odd in the adjective. "Reliable enough, I expect. Few drones hive in stewardships. We are obliged to him for his interest in us."

Greene, thinking himself better than forty understewards, grunted and went on with his supper.

The morning saw another parting, of father and daughter. It hardly seemed to matter that young Robert too was to say good-bye for the best part of a year. Confirmed in his increasing good opinion by Stoneaway, the elder Greene gave his boy a brief, dignified, and affectionate blessing and told him never to forget his manifold duties to himself, his parents, his College, and the Almighty, and then turned a little thoughtfully to Alice. It was an opportunity for a dissertation on the perils of the unknown world, the especial temptations of all young women, injunctions to fear God and hate the devil, but he feared it must be let slip. A very great love of his daughter seemed to fill the hollow of his breast, her helplessness as a child was recalled to him more vividly than for many years past, a strange possessiveness flooded over him now that he must let her go. "Be a good lass," he said abruptly, and kissed her. "Your mother and I——" He took his arms from around her. "Everything is ready?" In the decent tradition of his home he wanted the farewells over in private. "Good-bye, Alice. Never forget your mother and father for anything you want." With these inadequate words he led the way out to the horses. Copson and a serving man were already mounted, the baggage fastened. He wanted to kiss his daughter again, but instead swung his leg over Grimald's back, gave a curt and general salutation, and went at a walking pace from the yard, without looking back.

Copson sat silent throughout this awkward leave-taking, merely raising his hand to acknowledge Greene's farewell. Then he turned briskly to the others. "Mistress Greene—you are ready?" He and the manservant led the way off.

"The last of Norwich, Alice!"

"And the first of Braiding. Do you think this Master Copson will tell me something about it?"

"That is easily discovered." He watched her face for signs of grief, but saw none. "You are nervous?"

She admitted she was, a little. He described at length how he had felt riding to Cambridge for the first time, his meeting the Master, his room-mates, how he had put on resolution and held his own amidst strangers. "It is your own valuation of yourself that counts, Alice." He began to pass on advice given him by Sidney. "There is the world: what can it give you? Nothing, if it can ignore you. There should be something in us Greenes too good for ignoring, don't you think?" There was one thing he was not clear about. "You know, Alice, you are going here as a servant of a kind, and yet I am a friend of Sidley's, and he visited our house as a guest. How will it work out, do you think? Do you eat at one table and I at another?" He smiled at her. "Am I guest and you kitchen help? Do you have to make my bed and tip my jordan?" He patted his nag's neck. "Will you be married in a year, Alice?"

"Great heavens, no!"

"I don't doubt you'll get the chance. I never thought you were so pretty. Well, if the right man asks you——"

"The right man!"

"All women cannot be fidgety, Alice. If you had a good husband now, and knew it—if women do know it——"

"A woman always knows when she has a good husband. It is the man who never knows he has a good wife till he loses her."

He laughed at this feminine prejudice, and rode to catch up with Copson. "My sister would be glad to hear something of the house she is entering. It would be a kindness on your part——" From Copson's smile it appeared it would be a pleasure too, and Greene was led to reflect how he would respond to such a request for information on a dull journey by a pretty girl. A likeable fellow this Copson, he concluded, shrugging his shoulders. He stayed with the man-servant, asking questions about the distance they had to go, the condition of the road, its safety, the effect of the dry summer and autumn on the crops. The couple of times he looked back he saw that Copson and Alice were managing excellently without him. With a touch of envy, too, he recognised that Copson was a far better horseman than he.

They dined at the Unicorn, where everyone seemed to know Master Copson and be willing to serve him more quickly than anyone else, and then proceeded by the Spalding road on the second half of their journey. Greene again rode in front with the servant, whom he found a garrulous, cheerful sort of man, Alice and Copson continued busily talking in the rear. The hours were dragging when at last Copson called out from where he and Alice were lagging sadly, the serving man reined in his horse, and when the party had moved on close together for not more than ten minutes they rounded a thickly-wooded curve of a stream and saw a large mansion on a slight swell of ground rather more than a mile ahead.

Copson stood up in his saddle for the greater effect. "Braiding!" he announced proudly.

It was a large, flat-fronted, undistinguished house, with too many chimneys bristling comb-edged above it. Around it, and enclosing the whole of the slightly raised land, was a well-wooded park with a lodge at its hither gates. There was a second lodge, Copson informed them, on the far side. As they came nearer, there were tame deer to be seen moving among the trees. "Unlike the Italians," said Copson grandly, "we keep our splendour indoors." "You have been to Italy?" "Hearsay," he admitted, then: "London hearsay." "You have been to London?" "More times than I can count." Greene thought his tone condescending, but he had turned from him. "You will feed the deer, I know, Mistress Alice."

Mistress Alice! Greene frowned. "Mistress Greene is fond of animals and birds," he replied stiffly, and then wondered whether the others were mocking him. But who the devil was this Copson to be using his sister's name so freely? He must speak to her about permitting such liberties. He was her brother, her guardian now—a word in time—— The serving man had dismounted at the lodge and was holding his own and the packhorse. "Master Copson!" cried the lodge-keeper, an elderly man; "you are welcome home, Master Copson!" He ducked his head to Greene and his sister, who felt inferior even to lodge-keepers as they followed the long, straight drive. The nearer you were to the house, the larger it appeared; Greene guessed there was as much of it again unseen at the back; his unfamiliarity with such surroundings daunted him; he saw clearly that a baccalaureate could mean little to the heir to several estates of this kind. At the front of the house there was an incongruous addition to the original homely structure, an Italianate portico, and through this they entered. Straightway Copson led them by way of long tapestried passages to a small room where he left Greene for not more than two or three minutes, while he took Alice to the housekeeper. "You will be happy here," he told her, again in the passage. "You will not be without a friend." She recognised this as not flirtatious, and thanked him sincerely but with a certain breathlessness. "You must not be afraid, Mistress Alice. Or are you annoyed like your brother when I use your first name?" No, no, she was not annoyed. He knocked on a door. "Mistress Mako, I bring you Mistress Alice Greene." He bowed, smiled at both women, and went.

On the road Alice had heard such good accounts of Mistress Mako that she could not now be afraid of her. She curtsied.

"You are a pretty child," said Mistress Mako. She was of medium height, with iron-grey hair, about forty years of age, a managing woman.

"If it please you, Mistress," replied Alice.

"It does please me, child. I like none of your ugly, glum faces round about me, I tell you. You are all the way from Norwich?"

"From King's Lynn, if it please you."

"From King's Lynn, to be sure! My head is like a sieve to-day. Take off your cape, child, and sit by the fire a minute or two." She folded the cloak inside out over the back of a chair. "You are hungry?"

"Yes, I think I am, but I don't think I can eat anything."

"Hm, we shall see!"

She opened a door and clapped her hands for a maid-servant whom she sent to the buttery. While they waited and then while Alice ate and drank she asked a lot of questions and gave a good deal of information, though without saying a word about the family.

"Do I see her ladyship to-night?"

"In half an hour, child. I'll show you your room when you have finished that food you thought you could not touch."

"I get a room to myself?"

Mistress Mako nodded. "We are not short of rooms at Braiding."

She herself took Alice there. A prodigious distance it seemed, and made irretraceable by a number of turnings.

"But I shall never find my way about!"

Mistress Mako was obviously pleased by this tribute to the size of her house. "Yes, we do not run on each other's elbows here at Braiding."

At last she pushed open a door and signed to Alice to follow her. "You will have this room. Do you like it?"

It was at the back of the house and looked out upon much
the same kind of parkland as that they came through at
the front. She found that her baggage had been carried
there for her. Mistress Mako suggested she might like to
change her dress and offered to help her, partly from good
nature, partly that she might see what the valises held.
It was not until ten minutes or so before half past eight
that the two women had discussed the important matters
arising from even a first examination and Alice was fully
dressed again. Mistress Mako thought she looked charming,
and said so. But a little too much the puritan, she wanted to
add, walking all round her and touching here and there
the becoming but not stylish enough apparel.

And now they must go. Mistress Mako had a last regretful
glance at the garments laid out on the bed, and they were
walking through long corridors again. "Where is my
brother?" "Geoffrey Copson has seen to him. He is certain
to be with the family before this." Alice walked on, thinking.
So as Robin had jested, he was guest and she was servant.
Well, she thought (and Mistress Mako wondered why she
set her lips firmer), she had come here to take service,
and she would not court a snub. The household should see
from the beginning she knew her position. "I hope you will
find me useful," she told Mistress Mako. "I want to be
useful!"

Then they were in a large and gloomy room, its panel-
ling almost black, the few lights reflected dully from its
wooden floor. She hardly noticed the heavily framed
pictures, the soundless tapestries, the armour. "Through
there," said Mistress Mako, pointing ahead. It was then she
noticed two tiny pageboys, one on each side of the door
ahead. The one was smiling at the housekeeper, the other
opening the door inward into light and the sound of quiet
voices. Copson was coming out at that moment. "Courage!"
he whispered without stopping. Then they entered.

She saw Sidley first and her brother, then the gorgeous
dresses of the women, then the richness of the room, then
the man who must be Sidley's father. Robert stood, clumsily

half-turned towards her, uncertain what to do or say; Sidley gestured towards her with fingers wide apart, half introducing her into the room, half exhibiting her. At the touch of Mistress Mako's fingers on her elbow she curtsied to the ground, rose, and felt the same fingers prompt her towards the centre of the room. This was Sidley's mother, seated with straight back, dressed in black and white silk, her fingers covered with magnificent rings, jewels at her throat, and an elaborate collar high enough to frame the back of her head. A beauty once, but now her face was dreadfully ravaged with the smallpox, and, Alice thought, made almost monstrous by the use of paint to disguise undisguisable scars. "We are glad to see you, child," she was saying kindly.

"So you are Mistress Alice Greene?" This was Sidley's sister, the Lady Elizabeth. Alice curtsied once more, startled by her likeness to her brother. Like Lady Sidley, she was dressed in black and white silk, with a magpie ruff of bone-lace, but wore strings of pearls at her wrists and no other jewellery. Her shoes were silver. This elegance and glitter made Alice ten times more aware than any advice of Mistress Mako's of the homely cut of her dress, its plain material, its honest serviceableness and lack of distinction. Yet stubbornly she told herself she was a servant, and curtsied again, this time to Sir Ralph, seated near the fire. It was from the father Sidley and his sister got their looks. He had the same high, narrow forehead, the same dark brown hair, the same pale face and obvious lips. But unlike his children, he appeared stale and tired. Listening to his quiet words of welcome, she had the unpleasant fancy that all the time he was probing into the recesses of his own mind; that he was froglike, as though bred in tepid pools, scum-mantled, the encrustations of settling sand and smooth wet greenness upon him, his blood chilling the veins it half-filled. Suddenly his eyes fell to the outlines of her bosom, he smiled blankly, and horribly she imagined his hands like toads creeping over her warmth and whiteness. Trembling a little, she said a word or two in reply, and curtsied to Sidley, who nodded cheerfully, indeed half-bowed. There were perfunctory questions and answers; she was feeling very lonely and upset when the Lady Elizabeth rose determinedly and walked towards a brilliantly coloured pile of silks on a couch. "Do help me sort these!" she cried to Alice, who, receiving a nod and smile from Lady Sidley, was only too glad to cross over to her. "We'll arrange them by colours, shall we?" She nodded, unable to speak, and felt her eyes well with tears as under cover of the silks the Lady Elizabeth closed her thin fingers softly and protectively over her right wrist. "With my lady mother's permission, you can go, Mistress Mako," the young lady declared. "I shall want Mistress Alice such a long time!" Meeting Alice's eyes, she pouted. "We are going to be friends, yes?"

CHAPTER XI

In the months that followed her brother's return to Cambridge Alice was often to ask herself whether she was happy at Braiding. She always concluded by telling herself yes, and there were good reasons for her decision. She had left her narrow home and her increasingly difficult relationship with her father; she was part, however unimportant, of the larger world she and Robert longed for; she was treated with kindness and consideration at the best, with a friendly indifference at the worst; she had little to do and whatever guidance she needed in doing it. Yet she was not entirely happy.

For the Lady Elizabeth's sake she told herself she should be. That first night there was friendship between them, and it increased with the passing of each week. There was never any doubt whether one person wanted to see her. She soon found that Sidley's sister, with proper allowance for the difference of their station, had been reared even more shelteredly than she. Probably Sir Ralph's experience of women was the cause of this; he felt no one of them might be trusted, and illustrated the old paradox that a man can be proud of a loose-living son but tolerate not even the noonday heat to kindle his daughter. She had spent her sixteen years between Braiding and Leesome, and to Alice's amazement, who thought every member of every family boasting any kind of title must spend at least half the year at Court, had never been to London.

"My parents," she announced, whether satirically or not Alice could not determine, "think Ralph my brother represents the family enough abroad. I should find this Norwich of yours quite a huge city, I know. Do tell me about it, Alice dear!"

She did so, feeling the tables most oddly turned. Here was she, the homestaying daughter, bringing the outside world to this rich and lovely girl. "Not that there is very much to tell," she usually began, but it was extraordinary how she could always think of something new. She told of visits to neighbours and relatives, of weeks at Wroxham, of that never-to-be-forgotten fair she visited with her brother and the Lady Elizabeth's, of the fairs at Norwich too, of her mother and father, of the babies, of brother Robert himself.

"You seem to have seen so much," the girl complained. "Leesome is just like this. I do the same things at the same time, and there's hardly a new face from one year's end to another. I wonder why we don't visit. Since my mother had the small-pox three years ago—— I think it was kind of them to bring you here to me, don't you?"

"I think it was kind of you, my lady——"

"Oh don't call me *my lady* except when there are folk about! I feel sick to death sometimes with servants and servants and servants and never a friend! You will be my friend, won't you?"

"If you want me to be."

"But don't you want to be? Don't you want to be my friend?"

"Of course I do, only——"

"Only nothing, except when there are folk about! Now go on—call me Elizabeth!" Alice felt a difficulty. "Go on! Your brother is the friend of mine, isn't he? What is so odd about it then?"

"Very well, Elizabeth."

But the young girl was conscious of the restraint. "You don't call me Elizabeth properly! Why, why don't you?"

How explain the fear of inconsistent treatment, favourite to-day, in disgrace to-morrow? Yet there was never a hint of this with her young mistress, and in time she came to feel there never would be.

Her duties were so light she began to think she had been brought there entirely for Elizabeth's sake, as the child herself thought. She helped Mistress Mako in the early

mornings in solemn surveys of clean and dirty linen, in
light dustings of objects too precious to entrust to country
maidservants, in checking work done; and when the housekeeper discovered she could write with the same clear hand
as her brother's she employed her many an odd time on
the accounts she and Ferrers, the steward, had to prepare
between them. Ferrers, a rough-tongued but kindly old
man, she liked very much after the first shock of his animal-
frank conversation, and ventured to think if he were ten
or fifteen years younger he and Mistress Mako, who could
herself be more than becomingly broad of speech, might
have made a match of it. "Such handwriting is wasted on a
wench," he said rudely one day. "You are a bonny bit,
Mistress Alice, I doubt not, but you would be more credit
to yourself in a doublet and hose. As it is, I don't say you
would not make a tight little wife for a steward, and if it was
the old man Ferrers was still a young man, I don't say but
he'd have you in bed and——" "That will do, you nasty
old man!" cried Mistress Mako; "you get back to your own
quarters." "And why? Is a man old enough to be the lass's
grandfather to be shouted at for telling the truth that shouts
itself?" He looked at her in a way that reminded her of
the much more ancient William Beetham. "She'd make a
tight little wife for a steward, I say, with a hand like that—
or for an under-steward too. That's right, d'you see—the
lass shows ten times more sense than you, dame. She's
not offended. You are not offended, are you, lass?"

After the busy days at Norwich helping her mother and
the one maid, she seemed to herself now to lead an idle
life. "But you are not idle!" Elizabeth urged. "Look at
the time you spend with me. Let's go to my room now, shall
we, and look at all my dresses again?" Alice could not
persuade herself this was work. Taking dresses from their
drawers and wardrobes, draping them in falls of bright-
coloured silks over the bed, sitting helpless with admiration
in front of them, and changing one's mind twice a minute
as to which was most becoming: could she really call this
work? "You like the blue?" The blue took her breath

away. "But really, Alice, I think I like this yellow and gold better than any. Don't you think so too?" Fair consideration suggested it might well be the best, were it not for the flame-coloured robe worn with the orange petticoat, or indeed the green-and-pearl camlet bodice with its flower-sprinkled green skirt. Nor might the black and white silk in which she had first seen Elizabeth be so lightly dismissed— "Though I've had it two years now." Alice· was not so willing to admit this a fatal caveat. "It becomes you best of all, I give my word." "H'm," said Elizabeth. "Then there is velvet——"

There was; and satin and grogram and taffeta and hollands and lawn and cambric too. These were subjects for a twelvemonth's months. And sarcenet and tabbinet and tiffany and cypress and bombazin and stammel and an entrancing dozen others. No, the saddler of Norwich would never have called these dear debates other than the devil's work.

"Should I wear the blue or the black-and-white to-night, do you think?"

How easy to dismiss the results of Don John's death, argued so fiercely by Sidley that very day! The blue or the black-and-white? They shook their heads. If only one could wear both! "I'll try them on, shall I?" Alice drew the mirrors more to the light while Elizabeth undressed as much as she could without aid. "Unlace me, Alice dear." She tried on the blue. It was perfection. "You look so sweet, Elizabeth!" The girl threw her arms around Alice. "Then you said Elizabeth as I should always like you to!" They hesitated between pearls and brilliants! Oh, but it must be brilliants with the blue. She would wear the blue, that was settled. Nothing else could possibly—— "But we'll just try on the black-and-white, shall we?" This was the death-blow to resolution. In the blue undoubtedly she looked the prettier, but in the black-and-white more beautiful. A little older too—not a bad recommendation to just sixteen. The bone-lace ruff and the pearls, they helped. "I think you'll have to try them on, Alice, and I'll see what they look like on you." But Alice would not hear of such a thing. Besides, it would be a poor fit.

"Oh no, it wouldn't! I'm as tall as you are. Come on!" There was more unhooking. "The blue first!"

Elizabeth picked up the dress and held it out. "You are heaps better made than I am, Alice. I look quite thin, don't I?"

"But I am years older than you, Elizabeth. And you are so ladylike. Ladies ought to be slender."

"But not so thin as I am. Do put it on!" She clapped her hands with delight. "You must look in the glass! You must look in the glass!"

It was a revelation to Alice. The blue bodice fitted low and tight, the blue skirt swung loose and vast from the farthingaie.

"It doesn't look the same on someone else, does it?"

"Why, if Ralph saw you now, he would fall in love with the loveliest lady in Lincolnshire—in England," she added elatedly.

Alice saw the red blood in her face and neck, and bent over the hem of the skirt to hide from her companion. But Elizabeth went on talking: Why shouldn't the good Queen who they said liked to have the handsomest and tallest men around her in the handsomest habits, why shouldn't she have the most beautiful women in England too, and keep them and clothe them just because they were beautiful? —"And then you would spend your life at Court, Alice, and never, never care about things any more." She sighed, with sudden alternation of mood. "Perhaps never think about poor me here at Braiding."

"Of course I would, you dear child!"

"Of course you would!" Elizabeth began to laugh again.

Alice turned regretfully from before the mirror. "But I must take it off now."

"No, not yet! Isn't it lovely to be here with someone you like and wearing a lovely dress? I want always to make the good things last."

Ironically, at that moment there was her mother's voice at the door, and Lady Sidley came into the room. Never as then, fresh from the contemplation of her own and Elizabeth's beauty, was she so aware of the other's marred face. The thought was as strong as her confusion at being found so attired. For the second time she felt that betraying flush, and this time could not hide it as she curtsied.

"Oh, mother, mother!" cried Elizabeth, running to her; "I am so happy! Don't be cross. Say you won't be cross!"

"I am not cross, child. Why should I be?" She stroked her daughter's hair. "Be happy while you can. Beauty will not last for ever, nor happiness either perhaps."

"Oh, mother, mother——"

"You look both beautiful and virtuous, Alice," she said, coming towards her with her daughter. "I am glad you are with us and bring my Elizabeth joy." She turned to examine the garments laid out on the bed. "You have too much here, my child. You might consider——"

"May I really, mother?"

"Should a gentlewoman be selfish, you think?"

"Thank you, thank you, thank you! Then you must have the blue, Alice."

But this seemed a dreadful end to the afternoon. Did Lady Sidley think she—— Then she saw her smile and knew she did not. "But the blue dress—the one you love so much!"

"And I love you so much, so you must take it. She looks better in it than I do, doesn't she, mother?"

Lady Sidley's hand pulled at a brooch. "You are not to make each other vain." Near the mirror, she turned to look into it, and then abruptly left the room.

"Poor mother," said Elizabeth. "She was more beautiful than heaven till——" She ended what she was saying as though it were blasphemy.

Alice thought a lot about this tragedy of Lady Sidley's. From Mistress Mako she heard that since her beauty went she was a changed woman, never visiting, never willing to entertain. Mistress Mako thought she would never go to Court again. "Nothing short of a royal command—and who is Sir Ralph to receive that, pray? The boy now——" She told Alice of fearsome rages, now mercifully over, when even old servants were dismissed overnight for staring at her altered appearance, of high words between husband and wife, of the children's grief. "But what God gives, we must receive, is what I say." And she had come to think the same, with time. "Three years—you'd not know her now from then, Alice." Before a mirror, Alice would smooth the skin under her eyes, her cheeks, her neck and shoulders. She shuddered. One could only hope God would be kind. Politically, she never gave cause of offence by appearing to look or avoid looking at the afflicted lady. And at all times Lady Sidley was gracious enough to her, and her reserve she preferred.

And yet, with all this, she could not be entirely happy. Mistress Mako, Lady Sidley, in their degrees, yes; the Lady Elizabeth adorable; but the menfolk—no. Not old Ferrers—she found no offence in him, only rarely a blush despite his coarseness. But the Sidleys, father and son, and Geoffrey Copson, in their different ways all three distressed her.

Sir Ralph first—she could never free herself from her first impression of him as cold, froglike, pallidly lecherous. Not that she was frightened by him now as at that first interview when in fancy she felt his lean fingers dabble her. From Mistress Mako's remarks, gossip from more than one of the servants, and her own observation, she knew him burnt-out, incapable of aggression. "An old goat," said Mistress Mako with a wink, and pointedly allowed her upright index finger to curl down to her fist; "But he has called himself a fine man in his time. Half the pretty girls of the county—the kind that have no sense——" Instead of laughing she sneered. "Perhaps the young one——" Alice saw a warning in the housekeeper's sharp glance sideways at her, and flushed. "About Sir Ralph?" she suggested.—"Ah yes, Sir Ralph!" Mistress Mako unpicked the seam of a dress and talked. Sir Ralph was little danger to a maid now. She laughed with bolder face than Alice at her witticisms.

And yet, knowing this as she did, his pebbled eyes disturbed her whenever she met them. To look up from some task with the Lady Elizabeth and see his pale face turned towards her, his eyes blank, his expression as though he was groping slowly among the dripping weeds of unwholesome thought, never failed to set her heart a-jumping. Rarely she met him in a passage, when sometimes he smiled setly, sometimes ignored her, always troubled her lest he stretch out his easily-repulsed hands. Ignorance was no part of her training; at least she would not be terrified by the unknown; but Sir Ralph's was an uncomfortable stare over your shoulder, he saw you shrinkingly naked, it was annoying and, worse than that, shuddery to wonder what his speculations were. And worst of all in a certain mood, he was an aged caricature of his brilliant son. Oftentimes she looked from the one to the other with sharp distaste that so fair a tree might suffer an equal drying of its sap.

Sidley had not gone to London after all. She did not dare think herself the reason why. Yet there were indications, light straws puffed before a gathering wind. She remembered her talk with Robert the evening before he left. They had gone out into the park, walking several times as far as the lodge. "I hear, Alice," he said constrainedly, "that Sidley will not return to London for a week or two." He kicked his foot through a pile of yellow leaves. "This is a magnificent home, Alice." She agreed that it was. "I don't know," he began, after a short silence; "you are sure you are going to like it here?" She asked why he wanted to know. "I don't know," he repeated; "perhaps because I am now not so sure I myself like the homes of great men. There is splendour here, true. You are sure you would not prefer it back in Norwich with our mother, the children, everything you know so well?" She pulled at his arm. "I know what the matter is with you, Robin." "There is nothing the matter with me, Alice." "Oh yes, there is! At Cambridge you felt yourself Sidley's equal. The differences of wealth and rank seemed not to matter. Now they do. You are harassed because, as you said on the way here, you dine at one table and I at another, you are friend and I am servant. And perhaps you find yourself friend only on sufferance."

"No, no, Alice, you are wrong. They—why they treat me like an equal. Good God, I am an equal! It's not rank and wealth—I'm a scholar, and the scholar is welcome everywhere. I'm a bachelor of arts, I'll write poetry and set my name alongside Ariosto and Guazzo and Camoens. All this display of temporal goods—I am more than an equal, Alice!"

She assessed his lack of conviction from the heat of his argument. "Very well, you are then, Robin. Myself, I am a servant here. You must not allow yourself to be distressed by our relationship."

"As though I would! I told you Sidley is not going to London just yet, didn't I?" Once more he kicked up leaves. "You are going to stay here then? I think, as your brother, I owe you a word of advice, Alice." He was looking straight ahead, and she glancing sideways, was both moved and amused by the mingled righteousness, worry, and affection she read in his face. "Do you like Sidley, Alice?"

"In Norwich I thought him charming. Here I never think of him."

"You see, Alice, things would be different if you had not grown up so damned pretty these last few years. I never thought it of you as a youngster. Oh, you can laugh! It makes it very awkward, Alice."

"Makes what awkward?"

"My leaving you here, that is what. I want to think you are safe, Alice."

"Don't talk so foolishly! Are you afraid of Sir Ralph or Geoffrey Copson or Master Ferrers, our warty steward?"

"Oh, they are right enough. Besides, I think young Copson a bit afraid of me. No, Alice, I am thinking of Sidley." He took her arm. "You may think me a poor friend, but I ought to tell you——"

"That Master Sidley is fond of girls!" They stopped walking. "Then you need not. I know it well enough."

"You don't mean to say——"

"Of course not! I wonder if all brothers are as stupid as you and believe their sisters stop thinking when they are twelve years old? As though any woman in the world would not know on sight that your precious Sidley is a gallant and a fox!"

She could see that her brother was much relieved by this declaration. He said frankly that it eased his mind, and gave her one or two pieces of gnomic counsel which told her nothing she did not know before. "A maid's honour goes with her maidenhead, Alice. For God's sake, come to no shipwreck because of me."

"Because of you?"

"It was my talking brought you here. I can't forget that."

She remembered this talk now that she found Sidley home in October and November and December. Why then had he not gone? Braiding must be dull for him. He rode to hounds and showed a liking for the deaths of all kinds of creatures for entertainment, but was never recognisably a boozy country squire. Drinker and wencher though she knew him to be, she could not lump him in the same bundle with callers like Farmer John Scratton's son or red-faced Philip Round, who talked nothing but horses in women's company, nothing but women in horses'. These blunt-toed, mud-minded countrymen served for a day's hunting, but were less fitted to be his friends than Long Tom from the stables or Jake the kennel man. He was fire to their clay. It became apparent he had no friend of his own station; he did little visiting abroad. Sometimes when the days were too wet or frost-gripped for riding, he stayed indoors and read, talked with his father and mother, or spent hours with an Italian tutor who was perfecting his foreign conversation in readiness for his tour the next spring. It was the coming of this Signor Galanti which convinced Alice he would not go to London at all. Meantime, his conduct towards her was much what she had expected. He was a long way from the easy familiarity of Wroxham Fair and their tiny garden in Tombland; yet always treating her with more respect and courtesy than were due to a servant of any rank. He trod a fine line with as much dexterity as she. Had it not been for those worrying incidents——

One day he came into the housekeeper's room when Mistress Mako was about some other business. Alice was sewing near the fire. "A very domestic picture," he said curtly, and as she started to her feet: "Pray do not disturb yourself. Mistress Mako is not here?" He came over towards her. "How convenient an absence can be. Have you thought, Mistress Alice, how much better for the dragon if he had not guarded the golden apples?" She showed her bewilderment. "Because bold young men will take what they want, willy-nilly." He sat down on the other side of the fire. "You are diligent, Mistress Alice?" "I was taught, sir, that Satan finds work for idle hands to do," she retorted lightly, to cover her uncertainty.—"The very reply for a pretty puritan! And you have the right of it. What would you say if I tell you he is even now finding work for mine?" It was as though he had dropped a mask from his face. She rose hurriedly. "I must find Mistress Mako and tell her you want her." "Don't trouble yourself," he ordered harshly; "I must be going." He went, and this, though far from pleasant, she could ignore.

There was the night she heard the quiet tapping on her door. Sitting up in bed, hugging the clothes to her neck, she sat in the darkness, at first terrified, then really angry. The bolts were shot, she knew. She must speak to the housekeeper in the morning, to prevent rumours. But she did not. In the morning she could not be sure it wasn't a dream. Try as she would, she could bring it no nearer than a lifetime-old memory.

Then three weeks before Christmas was the afternoon when she walked into the banqueting room to light the infrequently spaced candles that were always burning there between daylight and bedtime. It seemed as though Sidley had followed her into the room. At any rate he was behind her with a suddenness which made her jump. "You are frightened, Mistress Alice?" She put her hand to her heart.

"I did not see you! I—it was the sudden way——" "Your heart beats faster than it should," he said, and put out a hand as though to touch her, but she moved her taper and cried out with alarm as the flame licked his fingers. "I play with fire; I must expect to be burned some time," he said coolly, gave her a long look in which there seemed more hate than desire, and with the first full bow with which he had honoured her since Norwich he walked away.

This was not an episode to ignore or treat as a dream. It remained vivid and raw-surfaced for a long time—like Sidley's burn, for foolishly he pretended he had no injury, and so neglected it that it needed poulticing and care for a fortnight. In each other's presence they thought the bandage the size of a stormcloud. It hung between them like a flag of war. The less forgettable because they never referred to it.

And Copson? He was a worry of a different kind. It was apparent to Mistress Mako earlier than to Alice that the understeward was falling in love with her. He found excuses for coming to the housekeeper's room in the hope of seeing her, he found duties which took him down passages along which she might be expected to appear, his pleasant, far-from-handsome face which at first had broken into easy smiles each time he saw her, now with smiles mingled an uncomfortable happiness. Ferrers, who discovered from Mistress Mako the way the wind was set, mock-grumbled at him for hours on end. "Body of all the saints, boy—if she worries you so much, wed her, bed her, and then attend to your duties again!" Copson implored Ferrers to say nothing of the kind. "Say?" cried the steward. "More doing than saying is what pups of your type need. God A'mighty, boy, you have only seen her this couple of months. Wed her, bed her, only don't neglect your duties!" With Mistress Mako—a widow—the steward—a bachelor— discussed the situation often and at length and generally with a pleasant bawdry.

"Though what he sees in a slip of a girl——"

"Or she in a slip of a boy——"

"When the world is full of fine women of fifty——"

"And fine men of sixty, Master Ferrers——"

"I'm not sixty, dame, make no mistake about it. I've kept my youth, I have. I should like to see the woman who'd dance the sheets with a younker, a bean-pod, a thin little pipestem, when once she had sampled me!"

"Well," said Mistress Mako slily, "you are still alive and my husband is dead," and left him to make what he could of it.

But throughout these early months Copson said nothing of love to Alice, though in everything except words he made his feelings clear enough: his voice, his laugh, his dawdling or hurry, the way he greeted her or said good-bye, his bringing her crusts and crumbs from the kitchen with an invitation to feed the birds or deer, his less frequent use of her name. With a pleasing extravagance he kept his hat off all the time he was with her. But he said nothing, until Ferrers swore to Mistress Mako that as Cupid was used to shoot arrows into some men's hearts he should aim at this time at young Copson's backside and jerk him forward to a declaration.

"And what does the maid think?"

Mistress Mako thought she liked the lad and nothing more.

"And what more is wanted?" asked Ferrers.

"Love, stupid!" cried the housekeeper.

"Never heard of it," said Ferrers. "Is it like the dropsy?"

Mistress Mako suggested one likeness. It puffed a man out.

Mistress Mako was right in her opinion, only if liking might be called great liking. Alice thought Copson the dearest man in the world. She knew him good and honest to the backbone, kind in all ways, and she felt for him an affection that came very near love. But she was sure she did not want to marry him—almost sure, anyhow. He was a little too—what could she call it?—not quite assertive enough to be her idea of a husband. He was too much the boy, despite the trust Ferrers placed in him. And yet if she refused him when the inevitable offer of marriage came, would she ever again know such a lovable man? If he were a little more like—she blamed herself furiously for saying it—like Sidley! A year ago in Norwich—but how different everything was here at Braiding. She temporised. He must not get the chance to love her, or at least he must get no chance to ask her to marry him. Certainly not for a long, long time. A word, a sigh, a downcast look, a minute's pleading, if such there were—she felt strongly her inability to cope with this new complication of life. Should she tell Elizabeth? Something held her back from doing so.

Yet it would be a wise match. Her life an assured one, a husband who loved her dearly, whom she liked more than any man she had ever met. With complete truth she told herself she was a fool to think above him. But if a man like Sidley—she remembered his squeezing her fingers at Wroxham Fair, and then his face as he drew his hand back from the taper-flame. No doubt of it, she was a fool. A greater fool for knowing herself one! There could be only one relationship for her with a man of his type and rank, and that she would never tolerate. So why not marry Copson and his ugly good-tempered grin? Because she was unsettled by her new freedom, because her standards of value were not quite perfected, because above all she wanted for a while to stay as she was, and because telling herself she was a fool made no difference.

CHAPTER XII

AFTER THIS FASHION the time wore on to Christmas. This was one of the occasions when the lady of the house could not avoid company, for her husband's position in the county and the irresistible strength of custom made Braiding the proper seat of the season's festivities. Even now the Sidleys saw little of their equals, but the farmers, petty squires, tenants, and dozens of servants gathered there each year and kept up the old ways. The mummers came over from Kelverton Marsh, there was usually a masque at night, that wanton monarch, the Lord of Misrule, never failed to wield his brief and irresponsible authority. There was certainly nothing niggardly about the preparations for the event. Under the supervision of Mistress Mako rooms not opened for months were cleaned and made ready, vast stocks of linen aired and freshly perfumed, and coarse blankets put in readiness for lesser men; Ferrers all but drove Alice and love from Copson's head with the thousand and one missions he thrust upon him, the calculations, and the overseeing. In the huge kitchens began the fierce industry which was to whirl to a destructive climax of eating and drinking. Lady Sidley and Elizabeth, with Alice's help, spent a couple of days deciding upon the gifts that would be presented to all who entered the house over the holiday. And there was always the problem of deciding what to wear at the masque, and the business of making up the devices. Alice contrasted this with the quiet Christmas of Tombland, and looked forward to the celebrations all the more.

"I think we work hard enough to deserve it," said Elizabeth putting daubs of red, green and yellow on a bird-like face of canvas and lath. "I don't think I like this bird after all. What else could I go as?"

They suggested one or two costumes and masks, but it was to be the bird after all. "I know I shall be happy whatever I wear," she admitted. "And you will be the Grand Turk, mother?"

"And carry a scimitar to strike off your heads!"

They laughed. "And Ralph?"

"He wants it to be a secret, I am sure, but I saw such a lot of green leaves and branches cut out in his room. Do you think he can be a tree?"

"Ask Mistress Mako. She is the sempstress."

But the housekeeper claimed privilege, shook her head, and they would not make her answer. Sidley's disguise was safe with her, and she always withdrew to her own room to work at it. It was so Copson came to the housekeeper's room one night with an appeal from Ferrers about the quantity of bread used that year, and found Alice alone.

"I don't see you so often now, Mistress Alice."

"We are both so busy, aren't we?"

"I miss seeing you, Mistress Alice."

"And I miss seeing you, Master Copson. You have been a friend to me—a good friend."

"You think I have? I wanted to be. Mistress Alice——"

"Yes, Master Copson?"

He laughed, going red in the face. "My name is Geoffrey you know."

She laughed with him. "So it is, isn't it? I think it a very good name too, Master Copson."

"Er—yes. You needn't call me Master Copson, really. I like my friends to call me Geoffrey."

"Thank you, Master Geoffrey!"

He looked around the room. "So Mistress Mako is not here?" He looked again, as though expecting her to climb out of a shoe or fall from a shelf. "Ah well, I shall have to tell Papa Ferrers. Mistress Alice——?"

"Yes, Master Geoffrey?"

He caught her eye and quickly avoided it. "You—you get all the exercise you need?" She saw him swallow. "You

might like some time to take a walk in the park. The
exercise is very beneficial, I believe. So Papa Ferrers tells
me. He is quite a healthy old man, Mistress Alice."

"So he is, Master Geoffrey."

"Yes. Well, if—if you decide you would like the exercise—
the fresh air—I should be very glad to escort you, Mistress
Alice."

"So that I shall become a healthy old woman, Master
Geoffrey?"

"No," he said earnestly. "So that you may remain a
beautiful young one!"

"But, Master Geoffrey——"

"Say you will come!"

She chose the fatal, easy road. "But I am too busy, as
you know. I am most grateful for your kindness——"

"Then when you are not busy!" He gave the fire a blow
which ruined its symmetry and sent out gushes of white ash
and smoke. "Say you will, Mistress Alice!"

"But I shall always be busy if you make a mess like
that!"

"Don't touch it! I'll clean it up. Where's a brush? But
say you will come! Please say you'll come!"

"Well, some time, perhaps." She felt ten years older
than this boy. "Won't Papa Ferrers be waiting for
you?"

He made a gesture of vexation. "I think he keeps me
running about the house in places where I may never see
you. If he knew you were coming out with me, Mistress
Alice, he would send me to Grantham for the week, I am
sure. As soon as you are free?"

"You are such a persistent young man! Yes, I will then,
some time when I am free."

"Ah! I'll hold you to it, remember." His grin redeemed
the homeliness of his features, made them handsome.
"And now I'll go back to my dragon!" At the door he
changed his mind and walked across to her once more.
"There is one thing I want to ask you now I have the
chance, Mistress Alice."

"I am too busy," she begged him. "You must go! I don't know what Papa Ferrers will say."

"He will have his chance in a couple of minutes. Christmas day——"

She was so relieved at these two words that she put down her embroidery.

"I don't know whether Papa Ferrers will let me join in the revels. He says I shall have to work for him."

"No, no—he is teasing you, Master Geoffrey!"

"But just in case he isn't—I'm going to join in all the same, Alice—Mistress Alice! Will you dance with me?"

"If you ask me. But you mustn't disobey Master Ferrers."

"You'll dance with me? Then it's settled. I'll see Papa Ferrers to the devil and back for that!" She watched him to the door and off he went.

Later she found an opportunity to ask the housekeeper whether Papa Ferrers would allow Copson to desert his duties on Christmas Day, and heard that he made the same threat every year and never enforced it. This year she imagined the old rogue had uttered it more firmly than ever because he knew his underling was making sheep's-eyes at Mistress Alice. "He's a lovely lad," added Mistress Mako, and when Alice agreed: "He will make some lucky lass a good husband, child," with which she also agreed, too calmly for Mistress Mako's liking. "For one I know of in particular," she snapped, and then repented. "It is not for me to say, my child, I know."

The two days before Christmas were such a time of activity as she had never believed possible. Guests were arriving constantly, including the mummers and morris-dancers, and she saw forty new faces a day. Mostly they were people of the locality, but two gentlemen with their servants sought their hospitality late on Christmas Eve with a story of unexpected difficulties on the road. They were travelling from London to Lincoln, and one of them, the son of Sir Godfrey Hurrish, had a slight acquaintance with the family. He was a courteous young man, with a fine tenor voice, and sang charmingly after supper to the old-fashioned rebeck and then to the Lady Elizabeth's lute. Clearly he was an acquisition, and Lady Sidley vowed it was gracious of the bad roads to keep him with them at such a time. His companion, Richard Canwelt, was of a graver turn, with a suitable melancholy baritone, who after one song stressing rather the miseries than the rewards of love, found his métier as a retailer of news. This he told several times over to different groups of listeners, and was quite untiring. These two were to share the second-best bedroom: the best, Alice knew from Mistress Mako, was used only for very great persons indeed; so while Canwelt opened his budget once more for the benefit of horsey Philip Round, and Hurrish was easily persuaded to sing something sweet and sad to the recorder, she and the housekeeper were busier than ever upstairs. Mistress Mako was as proud of Braiding as if it belonged to her, and left nothing of the more important guests' comfort to the care of her staff. "You are a girl after my own heart," she told Alice, one on each side of Canwelt's bed, tucking in the counterpane. "You would do the same when my back is turned, and that's more than I can say for the sluts of maids I have to deal with." They surveyed their work. "The men are like girls to-day," said Mistress Mako. "Pillows for their heads! What will it come to next?" But when in the steward's pantry she mentioned pillows and old Ferrers broke out into coarse jeers, declaring he would as soon put his cheek on a pair of fat buttocks, she changed her tune, called him a lewd old man, and appealed to heaven to know why young gentlemen should not have pillows to keep the blood from running overmuch to their heads. "No danger of that if their fathers 'ud fetch it out of their hides with stripes," cried Ferrers. The age was a soft one. He rubbed his nose with the back of his hand, meditating a strong saying. The young fellows you saw about the place to-day. Huh! you'd have the fathers brought to bed next! He scowled at Copson, then entering. Even when a lad loved a lass, he was afraid to take her hand, much less——

"Ay, we know all about you, you lackpenny lover of pap-ladles!" Mistress Mako interrupted him, and took Alice away.

In the morning the guests were roused with a broken consort of music and the voices of carollers. It was pouring with rain outside, so the instrumentalists and singers paraded the passages and halted for some minutes outside the principal bedroom doors till they were opened and those inside gave them good day or a god-be-with-you. Sir Ralph, less froglike than usual in a rich furred gown, and his lady followed after them and hoped their guests had spent a good night. With these courtesies and a sop of wine-soaked bread the hours were passed to dinner—with these and the giving of presents. But meantime in the kitchen there was the last but one scouring of ovens, the last but one broiling and baking, stewing and roasting, frying and boil-ing, mixing and stirring, carving and shredding, all with oaths and commands from the cooks. Alice was there in time to see the last of the mince-pies prepared: the flesh from a leg of mutton, three pounds of suet, pepper and salt, cloves and mace, nutmeg and a trace of ginger, currants, raisins and prunes, dates sliced and oranges; the whole to be baked in a pie-crust and served with burnt sugar and hot spices. This trifle was knocked off by a large man with red arms helping for the week; it went smack into the oven, and before she left he was chopping up chickens, rice and almonds for a massive blancmange. The heat there was unbearable. A hundred hot smells of meat, fruit, condi-ments and sweetmeats mingled sickeningly under the low roof, on the great ovens splashes of grease and water sizzled unendingly, the floor steamed like the hobs of hell, and clouds poured upwards from boilers and saucepans. A horde of boys and women in aprons stained with every filth from blood to dung ran at the biddings of their masters, who cuffed them, cursed them, kicked them, with spare breath and hands. Amid it all Papa Ferrers appeared. "It goes?" he cried to the head cook, who regarded him without respect. "It goes!" the cook bellowed, and reaching for a hanging carcase, hacked off the tail and flung it towards him. "If you can't eat it, wear it!" he shouted, and smacked the head of a small boy who had seemed afraid to laugh at his joke. Ferrers went off swearing, but only after a retort that made the maidservants scream.

Alice had not a moment to be with the family. As the guests left their rooms, these had to be cleaned and the beds made up. There was the laying of the table in the banqueting hall for some to attend to, the carrying of beers and wines to the sideboards for others, the mummers and dancers must rehearse over the stables—thirsty work, they needed waiting on—there were the singers getting in everybody's way, messages, errands, last-minute recollections, commands and countermands. Yet all there were joyous. Even the small boy with the smacked head knew that Christmas came but once a year. Ferrers was giving instructions for the last time to his pantrymen and table waiters. "Forget not the customs of the house!" he told them. "Forget them not, and disgrace not yourselves and me and Braiding, for by God's head if you do——" He left them to shuddering conjecture while he looked over the table. "Another dish of salt! a larger trencher! Fools! Scoundrels!" He criticised the placing of the holly and mistletoe: nothing like as good as when he was limber enough to see to it himself. "See here, dame ——" This was Mistress Mako, who crossed to him and was hugged and given a noisy and slobbering kiss on the neck. "You old goat!" she called him. —"Don't pretend you didn't like it. There's not a piece in the place but envies you, woman!"

And now it was eleven o'clock. First, through the doors at the lower end came those for the table running like the upright stroke of a letter T the length of the hall; and after these again such of the servants as rank and person warranted. They found their places without much shoving and quarrelling, and then stood respectfully for their betters. The doors at the far end were opened by pageboys in red

capes, and the company came in. To the high table went
Sir Ralph and his lady, his son and daughter, the guests
of the night before, local celebrities, stately, two by two,
while in the gallery above the musicians displayed their
art—or would have done had their efforts not been drowned
by the cheering at the lower table. Sir Ralph gave his lady
his hand and she sat down, then he himself, and then the
rest of them. His lifeless eyes rested on the company and
he gave a little nod. With that Ferrers signed to his men,
and walked stiff as a pike before his lord. Once he bowed,
twice he bowed, then stood a little aside as a servant with a
towel round his neck presented the first dish, a sirloin of
beef. Sir Ralph thought just one mouthful; Ferrers, using
the new Florentine fork with his left hand, carved as though
he dealt in diamonds, and the feast had begun. Slowly
the good things worked their way down the tables: beef,
mutton, coney, capon, pig, fish and fowl, one after the other,
the steward's men doing him the utmost credit. When
each dish reached the bottom of the lower table it was
removed for the benefit of the poor folk and almsmen now
congregated inside and around the lodge gates. There was
free conversation, but no rowdyism, and the musicians
supplied a tuneful background. Wines and beers were
massed on the sideboards, whence a dozen pantlings carried
them swiftly to the diners. There was venison of the red
and fallow deer, and poachers ate it without relish. There
were dainty eaters and dogged eaters, guts-stuffers,
bone-crackers, marrow-suckers, dip-and-splash-and-come-
againers. Ladies rolled their tongues and eyes, fat men
rolled their stomachs; there were belches, coughs, and
stenches; grunts and gross guzzlings; smacks and gnashings.
Then the great joints were thinned out with pasties, pies,
and tarts. Those still hungry went on eating, and for
politeness' sake the tight-bellied kept up with them. Manners
were improving on the lower table: After you, mistress;
after you, good sir; permit me to recommend; I find these
onions tenderer, my dear; a pot of beer, friend; your very
good health, master what's-your-name. Through the

buttery door came still more dishes. "I'll eat at Sir Ralph's table," said Jake the kennel man, "till my belly touches my eyebrows. More ale here!" Now they brought in rainbow jellies in the shapes of beasts, houses, trees, ships, what-you-will; rare-cut marchpane, suckets, fruits and marmalade of quince; conserves and gingerbread, codiniacs and florentines. "The first man to stop eating," said Jake, "may he be bunged for a fortnight! More ale here!" More than an hour had gone by. On the high table Ferrers had half a dozen times seen that water in a ewer, board-cloths and towels were offered to each guest. Alice saw with what dexterity Geoffrey Copson offered and voided the service, and hoped he would so impress Papa Ferrers that there would be no danger of his being shut out of the festivities later. Once she turned to see Sidley's eyes resting on her. He smiled as though amused, raised his glass to his lips with a slight nod, and appeared to toast her. Not seeing what else she could do, and relieved that the strain between them might now be at an end, she smiled back faintly, but took good care not to look at him again. How absurd to hold that episode in this very room against him! Let bygones be bygones then—but be wary. They were now coming to the dead end of the feast. Jake's belly was a long way from shifting his eyebrows but he could not go on much longer. Trifles, kickshawses hardly worth a decent man's attention, still came forward: nuts, pears, cream, good enough for boys maybe: many of the ladies would like to let out their stays, while men boldly loosed the waistbands of their breeches. Some were in need of fanning themselves, any number of other easement; and the jokes at the servants' end were making up in flavour what they lacked in subtlety. Those who had finished there hung with wonder on the finish of Jake's gargantuan meal, and in a way he challenged their interest. "Better belly bust than good beer go waste!" he admonished the quitters, and called a last, despairing time over his shoulder.

Then the doors at the top end were flung open without ceremony, and in rushed a grotesque crew of misrulers.

Their lord, clownishly attired in robes and a crown, dashed to the high table, snatched the wine from Sir Ralph's hand, drained it, gestured impudently, and with a nimble leap was on the table, his feet like boats among the frail glass and silver. "Oyez! Oyez! Oyez!" A fellow caperer was at his side, pulling out a scroll. "Silence! Silence for His Majesty The Lord of Misrule!" He began to read, or recite, with occasional ringing of a bell, His Majesty's commands. No man to refuse to drink ale; no maid to refuse to be kissed; there should be dancing and playing and singing and leaping; there should be absolution to every servant for any fault in the next twelve hours; no one to dare dispute the rulings of this most puissant lord. Alice saw more clearly than from Mistress Mako's words why the great hall had been stripped of its portraits and adornments. Furthermore, His Lordship commanded that the tables be thrust back, that all the company be about its own business for half an hour, and that all folk then reassemble to see the thrice glorious, orgulous, and incredibly magnificent and mediocre play of St. George of Merrie England and Bold Slasher the Turkish Knight. Two things only should they do first. Even His Lordship fell into an attitude of submission as Sir Ralph called to everyone to see his glass was charged that he might drink to the health of England's Queen. Down the toast went with cheers and gusto, and with a light-hearted smashing of glass by the more fashionable, and then the announcer called on Master Gilbert Hurrish to do his duty and propose the health and everlasting prosperity of the good knight Sir Ralph Sidley, his sweet lady, and his well-loved children. This was honoured with equal enthusiasm, for though the Queen was the Queen, Sir Ralph was giving them a good day gratis. Then the hall was cleared.

Alice and Mistress Mako had not begun to force their way through the crowd when they saw an alley cleared for Lady Elizabeth, who was coming towards them. "I have asked my lady mother and now I must ask you,

Mistress Mako. You can manage without Alice this afternoon? Oh yes, yes, I know she is to be free this evening, but
she will work ever so hard to-morrow—won't you, Alice?"
Mistress Mako looked at the pair of them. Yes, she could
have the afternoon free.

"You must let me come with you while you change,
Alice."

"Change, dear?"

"Well, of course! You must wear the blue dress
because I want all the men to see you and fall in love
with you."

Alice thought this a remarkable sentiment from an
unmarried girl, but made no comment as they hurried
off to her room. "Let's call in mine first, for I have something to give you," Elizabeth suggested, and they did so.
Panting with excitement, she pulled her to the bed and
showed her her Christmas gift, a carcanet in gold wire
for the hair. Her twenty years at home jumped up and
shook admonishing fingers at Alice as she tried it on,
after a long protestation that she ought not to accept it.
"But come along, dear—you simply must change your
dress!"

But this was delayed again while Elizabeth received her
present—a smock of hollands, made by Alice herself. It
was hailed as perfection in smocks. "It is so much nicer,
isn't it, to be giving each other presents like this than all of
a rush this morning." Alice thought so too.

They came back to the hall to find the floor space
cleared so far as possible, and a stage on trestles at the
buttery end. To help away the time the Lord of Misrule
and his companions, a score of tiny bells ringing on each
leg, were some of them chasing girls, some of them throwing
clumsy somersaults, some of them riding hobby horses and
tilting at each other with long sausage-like weapons made
of sacking and straw. Occasionally, the Monarch ordered
anyone he knew unpopular or a tyrant to be kicked up the
breech or, less severely, to kiss his imperial foot. Alice's
entry caused much interest amidst the small group to which

Elizabeth carried her. Her acquaintance for the more part had never seen her so dressed, strangers saw in her fine feathers and fine bird. Said Sidley, as though determined to atone for past faults: "Mistress Alice Greene is the sister of my College friend Robert Greene, who may yet become one of the most famous men of this fame-rich age." Philip Round made as though to edge his way to her, but Sidley calmly passed in front of him. "To you go some of the thanks for the feast, Mistress Alice." Confusedly she said no, she thought not, and wondered what lay aback of his smile, so masterful, knowing, and amused. "You could supply a feast fit for a king," he whispered, disturbing her with his ambiguities. As they waited for the mummers to enter, she knew he was just behind her and never taking his eyes from her. Her bosom burned for this, and she did her best to follow the witticisms around her at the expense of the Presenter. But she enjoyed neither these nor the mumming play. All the time her mind was on Sidley. It was after the fall of Slasher he leaned towards her so that he was pressing all down her side. "A memorable day, Mistress Alice?" Whisper though it was, she felt it alive with some unidentifiable excitement. She nodded, and he leaned heavier on her shoulder. "We must make it quite unforgettable, my dear." She could not resent the way he spoke to her, but was glad when he bent from her and towards his sister. "Shush-shush-shush!" she heard Elizabeth saying.

The play ended amidst a din of handclaps and bravos, the mummers got down from the trestles and were joined to the audience. Now for a time the Lord of Misrule's followers went around the hall offering to sell their badges to any who would buy, and then they saw the morris-dancers and a clever fellow playing the pipe and tabor at the same time, and even dancing to his own music. The hall was now lighted throughout, and it was early evening, and time for the gentry to withdraw before supper, which they did amidst cheers. Behind them the merriment increased, the hobby horses were out again, and in corners of the room there were bumpy games of hot cockles and hoodman blind which would last till the tables were set up once more. Alice was heartily glad when the ladies and gentlemen met again and went back to the hall. With women only she was more aware of her position on the edge of the group rather than of it. Supper lasted three-quarters of an hour and was enlivened by the antics of the misrulers, who acted, she noticed, with an impudence which always stopped short of insult to the Sidleys or the chief guests. That over, it was time to prepare for the masque. Many of the humbler guests felt they should take their leave and did so unobtrusively, the more independent-minded of the servants set about their own pleasures, only those remaining who must attend on their betters. In theory no one was supposed to know his neighbour till the grand unmasking towards the end of the evening; in practice, however, a number of disguises were known, and especially those of the host and hostess, for whom mistakes might be inconvenient. Sir Ralph was the Sophy, his wife the Grand Turk; Lady Sidley knew what her daughter and Alice and four or five others would represent, but her son had kept his secret. That there might be no unpleasant adventures she mentioned what she knew to Gilbert Hurrish and Richard Canwelt, who gratefully accepted the task of partnering the young ladies whenever they might with propriety do so. They went up to change while the tables were cleared away and chalk sifted on the hall floor.

Elizabeth had arranged that Alice should come to her room when she was dressed, and they would go downstairs together at the sound of the horn. Now as she walked on her own to see Mistress Mako for a minute before making her preparations she was stopped by Copson, who appeared so suddenly from a doorway near the housekeeper's room that she knew he had been waiting for her.

"Mistress Alice!" He appeared on the way to being dumbfounded by the blue gown.

"Master Geoffrey!" She dipped him the smallest curtsy, which he received with a bow.

"I have only now thought of it," he began. "You will be masked. I shan't know you!"

"But you are not supposed to know," she teased him.

"No, but I want to!"

"You think my disguise will be as good as all that?"

"Give me time and I'd find you in Venice a-carnivalling! But while I am looking someone else may get you."

"But why shouldn't someone else——"

"Because I don't want them to!" he said pugnaciously. "Because——" The door opened most disconcertingly behind him and three of the steward's men came out. "You are wanted, Master Copson." He gestured towards them. "Alice then? You'll tell me, please?"

"You look about for me," she told him, but was moved by the worried eyes that suddenly belied his eager face. "Look out for the black mask, if you know me no other way."

She almost loved him as he looked at her then, but hurried off before he could say anything more. With Elizabeth's and Mistress Mako's help she had made a frilly yellow dress, with tight-fitting black sleeves, and had a black mask to wear with it. She now put it on, and carrying her mask went to Elizabeth's bedroom and helped her get into a dress covered with feathers. Finally they tried on their masks and agreed they could never be identified. "For one thing we look almost ugly," said the younger girl. "Why, look—if we change masks, it makes no difference!" The horn blew a long and lively rally. "But, Alice," she cried, "you have forgotten to take the carcanet from your hair! Everyone would recognise that, it looks so lovely on you!" She handed it over to the maidservant coming back to the room.

At the hall door they became part of a thickening throng of masquers, who had to wait for a single entry and have themselves announced by the Lord of Misrule's lieutenant, that lively monarch meanwhile offering his loud-voiced

opinion of the costumes and their wearers. "Pantaloon!"
shouted the announcer. "Ay, grandsire," commented His
Lordship, "I ha' no doubt your face and my left slipper
would make a proper pair." "The Phoenix of Araby!"
"Where's a torch? Where's a torch to burn this Phoenix?"
He went scampering after the lady's tail and she screaming
with laughter over to the Sophy and the Grand Turk.
"His Be-Wived Highness King Solomon!" "Nay, your
majesty, those same wives of yours—here's an honest
man will help you keep them under." "Primavera!"
"Rascal," cried the monarch, "let's have honest English
here!" He hit his henchman over the head with his sceptre.
"None of your Don Portingo lingo in my court! None of
your sheep-gargle Italiano! What is this honest lady?"
"The Spring, if it please Your Grandiloquence." "And
that's a nice season, the Spring! Married men, gardeevoo!
Cuckoo, cuckoo!" In they came, Seasons and Planets,
Shepherds and Shepherdesses, Monarchs and Monks,
Big Noses, Fat Cheeks, only too many of them instantly
recognisable. His Lordship, darting about on a hobby
horse, herded them into files and then announced the order
of the dances, they took their positions, and now the servants
were allowed to flatten themselves against the walls at the
bottom end of the hall and applaud their skill. The dance
ended, there came forfeits and kissing games, hoodman
blind again, careering in a ring, His Lordship and his
men flogging them round with light and unfelt whips of
straw. Then another dance was called for, and Alice felt
her hand seized determinedly by a masquer all in black,
his face less readable than her own. He was Copson's build
but said nothing and he gestured fiercely and despairingly
towards His Lordship that he might appoint them partners.
Nothing could be less calculated to bring about his wish.
His Lordship imitated him, put his thumb to his nose,
dismissed him to the hand of the Three Graces (in one
body, however), and coupled the Americas with King
Solomon—"Who well knows how to manage a twilight
lass." But as he went—for it was Copson—"Alice," he

said; "do speak with me later!" She was too excited to reply.

King Solomon proved a nimble-toed majesty. Wildly happy, she saw, half-a-dozen couples in front of her, Elizabeth dancing with Gilbert Hurrish whom she recognised under his mask by a trick he had of throwing back his head. Where was Sidley? She could see nothing resembling Elizabeth's account of his leafy costume. The measure ended amidst the shouts of the servants and the dancers, she saw the sweat running down her partner's forehead and temples, his hands were damp; could they have a drink to cool them? "No, water!" she begged, as he handed her a glass.—"Cold comfort, princess!" "Isn't that the kind for to-night?" She saw the black masquer coming towards them, but did not see how King Solomon was to be dispossessed. It was a problem for Copson too. It was proving a desperately disappointing night for him. Try as he would, he could not get near Alice. The Lord of Misrule would permit no lasting partnerships, he was a brisk master of ceremonies as well as a mischievous one and kept his subjects on the move: it was Copson's fate to pass from lady to lady, and never reach his desire. The present gaiety, the fun of Christmasses past, seemed wretched things as he hunted her morosely with his eyes and thought how undeserving and ungrateful men enjoyed her nearness whilst he— damnation! here he was now, sad as a death's head, watching her with King Solomon. Who was King Solomon to have her company when he could not? Did King Solomon think of her all day and much of the night? Would King Solomon die for her? The devil sweep away King Solomon and all other partners too! Conscious of its uselessness, he remained perhaps a dozen or more feet from them, knowing he should go about his business, powerless to do so, a pin feeling the drag of the magnet, a compass needle swinging north. If the hall could only be emptied of these hampering, empty-headed, heartless revellers! He longed to be with Alice in the midst of a desert, on the unlittered shores of the Caribbees, on a ship in the middle of the sea. But she might at least give him a signal that she knew he was there. The least she could do would be that, surely! Perhaps she cared neither for him nor his misery? He felt like crying aloud: Great God, what a miserable place this world is! Then she waved her hand to him behind King Solomon's back, Ah! Whatever happened next he would—— Where was the Lord of Misrule? He must see him, he must implore him—better still, he must bribe him! Where? He saw him halfway across the hall talking with the King of China's Daughter, a well-shaped lady in yellow taffeta with a yellow mask and wig. Before he could move on his mission of corruption the great bell went once more. Rows of revellers formed a barricade in front of him as the floor was cleared for another announcement. "Your Majesty of Misrule," he could hear, "Sweet Imp of Infamy, King of Kinching Coes and Prince of Tosspots, Sovereign of Suds and Lord of Most Low Laughter—what is your vile pleasure?" The one-day potentate addressed his subjects with a slightly tipsy dignity. He decreed an elaborate game of forfeits, of a hare and hounds variety. Two gentlemen, one of them skilled in the disposition of the house, carrying red confetti, and two ladies, one of them knowledgeable, carrying white confetti, should be given a minute's grace, and then hunted by two packs: the active ladies should pursue the men, the active men should pursue the ladies. If the ladies were caught within twenty minutes they must kiss all the gentlemen: if the gentlemen were not caught, the ladies must buy them favours. Copson could have sworn with annoyance. What chance was there of seeing Alice amidst all this nonsense and separation? Unless perhaps they took no part in the chase—that was it! He hoped to speak with her as the older and more tired of the gathering made way for the division.

A full score of gentlemen lined up on one side of the room, perhaps a dozen ladies on the other. To Copson's chagrin Alice was among them. The spectators had retreated to the upper end. His Lordship paraded between them. "Of gentlemen, King Solomon and Red Harlequin."

King Solomon, Alice knew, was Egbert Scratton, so it must be the other who knew his way about the house. Was he Sidley? Somehow she thought not. "Of ladies, the Americas and the King of China's Daughter." Well, thought Copson gloomily, he might as well join in the hunt now, and sidled into the group. If all these cursed men were going to catch up with Alice and that yellow-wigged trollop —what idiot game was this for Alice to be taking part in? These young bucks in dark corners—he wondered Sir Ralph allowed it. How different it seemed from last year!

The hares took their bags of confetti. There was a blaring of suitable music from the gallery as they ran off through the top door, turning, King Solomon and Red Harlequin to the left, Alice and her companion to the right. She thought the directions would be her own, but where the passages branched the King of China's Daughter caught at her arm, pulling her in the direction of the kitchens, scattering a snowdrift of confetti around the corner. "Who are you?" she gasped, but the other shook her head and hurried the more. "Oh, but I shall die if I run any faster! Who are you?" The yellow lady slackened to a walking pace, put a finger to the lips of her mask, scattered more confetti. "But how do you know the house so well? Who are you?" A yellow gloved hand admonished her to silence. "But you frighten me! I must know who you are!" A long way behind them came the cry of the horn, she was taken by the arm and forced to run again, into rooms and out, until suddenly they came to a trail of white confetti she knew they had not laid. She was feeling breathless and alarmed. "I won't come another foot unless you take your mask off!" The King of China's Daughter then laughed, tilting up the mask by its chin. "Master Sidley!"

"No other. Do I make a handsome lady?"

"I——"

"We must hide. I'll tell you later."

"But the confetti?"

"I'll tell you later. Come along."

They were now in a part of the house she did not know very well. He opened a door, led her quickly through the room, out into another corridor, a few yards along it, and into a long chamber she recognised as part of the great wing at the back. "Oughtn't we to drop confetti?" "No, it has been seen to already." "Oh," she cried, "do take off your mask! It is so unchanging while you talk! It terrifies me." "Very well, I will. And you take off yours." He knotted their cords loosely and swung them in his left hand. He removed his wig too.

"Where are we going?"

"Just a little further."

Suddenly he had put his arm around her waist.

"No, no!"

"It is dark here. You may stumble."

"I don't think——"

"Why, what a little puritan it is! Do you remember Wroxham Fair, Alice?" He squeezed her to him as he opened the door at the end of the long chamber and brought her into a smaller narrow room, with windows almost its whole length. "We wait here, Alice."

Leaving her by one window he searched about for cushions and threw them on to the ledge. "Shall we sit?" "Don't you think——" "There we are!" He was seated too, leaning back against the window frame, and his arm was round her again, pulling her close to him. "From here we can see the chase." He explained how the trail had already been laid, running out of doors now that the rain was over, over the soppy grass, through awkward holes in the hedges, thrown lightly across quaky ground. "But it is too dark. They will never go!" "There are servants with torches at the right door, my dear. Would any man worth the name hold back?" She could not help laughing too. "And the ladies?" Arrangements had been made for them too. They would follow the red trail over three parts of the house and be brought at last through the buttery back to the assembly hall in time to see the return of the discomfited men. As each passed in, a gift would be thrust into her hand by Ferrers, disguised as King Neptune.

"But oughtn't we to go back?"

"We'll watch the hounds first. You know, Alice, you seemed to like me in Norwich much more than here."

She made a half-hearted attempt to get away from him. "It was different at Norwich, Master Sidley."

"It was better in Norwich. I believe you are afraid of me." She had nothing to answer. "Are you?"

"Why should I be, Master Sidley?"

"No reason at all. Look—the torches!"

She was leaning her back against his chest, and as she half turned to see more clearly his hands slid up from her waist. "Alice!" Her fright, her caution, her fear of him were all numbed by the unreality of the moment. The small yellowy-red flares danced below as in a dream, she heard her own breathing as from afar, the unaccustomed excitements of the evening that had run now swooned in her blood; in the morning none of this would have been. "Alice!" he said urgently. They were standing now, and she felt the hard strokes of his heart. She struggled but his hands were gripping her tightly and her struggles grew less. "No, no, think of——" "I can think of nothing but you! I want you, Alice!" She heard him muttering, his hands were taking all strength from her, when suddenly she came to her senses. "No!" she cried, and tore at them, lacerating the half-healed scar from the burning, and then she struck him sharply in the face. "So?" he said chokingly. "So?" There boiled up in him a madness after her blow; that burn on his hand—the whore! She'd not best him like that! The flouting of honour that she was Greene's sister, his humiliation—the white line of the moon emerging from black cloud struck down to her heaving and disarranged bosom. With a desperate hate of himself mixed with his lust, he threw himself at her and bore her to the ground.

Copson had recognised the hoax below and disgruntled turned back from the torch-bearers. Let the world do what it would, he could feel no worse. Tearing his mask from his face he went off to his own quarters. "Alice, Alice!" he was saying inside him: "If only you had spoken to me!"

CHAPTER XIII

WITH ALL THINGS good and bad the holidays passed out of town. Christmas ran on with rain to the New Year, the New Year with watery sunshine to Twelfth Night, Twelfth Night moonless and soon sped. Most of the guests left straightway after Christmas, those who stayed were away after the New Year, and men must wait till white May for the next rejoicings. But those gone by were not forgotten. For the gentry there were memories and more leisure, for the servants memories and a world of work; for Sidley shame and mortification such as he had never experienced, and for Alice that desperate and frightened misery of women which is beyond any conception of men. Sidley left Braiding two days after Christmas to spend a month with Gilbert Hurrish at Lincoln, hoping to lose, with absence from the scene of his outrage, the self-loathing that had engulfed him. A hundred wickednesses remembered, a thousand cynicisms, these could not help him. So complete was his revulsion from lust that those first nights his very body was horrible to him, his constant summoning of the event a call to feelings in which pleasure was not a millionth part, in which he could not find a trace of clean and healthy desire. This was his friend's sister, taken against her will, under his father's roof, pitiful, polluted. In this mood he cursed himself for his deed, his father for setting him no example, Greene for ever suggesting he help his sister to leave home, Coppinger for being the cause of his leaving Cambridge, Alice herself for ever coming to Braiding.

He did not see her before he went. He remembered some dreadful words of his as he left her in the gallery —that must be all she'd get from him till his return. But he had no need to avoid her. She had no wish to see him. Haggard and red-eyed the next morning, with the knowledge of iniquity stamped for ever into her flesh, she went doggedly about her duties. No, she was not well. She endured Mistress Mako's banter about eating too much, about too much rompsing and roaring, as long as she could, and then answered with an anger that convinced that wise woman she would be best left to herself. Sometimes she was on the way to convince herself that what she knew was a nightmare, still vivid with day; but this fact or that battered its way through any attempt at delusion, hard, aggressive, mocking. She did her work with her hands alone, hardly knowing which task she was about. Like Sidley, she too longed that time could move backward to some other course, that whatever is done must not remain for ever done, without hope of erasure or cancellation. She could not believe, looking at her hands, that they were still the same, unstained; she could not think her face showed no signs of her disgrace, even her skin must reveal outwardly her horrid infection. It could not be possible for a woman to suffer this ultimate degradation and it not be printed on her clear for the world to read. Yet she came to see it was so, and from this arose a desire for secrecy. It would not do to make an outcry. But she would leave Braiding as soon as she could. Not a minute longer than she must under its roof. She would go home again, help her mother, put out of her head the ideas that had led to her present plight. Life was full of things to be forgotten. A woman's life especially.

She was glad to hear of Sidley's intention, gladder still of his departure. That was one of her greatest trials spared her for a time. Maybe before he returned she would be home again. Deep down in the wells of her was something she expected never to forget: the hatefulness of men. She would never marry, never see, never speak to men. If Geoffrey came worrying her she would be merciless to him. She could never bear a man near her. Hateful creatures! Filthy creatures! She thought of them as great beasts blundering through the gossamer of women's finer lives, and wished for a world without them.

It was a week after Twelfth Night Elizabeth asked her to go to her room one afternoon. "I wanted to be alone with you, Alice dear. Are you unhappy?"

"No, of course not. Why should I be?"

"I couldn't know, could I? But I have thought ever since Christmas—you are sure?"

"I have been the same since Christmas as before it," she said grimly.

"It is my fancy then. I was afraid you might be getting tired of Braiding. I should not like it as much now if you went away, Alice."

"Oh yes, you would!"

"But you are not going?" She waited for Alice's denial. "No, no, you are not going!"

"Your mother could easily get you another friend if I did. Someone nearer your own station. Perhaps I will go soon."

"You don't like it here any longer?"

"Yes, I like it—I like you more than ever."

"Then I know you won't go! You are unhappy then?"

"I don't see why you should think so?"

"But you look unhappy so often. I watch you. You don't laugh as much, and you don't spend as much time with me, and you look worried oftentimes. Why don't you tell me what the matter is?"

She tried to jest away Elizabeth's questions, but the younger girl showed more persistence than usual. "Are you in love, Alice?"

"Certainly not!"

"I thought you might be if you are unhappy. Love seems to make a lot of folk unhappy one way or another, doesn't it?"

"Love!" said Alice.

"Not that it should. I think love was sent to make us glad, dear."

"Those who are lucky."

"Aren't you lucky then, Alice? You should be, because your sweetheart will be—so lucky I hope he knows it. In fact, I intend to tell him."

"You are talking idly, Elizabeth," she said agitatedly.

"I thought it might be love. I tried to think who. It couldn't be Ferrers, could it?" She laughed. "Or could it be Ralph my brother? I wondered."

"You must not say such things! I shall have to leave you if you do!"

"Sit down again, Alice." She put an arm about her and drew her to her side. "You may think me too young and silly and inexperienced. But I can think all the same. It's not Ralph, is it?"

"No," said Alice, harshly.

"Well, I think it is Geoffrey Copson you are in love with. And I think you are very wise. Forgive me—but Ralph would never marry you, dear. He could not." She seemed to give that time to echo and be heard twice. "But Geoffrey Copson is such a fine young man. You would be very happy with him, Alice."

"But I tell you I'm not in love! I want nothing to do with men! I wish there were no men in the world!" And to Elizabeth's amazement she flung herself on the bed, face in hands, and sobbed frantically. This confirmed her suspicions about a love affair not prospering, but more important for the moment was a way to stop her grief. Wiser than a man she let her cry for a time till she was less shaken and then offered her a handkerchief and put an arm around her once more. "I am a naughty girl. I have upset you dreadfully. What can I do to punish myself? Say something to me, Alice!" Her face against the younger girl's shoulder, Alice was tempted for a while to tell her troubles. But she did not. The less said the better. Bad was made worse by talking about it. "There," she patted her eyes. "I have been foolish."

"And I have been rude and naughty. You must think, dear, it was only because I love you."

And now it seemed to Alice that all her happiness would be to stay with Sidley's sister here at Braiding, with no Sidley, no Sir Ralph, no Geoffrey Copson even. To live old, and die a spinster and a virgin. That night she began to think how Sidley was going away for three years in the spring and might be from his home even longer. For three years at least she might stay here. As for Geoffrey—she would tell him she wanted nothing of him. Time was a great healer. She got out of bed before the mirror, looked at herself naked. No, she was the same. If she were willing to think so, she was the same. The hours of one day dripped like water on the sands of the last, confounding them; there were many days to come, slow-flowing and mergent. She saw the spasm twist her face, a screw of memory, but it did not last. She must not be her own worst enemy. She told herself the way the world wagged was the way to wag too. The same cool body, she felt now, the same cunning work-piece of the great artificer. So long as it was henceforward her own, it might be purged of pollution. Other maids had been as hard treated as she, and if they were wise kept a bright forehead to the sun. She must— yes, she must——

But within a week she knew the course of events was not at her will. Days of worry and doubt became days of fear and certainty. Again she got out of bed and brought the night light to the mirror, and ran her hands over her body. The same but not the same, she knew it now. Her agony of mind recurred greater than at any time since that Christmas night. She stayed there till she shivered, and then till her teeth chattered, fighting against belief, praying silently that she might be mistaken, then aloud in whispers that God would not be so cruel to her. "God, God," she gasped; "don't bring this upon me! You can't! Oh, let everything be right again, God!" She crept back to bed at last, huddling herself for cold, crying softly. Not a plan now unshattered. She could not stay here, she could not go home. What, what would become of her? To whom could she turn? Where, where, where the God who protected the innocent? The God of her father's house?

She must see Sidley. So much she decided, but made and unmade the resolution a dozen times. What could he do? What *would* he do? There was Elizabeth's voice to answer her: "But Ralph would never marry you, dear. He could not." The idea of marriage with him was abhorrent. But he must think of something, or she would—what would she? She did not know.

But all this might be trouble without cause. Think, think of that she must. All would turn out right. God would never be so cruel. Yet it needed little reflection to think of cruel things He permitted, according to her father even enjoined.

Should she run away? Now, before Sidley returned? No, she could not do that. It was the same whatever she thought of: she could not do it. If only the night would go! None but unhappy women know the length of a night.

Not that things were much better when it was day. She had never looked so drawn, and Mistress Mako suggested she go back to bed. But that meant inactivity, more time to worry; she refused, and then refused additional advice with this-to-Mistress-Mako-unsuspected temper of hers. "As you will, my girl!" said the housekeeper, sharply enough, and they were less friendly at a time when she needed friendship. Then later, to avoid Elizabeth, she did go to her room and because it was cold there went to bed. Mistress Mako, little inclined to encourage tantrums, sent up no supper, and hunger, with which she had never expected to be troubled, helped to keep her awake all the night. So she looked worse still, and was now alarmed by the housekeeper's curious glances. Clenching her fists, she told herself she was in danger of betraying her secret. She must be reasonable. She offered explanations which Mistress Mako accepted whole-heartedly, and was sent to bed as though a child, this time with a fire and a tempting table of food. "Get out of here!" the good woman shouted at Copson, diffidently entering after a knock at the door downstairs.

"The manners of the men!" she grumbled. "Must they always come thrusting their dolt-heads where they are not wanted?" She walked up to the bedroom with Alice.

"We women, child, must not be sharp with each other. We have too much to put up with."

Luckily she found Elizabeth less eager for confidences, as though somewhat abashed by the results of her former questionings. She forced herself to take the same interest in everyday affairs, and that carried her through the weeks that followed. Sidley's return she both dreaded and longed for. He was back in the first week of February, but they did not come face to face for some time. As often as the weather permitted, he was out riding; and he had the excuse of time to mend in his language studies why he should pass so few hours with the other members of the family. Besides, there was a household routine which made it possible for Alice and him to avoid a direct meeting. Her first sight of him was staring out of the window when she took the Lady Elizabeth a warm drink. He did not turn, and at the sound of her voice moved abruptly from the room. "Ralph did not see you," his sister complained. "You are such a mouse these days."

And then again came those nights of fearful anticipation, false hopes, and growing certitude. She did not show the effects of them so badly, however. Perhaps all the time she knew there was nothing but the one end, and that a bad one; conviction squatting black-spider-like in the recesses of her mind, contemptuous of butterfly longings in the web. This was beyond mistaking. Her fate was on her.

Again she determined to see Sidley. She was calmer now. She would use her wits to escape what befell many. She must not be thrust down under men's feet or not even God could help her.

She took the bold course and one afternoon went to his study where she knew him to be working with Gallanti. He looked up with irritation, concealing some discomfiture she thought, as she announced that his mother wished to speak with him at once. "Coming," he replied curtly, and she knew he would give her time to go away. Grimly, in the passage, she reminded herself this was not the worst kind of humiliation and waited for him to appear. Sure enough, as the door opened, he was casting a rapid glance up and down the passage. He saw her but would have gone by without a word.

"Master Sidley?"

He was doubtful of her and afraid to pass on. "Well?"

"I must speak to you."

"You waste your time," he said bluntly.

"Even so, I must speak with you."

She noticed a second time that rapid glance along the passage. "I have no wish to speak with you that I know of. In any case I cannot speak with you here. Where shall I see you?"

She felt herself stronger than he. "You may come to my room this evening."

Then he sneered. "I am still not interested, Mistress Alice Greene."

It was nothing to lose her temper over. "But you will come?"

He shook his head.

"I am with child. Will you come?"

"You lie!"

"I wish to God I did! That is how little I want of yours. Will you come?"

"You'll foist no pantry-boy's bastard on me, Mistress! No."

"I shall wait for you all the same."

"You bitch!" he snarled. "You'd trap me there!"

"Where else will you see me? I do not mind."

He hesitated only a fraction of a second. "I'll come at nine to-night. But mind you——"

She had already left him. Now that she was committed to action she felt surer of herself. And in those rapid minutes another illusion had been stripped from her. So this foul-mouthed boy was her brother's glorious Sidley, the marvel of the age? And she herself had thought very near the same! No, no, no, she must never lose her temper. She must be calm and strong and clever. This Sidley—not worth the leather of her oldest shoes. As contemptible as his father. Why, poor Geoffrey—— She forced her thoughts away from Copson. She must think only of herself.

The rest of the day hung heavily on them both. Sidley had gone to the stables and taken out a horse. He wanted to think, and he wanted to be away from people. A month gone by, all sense of shame had left him. It was like his first whore, and then his first seduction of a chambermaid. This was but another step. Had all gone well, by this time he'd be boasting of it. God! To preach his philosophy to Greene and then to rape his sister! There was a fitness in it. And it would do the —— no harm to be made a woman. Before he left Lincoln even, he could look back with a sort of amusement on his qualms. He was not the master of destiny he had for some time thought himself. He was but young in deed. A man of his stamp should be superior to remorse. All this pother! He struggled to attain a leprous joy in his own lack of morals. That upon his return home he should feel nervous and willing to avoid her, these were signs of weakness. She'd settle down, —— her! She'd be none the worse. Less pleasantly than to Robertus in Norwich, he swore it was not a woman's world. They must take what came to them and be damned. And now this! What should he do? See her to the devil? Tell black-faced lies? Have her bundled out of the house? Packed off to Norwich like a drab to have her brat at home? Should he? He shook his head. There was Elizabeth's attachment to her and his mother's increasing fondness. His father he cared nothing for in this—he knew the old lecher too well. And there was rumour. It would not do. She wasn't a peasant's daughter, worse luck. There was that damned brother of hers. He might be a nuisance. A tale to Coppinger and all the puritans, and from them to London maybe, to Sidney, Leicester, the Queen! Do what then? She shouldn't drive a bargain with him, damn her! Why wasn't this France? Italy? A lord was a lord there.

Someone to take the blame, that was the thing!

Some poor fool of inferior clay Patch up a marriage,

get the clown an office, legitimize the bastard on the way, wash his hands of them.

But who?

He snapped his fingers. The very man! In love with her, said Elizabeth. He grinned. He wouldn't deny the ass his leavings. In better humour he turned for home.

And yet he was far from self-assured when soon after nine o'clock he went stealthily to Alice's room. He was as concerned not to be seen as if it were an assignation with a jealously husbanded lover. He knocked and was at once admitted by a fully-dressed Alice. "You came then?" she said.

"It could do no harm."

She pointed to a chair, telling herself she must lose neither her head nor her temper. "Well," he said; "now I am here?"

"It is what I told you. That is all."

He fiddled with his shoe before answering. "You are not the first one to think yourself in trouble."

"This is no thinking. This is reality."

"Well, for God's sake, sit down! It's no reason why you should be standing there like the queen of the may. You want to say it is my fault, do you?"

"It is your fault!"

"Say it is, for the sake of argument. I admit nothing, mind, but say it is—what do you expect me to do?" That she should look frightened, ashamed, haggard, yes—but her look of contempt, he would not tolerate that. "Do you expect me to marry you?"

"No."

"How reasonable you are! How well you have it worked out! Well then?"

Her face was beginning to work. "You got me into the trouble. You must get me out of it."

"Must? I like that *must!*" They sat silent for a quarter-minute. "How do I know——?" he began.

"Go on! Say it! You—— Oh, I hate you, I hate you!"

That she should cry so bitterly alarmed him. If anyone came past the door and heard and knocked and asked questions—— "It is no good crying, Alice! I believe you—there! Don't keep on crying. I believe you, Alice—I can't say more than that." He put his hand on her shoulder. "Only tell me what you want me to do! I want to help you, Alice."

But this apparent yielding brought Alice a greater desolation. What could he do? This was the question she had all the time left without an answer. But he must do something! "I could never marry you, you know that." Safe in that knowledge he made his voice sound remarkably as though he would like to. "My father and mother—but it is impossible!"

"Then you will help me?"

"Anything! Now here, dry your eyes." He was glad to see her calmer. "Have you thought of anything?"

"I can't," she confessed.

"You are certain about the child?" he asked after a pause.

"Oh don't let us——"

"Well then!" He paused again. "You don't want the child? It might be possible——"

She looked up.

"I know of a woman——"

"No," she cried, "No! I won't!"

"I was thinking only of your good." He gave way before the horror of her eyes. "It is hard to help you, Alice."

"You would help me into a grave!"

He dropped his eyes. She shuddered. "I wondered, Alice, whether you might like to come to London with me when I leave here next month. I could set you up comfortably and leave you money against my return." Knowing she would not accept, he outlined his scheme rather indifferently; and she, listening, was thinking of herself unsupported in that great unseen wilderness of London. It was death she saw, perhaps death not soon enough. No, she would have nothing of it. "It's very hard trying to help you," he complained once more, and sat staring moodily at the bed.

Then at last he said: "You are in love with young Copson?"

With that she saw what he was going to suggest. Yet she did not stop him. "You are thinking of this late, Master Sidley!"

"Not too late. You are in love with him?"

This was a new kind of shame. "Perhaps. Perhaps not."

"He is in love with you!" He laughed for the first time that night. "The whole household knows as much."

"It has nothing to do with me now," she answered, her shame stronger.

"I think it has, Alice. You could be very happy married to him."

"After what you have done to me? You think any man would want me now?"

"I do, Alice. Do we understand each other?"

Think of yourself! Think of yourself! That was the way of the world. She heard him saying: "Why not marry him, Alice?" And he would marry her, as soon as she liked. And when the baby was born he would be loving her so much he would not put her away. Even a seven months' child—she caught at these hopes—it was not without parallel. If they could marry at once, at once, the miracle might happen. And in any case, once she was married, did it matter? "Why not marry him Alice?"

"He wouldn't want me now."

"Ferrers won't live forever. He'll become steward here. He will want you!" She'd agree, he knew she'd agree. "I'll get my father to promise him the succession as a wedding gift; and if it is in my day, not my father's—so much the better."

For some time they sat there, another silence between them. Suddenly she cried out, as though against her will: "I won't marry him unless he knows, and still wants me! I won't be so unfair!" He argued with her, demonstrating the folly of her attitude, but she remained unshaken. "Then

let me tell him," he begged. And, still with this new shame
warm in her, she agreed.

Copson saw her three days later, when she had had plenty
of time to think about her future if he did not marry her.
It was little short of panic possessed her when by his face
she could tell Sidley had spoken to him. "I must speak with
you, Alice," he said, as though echoing her own words to
Sidley. She could only nod. "I'll wait for you as soon as it
is dark by the five elms." She nodded again. Then, impulsively, he kissed her hand and hurried off, leaving her red-
faced, then white, sick with the heavy beating of her heart.

He was there waiting for her. Without invitation they
started to walk, their unhappy minds seeking the slight
comfort afforded by that much use of their bodies. She could
not bring herself to speak, and he, vainly beating about for
some beginning that would not be harsh or crude, could
find none. But long silence was impossible. "Master Ralph
saw me yesterday morning," he said finally. After waiting
for her reply, he asked: "Was what he told me true?"
He took his answer from her silence. "Alice, I've been in
hell since then."

The dark had never been so kindly. Here, between the
tall pillars of the trees, they could hardly see each other's
face, and this was well, for she was thinking of herself as
such another unstruggling calf as she had seen a hundred
times led off to the slaughter-houses behind Norwich
Market Place. What must happen would happen now
without and despite her. "Alice," he said quietly; "I
don't care. Will you marry me?"

They went on walking. "If you want me to."

He had expected something more telling. "Yes, I do."

Perhaps she too had expected something more telling.
She made no reply.

"When shall the wedding be, Alice?"

"When do you think?"

"Soon. As soon as possible. I must see your father and
mother first."

She had thought of that. "They may not want an early wedding. They may want it at Norwich in the summer."

"I think I can persuade them. It is true, Alice, about the child you are going to have?"

"It is true," she said, hard-voiced. With one of those flashes of insight granted her of late, she had seen that whatever became of their lives she would always have in her heart something of contempt for Copson, the taker of leavings. Though he did it for love—and she thought he was doing it for profit too—she would still despise him. Not with a constant scorn, but when they quarrelled, when they grated on each other, when between them came those discords she knew in the lives of her own father and mother —then he would appear the meaner for what he was now doing. "I only want to ask you one question, Alice." She waited. "Master Sidley (Why need he say *Master* Sidley?) said he was entirely to blame." She heard him gulp. "That he overcame you against your wish."

"He did."

She sensed his gesture rather than saw it. "Then I forgive you, and we can forget about it."

He forgave her! And had he been generous enough to forgive *Master* Sidley too? Forgive, forgive, forgive—the word blew helter-skelter down the avenues of memory, back through two months of almost unendurable misery and shame, to hateful Christmas. This was a fine Christian charity, to forgive the innocent! But there was nothing she could say. She was not feeling the relief she should. She wished she were in bed, that she might not have to talk or walk or think, only wash away day with sleep. Bitterly she went on to wonder whether he was waiting for thanks. These two months—she felt a change in herself as great spiritual as physical. Perhaps such things went together? A maidenhead lost—a symbol—did it mean the loss of spiritual freshness too? Let the fault lie where it would. She could not say. But she knew she had hardened and thought she would not change again.

"You are very quiet, Alice."

"I am, Geoffrey. I know. I don't find it easy to talk."

"You want to marry me?"

Copson felt that he was doing a noble thing and that he was unappreciated. He knew now he loved Alice more than he had thought it possible for man to love woman, and he had driven himself as near knight-errantry as under-stewards may do. And not for profit. Sidley, true, had mentioned the stewardship after Ferrers, he had spoken of the expenses of the wedding after a fashion that suggested there would be no checking of pence, he had hinted at the value of his favour; but without all this, Copson told himself with a conviction so near truth there was no telling where the one ended and the other began, he would have married her. He, like the youthful Greene, was not without his day-dreams, his passion for sacrifice, his longings that monsters would tear him but spare his mistress; but, unlike the youthful Greene, he had a chance to live them. His monsters too were of the most fearsome kind: ill report, neglect or cruelty, the human pack hounding Alice down to hell. Even his sword-chop through their maws might not account for them. Yet now, thinking over his twenty-four hours of bewilderment and agitation, he could not realise that his had been a free choice, while Alice in her two months of trial had none whatever. He had expected tears, an outburst, their arms around each other, fine sentiments, and much, much gratitude. How many men would marry a ruined maid, father another man's child, expose themselves to gossip, reproach, misunderstanding? Surely he deserved credit for this. But here she was taking everything in so matter-of-fact a way.

"You do want to marry me, Alice?"

How make the proper response? "Of course I do, Geoffrey! I don't know what I should do without you! I've been—I've not had an easy time either."

"Poor Alice!" he said.

Something was needed to ignite his real love for her, her great affection for him, strike out the one spark that would explode it and kill for a time all their reserve and blundering.

"Let's stop walking, Alice." He remained in the tree-shade and put his hands on her shoulders. "It is a strange thing we are doing, Alice, I can see that, and I can see it might turn out badly but for one thing. I love you, Alice. I have loved you ever since that day I saw you at King's Lynn, since I rode with you here the next day, ever since then I've loved you. If you love me too, everything will go right for us. Do you?"

She could not keep her composure face to face with him. "I am so ashamed, Geoffrey. I am so ashamed!"

"Never mind that, sweetheart. You love me?"

She cried out again that she was ashamed and that she wished she were dead and that she loved him, but he took her into his arms, feeling a new pulse of manhood through him, tremendous pity and faith and strength, proud as he held her that he was doing so fine a thing. There for a while in the darkness, space as it were billowing away from them across parkland, meadows, the sightless acres of the county, he found complete joy. Even her trembling was sweet, shadowing the darker his own rocklike masculinity. He began to talk, his voice low and leaping from phrase to phrase: how much he had loved her, how he had always worshipped her, how beautiful she was, how happy he wanted to make her. She must not be afraid any longer, nothing should harm her, for her sake he'd pull down heaven from on high. And so, for a while, she clung to him, forgetting the past, thinking of his dearness, protectiveness, this solidity of once-hated man on which a woman could lean. She too found words: she would never forget how good he was to her, she would spend her life to make him happy, all the world could do would be but kitten-scratches so long as they could hold each other. She said how she had hated all men, how desperate she had been, how different the future was now. Then, since these ecstasies are only moments, their taste fast-dying from the tongue, they descended anew to a discussion of what they must do. They began to walk again, constraint gone. His arm was around her waist, and then hers around his; thigh and hip, breast and shoulder they fitted one to the other; as though instinctively they left the colonnade of elms, finding pleasure in each other's smiles in the moderate darkness. Nothing should spoil their life together. He would go to Norwich at once and get her father's permission, the wedding should be next month at Braiding, how quickly time ran by! "It will be our baby, Alice," he told her; "yours and mine." And then he started to laugh embarrassedly.

"What's the matter with you, Geoffrey?"

A second time they stopped walking. "Have you thought, Alice? I've never kissed you!"

"Well—poor Geoffrey!"

"That's vanity, if you like!"

They kissed, a little clumsily at first, but his arms tightened and tightened, he felt her bosom compact against him, his blood grew hot, and he was masterful when at last he let her go.

CHAPTER XIV

COPSON SHOWED HIMSELF no dawdler. That same week he left for Norwich to see the Greenes, and carried with him letters from Lady Sidley and her son, recommending him strongly to their favour. Greene was not inclined to be nice about his son-in-law so long as he was a decent man and could keep Alice in a fair station; Jane took to him at once, so there was no need for debate. He could have Alice and welcome. But the wedding? They would like it at Norwich in the summer, as Alice had suggested. Copson, however, had a reason and an argument for everything. It was the custom at Braiding for servants of good rank to marry from the house, he had no father and mother himself, and looked with the keenest sense of gratitude to his lord and lady; he could not go against their declared preference. Besides, they perhaps did not realise in what high regard their daughter was held at Braiding, the close bond—he thought he might, without disrespect, use the word affection—between their daughter and the Lady Elizabeth; he was sure she would be both hurt and insulted if she could not assist at the ceremony; he told them with as careful words as he could find that the Lady Sidley had no liking since her misfortune for travelling abroad. He understood that her ladyship's letter contained an invitation to the Greenes and such members of their family as they thought fitting to spend some time at Braiding before and after the event. Yes, said Greene, tapping it against his knee; that was so. It was gracious and kind of her ladyship. No doubt Master Copson would wait a day for their deliberated opinion? Late into the night he and Jane lay talking this over, Jane seven months gone with her third child in less than three years. She could not go to Braiding, that was clear. But her husband could, and maybe Robert could get there from Cambridge. They would be enough to

represent the family. How much Jane would regret her
absence she alone could say, but for the moment her
husband was not thinking of that. "I wonder whether the
wedding is somewhat more hurried than is decent," he
said to her, but she had no patience with him. "Hurried
to old married folk like us, but not to young bloods, I'll
wager." Well, yes, he agreed.

So he told Copson after breakfast the next day he would
come to Braiding for the wedding. He hoped then to express
his consciousness of Sir Ralph's condescension. One favour,
however, they did ask. The girl's mother——Jane had a
long talk with him after her husband had gone to his workshop. "You see how it is with me, Master Copson," she said.
"I shall be delivered again while my Alice conceives.
You love her?"

"As God is my judge I do!" "Then you will know how
much I want to see her, for I love her too." He swore he
would bring her to see her mother within a week. Come hail,
or rain, or snow. There was talk about the dowry too, though
he vowed he would take the girl in her shift, if need be.

Back at Braiding he told Alice all this. Her mother with
child again was dreary news to the girl. "Did she look
well?" Oh yes, very well, all things considered. "Poor
mother! If she knew that I too am with child!" Copson
rallied her and forced her to think of practical matters.
There was no difficulty in obtaining permission to visit
her home. All at Braiding thought it a very proper thing
to do. "I don't know, child," said Lady Sidley, "whether
your father would consent to it, and so I do not wait. I
have here a charm which I wore round my neck when
Elizabeth was born. Ask your mother to wear it when
her time comes." She saw Alice turn the odd-shaped
trinket over and over in her fingers. "Don't be afraid, child.
I know it sovereign." She thanked her mistress for her gift
and kind thought, and took the charm with her when
she set off with Copson and one of the maidservants. At
the first opportunity she put it, not without a grimace,
round her own neck.

She came to Norwich with a clear mind. Not without qualms of desire to see her parents again, not without an upsetting homesickness, but her mind free from all worry about her condition and the general imposture of the next few months. Whether ever again she would ride home without the prospect of blame and coldness she could not tell, but she set all thoughts of the kind behind her. The slender spires spurting into the air pricked her heart with love to-day: to-morrow must wait. To the clack and rattle of the horses' hoofs on the cobbles of Tombland she thought of herself leaving home six months before and how in the meantime the stuff of life had wrapped itself around her. A sense of the inexorability of things experienced, the frailty of all that is good, helped her to the rush of tears that burned her eyes as she saw Robert and Jane waiting for her. Crying, with her head on Jane's shoulder, it seemed to her that for an eternity she had done nothing but cry; and cry she must again, with joy, with sorrow, and soon with her gift of life to the baby in her womb. Copson, watching, and her father too, were powerfully affected; Greene by the strong and inescapable ties of blood and seed; Copson by his sympathy with these two mothers, sharing a life from which he and Greene were hopelessly shut out.

They were at Norwich four days—to Jane days of heaven-sent rain which kept them indoors almost every minute. Copson was all a future son-in-law should be, not less so because he left mother and daughter together such a lot and busied himself with Greene. Alice was so happy that she actually found it hard to believe her marriage was not all it seemed. Sidley and everything he stood for counted not at all here; talking with Jane over endless trifles, helping about the house, nursing the children, Anne now two years old, Tobias one, she felt that by leaving the scene of her distress she had destroyed it. It was only by deliberately thinking on the betrayal that must follow with the months she could reconcile herself to so speedy a return. Several times she was tempted to tell her mother she was pregnant, naming Copson as the father, but this seemed so unnecessary a slander against one who was really her deliverer that she always decided it was preferable to deceive her mother. To-morrow, and the days after that, they would come soon enough.

It was on the morning of their last day she gave Jane the charm. "If you believe in such things, mother."

Jane said the most startling thing she had ever heard from her. "Why not? Women had babies before Jesus was born." She was confused straightway after, but took the charm and put it carefully in her pocket. "Noah did not keep fleas out of the Ark," she defended herself. "All things have their uses—even charms."

"You don't think father——"

"It doesn't do to tell the men everything," her mother said half-seriously to her marriageable daughter. There was a slight but distinct difference in their relationship already. "You will come and see me soon after?"

"If I can, mother."

"Oh, you will be able to, Alice." She sighed. "I wish I could come to see it, but there you are."

They fell into talk of intimacies till they were joined by the men. In no time, it seemed to Jane, they had ridden out of sight. "When will I see her again?"

"Go over when you are strong again," her husband comforted her. "Yes, I find this Geoffrey Copson a good young man. I see no reason why it should not be a good match." He sought a final sentence. "A decent marriage is a pleasant thing in the eyes of God."

Back at Braiding there was plenty to do for everyone. Master Ralph was leaving for the Continent in a fortnight, the wedding would take place not a fortnight after that. "Are the young men eager?" Ferrers asked Mistress Mako. "Explorers both, and perdition seize my uncle's soul if I know in whose shoes I had rather stand! Eh, dame, I'll wager you haven't forgotten the shaking of your own sheets, have you?" "No thanks to you, you bawdy old ruffian," she retorted. He bent to bring his eyes level with hers. "He was a fine sprig that husband of yours. God, how we

sighed to see him bend in six short weeks! As a bachelor
I've held my place at every feast, but there is a diligence
about marriage I never fancied." Most of this Alice and
Copson heard. "The man has no shame!" cried Mistress
Mako.

The night before Sidley left all the servants were called
into the great hall for a ceremonial farewell. Sir Ralph,
blank-eyed and apparently indifferent, gave the toast of
his son; it was drunk and the son was cheered vociferously.
Three years, they said excitedly; three years was a long
time of it. Ferrers remembered what the Grand Tour had
done for Sir Ralph, but had too much sense to offer confidences. "They ha' plenty abroad for such as he," he
muttered to Copson, nodding at Sidley. "I don't doubt
he'll have a grand time of it, and bring home fine clothes
and fine manners and maybe something he'd rather be
without. For your own ear, understand!" With a shocking
lack of tact he added that the young master on all his
journeyings would not find a girl as soft between the
sheets as Copson's bride-to-be. "And I know!" Copson
shut his ears to some of this, his heart to more. Later, he
heard that Master Ralph wished to speak with him. It was
a peculiar interview. As though there were nothing between
them, Sidley talked big about wishing him well. Their
boy (he took it for granted the child would be a boy) should
never want for anything. He had spoken to his father about
the succession if anything happened to Ferrers while he
was away, and Copson need have no fears. He would not
see Alice in private, but he wished to mark the occasion
with a gift out of the ordinary. Here it was, a bag heavy
with money For one absurd stroke of time Copson thought
to dash it into his calmly dictatorial face. It was like the
price of his wife's body. Instead, he took it, bowed low,
murmuring indistinct words of thanks. Sidley half-turned
from him and he saw that the interview was over.

He went straightway to find Alice. She was in the housekeeper's room, but Mistress Mako made it easier for him by
claiming she must give orders to his blockhead of a master.

Alone with her, he pulled out the strong velvet bag. "From *him*," he said.

He dropped it on the table with a crash. "Oh, Geoffrey, Geoffrey—why did you take it!"

"How could I refuse?"

The worm mistrustful scorn stirred in her heart, but she saw the justice of what he asked. "It would have been better, that is all. I know you couldn't."

He picked it up and let it crash down again. "I'll put it away. Whatever it is, there is no reason why the child should not enjoy the use of it. We need never touch it."

She thought how rarely servants could make a gesture of renunciation. "That will be best," she agreed. "Yes, put it away and let us never think of it."

So Sidley went, with his servants and his baggage. There were plenty to holla for him, as many to scrabble on the ground for the handfuls of silver he flung about him. Copson and Alice, as was their obligation, were present to wish him god-speed. He ignored them, and though they could expect nothing else, yet it annoyed them to see him ride off like a prince from amidst lackeys. The bag of money was present to their minds: the son of the house had taken his pleasure and had paid for it. Why should he not ride off? No doubt he was thinking himself a magnanimous young man.

"Well," said Elizabeth, turning indoors again, "now we must give all our time to your wedding, Alice. I want to be busy for your sake, and because it will help us to forget that Ralph has left us."

She did busy herself too, as did Lady Sidley for the same reasons. Sir Ralph alone of them let the light and dark glide under his toad-eyes, as though grief at parting and joy at wedding were infinitely small things. Alice still looked up to see those eyes upon her, their only message a hint of scum-strewn thoughts; she still passed him in passages or entered rooms where he sat reading, and was glad to hurry away, but she had no ground of complaint against him. If he took pleasure from her, at least he confined his exploits to

regions of the mind. Once only he spoke to her apart from
civilities during those weeks before her wedding day. Quite
unexpectedly he looked up from a book he was reading one
day when she had taken wine to his private room, a task
she had once shrunk from but now performed with indifference. "There is in that happy country France, Mistress
Alice," he said drily, "a custom called *le droit du seigneur.*
It is as well it does not obtain here at Braiding. I should
find it impossible to rise to the occasion." That was all,
he was back at his reading, she made a dozen guesses at
what he meant but had forgotten even the sound of the
strange words, and said nothing of it to anyone. One thing
she was certain of, though: whatever it was, it gave him
a relish to say it.

But if he was so neutral, his wife and daughter made up
for him. Copson had exaggerated little if at all at Norwich.
They put their own hands to the wedding dress and insisted,
without   knowing   what   mixed   thoughts   followed   the
announcement, that it was Ralph's wish the event cost
neither Copson nor Alice a penny. "You are going to be
so happy, dear," Elizabeth said time and time again.
"Your husband is such a fine young man! And I shall be
here," she concluded, laughing, "to see that he treats you
as well as you deserve." She looked forward greatly to the
arrival of Greene father and son, and made herself particularly affable to them. Greene the elder was in need of
affability, for he felt thoroughly out of place in these surroundings. He had expected a household more godly, more
in keeping with Sidley's original splendidly sober appearance at Norwich, and though he would not admit it even
to his son he felt ill at ease with the gentles. But he had
the quiet competence of speech and manner that allowed
him to conceal discomfort, and Lady Sidley herself thought
fit to remind Ferrers not to offend the grave gentleman.
Robert Greene, bachelor of arts, was naturally delighted
to escape from Cambridge. He had been given a week's
leave of absence to mark the Master's appreciation of his
continued good behaviour. With him he brought the kindest

thoughts of that perfect friend Coppinger, who regretted
that he had never met Mistress Alice Greene in the days of
her spinsterhood but was pleased he might now look forward
to a happier meeting with her and her husband. He spent
a lot of time with his sister and Elizabeth, talking about his
College as though the Court were a dungheap and London
a farmyard. And as it had once been all Sidley, it was
now all Coppinger. "I never heard Ralph speak of him,"
said Elizabeth. "No," said Greene briefly, and asked
whether she and her lady mother had yet read Master
John Lyly's *Euphues*. They had not? He was amazed. They
had not even heard of it? Why, the country could not get
it quick enough, it lay in every lady's closet, the scholar
pawned his gown for it, it won the warrior from the field
of Mars. Not read it? He had a copy in his bag. He never
failed to read ten pages before he fell asleep at nights. He
begged that the Lady Elizabeth, with the gracious permission of her noble mother, would do him the honour to
accept his copy. One thing, though. He was by no means
sure his father approved of writers like the elegant John
Lyly, so perhaps they would say nothing of its source. But
what would he do for his bed-cap if he gave her the book?
Feeling delightfully flattered, Greene began to hum and
ha and finally told them he was himself in intervals between
study (he coughed) composing a romance which he hoped
would be in no way inferior to anything produced by the
witty, learned, elegant, moral, recondite, but not neces-
sarily unique John Lyly. Elizabeth was not sure whether
this was unworthy of him or a marvel, but gave him the
benefit of her doubt. What was it called? When would it
appear? How long would it be? How much would it cost?
It was with difficulty Greene forced himself to remember
the romance was hardly started. But if all the world greeted
it with the same respect and eagerness as this pale-faced
young lady, he would be the loudest note in Fame's sweet
trumpet. But as for profits, well—Elizabeth must have a
copy, so must her mother, her father would surely take
two, and then there was Ralph. Five copies in every country

mansion throughout England—that was ambition! He thought Alice was regarding him a little satirically from where she stitched, and came down to earth. Coppinger would buy one, he thought five minutes later.

The wedding took place on a Wednesday, at the Parish Church. The day was fine—the sun shines on a sunshine maid, said Lady Sidley—the ceremony impressed Alice's brother greatly, for it was his first wedding. They went back to the house for an enormous meal which lasted for hours, and at which most of the men and three or four of the women became very drunk indeed, before it was time for the bride to be put to bed. The jests became increasingly frank after she had gone with the ladies whose privilege it was to undress her, and Copson had a trying time of it from Ferrers while he waited the correct interval. "Send for me!" Ferrers kept shouting from the far end of the table. "If you need help, send for me!" He caught sight of the elder Greene but was too drunk to know he looked displeased. "Ay, dad," he bawled, "thou'st bred a pretty bit for this young cockerel to whet his beak on!" It was release from gaol for the blushing Copson when at last he could leave the table and, attended by his men, go to his wife. Some of his attendants were roaring drunk, it was only the protests, even the blows of the others that kept them from seeking the bride's garters, and they sang bawdily for ten minutes outside the door before her brother and his well-wishers could force them back to the drinking. It was everyone's opinion it had been a wedding worthy of its ancient setting.

The morning came, and the young couple had to face the immemorial jokes. Alice took it all very well, laughing and blushing, but Copson looked so worried that he was well-nigh driven out of his wits by midday. Ferrers, as might be expected, was a fountain of lewdness, and absolutely disgusted the bride's father. He was glad he was leaving on the morrow. This Braiding Hall was no place for him. It could not come too soon, the morrow.

And then it was to-morrow and he taking leave of them.

His son Robert was going with him to Norwich to see his
mother. He would be two days over his time getting back
to Cambridge, but he had the excuse that his mother was
soon to be delivered, and not a Master in Christendom could
look twice at a story like that. And so they went, the heavier
for a load of greetings and messages, the lighter, in the
case of the son, of a copy of *Euphues*.

"You like Geoffrey Copson?" he asked his father.

"He is well enough—but I tell you what, Robert. I have
no liking for Sir Ralph." His son knew there was more to
come. "Geoffrey Copson is well enough, but Sir Ralph—
if you are ever to see an orange sucked dry by the devil,
you will see Sir Ralph!"

CHAPTER XV

ALICE DID NOT go to see her mother after her marriage. Throughout April and early May it proved impracticable, and then there were good reasons why she should not though she could. Indeed, she and her husband waited now daily for signs that Alice's condition was known to others. Life at Braiding was so closeknit that deceit for long was impossible, and sure enough before the end of May Alice suspected gossip. It was a dropped voice, the women's eyes resting on her shape, a turn of the head to stare, a not ill-natured smile, a grimace from Mistress Mako, the calm regard of Lady Sidley, the well controlled but yet visible surprise of Elizabeth. It was Mistress Mako who at last made a declaration. "Maybe you will follow your mother this year?" she asked boldly, the day a messenger had called with news of Jane's safe delivery. "Maybe," Alice agreed, hot as fire. "That's a lively young husband of yours!" Mistress Mako jested, and went into reminiscence of her own childless marriage. "Anyhow, my child," she concluded suddenly, "wedlock is a great comfort." Something in her tone fetched that hot blood back to Alice's cheeks, but the housekeeper patted her shoulder. "It will be the early winter?" she asked, matter-of-fact. Denial was useless. She nodded. "Or before."

Frankness now seemed best. She was sewing with the Lady Elizabeth that same afternoon. "Elizabeth," she said calmly, "I am going to have a baby."

Elizabeth was not at ease. "You are?"

"You knew, of course?"

"In a way I thought I did. It is going to be lovely for you, Alice!"

"Yes"—a far from rapturous agreement. "It will be born at the end of September."

"Oh," she exclaimed, and shut her mouth tightly. She had tricked over the ancient arithmetic.

Alice felt the estrangement as they both bent over their sewing. There was a quarter of a minute's silence before Elizabeth began: "Then——"

"Well?"

"Then you were not married, Alice?"

"No." She fought down the rebellious instincts which tempted her to shout aloud the truth to this half-disapproving sister of Sidley's. "No," she said a second time.

"Well, you are now," was all Elizabeth could think of to say.

"Yes, I am now." But not to your brother! she wanted to shout, and shake her as she did so. She stood up. "With your permission, Lady Elizabeth, I will leave you."

Elizabeth watched her to the door in voiceless misery. "No, no," she cried; "don't go, Alice! Don't go and leave me!" She ran after her and clung to her. "Oh come back! Come back!"

It ended in tears on both sides, implorations, and then apparent reconciliation, but Alice had the occasion stored in her mind, nor would she ever forget it. With half truth only, Elizabeth explained how hurt she was Alice had not confided in her before, nor had her appreciation of the impossibility of confidences helped her; but Alice could not overlook that deliberate checking of the calendar, that uncomfortable silence. Who was the sheltered Lady Elizabeth to pass judgment on her? She was seeing, too, that there could never be the same friendship between them now she was married, child or no child.

She went to see Lady Sidley as part of her duty, who heard the tidings without surprise. "When I put you to bed, Alice, I said to myself: Here is a wedding three months late. You need not be confused. You are not the first and you will not be the last. I do not countenance loose conduct for one moment, but I know you are not loose and you will never give occasion for further gossip." There followed some advice, stately and moral, but before the interview ended Lady Sidley was taking so much interest in the coming of the child that she forgot most of what she had said and treated her most motherly. Yet in the months that followed she saw to it that her daughter and Alice spent less and less time together, and in early September announced she would arrange for the services of a new companion. Alice's motherhood, she explained to Elizabeth, and her duties would henceforth prevent their seeing much of each other. Besides, Alice was now much more the wife of Copson, a servant, than sister of Robert Greene, Ralph's friend; and life was perpetually demanding these adjustments.

Copson and Alice were happy enough as it drew on to her time. Copson had been the victim of much coarse chaff, but none of it meant to wound him; Alice too had been put to the blush by the women of the household, but they were without exception friendly; and they were both conscious of a lightening of heart now that the situation was known and accepted. Her greatest trouble now was that she had not sent to Norwich to invite her mother to her lying-in. She contrasted her deceit with the prompt and expensive despatch of a messenger from Norwich after the birth of Susanna in May; she told Copson a dozen times how hurt Jane would be, but when he finally offered to ride over to Norwich himself and fetch Jane back with him she refused in panic. She had a terror lest her father should come to curse her; terror too lest he and her husband quarrel and come to blows. She tried to still her conscience with vows to send the very next day.

Copson sat with her alone for an hour that last day. "You are afraid?" he asked.

"Only a little bit, because it isn't yours. I should not be afraid at all then."

"It is mine," he said determinedly. "Think that! And be brave."

They were full of love for each other. "Dear Geoffrey!"

"Dear Alice!"

"I don't know," she said. "But if I die——"

"No," he cried. "No, Alice!"

"I don't expect to! This creature is eager for the world and will enter it easily." She laughed before continuing. "But if I did, Geoffrey, you could know that I've not been ungrateful, even when I have seemed so."

He was so affected that he had to fling himself down, his head across her knees. If Sidley's child killed her —no bodied idea came to his mind, only shapes monstrous, amorphous, murderous. "Not Sidley's child!" he muttered in agony. "No, dearest," said Alice. "Yours." It should be their secret. Not even the child should know.

The child was born on a Wednesday, the day of their wedding. As she had said, the youngster was eager for the world and entered it without hesitating. Mistress Mako and Lady Sidley were there to assist the midwife, who had made her hand more cunning by drinking spirits. Maybe this had confused her thoughts, for to the astonishment, of both women she said distinctly: "Ay, ay, ladies, I recognise this Sidley head!" Startled, they looked at each other, and then, fascinated, at the crinkled child. The housekeeper expected a fierce reproof from Lady Sidley but none came. All she said was to Mistress Mako herself, that she would be upset if there were any repetition of the sentence, which the housekeeper interpreted as a command to keep her mouth shut. But it could not keep her from thinking, and think she did. It was her privilege to tell Copson he was father of a boy, and later to seat herself in her room and give details of the confinement to the open-mouthed womenfolk, but the midwife's saying, though she dared not repeat it, she could not forget. It was a drop of sour in the day's sweet.

But for Alice with her baby there was no sour. None for Copson either. Yet.

The months went quickly round. Lady Sidley saw that a message went to Norwich with a ballad-singer bound that way, but no reply came back that winter. Alice could only imagine that her father had prevented her mother sending her word, and knew, however unpleasant it might be, Geoffrey must ride over in the Spring. To know where you stood—that was the thing. The companion for Elizabeth had arrived from Lincoln, sent on the recommendation of Lady Hurrish—a thinnish woman in the middle twenties who, to give her her due, was uniformly civil—and Alice imagined that part of her life ended for ever. It was a pity, but nothing for tears. With a certain smugness she was beginning to feel herself superior to any woman without a baby, and he needed all the time she could spare from her household tasks. When the good weather came they would probably shift their quarters to two rooms at the far end of the wing at the back, and she was looking forward to the change.

It was at the end of February that Ferrers came to the housekeeper's room with a grave face. "You hear your share of gossip, dame, I'll be bound," he began after short greetings. She agreed, her face grave too. "Then this will be no news to you, I can see." He spoke of sneers among the men servants that must lead to serious trouble if Copson heard them. "The boy is quiet, he is bashful—or so we thought—but he'll not take this without his dagger out. I'm not sure what to do, dame." She asked him what he thought of it himself, and he shrugged his shoulders. "You saw Master Ralph a baby, dame?" He watched her. "I can't think it the household air, dame." She spoke a long time with him. "Well, what is it?" he asked, and gave the cuckold's sign, the index and ear finger erect from the fist. No, no, she couldn't believe it for one moment. "She has not deceived the lad then?" It seemed still harder to believe that. "Dame," said Ferrers harshly, "believe what you will, it must be bad. Shall I tell him?" That seemed a dangerous thing to do. Do the easy thing: leave bad alone.

"I am not easy in my mind," he said unnecessarily.

Soon neither Alice nor Copson could be easy. The remarkable and increasing likeness of the child to its true

father frightened them. All their plans were being brought
to nothing. Great trials overcome, they saw a greater one
ahead, swiftly upon them. There had begun the same
significant smiles, stares, whisperings, but now they were
malicious, they could not be too cruel. They must expect
jeers not chaff, abuse not jests. Inevitably they began to
speak harshly one to the other, not with any intent to
blame but because of the strain on their nerves. Copson
would declare passionately it was no fault of his, Alice
twist his words to mean it was fault of hers, and so they
wrangled, fell into sullen silences, ignored each other for
hours, became reconciled and defied the world, only to
quarrel again before the day was out. These differences
grew more violent.

"Maybe," said Alice one morning, "you would prefer
it if there were no child."

"I wish it to God!" cried the goaded Copson.

She hugged young John to her breast. "Then let me
tell you I'd rather have him than have you—so how do
you like that!"

"You would? You would, would you? And perhaps
you'd prefer his cursed father too! Damn him! I hope
his body and soul are stinking before this! I hope, I
pray to God, the flames of the stews consume him, I
hope, I hope——" He dashed his fist against the wall
with rage and saw her sneer at him. "Don't laugh at
me!"

"You are not amusing enough—is he, John?"

"By God and by Jesus," he swore, "you'll drive me too
far!"

"You are acting like a child."

Wild with mortification, he left the room, leaving her
with a contemptuous bitterness for him and complete
detestation of herself. Within ten minutes he was back
again. "For God's sake, Alice, don't let's quarrel! Haven't
we enough to face without that? Say you are sorry! Say
you are sorry!"

"Am I the only one to be sorry?" she asked coldly.

"Oh, what does it matter who is sorry? What does it matter?" Baby John was put down to cry if he wanted to, they were in each other's arms, tears helped them, never mind, he washed his face again, by God he'd stick his dagger into anyone who said a word against his Alice. "You are not sorry you married me?"

"I'd marry you again to-morrow, and again the day after!"

"Lovely Geoffrey!"

"Darling Alice!"

The inevitable clash came in March. Copson drew his dagger on the reeve who accused him bluntly of selling his wife's flesh. Mercifully it turned aside and outwards on the rib, but news of the attack spread through the house in a matter of minutes. The wounded man was taken to his own cottage, swearing vengeance, and Ferrers made it his responsibility to report what had happened to Sir Ralph.

"And the nature of the slander?" asked Sir Ralph, grinning. "Out with it, man."

"Then with all proper respect, Sir Ralph, all the servants—all who see the boy—say he is a Sidley and none of Copson's."

"And they think that a disgrace?"

Ferrers ducked his head as though a blow had whistled over it. "You think there will be further disturbances?" He did. "Take me to the child," said his master.

Ferrers shortened his stride to keep respectfully half a pace behind Sir Ralph as they walked to the Copsons' room. He wished he could send some message ahead of him, but there was no chance of this, and he had thrown open the Copson's door and announced the caller in his best steward's voice. They made a better showing than they often did. Deplore it as she would, there was something very satisfying to Alice in this deed of her husband's. It showed him willing to fight for her. He was standing near the window and had evidently been knifing the reeve once more for her benefit; he was very pale, but her face along

with a host of other emotions showed undoubted exulta-
tion. The boy was in his cradle in the far corner, behind
Copson. They wheeled to the door at the steward's announcement, Alice getting to her feet, and confusedly
they bowed; but Sir Ralph went between them to the
cradle and looked at the boy. Ferrers three-quarters closed
the door behind them. There were to be no sightseers.
Sir Ralph stayed there some half-minute. "H'm!" he said,
and then turned to the door. "My compliments to my lady
and will she join me here. Go yourself, Ferrers." He went
back to contemplation of the boy, turning his back on the
couple standing there. Copson looked as though he would
speak, but Alice, agitated though she was, had sufficient
presence of mind to motion him to stay quiet. They had
five minutes of this constrained waiting before Ferrers
came back with Lady Sidley. "You were gracious to come,"
said Sir Ralph perfunctorily. "You have seen the child?"
She gestured without crossing to the cradle. "You did
not see fit to tell me?" She flushed at his tone. "You
would say you lost discretion with your beauty," he said
icily, disregarding the others. "You would make a fool
of me in my own house?" Anger seemed to sprout on him.
"We have under one roof a maid loose in the hilts, a poor
pimp, a faithless steward, and a wife who would be glad
to leave me in my ignorance. Did you think, fools! I should
know nothing of it?" Ferrers opened his mouth to speak
but a pointing finger made him close it. "I tell you this
much: the boy shall have a place here, his mother and
her husband for his sake. Not one of you shall speak a
word of this to anyone; and finally, Ferrers, you will tell
your gossips and scandal-bearers that the next to talk
shall go, whether his service is a day or—listen, sirrah!—
fifty years. As for the idiot with the knife in his ribs—tell
him, Ferrers, he may hold his peace or leave my house.
Is everyone satisfied!" They were silent as his eyes went
from one to the other, with no more respect for his wife
than his servants. "Come then, madam." They went out,
followed by Ferrers.

For a time they were too stunned to discuss Sir Ralph's words and action. Then Copson alarmed his wife by saying he thought they should go.

"Go?"

"Leave Braiding."

"But whatever would we do, Geoffrey? We could not go to my home."

"It would be no better there. It could be no worse. Let's go to London, Alice, and live lives of our own." He dwelt on the miseries of their position, the daily gibes that were breaking his spirit, his fear that he would lose his self-respect, the way everybody thought of him. "We can never be happy here, Alice, I know it."

But she clung to the known, however bad. It was easy to make Sir Ralph's speech out worse than it was. Things would be better from now on, if only because everybody understood the situation. Later perhaps, when Sidley came home, they could get appointed to another household. In the meantime they must stay here. It would be madness to go to London without prospect of employment. Besides, it was only fair to the child.

"And what about me?" Copson asked. "Must I stand being called a pimp by that old swine?"

"You are too handy with your dagger," she flattered him; "you do not think before you act." This pleased him, she saw the jerk of his chin. "You are lucky to have me to think for you, hothead that you are. London is bigger than a reeve, or even two."

They talked about Sir Ralph's treatment of his wife. The same conclusion came into both their minds but neither spoke it. Finally he admitted that he had been hasty. They would remain at Braiding and hold their heads as high as anyone. "You don't mind that I drew my dagger?" he asked, angling for praise. "Mind!" she cried. "It was wonderful of you!" Self-esteem poured with the blood through every vein as he heard her. "I'd have killed him, you know, Alice!"

Chiding him for a desperado, holding the right hand

that had driven not quite home, she tried to think back to that quiet Alice Greene who had lived for twenty years in Norwich. She could not. Do as she would, she thought herself committed to a life of stratagem, calculation and struggle. Even Copson seemed outside her, an instrument. Only the boy could share her heart. Yet she was the same Alice Greene. It was circumstance, she felt, that made destiny.

She never saw Elizabeth on the old intimate terms now. Not only was there the companion to take her place, but undeniably they had cooled to each other. Frequently she asked about the child, but hardly ever came to see him, her use of Alice's name was each month a shade more patronising; Alice for her part found it easy to shade her usage to a respectful *Lady* Elizabeth, and was not checked. No matter, she had all she wanted of the Sidleys' at her breast. Young John's lips clasping her nipple, she would look down on him with a tender and yet fierce love, rejoicing with each suck that drew strength from her, telling herself she and John—no matter for the rest of the world. She and John! And her husband—they were not quarrelling now. They were in league against a million. Even at those times when she felt no love for him, she knew him good and indispensable to her. She must bind him to her for her own and for John's sake. He showed every sign of affection for the youngster, but had given over the pretence of calling him his own child before her. He had matured five years these last twelve months.

In June he gained permission to go to Norwich to see his parents-in-law, and this time the Sidleys sent no greetings to a servant's father and mother. He was there two days and then hurried back to tell the anxious Alice the tidings. Robert and Jane still thought Copson the boy's father, and Robert made no attempt to hide his disgust at their anticipating their marriage. He had gone off somewhere and not said good-bye; but Jane was rather glad of that than otherwise, as it gave her an opportunity to talk privately with her son-in-law. She had nothing to say

of blame—what was done was done—and Copson told
how she asked a hundred questions about her daughter:
her pains, her flow of milk, the weight of her child, his
colouring, how much hair he had, how much work she
did, whether she was happy all the time or only twenty-
three and a half hours of the twenty-four. As for the messages—for the next two days Copson was pulling up short
with: "That reminds me; I ought to have told you, Alice;
Ah, yes, she told me to tell you; While I think of it." There
were rules of conduct, maternity hints, advice about diets
and binders, so many good wishes and kisses, and much
information. Jane was well again after Susanna, who
appeared a sickly child. "She cried, Alice, and said how
much she wanted to see you." "Poor mother! I don't
know——" The least she could do was give a tear or two
to the same store. "Don't fret yourself," he ordered, kissing her under the eyes. "We'll go over next summer without the boy."

She asked him whether her brother knew, but he had
forgotten to find that out. Still, she was not much concerned about what Robert might think of it. Not until
he knew about Sidley. Then it might be awkward. But
when that day came she intended the awkwardness to be
other folks' more than hers. And she assured herself it was
so far ahead she would waste time to give it a second's
thought. Sidley himself might be home by that time—
a much more serious problem. She agreed gladly with her
husband. "Next summer!"

It was not to be. By September she, Copson, and the
child were in London. They had fled the house, from Sidley's father.

It was during mid July, when Copson spent almost
every day and many nights away from the house collecting and paying dues, she grew aware of and then alarmed
by a change in Sir Ralph's attitude towards her. He came
occasionally to see her son, but had hitherto had nothing
but the barest good-day for her, though his following glances

were becoming more disturbing. This one day, however, he came in when she was suckling the child. He laughed with a deprecatory gesture as she went to draw the covering over her bosom. "The rascal is hungry!" he said thickly, and then horrified her by trying to put his lips to her breast. She was on her feet, quivering with fear and rage. "Get out!" she said viciously. "Get out!" For only the briefest note of time he let her look through his eyes into the stirrings of his heart, then they were pebbled as usual, meaningless. "You forget yourself, child," he said mildly, and sat down. Instantly she had swept a shawl from beside her, and was through the doorway before she had time to wrap it round the child and herself. Five minutes later she returned. He was gone, but it left her in a turmoil for hours. He was all she had thought him at first, she knew it. Henceforth the sight of him would be abhorrent as contact with a reptile. Would she never again find that old uncomplicated life and be free of doubt and fear and the ever thickening battle with circumstance? Now she must debate whether to tell her husband. Yes, no—now one, now the other. Would they have done wisely to go when he said? What would come next?

She decided not to tell. A week went by and she saw nothing of Sir Ralph; a second, and a third. It was now the second week of August, when Copson made an annual visit to London for six days on business. The year before he had been excused because of his wife's lying-in, but Ferrers had only abuse for his deputy, and there was no reason why he should not take up the duty again. He always stayed at a quiet inn, the Glove in Paul's Chain, not a hundred yards from the Church. He would pass through Cambridge, but he and Alice decided it would be better not to see her brother. He set off on the Tuesday at daybreak, with one man, and she settled herself without misgiving to her brief widowhood, perhaps glad of the unbroken companionship there would now be between her and John. As far as Cambridge she knew him completely safe, and there he expected to find company for the more dangerous part of the journey During the afternoon she passed Sir Ralph as she went, boy on arm, to speak with Mistress Mako about a household matter. She thought of turning another way, but wisely decided to go past him with as brief a curtsy as she could. Her reward was a smile, which she found both pitiful and repellent, it was so abject an expression of useless desire. She did her errand and after a time spent with the admiring housekeeper went back to her room. It was late into the evening, the boy had been asleep for hours, when there came a slight knocking at the door; it opened, and Sir Ralph was inside it. Trembling, she jumped to her feet. His face showed much of his mission. "No," he half-said, half-whispered, "don't be frightened! I wouldn't hurt you, my dear." She put a hand to her heart. "No, no," he kept on saying; "I wouldn't hurt you. I wouldn't hurt you." His hands, spread out placatingly, trembled still more than her own. "I have money, child, I have money. I can give you so much!" His chilliness, his bleak indifference, were gone. "We can do so much for each other. You can please me and I can give you money." His voice was too high-pitched to sound entirely sane. "Will you go?" she panted. He shook his hands. "You don't understand. I want you to be kind to me. Look!" He dipped a hand into a pocket. "Look!" He had drawn out a necklace of silver, with a flashing stone at the end. "For you!" He came nearer, and nearer again as she retreated a pace. "A handsome chain for a handsome neck. A lovely stone to lie between your breasts Will you wear it? Shall I put it on for you?" He motioned towards her, but she shrank away from him. He began to blabber that he would ring her breasts with diamonds and heap her belly with gold, if only she'd be kind. He shivered with the ignominy of his impotence, but went on begging for a full minute. Her teeth were clenched hard and she shuddered at him, shaking her head. "Don't forget," he said shrilly, "I can turn you out of house and home. You had better!" Her expression told him that would not do, and he held out the necklace once more. He held his pride

out with his price, and she scorned them both. Suddenly
he tried to wrestle with her, but she was stronger than he
and pushed him off and struck him as she had struck
his son. Even then she remembered, and there broke into
her mind the strangeness of such a repetition. This one at
least could not harm her against her will. He made to come
at her again, a ludicrous thread of blood running from his
right nostril, but before her uplifted hand could fall he
desisted, not too mad to know the impossible. He looked
fool and knave, not even a man, a straw-brained, spindle-
shanked, dry-lipped, water-blooded old fumbler, and he
knew it. He felt the wet run over his mouth and rubbed
it away with the back of his hand, starting at the red stain.
She saw him make a deliberate and powerful effort to
recover himself, his trembling ceased, and for a while
they regarded each other in frightening silence. Then
without a word he flung the necklace into her face and
walked out. John had been disturbed and started to cry,
she took him up and rocked him in her arms, more to
soothe herself than the boy, and tried to get her head clear
enough to think what she must do. She could not stay,
that was certain. She identified herself with Sir Ralph's
thoughts more clearly than she could control her own.
After such humiliation, such a frantic display of his weakness, he would be too dangerous to share a roof with.
She must go. And with her husband away, she must trust
to herself. Despite her experience she felt she was being
absurd as she dragged some of her furniture across the door
to secure it. John slept through this, and then she began to
turn out her own and her husband's possessions. Their
moderate store of money she heaped together with trinkets
that promised to be of any value. Once or twice she kicked
Sir Ralph's necklace out of her way, but eventually bent
down and held it up to the light. She threw it aside again,
but not to the floor—on to the bed in the other room,
very near the other valuables. With her husband's things
she found the velvet bag given him by Sidley. The thong
was pulled so tightly and knotted so intricately around its

neck she could not open it without cutting, so she let it
be and threw it with the other things into her bundle. She
felt now she had the irreducible minimum, and was shocked
by its weight. She could not carry so much and the child
a hundred yards. So far she had not even considered how
she was to get out of the house, much less how she would
reach London. Vaguely she thought she could get a horse
from the stable and somehow make her way to Cambridge
and trust to Robert to do the rest. The Glove Inn, that
was it, The Glove Inn, Paul's Chain. It seemed an infinite
distance away. Perhaps she ought to stay here. She thought
again of Sir Ralph, the slithering blow of the chain on her
face. She must go.

She slept for a few hours, after all, but was waiting before
it was light. Quietly she worked the corner of the side-
board from the door it held, and with her bundle stepped
out into the passage. She made the journey successfully
to the nearest side-door and drew the well-oiled bolts.
Leaving her bundle she went back for the baby. He stirred
and whimpered, but fell asleep again in the renewed warmth
of the shawl. It was now she knew the madness of what
she was doing, and yet could see no alternative. With the
feeling that she was irrevocably committed, she went along
the passage a second time to the side door. She had closed
the door behind her and was taking up her bundle when
a shadow moved from shadows. "Well, Mistress?" Her heart
almost leapt from her breast. It was Ferrers. They were
about equally stupefied. He had a cocked pistol in his
hand. "You, Alice!" Incoherently, yet not above a whisper,
she began to beg him to help her, to help her husband.
He shook his head. "I can't do it! I should be failing in
my duty. I don't know what is in your bundle. I can't
do it!" "But open it and see!" she begged. He still shook
his head, with slow and weighty motion. She began to tell
him about Sir Ralph, entreating him by all he held dear to
help her, and this obviously harassed him. "Last night?"
He burrowed into his ear with the forefinger that had crooked
about the trigger. "Come back to your room, Alice." She

begged him the more. "If I am satisfied, I'll help you," he said angrily. He caught up her bundle. "Come along." There was nothing else to do. He thrust home the bolts and saw her through the passage again. "I'll make time to see you, lass," he said roughly, and then, more gently: "You'd not have gone a mile on your own, you can see that."

She was alone in her room, exhausted after the excitement, aching with a sense of her futility. What could she do now? She was tempted to throw herself on the bed and care not. But not for long—she must go about her work this day again as though nothing were the matter, and had not Ferrers said he would help? This braced her, and she wondered how soon she could see him. This was almost as soon as the household began to stir. He came along to her room, knocked, announced himself, and when she showed her head, said behind his hand: "Don't be a fool, Alice. Ask her ladyship to let you visit your parents." She shook her head at this. "Then there is no helping you against your will," he said, frowned, and went off.

Within an hour she saw his solution the only one and went to see Lady Sidley. Her ladyship showed irritation at her request and treated her with a new rudeness. They were not used at Braiding to consult the wishes of maid-servants, they had no wish to get a bad name for women-folk gallivanting the countryside, she saw no reason in what she was asking. Alice was at point to tell her she could not keep her at Braiding against her wish when she asked curtly whether the child was to go with her. Yes, she replied, he was. His grandparents had never seen him, and it was fitting they should. Lady Sidley came near sneering. "He's my baby," said Alice hotly. "I love him if no one else does!" She was asked when she wanted to go, and said the next day. And for how long? She would be back before her husband returned from London. She had not seen her mother for eighteen months, she added, blaming herself for her hypocrisy. "Very well. Tell the steward to send an armed man with you."

She told Ferrers she was setting off for Norwich that morning, and would he see to horses and an escort for her. Impassive of face, he said he would: and half-an-hour later she was riding through the lodge gates, baby, bundle, and all. There had been no farewells, not even with Ferrers. Her escort was one of the steward's men, delighted with this break in the monotony of his service. They were about three miles from Braiding when she said to him confidently: "You know the way to Cambridge, of course?"

"Norwich, mistress," he corrected her.

"No, no, Bufton. Cambridge!"

He reined up. "Wait a minute. Aren't we going to Norwich?"

"Of course not! Whatever gave you that idea?"

"Master Ferrers did. Who else?"

"I'm surprised at you, Bufton, I heard him telling you myself. To see my brother, that is where I'm going."

He knew she had a brother at Cambridge. "I could have sworn——"

"Please, Bufton, let us ride on. I must reach an inn before my baby wants his feed again."

"Giddy-up," he said to his mare. "You know, mistress, I could have sworn——"

They were at Cambridge on the second day, Bufton much surprised by her desire to hurry and still dissatisfied he was not being made a fool of. She put up at a small inn on the edge of the town and sent him to fetch her brother. Greene received his tidings as though they were gunshot. He made a hurried explanation to Coppinger, rushed to get permission to leave College so late and, having been told he must be accompanied by a master, went back once more to Coppinger, who willingly agreed to go with him. Bufton felt like a brown moth with two blackbeetles as they set off to meet Alice. He was full of information about the journey down, but said nothing about the scandal of the child's parentage, though tempted to do so for his own importance. He kept on saying he

couldn't have looked after her better had she been the
Queen's Own Majesty whom God bless and whose health
he was always pleased to drink, till at last Greene cut him
short in this loyal sentiment and told him he would not
be forgotten.

Coppinger waited downstairs while brother went to
sister. Climbing up to her room Greene was wondering
what differences he would observe in this sister wived and
childed, and why she should be there in Cambridge. A
quarrel with her husband seemed unlikely, and in any case
why Cambridge? He pulled at his ear. Awkward, very.
At any rate he had decided that the birth of her child so
soon after marriage was no reason for indignation. He might
have company to Norwich after all.

He was to find her will stronger than his, though the
trial did not come during those fond minutes when they
embraced and found only trivial words for each other, of
their amazement, their delight, the way they looked,
when last they had heard from home.

"I came to you because I want your help, Robin."

"Why, Alice, no one has called me that since I saw you
last!"

"No?" She frowned at him. "You must help me,
Robin."

"I must?"

"Yes, yes, you must! You must! You must, Robin."
The tale of Sir Ralph's wickedness broke on him like a
wave. "I had to come, Robin!"

"You had, Alice—unless you went home. Why didn't
you go home?"

"Because my baby was born too soon to please its grandfather."

"Oh come now, Alice," he remonstrated. "I've said a
lot against dad in my time, but he wouldn't hold that
against you now you want help." Truth to tell, he felt the
situation too much for him. It was absurd she could be
sitting there telling him such a thing. What the devil was
he supposed to do? If her husband had only stayed with

her instead of rushing off to London——"You ought to go home, Alice, if you don't intend to go back to Braiding."

"You think I should go back?"

He wriggled at that. "I didn't say so, Alice. Don't be so quick there's a good girl. But it is one thing to run away; another to fit in somewhere else. I think you ought to go home. I don't like the notion of your staying at inns like this. It's not as though you had your husband with you."

She was exasperated by his stupidity. "Will you take me to Geoffrey in London?" she asked plainly.

"Well, he is your husband——"

"So he is! Will you take me?"

"It's not as easy as all that. You come here so full of your own news you don't give me a chance to tell you mine. I am leaving for home to-morrow, Alice." He laughed as though expecting her to feel relieved. "So you see how handy it will be for you?"

"Home?" This was irony! She checked her feeling of helplessness. "Then you will not be taking me?"

"To London? I don't see how I can. It is too important, Alice. I am going to Italy in a couple of weeks."

She heard this news with indifference. What was Italy to her? "If you won't help me I must find someone who will, that is all."

He started to tell her how convenient it was he was going to Norwich. They could go along together. To her husband he gave not a thought. He had spun his plans with such satisfaction to himself that he was annoyed when she angrily refused to listen any more.

"But you ought to be home, Alice! I feel most uncomfortable at the idea of your riding about like this, with just a servant behind you. When I think of all the people you are bound to meet! I tell you what, Coppinger is downstairs—shall we ask him?"

"Can't you make up your mind without his advice? And what did you bring him here for?"

"I couldn't come without him. It is all very well for you, Alice, but the situation is full of difficulties for me. I should feel it my responsibility——" She turned from him so impatiently that he fell silent. When he spoke again it was with less assurance. "Edmund knows all about London. I have never been there. Don't you think we could ask him?"

"I'll go without you!"

"He may know." He sighed, at the door. "If it had been any other time, Alice!"

They found Coppinger the very man. He told Alice how he thought of her as an old friend, he had heard so much about her from her brother. Greene was grateful to him for saying he, Robert, was never tired of singing her praises. And he neither asked questions nor showed curiosity. She wanted to get to London. Robert could not go with her. That was enough. There was a party of assessors going back the day after to-morrow from Pembroke Hall, who would certainly admit her to their company. "Grave men," he said, smiling; "they will not ride too fast." It was the first exhibition of thoughtfulness and courtesy Alice had met with for some time, and her heart warmed towards the puritan. She grew less defensive, smiled back at him, laughed with her brother. She became willing to hear about Robert's Italian journey. As Coppinger told her about London, too, for her as for Robert the names burst brilliant as night fireworks: Parliament House, Westminster Hall, the Court, Charing Cross, Cheapside, St. Paul's, the Tower. She was buoyed up by a sense of adventure she knew indecent in woman. She and John—she started and looked to where the child was fast asleep in her bed. They must not see him. She yawned, pretending greater exhaustion than she felt, and Coppinger took the hint. He would see about her admittance to the assessors' party first thing in the morning. Yes, her brother would see her before he left for home. They said good-night.

Walking back to College, Greene reproached himself

half-heartedly that he was not accompanying her to London. "Any time but this, Edmund," he kept saying. "But it had to be now when I have this glorious chance to visit Italy! Life is like that, Edmund."

Coppinger shook his head. "Any other time!" Greene complained.

CHAPTER XVI

GREENE'S PROSPECT OF visiting Italy he owed
to Harrison. The former envoy had been sufficiently interested in him after the scuffle at the Rose to permit infrequent visits throughout the two years following Sidley's
flight from the University. He certainly amused himself
at Greene's expense and never failed to satirise his oft-
expressed ambition to be superior to all the saddlers that
ever lived. Their talk together, he came to see, was an odd
contrast. Greene lived in the future, he in the past; and
while he rallied the young man on his dreams and im-
practicabilities, the other drew on his experience and
wisdom. This provoked his raillery the more, but it flattered him too. In Greene he found amiability and a quick
spirit. He was full of promise. Nor had he forgotten Greene's
hands round Hunter's throat. Not a backward lad, by any
means. He came to think that if and when opportunity
offered he would be willing to help him.

The opportunity came quicker than he expected. At
the end of July he was sent for to Court, received by his
Queen, and told that she had work for him to do. Half-
sorry, half-delighted, he expressed his unworthiness and
his eagerness to serve. He was needed for a mission to Genoa
to bargain for better treatment for English merchants at
that port. If he succeeded there, he should proceed to
Leghorn before winter on the same errand. The general
terms of his venture were given him by Burghley, and secret
instructions about the granting of a loan to the Genoese
in return for contingent aid which no one but he, Her
Majesty, and her Council knew anything about. It was
from Burghley too he learned why he in particular had
been chosen. The most powerful man in Genoa, Burghley
assured him, was that Cesare Spinola who had been with
him on his famous journey to Cathay. Between such

friends all things were possible. He shook his head when
he heard that Harrison had not corresponded with his
fellow-traveller for more than ten years. He said moreover that Her Majesty was minded to repair the neglect
that had followed his previous mighty though unsuccessful
journey. A knighthood would suit well the English dignity
abroad. Harrison—soon Sir John—listened more than he
talked, as the details were settled. They must sail on the
first day of September. There was no reason at all why Sir
John should not take with him a young man from Cambridge, skilled in the Italian tongue, with a gift for fine
penmanship. But no unlimited expenses—let that be
understood. There was no money to burn in England,
though fools were always grumbling. A fair allowance—
but there, Sir John had always been noted for his discretion. He would know, without need of more words.

Thus it was that Greene received his letter from London
asking whether he was prepared to spend at least three
months and possibly the autumn and winter in Italy.
His excitement knew no bounds. This was the dream of
dreams come true. All he had sighed for over Ariosto,
all he had envied the brilliant Sidley, was now his. Genoa
and Leghorn, true, were lesser names than Venice and
Rome, than Florence and Bologna, but his mind was
unconfined by them. His foot on Italian soil, who knew
what might lie ahead?

"Edmund," he cried when first he saw him, "I'm going!"
He could hardly understand that the cry needed amplifica-
tion. "Where? Why, to Italy, Edmund!"

He walked jerkily up and down, gesticulating; he paused,
before the bookshelf, patting the Italian authors with
nervous hand, conjuring with fast-running words a score
of visions for his listener. So jubilant was he that even
the grave Coppinger was affected. When? Whither?
Whence? Wherefore?—these were words that struck a
rock to produce torrents: the time, the means, the manner.
Anyhow, he must see the Master. He did, and found that
Harrison had sent him word of his mission, and that he

craved permission for Master Robert Greene to go with him. So much was settled. Howland would not be sorry to see the last of Harrison. He could find as good a lecturer, and he might prove a friend at Court. Yes, Robert Greene might go.

But first he must visit Norwich. He had not seen his mother and father since the wedding at Braiding, he had never set eyes on the infant Susanna, dead these eight months, he was forgetting what Anne and Toby looked like. He must go home with this incredible news that their son was to accompany Sir John Harrison on a diplomatic mission to Genoa. And Leghorn! He would need money too. No time to waste, the weather was good for travelling, he would set off on Saturday. Sir John's messenger had gone back to London that same day with his acceptance. The time was topsy-turvy; either it fled from him or loitered. Clothes too. Ideas came to him in no order. But he was going to Italy!

It would be a good thing when he was in London. Still better when he was on shipboard. Here in Cambridge, home at Norwich, the journeying: how much better when there was no possibility of accident or error! Would they sail direct to Genoa or go overland through France? Would they do this? Would they do that? He must practise Italian conversation every hour of the day.

No wonder he was nonplussed at Alice's arrival. He thought vexedly that night: Why can't women who are married stay in their proper place? Sir Ralph—he could not believe it of him. Though if it were true and he ever again set eyes on the old devil—he allowed himself the usual heroics. But Edmund had promised to see to all that. Italy! Italy! He saw marble palaces rising from a blue and white-foam sea, rainbow cathedrals climbing a blue and white-cloud sky.

He saw her for half an hour the next morning. It was very early, just after daybreak. "You will be all right, Alice," he said three or four times to assure himself. Now that his departure was at hand, he felt mean. His sister going to

London—— "You will be all right, Alice." Uncertain though she was, she agreed, on the surface calm and confident. "You won't tell father and mother you saw me?" "Why not?" "Because I ask you not to." He thought a moment and promised.

"I am sorry I did not see young John. Still asleep, is he?"

She nodded. They were at the entrance of the inn-yard. She was running no risks. "He sleeps a lot. Babies are as lazy as Cambridge scholars."

"Little you know! When will you be going to Norwich, Alice?"

"Soon. As soon as we get settled."

He believed the lie. "Mother would like to see you," he said rather absently. "Shall I tell her?"

"You have just promised to tell them nothing!"

"Why, of course! Hm. I was thinking."

"Well," she said; "good-bye."

"Good-bye, Alice. Look after yourself. I am glad you met Edmund Coppinger. He's a wonderful fellow, Alice."

"So was Sidley. Good-bye."

He stared at her from horseback. "I might see him in Italy. You never know."

"You might," she said. "Good-bye."

"Wish me good lucky in Italy!"

"Good luck!"

"Good luck, Alice! I am sorry I did not see the baby." He left her with his head so obviously full of his own concerns that she believed he felt not a qualm on her behalf. She did not look up the road to see him disappear but went back to John. Now that she thought of it, she was certain he would tell all he knew before he left home. No matter, her life was no longer her parents'.

Greene had congenial company for two stretches of the road. There was the middle-aged man who spoke with authority on Italian manners and maladies, and the young man who lost himself in admiration and envy when he heard where Greene was going. If anything, he drank too much with this second, and almost fell asleep during the hot hours of the afternoon. It was surprising the sense of superiority one got from being able to talk about Italy to obvious stay-at-homes.

His news came as less of a shock to his parents than he had expected. They seemed surprised, nothing more. Perhaps because they had seen him at such rare intervals during the last five years they were accustomed to the idea of long partings. Jane, he found, had only the vaguest idea of where Genoa and Leghorn were to be found, and Robert knew nothing of them save that they were Italian, and therefore immoral. His son's upbringing would stand him in good stead in both places. He attempted good counsel that evening, and his son, nodding every now and again, saw fit to agree with all he said. The way of the transgressor was hard, he knew it; and was sure that his sins would find him out. As he sowed so also should he reap. Yes, father.

"Of course, I shall need some money, father."

'Your expenses?"

"All official expenses are paid," he said glibly. "But I need fitting out before I go. My clothes——"

"What is wrong with your clothes? They seem very decent and almost new to me."

He saw that explanation was going to be hard. When he pointed out that he would not be clerk all the time and that he hoped to mix with good company, he saw his father's eyebrows come down in that formidable way he remembered from almost twenty years before. But the Englishman abroad must not disgrace his nation. Surely his father would not wish to see his son the only shabby one of an assembly?

"Your wages?"

He did not know what they would be. In any case, they must come too late for him to fit himself out in London He needed a capital sum to establish letters of credit on the famous bank at Genoa.

"How much?"

Diplomatically he suggested twice as much as he expected to get. Then he and his father might simulate frankness and good feeling and hit the happy mean. Instead, an inexorable puritan logic beat him down to a quarter. As though it were a matter of no consequence he asked whether Grancher Beetham was still alive. The old man might well help his favourite grandchild, and that red-headed image of himself when a boy.

Italy, he felt certain, was no place for a man without money in his pocket. Cambridge now—but this was altogether another kettle of fish.

He went moaning to his mother the next morning, in exactly the spirit of his old-time candy begging. His father didn't seem to appreciate what a wonderful opportunity he had. "You see how it is, mother? Why, I might have lived to be a hundred and never seen anything like it. Who knows what it may lead to?"

"Yes, that is so," she agreed, and planted Tobias more firmly into his chair. "Your brother Tobias will keep quiet all the morning if I give him a pickled onion to suck."

"It can't be very good for him, mother, can it? But about Italy—as I was saying——" He sketched for her gem-like cities, marble mountains, winey rivers, purple fountains. He peopled the land with grave scholars and their grave disciples, with learned statesmen and their learned clerks, with solemn merchants, valiant warriors, divines. He communicated to her his vague fear that amid all this Robert Greene, son of Robert Greene, would creep impoverished, ill-clad, not exactly hungry, but nearer Duke Humphrey's than Dives' table.

"Come on, mother, you must have some money somewhere."

"The idea!"

"If you have, I know you'll let me have some of it. On loan—is it?"

She protested sharply he must see his father.

"*Him!* Come on now, mother—once I start to earn my living I'll see you repaid."

"I don't want to be repaid!"

"Of course you don't! You have some money then?"

She grew confused with this pleading of his, as though he was still a small boy to be bribed and clouted indiscriminately. "Now don't you come bothering me! You are not too big, mind, to have your head smacked."

He knew he had won. "Where is it, mother? In the purse?"

"Certainly not!"

She laughed at him, helpless against his cadging. "Very well, I'll see what I can do for you."

It was that afternoon, while his father was about the town on business, he told her how he had met Alice in Cambridge. He did this without having intended it in the least. The tidings came up like spittle under his tongue, and then the secret was out. Instantly repentant, he watched his mother's expression change from disbelief to alarm. "And you left her there!" she reproached him, and seemed not to be listening to his defence. "Why did she leave Braiding?" He hummed and ha'd, pretended he did not know, cursed the blabbing tongue which had ruined his stay. For the first time he felt his mother would not forgive him in a hurry. To save himself he began to lie. She had a woman servant and a man with her. Copson must have preferment in London. Besides, she was joining the company of assessors from Pembroke Hall and Coppinger was going to London at the same time. Yes, he would be seeing her before he left for Italy. The address? He had it written down somewhere inside one of his books. In any case Coppinger would know it. Too late he realised he had destroyed his mother's peace of mind and could do nothing to restore it.

He was glad now he was leaving the next day. To make things worse his mother insisted on telling his father about it when he returned. "I shall be surprised at nothing I hear of her," said Greene sternly. "It is no subject for talk." Evidently Alice had known better than he her welcome at

Norwich. He lay awake a long time that night thinking over the tangle of Alice, his mother and father, but got no further than a series of useless ifs. But he had been a fool to talk, and had broken his word to Alice. He did not feel eager now to see her at the Glove Inn before he went abroad. He felt her first words would cut through his betrayal like wire through cheese. But if his father would only this, if only Copson had not that, and Alice herself, and his mother—oh, to hell with the problem! he thought angrily. Wasn't it enough for a man to look after himself?

The shadow of a household difference hung over his departure. He could see that his mother was desperately unhappy about Alice, his father pig-headed. He felt uncompensated by money in his purse and a draft arranged through Portington's wealthy father on a London house. Why this family squabble? Why couldn't they all be on good terms? He was tempted to speak with his father but could not bring himself to the necessary state of resolution. His mother he saw alone for ten minutes. "Please don't fret, mother. She said she would be visiting you soon." Jane looked ready to cry. All these upsets coming at once—— "Did she really, Robin?" He patted her shoulder, feeling miserable himself. "She'll come, mother. If she said she will, she will. You don't know how much more determined she is these days." "If she only would! And then there's your father!" "I know." Greene had never disliked his father so much as that moment. "But he'll change, mother. Whatever he says, if she were to walk in here now——" Jane sighed, hoping she would; her son was checked by the futility of his own words. Then she groped behind her preserves. "This is the money, Robin." "I was only joking, mother," he protested. She shook her head. "I thought that if Alice and the boy are in trouble, you might give as much as you can spare to them." He kissed her. "They can have every penny of it, mother!"

So he made another parting. He was riding with three Thetford tradesmen for the first part of his journey, and hoped to join a strong enough company at Cambridge to pass through Epping Forest without disaster. The children and his mother were kissed, Jane many times, he gripped his father's hand, almost at once he was meeting his fellow-travellers, and then the city towers were vanishing behind him. For a time he was wretched, but eventually began to brag to his companions who treated him good-humouredly. Soon he felt the sun shine for him alone. He was twenty-two years old, and could stuff the world like a tennis ball into his pocket.

After a night at Thetford he pushed on for Cambridge without mishap. He made arrangements to change horses at the Rose, and spent the night in College with Coppinger. They had much to talk about but nothing they had not already discussed a dozen times. Once or twice Greene did think it would be jolly if Portington and Callimet were asked in for half an hour, but Coppinger did not suggest it and he himself was unwilling to. He asked about Alice. She had gone away quite safely. He was relieved to hear there were three other women travelling with the assessors —better still, they were married women travelling with their husbands.

Good luck kept with him. He heard from the porter that there were six of Lord Hunsdon's men leaving Cambridge for London the next day, and before he went to bed had arranged with their leader to join them on the road. They were straight for town, but it would take them the best part of three days to get there. Greene, recognising that delay meant safety, and thoroughly alarmed by all he had heard of the dangers of the Cambridge to London road, was content.

During those three days the players opened up yet another world. Their leader was James Candler, who from his talk had been part of theatrical history for thirty years. He had appeared in miracles and moralities, interludes and chronicles. He had tales of the Saracen's Head in Islington, the Red Lion in Whitechapel, and the Cross Keys in Grace-church Street; he had acted in the revels at Court, and knew all the vicissitudes between a bed of earth and silk sheets. Then there were Kit Cornish, Fabian Penton and John Shanbrooke, liars possibly, but men of strange and plentiful experience, and the boys Arthur Shealden and Harry Totnell. Alongside the youngest of them Greene felt himself a slugabed, alongside the grown men he was most uncomfortably a child. They had, been up and down the country, from border to coast in each direction; they knew London like the backs of their hands; they laughed at the names of ladies, spat at the names of lords; they assessed the worth of actors and inns. They dumbfounded Greene with a flow of talk light or serious, discursive or practical, bawdy or impassioned. He thanked God that by a reference to Italy he could demand some kind of equality.

"They told me in Nuremberg," said Penton casually, "that at Venice they have women actors."

"No, no," remonstrated Candler; "you were deceived, Fabian."

"The idea is monstrous," Shanbrooke interrupted indignantly. "It would be the end of the art. The only place where women should play is——"

"In bed," cried Totnell.

Shanbrooke pointed to the boy's chin. "If you get goatish, boy, you are unparted. Don't forget!"

Greene called over to Penton: "You have acted in Germany, Master Penton?"

"I have, and hope to again." He boasted to all of them that there were no actors like the English, no theatres like theirs, no plays. "I drew tears at Nuremberg, masters, till the townsfolk fled to the Schloss for dry land. I drew laughter till the sausages fell out of their skins at the Bratwurstglöcklein. I drew sighs that wafted the roof from the Lorenzkirche, groans that fetched the midwives from all Wurtemburg."

"A holocaust of art," Cantler suggested.

Lumbering along at a wagon pace, they set the slow miles behind them. At both the inns where they put up for the night Greene noticed that the older players were known and apparently liked. He sat up with them late, and wanted to treat them to all the beer they could drink, but the older men insisted on paying their shot. No one of them had visited Italy, but Cornish as well as Penton had been to France and Germany, Candler to Denmark as well. "They love us English overseas," he was assured; "they think us all fools and rich—even players. They will buzz round your head like flies, hang on to your tail like monkeys, offer you wine and women, and willingly kiss your breach for a groat." Their words were oil to the flame of his desire; he slept confusedly each night, dreaming of Genoa and the cities he hoped to see.

The other side of Epping Forest the players diverged towards Edgeware upon business, and Greene kept with them. Thence they went across country and the most infernally dusty cart tracks till they met the main Uxbridge Road, three or four miles from the city. "Your first visit?" Ashamedly Greene confessed that it was. "Pooh," said Candler, "there must be a first for us all some time or other: the first time on a stage, the first time to marry——" "Even the first time to die!" jested Shanbrooke. But Candler, a native, displayed as much as could be seen of the city to Greene, who stared and listened with thumping heart. Candler's ability in his calling might be judged from the gestures with which he indicated St. Giles's and then Covent Garden, Holborn, and Clerkenwell with his left hand, pointed dramatically towards Charing Cross with his index finger, and then made a magnificent display of palm and back to illustrate the features of Westminster and Whitehall. He was map-maker, architect, and painter in one. "You know where to go?" he asked at the Cross. At least he knew where he wanted to go: the Glove Inn in Paul's Chain. And in the morning he must find Sir John at a house in Fetter Lane. "Here, boy"—this to Totnell— "you have time to take Master Robert Greene to Paul's Chain?" "Time and will enough," the boy replied smartly. They made farewells, cried out for further meetings, and then Greene was following Totnell into the Strand. He was a friendly lad, but nothing like the guide Candler was.

Occasionally he nodded in the direction of some notable building, jerked his thumb up or down a side street, but his interest seemed rather in persons than places. He told the only half-attentive Greene of his plans to celebrate his return from the country, of the fellow-actors he would be seeing again, of the girl in Turmer Street who loved him. So they passed under Temple Bar, through Fleet Street towards the Church, and then into the Chain, where the boy reined in before the sign of the Glove. He took the coin Greene offered him and went off whistling cheerfully, leaving Greene to enter the inn and ask for Master and Mistress Copson.

He had his first shock. They were not there. Mistress Copson had arrived six days ago with her child and three days later her husband had taken her away. They had no idea where. Greene was rubbing his forehead at this news when the landlord suggested he might be staying there overnight, and because he could think of nothing else he agreed. As though to do him a service the landlord told him he was in the very room used by Master Copson before the arrival of his wife. "Send up a good meal," said Greene to that.

While he ate he thought, and performed a twofold digestion afterwards. How to begin to look for them he had not the slightest idea. Besides, it was still not more than early evening and there would be three hours to dark, and he wanted to see something of the city. What good was there in worrying? Copson was a reliable man. He would make his way. He called the landlord and obtained directions for an evening walk, larded with warnings. "You make the city out a forest," he chided; "a forest of wild beasts." The landlord dipped his head to think this over. "And I wouldn't be so far wrong if I did. There's plenty of beasts here, from the female serpent to the black boar of the woods. I mean it kindly, young sir." Greene hesitated whether to give him thanks or a snub, but chose the fairer course and bade him good evening before leaving the inn and turning left to where the great square tower of St.

Paul's dominated the house and inn roofs. The roadway was worse than that he had lived on at Norwich or that in front of his College. A kind of high-water mark of decaying refuse showed how during heavy rains the water must come flooding down to the river, lapping the very doorsteps of the tall narrow houses. There were holes in it big enough to take a coffin, and he guessed it hopeless for a coach. Around St. Paul's he saw the celebrated yard, home of idlers, riff-raff, tricksters, and occasional honest men; he made the circuit a couple of times, but when a leery fellow in red hose brushed against him and began to speak of the weather he thought it time to move on. He took a direction of an elderly man for Fleet Street, and was soon retracing the way he had come earlier with Totnell. The street he thought exceptionally crowded for the time of day. Young gallants, gay as peacocks, took the wall of sober-suited tradesmen and their wives; porters and messengers, some in russet, some in the liveries of their masters, hurried by; there were the steel breastplates of soldiers, the dark robes of scholars, the fur-trimmed cloaks of merchants, procession-like. Frequently he passed drunken men, singly or in twos or threes, once or twice brisk companies led by a brilliantly-dressed lord (so he judged) making their own way without ceremony through the press. As at Paul's, there were women parading up and down or waiting at the doors of drinking houses, many of them stale and ugly under the ceruse, but a surprising number handsome, sprightly, and young. There were beggars a-plenty, crying out that they had lost an arm, a leg, an eye, a nose, in Her Majesty's service, brandishing scrolls, beseeching the sweet young masters, the gallant young men, the most reverend sires, the fairest dames of Fleet, to give them alms. Among all this Greene felt nervous and gay, with a hollowness in his stomach as though he had not eaten for a long time. For this was Troynovant—the New Troy.

He shook his head impatiently at women and beggars alike, and was not distressed to hear himself cursed a time or two. Scraps of conversation, magic as incantations, met his ears, and from these or mere appearance he gave men characters, ambitions, offices, and ideals. The fat grocer, thinking on butter and his fat wife; the lean-jawed playwright, his head chockful of rant, his tongue a-drip with wet tags; the student, hacking at life in London with the blunt tools of his disputations; the black-eyed lover, the deepoathed soldier, the miser thinking of his money-bags, the spendthrift, too; he saw these time and again thrusting, sidling, manœuvring past him. He was now back in the Strand among the taverns, the signs thick as leaves over the doors: pelicans, cranes, coaches and horses, dogs and ducks, bunches of grapes, armorial designs, most of them painted or enamelled. Suddenly he was stopped by a quietly-dressed young man, who spoke to him with every appearance of surprise. "Surely," he asked, "you were at the University?" Greene looked at him with open suspicion. "I was," he said coldly.

The other laughed. "You doubt me, I can see. You do wisely." He waved his hand. "Among all these——"

He was a short young man, with a frank and merry expression. To Greene's eye he had student written all over him. "You have not recognised me, I can see," he was saying.

"No," Greene admitted; "I have not."

"We were at different Colleges. You were at—Christ's, was it?"

"St. John's," Greene corrected him.

"Ah yes! I was at Pembroke Hall. You remember Pennybread?"

Greene did not, nor one or two others mentioned. "You were not among the gravest then," he was told. The student, as he judged him, went on to talk easily about Cambridge and life there till Greene knew him genuine. "You must excuse me that I stopped you. I am in London and have few friends. A face one recognises in this great town—one cannot help oneself." He motioned with his hand down the street and they began to walk again. "My name, I should have said, is Ingpen—Cuthbert Ingpen. You remember it, I feel sure." He pulled a face. "So poor a thing is College fame. I was not unknown in my day there." Soon, apologetically at first, he was pointing out the sights to Greene, had drawn from him that it was his first visit, that he was a bird of passage to Italy. His expressions of envy put Greene in an excellent mood. "But shall we drink a glass of wine?" he asked. Greene was suspicious at once, agreed warily, and kept a hand on his money in the Wise Men; but Ingpen was pleasantness itself, drank to the Italian venture, insisted upon paying the reckoning, and they went into the street again. Greene felt better after that. Had there been a plan to deceive him the tavern was the place for it to be carried out.

"You have been down to the river?"

He had not, so his new friend first got from him where he was staying and then led him down from the Strand bridge to the open walks past Arundel Place. This was heaven to Greene. The river was corselet-grey under the late sky, alive with row-boats and sailing vessels in criss-cross patterns. As they walked Ingpen showed him back to the right the bold crenellations of Somerset House and the Savoy, then Duresne Place, and then, on the great curve of the river, the massed buildings from York Place to Parliament House. Opposite them the long-deserted flats of Lambeth Marsh showed nothing of comparable interest, but left again on the other side were straggling lines of houses, on their own side the fields to Water Lane and Bridewell, and the piled background of the city. Ingpen's finger flickered snake-tongued from point to point; he was better than Candler even, for he found lines from Ovid and Virgil to adorn the scene, happy comparisons between the Troys, Simois and Scamander and Thames. He had many a pretty remark of Amphion and his like, and Greene grew comparably classical.

They kept to the water's edge as far as Water Lane, and then passed over stinking Fleet Bridge to the hill. Once more Ingpen suggested they drink and Greene was agreeable. Ingpen thought the taverns on Fleet Street would be too rowdy by this time and led Greene into Blackfriars where he knew a quiet place for gentlemen, the Three Cocks Tavern, and here he let Greene call for a pint of sack a-piece. They drank it very leisurely, and then another, and Greene was about to call for a third and last when Ingpen leaned forward confidentially and said: "Keep up your money, friend. I know how we can get our wine free." "You do?" He nodded. "You see this gentleman who has just come in?" Greene looked at an ingenuous young man, with straw-coloured hair and light blue eyes. "What of him?" "He is a city fool, Master Greene, and such should always pay for scholars' drink." Greene felt the thrill of an adventure. Besides, Strawhair could afford it.

"Good evening, sir," said Ingpen courteously.

"Good evening to you, gentlemen." His voice was straw-coloured too.

They passed a few sentences. "Ah well," said Ingpen, "poor scholars grow thirsty like other men. Drawer—wine here. I tell you what, sir—shall I give you a pint of wine or you me?" Strawhair said he cared not either way. "Then let us play a hand of cards for it," suggested Ingpen. Strawhair languidly agreed. "What game?" "Mum-chance?" Strawhair said it was all one to him. "But you will excuse me first, gentlemen. I have a visit to the back."

Ingpen leaned closer to Greene. "You don't know this game? They call it decoy at Cambridge. He shuffles and I cut. When I cut I'll show you the bottom card of the rest of the pack and you call that for me. You understand?" All Greene understood was that there was some kind of trickery afoot, and that he was part of it. "The bottom card of the whole pack, remember," Ingpen had time to remind him once again.

Strawhair now returned with the cards. "Who is to shuffle?"

"You may, sir," said Ingpen, "and I'll cut. I prefer honest dealing." He made a fine cut of seven or eight cards from the deck, set the rest of the pack on top of it, and

Greene sitting on his left had a glimpse of the four of hearts. "I think," said Ingpen, "with your permission, sir, I'll let this honest gentleman name my card for me. To show there is no deceit." The whole process was now clear to Greene. The four of hearts was seven or eight cards from the bottom of the pack, and when the cards were drawn the odds were between sixes and sevens against Strawhair.

"What card?" he asked, as though ignorant of everything to do with cards.

"Any card," Strawhair assured him.

He felt Ingpen's foot press against his. "Just call any card?" he asked again.

"Yes, any card. You are no player, I see, sir."

"Oh well," said Greene, "the four of hearts."

Strawhair chose the Jack of Spades, the cards were drawn face up, and the four came out in seven draws.

"You win, sir," said Strawhair, laughing. He called the drawer and gave his order. "But you will give me my revenge, sir?"

"I had thought but one cut, sir," said Ingpen.

"No, no, you'll give me my revenge!"

There seemed no way of refusing. Strawhair shuffled, Ingpen cut a fifth of the pack, Greene saw the King of Clubs, called it, and it won. "That's a quart," said Strawhair. "I tell you what I will do with you, sir—I'll vie you two quarts on the next cut."

Ingpen frowned. "I am no gambler, sir. You had your chance of revenge. Besides, we have no use for so much wine."

Strawhair agreed this should be the last call. Naturally enough, he lost. Ingpen, however, gave him no time to order his losings. "I have no wish to take it." To Greene's admiration, he explained to Strawhair the trick they had played on him, and Strawhair, after a moment's thought, took it handsomely and insisted on getting the wine to share amongst them all the same. He proved a most interesting companion, they withdrew to a small private room to drink, and half an hour slipped by quickly as they showed each other card tricks or told fortunes. They were about this when the door was opened abruptly, and a stout, red-faced man came into the room. At once he was full of apologies. He had an engagement with a friend, he had thought so-and-so, he begged their pardons. "No need for that, sir," said Strawhair mildly; "we shall be glad to offer you a cup of wine, if you will accept it." Redface was eager with thanks, accepted the cup, and drank to their very good health, requesting immediately afterwards that the gentlemen should drink with him in turn. "I know scholars, masters," he told them; "I have a boy of my own at school and he shall to the University when it is time." Greene liked the old fellow at once, and still more after Redface had asked his advice upon the better University and the best College. "St. John's College, eh? I'll not forget your kind advice, young master." Then Redface noticed the cards. "At cards, gentlemen?" Only in sport, they told him. "The only way to play cards," he warned them. "How now, though, shall we play for a pint of wine till my friend comes?" They all three looked at each other, and then Strawhair, grinning, said he would hold him for a pint with pleasure. "What game?" asked Redface. Strawhair grinned at Greene, sitting on his left. "Mumchance," he said. "Mumchance?" cried Redface; "what boy's game is that?" Strawhair explained the simple shuffle and cut, and Redface held himself content. Yes, anyone could call so far as he was concerned. The best of five cuts should decide.

"Ace of clubs," said Greene. It won.

"Seven of hearts." It won.

Strawhair made too thick a cut. Redface won with the ten of spades.

Strawhair, as though to coax him, made a half-pack cut and lost the second time.

"All or nothing!" cried Redface. "Tray of diamonds," called Greene. "Queen of hearts," called Redface. They drew the cards, and the tray came first. Redface ordered Strawhair his wine. He sat quiet a few seconds and then shuffled his cards resolutely. "I'll play you a shilling cut, sir," he offered Strawhair. Strawhair winked at Greene from behind his cup. "Taken!" In five cuts he won three shillings, only one going against him. In ten cuts he was six shillings to the good. Then Redface smashed down a heavy purse on the table, swearing he would break his bad luck or lose the lot in the attempt. Greene called the nine of spades, Redface the knave, and the first cut was pricked and set aside. Redface, looking mighty flurried, smacked down his hand as loud as his purse. "I'll vie a shilling on my stake!" "No, sir, that was no part of our terms," Strawhair objected. Redface thrust his chin forward. "You'll not revie?" Most decidedly Strawhair said he would not. "Will any other gentleman revie?" asked Redface. Warm with wine and feeling Ingpen's foot press his once more, Greene said he would and changed places with Strawhair.

"Two shillings," said Redface.

Greene pushed a shilling forward.

"Three."

"Four."

"Five."

Greene was alarmed now, but knew his card would be the fifth turned up and therefore with a twelve to one chance of winning. "Six."

"Seven."

"Eight."

"Nine."

"Ten."

"I'll see you," said Redface.

They drew. The top (formerly the bottom) card had been pricked, three more cards and the nine of spades appeared. The very next card was the knave. "Did you ever see the like of it, gentlemen?" Redface begged.

Greene scooped over his winnings. He had been drinking moderately for more than an hour and was ten shillings richer than when he entered the tavern.

"Again!" cried Redface. Shuffle and cut. Greene won four shillings.

"Again!" Greene won three shillings.

"Again!" They vied to eight shillings and Redface won.

"Again!" Vie and revie. Greene won six shillings.

Redface mopped his forehead. "Such luck! Did you ever see the like of it, gentlemen?" Greene, unlike your true gambler, was pocketing his winnings after each play.

"Again!" Redface shuffled as though he'd get the pictures off the cards. Strawhair cut thin, and Greene saw the bottom card of the rest of the pack as he dropped it over the cut. "Prick the first card," said Redface. The pack was turned face upwards, the top card removed.

"Two shillings."

"Three."

"Four."

"Five."

"I'll vie it to ten," said Redface.

Greene shook his head. "You are past the stake, sir."

There was a mannerly argument among all four before Redface established his point. And then, as he lifted wine to his mouth, Greene saw a frightening thing. Ingpen had made the tiniest nod to Redface. It came to Greene like cold water that he was in danger. "I'll see you," he said quietly. "Double up!" cried Redface. "No, sir," Greene said steadily. "I'll see you."

He won. For the first time he left the money on the table. He saw now the absurdity of any gambler allowing a constant arrangement of shuffle and cut and a third-party caller. He must get out quickly. "Again!" cried Redface, as it seemed to Greene inexorably. "With pleasure," he replied, and made to gather up the cards. "But with your permission a journey to the back first." Ingpen and Redface got to their feet at the same time. "I think I may safely leave my winnings on the table," Greene said, smiling. His cap was beside him, he set it by the small pile of money, and made for the door. Redface sat down again, but Ingpen said something about having the same errand and started after him. Quickly Greene pushed the door to in his face and stepped swiftly through the public room. He heard Ingpen's voice as he reached the outer door, and then he was through it and hurrying in the direction of Ludgate. He was trembling. He looked behind to see if he was pursued and saw Ingpen first and then the other two come out, and as they shouted he had taken to his heels. In desperation he ran towards four or five young men standing forty yards higher up the street. "Gentlemen," he gasped, "there has been an attempt to rob me. Stand by me!" The pursuers were up before they could ask questions. "Well, gentlemen," said one of the young men, "who is victim, who is thief?" Ingpen and his companions burst into accusations against Greene. "Well, sir?" the same young man asked him. Greene blurted out his story.

"You are of St. John's College?"

Greene was. He talked fast.

"And you of Pembroke Hall?"

Ingpen nodded.

"You are a liar. I was there myself." He turned to his companions. "Shall we hold them all for the justices in the morning?"

As at a signal Ingpen, Strawhair and Redface were in flight. There was no attempt made to stop them, just a stone or two thrown after them. The young men bowed to Greene and told him they were happy to have helped him. There was an exchange of names.

"And you were at Pembroke Hall, Master Panning?"

Panning laughed. "Not I. But I thought to rouse Ingpen by the statement. Shall we recover your cap?"

It was still on the table at the Three Cocks, but the money had been taken from beside it. For his greater safety Panning and his friends then accompanied him back to the Glove Inn, and there, over yet more wine paid for out of his winnings from Redface, he heard much of the thieving barnard's law: the taker, whose part was played by Ingpen; the verser, played by Strawhair; the barnard or barnacle, played by Redface. He had fallen for one of the oldest tricks in the world, and it needed much commendation of his finesse and daring from his new acquaintances before he could rid himself of the uncomfortable knowledge that he had acted the fool's part to perfection.

But, counting over his money when he went to bed, he half-hoped to find another Ingpen on the morrow.

CHAPTER XVII

THIS FIRST-NIGHT ESCAPE from conny-catchers
was Greene's only dangerous exploit before he left London.
Sir John, on whom he waited next day, had a little work
for him to do in the mornings and occasionally expected
his attendance at other times, but he had opportunities
enough for sight-seeing and now used them circumspectly.
In the safe company of one of Sir John's secretaries, a man
about thirty and named George Somerset, he walked the
streets till he was tired and paid visits to institutions of
national or historic interest till he was tireder. Now, at least,
the Tower, Westminster Hall, Baynard's Castle and the
rest were more than names to him. He saw, too, a bear-
baiting south of the river which Somerset reckoned the
bloodiest and best of the year—Belcher and Black hanging
from Bruin's dripping muzzle, broken-boned Belfont creeping away to death—and one afternoon they went to a
performance of *A Warning to Wantons* at the Curtain in
Moorfields. Fresh from the University plays, he found
neither piece nor performance satisfactory, bragged to
Somerset of the Cambridge *Fulgens and Lucres*, and set
light by his eager defence of the London practitioners.
Then one memorable morning they had an entry to the
Court and were privileged to fall on their knees as the
Queen went by to Chapel. Before her, like a field of daisies,
went a score of noblemen, then the chancellor with his
seals in a purse of red silk, flanked by officers bearing one
the royal sceptre, the other the sword of state in a red
scabbard; then Her Majesty herself, in a dress of white
silk with a scarlet mantle, her train borne by jewelled
ladies, her escort fifty gentlemen pensioners with gilt battle
axes—a gallant, glittering procession, and one he talked
about for hours. If anything, he had expected Elizabeth
to be more beautiful of face, but dismissed his sense

of shortcoming as though it were treason, compelled almost to worship by her stateliness, her splendour, her easy Olympian air. This was a Queen indeed! And this a nation to be part of! He was proud to be an Englishman, and would not have swopped that title for a foreign dukedom.

Somerset gave him good advice about his wardrobe. Admittedly advice that was expensive to follow, but he had the money and the inclination. Somerset, though no dandy, was a man interested in his appearance and well-versed in fashions, and he superintended most of Greene's orders at the Exchange and on Cheapside, with threats what he would do to the tailor who skimped or miscut or was late with delivery. He carried off small samples of materials, explaining to Greene that tailors were offal among rogues, and that there was no trickery beyond them. The result of all this was that Greene soon possessed several changes of clothes richer and more colourful than he had dared possess before. He went to a good barber, who cut his red hair long and carefully as a worthy setting for a handsome face—so he said, and Greene, staring into the mirror, saw no reason for disbelieving him. Feeling ten times the man he had been before the metamorphosis, he went with Somerset for a saunter around Paul's Yard, and felt unalloyed happiness when the women ogled him and the seated men appeared to envy him his clean calves. He made the thrilling discovery that the body is more than a clothes-horse or a line for washing. Henceforth he would take care to cover it as handsomely as it deserved.

Of his sister and Copson he saw and heard nothing. Inquiries seemed so pointless that he made none. He thought too that his spending on dress had taken so much more than he expected that he would be embarrassed to pay over the money given him by his mother. And Copson was a reliable man—hadn't they always thought so? He was not the sort to come to harm. Probably they were back in Lincoln before this, her silly story about

Sir Ralph dismissed for what it was worth. And they always had a home at Norwich. Why worry without need?

On Sir John's advice he deposited all his money except what he needed for day-to-day expenses with the London representative of the St. George's Bank of Genoa. It made a most useful sum when he could add to it his first advance from the Treasury, and it would not have been really difficult to help Alice had she been found. But in Italy a man would have uses for money. He counted his nobles like a prospective spendthrift.

Those last days of August were almost too short for him to savour their newness. They slid behind him brief and bright as winter sunshine. It had been Cambridge, Norwich, London—swift-moving panorama of scenes and faces and interests—and now it was London, Tilbury, the ship, sea-sickness and all, till they made Genoa late one evening and he had his first glimpse of Italy as the sun sank behind them. A glimpse of a noble city crowned with fortifications, mistress of the mackerel-backed sea before her and the rounded Ligurian Alps behind. He walked the deck impassioned, as though before him lay his promised land, the mother of cities, the matrix of the Western World. Not Genoa, but Italy—the home of poets, fair nurse of painters, sculptors, builders, nourisher of the arts. "A dissolute land," said Sir John, signalling to him; "a fountain of abuse, the ruin of youth, the grave of much young manhood." The metaphors chopped and changed through Greene's head, noble and degrading in turn. He raised his hand dramatically. This was Italy—the New Circe so bitterly inveighed against by Ascham and the graver sort, so much more potent than the rest of the world for good and ill as a sword is more than a needle. He watched till darkness masked the city but for its eyes of lights, the water slapping like the wet palm of a hand beneath him, a tuning fork for thought.

They put into the pincered harbour by ten o'clock next morning and waited on board while messengers took Sir John's greetings to the Duke and in return brought him.

an invitation to dinner. For the first time in his life Greene had the odd experience of shifting from shipboard to firm land as though from stability to an unfirm element. He was not one of those chosen for the dining party, so instead he and a few others hired a guide who led them through the narrow, high-fronted streets of the city and discoursed in a barely intelligible mixture of Italian and English on the chief sights. Before the afternoon was out he showed himself an unblushing agent of the bordellos, and ever and again on his circuits brought them to the same disreputable district where low-bosomed and somewhat flyblown ladies waved to them from balconies and on one occasion kicked off a shoe or two for the boldest to retrieve. The clean magnificence of most of the town impressed Greene deeply, and he felt something very near contempt for those of his companions who were promising themselves a bawdy night of it. Were there men to whom Italy meant no more than this? These marble-fronted palaces, these galleries of life and colour, these squares rustling with silks and sweet talk—were men so base they could desert them in a day for a bait of haltered whores? He felt England was on trial in his person and behaved with a Cambridge sobriety, even over his wine. With more appreciative companions he would have recited passages from Tasso and Ariosto.

Very quiet days and weeks followed. Sir John was an unspectacular envoy but not one to be worsted. He had been offered and accepted a suite of rooms at the Palazzo Spinola, and much of his time was spent in long and tiring consultations. There were festivities in his honour, which he attended with a sufficiency of dry smiles and protestations that his hosts were too gracious, but Spinola knew his tastes unchanged from harder days of old and spared him all he could. Sir John preferred to talk about their early travels and trials, he even undertook long walks alone with Spinola when that busy man could spare the time, and no doubt hoped for gain from sentimentalities. How his negotiations were proceeding he kept under his hat, both for his stated and secret ends. Greene, lodged at the Gifts of God, a neat and vine-decked inn not far from the Palace, composed letters, addresses, compliments and thanks, and worried his head little.

An unforeseen result of his ideal behaviour of the first week was that he established an inconvenient reputation for gravity at the inn. It did not take him long to see that these Genoese had no wish to be idealised. They were a gay and kindly people, no more rapacious than Englishmen, and every man he met was neither a poet nor an admirer of poets. Many were young business men, dreaming not of Jerusalem Freed but of cargoes, port-dues, bills of lading half the day, and wine and girls and the bloom of life the other half. They would have raised their eyebrows in polite bewilderment had he declaimed the verses nearest his tongue-end. It was much later, only a week or two before they left Genoa for Leghorn, that he came into touch with members of the University there, and found his rhapsodists and humanists, and more than one pedagogue and wiseacre. Meantime he was vexed when one night his landlord brought his supper to his room, apologising that the young men downstairs were rather too happy for the approval of the sober-sided Englishman. Eating solemnly and caressing the beard he was now rearing, he saw that he had been a prig. Who was he to sit upstairs while the wine went round below? It was irksome and it was silly. What an ass these good people must think him! And the worst kind of ass—a young ass, a grave ass, a puritanical ass. He kicked the table leg, and then started to laugh at his asininity. Do what then? He feared something desperate would be needed—jump out at the landlady, chase the maids into the cellars, come home drunk and ringing a bell, throw stones through the stained glass of the Duomo. Two nights later, when Bando again brought him up his supper, he startled the good man by sending his compliments to the drinkers downstairs and requesting that an Englishman who loved their country might join them for an hour. Two of them waited on him in person and with high-flown language begged him to honour them below. He descended, there were salutations and praise of all things English and Genoese, the drawer had a busy time, and Greene between whiles saw Bando and his wife peeping at the portent—Signor Longchops of London actually kicking up his heels and enjoying himself. Next day, fumy with wine, he felt confident the couple thought more highly of him, the maid on the stairs curtsied to a man not a eunuch, he thought he'd ruffle it more and slipped an arm to her waist, thought to call her a pretty tomtit, knew not the Italian, but kissed her twice instead. She showed no resentment, so smoothing his beard he went on his way with frequent and pleasant remembrance of her lips. Beelzebub had thrown him a life-line and he snatched at it. When his English comrades, fresh from facile triumphs and prodigious drinking, bragged of their virility and liquor-content, he began to smile mysteriously, coughed at the right moment, and soon had them thinking him a Will Sly, a Chaseskirt. He jested, hinting that the pick of the men found the pick of the girls without wasting shoe-leather. To show him he was right, his landlord, fat, fatherly, respectfully familiar, suggested to him one evening that Benita was a sweet-natured maid, and when Greene, remembering stair-encounters, agreed, came out plump with it: that for a couple of ducats for herself and a consideration for the good name of the house she would make no objection to a change of sleeping quarters. Sleep with that fine girl! He could not resist temptation, and just as the nights grew cooler found a glorious warming-pan. It was a convenient and on the whole respectable arrangement and saved him from perilous excesses in the stews; and though his natural generosity led him to treat the girl well and buy her presents to keep her happy, it was comparatively cheap. Life was certainly more agreeable in the part of jolly than sober Englishman.

All through the winter it continued so. At last Sir John was successful for all the world to see, and in December dictated to Greene a letter which was sent overland through

France to England. His scribe was sorry to see it go, for it meant a remove to Leghorn as soon as the weather permitted, and then maybe a quick return to England. He would be sorry to leave this city for which he now felt almost a native's affection and the inn that had sheltered him so well for many months; he would be sorry to leave Benita. Though his blood was hot too often there was not a grain of brutality in his heart, he had become fond of the girl and her ways, and would not leave her like an old shoe or outworn convenience. But by the end of March they had made their adieus and taken the coastal road to Spezia. "Good-bye, Benita," he told her that last morning; "I'll be back again one day." He did not believe it, neither did she, and he was affected by the tears she shed. She made none of the easy protestations of the harlot, had her short cry, dried her eyes, took his splendid gift of ducats and went off to her room to hide them, leaving Greene the better that someone would miss him, for however short a time. The first day of absence he thought of her for hours, fondly and with desire, but thereafter except for a twinge now and again at night her memory was a quickly fading one. Indeed, the vileness of the road to Spezia was enough to drive most things from the mind. For the most part it ran through desolate country, for miles was hardly recognisable amidst bogs and rocks, and a dozen times a day they had to haul the wagons out of holes or help the oxen to get them over humps. Fretting, Greene looked oftentimes to the smooth sea, contrasting it with the jags and crags of their uneven way, wondering why in the devil's name Sir John had not taken ship for their destination. It was the coming of a savage storm from the south-west and then west and north-west, shutting the sea from their view with tempests of rain, deafening them with its pouring winds, that convinced him they were better off where they were. It lasted twenty-four hours, beleaguering them in a cluster of miserable fishermen's huts, and making their road even more difficult. They did twenty miles in the next three days, with a burden of impatience and bad temper heavier than

the wagons. With patriotic zeal he cursed the Italian idea
of a road, forgetting that most roads in England were every
bit as bad, until Sir John told one night of riding between
Reading and London and finding a hat on the muddy road;
he picked it up and found a head inside, and when they set
to work with shovels they found a man seated on horseback.
It was an old story, but new to Greene. Sir John, to beguile
the time, told too of eastern armies engulfed in bogs worse
than Serbonian, of the flooding of yellow rivers with
ten thousand lives lost in a night, and—more cheerfully
—of the glories of Roman roads as good that day in
Italy as when their indefatigable makers laid their strong
foundations.

They were in Spezia a week and then pressed on by way
of Carrara and Pisa to Leghorn, a town not long awakened
from the quiet of centuries by the sharp alarum of the
Medici. They saw everywhere the mason, the shipwright,
and the soldier, and a more varied population than at
Genoa: Frenchmen, Spaniards, Teutons, not infrequently
a Lowlander or tall Scandinavian, a few Englishmen and
many Jews. Fine buildings were in the making, a start
had been made on the fortifications, there was talk that
money was forthcoming for the construction of a harbour.
Huge blocks of marble bulked among debris with an incongruous mass and dusty beauty, emblematic of the town that
was supplanting this one-time huddle of huts. A crude and
money-grubbing spirit seemed in most men there. Its
history lay ahead. Greene thought meanly of it after Genoa.
The graces of life were absent.

Here Sir John had a long but not difficult task inter-
viewing men who might be more important later than they
were then. Within a fortnight it was clear to him he was
ten years, maybe twenty, too early. He walked like a rook
amidst the activities of the shore and decided there would
be no harbour worthy of the name this side the new century.
There seemed little to be done except make useless promises,
receive useless assurances, and take steps for England.
He spoke about this one evening to Greene who was attend-

ing him on his way back from supper with the two Consetti, father and son.

"You are ready for England?"

"When you will, sir," Greene answered doubtfully.

Harrison looked carefully for a good footing. "You like Italy?"

"Genoa, yes. Leghorn not so much."

"Hm. This, of course, is not Italy. You know the proverb about Naples? Then there is Rome. And Verona, Padua, Florence, Ferrara, Venice herself. Bologna—a dozen cities yet." He stared with distaste at where the sea must be. "This will be something one day, I believe, but hardly in our time."

"While Rome was great before London was dreamt of!"

"You want to see Rome?"

Greene shrugged his shoulders. "When a man is so near——"

"Then why don't you?"

Greene looked at his master fearfully. "If," he said, "—I don't see—— If I——"

"Vocal to the intelligent alone," said Sir John calmly. "I give you leave to stay a year. Your papers will bear you."

Greene stammered thanks and Sir John changed the subject. But the next day he referred to it again and asked Greene whether he had made up his mind. He had. Sir John suggested he make inquiries for a party travelling to any one of the famous cities and endeavour to join it. "As a money-maker," he advised, adding that the Consetti were soon bound for Florence. Would Greene like him to open the matter with them? He cut short expressions of gratitude. "You'll probably make a fool of yourself here," he told him. Three days Greene lived in a fervour of expectation and then heard from Sir John that the University of Cambridge might rejoice that another of its sons had found useful employment. He could accompany the Consetti to Florence and act as tutor in English to the son Giovanni. Greene was so elated to hear this he went

off walking for five hours and exhausted himself pleasurably.
This he thought would save him from celebration, but
in the evening he found it impossible to stay indoors, his
tiredness left him and he went out to a tavern, where a jug
of wine, working on his excitement, sent him sufficiently
towards intoxication for him to drink still more, and
eventually he was brought home by an obliging gentleman
who went through his pockets on the way and even took
the brooch from the front of his hat. Next day he considered
himself lucky to be home at all, not stripped and with a
dagger through the carotid behind a lump of masonry.
It was an insight into the Italian character that before
noon his guide of the night before turned up at his lodging
and claimed largesse for his kindness. He was a grinning
scamp and denied all knowledge of Greene's empty pockets,
so to get rid of him with the least fuss he crossed his hand
with silver and then threatened to kick him downstairs.

Not long after this episode a boy arrived to ask him to
wait on the Consetti the next morning at nine. He drank
nothing but a cup of white wine that evening, went to bed
early, and did not go to see them till the barber had spent
almost an hour on his face and head. So carefully had he
dressed that he might be a bridegroom, not a tutor, and
his bearing was very nearly that of his first days at Genoa.
The Consetti had taken over the whole of the first floor of
their inn, for the father was making a new fortune from the
building and development of the port and the son getting
a training in business matters. Greene found himself treated
with considerable politeness. It was clear Sir John had
extolled his learning and manners. It was probable that at
some future time young Giovanni would be going to England
to look after unnamed interests of his father, and he declared
it a privilege to study the language under the distinguished
Signor Greene. If his proficiency in English even
approached that of his master in Italian he would be more
amazed than satisfied. The boy was seventeen years old,
and despite the grace of his ways Greene judged him too
much his father's darling for the good of his character.

For once he felt old and wise, and enjoyed the rare sensation.

It was now the middle of July. Sir John was ready to depart, but the Consetti would be in Leghorn till early September and the immediate prospect was deadly dull. He sighed for Genoa. Sir John went, with too much good advice left cynically behind him, and he sighed still more. What was there to see in Leghorn day after day? For two hours, three at the most, he waited on young Consetti; the rest of his time was gapingly his own. Consetti soon proved himself not the easiest of pupils and showed an aptitude for forgetting a twenty-times-repeated phrase which suggested his heart was not in the work despite his fine words. He seemed willing enough to ask questions about England, but only in the Italian tongue. He surprised his tutor by asking lewd questions about the English women, and when Greene dubiously mentioned his father's displeasure told him with an air of boredom that he had been allowed a mistress ever since he seduced one of his mother's chambermaids at the age of fifteen. Oh yes, here in Leghorn whenever he found the time hang on his hands—his father too, of course; what did Signor Greene expect? Were things so different in England then? Without using language that would guarantee his dismissal Greene found it hard to explain. The New Circe had stripped from her face a second veil, and a blemish or two were now to be seen.

A break in monotony, but one he could have done without, was an expedition at the beginning of August to the quarries at Carrara. On the return journey the elder Consetti left his son and Greene at Pisa for a fortnight. This proved disastrous for Greene. His charge showed himself elegantly vicious, visited bawdy houses night after night on a round of debauchery that put rings round his eyes in a week, and Greene at first hesitantly, then with a fatal acquiescence that it was only an episode, kept him company. What he could not endure were Consetti's hints that he was afraid or that he lacked virility. It was a mercy that much of their money was stolen and that for five days they had only their inn charges and so repaired their damaged bodies. The episode left Greene with a disgust for himself and Consetti but a sharpened appetite in lust. It was so easy to surrender. God! Jogging back to Leghorn under a blazing sun he mopped his forehead and swore to pull himself together even if he had to leave Consetti's service. And yet the memory of the women he had embraced would not leave tormenting him. If only a man had never started with it! Once you knew—he writhed. It came to him with the force of a revelation that he might spend most of his leisure writing, and maybe at his return to England benefit his purse and reputation. When he remembered his romance *Mamillia*, the first part of which was by this time entered in the Stationers' Register—why not a second part now, before he left the town? His recent debauch had taught him enough about his own besetting weaknesses for him to see he must keep his mind otherwise active, so back in Leghorn he kept indoors, fought down his temptations, and composed busily as a narcotic to passion. Verse too. Was he not in a land of poets? Did Dante and Petrarch deserve no more than that their native land should be the common sewer of the earth? Great men must help him. They and Boccaccio and Machiavel. To forget——

And when he got back to England, would he not show them! *The Fall of Princes, The Shepherds' Calendar*—by Apollo and his brother he'd show them! Once in Florence, treading the sacred soil——

The city itself dazed him. That anything so wonderful could exist in stone and marble confounded him. That, late autumn, under a magic sun, he inhabited an enchanted city. To save it from destruction he would have laid down his life. It was as though every street and square, each palace and bridge, spoke to him with the voice of poets dead, as though great men of the past, varied as da Vinci and Vespucci, Michael Angelo and the Medici, waited to talk on every corner. He had never dreamt a place could be so alive with memories; that it could add to a present splendour the glory of so magnificent a past. A ghost-rich city this Florence. Could a man ever tire of it? Toiling up the curled paths of the neighbouring hills, whence one could look down to the concise beauty of its colouring: cypress almost black and the dusty sage-green of the olive trees interspersed with red-brown houses, the yellow river banded by its dark bridge-strips, and behind it the wooded hills starred with private palaces, and behind those again the sky, deep blue at noon, shaded to mother-of-pearl with the coming of the twilight. Or starting from sun to chilling shade, from shade to hot sun, as you skirted the grim straight walls of the Palazzo Vecchio; then stepping back for upward gaze at the battlements, double-dog-toothed or square for Guelf or Ghibelline, and the indomitable upward jag of the strong tower. The pale harmonies of the Cathedral and the Churches, set stately in their open places; the colonnades of statuary; the goldsmiths' shops; the shops of the makers of weapons—he loved them all. And most he loved the Old Bridge, narrow, huddled with men and mules and carts, because there, suspended over Arno, he seemed the centre of the city, its immediate clustering of dwellings and monuments, and the soft amphitheatre of its hills. Even under the greyest skies of winter it offered its comforts of red and brown.

Yet here, in this paradise of his soul, he could not avoid the serpent. He was living in an immoral household, surrounded by beauty that roused his sensuous nature to worse ends. The Consetti, father and son, kept mistresses, he heard gossip about the lady and believed it well-founded. Lasciviousness was in the air he breathed, the spiced foods he ate, the brilliant-hued wines he drank. In the Palace galleries nude women spread their opulent beauty for him on the walls, in a riot of reds and whites and blacks, their marble breasts and haunches met him at every corner, the cunning work of masters. It was as though the old struggle in his heart between the influences of Coppinger and Sidley was being fought out again, Coppinger less attractive than the literary and artistic associations of Florence, Sidley less attractive than its insistent call to self-indulgence.

Oftentimes his early training, his father's counsel, recurred
to his mind, and he would come home from the bagnio
almost frantically ashamed, but it was never long before
he went back again. He found it matter for detestation that
at certain houses he was well known by the end of the
winter. They knew his favourite girls, there was a room
instantly ready for so good a customer. There were times
when he could deceive himself that this winter in Florence
would free him from dangerous constituents and that he
would be his old self the day he left it. Other times when
he imagined himself a gay pagan snatching happiness under
southern skies, hand in hand with Bacchus and Venus.
Other times when he appreciated to the full how sordid was
his way of life.

One day he accompanied young Consetti on a walk
through the city. They were crossing the river by the Ponte
Vecchio when they were passed by an old man and a young
girl, possibly his grand-daughter. The child, not more than
fourteen years old, had the purest face Greene had ever
seen on woman. As they drew near she noticed Consetti's
bold and coarse glance, flushed slightly, placing her hand
on the old man's sleeve, and kept her eyes on the ground
as they went so silently by. This filled Greene with a greater
shame than he had known throughout his life. He felt
Consetti and he were deformed in the child's sight, that
honest soil went foul at their footsteps. That girl—a hundred
madnesses ran through his head: If he could die for her there
and then! If he could give her all his money, keep her
ever unsullied from the world! With an aching throat he
swore to himself he would never visit bawdy houses again,
and spoke so harshly when Consetti made the swinish and
inevitable remark that that young man fell angrily silent.
A hundred yards further on he tried to turn it into a jest,
but Greene retorted savagely that swine though he might
be in the stews, he hoped God would blast him the day
he forgot his regard for pure womanhood. Consetti sneered
at him, and the next day at lessons treated him with insolence
and disdain.

His relations with his pupil grew less amicable weekly after this, and he began to think of change. Once away from the Palazzo Consetti he would reform, shut his ears Ulysses-like to the sirens of the public ways, fill his heart with things sweet and fresh, and among other things go forward with his writing. Besides, he would not endure a dirty little fellow like this Giovanni to treat him like a menial. An English student was worth a cartload of Italian financiers. He counted his money and made inquiries about parties bound for Venice or Rome who would take an Englishman along with them cheap. And then chance sent him to Venice in the late spring.

He was at the foreigners' tavern near the Ponte alla Carraja one evening, drinking alone, when an authoritative-looking man in black dropped a satchel which burst open, sending coins rolling under the legs of the tables. Greene busied himself in gathering these together and handed them to their owner, who had done no more than stiffly retrieve his satchel. He nodded and explained that a wound in the back did not allow him to bend, and remarked that Greene was an Englishman.

"My appearance or my Italian?" Greene asked, laughing.

"Who could mistake an inhabitant of that gallant island?" the other replied courteously, and begged Greene to join him over a bottle of the best wine in Florence. Yes, he knew London. He had been there as a young man, and no doubt it had altered greatly by now. He gave his name as Castelvetro, and for a time they talked about places they had both seen. Castelvetro expressed great admiration for the English, for whom he foresaw a greater future than most southerners were inclined to admit. He made the daring speculation that as the New World of the Americas increased in importance English ports would be more advantageously placed for trade than any others. What the English needed above all things, however, was the quick spirit of the Italians. Their doggedness and practice in the useful arts were not enough. It would be a good stroke of Her Majesty's to send English students to the great Univer-

sities at Bologna, Genoa, and elsewhere in the Peninsula
that (he did not wish to offend the signor) their clay might
be moulded in the brave Italian fires. He doubted whether
England had yet fully experienced her renascence. Among
that solid people there were vital men, he did not doubt it.
Some years ago at Vienna he had met Sir Philip Sidney,
his ideal among courtiers, wits, and scholars. He welcomed
the Englishman abroad. It destroyed that insularity which
in itself led to stupidity. Yet he thought it a pity so many
travellers abroad showed more aptitude for foreign vices
than virtues. He had travelled from Prague to Vienna last
year with an Englishman—not a man of Sidney's stamp,
let that be clear. One whose charms were of more account
than his merits.

"I might know him," said Greene, to give the impression
he knew everyone worth knowing in England.

"Sidli—yes, that is right—Sidli." He raised his eyebrows.
"You do know him then?"

"Know him! Ralph Sidley? Know him!" He was
Sidley's best friend. He had hoped to meet with him in
Italy. Where was he now? When had he seen him last?
Where left him? The Italian was pleased to repay Greene's
kindness and submitted to a dozen questions. He had met
the Englishman in a small company travelling from Prague
into Austria. He was staying the winter at Vienna and then
coming to Venice and so by way of Florence to Rome and
Naples. He had expected to spend the summer and early
autumn at Venice. An intrepid traveller, he had gone
further afield than most of his countrymen who undertook the Tour, away past Warsaw, travelling for months in
perilous places before making a circuit to the north of
Hungary by way of Prague. Like a wise man he had kept
Italy to the last. The epicure's touch. Yes, he was certain
about Venice.

This gave Greene plenty to think about. Should he stay
at Florence and hope to find Sidley as he passed through?
What if the traveller changed his mind and took ship around
the coast? Castelvetro had heard him speak of Sicily as

though he meant to visit there. Would it not be better to
go to Venice? Otherwise he would never see that city,
and to return from Italy, Venice unseen, was contemptible.
And the Consetti—could he endure them another six
months?

He made up his mind: He would visit Venice.

CHAPTER XVIII

GREENE WAS IN Venice when the June skies flung
their dark blue arch over that jewel of the dark blue sea.
He had come there at his own expense by way of Bologna,
Ferrara, and Padua—a fortnight's easy journey. Each
league of the way tempted him with offers of what lay
beyond, each city drew him to stay within its walls; yet
always fellow-travellers said: This is good, but think of
Venice! The half-caught vision of its splendour haunted him
like a new Grail. What was one lifetime in a land like this?
And Sir John had allowed him till July! Riding down the
wild valley to where the spires and bell-towers of Bologna
thrust like needles amidst their brick walls, he shook his
rein for joy. He was in Italy! Sir John could do his worst
when he returned to England. If he could find Sidley and
put money in his purse, he cared not. This Ferrara, a little
melancholy under neglect, charming as a pensive beauty;
this Padua, wearing learning like a rich robe—O Jupiter,
O Bacchus, he was in Italy! England must keep her rain-
dim counties for another year. Free from the Consetti and
their purple brothel of a palace, he found life lovely as these
warm Italian landscapes. If he had not been such a fool
at Florence and still had the money so wickedly poured
out on wantons, he would be without a care in the world.
Unless he found Sidley at once he must look for employment in Venice. He had letters from Sir John and the
Consetti. Some great family, with a son in need of English
—it should not be hard.

He was in Venice six weeks before he met Sidley—not
long enough for him to emerge from the state of bemused
delight he was thrown into his first day there. With an
enthusiasm keener than that with which he had greeted
Florence he swore he had rather be a menial here than a
prince elsewhere. Florence had been rich and glowing with

tender harmonies of colour, but Venice was brilliant and vivid and dazzling. Nowhere had he seen skies and water so blue, such an intense sunlight to bathe the creams and pinks and blues of the marble-fronted palaces or the glittering cavalcades of peacock-people. There was a perpetual assault on the eyes, from the rapturous blue and gold of San Marco to the striped awnings of the gondolas, from the sun-pierced spray of the cobalt rollers crashing on the yellow sands of the Lido to the naked brown backs of sailors on the quays, from the spiral splendour of arches and bridges to the unending rainbows of passengers under and over them. For rest you must seek the narrower waterways, where between high impassive homes of princes the black face of the canal was picked out with silver or wait till night flung her irradiated cloak of starry darkness. To be English, superior to these Venetians, and yet possess their city of sea-veined marble—that was heaven. Surely no mortal mistress could so lure a man and keep him thrall?

He found enough employment to keep him in necessaries and rare luxuries without having to pledge his twenty-four hours a day. His letters of recommendation brought him tutoring in two families—two hours each morning with the young sons of Gaspari del Firenze, two hours in the late afternoon with an elderly spice merchant who was going to England in the autumn. Gaspari had asked to see his papers and pointed out that Greene was required to return to London in July, but Greene won him over by protesting that the prospect of no displeasure to come should deny him the felicity of seeing the Queen of the Adriatic. Gaspari laughed, then frowned, said sadly that the Queen had shed her best robes, but laughed again when Greene retorted that the test of queenliness might lie in naked beauty. Maybe Greene was right. He too loved his city with a prodigal love. He would not send the Englishman away. Sometimes he talked with him for an hour after Greene had finished with his sons, he led this eager admirer through homes and palaces he otherwise could not have seen, pointed out where treasures might be found for the eye, and once by the water-edge delighted and amazed his listener by an impassioned eulogy of his city's past. Greene attended him almost dazed by the beauty of his voice and words, and henceforth a scroll, a carving, a scarred pillar were eloquent to him. He had found lodgings at a tiny inn on the Merceria, from which indeed he could see nothing but the opposite frontage six yards away, but this was no hardship. It gave him privacy, and yet he was within a stone's throw of the Piazza San Marco and the centre of the city.

Gaspari was a father of a different type from Consetti. Greene came to feel affection as well as admiration for him. He liked his pupils too, unspoiled lads of nine and eleven. The elder boy showed such aptitude and progress it was a pleasure to work with him.

Many times he was hard put to it not to spend money on sensual pleasure. He had seen no women like the courtesans of Venice, nor had the common report of them as the most famous and perfect of their profession prepared him for the actuality. Their numbers appeared out of all proportion to the population: they were to be found almost in state at the theatres, no piazza was without them, they had the entry of the best places of resort. To step into a gondola without giving the boatman an immediate direction was equal to an order that the fellow take one to the house which paid him commission. They walked in women's costume, they rode breeched like men, they plied every waterway. Most of them had yellow hair low on the forehead and dressed in the shape of two horns six inches high standing up above. On the head they wore nothing but a veil of black crepe or hollands, falling down before and behind, and this transparent enough to show their faces, necks, and shoulders. At times indeed their bodies were visible through a kind of gauze to the navel or the small of their backs, a dreadful temptation to men far less susceptible than Greene. On their feet—under them rather—they wore chopins as much as a foot in height, so that when they walked it was necessary for them to have the support of a man's arm or be helped along by a handmaid. Of them the proverb ran: *Grande di legni, Grosse di straci, Rosse di bettito, Bianche di calcina*—Tall with wood, fat with rags, red with painting, and white with chalk. One peculiarity of their profession was that they might never wear pearls, and a frequent invitation they used was to raise their veils so that any man interested could see their uncovered throats adorned with huge, multi-coloured glass beads. He dubbed them serpents by land, sirens by water, destroyers at all times and in all places, and at the cost of occasional unhappiness kept from them.

He was making constant inquiry in the most likely parts of the city whether inn-keepers, porters, gondoliers or money-changers knew of the arrival of an English lord Sidley. For six weeks without success; and then one fine afternoon when clouds tempered the sun and a cool breeze blew in from the long flat shore, he heard from a boatman who often took him about the canals that a large party had arrived that morning by ship from Trieste. This seemed a likely route for Sidley to take from Vienna, and all the rest of the day, apart from his two hours' tuition of the merchant, he went from hostel to hostel in the San Marco district. He did not find Sidley, but at one of them had conversation with a Hungarian who had crossed from Trieste in company with an Englishman whose name he did not know. Greene described the man he was looking for. Yes, that would be he, though this particular Englishman was growing a pointed beard of French cut. Fingering his own sword-point of growth, Greene thought little of this. Yes, the Hungarian had particularly noticed the high forehead, the pale, clear complexion. No, he had little luggage.

Greene went home most excited. So Sidley had arrived! He imagined his surprise at finding Greene there in Venice, and did not doubt his delight. A fellow-countryman, a friend, in a strange land. Why, Greene knew enough about the city to act as guide, and was honest into the bargain. This would be the tables turned on that unexpected meeting

at the Red Lion in Norwich, where he sat measuring the
time by drinks of beer and Sidley appeared like a prince
from the blue. Proud? He gloated that Sidley should find
him in Venice. Sidley might be richer, he might find his
road smoother, he might even fare further afield, but after
this meeting he must recognise the stuff Greene was made
of, must recognise his equal in talent, his superior in determination. Greene felt quite homesick for his friend.

He had to wait almost a week before he found him, and
then by accident. By that time he was alarmed lest Sidley
had made no stay in Venice, had pushed on through the
North Italian plain, or south-west to Florence and maybe
from there to Rome. Before such a shattering of his plans
he would hardly know what to do. And then one evening,
on the Canalazzo, he saw him. The short pointed beard
altered him hardly at all, the thin line of the moustache.
He signalled frantically to his boatman to put about.
"Sidley!" he shouted. The other turned, his hand on his
dagger, and looked at Greene. To his amazement, he sat
still where he was. "Sidley!" he shouted again; "don't
you know me?" The distance between them grew less.
Sidley's hand was still on his dagger. He looked on the
alert. The smile died from Greene's face. What could this
be? "I have been looking all over Venice for you," he said,
putting out a hand to Sidley's gondola, and feeling very
foolish. Sidley nodded. "And now you have found me?"

Greene had expected raptures, a putting to land, embraces.
"Why, Sidley, aren't you glad to see me?"

Then Sidley laughed. "I have been foolish, Robertus. I
don't know what came over me." He gave an order to his
gondolier. "Follow me, Robertus." He waved his hand
like a happy man, and shouted inquiries to him in English
as they were taken to their tavern. But for the shock and
disappointment of the first minute or two Greene would
have held that short passage along the sunny canal as among
the happiest hours of his life. There was his friend; here
was Venice: he loved them both, and surely they loved him.
Sidley, he thought now, in contrast with his momentary

hostility (that did not seem too strong a word for it) was even hysterically glad to see him. Disembarked, they flung their arms about each other, Sidley hammered him on the back and chest till even Greene thought him immoderate, and passers-by stopped without pretence to watch them.

"Didn't you recognise me, then?" he asked a few minutes later.

"I was startled. I must admit it, Robertus—I was startled. In a foreign land, to hear your voice shouted by a red-bearded ruffian——" He laughed. "How did you leave your sister?"

"She is well enough," said Greene, paying no real attention to what he was asked. "She was two years ago, anyhow. Were you ever so surprised in your life before?"

"A shock, Robertus—it was a shock." His expression changed a little under his smile. "You have been looking for me, you said?"

"I heard you would be in Venice this summer." He went into long explanations of what he had heard from Castelvetro.

"Ah yes! A papal envoy, Robertus, that Castelvetro. Travels three hundred and sixty days of the year and sleeps the other five. Leap year troubles him worse than the plague, Robertus." He watched Greene pour out wine. "You did not come from England expecting to see me, hm?"

"Hardly, Sidley. I hoped, as I told you, but as for expecting——"

"No news you were bringing out for me?"

"Of course not! Nothing of any moment has happened there, Sidley. The usual plots and executions—— Why do you ask?"

"No reason. My curiosity, nothing more." He looked at Greene and shook his head. "I can't believe it, Robertus. Strike me down to hell, I can't believe it!"

"Believe what?"

"That you can be sitting here in Venice in front of me,

drinking wine out of a green glass, your elbow on a marble-topped table. It is beyond me, Robertus!"

"Well, don't shake your head right off. You will need it again."

"Come on," Sidley invited him; "start at the beginning. Tell me everything." He heard the word Genoa. "No, right back at the beginning, man! Start with Cambridge. Start with friend Coppinger."

One thing Greene did not tell him: that Alice had left Braiding because of his father. He feared it might wreck their friendship, and mentioned her only once, and then to say he understood she and Copson were very happy together. He held it kind of Sidley to express his pleasure at this, and then pushed on with his story to the end. "And you?" he asked.

Sidley had little to say about his travels, and that mostly a confirmation of Castelvetro, to whom he must have spoken more freely, Greene judged—not without jealousy.

"And the future?"

"Yours first?" Sidley countered.

"I shall have to return soon. I wanted to see Rome first, though."

"A commendable ambition. I hope to see it myself. It will have to be this winter if I do. I return to England in the spring." Greene waited for an invitation to accompany him, but it did not come. "You have not grown tired of Venice?"

"Not in a thousand years!"

"Your papers though, Robertus—you say your passport is over-run." He looked grave. "You came to Italy on a diplomatic mission, remember."

"What odds?" Greene saw no reason to pull down the corners of his mouth.

"Your future, Robertus? It will be a poor recommendation. I speak as a friend."

"You mistake me, Sidley. The passport and other papers are for the use of Her Majesty's subjects on Her Majesty's business. It is not high treason if as a private person I go where I like for as long as I like. It only means I cannot call on Englishmen abroad and demand their help."

"I see. I must seem officious. I am sorry I spoke as I did." He called for the reckoning. "What shall we do to-night to celebrate our meeting? There is no masque, no carnival? They tell me the women here are the cream of the earth. You, naturally, know all to be known that way. Where is the best house?"

Greene shook his head. "No, Sidley—not that. Anything else, but not that."

He resented Sidley's amusement. "Don't preach, Robertus. The stallion of Florence to speak so!"

"I thought you might like to see the places of interest, Sidley. I know enough to be your guide."

"Some other time! Not a palace but will be here to-morrow. Not a church will run away. You call this friendship?" Then he gave way. "We'll strike a bargain. You take me where you like for the rest of to-day, and I'll take you where I like to-morrow. You agree?"

"You will take an unfair advantage of me, Sidley."

"Not I. To prove it I'll let you pay the reckoning for the rest of to-day and I'll see to it to-morrow." He leaned sideways. "Who is that lady?"

Greene said he did not know her from Eve.

"I'd find means of knowing them apart," said Sidley.

It was a quiet evening they spent after all. Next day Greene had his pupils to attend to in the morning, but decided to leave his merchant in the lurch. He went to Sidley's lodgings for dinner at twelve o'clock, and was afterwards dragged willy-nilly to the theatre. Sidley had been there two or three days before and took no interest whatever in the performance. Greene now saw those women actors of whom Fabian Penton had spoken between Cambridge and Epping Forest, and despite his prejudices had to admit they did as well as the men—praise tempered by an adverse judgment on the standard compared with that in England. Even at the Curtain that night with Somerset he saw better than this. From time to time he

nudged Sidley to tell him so or to comment on the poorness
of the raiment, the inadequacy of the staging, but Sidley
in return pointed out what a superb woman she was who
played the part of the queen and then went back to his
study of the courtesans seated in the two little galleries.
As always at the theatre they sat without men, so heavily
masked it was impossible to discern a single feature, or
tell whether they were comely, ugly, old or young. Again,
most of them were so girt about with linen that they looked
unnecessarily fat—a testimony to the national taste. It
was evident he proposed to wait on a couple of them at
the end of the play. "Consider each one a Juno," he said
in English. "Consider each one a death's head," replied
Greene, and though he knew they were in the wrong,
scowled at the hists for silence. But at last they applauded
as much as anyone and stood up to go.

"We'll wait outside," said Sidley.

"No," said Greene; "I think we shall do better to return."

"You are not afraid are you?"

This rankled. "Of course I'm not! It is just that——"

"Save your breath!" Sidley told him rudely. "I am
disappointed in you, Robertus. Where's your spirit, man?"

The women were coming out, removing their masks and
their short black cloaks of taffeta. Greene found his hands
quivering.

"The three graces there, Robertus. Are they not charming? You observe the delicacy with which they await our
compliments? How skilfully they offer themselves and yet
do not court rejection?"

Before he quite knew how, Sidley had manœuvred the
five of them together, and was discussing the play as though
he had watched it throughout. The women were mistresses
of their art, and Greene, feverish though he was so near
their cleverly revealed charms, had to admire the address,
the dignity even, with which they bore themselves. Those
crude words *drabs*, *trulls*, and the like seemed out of place
here. They had breeding, assurance, and as he found on
the way to their place of call, no little culture. It was harlotry

with the manner of royalty. Their table behaviour was as elegant as anything Greene had ever seen. He was confounded by the paradox when, after supper was over and they had suggested a visit to their own quarters, each lady took pains with her skirts as she took her place in the gondola, and the oldest of the three tapped Sidley's hand reprovingly when he attempted a liberty. In a way so modest a beginning comforted him, for he had all along been uneasy. Inside the bordello there was a change, and when at length he and Sidley made their sorry ways home, he knew he had sunk to a deeper degradation than ever before. He was an uglier animal now than he had ever been in Florence, and could not help thinking, and bitterly, about the girl he had seen there on the Ponte Vecchio. Her face, calm, radiant, inexpressibly innocent, was with him as he cursed his own loathsome knowledge. This hateful world! Why not everyone pure? Everyone good? This horrible difference of the sexes! Said Sidley: "All my learning, Robertus: *Omne animalia post coitum triste*—such grave repentance of the sin-exhausted!" To Greene he looked ugly and vile. He was glad to leave him. Alone, he went so far as to threaten half-heartedly to throw himself into the canal, and perhaps his rejection of the idea, by provoking an ironic detestation of his weakness, helped him over his bad hour. The next morning, as ever, things seemed different again; he sucked in the sunshine, and was forced to admit that the women he passed on his way to the home of del Firenze, far from repelling him, struck home through his eye to his pulsing blood. For the next few weeks of high summer he followed in Sidley's trail, and did himself much harm.

Then midway through August, when he was thinking each day to tell Sidley they should go to Rome, his companion embarked on an adventure beside which these brothel-hunts were venialities. At a brilliant ball and masque at the Palazzo Ducale he saw the daughter of Pauluccio Caranella the merchant prince, and cold-bloodedly proposed her seduction to Greene. Greene very nearly went on his knees to him once he found it no jest, begging him to think of his safety as well as his good name, which might survive a deal of lewdness in a foreign land but must be lost for ever by a social crime. But Sidley swore he was tired of virtue measured by livres and would try a notability. Had Greene eyes in his head? Had he never seen the lady at church? Had he not seen her escorted through the town with as much ceremony as a Sultan's daughter? Was she not fit for any man to attempt? "You love her?" asked Greene, and had a leer for his answer. This was sport keener than the fox could give, more dangerous than the bear. Sidley swore it gave an edge to existence.

"I tell you now, Sidley, I shall do nothing to help you."

"Who asked you? D'you think that when at last I slip between the lady's sheets I want to find the imprint of your head on the pillow? Fine help I should get from you! And as for your preaching—I tell you frankly, Robertus, it comes ill from you. What have I done that you have not?"

"I have never wronged the innocent," said Greene, conscious of his priggishness and yet feeling it justified.

"You have not? And how do you know what you have done? And how do you know what you will not yet do? Don't cant, man! Did you learn these pious words from Coppinger on a cat-night out together?"

"You have no call to say that!"

"Have I not then? These puritans! Blood of Jesus, I'd be the last to trust one of them near a girl of mine! Besides, this Fidelia Caranella—what d'you think she is? Some lily-navelled nun? You waste your time thinking so. She is like all the rest. You ought to know women by this time. You ought to have more sense. You have had enough to do with them, God only knows!"

"I have? You forget, I think——"

"I forget nothing. For Christ's sake, Robertus, act like a man of your age! Not a straw-stuffed calfskin, a sheep with sawdust for guts! A mere farthing's-worth of hay-fed rabbit! All these women in Venice—it goes into the bone of them with the sun. All women——"

"Our sisters?"

"Even they——" He broke off, warned by his fellow's face. "No, not they. You are a fool, Robertus. You make me say things—— Go away. Leave me in peace, to think."

"And Rome?"

He waved his hand impatiently. "Later. I'll not be long. A fortnight at the most."

But he was wrong. At the end of a fortnight he had made many presents to Fidelia's waiting-woman but had not so much as seen the mistress except at public worship. A second fortnight passed, enraging Greene, who feared the coming of the bad weather. Sidley was now in a perpetual bad humour, conscious that the waiting-woman or the Caranella or both were amusing themselves with him. He ran over his expenses with the helpless Greene and vowed he'd enjoy the bitch if he had to knock her down in the street to do it. His gallantry was revealed for what it was— vanity and lust. "And Rome?" Greene asked. "After! I'll not be made a fool of! A necklace, two bracelets, the pearls for her ears, a parcel of gold——" Greene inwardly jeered at him for reckoning up his outlay like a tradesman, but the time still went by, and he had not enough money to take him to Padua on his own, much less to Rome. The merchant had gone abroad, that source of his income dried up, and he was in debt to his landlord. He must wait on Sidley's pleasure—in this case his displeasure. Their relations were now a long way short of cordial. They saw less of each other. In varying degrees they despised themselves and each other.

Finally one afternoon Sidley told him sulkily he had determined the position of the lady's bedroom and meant to get into it. Greene shrugged his shoulders. The whole affair seemed now a farce. More like a puppet show than life. Such a lack of proportion—could Sidley be sane, he wondered? When he could find fifty women in an hour! Nevertheless, he called round at Sidley's lodging first thing the next morning to see what success had come his way. He had not yet come home. In the afternoon he called again, and still he had not returned. Sidley's landlord knew him well enough to offer him wine which he would charge to his lodger's account, and he sat there till dusk, getting more alarmed with the passing of each hour. The next morning he was round once more, but there was no news of Sidley. The landlord seemed indisposed to worry; he hinted at Sidley's gallantry, and in any case he had enough security in the baggage to pay the reckoning ten, twenty, thirty times over. Greene could not decide the best thing to do. Common knowledge of the exploit was the last thing he wanted. He decided to wait a third day, and that was unproductive as the two before it. Now he must do something. He did a brave thing. Telling his own landlord where he was going, he went to the Caranella home and asked for audience with the head of the house. His suspicions were strengthened, his fears increased, when this was granted him with a promptness his insignificance did not deserve. He was led to a small but richly-decorated room, where Caranella was waiting for him. It was none the easier for Greene that he had to speak first.

"My friend——" he began clumsily, and halted.

"Is a fortunate man, I doubt not," said Caranella softly. He was a white-haired man, but not more than forty years old. He sat on the far side of a writing desk and played with a pen when his eyes were not on Greene's. "Your name is Signor Roberto Greene, is it not?" Force of habit brought a bow from Greene. "And your friend?"

"Sidley—Ralph Sidley—an Englishman."

"What of this Signor Sidley?"

"He is lost."

Caranella seemed amused. "Am I a dog to smell him out, Signor Greene?"

"I thought——"

"You speak Italian very well, Signor Greene. You have been in the country long?"

"Monsignor——" He could not go on speaking. He was frightened.

"You like this city of ours? You Englishmen usually do. Sometimes one of you likes something in it so well that he can never leave it, eh?"

Greene did not like his role of mouse to Caranella's cat. "Sometimes," he agreed.

"How old are you, Signor Greene?"

"Twenty-four, monsignor."

"You look older. Maybe you live hard, hm? Well, it is an age when one has attained wisdom, if ever one is to attain it. You, for example, would not wish to stay in Venice and never see England again?"

"No."

"Then no doubt you will be leaving us quite soon." He looked up from his pen, mocking Greene.

"When I know what has happened to my friend."

"Now with all respect to you, Signor Greene—I judge you a student. Your friend, as you call him? A student?"

"A lord's son," said Greene firmly. He thought a stronger lie might be useful. "A great lord's son!"

"Usually such are more esteemed but less estimable than students. Do not deceive yourself, Signor Greene— I give you the benefit of a lifetime's observation—lords' sons are no friends for you."

"But you know where he is?"

"You are impatient! But you need have no fears, Signor Greene—yes, I know where he is." Greene tried to carry himself with dignity but felt too helpless. "He is receiving the best of attention, I assure you."

Murder, torture, imprisonment in some dank dungeon below water level—these things flashed into Greene's mind. "What do you mean?" he cried.

"What I say. The best surgeons in Venice are attending to him."

Greene moved agitatedly up and down in front of Caranella's desk. "But I must know! I must know! Monsignor——"

"Your devotion to this worthless fellow is wasted on him, Signor Greene. He does not deserve it. He would

not even thank you for it." He stood up. "You are satisfied?"

"No, no! I must know what has happened!"

"There are no *musts* in this house except mine. You
will excuse me, Signor Greene. I will ring for you to be
taken away."

"But where?" Greene demanded. "Not——"

"To your inn—where else?"

"But Sidley? What of him? A fellow countryman—I
must know!"

Caranella had broken the point of his quill. He spoke
more harshly. "You have my word he will be returned
safely to his lodgings in a week or two. You can ask him
for details. You may go."

Greene found a serving man at his elbow. There was
nothing else to do, so he bowed to Caranella, who nodded
his head, and was relieved beyond words to find himself
safely out of doors. He called back at Sidley's lodgings as
though he might be there after all. He determined to seek
out the officers of the town, but found reasons why he
should not. If Sidley had been marked for death he would
be dead before this. Why make scandal where none had
yet appeared? What would his own life be worth if he
interfered? He came to feel that wherever he went he was
being followed by an agent of Caranella's. Seeking comfort,
he tried to persuade himself that all was well, maybe that
Sidley had hurt himself and was being cared for, that
Caranella had nothing else in view but to avoid gossip.
That must be it! Sidley had fallen or slipped or been
wounded, there would be a week or two for healing, and
then he would find it best to leave the city. And Greene
was expected to go too. It might yet be Rome for the winter.

Or it might not. He went to the Palazzo Caranella a
second time but did not get past the servants. He now
believed that Sidley's landlord knew more than he was
prepared to tell, for he had grown unwilling to discuss
his lodger's absence and strongly advised Greene against
going to the authorities. All would be well in God's own

time. He would come back. "How do you know?" Greene asked him point-blank. "Have you heard anything?" He got himself out of the room with a rambling sentence about hearing more than one saw, and seeing more than one said.

Then one day at the end of the month the padrone met him with smiles and a shower of spittle. The Englishman had returned. He was in his room. Would Signor Greene——

"Sidley!"

He was seated on a couch with his legs up and did not move. "Well?"

Greene stammered at him, shook his hand. "What happened? When did you get back? Where have you been?"

"You should know!"

This was a second meeting with Sidley in Venice when things seemed wrong between them. "But, Sidley——"

"You had to go interfering, had you?"

Greene hesitated whether to strike him or walk out. He did neither. "I was alarmed for you. I had no other reason for entering the Palazzo. I cannot regard it as interference."

"I'm sorry, Robertus. I should not have spoken so sharp. Forget I did so, will you?" He shifted his legs. "I've been in trouble, Robertus. I am like a bundle of snakes inside me. Get yourself wine. I'm sorry."

Listening to his jerky sentences, Greene decided to forget. "They told me you were sick. A wound, was it?"

"A wound."

Greene shook his head over him. "I knew ill would come of it."

"Well, for Christ's sake don't croak over it!" Sidley controlled himself once more. "You must let me shout— I can't help myself, apparently."

"You are hysterical, Sidley. I don't like that high pitch of your voice."

"It will go." His face twisted.

"Of course it will. You will be your own man again, Sidley. Where were you wounded?"

"The groin. With a sword. It is almost well. I am leaving here, Robertus."

"Rome, is it?"

"I am leaving Italy, and may hell sink it in the sea!"

"But, Sidley——"

"Am I my own master?"

"It was just that I——"

"I'm going!" That same hysterical note. "Go to Rome yourself if you want to!"

His words, his manner, his ingratitude, all hurt Greene equally. "What in heaven's name is the matter with you, Sidley? You may have had a trying time——"

"Oh Christ! Christ!"

The agony in Sidley's voice cut razor-edged through his fatty wonderings. "What happened, Sidley? For God's sake tell me what happened?"

"Will you go! Will you get out! Will you leave me to myself!"

"As you will." He went from the hostel to his own lodgings, puzzled for Sidley's sake, anxious for his own. It was now he realised how implicitly he was relying on Sidley to settle his small debt and take him to Rome. If Sidley kept to his word and left Italy—could he go with him? For a while he considered this change of plans dejectedly, and then looked for its brighter side. He could go back to the University and take his master's degree next summer and then, experienced and qualified, either find a post as guide and tutor to a youngster visiting Italy or hope for Harrison's good word to get him a secretaryship in London. He remembered Caranella's suggestion that he would soon be leaving Italy; and it had all the strength of a warning. The death rate was high in Venice for those who offended great families. That was why Sidley was going, no doubt. He had been taught a lesson, and would never again talk so glibly of the world as his orange. A sword-thrust through the groin, hysterics, ignominious failure in

a field where he had always boasted his prowess, a friend to
witness it—he thought with a start that Sidley might now
come to hate the sight of him. Tears of Christ! he'd be begging his way home yet. If only he had saved his money!
If only he had not been with the Consetti in Florence!
If not with Sidley here in Venice! Coppinger was right—
it was ill company that ruined a man. Still, he must bear
with Sidley a little longer. Rome or England—he must be
helped to one or the other.

He called on Sidley the next day. The would-be seducer
of Fidelia was more civil to him.

"When you leave Venice, Sidley——"

"Italy, Robertus."

"I am wondering whether I can come part of the way
with you." He saw no particular welcome in Sidley's face.
"The truth is, I have no money. And I owe a reckoning
here too."

Sidley hesitated. "I'll pay that for you with pleasure,
Robertus. But I thought you were set on Rome, not
England?"

"I shall have to go through Padua, in any case."

"Yes. You had better come as far as Padua then." The
first two fingers of his right hand were drumming on his
lips. "You can go south, the way you came, from there.
You might stay in Florence a while?"

There was no mistaking this hint. Sidley did not want
him, and he knew enough of Sidley to be sure this meant
he would not have him. But there were dozens of Englishmen at the University at Padua. He might get help here.
"Padua then," he agreed. "When do you start?"

"A week ahead. I shall be fit for a litter by that time—
maybe for short stretches in the saddle." Greene felt that his
lack of means had introduced something of master and
man into their talk already. Other of Caranella's words
recurred to him. He was a memorable talker, that Caranella.

They left Venice in exactly a week and were in Padua
two days later. After all, Sidley travelled the whole distance

by litter. Any reference to his incapacity infuriated him.
There was too great a reserve between them for a continuance of friendship, so at Padua Greene intended to
ask him for a loan sufficient to make him independent for
a while and push on ahead of him to Genoa. Thence he
would take ship for Marseilles or Narbonne, go overland to
Bordeaux, and there get passage in a wine ship to England.
It was likely to be a long and rough journey, but he was
too much the beggar to be chooser. But more happened
at Padua than he had bargained for. They found it
impossible to get adequate lodging in the city. The University had received its new students and there was an imperial
conference in session. The place was a-crawl with civic,
ecclesiastical, and military leaders and the followers, useful
and parasitic, they could not move without. They dragged
their way from place to place, with offers of nothing better
than hay in the loft and not even that to themselves, till
their tempers were short and their forbearance shorter.
At last, for an extortionate price one fellow agreed to
arrange for two soldiers of the Neapolitan legate to give
up their room. Now came an unexpected difficulty: Sidley
held out for the room to himself. Greene indignantly
asked if he was to sleep in the gutter, and Sidley retorted
he cared not a harlot's oath where he slept so long as it
was not in his chamber. He almost threw Greene a gold coin,
before curtly ordering the porters to separate the baggage,
and Greene, not making too fine a point of honour of it,
accepted and started on a trudge of his own. He tasted to
the full the miseries of dependence on another man's purse.
The first place that offered him the stable was good enough.
The porter's dues had been paid by Sidley and he had
nothing in the way of small change wherewith to add a tip—
scowls and mutters from the men, resentment on his part.
He lay awake for a long time, thinking about the change
in Sidley, until suddenly he saw the truth of it. Sidley's
treatment by surgeons after the attempted violation of Fidelia
Canarella, his high-pitched outcries, his inability to sit a
saddle, his refusal to share a room. "As God is in heaven,"

he said excitedly, sitting up in the dark, "he's been gelded!"
For a minute or two he felt sick, with an indescribable
ache through his teeth and jaws; felt the silence as something terrible and palpable. Then he lay back fitting a dozen
hitherto unrelated details into a cruel and readable pattern.
Yes, by God, everything fitted—Sidley had been doctored!
A dozen brutal metaphors made him grin. He simply could
not help it. Nothing else in the world could be so loathsome,
so pitiful, and yet so ridiculous. He called himself an unfeel-
ing monster, but could not, did not try to forget Sidley's
snubs and insults. And all at once he was sneering at the
woman-hunter shorn of his weapons. A eunuch! It was
rich—Sidley of all men a eunuch! Cut like the poorest
little devil of a Roman choir-boy, like a tomcat, like a horse.
He took an ignoble revenge in the next ten minutes for the
subjection in which Sidley had held him so long. Why
hadn't Sidley listened to him in Venice months ago?
But he must always have his own way, and now God
knows whether he was paying for it. He would never think
of him again without contempt. Poor devil—call him that,
yes, but who could help despising him? And laughing at
him? It was going to be hard for Sidley.

He thought about his own prospects too. He wagged
his head. He must keep in with Sidley all the same.

In the morning he went to see him. Half-friend, half-
lackey: half-pitying, half-contemptuous. He contrasted
his appearance with that first sight of him at Cambridge.
The fellow looked fifteen years older, not five. He had
aged these last few days. The beard and the moustache
—not those so much—the lines in the face, the haggard
expression, the eyes.

"You find me interesting?" It was Sidley, near a snarl.

"I was thinking we both get older," he said mildly.

"You don't expect to get younger, do you?"

"No. Five years can be a long time, that is all."

"You find me so hellishly different?"

"You need not be so sharp, Sidley. A cat can look at
a king."

"So long as you are the cat," Sidley said unpleasantly. "When do you leave for Rome?"

"I may not go there after all."

"You'll be a fool to stay in this—this pit of a place."

"I thought I might make my way back to England."

Sidley showed his displeasure. "Now, or in the spring?"

"Why not now, Sidley? I have been frank enough with you. I have no money. Why not let me travel with you? If you won't take me as a friend, let me come as secretary, servant, what you like."

"I don't want a secretary or a servant."

"And you don't want a friend—is that it?"

"Since you ask me, I prefer to travel alone."

Greene choked down his bile for the last time. "Will you lend me enough money for me to get home myself?"

"I can't, Robertus."

"You mean you won't!" He hit a glass from the table, so enraged was he. "To think that for a year I made a god out of you and now you show yourself the poor thing you are! By God, Sidley——"

"Remember yourself, Greene! I take insults from no one. Certainly not from the brother of a servant!"

"Servant! No servant of yours! She left Braiding long ago because of your old goat of a father—the lean-shanked old monkey, the slime-gutted old toad that he is!"

"And the sooner the better! We want no trollops at Braiding, I'll tell you! None of your——"

"Trollops, is it! I'll ram the lie down your blasted throat!"

He moved towards Sidley who snatched at his dagger. "Keep off! I'm fastidious whom I use this on," he sneered.

Greene halted. "And when my time comes I should like to be killed by a *man*," he said slowly.

He watched Sidley's face change. "You said?" he asked stupidly. Then he leapt at Greene who was only just in time to catch his dagger arm. For a moment they closed and swayed, and then Greene, stronger and heavier, had thrown him off. He jumped up again, screaming with rage, shrill, falsetto, but as though he suddenly heard himself, broke off and began weeping. Great shame and pity came to Greene now. "I'm sorry, Sidley," he said. "I'll go."

"No, don't you go, damn you!" This was another change of mood. "I'll not let you go!"

There was a hammering on the door. Greene kicked Sidley's dagger under the bed before opening it. It was the padrone with half a dozen followers. "What dreadful thing——" Greene drew on his imagination. It was the stabbing pain through Signor Sidley's wound. It took him this way every so often. But the landlord was not satisfied until he had entered the room and had confirmation of this from Sidley himself. Then he was all gesture and gabble; he knew the best surgeons in Padua; he could be trusted to do a thousand things. Greene pushed him out of the room.

"How did you know?" Sidley asked. Greene saw the torments of hell written on his face.

"It is true then?"

Sidley nodded. He began to sob.

"How did it happen?"

He had gone to the Palazzo Caranella and found a rope waiting for him. Once inside the house he was seized and gagged and maimed within an hour. Caranella had seen him the next day and told him to leave Venice as soon as he was able. Otherwise his plight would become known to the curious. During his short recital Sidley acted very like a madman, but once calm enough to think, he had seen that no idea of revenge should tempt him to release the jeers and contempt that must follow him for the rest of his days. Had he been free during his stay at the palace he believed he would have killed himself, but now he lacked courage for it and clung to life. He begged Greene to tell him how he knew, whether he was the only one, would he take oath never to let anyone else into his secret? He would take him back to England, he would maintain him for life, he would pay him half his fortune, anything if only he would not tell. Greene saw the idol of his College days, that very pattern of the young man of the world, in tears before him, abasing himself like slave before bashaw. He became calmer when Greene reasoned with him, showing that no one else need ever know, that he had not thought of it himself till last night, despite the knowledge peculiar to him. His voice? He jested at Sidley's alarms. An old wives' tale. He looked and sounded as much the man as ever. Neither of them saw the inadequacy of that guarantee, and eventually Sidley was wiping the tears out of his eyes. He even found it a relief to talk about the life ahead of him, snatching at the thinnest straws of hope with Greene's warm encouragement. Full friendship was theirs again, except that Greene appeared to take the lead more. Just one incident there was which Greene would not forget till his dying day: Sidley, after physiological details, showing something of a laugh at his dreadful and yet ludicrous loss. It made Greene almost sick with pity for him, and haunted him a night or two. Of course he would now share Sidley's room. He would understand now why Sidley had been so consistently unkind.

They were in Padua a week, and then Sidley announced himself fit for the road. There would be no litters henceforth. They must hurry to Genoa if they were to reach England that year. Several times they were advised to give up the notion and stay in Italy till the spring. They might already find the Ligurian passes closed to them. Then what of the way Greene had come through Bologna, Florence, and the valley of the Arno to Pisa, and then that fearful coastal road? "We shall be there while we argue the matter!" said Sidley, and they left in dry weather for Verona. They reached it in a day, turned south-west for Cremona, and followed the Po till they met the road for Alessandria, where they spent their fifth night and hired armed guides for the mountain roads. These proved passable, and although their rate of progress was slowed down they rode into Genoa in another two days. There was a ship sailing for Marseilles three days later and Sidley reserved their places. Greene told Sidley frankly why he wished to put up once more at the Gifts of God, and saw only this much sign of jealousy that the other reckoned he would stay elsewhere. So here he was, early in the evening, riding like a lord to the well-known street under the Palazzo Spinola. It was like a home-coming. Bando went so far as to kiss him on both cheeks and Greene was equally courteous to his wife. "Benita! Benita! It is your Signor Roberto!" There was a hurry and scurry, he heard feet pelting madly up the stairs—no doubt Benita on her way to make herself pretty for him—he spread his arms before the delighted couple—"Home again!" he cried. The wine was on the house—a glassful each of *lagryme di Christo*—why, cried Greene, does Christ not shed such tears in England too!—the toast was his safe arrival and the continued prosperity of them all, he was taken to his old room, there was another pelting of footsteps, down, up, along the landing: "O Roberto! Roberto mio!" The host withdrew. "Benita! I came back! My pretty one! My dove!" So, he felt, must an honest man return to a loving wife. He kissed her a score of times, gesticulated like a fool, gabbled without sense or continuity, asked questions that wanted no answer and did not hear when the knock came at the door to herald his supper. She must sup with him, he would hear of nothing else. Happy? He had not been so happy for months. The whole round of foulness from Pisa to Venice mattered nothing that evening. He would not be lying had he sworn he loved the girl, and it was that which singled her out from the more beautiful (some of them), abandoned, and complaisant women in whose embraces he had explored a universe of sensation. Eating, drinking, laughing, bragging unashamedly, he felt the wholesomeness of it like pure night air after a stinking stew. There was more than a passing of gold between them—regard and kindliness, a desire for the other's happiness too.

"You are happy to see me, Benita?"

Happier than birds when their little ones come from the eggs, she told him; and he knew he could believe her.

"You have had many women in Italy?" she asked, not scoldingly, but matter-of-fact.

"Benita, my love—of them all I remember only you!"

He was laughing when he began his answer, but she saw the quick tears gush to his eyes, and he took up her hand and kissed it. "Why, Roberto!" He was thinking: the creature I've been since Genoa last! If only the badness of those years could be expunged, and only the loveliness remain. Well, God helping, in the future there would be a difference.

The two days that followed were too happy for long lasting. He felt younger, more boyish of heart as well as of body; undoubtedly his three months' abstention from vice had contributed to this, and now with Benita he was free from that rancid lust which had turned his stomach with useless regret and self-hatred. Even in so short a while he enjoyed the peace and decency of permanence. She was not something to use. He had delicacy enough to believe she did not want his money, and spent an hour among the goldsmiths to find a small brooch with admittedly inferior but still expensive stones in the shape of a letter B. It was Sidley's money, true, but he would have done the same had it been his own.

He spent the last evening with Sidley, who appeared distraught and uncertain of himself now that their departure was at hand. Greene found him in turns eager for news and absent-minded, and it was during one of these eager spells that he suddenly asked him what he meant when he linked Alice's name with Sir Ralph's. Greene hedged for a time, but he pressed him, insisting that frankness was best, so it ended with Greene telling him all he knew.

"So she came to no harm?"

"None. It was no fault of yours whatever your father attempted. It shows again what I have learned for myself in Italy—how ugly these things can be. But it is best to forget."

"There is nothing else to do with the past, Robertus." He ran a drop or two of wine on a cloth and mopped his forehead. "The good things are past recall: the bad—who wants them? We must school ourselves to forget. You saw her child?"

"I can't remember, Sidley. Not the kind of thing you do remember, is it? He would be like all other babies, I fancy. Why?"

"No reason, Robertus. Except that it is hard to think of people one knows like that becoming fathers and mothers. I ought to do something for them, though."

Greene now spoke to him a couple of times without getting much by way of answer. Finally he said he must go. "No, no," cried Sidley; "you mustn't go yet! It is too early. I've got the devils, Robertus—stay here an hour yet!" He began to talk blunderingly about his return to England, how he must act to hide his infirmity; again and again he asked Greene whether anyone else could know. "You are a good friend, Robertus." He mopped his forehead continually. A second time he begged Greene to stay longer, but at last appeared to see reason. "Your Benita, I know! You'll want to get home to her. Go on then! You lucky devil!" He began to laugh excitedly. "Perhaps I'm not done for yet. Good night then, Robertus." He insisted upon coming with him for fifty yards. The oddity of his conduct was a problem to Greene. He kept him talking in the street despite his own bare head and the freshness of the hour. "You will be in time in the morning? You will not sleep too late? You have plenty of money? At daybreak, don't forget. There must be no waiting!"

"I won't forget. Good night, Sidley."

The other still held his sleeve. "What was I saying? Ah yes, you are going then, Robertus?"

"You had better go too. You are shivering, man."

"Am I? I don't feel cold. Look, why not come back and spend the night with me?"

"Impossible! What would Benita say?" He laughed.

"I am serious, Greene." He noticed the change of name. "You'll come?"

"I cannot."

"I beg you to come!"

"Impossible! Get back indoors. In the morning?"

"You won't come?"

"What is the matter with you, Sidley! No, I won't come. Once and for all—good night to you!"

He turned away. "The morning then," said Sidley behind him; "and what it brings forth."

Half-heartedly he cudgelled the question of Sidley's sanity as he walked along the narrow street. The stars were shining but gave little light. Benita he thought would be sleeping now, and he determined not to wake her. His packing was done, his bills paid, Benita's present hidden in the——

Ah-ah-ah-ah! He was trying to shout but no sound came through his wide-open mouth. There was an arm garotting him, and he felt a lightning stab of intolerable pain run through his back to his chest.

A million years later he had a half-second of consciousness. There was something hard at his back. He was cold.

He woke again after the flight of aeons. He was in a bed. He closed his eyes. Endless darkness flooded over him.

CHAPTER XIX

HE WAS FOUND early in the morning by two boys behind a wall in the Old Town. First they examined his pockets, but these had been emptied, and then they went to give notice of their discovery. Luckily, among those who hurried to the place, there was one who recognised Greene as the Englishman staying at the Gifts of God tavern. All Englishmen were known to be wealthy and lords' sons, so they took more trouble with him than with one of their own nationality. One of the two boys ran on to the Gifts of God, the other walked with the funeral party, so that whatever the source of award they might be ready with a claim.

At the inn the news was received with proper amazement and sorrow. The inn-keeper and his wife liked Greene more than most who stayed with them; and they thought his credit good. Bando, throwing up his hands, cursing the outrage, taking measures against Greene's arrival, could yet think that if the English signor died—well, there was his baggage, there was his money, there was his rich friend milord Sidli. The fine sheets were whisked off the bed, poor ones brought forth to take the blood-stains, water fetched from the fountain. As for a surgeon —someone must run to milord Sidli's lodging and see whether he would take full responsibility for necessary expenses.

Away went the messenger. He was back in twenty minutes. Milord Sidli was overcome with horror, he was the colour of grass, the sweat ran from him as from a hard-pushed horse, his eyes were the size of rose-windows. His tongue stuck, his hands shook like a wheatfield, there was—— "But what of the surgeons?" Milord Sidli would pay for everything.

"Benita, my lamb——"

All these callers—the inn did good business for an hour. She served downstairs, wincing at much of the talk. The surgeons arrived, two of them, black-garmented, to frighten Death with his own colours. Greene's was one of the few cases for which they prescribed no bleeding. In any case he would die. The skill of Guglielmo Manucci and Francesco Aconti would be wasted on him. They explained to Bando and his wife that the patient was a grapeskin—all the blood and pulp sucked out. Any time now they might throw him to the ground. Said Bando: "It is so sad for you, Benita child, so very sad! And for the gallant Signor Greene, so sad too. But it is the will of God—well, well, well!"

The brief rush of serving over, the clamorous boys told to return the following day and finally clipt over the head, and Bando having withdrawn with sufficient headshakes to make his teeth and brains rattle, Benita went up to Greene's chamber to see him. The blinds were down, the room dark, the air unclean. She went and bent over him. His beard pointed straight down over the coverlet, his red hair was screwed all ways on the pillow, an untidy halo for his white face. She too felt he would die, and cried for a time for him and for herself, for he had been good to her. But there was work to do, and sorrowfully she gathered up her few belongings there, and took them back to the room she usually slept in with the other women of the inn.

But where was milord Sidli? Bando, his wife, and Benita began to suspect the same truth after another hour. They knew that he and Greene were to leave for Marseilles at dawn, but surely that arrangement would fall through for both now that it had fallen through for one? The English were so stolidly faithful a race. At last Bando sent his same messenger a second time to Sidley's lodging. He came back headlong. Milord Sidli had gone.

"Gone?" cried Bando, and his wife echoed: "Gone." Benita heard, and the word to her was as something half-swallowed sticking in the throat. Gone without a word for Roberto? "You are a fool!" cried Bando. "Get to the harbour and find whether the ship has sailed, and whether this Sidli was on board." He called on God, to know whether He had ever heard the like, and had the chance to call on Him again when the boy returned with news that milord had left for Marseilles as arranged. This was unparalleled, incomprehensible, incredible. Now, cried Bando, the Gifts of God would have to bury him.

It was time to examine the baggage of the soon-to-be-deceased. He and his wife climbed upstairs once more and called to Benita to help them carry the stuff elsewhere that the dying man might not be disturbed. It occurred to Bando he might need a witness to what he was doing, so Benita stayed with the couple as they opened and searched. There was a small handful of Sidley's gold, which Bando counted with satisfaction, and little else of value till the brooch with a jewelled B tumbled out from the sleeve of a doublet. It was to the inn-keeper's credit in this life and the next that he resisted the impulse to slip it into his pocket and instead held it up for his wife and the girl to see. "It might stand for Bando," he said, scratching his head; "but somehow I think not." He passed it up to the girl. "This Signor Roberto was fond enough of you, Benita." She stood irresolute with it. "He meant it for you," said Bando's wife. "Be wise, my girl, and put it away before the officers make an inventory." She pinned it inside her corsage, feeling with passionate satisfaction its friction against her skin, and later in whatsoever privacy she could get took delight in taking it out, handling it, admiring it, watching the light flash from it, tracing with her finger the outline of the letter she had been told stood for her name. That Roberto should die seemed doubly terrible now.

But the following day he was still alive and knew them. He took a mouthful of wine, as much of soup. He took more the day after, and though Manucci and Aconti spoke over him in Latin it had no ill effect. He began to recover, crawling slowly from the yawning mouth of darkness. Pulp came back to the grapeskin. Benita without a word to anyone poured the surgeons' concoctions into the privy and gave him soup and wine instead; she shifted his garments and bedclothes; watched over him protectively. In time he came to ask questions, the blinds were drawn back for what sunshine there was in the day, new blood seeped through his thirsty veins. He relied on Benita like a child on its mother, and with the confident selfishness of the invalid made her sit by his bed for hours, quietly talking to him or in silence holding his hand. For him she was warmth and protection, the safe healing of familiar things.

"Benita, heart of my body," he told her one day; "but for you I should have died." She shook her head, laughing. "Oh yes, I should! Because of the way you have looked after me, and more than that—because you gave me something to live for."

It was something for her to think of. And it made her happy.

He asked after Sidley. He had gone then, indifferent? What was at first unwillingly suspected hardened into certainty. Sidley had arranged for the attack upon him, wanted him dead and his secret with him. Well, he swore, wriggling in bed to see how much pain was still in his wound: I'm not dead, and I don't intend to die, and I'll be revenged on him yet. But most of the time he felt too indifferent about him to care for revenge. His former idol was like a figure in a puppet show: The Lincolnshire Gelding—rather than a flesh-and-blood man of his knowledge. Poor contemptible Sidley, with such lessons learned in Italy that he could arrange for the murder of his friend and return to England unmanned. Looking back now on his Cambridge infatuation with this clay-footed god he laughed at his folly and lack of judgment. And if he wished, he could arrive at Braiding, Leesome, London, wherever the pitiful creature might be hiding, and break his hopes of happiness like sticks across his knee. He thought he would never again think any man better than himself.

He had plenty of time for thinking. The assassin's knife, though driven by a botcher, had skewered him like a fowl, and there were his surgeons to contend with. They did their very best to maintain their reputations for accurate prognostication, little content a foreigner should live in their despite. But the constitution he had inherited from generations of clean-living men and women, and Benita's care, defied them. Their syrup of earthworms boiled in milk was committed to earth; his stomach threw up a restorative of dried grasshoppers and the ordure of pigeons. Manucci's favourite remedy of a new-killed rat split open and applied to the naked wound was fortunately objected to by Aconti, who favoured bathing with the patient's own urine, in which ants had been allowed to soak for exactly seven hours. At one time it looked like a compromise of bathing and poultice, urine and rat, but Manucci suspected Aconti of newfangledness and Aconti knew Manucci an old stick-in-the-mud; and their mutual distrust worked to Greene's advantage. Wine for blood, fish for brain, meat for flesh, and eggs for seed, was Benita's wiser faith. Blood and brain ran a faster race than the other two, and he had plenty of time for thinking.

He commended Bando's discretion in searching his baggage. The money was holding out? Bando shrugged his shoulders: a Christian's duty was clear. Besides, he had not yet changed the last ducat, and there were English students at the University from whom, no doubt, Signor Greene would receive the help always accorded so generously by one Englishman to another. He shrugged again. Almost always, might be nearer the mark. "Your friend milord Sidli, Signor Greene—if he ever deserved such a name— after he had promised to settle all expenses—has God in his heaven ever seen the like of it?" "You shall not be the loser, friend," Greene promised warmly; "This generosity of yours—I shall not be content to leave its reward to the world to come. I am not without influence——" He bore in mind the hint about the English students at Genoa. For there was more to do than pay his shot—he must find the money to get back to England.

Benita was very confused when she had to explain that the brooch found among his belongings had been given to her. He pretended severity and then, when she looked distressed, came out with the pleasantry that he would never forgive Bando for denying him the happiness of giving it her in person.

"But I'll give it you now," he promised, and took it from her hands. He explained the significance of the ornamental letter. "I had bought it for you, sweetheart. You knew that. You see, even Bando knew how much I am in love with you. And now I'll pin it over your heart." Flushing a little, he kissed her bosom and then her lips. "If I had died, I am glad you would have had something to remember English Roberto by, Benita."

"I should have remembered you. You are a dear man to me, Roberto."

"And you are the dearest one in the world to me You have given me my life. Given me something as great, too." He told her haltingly of the wickedness that had marred his life since he came to Italy. "But with you I have been able to respect myself once more, Benita. Knife or no knife, I am better in mind and body than I was three months ago."

He came to sentimentalise his relationship to her. Thus late he found again that he had not lost that power of make-believe which had put him to worship of Mistress Petherill. The best of love, he called it, this free adoration. When else could a man be so happy? Yet one afternoon he knew her—to her mind the end of his convalescence. It was then the end of December. They took up their decent man-and-wife life together.

Still, there was the problem of money. Bando gave him a reckoning which showed him all his ducats were gone, and that he even owed the house a small sum. Something must be done. He explained as much to Benita, and was embarrassed when straightway she offered him some of her savings. He expostulated that he could not rob her, but she told him it was not a coin more than he had given her during his first stay in Genoa. "Oh well," he said at last, "if we can look on it as a loan——" He felt that if he could lay hands on a thousand pounds he would use it to buy Benita the most magnificent inn in Italy. Nothing should be too good for her. He tried to find those in need of English lessons, but none wanted them except free; he obtained a little clerical work, copying lists for winesellers, bills for merchants, he wrote a number of love-letters for young men, but came nowhere near a thousand pounds. Unless something came his way soon, he would have to try the students.

Meantime, he was working at the second part of his romance *Mamillia*. The first part, long since entered on the Stationers' Register, had been pure Lyly; this second part showed Sidney's influence as well. Not that he had read the *Arcadia*, but what he had heard of it at the University had bred in him the desire for romantic entanglements and resounding sentiments. To a Benita who never grasped that their story was not true he explained how Pharicles had loved both Mamillia and Publia, and fled to Spain because he could not make up his mind between them. Now, in the second part, poor Publia had died in a convent, but not without leaving her fortune to the unworthy Pharicles. Mamillia, too, stood to inherit untold wealth but only on condition she did not marry Pharicles. "But why bother to marry him?" Benita asked. "Why shouldn't they take joy in each other and keep the money?" This was not easy to explain, without stressing the significance of that legal permission to take joy in each other he and Benita had dispensed with. She was worried too during the weeks Greene left Pharicles in prison at Saragossa, at the suit of a harlot whose blandishments he had spurned. "But couldn't you borrow money from him?" she asked once. He tried several times the impossible task of explaining that the noble Pharicles and the nobler Mamillia were creatures of his own brain; then he began himself to think of them as alive.

He was writing verse too. Light, airy verse, with an anatomical bent, again rather in the vein of his adolescence, with a wealth of platitude and imagery. All lips were ruby,

every cheek mingled the lily with the rose, necks were
stately, and bosoms of snow; the hand to Hebe and the foot
to Thetis. Mercy was seated in each lady's face, Love
hung his trophies 'twixt her breasts. He discovered with
a shock that according to one poem the lady, though
fathered by Cupid, had suckled Venus. An hour went
quickly, so occupied. He wrote a number of copies too,
about the pleasures of content; and recited them aloud for
his instruction. Money to live on and the price of his passage
to England, and he would be completely happy. He had
been near enough to losing it to know the loveliness of
life.

The first ugliness came when Benita told him one day
that Bando had ordered her to transfer her person to the
room of a plump young man from Alessandria. Greene
was no longer a guest who paid his way, and must not expect
luxuries. But his dagger was out before she could finish
telling him, and he was swearing he'd have plump-cheeks
by the throat and Bando by his stubby nose. This seemed
to her foolish behaviour; she said so, and he calmed down.
Nevertheless, staring out of the window one moment, staring
at her the next, he felt as much indignation and disgust as
if he had been asked for the use of his lawfully-wedded wife.
Who was this Bando? And who this lump of Alessandrian
fat? This whey-brained, butter-livered, cruddle-blooded
sneaker after better men than himself? He'd show them
whether Robert Greene, Englishman, could be treated
so. The sooner Bando realised—suddenly worry was joined
to his anger and indignation—if Bando proved awkward,
the awkwardness would trouble Signor Greene most. "I'll
get money, Benita," he said. "Leave your things here,
and if Bando says anything——" "Yes?" "Oh, nothing."
He sat down on the bed, frowning.

"What are you thinking to do, Roberto?"

"I shall try the Englishmen at the University."

"Are they generous?"

"On the devil's work, probably."

"You know none of them?"

"None."

"Then they will give you nothing."

He thought it very likely.

"Then I must go to the Alessandrian."

But he stamped and swore at the very idea. "Don't you love me, Benita?" he asked at last.

"But love is not enough, Roberto, unless——"

"Unless what?"

"Unless you and I are like your friends Pharicles and Mamillia."

"But God and all his angels, Benita," he exclaimed, "I can't marry you, if that is what you mean!"

She had known as much. "Then what are we to do? I take orders here, not give them."

"I'll see Bando," he said. He did so, his manner shifting from humble to arrogant and back again. The landlord was sympathetic but businesslike. There had never been anyone under their roof he and his Emilia liked better than Signor Greene, but the Englishman must realise that to run an inn in Genoa, with all this competition—well, there it was, the Alessandrian wanted a girl, he had made the most careful inquiries before settling on the Gifts of God, and Signor Greene must admit that the same arrangement had been made in his own case. The jolly landlord suddenly appeared to Greene in the guise of a wicked old pandar, his wife a bawd. What was this cursed land of Italy but one vast brothel? If only he had money to go home!

He kept Benita that night, and the next day he went to the University to ask after the English students. There were only three in residence, and no one of them had money to spare. Ganbow, tall and stout; Fenn, with a kick in his speech; Baldwin, dirty and short-sighted—no credit to the nation. He blushed for them as Englishmen. It was later he came to see that they must look on him as both rascal and waster, and were as much on their guard against him as he should have been against Ingpen on his first night in London.

Ingpen! But confound it, he knew no one to rob. Card

tricks, the art of the barnard, the barnacle's law, the verser, the setter, the high law—he saw no way of profit. Impulsively he set off for the Palazzo Spinola and asked for audience with Sir John Harrison's friend, Cesare. He had been a fool not to think of this before. It was a form of cozenage, but hang it all, he was picking no one's pocket. If nothing came of it, it was only breath wasted. A grave man saw him at last, one of Spinola's secretaries. His business? He was a secretary of Sir John Harrison's. With satisfaction he noticed a quickening of the other's interest. He had been unfortunate. He gave an account of his adventures at Genoa. Really? The other was impressed. Would Signor Greene be kind enough to call back the next day? In the meantime—a little help? Gold changed hands. "I remember your face, I think," the other was saying. "This will interest His Excellency. To-morrow then, Signor Greene."

He went back to the Gifts of God cock-a-hoop. He called Bando his honest friend, placed a gold coin on the table, and spoke briefly about his influential friends at the Palazzo Spinola. To-morrow—to-morrow he expected to be in a position to do wonders. In the meantime—he felt confident honest Bando would find other pasturage for fat-face from Alessandria. Bando agreed willingly. "You understand, Signor Greene, that only necessity could force me—in any case, what is Alessandria to Genoa? A mere cowshed! But there, you saw it yourself." "A dunghill, Bando—a dunghill." They felt the warming influence of bright gold like a June sun in January. Late that evening Greene dropped his second piece of gold down the front of Benita's shift, they struggled amorously when he tried to get it back again, and were as happy as kittens. Later still, her head pushed into his shoulder, her breath passing warm across him, he philosophised upon the meaning of value, noting that not only did other people esteem him more but he esteemed himself more for the possession of a couple of bits of yellow metal.

Next day, at the Palazzo Spinola, he was informed he might have audience with Cesare himself during the afternoon. He was not short of time and waited patiently at the palace, sharing the meal open to all comers. His interview was not a long one but was pleasant. Cesare was pleased to do something for Sir John's sake, and Greene's compliments to the glories of Italy and Genoa were well-timed and helpful. To Spinola's remark that he must have other than happy memories of Genoa he was able to reply with conviction that nowhere in Italy had he been so happy. Spinola was glad to hear it. "And if now you return to London, you must be good enough to carry a letter to my friend Sir John." Greene would be charmed. He said nothing of passage money. "I think, Signor Greene, Genoa owes you something." He rang a little silver bell, and the grave secretary entered. Spinola merely nodded his head, he went outside again, to re-enter with a silk purse carried on a red silken cushion. Spinola stood up, the Englishman did the same, there were gracious words on all sides, and the purse left the palace with the elated Greene. In three weeks' time there would be a ship for Narbonne in which passage would be reserved for him, the letters would be written before then, he would be in London for the spring, what a marvellous world it was! He eyed the women on the balcony of a noted house with the assurance that comes of money in the purse, smiled and waved his hand to them, but passed on his way to the Gifts of God, where in his room he counted what had been given him. There was more than enough for necessities, his dues at the inn, a present for Benita, the return of her loan. Calling up Bando he settled his bill to date, adding a coin or two for luck, and watched with amusement and satisfaction the new standard of civility reached by the inn-keeper. "Yes, Signor Greene. No, Signor Greene. Some wine sent up, Signor Greene? A fowl perhaps?" The house was Signor Greene's for a chamber pot, if he wanted it. He could not have obliged Bando more than by spitting in his eye.

He told Benita he would be leaving for England in three weeks' time. "You will be sorry?"

"Very sorry, Roberto."

"You will miss me?"

"Oh, Roberto!"

The time raced by. Apart from those wearisome weeks in bed, it always had. In his finest clothes he called at the palace several times and was privileged to inspect its treasures, and especially its pictures and books. In the library he handled manuscripts and quoted Ariosto to the taciturn young man appointed to wait on him, and finally, encouraged by his silence, made a number of uninformed and reckless statements about Italian poetry in general. He enjoyed himself thoroughly till a remark or two showed him this same taciturn but respectful fellow knew twenty times more about the subject than he and was probably laughing at but tolerating his ignorance. This made him silent as the other. Still, while in the palace he acted as though he kept hens in a better one, and so acquitted himself as an Englishman should. Now that he had money, the town was as convenient as his own backyard; the Gifts of God was the sweeter for the removal, after one week's stay, of the Alessandrian; he was master of his fate again.

Only once did he put himself in trouble's way. He was sitting with wine one evening, feeling himself the biggest bird in the coop, when he was invited to take part in a card game. Foolishly he did so, to suspect after a quarter of an hour that there was too much manipulation going on to promise well. He resorted to his old technique of leaving for the back, and as in London knew he was followed. This time he acted differently, waited at the door, and as his watcher stuck his head out smashed him hard between the eyes with a stone he had ready, vaulted the low wall into the adjoining garden, and hurried back to the Gifts of God. For an hour there he bragged to Benita of how clever he had been, but she was worried for him, telling of revenges and stilettos, so that his confidence oozed away, and when next he went out after dark it was hand on dagger hilt, eyes open for cross-biters, versers, setters and oaks, his head going round like a marionette's at a footstep on the cobbles behind him. It would be a good thing when the day came for him to leave.

And come it did. He relished his feeling of honesty as he saw his baggage carried from the inn. Every debt paid. Not a chalk mark against his name from one end of Italy to the other. Good-bye, good-bye, good-bye.

"Where is Benita?"

Bando spread his hands. "She will miss you, Signor Greene. We shall all miss you. I think my wife will cry. I think I shall cry myself."

Her sense of drama had sent her upstairs to his room. He kissed her long and hard. "Look, Benita——" His hand went into his pocket. He was thinking: I can always get more. He pressed more money into her hand. "Good-bye!" He hurried off and did not once look back. It was over.

He had Spinola's letters on his person. Going on board he pressed his hand to where they were secured. Good-bye, Italy—things might be much worse. And so much lay ahead.

He stood astern to see the land dip behind him. Soon, except for memories, it was gone.

CHAPTER XX

H<small>E WAS IN</small> London by the spring, glad of the letters from Spinola as an excuse for seeking out Sir John Harrison. He went first to his old lodgings at the Glove Inn, and the next day made inquiries for Sir John at the house in Fetter Lane. But the former envoy and Fellow had moved, and he was a day or two discovering him near St. Mary Rouncival.

He found Sir John altered for the worse—a rook with the croup. He was swathed in a great furred gown and complained of the wet, cold winter which had given him no chance to recover from an ague of the year before. "As for you, young man, I don't know what to do with you. Why didn't you come back from Florence as arranged?" Greene admitted that his excessive love of Italian culture had made him stay longer than he should; but this last year—he could not be blamed for that. He gave a fairly truthful account of his adventures at Genoa, ending with a compliment to Sir John that his name was so well known throughout Italy that succour followed the mention of it. "Ay," said Sir John; "I can see I have been a convenience." He looked Greene up and down. "Like most other fools, you learned one lesson out there, I can see."—"I did, sir?" "Ay, you are prinked out like a lousy dancing master. Saints help us! these velvets and silks, these reds and yellows— why don't you cut your hair a bit shorter?" Greene remembered not to pat his well-dressed locks. "I thought it suited me, sir," he confessed. Harrison shook his head. "You look more like a sunset than a man. Go to court like that—I don't know whether they will throw stones at you or make you a gentleman of the chamber. They are idiots enough to do either." He asked a number of questions about Italy. "You sought out the men of note wherever you visited?" It was necessary to explain. "I know, I know. Bawdy-house to tavern, tavern to bagnio, back to bawdy-house again—the same miserable story! You thought London looked dull, did you, when you got back?" But Greene spoke well and long about the glories of his native land, and would not have that it yielded to anywhere in the world.

On his return the next day Sir John asked him his plans. By this time Greene was growing used to the idea that there were plenty of helpers in the world and that something would be done for him again. Sir John might still be in need of a secretary—might he? He was disabused. "You must go back to the University. This city is cluttered with half-taught cubs like you, who all think there is nothing left for them to know. Back to Cambridge for you, sir!"

If there were no immediate employment in London, this squared with Greene's own wishes. He saw himself a man of mark at the University, with tales to tell in spread ears, with freshmen proud of his company and masters quick to consult him. He asked Sir John whether he might have a letter to the Master, authorising him to take up his studies straightway and proceed to his examination that same summer. Sir John sourly agreed that he might, and that the sooner he was on his way the better.

He was at Cambridge within the week. His interview with the Master was less of a triumph than he had expected. Howland greeted him without fuss, read Sir John's letter, and said there would be no difficulty but that Greene must expect no special favour when examined. He must stand or fall by merit. Greene, who had expected to dazzle this home-staying man with a dozen racy reminiscences, agreed humbly that diligence was best, answered a couple of questions about Sir John, not himself, and was dismissed. He went to his old room to find Coppinger. Instead he found a stranger, a youngster the cradle side of twenty, lying on Greene's old bed, reading a pamphlet.

"I interrupt you," he said politely. "Does Edmund Coppinger keep this room still?"

The other swung his legs and stood up. "He does not. He herds with Eggerton, for community of soul."

"Hm," said Greene. "This is my old room. My name is Robert Greene, of Norwich."

The other was a brisk-moving young fellow, with a face both hard and cheerful. "My name is Thomas Nashe, of Lowestoft. I am at your service, sir. I have heard of you."

"Nothing but good, I trust. I am glad to make your acquaintance, Master Nashe. You are new here?"

"I have gathered no moss. This is my second year."

"Ah yes," said Greene tolerantly. "Second year to be sure." He looked around the room. "How little the immovable changes. I shall be your room-mate for the rest of the session, Master Nashe. I hope we shall be good friends."

Nashe hoped so too, and then Greene went off to find Coppinger. It was strange to be among these surroundings again, monastic after eager years. What roosters they were! Foot-tied nags in the home fields. Whilst he——

He knocked, and was invited to enter.

"Edmund!"

"Of all men under the blue sky—Robert Greene!"

"Good day, Master Greene," said Eggerton, greeting a friend's friend.

They embraced, stood off and looked at each other, embraced again. Greene felt his cheeks pouched up in a permanent and idiotic smile, goblinlike. There was no cold edge to Edmund's delight, and Eggerton like a good soul made excuses to leave them together. For the first time Greene really felt himself the traveller returned from far countries. This was how people should be: amazed, delighted, with torrents of questions and proper recognition of one's importance. He swelled.

"You find me changed, Edmund?"

"Older. As though Italy was exacting, Robert."

"She was. But I have lived—I've lived, Edmund. The things I've seen! The things I've done!" They stayed there

an hour talking, Greene being brought up to date with
College news, and in return talking with a vague magnificence about himself. Portington had gone down, Hadman
was dead, Criddle too. There had been a whiff of
plague through the town two years ago, it had taken
many. Callimet was still in residence, but grown wilder.
Coppinger shook his head: there was little hope for
Callimet.

"And you, Edmund?"

He had been elected to the Fellowship vacant after
Hadman. Congratulation followed—who was Hadman
to stand in a friend's light? As for Criddle—no, he could
hardly pretend to be sorry for Criddle. The fellow had had
him birched.

"You saw Sidley in Italy?"

Greene laughed awkwardly. "I met him, yes. In Venice.
We were together for a while. He left Genoa before I did.
I think little of him now, Edmund. You were in the right,
I know that now."

"Then your Italian journey has not been without profit.
I tell you, Robert, I feared for you that year he was in
residence."

"You are my best friend!"

Edmund smiled. "But the discipline is worse, Robert.
I don't know what the end will be. What room are you
in?"

"The old one. I found a youngster named Nashe
there."

"Nashe—I know him. An acid-toothed baby but not
among the worst. I heard him tell the Master he hopes
to become the English Juvenal. He would!—just sixteen
years old, his brain like a handful of spiders, as much
knowledge of the world as a sucking-pig. Juvenal!"

Greene laughed with him. "We all know everything at
that age, Edmund. I was as bad myself. But I am still at
the University, still proceeding *eggregie dunsus* to a master's
degree." He did not get the denial he wanted, so changed
his tune. "The difference three years make——"

He spoke about them at length: how much wiser he was.

He found it easy to take up his University life again. The two years of sound study he had shared with Coppinger stood him in good stead now, and matters learned and not entirely forgotten were quickly fresh again. And he had Coppinger's guidance whenever he needed it. His mind was nimble and acquisitive, he had the examination trick of so mastering subjects for a given day that a month later he might never have heard of them, he could put his thin store into big barns. His greatest temptation to idleness was young Nashe, always prepared to listen, though sometimes sardonically, to his tales of Italy. For his sake Greene drew on his imagination and recorded all he would like to have done as faithfully as much of what he had. He could be freer with him than with Edmund. Nashe made no objection to girls and knives and cards. When at last Greene condescendingly told him that he had in his bag a tale on the model of Achilles Tatius he begged to be allowed to read it, and soon confided in him that it was his ambition to make one more poet for England. He was thus the first judge of the second part of *Mamillia*. It was upon a hint from this bright youngster that he inserted into the body of the work some deplorable hexameters against the women of Sicily; and it was he who spoke so highly of the old lines from Guazzo and approved their morality with all the earnestness of sixteen. He proposed before he left the University to show the folly of women, the brutishness of men, the evil of new ways, with more force than anyone since Juvenal. Verse or prose, it was all one to him. Greene found him a promising lad, especially when he made it clear he held Greene one of the hopes of the reign.

On the first of July he became a master of arts in the University; and six days later entered the second part of his *Mamillia* on the Register, from Clare Hall. He now made preparations for his visit home. The first time he had

seen them for three years. Then on to London and
fortune!

He was in Norwich by the middle of the month, to find
little changed save the size of the children. His father—
the same. And his mother. But it came as a shock to
find they had heard nothing of Alice and her husband since
the late summer of 1580. "We know nothing of your sister,"
said his father to his eager question, with "Neither do we
want to" implicit in the words. He stared from him to his
mother who hung her head, but not before he had seen her
sad eyes.

"Mother," he said to her later, "don't you want to know
about Alice?"

"She has never sent us word or come to see us, Robin.
What can we do?"

"But father ought to go and look for them."

"Your father won't, Robin."

He knew that tone of miserable acquiescence with what
her husband thought fit. "Well, I'm going back to London
this autumn. I'll find out something about them, mother."

"You won't go away as soon as that, will you?"

He laughed at her alarm. "I have my way to make in
the world, mother."

"I know. You have been a good boy too—the way
you have done things. I know how proud your father is
of you."

"Yes. But you will make me conceited with praise,
mother."

He found she was glad to have someone to talk to about
Alice. "She's stronger-willed than you might think, Robin.
There is a lot of your father in Alice. If you do find out——"

"I shall let you know, mother, never fear."

"I wonder what her baby looks like by this time? He
would be near enough Susanna's age, if Susanna had lived.
You know, Robin," she went on, wiping her hands clean
before mixing dough, "that is the worst of it—we don't
know what may be happening to them."

"They are safe enough, mother. I remember the first time I set eyes on Copson—'That's a reliable man,' I said. I said it to father and Alice at the Howard Arms in King's Lynn. He is just the sort to do well for himself and for Alice too. He is probably a steward by now." He skirted past his old lies. "Out in the west, where they went——" He coughed.

She was filled with horror to learn he had been stabbed at Genoa, and he had to bare his back for her to see the scar. "Doesn't it hurt?"

"Only when there is rain about," he explained, like a veteran of the wars. "It will take more than a dirty-nosed Genoese to kill me."

"You must not talk about killing, Robin. It is unlucky. You can laugh, but there was Henry Hutchins up at the Market only two years ago——" She recounted the fate of the unhappy Hutchins, and the ominous words that had made it remembered.

He was staying at home till the end of August. He told his father he was certain to get secretarial work with Sir John Harrison, who had taken him to Italy. Yes, Sir John thought very highly of him, and well he might. He had no wish to boast, but speaking between ourselves, father— he invented an episode to show the worth of his services to Sir John. "You found Italy all it is said to be, Robert?" "There is much exaggeration, father." "Oh well, if you are set on going to London I suppose you will have to." Greene was afraid to ask about his sister.

One thing he did owe to himself. He must visit the Red Lion. Mistress Petherill would be, let me see, he counted: thirty-two in '78, she'd be thirty-eight now. Some women were neat enough at thirty-eight, but he warned himself against too high expectations. He dressed in his yellow and red one afternoon, spent twenty-five minutes brushing his hair and beard, asked his father for some money, and set off for the inn. In the fields he laughed at the boy Robert going that way, dry-mouthed, afraid of the woman, afraid of his own shadow in love. Since then, what a change!

He took out a small mirror and after a quick glance to see whether anyone could see him admired himself in it. He was content to admit it—he was a handsome man. Tags from his letters to her, his poems about her, ran through his head, and he jeered at some of them and thought others good enough for future use. He had been a precocious lad and no mistake. Perhaps the Grand Master of Pandonus and the wise Forbrantine, Culius the curiously-learned and the almost divine Menocrates had stood at his shoulder that last month and helped him to his degree. Between them they should be able to rout the members of the examining board. He stroked his beard, admired its softness; he would let Neaera see what she had missed.

He did not visit Nat this time but went straight into the familiar taproom. Exactly as he had expected it: the tables in the same places, the same benches, the same drinkers, the same drawer attending to them. He called for wine and set his bonnet on the table. Near him sat a young man, five or six years his senior, whose face was familiar to him. They looked at each other for a moment or two, and then remembered simultaneously.

"It's young Robert Greene!"

"It's Adam Bolton!"

In the hope of impressing the bumpkins and Adam, Greene threw a snatch of Italian before him and then they shook hands. Where had they been? Bolton was impressed in a most gratifying manner when he heard of Greene's travels. He himself, as Greene had long expected, had settled down in Norwich as an imitation gentleman. But he was as harmless as ever, and made Greene laugh good-temperedly at his boastful nods and winks. He was still the same mad wag, the same Old Adam. He couldn't help it if he had the best horses and dogs in the county, and if his cellar was the best in Norwich, and as for the girls, well—he made brushing motions of his hands, like a man plagued with flies—a smirk, a nod, a wink, damn, he supposed there was something about him, that was the way of it. He explained to Robert—he did not mind if he called him Robert?—he explained that there was a quality, and either you had it or you hadn't, and he had it. "I try to keep them off, Robert, but you know how it is— you are a fine-looking fellow yourself. Remember that Constant woman?" He showed Greene that he lived as pleasantly in the past as the present. "Remember how we used to have a drop to drink, Robert? How you used to write that poetry? Blood of Christ, Robert, you were a clever youngster. As for me, I never worked at the learning. Always after pleasure, Robert—like a duck to water or a pig to swill. Pleasure always at hand. How long you staying in Norwich, eh?" He thought he might take a trip to London too. The girls in Turnbull Street, the sign of Blind Cupid— but there, Robert would know all about it himself. "How is your sister, Robert?" In London, she too? "Isn't it surprising the way folk get about? Ten years ago, look how we were all in Norwich, and since then where we've been. It is remarkable when you come to think of it, Robert."

But where was Mistress Petherill? Where the peerless Neaera? He was not dressed in red and yellow every day of the week. "That's a fine outfit you are wearing, Robert. Is that the Italian cut?" Greene took some trouble over his answer, displayed his sleeves and stockings, the shape of his shoes. "But the shoes I saw in Venice, Adam— you'd hardly credit it. On the courtesans there." Adam's ears seemed to move forward like a dog's when he hears a knife sharpening. "Let's have our own room upstairs, Robert. We can talk better there."

They went up to a room looking out on to the yard. He saw Nat come out from the stable, leading by the hand a little boy and girl. He looked a lump of good earth, and English. "These courtesans now, Robert?" Ah yes. Nat looked just right in his setting. Those must be his two children. Those times when he and Nat and the Wotton boys and the Hayshams from Bratton used the trick of the dice—it occurred to him that Adam had a long purse and might pay for attention the month he had in Norwich. "Yes, Adam, as I was saying——"

They sent down for more wine—at least, Adam did.
"No, no, Robert—the wanderer returned—we can't let
him pay for his drink. I may not have been to London for
a year or two, but we keep our manners down here, Robert.
So they don't wear anything except this veil, you say,
down to the waist, eh? What a country it must be, Robert!
Nothing widens the mind like travel. I don't know that it
wouldn't be worth while yet for me to go abroad. I've got
money enough, of course. I'll never want for that, Robert."

They drank off that bottle and sent for another. "Now,
in Florence, Robert—what would you say was the most
remarkable thing you saw in Florence?" Before Greene
finished telling him, they were both calling it "Flawnce."

They had more wine. "Now, talk'n 'bout Ven'sh 'gain,
Robert——"

"Well, in Ven'sh you shee—when you get Ven'sh in
firsh plaish sh'all warrer, shee Adam!"

"Mosh' remarkable!"

"Yesh, sh'rather remarkable, as you shay. Now, as I
was shaying——"

"Mosh' remarkable, Robert. Sh' mosh' remarkable
thing I ever heard, Robert."

"Yesh, it ish remarkable, Adam!"

"Mosh' remarkable! I don' remember ever hearing
anything more remarkable."

"Thash right, Adam."

After a time their conversation gave out and they felt
very sleepy. However, they shook this off and decided they
must make for home. "You'll come along with me, Robert?"

"What about your mother, Adam?"

"Dead," said Adam sadly. "She'sh dead, Robert. I'm
an orphan, thash what I am, Robert." He shed a tear.

Yet they sang in harmony as they left the Red Lion and
crossed the fields. Each felt the other the second most
remarkable man in the world. It was surprising how that
adjective kept recurring. They sang as they entered the
town, and through the streets to Adam's house, and created
a stir. Greene in red and yellow was no inconspicuous

figure sober; drunk he was noticeable at cannon-range. For such burghers as he saw he felt the contempt of the man who has been to Italy. He snapped his fingers once, and tried to snap them a dozen times.

He remembered little of what happened at Bolton's. There was more to drink, and he had the fuddled recollection that they both grew smuttily confidential. Anyhow, it could not count as sin, for they knew not what they did. But next morning, waking to find himself in Bolton's house, he had a salutary fright. What would his father say? No doubt he would know already. It was a pity he had to account for every action, a grown man like him. And what a difference it made to be home! As he explained to Adam, in Italy or London a man was a man; at home, a child. "At least," said Adam, "you are not an orphan."

Approaching his own home, he half wished he were. His mother's grief or his father's anger—which would a man the sooner bear? And he a grown man, stabbed in the back, gone on diplomatic missions to Italy.

"Well, mother," he said reasonably, when he entered the atmosphere of disgrace, "it's no good looking at me like that. I suppose you've heard?"

Yes, they had heard.

"Well, mother, you know how it is. We all make mistakes now and again. I can only say I'm sorry."

He managed to win Jane round to his side by throwing the blame on Adam Bolton. "I don't know what sort of wine he bought, mother, but it knocked me down in an hour. I haven't been drinking for so long, that must have been the cause—that and the heat." Once on this tack he remembered he had felt queer earlier in the day. From his wound, it might be. In any case, it would be unfair and unmotherly to blame him.

"But, Robin, you mustn't grow friendly with that Bolton man. You haven't forgotten what happened when you first came home drunk, have you? And you only fifteen. You'll promise?"

He promised. "How has father taken it?"

With a brow like Rising Castle, his mother told him. "Where is he now, mother?"

He was in the shop.

"Then I think I'll keep out of his way for a bit. You might just tell him how I felt though."

They met during the afternoon. Greene was hoping to slip out of doors (he had wanted no dinner), but by bad luck found his father airing himself at the time. He saw that famous brow. He had to listen to a sermon and sad reproof, knowing all the time that Old Vose was eavesdropping three yards away. When at last he walked off he was rebellious and even contemptuous. If he wanted to see Adam Bolton and let the ass pay for his wine, he would do so.

He did, a number of times, and he went out to the Red Lion again before the week was out. This time he saw Mistress Petherill, and being not without standards thought her a pleasant piece. Old Goring had not been such a bad judge. With Bolton he discussed her as though she were a prize cow and they the umpires. They decided they ought to possess her in turns, but the reality was she wanted neither of them. She took the wind out of Greene's sails by remarking that he was quite grown up now; and when, to sustain his reputation with the Old Adam, he tried to snatch a kiss, she eluded him without difficulty and was away from the room. They found excuses easily enough, and drank more than they wanted to, to keep reputation. Englishmen were expected to come back from Italy ruined in mind and body, to drink between drinks, to devour women like blackberries, to be fantastic in behaviour, quick with an oath, quicker with a weapon; so for Adam's benefit Greene acted a part. Lewdness and blasphemy were the staples of his talk; he was ranker than the Red Lion midden.

He found Nat below him now. He would have spoken to him had it been possible for their talk to be in private, but the first time Nat saw him was as he entered the inn yard with Adam Bolton. He touched his forelock, muttered

"Good-even to 'ee, masters"; Greene said "Ah, it's you, Nat, is it?" and that was all. So he made no inquiry about Susan and the children, and was guilty to know it. Still, Nat cared not a bean. He knew his place and was content to keep it.

In this way the days drew on till he must leave for London.

"And if you get no employment?" his father asked.

"I'll not trouble you again. I am launched on the world, father. From now on I sink or swim myself."

"We shall see," his father replied, as one far from convinced.

But his mother said: "You will let me know about Alice, Robin?" He promised. "And you'll not stay away so long?" "Not this time, mother." "When will you be home then?" He shuffled. "It's hard to say. It depends on so many things, mother. But you must not be miserable when I'm gone. I shall be thinking of you just as I was in College and in Italy."

CHAPTER XXI

When he reached London before the weather broke he had almost three pounds in his pocket. This was to last him till he found good employment and settled down to a useful way of life. At Cambridge he had once more received Coppinger's good wishes and an invitation to call on his father who lived near St. Botolph's, but for a time at least he had no intention of doing this. For sentimental reasons he stayed at the Glove, in Paul's Chain, and waited only one day before paying his respects to Sir John Harrison. Setting eyes on him: He'll not be a patron for long, he thought disappointedly. Though the weather was far from cold and a big fire burning in the grate, he was muffled up; his shoulders folded inwards across his chest; he spat continually into a jar at his side and wiped his mouth with small squares of linen. He waved aside Greene's well-wishing with contempt.

"You had no more sense then than to return?" He shook his head so like a bird that Greene imagined him rooting into his feathers for livestock. "And now, like the rest of the young men, you'll be expecting me to do something for you, eh? Well, maybe I will, and maybe I won't. You know, young man—or perhaps you are too much of a fool to know—it seems a great thing to become a knight, to blossom forth a dingy flower among these stocks and stones, to dangle in court-attendance like a thin chain round a fat woman's neck—it seems a great thing to some of you——" He had to spit and did not go on with what he was saying. "I'll see if I can recommend you. In the meantime, what can you do for yourself?"

"I thought to write, Sir John."

"God help us, you did, eh? To become one of a crowd of farthing-candle hirelings, and rub shoulders with players, beggars, rogues, rascals?"

"I thought——"

"And what did you think with? I tell you now: If your ambition is to write, you are condemning yourself to poverty and neglect at the best, to persecution and defilement the likeliest."

"But I thought, Sir John—men like Master Edmund Spenser, Master Lyly, Sir Philip Sidney, Sir Walter—men at Court, men in Her Majesty's employ, their praises in everybody's mouth—it seems to me there is honour and profit in following such as these."

Sir John shook his head. "For one happy, a hundred miserable. For one who prospers, a thousand who starve. Edmund Spenser, you say—have you an Earl of Leicester to help you? Sir Philip—have you wealth and family? Sir Walter—I think it still a question whether the Western Hemisphere will be kinder to Sir Walter than to his cousin Gilbert, and his heart lies there, however much he plays with sonnets for the goddess of his life. As for your Master Lyly—is he still in fashion?" He waved aside Greene's attempt to speak. "I know little of these matters. But what I do know speaks loudly against the folly of writing."

With this Greene had to be satisfied. He met Somerset once more, was complimented on his changed appearance, but so changed the drift of their talk that he discovered Sir John never went to Court and that he had seen little of influential men this year or two. This was something to think over. What would he do if Sir John could not help him after all?

Then there was the finding of Alice and Copson. Apart from a chance discovery, he had no idea how he might get into touch with them. In a city so mighty it was difficult even to begin. London sprawled like a world of its own from the Abbey to Hog Lane, from the river to St. Giles's, to Clerkenwell, to Shoreditch. Why, there must be a quarter of a million people there! He explored it those days of early winter, tramping scores of miles, mapping it in his mind, setting the points of its compass. His was the thrill of travellers in virgin forest or over windy plain, among the stark

mountains or the thin-finger valleys. He sought for the
heart of the town like Spaniard for El Dorado. One morning
he set out from Paul's Chain for Westminster, the next for
the Minories or the Bars beyond Aldgate; one day it was the
open windmill-dotted fields of Finsbury, the next the packed
rottenness of Little Britain. From the noblemen's palaces
facing the Thames to the crazy hovels of the poor he went,
from the gaiety of mansions to the furtive misery of slums;
he saw the inns, the shops, the markets, hospitals, churches
and gates. The fleshless heads on London Bridge, the bellowing of bulls at the baitings south of the river, the rapacious
buying and selling of Smithfield, the wherries, the drays,
the lions at the Tower, these became part of his London
in short time. The coloured bustle around Whitehall,
where insolence and servility went gay in silks and furs;
the green emptiness of Spitalfields, where honest men went
not after mid-December dusk; the furtive greyness of Turnbull Street, the lair of vicious drabs—he knew them all.
And from the hundred extremes of this queen among
cities he felt the pulse of blood, the throbbing of a heart,
the stirring of unforgettable, tangible life. Venice, yes.
The pride of wealth, of luxury, of ostentation, city of palaces,
Venus of the blue water, brilliant under the hot sun. And
Florence—where yellow Arno crawled under her red bridges
and between the red-brown homes of princes. Genoa too—
these gave sharp memories like the turning of a blade
by firelight, but now he would love London. With rain,
with snow, with mist, with heavy skies—like a hive, like
an ant-hill, this heart of the coming nation. Great men to
pass in the streets, Burghley, Walsingham, Haddon, statesmen like cherries on a harvest branch; captains of ships
back from the edge of the world, from freezing in infernos
worse than Ugolino's, from roasting under copper skies,
from peoples red, black, yellow and brown; Hawkins,
Frobisher, Cavendish, Drake—who knew when he would
jostle them in the streets? The square-built stranger you
followed down Forster Street might be mercer or mercenary;
that haggard beggar you threw a coin to—why, the amazing

thing was that his tale might be true, he might well have lost his leg to a cannon ball and his thumbs to the Inquisition. And it was here in London that Whitgift was grinding remorseless as the mills of God at non-conformists, dragging them from conventicles, flinging men like hens into the Clink, into Newgate or the Marshalsea, botching up sentences while they putrefied in prison, the universal butcher. Hear one side of the question from one man, the reverse from another: argument, anger, remonstrance, gibe. Blows. And as for foreign news—more here in a week than at Norwich in a twelvemonth. Alençon cooling off, poor little monkey, and who's the next fool for a royal marriage? Spanish forces moving towards the Flanders coast, the French Mary meditating war, the Scottish Mary meditating death; reports from Ireland that by the year's end two thousand men of rank rooted out, Desmond slaughtered on his own hearth-stone, humbler men stamped into their bogs to suffocate, babes crying for the breast silenced by heavy English heels; death, death, death to all but true-born Englishmen and their allies. And men conscious they were part of a great movement; that infallibly and in the teeth of Spain and Papacy, a great future lay ahead for Englishmen, and that it would call for blood, for death, for sacrifice. And most men willing and ready to cry "Long Live the Queen!" Even the poor devils her victims, many of them, lifting up their bleeding stumps, groping for their cropped ears.

Greene, his money growing steadily less, moved through all this. He had no employment as the winter wore on. Still, if a man was careful—he made calculations. Soon Sir John would be better, or dead, and then something must be done. But how find Copson and Alice?

He met an old acquaintance towards Christmas—John Hunter, the soldier who had bested Sidley at the Mitre the time they grew acquainted with Tartary-Harrison. This time too the meeting took place in a tavern. Hunter knew him at once, knew his face at least, and spoke the first word. Of course Greene remembered him! They laughed together at past history. Yes, Hunter knew Sir John was in town. Yes, he knew he was low in health. Yes, he thought he would die that winter. Pooh, he could tell—he'd seen plenty go the same way. "It's a maggot you get in your bones in China, Master Greene—a little yellow maggot, wouldn't be bigger than a dog's eyelash, but he eats his way right to the spine, for the marrow of course, and then you waste away." Drinking at Greene's expense the soldier of fortune told stories, probably invented, of episodes in Sir John's service, with no hampering details of day or place. And the young fellow who broke the bottle? He heard that Greene had been to Italy. Yes, he had been to Italy himself, two years' campaigning with the Papal Guard. He laughed at Greene's surprise. "They pay well enough, and there are times when that is the first thing you look to." He had another drink at Greene's expense, and soon had called over a couple of his friends. Greene was so pleased with Hunter's account of his, Greene's, behaviour when first they met, that he stood them all a drink before he had time to count the cost. Still, he felt repaid by the excellence of the conversation that followed and before they parted with good-will had made up his mind to become a soldier and probably a lord-general. It was the next morning, counting his money and finding himself six precious shillings out of pocket, that he knew with a change of companions his ambitions might well have been to become a sailor and probably a lord-admiral.

This same month he made a couple of only half-determined attempts to obtain service with men of rank, but he was abashed by the competition that must be faced. As Sir John had told him, London seemed full of pen-wipers, and he came to consider the prospect of raising a loan and returning to Norwich and saddlery after all. This was detestable; he blinked his eyes and counted his money again. Finally, a few days before Christmas, his money almost run out, he remembered Coppinger's parents and thought he would lose nothing by calling on them. It was not impossible Edmund himself might be there, and he had never borrowed a penny from Edmund yet.

So on the twenty-second of December he left the Glove Inn and went by way of Friday Street into Cheapside and so along that splendid thoroughfare to Cornhill, and through Aldgate past the church to the Coppinger's house near the Bars. There were a dozen small shops before he reached it, projecting forward into the street from the houses which rose two and sometimes three floors above them, and lighted by large, protected windows in the roofs. Loitering, with the uncertainty of the man not quite sure he should be about his errand, he was tempted to buy by some of the shopkeepers, but shook his head. He might be in a better position to spend on his way back.

He made an inquiry of a shopkeeper, and then a second to make sure, and then he was knocking at the door. "A friend of Master Edmund Coppinger's," he announced himself to the soberly-dressed servant who appeared, and was shown in at once. It was Edmund himself who appeared first, to Greene's surprised delight, and his own. There was hardly time for a greeting, and then—"Mother! Father!" he was calling; "Here's a visitor! Here is Robert Greene!" It was certainly a flattering welcome. Charles Coppinger was a man almost fifty years of age, a little older than his wife. He was obviously Edmund's father, the same build, features, bearing. Charity Coppinger was such a kindly woman as Greene's own mother, and at first he found her undistinguished. There was such a swirl of questions too. Had he eaten? Had he come far? Was he cold? He would stay with them? The father and mother left the young men together as soon as they well could. "You'll want to be talking," said Charity.

"Do we?" Edmund asked, smiling.

They clashed on the same exclamation. "You here, of all the world!" And then they found nothing likelier. Why shouldn't Edmund be in his own house at Christmas? And hadn't Robert promised to call there?

They talked for almost an hour without interruption. Greene told of his lack of success in London. "I haven't earned half a pistole, Edmund. Half a pistole, I said? Not a penny. Not the price of a lead button. They don't want me, Edmund. I don't know why. I thought——" He broke off to ask: "But what are you doing away from Cambridge? I didn't expect to find you here. Why then?"

For once Greene knew he was getting not a lie but less than the truth. "I just came," Coppinger told him. "I had not set eyes on my parents for a long time. I needed a change of air and company. Those handsome College walls, sometimes they hem a man in. And I had some business to attend to." He gestured. "So here I am."

Greene drew a long bow. "I hear that the Archbishop is a bad man," he said insinuatingly, and then was ashamed of himself and wished he had not spoken. He tried to turn it into a jest. "At least he has done nothing for me."

"There is so much we must do for ourselves, Robert," Coppinger told him gravely.

This made Greene not so comfortable. There was a criticism in the words, he felt. "I know," he agreed. "But I'll make a start soon, Edmund, never fear."

"I meant nothing." Without much skill Coppinger changed the subject. "So Harrison will die, you think?"

Later they went into a handsome room for a meal, and Greene was invited to stay with them over the next week or ten days. Edmund was now all smiles again, and he was glad to accept. They would walk back to the Glove, the two of them, and fetch along the few things Greene would have need of. Greene preferred this arrangement to sending a man, and after the meal and grace they set off.

"I am sorry for what I said about Whitgift, Edmund," Greene had the fairness to say, as they were walking. "I must learn to mind my own business more."

Coppinger waved his hand. "It is forgotten. And I like the man, Robert, no more than the rest who think my way. That is no secret. Sometimes a man thinks—the same kind of thing you thought, no doubt—it is a poor thing to live behind a fellowship when the world has need of one. I know this, Robert, that before long there will be need of men to testify to what they believe and hold dear. What will we do then?" he ended abruptly.

Greene swung his hands together. "I shall most certainly do nothing, Edmund, and all politic men will do the same."

"But all men, thank God, are not politic. If England has Whitgift, she has had Hooper; if Scotland had Beaton, so too she has had Patrick Hamilton and George Wishart; from Wales came Anthony Kitchen and William Hughes, but will men ever forget that she gave us Rawlings White? These men were not afraid. And I remember now how so short a time ago John Copping and Elias Thacker were hanged at Bury St. Edmunds because they would not profess what they did not believe."

Coppinger's words buffeted Greene's ears like a roaring wind. "We'll not speak of it, Edmund!"

"I cannot see why not. Can any man doubt the way the faithful must tread? We are near a persecution as severe as the Marian. If a man's faith——"

"We'll not speak of it!"

Coppinger looked sideways at Greene. He knew his friend afraid for him. In his heart there welled up pity for he knew not what—in part a self-pity that he later despised as weakness. This fair world all around one, the goodness of God—and men must spoil it all. "Very well, Robert," he said; "we'll say no more, if you would have it that way."

For a while they walked without speaking, but through Greene's brain roared the devil's pun: Hanged at St. Edmunds, John Copping and Elias Thacker, *Edmunds*, *Copping*, *Edmund Copping*, *Edmund Coppinger!* And again to mind came the picture of Coppinger that night at College before Sidley came. "I have God on my side," said Coppinger, his face a-glow. And the vision of martyrdom came again, wrenching Greene near sickness, before he could look at Coppinger and pass some trivial remark about the street they were walking along.

It was before he left the Coppingers' that he found Copson. It was the accidental meeting he had now pretty well forgotten to hope for. Who knows, he told Coppinger, whether he and Alice are in London at all? And Copson was such a capable fellow. He'd manage, if anyone could. Yet he always ended, it would be cheering to know things were well with them. And now on the last day of the year but one he turned into a shop in Bucklersbury to buy a pennyworth of ginger as a sweetmeat and there was Copson waiting to serve him. "I want——" he had begun to the bent back, and then he gaped as the other stood upright and turned to him. "Great God above us, it's you, Copson!"

In a way it was like his meeting with Sidley in Venice. "Yes," said Copson, with more wariness than enthusiasm, and Greene even in his excitement noticed the deliberation with which he was regarding him. "I've been searching for you all over London," he said inaccurately; "But where is Alice?"

"She's very well," Copson replied, more or less evading the question.

They shook hands. "You help here?" Greene asked suddenly.

"No," said Copson grimly, as though reading his thoughts. "It is my shop." He looked around, following Greene's eyes. "You have a shopkeeper for a brother."

"As though I care!" retorted Greene magnanimously. He picked up a small package as though not aware what he was doing. "I—er—But where is Alice? Where is *she*?"

"She is out visiting," said Copson.

"Ah!" He put years of longing into his exclamation without in the least impressing Copson. "By Jupiter, I can hardly wait to see her!"

"You will have to," said Copson.

"And the boy? How is the boy?"

"There's nothing wrong with the boy. He is out too, with his mother."

"But, Copson, tell me, what have you been doing these three years and more? And where have you been? How long have you had the shop? And how did you manage when Alice came up to London that time?"

"It's a long story," said Copson, and rubbed his chin.

Greene was peering forward. "You look older too."

"So do you."

"Yes, of course, I've had a busy time these past years. What with Italy, affairs at Cambridge and home, and the last six months in London." He laughed briefly. "Yes, I suppose I do look older."

"Yes, you do."

They were still standing in the shop. Why didn't Copson ask him into the house above and behind? Strange, surely! "You live here?" he asked.

"Yes." Copson was evidently taking no hints.

Greene felt thoroughly dissatisfied. "How long have you been here?"

"Here is a buyer," Copson broke in, and he left Greene standing idly while he attended to an elderly woman. Greene watched him weigh out a portion of spice. Wrapping up ha'porths for all comers—Good God!

The elderly woman went. He tried to look busy. "Then I'll call back to see Alice?" he asked.

"It had better be to-morrow," said Copson, moving towards the door.

"You'll tell Alice?"

"I will."

Greene had a feeling that he was being turned off the threshold. He was irritated in the extreme as he turned left past the church into Bearbinder Lane, and puzzled too. What an afternoon!

So he exclaimed to Coppinger an hour later. He explained why. "I just walked in, Edmund, and there he was! An odd thing, though—I never think of him by his Christian name, Edmund." He thought a moment. "Hang me, he never even asked after my father and mother. What d'you make of that?" He proceeded to talk a lot without saying much.

Next day he was at Bucklersbury by eight o'clock. He

thought excitedly: I am going to see Alice! He felt his heart thumping.

This was the shop. Alice!

"Where is she?"

Copson opened a door. "Alice!"

He heard a cry in answer.

"It's your brother. It's Robert!"

He motioned Greene inside, and it was immediately behind the shop he met his sister. "Alice! Is it really you?" He felt ridiculous because of the break in his voice. By God, he loved this sister! "Why, Robin! Robin!" They flung their arms round each other.

"I haven't been called Robin since I left home," he said at last.

"Home! Oh, how is mother?"

"She wants to see you, Alice. You've never been! Why haven't you been? Why haven't you been to see her, Alice?"

"Not because I don't love her. I've thought about her —you don't know how I've thought about her!"

"But why——"

"I know I haven't been. It's the way things turn out, Robert."

"Didn't I say——"

"Robin, then!" She took his arm and led him into the little living room above the shop. "You look stouter, Robin."

"They have been telling me that all my life. I am not the only one either!" He held her off at arm's length. "You do look well, Alice!"

The girl had become a woman, fine and full-grown. He thought that maybe some of the old brightness was dying down inside her. But that was only because she appeared calmer and married.

She laughed. "It's not because I get an easy time. But Robin, it seems no more than yesterday since I saw you last."

"Not to me, Alice. More like an eternity ago. You can't think how I looked for you and your husband!"

"You did?"

He let a gesture answer for him. It embraced half the world. "And mother is well?" she asked again.

"She doesn't grumble, as you know. Father is very trying sometimes, I imagine."

"Poor mother!"

"You ought to go and see her, Alice. Why in heaven's name haven't you?"

She manœuvred him into the shop before he could press for an answer, and there the talk was mostly of Greene. It did not occur to him that the conversation was being managed for his benefit, and with one or two interruptions because of people coming in to be served he gave them a detailed but not full account of all that had happened to him since he last saw Alice at Cambridge. But he was not too taken up with himself to miss their glances when he mentioned Sidley—peculiar glances they were too. Sidley's father, he thought, and his share in bringing about their present situation——

"And what about you?" he asked at last.

He saw another exchange of glances. "I'll tell you upstairs," said Alice, and Copson nodded.

Back in the living room Alice said: "You have never seen John yet, have you?"

No, he hadn't.

"He is in next door with the neighbours' children. Wait here and I'll fetch him."

He waited an unexpectedly long time, and wondered whether she was talking with her husband in the shop. He had come to feel there was some mystery in the air. Then she returned, carrying the child.

"Is he like you or Geoffrey?" he asked jocularly.

"You had better look." She held him up. "John, here is your uncle Robin."

"Hullo, John," he said affably. "Great God, Alice!"

She watched his face with a hardness he had never suspected in her. "Well?"

"But, Alice, this is not——"

"Stay here." She turned and took the child from the room, as he thought to Copson in the shop.

"Well?" she asked again, when she returned.

"Alice, may God judge me, I don't know what to say! I've stood here—— This is Sidley's child! You never let that dirty little brat——"

"You have changed your mind about him, then?"

He walked across the room. "I am ashamed of you! I never expected to see the day——"

"The less you say, the better. It is all ancient history to me. I need no telling from you or anyone else. And I'm sick to death of you men and your damned righteousness! You are the same as your fine father, I can see!"

"Great God, it's not a matter of self-righteousness! It's a matter of ordinary decency. Anyone can see that."

She looked so furious he felt half afraid of her. This placid woman, as he judged her. "Will you listen?"

"To let a fellow like that—a common whoremonger— have his way with you! I'd rather see you in your grave, as God's above me I would!"

"There was no letting," she said bluntly. Her words crashed like blows to his head and heart. "If you know what words mean, then know your good friend raped me!"

He could hardly realise what she was saying. Then he began swearing dreadful oaths, invoking hell and damnation, using the language of the stews. If ever he set eyes on that blasted Sidley—he stamped up and down the room, saying the things he felt he ought to say, and for a time she listened, thinking how like his sex he was with his useless heroics, controlling her own temper that she might the better manage his. "Will you listen to me?" she asked suddenly, dragging him back to reality.

He sat down. Then he stood up again. "And that weak-kneed bastard of a husband of yours——"

She slapped his face till his head rang. "Don't you dare say such a thing!" she choked. "You—you——" She could think of nothing bad enough to meet his case.

And then he wanted to laugh. It was all so silly—so unutterably silly. The stage had shown nothing like this. His cheek was stinging most painfully. He sat down once more.

"Will you listen?"

He rubbed his face tenderly. "Half London must be listening, I should say. Go on, Alice—tell me."

She began to tell him about what had happened at Braiding, calm enough now. Then on to her arrival in London and her finding her husband at the Glove Inn— "Yes, where I've been staying," he muttered—and the steps they took to safeguard their future. How Copson had failed to enter a great household, and so, instead of letting their money dwindle to nothing, he had bought this shop and made a living out of it ever since.

"Did it cost much?"

"Geoffrey was not a foundling," she answered sharply.

He grunted.

"And that is all. Except that you know now why I have never gone back home." She watched his wiseacre nod. "And two years ago I had a second baby."

"Why, Alice, I'm sorry!"

"It died within a month. You said something against Geoffrey just now, Robin——" He shuffled. "Never mind. There must be plenty who have said hard things about him. They don't matter, after all. He stood by me when no one else would—I haven't forgotten it. That is why"—she began to cry—"that is why I'm sorriest his own boy died."

"Don't cry, Alice! I didn't know what I was saying."

"He has not had as much as he deserves—Geoffrey. That is all." She cried quietly for a time, and her brother felt his own tears womanishly near. "Well, that is our story, Robin."

"Never mind, Alice." He kissed her cheek. "You may have a dozen children yet, and you can call them all Geoffrey!"

She laughed a little at that. "I may," she agreed. "But it's a long time now, Robin."

"It must be that husband of yours," he jested, and more laughter eased them. "I'll tell him, never fear."

They went down to the shop together. Copson was there on his own. "John is next door," he told them, looking only at Alice.

Greene felt a gesture was expected of him. He held out his hand. "I am coming back for a talk to-morrow, Geoffrey." He found it easier now to use his brother-in-law's name. "You've been good to Alice. I want you to know——" He found he had no words ready, Copson looked so tired and happy, so he gripped hands hard, kissed Alice, and set off for St. Botolph's, walking fast and importantly, and thinking confusedly over all he had heard. "Great God," he said aloud, "what a world it is!"

CHAPTER XXII

When, more than a month later, his wife told him her brother had asked whether he might come and lodge with them, Copson was displeased. He did not much like Greene, he was sorry he had ever found them out, and he detested the idea he might now come into contact with the rest of the family. "Has he any money?" he asked suspiciously. It appeared he had not. "Hm. When relatives seek us out," he grumbled. She retorted that it was unworthy of them to bother about a few shillings a week; he shrugged his shoulders and held his peace; and for an hour or two they were constrained.

"All right, Alice," he said at last, coming into the living room, "let him come if you like—only for God's sake don't you and I quarrel again."

"He will soon be gone," she consoled him. "I don't know how it is——"

For she was glad to see her brother again, glad to see anyone who had news of Norwich. It was so long since last she had news of her mother and brothers and sisters. Poor Jane! How many times had she reproached herself for never letting her know, leaving her in sorrow and uncertainty. With a child herself she understood the longing of mothers, could guess the ache at Jane's heart, and yet it was always: No, we can't let them know; no, we can't go to see them; no, we don't even know if they are still alive. And so, oftentimes she was depressed and Copson irritable. Why not forget about them? he demanded. Had they not their own lives to live? Their success to dream of? Had he not given every minute of the day to her and hers? Anyone listening would think she had no one in the world to hear her sometimes! Sulks, passions, recriminations, they knew all these in the years that followed her flight to London. It was his burden that he loved her more than life itself and yet was not free from self-pity; hers, that she loved him and at times a little despised him. And her tongue could be a sharp one, and cruel to him. "Then why did you marry me?" she would ask him, in these quarrels. Infuriated though he might be, he had never made the ignoble, unforgivable retort, and after reconciliation she recognised this and hated her own meanness of spirit. Poor Geoffrey, dear Geoffrey, darling Geoffrey! he was all these then; she embraced him with as much love and protection as she did John, and swore to herself she would never again be unkind to him.

Was he happy? Sometimes she did not care. Sometimes she would have given him the sun from heaven in her gratitude. "Would you marry me if you had it all to do over again, Geoffrey?" He swore in these moods that he would, that he worshipped her, that he'd give his life for her with joy and pride. Holding each other, as that first night at Braiding, they felt only the glory of self-sacrifice, of suffering for each other, a great contempt for the world, the desire to live without it. But later would come new misunderstandings, lacerations of spirit, his anger, her contempt, she staying upstairs to nurse John and scorn her husband and herself, he down in the shop with the black adder round his heart. The mention of her home was the chief cause of these wretched quarrels. Bitterly he would think: Who at home would do for her what I did? What welcome would she get even now from her father? Why couldn't she be happy with him all the time? And now, if this brother of hers came to live with them, it must be worse. Talk about Norwich and the family, talk about any and every cursed thing except him and all he had done for her. And Greene was a fool. He had been to the University, he had found someone to pay for him to go to Italy, he felt himself of better clay than his brother-in-law. That first day in the shop—God and Paradise, he thought with equal resentment and contempt, that a fellow like that, a dressed-up College pudding, should put on airs with men like himself, who had been through a hot fire and not without burns. On the strength of two-pennyworth of book learning, some facile gab about places abroad, and a red and yellow suit of clothes. And now he must come to be carried on Copson's back. Damnation then, must he!

"All right, Alice—let him come if you like. Only for God's sake don't you and I quarrel any more!"

This new supply of food and shelter seemed heaven-sent to Greene. His money was quite exhausted, he had hung hopefully but in vain on his expectations from Sir John, and Coppinger had returned, unsolicited, to Cambridge, where Greene suspected he was to work at a tract for the times. So what more natural than to turn to your own family? Beggars were limited choosers, and something must come his way soon.

He did not hope that more than Copson. And the sooner the better.

He was with them in Bucklersbury for just over two months. By that time they were all, except young John, tired of the arrangement. The child was delighted with his uncle, who tossed him up into the air, rolled on the floor with him, told him stories, and took him out for walks. Not that Greene had any particular liking for children, but he thought it would please Copson and Alice if he made much of Sidley's child. All he did, however, was make Copson jealous. While he had to work in the shop and find food for their four bellies, that red and yellow oaf had to be dandling the boy upstairs till he thought more of him than his own father—for such Copson regarded himself. He made a grievance of it, the worse because he had to keep it to himself for fear of appearing foolish. And for conceit— had Greene his equal? Jabber-jabber about Italy—if he liked it so much why hadn't he stayed there? And these scribblings of his—how could a man waste time so when there was work to do in the world? Unless, of course, he had some poor fool to do the work for him. He smiled sourly, thinking himself that poor fool.

Alice too found eight weeks of Robert as much as she wanted. At first it was delightful to sit and talk of home and the past, to revive a thousand pleasant memories, but no one can be talking all the time, and Robert took surprisingly little interest in the past of anyone except himself. Here, true, he was prodigal of recollection. The things he had seen and done were sweet to his tongue—such as he chose to speak about, anyhow—but they were less sweet to other folks' ears. He seemed not fully to understand that she was very different from the girl who had listened to his ambitions those summer weeks at Grancher Beetham's, and that her experience was greater than his in those things that make character. Life at Braiding, the catastrophe and trials there, London, the winning of a livelihood, elemental child-birth and motherhood, marriage and wifehood—what had he to set against these to justify his airs? He had skimmed a score of dead books, had seen a dozen cities, had gone after the girls—some of them perhaps as ill-used and less fortunate than she herself—and that was all She couldn't very well tell him to go, but if he suggested it there would be no opposition.

As for Robert Greene—he was wasting precious time. He knew it. Copson didn't want him very much, that was easy to see, and once he got his money from the bookseller for the first part of *Mamillia*, he'd be off. He knew exactly what he was going to do. He was only waiting for money and fine weather, and then to Braiding to give Sidley the shock of his life. There was a strange border custom those Scottish undergraduates had told him about, the paying of Black Mail by farmers to buy off raids and persecution —he frowned, thinking that Sidley owed him something for that attack on his life, and this looked like the time to collect it. He tried to imagine the scene when they met. Did Sidley know he was still alive? He rubbed his hands together.

He felt little excitement over the publication of his first book, partly because he thought less of it than three years ago, partly because he had its sequel ready. Further, he was planning a work that should out-Lyly Lyly himself —*The Card of Fancy*. Yet he came home rather drunk one afternoon in mid-April to tell them he had been paid for *Mamillia* and that *The Card of Fancy* was to be entered on the Register. He pressed money on Copson, and when he would not take it folded it into John's chubby fist, and was very expansive and good-natured.

"And that leaves as much for me," he beamed.

"And what use will you make of it?" Alice asked him.

He put his finger to the side of his nose. "I'm going on my travels again, sister."

"With three nobles?"

He tapped his nose knowingly. "Why not?"

"And when are you going?" she asked him outright.

"The day after to-morrow," he said. Then—"I was forgetting. Here is a copy of *Mamillia*. You keep it close, Alice. It may be your proudest possession one day. I wonder if they'll buy one or two or even three at—chrrm!" He coughed to cover his secret. "Yes, I shall be off to-morrow."

"Where are you going?"

"Ah, wouldn't you like to know? What if I said Coppinger at Cambridge, that's who I'm going to see?"

She said to Copson in bed that night: "Is that fool of a brother of mine going to Norwich, do you think?"

He had been wondering the same. "He'll be sober in the morning. We can find out then."

"But, Geoffrey——"

"I wish to heaven he had never come here interfering! If only we could be on our own, free of everybody, not caring about them, then we'd be happy enough, Alice. If he goes home blabbing——"

They lay silent for a while, thinking. He would go home and talk, and he was fool enough to tell everything once he grew confidential, and then what would happen?

"Your father will never visit us, Alice, and he won't let your mother do so. Everyone will be that much less happy. If he liked Italy so much why in hell's name didn't he stay there, that's what I should like to know!"

She turned on her side and stretched her arm across his chest. "If he went to Norwich and told, Geoffrey, and mother never came to see me, I should have to go to see her, dear."

Oh, God, he started to think, now it must start all over again. "You know I am sorry for her, Alice. I liked your mother, but if you go home—how could we do it, Alice?" He opened his eyes in the dark. "Alice, are you sure you love me? You do? Then don't let us worry about other people. It's other people—it is they make all the mischief in the world, not you and me. Let's live for you and me and the boy. Go away from here, if you like. I'll find a way." Vague dreams—go to Braiding and demand help, get service with such-or-such a one, move to Bristol, to Chester, to Carlisle—only keep away from other people. Where their story would be their own, where she would think only of him. Lying there, her arm around him, he felt a boy again, full of the wildest longings of love, ready to dare all things. He would like to sell the shop and take the money, the filthy money they took from Sidley, fling it into the river, and then maybe, relying on themselves, life would be better, she'd be sweet to him always as now sometimes, he would hold his head as high as any man, all the things he had thought over—— "Alice," he said hoarsely, "as God's my judge I love you and always will. Be kind to me always." She drew him towards her, pillowing his cheek on her bare breast, stroking his hair, murmuring all the time. She had been unkind, she had been so cruel to him, all the bitter and unfair things must be forgotten though, from now on she must cure herself, and always, always he must know that whatever she said did not matter, that he was the one, that she owed him her very life. Soon he was entirely happy, his mind blank to the thought that this had happened before and would happen again. Dear Alice! To think her happiness depended on him! If he had to kill for her—— Heroic thoughts and tender sent him to sleep at last, her breast wet from his open mouth.

She asked her brother in the morning whether he was going to Norwich. He said No, most emphatically. "Because if you do, and if you tell——" "What?" he asked.—"Oh, nothing. You'll have sense enough to see without telling or none at all, I suppose." He complained that was ungracious of her, and explained he was off to see about his future. He pointed out that he was almost twenty-six and unprovided for. He was for Cambridge. Reports were in that the roads were passable and a strong company was leaving at dawn the next day. Yes, he had arranged to hire a horse. At least, he thought he had, but since he was admittedly a little fuddled at the time it might be as well to go across and verify it. He did so, while she told her husband she thought they need not worry about him. "I am worrying about us," Copson said curtly.

He was up before daybreak the next day, and off he went with kisses and handshakes and relief on all sides. The meeting place was the Red Lattice yard below Strand Bridge, a hostelry well known to Greene. He sat for a time at a window-table with a pot of warmed wine, watching his companions assemble. There were three or four College men, only one of whom, Hargreaves of Christ's, he recognised; there were four soldiers, evidently on Her Majesty's service, and several travellers whose precise status and calling it was not easy to guess. There would be a number of women in the party, one of them with two young children. But no more Uncle Robining, he told himself, and swallowed wine after rolling it round in his mouth. Ah well—he called the maid, paid his score, gave her a halfpenny for herself, and took the kiss both he and she expected for it. He went down to the yard.

Hargreaves of Christ's knew him not, nor did he care. As they made their way from the inn yard, Greene was well to the front with the soldiers. For a time they talked among themselves, but he worked his way into their conversation and enjoyed the next few hours. Certainly they laughed at his horse, but he had already laughed at it himself, so took no offence. He listened when two of them told how they had been in a company attacked by robbers some twelve miles from the city not a month ago, and appreciated their jests when eventually they passed three bodies strung up at the wayside as a warning to other evildoers. Their clothes had been ripped up by the birds eager for their flesh, and altogether they were a comical sight. The soldiers speculated loudly which parts of them the birds found the greatest dainty. Their leader, a fellow named Bart, told of dreadful things done a-pillaging, calmly, as though lust and rapine were the nails of his fingers, and Greene invented an Italian tale of revenge for them. It seemed no time before they stopped for food and to bait their horses. Greene, the most sociable of men, walked in and out of the company, introduced himself to Hargreaves, who seemed uninterested, and encouraged some of the men travellers to talk. One fellow was on the first stage of a journey to York. Yes, he understood the four soldiers were bound for Berwick. Yes, he had paid a small sum for protection. No, he knew all about their tricks; he wouldn't let them out of his sight. Another was bound for Edinburgh, where his cousin was a merchant; another for Hull; a third, strangely enough, for Norwich. "Hm," said Greene, "Norwich, eh?" He gave him a line of Latin, and the fellow stared. He saw the mother of two, the wife of a traveller to Cambridge, and nosed his way into position to take stock of a girl in company with a delicate looking man not without dignity. Pretty, he thought, eyeing her more like a horse fancier than a gentleman; but a little thin for his taste. He went back to discuss women with the soldiery, but found their brutality too much for him.

For a time he rode with the Cambridge men, swapping erudition and scholastic jokes, and trying to look as though he understood the Greek with which Hargreaves and his companion Fletcher enlivened their discourse. He saw now that you had to keep in touch with a language or you forgot it all, but lest these stay-at-homes triumph over him, he let Italian—and no lingua turistica either—flow with the spittle from under his tongue. Then Fletcher began to ask him about Rome, and rather than admit he had not been there he had to be brisk in lying. The despoliation of the Pantheon, the decoration of papal churches, the view from the Capitoline Hill—he was nimble, and when Fletcher again unloosed the Greek he was so proud of because Ascham had been his tutor, he looked knowingly between the ears of his horse, sighed, and nodded gravely three or four times. "Florence too——" he said, and escaped to safer ground.

About the middle of the afternoon came one of the decisive happenings of Greene's life, quite unheralded. There was a call from the back of the party, for the others to halt a moment. The reason, they found, was that one of them had been taken ill. It was the father of the girl whom Greene had thought too thin. It was the occasion for a telling display of human selfishness. The soldiers had their mission and must proceed with it; those who relied on their protection must keep up with them. Could the man Fernley keep up with them too? It was clear he could not. Most agreed this was a pity, but what could they do about it? Bart helped them to a decision by stressing what a dangerous part of the road they were on, and Fletcher eased their consciences by recalling that there was a house about half a mile further on where the sick man might find shelter. In the meantime—farewell, fieldfare! "But we can't leave a sick man like this," Greene expostulated. He found he was speaking for himself.

The cavalcade was on the move. There was no lack of good wishes. Greene pulled at his beard. "If you will permit me, mistress," he said finally. "And you, sir——"

Fernley was crouched forward over his horse. Thanks were beyond him. His daughter was pouring something from a small bottle into a cloth for him. "You are more than kind, sir. I don't think you ought——"

"My name is Robert Greene. I am a student of Cambridge —at least, I was until last year—I do hope you will allow me to help you."

She seemed a brave girl, but her hands were shaking. "Let me," said Greene, and took the bottle and cloth from her. It was some acrid, vital stuff. He pressed it to Fernley's nose just as he fainted and would have slipped from the horse had not Greene taken his weight. He shouted after his retreating companions, and as he manœuvred to get himself and his burden to the ground had the satisfaction of seeing two riders coming back to them. Now they would be all right. The riders came within twenty yards before they reined in their horses. One of them was Fletcher.

"The man is sick," Greene cried. "We must get him a litter." He stared at them, getting angry. "Why don't you help?"

Said Fletcher: "I think I should tell you, Master Greene, one of our companions reports the plague in St. Benet's last night. You must look out for yourself. Leave this poor man and make your way back to where you may be examined."

The hair bristled on Greene's scalp. The plague! He looked with horror upon Fernley in his arms, and at the girl. "You are lying!" he shouted fiercely. "I warn you, Master Fletcher, and the rest of you, that if this man dies I shall see you are held responsible."

"It is our duty to avoid the plague, not encourage it, as you know yourself."

Greene saw the scene as though he wished to paint it. The tragic little group in the foreground, behind them the two mounted men, and in the background the fidgeting company he had been on such good terms with that morning. The road was dry and open, the brush cut back for fifty yards and more.

"Make a litter!" he shouted to them. "This man is unspotted. There's no plague!"

Fletcher raised his hand. "You have been warned. God be with you."

"Don't go!" Greene shouted, almost in a panic. "We are coming with you."

Fletcher checked his horse. "You cannot. If you try to join us you will be shot down. Go back to where you can be examined." He rose in his stirrups for effect. "And let the dead bury their dead."

They were riding back to the main group. Greene dug into his heart for oaths and found them. This was the most ghastly fright he had ever known. Suddenly he pushed Fernley from him, his feet were caught in his stirrups, and his body fell to hang head downwards on the road. The girl gave a weak little scream, but Greene had flogged his horse madly with his gloved hand and was galloping back along the road. The Plague! The Plague! The Plague!

But in half a mile at the most he stopped. He sat for a while looking at his hands as though he expected to find them breaking out with pustules. Slowly he found resolution. He must go back. The man was not suffering from the plague. Even if he were, there was the girl. What a child she was! He did not know why, but again he saw before him the face of that girl on the Old Bridge at Florence. He must go back. He shivered, but there was no longer any doubt in his mind. He turned his horse.

Drawing near he saw that the girl had released her father's feet and had dragged him to the roadside. The two horses were cropping grass, sixty yards away, untethered, unhobbled. He galloped up, thoroughly ashamed and still very frightened, dismounted, and crossed to where Fernley was lying with his head in her lap.

"I have come back," he said. "I should never have gone. You must forgive me."

She seemed too frightened to reply, but she let him help her to her feet. "We can't stay here. We must get on to shelter." He studied Fernley's wrists, looked carefully under his eyes, for he was still hardly conscious. "This is no case of plague," he announced confidently. "It may be——" He did not know what it might be, so stopped short lest he reveal his ignorance. "How are you now, sir?"

"I was dizzy," said Fernley. "Something I have eaten, I think. We are much obliged to you, young sir."

"You will not think so later," Greene assured him. "You think you can sit a horse now?"

He thought he could. But before they could move him he began to retch violently, and then was taken with diarrhœa. Greene now thought it best to make for the house they had been told lay ahead and get help to shift him. He explained this to the girl, wondering whether she would think this a new desertion, and then set off. He had to go not a half-mile but three times as far, and then it was to meet with a barred gate. He had not time to call out before the door of the house was opened, and a man stood there with two dogs. He had a cudgel in his hand. "Be off!" he cried out, "or I'll set the dogs on you." Greene tried to explain that he wanted help for a sick man. "The plague!" the other shouted back. "You'll get no help here. Be off with you!" He pointed the snarling dogs at Greene, who had to retreat, cursing those who had spread this unnecessary alarm. What sort of message was he to make of it to Fernley and his daughter? And what in God's name were they to do?

He turned back to the house and called out. The door opened so promptly he knew he had been watched. "Will you sell me food?" he shouted before the other could threaten him. He spun a silver coin into the air and relied on profit more than charity. "Throw the money over first," the householder invited him, but he refused and asked that food be placed outside the gate, while he withdrew, and then he would come back and throw the money up to the door. This was their arrangement, and Greene had his first piece of amusement for some hours when he saw his supplier pick the silver up with a tongs made of wood. It was usury, for the food was half a loaf of bread and a small piece of bacon. With this he set off for the Fernleys, convinced that by this time they had given him up.

Bearer of bad news though he was, the girl greeted him with relief. Her father was now most helplessly ill, suffering

frequent purgings and sickness. The one good thing was
that Greene could see no sign whatever of plague about
him. No travellers had gone by, though they were on the
high road, and Greene realised with dismay that any such
saluted by their late companions would certainly give them
a wide berth. He realised too that the day was passing,
and that in an hour or so all hope of passers-by must be
given over. He fumed at the ridiculousness of it, that on a
highway of a great kingdom a man might lie down and die
before anyone came to succour him. "What can we do?"
the girl begged him several times, but he had no satisfactory
answer. Mistakenly he had left it too late for them to retrace
their steps and was gambling on help which now appeared
unlikely to arrive. If only Coppinger were here! Edmund
would know exactly what to do.

He had almost made up his mind to strap the now useless
Fernley on his horse and set off, even if the jolting killed
him, when company approached from the London side.
They were three men riding together and stopped at Greene's
hail, and were willing to help. The oldest of them examined
Fernley closely, and diagnosed such an inflammation as
had carried off his own father—an opinion he expressed
incautiously in the daughter's hearing. Greene patted her
shoulder, and then they set about improvising a litter.
He was not in the least frightened now that there was no
danger of the plague, and felt wonderfully capable and
protective. Though if Fernley died—— He remembered
with surprise that he knew nothing of the pair's destination,
nothing of their affairs. He now rode alongside the child,
for she seemed little more than a child to him, and asked
such questions as he thought necessary. They lived in
Lincolnshire, just below the church at Hartop. Why, he
knew Hartop well! Actually he had been there once, it
was not more than ten miles from Braiding, his own destination. It made them feel old friends, and their ordeal
together and its searching inquisition into strength and
weakness had already prepared the way. She must let him
help. It was no trouble. But the way he had galloped back

that afternoon—could she ever forgive him? It was cowardly and base of him. But she was just enough to forget the horrid predicament of her father hanging from his horse and told him that to return was brave beyond words. He made his disclaimers but was pleased all the same. "You are quite a child," he said suddenly, anciently twenty-five. She smiled at that.

They put up for the night at the house where Greene had met his churlish but justified welcome. After some argument their host expressed himself satisfied that the sick man should enter. The leader of the three, who gave his name as Bates, shook his head as he helped put Fernley to bed. "He'll go," he said laconically. They tried him with a milk dish, but he threw up what little they forced down his throat. Greene lay awake for some hours wondering what to do if, as seemed certain, he were worse in the morning. He muttered to himself, thinking how he had made the responsibility his own, thinking too of the girl in Florence and how it would be an atonement for much that was ugly in his life if he helped this innocent Mistress Fernley. Thank God he had reformed greatly since his return from Italy. He had learned his lesson, he told himself. He might in the past have driven some poor devils further down, but this time he would be a lifter. These thoughts stayed with him till he woke again, and though the issues then seemed more practical he had decided his line of conduct.

Together with Bates he went in to see Fernley before it was light. His disease was running a rapid course, and he was worse. Move for home or keep him there, was the problem. Mistress Fernley had no way of making up her mind which would be best. "He must stay here," said Bates. Greene counted his shillings and pondered. "You must be a brave girl," Bates told her kindly. "You think you can be?"

"Of course," Greene answered for her. "Hasn't she been brave all the time?"

Money was always a problem. How short of it he was

already! Really he should be pressing on to Cambridge, where Coppinger would help him forward to Braiding if he told him he was making for Norwich. But he saw the girl's eyes as Bates and his companions said good-bye. No, he would stay here with her. He told himself many times he was a fool to do so, but relished the difference from other times he had called himself a fool. Then he had been about the devil's work: this was Christian charity. He was the Good Samaritan.

"Shall I stay with you and your father, Mistress Fernley?" he asked her, in Fernley's room, and she answered timidly: If he would be so kind. He came to feel she did not like their landlord and he could not help coming to think her even prettier. She was not much higher than his chin, and very slender, with a girl's arms and bosom. He had met before women whose stock-in-trade was an appeal for protection, a charming simulation of helplessness, but he knew this was different. She *was* helpless. She was dark of hair and eyes, unfashionably so, but he thought it made no odds. But I am a fool, he assured himself several times. He found a satisfaction in telling himself he was a fool, and then arguing he was a noble fool.

They administered several homely remedies to Fernley, without doing him any good, and Greene made it his business to appeal to each company of passers-by whether there was a doctor amongst them. There were busy-bodies a-plenty, who came inside, wagged their heads, passed a desolating opinion and then rode off, but no doctor. By evening Greene knew this would make no difference. Fernley would die. He felt not the slightest sorrow for him, either. It would be his duty, though, to take his daughter to her home. This idea gave him a not displeasing melancholy feeling. Poor child! He began to rehearse his part in readiness.

That second night he was roused by the man of the house shaking him. He sat up, confused, and heard crying. "What has happened?" he asked. "Gone," said the other; "the gentleman's gone." He jumped out of bed, reaching for his clothes; he dressed and hurried to Fernley's room. Dorothy was sitting by the bedside, weeping and rubbing her father's hand. Such useless comfort as he had he essayed, but she seemed not to be listening to him, and his fine speeches were wasted, some of them not even delivered.

CHAPTER XXIII

NEXT DAY GREENE hurried on to Cambridge and was lucky enough in the state of the roads to get there before dusk. He had gone to seek Coppinger's advice, indeed his help. His landlord, once he was assured of his money, had made arrangements to get a carpenter at work and find the nearest parson, and his wife would try to console Mistress Dorothy. Could Coppinger return with him? He found Edmund at the College, newly returned from lecturing in the Schools, and gratifyingly pleased to see him. He listened, not without puzzlement, to Greene's story. He did not see how Greene could have acted otherwise, yet he felt it something of a fairy story. He thought the girl must be very beautiful for Greene to act so, but dismissed the thought as uncharitable. To Greene's direct question whether he thought him a fool he found a proper answer, and pointed out how often the right course appears a silly one to those not called on to take it. He did not see what purpose there was in his travelling, but "Yes," he said, "I'll come with you, Robert." Greene stayed on at the College till the porter came to turn him out, for a time with Coppinger alone, for a time with young Nashe too, who came in looking like a hungry dog. He had missed his lecture with Coppinger, and had some fantastic excuse which the other accepted. "A lively lad," said Coppinger, after he had carried his thin jaws back to his own quarters. "I think he will do something—on the other side." Greene looked up. "Ah yes," said Coppinger, "not the puritan side, I meant, Robert."

He left as Eggerton was coming in. "I am glad you called here to take him from his work," said Eggerton. "Study, lectures, writing—never a whole day free. What will he make of himself?"

"Something memorable," said Greene perfunctorily. "In the morning then?"

They were on their way at dawn. "You have never seen this girl and her father before?" Coppinger asked.

"Never."

"There is no interpreting life by human judgments only," said Coppinger.

"No. But all this work of yours, Edmund—is it necessary?"

"Eggerton exaggerates."

"Maybe. I've been hearing talk, Edmund."

"You have?"

"Yes. In London. Talk of a counterblast to the Whitgiftian system. To come from Cambridge here. Am I meddling?"

"My dear Robert, of course not. Say what you want to say, do."

"Then are you mixed up in it?" He did not wait for an answer before he continued: "For God's sake, Edmund, go warily. Think of Waybridge and Harmon and Baines—rotting in the Compter these seven years and never a charge against them yet. There are wicked men on the Bishops' bench, Edmund."

"I know it."

"It must not happen to you, that's all."

Coppinger smiled at his earnestness. "You are a dear fellow, Robert, and I love you for it. But don't worry about me." He looked away. "What I do—I think what all men do—is not entirely of their own will, Robert. No man of his own will would burn at the stake or hang in chains or see the pincers come near to tear out his tongue. Yet men do burn and hang and suffer mutilation. God or the Devil, one or the other will always help, Robert. All we can do is be careful which we call on."

"You are writing then?"

"I ask you as a friend, Robert—never ask such questions. They do no good. They may do harm."

"I won't again."

"Are you offended? You ought not to be. You have your way to go, I mine. If the ways cross, who will welcome it more than I? But they are not likely to, Robert. So don't be offended."

On the ride back to where Fernley lay dead, Greene indulged in an almost Catholic confession. He explained uncomfortably at the end of it why he was now acting as he was. "Faith and works," said Coppinger. "No one can doubt that both are better than one." He asked about Sidley and was glad Greene had no news of him. They talked about their families. "I must call on your sister when next I am in London." But Greene hoped not.

They found at their journey's end that Fernley was to be buried in sacred ground next morning. The coffin maker had known by experience that you must get these inflammation corpses into the ground pretty quickly. To-morrow morning would be late enough. Dorothy had not broken as much as Greene expected. Evidently he had underestimated her strength. "Why, Robert, she seems such a child," cried Coppinger, at the end of their interview. "As I told you," countered Greene. Coppinger looked at his right thumb. "You did right, Robert. You could not leave this child in the lurch." They discussed her case. She had no relatives nearer than Wirral, no one dear to her there. She would first return to Hartop, she had said. There was an old family servant there. "By the way," said Greene, "I must not forget to give you a copy of my *Mamillia*, either."

They followed the wagon over a dreadful road to the little churchyard next day. "I am Edmund Coppinger," Coppinger announced to the vicar who conducted the service, and there could be no doubt his name meant something to its hearer. The service was the better for it. "An honest man," said Coppinger, after a little talk apart with him. "He will see that all is done as it should be." Greene meditated. It was hard to believe that Edmund, cooped up at Cambridge, was making a name, and he still the veriest nobody.

They had persuaded Dorothy to go as far as Cambridge with them the next day, and because she trusted them she agreed. It was a sad leave-taking, they knew, but there was nothing they could do more than they had done. Dorothy had an extra source of grief in that her father must lie so far from the people who knew him. "He is as near God there as elsewhere," Coppinger said kindly. "Nearer than we now standing here." He was a splendid companion, as Greene knew he would be. Reliable, tactful, considerate. He knew exactly the right things to say. Greene imagined a kind of radiance about him.

Coppinger returned to his rooms for the night, and Greene and Dorothy lodged at different inns. Coppinger had commended Greene for offering to conduct her to Lincolnshire afterwards, and had seemed glad to help him out of his money troubles. He would see them before they set off. "And you will be passing back through Cambridge to tell me the news?" he asked at parting. Yes, sooner or later. He might go home to Norwich first, but never fear he'd be back one of these days. "Good-bye, Mistress Fernley."

They had found two fellow travellers. "Good-bye, Master Coppinger. I shall never forget how kind you were to me."

Coppinger gave the credit to Greene, and waved to them riding down the street. "I think your friend the loveliest man I ever met," she told Greene. He replied carefully, inviting praise for himself. Soon he noticed that their two companions were thinking him a lucky fellow to be squiring Mistress Fernley. Her clothes were sober, but not entirely black under her new cloak. She was a pretty child, he told himself once more, and to take her mind from her loss began to talk about himself in the highest terms. She asked one or two questions about Coppinger, but he usually answered with: Yes, I remember telling him, or Yes, Edmund and I often used to discuss that sort of thing; and then Edmund would be pushed out as Robert grew bigger in the narrative. But all this served a useful purpose, for he was an entertaining enough talker, with the great advantage of being in love with his subject. She did cry once or twice during the day, quietly to herself, but the novelty of her situation and company worked wonders. She told him calmly enough she would probably seek service in the neighbourhood, for she was sure her father was not a wealthy man. There were the Rounds and the Vincents, and the Vereys and the Sidleys—with any of whom she thought she could get some post fitting a gentlewoman. With the Sidleys? thought Greene. No, by God, he wouldn't see her go there. But then he laughed. There was no danger.

They stayed the night at a cluster of houses ten miles nearer than Peterborough. Greene shared a room with the two men. He was growing excited now at the prospect of seeing Sidley again. It had been easy charity after all, this to Mistress Fernley, and he would willingly go to greater trouble on her behalf. No doubt if he mentioned her case at Braiding—he felt quite the dispenser of favours. And he would see that Sidley did what he should for Alice and the boy as well as for himself. He should be as great a benefactor as Whittington, like it or not. She was a pretty child, this Dorothy.

They were at Hartop by the end of the next afternoon. The homecoming upset her more than anything since last she saw her father's face, and Greene did not intrude upon her now. He told her he would call to see her in a couple of days, and pressed on for Braiding. He arrived there soon after darkness.

For a time he was too nervous to go up to the house. Perhaps the morning would be a more suitable time? He dismissed these temporizings and went forward. "Master Robert Greene of Cambridge to see Master Ralph Sidley." The servant looked at him with interest. Oh yes, they remembered his sister's story.

Would he wait?

Those same pictures on the walls. How little most things changed. He heard the door open behind him and turned to confront Sidley. He still had the pointed black beard, the small mustachios shading the too full lips.

"So it is Robertus Greene?"

He knew now that Sidley must have known he was alive and in England.

"Are you surprised to see me?"

"Very."

"And far from pleased?"

"I would not say that."

"That is gracious of you! I thought I should be the last man on earth you'd care to have visit you."

"And why?" Sidley motioned him to a seat. "What brings you so far out of your way?"

"Just the wish to see you."

"I ought to feel flattered, Robertus, but somehow I do not."

"You are still yourself, Sidley, I see." He wished to break these frigid sentences with the harshness of his mood. "Though not entirely yourself."

He saw a stiffening of the other's face. "You were saying?" said Sidley.

"That I wanted to see you." He stretched his legs the more comfortably for Sidley's self-betrayal. "Because I think we have a good deal to talk over. When I think of it, Sidley—a lot has happened to you and me since I was last at Braiding. The past has left its mark on both of us, has it not?"

Sidley looked at the floor. "And if I don't want to listen?"

"I think you will listen."

"There are servants here, and very strong in the arm some of them."

This was better, Greene thought. "Nevertheless, you will be wise to listen, Sidley."

"Go on then."

"I will. You never asked what became of me in Genoa, Sidley?"

"Why should I? You are old enough to look after yourself, aren't you?"

"You knew, more likely! You took ship the morning you had me stabbed, did you not?"

"I don't understand you, Robertus. You have been stabbed, you say? How did that happen?"

"I have depositions from the harbour master, from my innkeeper and yours, from the captain of the ship you sailed on, and from——" He ended his tremendous lie without adding the assassin and so ruining it. "My God, Sidley, you've got something to repay me! You've got more than me to repay in my family. You've got a lot of the foulest wickedness to see righted—and I'll see that you do!"

"You need not walk about so excitedly. You are talking like a fool, Robertus."

"Am I? We'll soon see who is the fool—me or you—man or gelding!" He snapped his fingers. "How d'you like that, my fine gentleman?"

"Be quiet, damn you! Don't shout, you blasted——"

"You don't like it? Then adopt less the hoity-toity attitude, will you? I'm not here begging, can you understand that? I'm here for justice. I've got your knife wound in my back, my sister is rearing your bastard, I know you for the thing you are. I'm not here begging, d'you hear?"

Sidley waved his hands irresolutely. "Only for Christ's sake, don't talk so loud, Robertus. We can discuss the matter without shouting, can't we?"

"I am glad you think so. I had begun to doubt it."

"The shock has been a great one. Sit down, Robertus, do sit down! I know I have not done as I should by you and Alice. What do you want me to do?"

Greene suspected his victory too easy, and yet what other end could he look for? In all his rehearsals of the scene he had come brutally to the point, and Sidley had capitulated, even grovelled. And now, this furtive-looking half-man in front of him, was he to be trusted? He must be very careful.

He began his set speech. The attack on his life in Genoa had given him the expenses of a winter there, he had been forced to borrow money and had not repaid it, the delay in his return had cost him preference to a post under the Lord Admiral, he had not prospered since, and he could not lay the responsibility to his own charge. Then there was his sister. Had Sidley even thought—and he was saying nothing now of the unspeakable vileness of his conduct— had Sidley even thought what it meant to be cut off as she was from the rest of her family, to live a hard life in London, never seeing a soul she wanted to? And poor Copson? All his prospects in life ruined, and forced to become a mere seller of condiments. In short, he hoped Sidley would see where his duty lay. He referred constantly to principles, ideals, justice and fair-play, watching carefully the while for Sidley's sneer, and satisfied not to see it.

"I shall have to think about it," Sidley said after a short silence.

Greene admitted that was fair enough, adding—"Till when?"

"To-morrow I should make up my mind what to do. You'll not believe me, Robertus, but the day I heard you were still alive I thanked God as I had never done for anything before. It was the pain and humiliation that drove me to it, the shame that devoured me and rid me of every decent feeling. The misery and torture I went through afterwards—you won't believe me, I know—I can't think your sufferings, whatever they were, could compare with mine." He clasped his hands, unclasped them. A fine range of emotions coursed over his face: remorse, despair, doubt, self-pity; but Greene had seen Sidley do even better at Genoa.

"How is the boy?" he asked suddenly. And Greene told him. "I must see him," he threatened, for threat it was to Copson and Alice. "He looks like me?"

"More like you than Alice."

Sidley rang for a servant, who brought wine. "Shall we drink to him?" Sidley seemed shy proposing the toast, but Greene seconded it worthily and commended the wine so highly that he was invited to finish the bottle. Sidley asked

Greene where he was staying over night, heard that it was at the Crown, and did not ask him to put up at Braiding. "I'll come along to-morrow morning and see you. What you have told me about the boy makes me think a lot." It was a little later he added: "Don't take it amiss that I gave you a cold reception. If only you could know, Robertus, what it means to me to have you sitting there!"

Greene could not rebel against the unexpected turn of events. They were talking quietly, as though about College affairs. He accepted Sidley's excuses with a deprecatory wave of the hand. How the gay fellow had changed! He was a drab man now all right. With a tendency to put a whine into his voice occasionally. But he must be tolerant. Sidley was in a bad way, and he was evidently meaning to do much for the Greene family. Another glass of wine and he felt most kindly towards him, like a good schoolmaster towards a boy who has given him trouble. One could beat the offender unmercifully, get the hide off him in patches, but why? How small, how poor, how weak the rascal seems. How appealing to magnanimity.

"You understand," Sidley could bring himself to say at last, "you understand it will be difficult for you to meet my family?"

He understood. He understood too it was time for him to go. There was no taking of hands.

A thought came forcibly to Greene. "You will send a servant with me back to the Crown?"

Whatever Sidley thought, his face showed nothing of it. It would be the least he could do.

Greene stayed late in bed the next morning, with plenty to think about. He was at the beginning of his fortune, undoubtedly. He would be going back to London like a prince, with money and promises for himself and the three Copsons. He was not hypocrite enough to play the moralist, though he did tell himself now and again that the man who took his pleasure must be prepared to pay for it. Not that Sidley would do any paying without his special

power to force him. That he should be aware Sidley had
been gelded was the bare palm of the hand of providence,
revealed for good. And how Sidley had changed! He had
a sop of wine and bread before getting out of bed.

Ten o'clock and no Sidley. Eleven o'clock and he called
the landlord in to share his drink, and listened to local
gossip. Yes, there were big goings on at the Hall now
that Master Ralph was leaving for America. Greene
gulped. For America? Yes, he was going out as part of
a colony to America. He would be a prince, at least, out
there.

Greene hurried up the lane towards Braiding. Thrice
damned fool to trust one word out of Sidley's mouth! As
though he had not had lessons enough. He would find him
gone. He knew it. And what the devil was he to do then?
What a bungler! What an ass! What a clown!

They seemed to be expecting him at Braiding. Yes,
would he wait some minutes? Then a servant appeared to
lead him elsewhere—to Sir Ralph.

"I remember you, Master Greene. You wish to see my
son, you say?"

"I did see your son last night, Sir Ralph. I was to see
him again this morning."

Sir Ralph was laughing at him, he could tell. "You must
be mistaken. I did not know you were in Braiding last
night."

"Nevertheless, I was. Is your son here now?"

"I am entirely his manager, Master Greene. What did
you wish to see him about?"

"Private matters. He would not like them discussed."

"They cannot be so private that I know nothing of
them. If you will jog my memory——"

I should like to jog your rotten ribs, Greene was thinking.
He had the foolish idea of rushing from the house, getting
on horseback and galloping like mad along the London
road to catch up with Sidley. Then he saw that he might
well get into trouble for the last time if he did that.

"I wanted to see him about my sister."

Sir Ralph covered his pebble eyes with his unpleasant hand. "Your sister? I think I remember her even better than I do you. A handsome girl, was she not?"

That this paper-guts should be a connoisseur! "Your son thought so."

"We all thought so," said Sir Ralph.

"If you know as much as you say you do"—Sir Ralph pretended to start at such rudeness—"if you do, you'll know that he is the father of her child. That is why I am here."

"You are?"

"And I demand——"

"You demand!" The old villain was laughing at him. "Oh, and what do you demand?"

"Justice," said Greene.

"An excellent lady, though blindfolded. Like other ladies—like your sister, Master Greene, evidently—she too has her price."

"That's a damned lie!"

"But I assure you, young Master Greene, I have bought Justice many a time, and I am well able to do so again. That is worth remembering, don't you think?"

"I am not interested in what you have to say. What is your son going to do?"

"I thought you were such friends!"

"Until I knew him for what he is."

"Does paternity make so much difference?"

Greene began to lose his temper. Wasn't this old lecher supposed to have driven Alice from Braiding? He grew hot at the thought. "Like father, like son," he said bluntly.

"Is it any credit to your sister she should admit us both?" Sir Ralph countered, sneering.

Greene's dagger was half out of its sheath, but he thrust it back again. "I must see that you and your family pay for that," he said quietly.

"You will, Master Greene, *young* Master Greene?" He rang the bell near his hand. "You may leave the house either on your feet or the shoulders of my servants." So

prompt was their entry that they must have been waiting
outside the room. He motioned them out again, "As for
your sister's brat—it may be my son's, it may be mine,
it may be the kennelman's, or it may be that fool Copson's,
for she was as common here at Braiding as the road from
Cheapside to St. Paul's." Greene, panting to keep himself
from folly, sensed him mad with hatred of his sister. "You
are a meddler, Master Greene, and meddlers never hear
good of themselves. That is as much as you shall know—
that your sister is a whore, that her body was a sewer to
the whole of this estate, and that her bastard, as it was
denied known father——"

He jerked the bell as Greene rushed at him, and dodged
ludicrously round the table. Greene struck him once,
twice, heavy blows on his head, before he was seized by
those entering, swung off his feet, and carried off with
many a hearty thump and oath. He thought he heard Sir
Ralph laughing and squeaking, but when next he knew
what he was about he had more to think of than Sir Ralph's
laughter. He had been flung on to the midden, his head and
limbs ached to desperation, he was afraid to move lest he
discover broken bones. In a minute or two he discovered
that some serving girls were watching him from a low
balcony on the right. Without knowing why, except that
they were identified with his enemy's house, he shook
his fist at them, whereon, secure as they were, they laughed
and jeered at him, and a couple of them made a world-
old gesture of contempt. "You —— ——" he ground out,
just loud enough for them to hear; "You —— ——." He
picked up slabs of dung and began to hurl them at the
women, who fled, but this brought out a hairy man with
three dogs which he set on Greene. His bruises considered,
he ran fairly well, and if his clothes were ripped and his
flesh nipped half a dozen times he had the slight comfort
of kicking one dog in the ribs and another full in his wicked
teeth. "Take that, you——!" he cried with a real joy of
battle, and heard the whistle that called them off. Then
he went limping towards the Crown. But his troubles were

far from over, for the landlord refused him admission, on Sir Ralph's instructions he guessed, and flung his belongings out of doors to him. He stood there irresolute. What could he do? He decided he must go to Hartop.

The journey to Mistress Fernley's cottage was not the nightmare he expected, but it was bad enough. He turned in by a sheep-fold half a mile further on and tried to clean himself, but could do little with handfuls of grass except smear himself worse. Further on again, with the help of running water he made his face fairly presentable, but knew that one of his eyes was growing darker. He suffered the mortification of being stoned by jeering small boys at two places, and there seemed to be absolutely no charity in the county. Those he passed must look on him as a beggar who had met with his deserts, and soon he gave over his appeals for help and trudged stolidly on his way. He was hungry too, and thirsty, but not for water. What if he got no shelter at Mistress Fernley's? What ought he to do about Sidley? What could he tell the Copsons? Was there anyone from whom he could borrow money to get him home? The best question of all was: Had he drawn blood from that old beast Sir Ralph? Once again he felt his fist coming down hard on his head and hoped he had split the old devil's skull.

But what if he got no shelter at Mistress Fernley's?

It had to rain, of course. Misty stuff at first, with assurance of no ceasing. God, he was tired! And that jakes-scraping Sidley would be well on the way to London by this, and maybe he'd never see him again, and all his fine hopes blown off like thistledown. Thank God for the comfort of strong chesty oaths. He'd get his own back on the Sidleys before he finished. He speculated that Sidley, too, had a sister. He kicked at a stone in his path. He'd just like to get the bitch behind a hedge, that was all. He'd square off accounts then. Huh! Hardly had he thought so before he knew how unworthy it was. No, he wasn't the man for that kind of revenge. God, but he was tired! The rain had thickened to a steady drizzle, wetting him through, and his shoes squelched in mud. At least it would discourage travellers and make him less of a show. His right eye was almost shut now. He dare not think Mistress Fernley might not be at the cottage. He listened to the sound of his feet: pash, pash, pash, slish, slish, slish. What old Sidley had said—not a word of truth in it, he knew. The old goat had wanted his way with her, and she had beaten him off, bloodless old wheezer that he was. He had hammered him over the skull, anyhow, and made him scuttle round the table like a youngster with his bottom bared. Lost his dignity he had. And there would be a reckoning yet, never fear, there'd be such a reckoning! Slish, slish, slish. Was ever man so tired? What did his face look like? And the stink on him! Phew! He was like a walking privy. What a noseful for Mistress Fernley! Like the back-end of a fig-eating donkey. Faugh! His gorge was rising at it. The rain made it worse, released effluvia, undid the reticence of desiccation. Slish, slish, slish, through the pools and puddles. He would write about it one day, perhaps.

He began to think about what he would write next. He forgot his aches and smells for incantations. *Arbasto* and *Morando* already planned, and the *Tritameron of Love*. He'd show those Italian tale-tellers! What was that story in Boccaccio of the bitch who got her lover stark under the tower, till he almost froze to death? This was the first time for him to feel sorry for the fellow. Might all such bitches— Faugh! The stink! Urgh-urgh!

Such a pretty child she was. So gentle, so sweet, so unspoiled. On this wet day, trudging along with only your aches for company, you knew just how delightful she was. Dark eyes she had, sweet eyes, pitying eyes surely when her knight turned up so woe-begone. She would see to him, get him food and drink, find him a place to rest, talk him into self-esteem, reinstate Lincolnshire in the eyes of the Lord. Remember that girl on the bridge in Florence? Young Consetti—a fine one he was! An ulcer among men. He and Sidley a pair well matched. Boils on the groin of

humanity. And what a wretch he too had been! Those
Italian years. The New Circe indeed. Young men should
never leave their own country, settle down they should,
marry, be decent in their living.

He was at Hartop. And not too soon. He remembered
how you turned past the trees here to reach the house.
What if she did not know—— He knocked at the door.

A middle-aged woman answered it. "Go away. We want
no rogues here."

He wedged his foot between the closing door and the
joist. "Tell Mistress Fernley that Robert Greene wishes
to speak with her, will you?"

"Indeed I'll not!"

He groped for money. He would like to be kicking the
coins right up her backside, not greasing her palm. Tiredness
was a mantle from his shoulders to the ground.

"Oh, Master Greene!"

It was the girl. "I have been in trouble," he said. His
one sound eye filled with water, he was so sorry for himself.
He had been a fool to come here. What a fool he'd been!

"Poor, poor Master Greene!" The door was wide open,
her hand was on his sleeve, pulling at him. "Anna! You
must come at once and help!"

"I'll make a smell," he muttered, entering like a sheep.
Kindness, he knew, would loosen his tears. And he thought
himself such a leather-heart!

It was a quiet and clean house he entered, plainly
furnished, and without decoration, low-ceilinged and dark.
There was a small fire, but red and cosy, and altogether
the most attractive fire he had ever seen. The amazed
Anna stood to watch her mistress leading in this dungy
tramp. "Hot water, Anna! Quick!" When Anna did not
move briskly enough she repeated the order sharply.
It was now he noticed they were both in the deepest black.
He tried to admit he had been inconsiderate in coming
when he did, but she begged him not to say so after all the
kindness he had shown her. "But I can't stay here," he
expostulated; "I smell so." "Have you no other clothes?"

None, he had to confess. "Then you must take some of my father's," she had told him, too quick for repentance. And so it was. He was taken to Fernley's room, where the presses were opened for him to take his pick, and a tub was carried up and filled with water by Anna. Ashamedly, once on his own, he removed his rags, and doing all he could not to spill water over the floor wiped himself down with wet cloths and towels. He should never have come here —he could see that now. It had been quite unpardonable presumption. Rigged out in the dead man's clothes even— what a shock for his daughter. He felt the absence of ease that accompanies other men's garments. As though he hadn't the price of a shirt to his back! It worried him to think that neither had he. There was a tiny mirror on the far wall and he went to examine himself in it. He had a shock. A thin slit was all that appeared of his eye amidst great purple swellings, and there were contusions elsewhere on his face. He'd cut a fine figure downstairs.

There was a meal waiting for him, and though she ate nothing Mistress Fernley sat to table with him. There was bread and cheese and boiled bacon, cold, with magnificent streaks of white fat in it, and pickled onions, and the choice of wine or beer. He wanted to begin explanations, but Anna stood respectfully near, and he did not wish her to know of his adventures. Without real sympathy they might appear comical. And he would never forget that he had to bribe her to give his message. So instead, he detailed some of his injuries and set the women debating what they had in the house likely to do them good. Anna suggested burning for the dog bites, but Greene preferred death should it betide. He looked at the poker a long time, thinking what pleasure it would give him to try such a remedy on Sir Ralph.

The pleasant half-light of the little room flattered Mistress Fernley. Her face was white and small amongst so much that was black. She was so attentive to his needs, so obviously pleased to repay what she considered a huge debt, that Greene's spirits improved. He came to talk more animatedly, his jokes made himself laugh and Mistress Fernley smile and then laugh too. The ointments and compresses already applied were remarkably soothing, his tiredness was almost a luxury now. Ah, he sat back from table and at her invitation turned towards the fire, letting its warmth play with temporary healing on his legs and trunk. Soon Anna would go about her business, and then how he would explain!

CHAPTER XXIV

Greene arrived home in Norwich about five weeks later. He was a far from elegant figure, in Fernley's not quite fitting clothes and riding a horse with a curve in his back. This did not in any way affect his mother's welcome, but it raised his father's suspicions. He told as little as he could about himself. No, he had no regular employment, but he was not in debt—yet. At least, nothing worth mentioning. Jane, horror-struck at the notion of owing any man, found opportunity later to ask him how much, and from that small store she was always saving from her housekeeping against a time of need gave him the stated amount, with orders that he was not to spend a penny of it save for the one purpose. He promised this solemnly and meant to keep his word. "Did you find Alice?" she asked, with little hope of a good reply. No, he had not found Alice, but he had met a man—he began to spin lie after lie about this chance meeting and how the man had told him Copson was in good service in the West Country, and that his wife and child were both well. Copson was a steward and Alice a housekeeper. They must find it difficult to get even a day to themselves. He explained to his mother how unreasonable lords and ladies were, how they cared not a pea for the private lives of their servants. The man's name? One lie more was neither here nor there: his name was Sennington, his home was somewhere near Bristol, and one of these fine days Alice would be here in Norwich and they would not know themselves for joy. Jane thought this unsatisfactory, but "It is better than nothing," she concluded philosophically. Her thanks made Greene writhe.

"And about yourself, Robin?" she asked. It was a long tale he had to tell her. Somehow—he could not understand how—his worth had been unappreciated. Mind, he had a

printed book to his credit, and a considerable supply of
manuscript. It was only a question of time. "What would
you say, mother, if I settled down, married, gave up the
idea of London?" He hurriedly explained he had no one
in mind, but some decent girl or other—there must be plenty
of them about. "And how would you keep two where you
can't keep one?" Jane asked blankly. He fingered his
beard. There was his father's business, wasn't there?
He did not want to stand in Tobias's light, after giving his
father to understand he was not eligible for saddlery,
but surely the place could support more than one son?
"So you would be thinking to live here in Norwich for
good?" his mother asked. If he married, yes, he thought
so. Apart from Alice returning home, no prospect was
nearer Jane's heart. She was already thinking how the
bedrooms might be arranged, when he said: "In any
case, I could stay here in Norwich and write, even if
there was no room for me with father. There is plenty
of money in writing, mother, once you get into the way
of it."

It was not so easy to explain the past and future to his
father.

"Where did you get those clothes?"

"I bought them cheap, father."

"Whose clothes were they before they were yours?"

"An honest gentleman's."

"Hm. You had better get something made for yourself."

"Thank you, father."

"And then you had better think of making the money
to pay for them. In the meantime, I will advance the
money to you."

That was satisfactory enough. But—— "You found
no employment?"

He began to tell how Sir John Harrison had disappointed
him by falling ill and then dying, how there was so much
favouritism at Court that it was hard for an honest man
without money to get on. "The secular world, father, is

like that in orders. There is not more plurality under
Aylmer and Perne than at Court. Provided you have the
right man's ear there is no stopping you, but if you have
not——"

"Quite so. Do you ever expect to have the right man's
ear?"

Uncertain what answer his father needed, Greene fell
back on a sentence of Coppinger's. "You know what they
say, father—God and the Devil are always ready to help.
It is only a matter of calling on the right one, don't you
think?"

"You should be an authority, my son, by this time,"
said Robert the elder.

And the future? "To tell you the truth, father, I am unsettled in mind. I don't quite know what I want to do.
I find myself more or less in the position of Menocrates—
you remember?—at the beginning of his career. I could
go into the Church, I know."

"You mean a Reformed Church, when it comes?"

"More or less, father. Or I could set about making a
living by my pen."

"Not under my roof, Robert! If all the scribblers of the
day were taken and set to useful employment, we'd not
have the times we do. I thought your experiences already
would have put such nonsense out of your head."

"Or I could stay home and put my energies into your
saddlery, father. I imagine that is the course that would
most please mother."

The elder Greene thought this over for a day or two.
"Very well," he said at last; "if you want to help me, you
can. What is this your mother was telling me about your
saying you might get married?" Greene explained that he
had mentioned it as a distant possibility now that he was
minded to settle down. "Because you'll need a different
stroke about you if you take a wife, you realise that? No
more wasting time and substance, but work and prayer
and more work and steady living." He agreed without
argument.

For Greene had fallen in love. With Dorothy Fernley. To an extent he could see how the unlikely thing had happened, but always he must confess that something was intermingled that defied explanation. His pity for her, the extraordinary conditions in which their acquaintance had begun, his recourse to her after his ejection from Braiding, the uncertainty of her future and his, the charm and intimacy of those first days at the cottage, the growing delight in her presence that had kept him at Hartop long after he had any possible excuse for staying there, the genuine desire to do away with the evil of earlier days and devote himself to the service of an ideal—all these had counted. Beyond them he knew something incalculable and hitherto never experienced. The adorations of his boyhood, the genuine tenderness of his regard for Benita, the remorseful girdings at his own vileness that had followed his Italian debauch—this was quite different. At Hartop, the way he was going clear to himself, he had found a new happiness in his relationship with Dorothy, his almost sexless devotion to her. It was a revelation to him that after all the sordidities of lust he was still capable of love free from sensuality. Even the old way of looking at women— that seemed unthinkable with Dorothy. The curt masculine judgments, brisk assessings of partners in bed, were merely shocking. The things he had said, the things he had thought —Great God, anyone could tell this was different! And part of it all was the feeling that by a pure love for Dorothy he would wash away all the faults of the past, cleanse himself, and start afresh on a quest of eternal beauty and the worth of life. He had sense enough to know that men like Edmund Coppinger, if they loved, would find greater happiness with women than he and those like him, reeking with sexual experiment though they were. And now he would be back with them, his false start forgotten, a glorious race ahead.

So far as there had been any courtship, it was a strange one. Her father dead so recently—neither wished to forget it. Anna was too faithful a duenna, and no conviction

of the wisdom of her presence could make it other than an
annoyance. They were hardly ever alone, and then for
such brief intervals. He talked about Cambridge, about
Italy, about London, with a fine flow of coloured words;
he talked about himself; usually she listened, though for
her part she told something of her quiet life with her father,
the reasons for that one short visit to London, her father's
virtues, and something of those kinsfolk in Wirral to whom
news of his death had been sent. She thought she could
just manage the cottage if all went well, and if not, there
was the chance rather than the choice of service. Greene,
only half listening to her plans, was making up his mind to
find a regular income and assure her life. If only he had
money, how pleasant to settle here at Hartop and let princes
and counsellors, prelates and conquerors go their perilous
ways. Amidst a kind of rustic innocence, with the music
of a brook, the bleating of lambs, the dancing of red-kirtled
maids in summer, the dull shuffle of shoes through snow in
winter: in their season the bursting buds, the delicate sheep-
cropped grass, the ceremonies of May and Harvest-Home—
the wains draped with flowers, the horses gay with aromatic
herbs, the healthy hinds stuffing the good cheer—the
placid joys of ingle-nook and sanded floor, with mirth and
story and kindliness, and warm, sweet-smelling beds at
end of day. To think so with Greene was to write, and with
a hitherto unparalleled burst of inspiration he set down
on paper a dozen poems which he thought the best he had
ever composed. Some of these he read to Dorothy and
Anna, who voted for the shepherd's wife's song as the one
with the prettiest moral.

Unfortunately, reality would keep breaking in with
reminders of his pennilessness, and at last he announced
that he must go back to Norwich. It was Dorothy's agitation
at this statement which encouraged him to ask permission
to return to see her, soon.

"I may?" he asked that evening when for a few minutes
they were alone. "I may come back and see you again,
Mistress Dorothy?"

"Will you?" Surely he detected pleading in her voice?

"You will let me?"

"You will come?"

"And you are not going to be unhappy while I am away?"

She smiled at that. "Who can say how one will be, Master Greene?"

"You must promise." He looked from the fire to her. "Your happiness is precious to me."

"I promise then."

"You make me happy when you say that. And the future—never worry about that." He wanted to say more and pledge himself, but a hateful and unworthy caution kept him from the decisive words. "The future is never terrifying when it becomes present." She looked away from him, and he from her. "And when we say good-bye now—no, I don't know what I meant to say!"

Anna entered to save him from worse blundering. She, he guessed, would be glad to see the back of him. He revealed his mental commitments by vowing there'd be no room for Anna in any house of his.

He left two days later. How much of life was good-byes and greetings? Some of the neighbours were staring over the hedges at his departure, and not for the first time he reproached himself for his indiscretion. Who knew what might be in the heads of these clods, these dung-boots? On his horse with the curved back, in Fernley's clothes, under the fresh sun, he reproved the world for not being better-thoughted.

And now in Norwich he settled down to help his father. The poems of pastoral life he had left with Dorothy, half-intended as a pledge that he would soon return. The writing he must do now was tiresomely different. He was a beautiful hand-writer, so Greene the elder set him to ledgers and accounts and to designing capital initials for transfer work or embroidery. Occasionally he went around collecting

debts, and was surprised by his moral righteousness before
bad debtors. What of equity, justice, the foundations of
commerce and industry? Had men no shame? "Why
not commit the man Jennings to gaol, father?" he advised
in one case.

He met Adam Bolton, naturally. Adam had thought
better of it after all and not sought to enlarge his mind
by foreign travel. Mother Dowse's, behind the Market
Place, was as far as he need travel for his particular
kind of enlargement. "I tell you, Robert, she's got
just the girls there for men like you and me. And it's
open house for you, remember—not a penny piece shall
you pay." Greene shook his head. "Nothing to be afraid
of, man. I *know*." Greene still shook his head. "What's
the matter then? Once bitten twice shy, eh?" "I've
changed a lot, Adam. It no longer appeals to me." Adam
thought over this unnatural state of affairs. "It won't
last," he vowed; "Never does once a man's been over
the tiles. You always start thinking about the girl at the
Red Lion or that other one in the field near Wymondham,
and soon you can't help yourself. So when you grow a
bit tired of virtue—don't forget the Old Adam, eh?"
He dug into Greene's ribs. "No offence meant or taken,
Robert lad. I'm an understanding fellow. I've been about
a bit. I know one end of a horse from the other, eh?
Since I was a youngster that high, I've known what was
what. You can rely on the Old Adam, and don't you
forget it." His wink showed Greene that Adam would
believe nothing but that he stood in fear of his father now
he was working for him.

They met frequently, Adam usually making some
such invitation. He *knew*. He said he did, so he must
have.

He met Mistress Petherill again. No denying it, there
was still something about her. He repeated proverbs about
the old fiddle, though Mistress Petherill was far from old.
Perhaps it was because she had been Neaera that he would
never lose interest in her. She sensed at once that he no

longer wanted to flirt with her, and they gossiped together for more than half an hour one day in late July, laughing shamelessly at Adam Bolton, and finally laughing together at Greene's earlier immolatory passion for her. He said the proper gallantries, but less than half meant them, and she less than half believed them. He learned with a shock that Nat's Susan had died in childbirth last year. Poor little Susan! Poor little dumpy Susan! And his old friend Nat too. He must see him without fail. He had been ungracious to Nat and news like this made him sorry for it.

He made no delay and saw Nat that afternoon, in the self-same loft over the self-same stables. There were the horses, their rumps glistening towards the doors, their heads inclined to the mellow shadows of the mangers, their feet clip-clopping the cobbled flooring; the same dogs were there, Flame the white-headed sheep-dog, old and lazy, Benjamin the mongrel, his purpose in life more than anything else to keep Flame in good temper; the strong sweet smells of fodder and manure and the breath and sweat of clean animals; there was Ned in leather and fustian rubbing at a piece of harness.

"Hullo, Ned?"

"G'day to 'ee, Master Greene."

Greene wanted to say No, don't call me Master Greene; call me Robert, as you used to—but he did not. The ranks and orders of men were fixed as those of angels. "I hear you have had a sad loss, Nat."

"Ay, I have."

"I wanted to see you and say how sorry I am."

"Thank'ee, Master Greene."

"I have been away. I seem to have been away an eternity, Nat. I hadn't seen Susan since I was just a youngster. It shows the way the world goes—how we are young one day and old the next. All the strange things that happen in between. How is the boy—young Nat, that's his name, isn't it?"

"There's naught wrong with him, Master Greene."

In another couple of minutes he came to see that he was no part of Nat's world and would not be permitted to intrude into it. Nat was strong, God had built him slow and strong, he could take the most tremendous blows and keep square on his feet. Going back across the yard, discontented, Greene saw the child young Nat, just such another piece of sound timber, waddling rather than walking towards the stables. He gave him a half-penny, which the lad accepted gravely and with no more than a bare thank-you. Hardly off pap, he looked an ostler already as he disappeared past a chestnut horse. What was this quality men had who never ran after the world's gauds? Coppinger as one form of it, Nat as another. And those without it, like Bolton the wencher, the Sidleys father and son, great men like the Archbishop, all frantic chasers after disillusion. He must leave those ranks. With Dorothy it would be different.

And he thought too: Robin, Robert, Master Robert, Master Greene—not an honourable progression, this aggrandizement of title.

In August he told his father and mother he was going into Lincolnshire. His father pulled down the famous eyebrows, and Jane said tremulously: "Not to that place——"

"Be quiet, woman!"

"No, mother," Greene said gently, as a rebuke to his father; "not to Braiding. To Hartop. To someone I know there."

"I don't like your Lincolnshire friends," Greene senior said harshly.

"You know nothing of this friend, father. I should have told you before. It is the girl I want to marry."

"Why, Robin!"

"Marry!" said his father.

"Yes, mother. I know I am to blame. I should have been more open, I know, but there were so many things to explain, and I had to think carefully first."

"Who is this girl, Robin?"

With many of his facts in the wrong place he explained. "And you actually lived in her house, with no folk of hers there, for a month! What conduct was that, Robert?" His dislike of his father in his awkward moods grew stronger than ever. He looked from one parent to the other. "I may tell you again," he said rebelliously, and left the room and the house.

It was to Jane he emptied his heart later. "Mother, you'll understand, I know." They were in the kitchen, she with her hands in flour, he seated on the corner of the table where long ago he had waited for candied peel and bits of fruit.

"You did nothing wrong, Robin?"

"Mother, as God's above me——"

"Because a marriage started like that more often than not turns out badly—that's why I ask. You can think of examples round here: Tom Birch and Fred Hopewell's daughter, and that girl of Anthony Gissing's who married the man from near your grandfather Beetham's."

"But it's not like that, mother! I'd die before I would do her a wrong. I'd cut my hand off before it should offend her. You don't realise, mother—there has never been anything like this before. Never in the history of the world! I love her, mother."

Jane began asking questions: what was her name? who were her parents? what were they? could she cook? was she beautiful? was she as pretty as Alice, for example?

"Oh, I've never compared her with anyone, mother. She's—oh, I don't know what she is! There aren't any words, mother, and that is all about it." Blunderingly he began to show how unique she was.

"Well, Robin," she said sensibly at the end, "I can see you will marry her, whatever your father says, so I must talk him round a bit, don't you think?"

In reality Jane was delighted at the idea of a daughter-in-law. If in addition she could have Alice home, she would have nothing in the world to ask for. She asked Robin whether he would be bringing his bride to live in Norwich, and he, though uncertain of it so far, promised that he would. He did not want his mother's enthusiasm cooled.

"Of course," he said, "it all depends on whether she will have me." But it was inconceivable to Jane that any girl should not want her Robin, and she regarded the matter as settled.

The talking round of Robert Greene the elder must have been done with skill, for he raised no further objection to his son's journey and even asked one or two proper questions. Would his son like him to ride over in ceremonial fashion and pay his respects to his proposed daughter-in-law? But Greene suspected this was merely a dodge to investigate with a view to prohibition, and suggested it might be left till his next journey. This time on a horse without a curve in his back he set off early in the morning, with messages from his mother to Dorothy, and the strongest welcomes he could frame for her to spend a season with them at Norwich. "Quite so," said his father, as though he had forgotten all about the matter.

So there he was in August, riding the same narrow road through Hartop to Dorothy's cottage. He was not vain enough to think the stir among the neighbours at his coming entirely complimentary. No doubt tongues had swung loose on their hinges since he rode away. Pigs! Now knock, knock, knock at the door he had arrived at in such a pickle last time. He had driven himself to an agony of anticipation. Anna answered it. He would like to fling her out into the garden. "Where is your mistress?" She gawked at him. "Where is your mistress, I say?"

He pushed inside.

"Master Greene!"

"Dorothy!" He checked. "Call me Robert. Don't call me Master Greene. Call me Robert. Is it really you? Is it you, Dorothy?"

He had her hands in his, to press them, to kiss them. "Master Robert, you ought not!"

"I ought and I will!"

"Will you take off your riding boots?" asked the scandalised and inexorable Anna.

"Have I been a long time?" he asked later, calmer now the two of them.

"But I knew you would come," she told him.

"Of course I'd come! Hasn't it been my one thought all these weeks. Have you ever been out of my mind? Anna," he said firmly, "will you go away?"

"Not unless Mistress Dorothy tells me to."

"Then go, Anna, because I do ask you."

Greene sighed. "The sight of her about the place! How can you endure her?"

"She is kind to me."

"Then I must endure her too. But we won't call her back just yet, all the same. I have something to ask you, Dorothy —will you marry me?"

"But, Robert!"

He fell on his knees and buried his face in her lap. "You must, you must, you must! I shall do something terrible if you don't. I shall not live if you don't. Say you will, Dorothy!"

She furrowed his red hair with her hands. "You are such a rash man, Robert. You come rushing back, and before you are in the house five minutes——"

"But I can't help it. I'm in love, Dorothy; I'm in love with you. That is why! You must say yes! You must." The words came tumbling from his lips, how he loved her, how he could not live without her, how he needed her, how he thought of nothing else but her, how he asked only to make her happy, protect her, lay down his life for her. Would she then marry him? Would she? Would she? His unseized ideal had made him drunk; he knew panic at the idea that he might not be allowed to give his life for her.

She was stunned and delighted by all this. However much you had expected, even planned, this was almost frightening. Love and the desire for security pulled her to him. "Your father and mother?" she asked. He satisfied her with quick babblings. "Yes, I'll marry you, Robert."

It was the first time for him to kiss her. He had heard from Alice, defending Copson, that he had not kissed her until after their pledge of marriage, and the coincidence came home to him now. But Copson as a husband—he would be fifty times the husband Copson was. By all hell-flames, his brother-in-law should be no better than a wifebeater alongside him, Robert Greene, the happiest man the sun had ever shone on. He looked at Dorothy as though she were too delicate to kiss, as though the very breath from his lips would melt her away, but she was still there when it was all over. And if anything looking the better for it, too. The kiss had grown rather less spiritual as it went on. "Shall we sit down and talk?" he said.

What happy hours those were! One after the other ticking off in unheard seconds, while they deliberated the amazing future. All the things they would do, all the marvellous things that lay ahead, incredible prospects of realisable delight. The long summer evening drew to a close and still they were talking there; the red sun glowed farewell among his amber clouds, and still they were talking; greyness made the world its own, deepening with the beginning of night, and bats wheeled up and down the chilly air, under the first stars. "Are you cold?" he asked. No, she was not cold. They were afraid to move, for once this day was over its like could never appear again. Anna must have gone to bed, offended; there was not even a taper to light them when they rose. Happiness fully understood at the moment of its complete-ness will turn to melancholy, and it did so now for these. "I'll sleep down here," he said.

He opened the door after she had gone upstairs, and looked into the garden, loath to sleep and end the joy. An owl was calling in the great trees to the right and another answered from far behind the cottage. "Help me, God," said Robert Greene, "and make me a good husband."

CHAPTER XXV

In the late summer of 1586, eighteen months after his marriage, Greene, in Tombland, Norwich, could cry out with the vehemence but without the conviction of Job that no man was so sorely tried as he. What a mistake it had been! How everything conspired to make him miserable! Doll, Doll, Doll, if only we had stayed to think; if only we had known!

It hardly bore thinking on, this position of his. If only there were remedy—but there was none.

"Doll," he had said—he had given up counting how often—"won't you come to London with me?"

It was impossible. He must be mad to ask it.

"But, Doll, God knows I've told you often enough— I shall go off my head here at home. I am sick to death of it. I must get away!"

And he had thought her weak and tender, without will-power. Never again would he set up as judge of character. "You must be sensible, Robert. How can we go to London or anywhere else? How would we manage with Kit?"

"Kit?" He swallowed. "You use him as an excuse for everything. The child has turned your brain. You are a different woman since you had Kit. Don't I love him the same as you do? Don't I? But I don't lose my head over him. I can still see there is a world around me. Whatever I want, it is always this 'What about Kit?' As sure as hell goes deep, Doll, I'm getting sick to death of it."

Prim, tight little mouth, impatient snap of the head. "If you want to talk that way!"

"Now listen, Doll. I'm sorry if I shouted. But I'm upset. I'm getting to the end of my tether. Let's get away from here. That is all I am asking."

"But I'm happy here, Robert. You ought to be too. You have your work—writing work, the sort you wanted——"

"Pah!" To think he used to read her those lovely poems of his! Might he as well have read the household accounts? "Pah!"

"You are so unreasonable. I don't know why you have changed like this. When we were at Hartop nothing would do except sell up and come home here to live, and now we have come and I like it and want to stay, it is all this talk about going to London where we should not have a rag to our backs in six months' time. You talk so childishly sometimes!"

That hurt him. "I do, do I? It's you talk childishly. Why, anyone would think to hear you sometimes you were still a girl and Kit your sawdust dolly. All I can say is it has been a good thing for you that you have had me to think for you and work for you. When I remember——"

She was ready to cry now. This irritated him still more. Why settle an argument with tears? Always wanting the unfair advantage, making him feel he deserved hanging, women's weapons, all deliberate, just to score off him. "It is nothing to cry about," he said brusquely. "The question was: Will you come to London with me?"

"No, I won't! And that's that."

"You think so? Don't forget this, Doll—I have as much say in the matter as you, more perhaps, and I want to go to London, and I'll go yet. So you think it over again."

"You can, if you like, but I'll not go, Robert. I'm going to stay here where I'm happy with Kit."

"You never think about being happy with me for a change, do you?"

"Of course I am happy with you. You and Kit—it is all the same, isn't it? You *are* childish, Robert."

"Am I then?" The argument beat to and fro over the same ground. He wheedled, spoke firmly, even made demands, wheedled again, but her mind was made up. She was very well in Tombland, and in Tombland she meant to stay. Christ! thought Greene, I must be a good husband when you think of the men who'd drag her by the hair to London if they really wanted to go. But there it

was—he couldn't play the bully. He could never be his
father's kind, his word law in the house, scowls for his wife
and blows for his children at the slightest upset. He pondered.
Doll had revealed herself the stubbornest thing in petticoats, and yet once he had thought her the yieldingest little
thing, unable to shoo a calf out of a garden. She would not
budge for him. Back there at Hartop, if he had said 'Jump
in the river!' surely she would have jumped, but this last
year in Norwich—what a change. Just as everything else
changed: ambitions, feelings, circumstances.

He was bored. He was sick of life here in sleepy Tombland,
with nothing to do but watch the children going to school
and the worshippers going to the Cathedral. Sick of the
dull round of copying, crediting, and collecting; sick of the
same faces on the same streets; sick of the same stupid voices,
the same silly greetings; sick of the household round too:
up in the morning at the same hour, to work with his father
at the same hour, passing the same places at the same hour,
feeding at the same hour, listening to his mother and Doll
discussing the quality and quantity of milk, the colour of
Kit's napkins, the vicissitudes of tooth-cutting. Sometimes
he wanted to stand up and shout: "Is there nothing else in
this magnificent and only once-visited world to talk about
except the baby!" When you knew of the present dangerous
turn in the Low Countries, Leicester encamped before
Zutphen, the fate of Protestantism in the balance; when
from the New World came strange reports of Raleigh's
settlements, rumours of El Dorado, mountains of gold, and
home to Norwich itself the potato and tobacco plants;
when in Spain and the Indies men heard of the new Enterprise of England not long to be awaited; when these last
few days had seen the arrest of Babington, Barnwell, Salis-
bury and Jones, and the exposure of their plot to assassinate
the Queen's Majesty and put Scottish Mary on her throne.
Might not a man expect in his own home to hear of something save his child? Yet he loved his son, he told himself,
as much as father ever loved son, loved his soft red moss of
hair, his blue eyes in his pudgy face, his fatly helpless hands

and feet. But to dote, to rave, to surrender your self-respect
—why do it? Jane laughed at him to his face when he
expostulated they would spoil the child, make him a girl,
a mere simpleton. She was as bad as Doll every bit. After
the children she had brought into the world and reared
you'd think she would be sick of the sight of babies.

If he did not love Kit and Doll so much, he told himself,
matters would be simplified. If one morning Doll were to
tell him she had grown to hate him, that she detested his
very presence, that she wished he'd take himself to the devil
for want of a better friend—the future would be simpler,
no denying it would. He thought he'd be off.

He came at last to speculate on the course of his life had
he not married. If instead of hiding himself here in Norwich
like a worm in a dunghill, with nothing to do but grow fat,
if, instead, he had spent these last years in London, where
men with not a tenth of his ability were in demand, what
might he not be by this time? His poetry alone would have
carried him into some great man's favour; Her Majesty's
affection for wits was well known, he would have come to
her notice, found some easy and well-paid post, become
a man of mark, a big frog in a bigger puddle. Surrounded
by colour, wealth and movement, making a splash like the
rest of them.

Had he made a mistake?

It was a decisive day when he admitted to himself, not
without shame, that he had. He had been carried away
by his better nature, that was the truth of it. He had sacri-
ficed himself for Doll's well-being. Was it right that a man
who could offer the world all he could should stay
undistinguished far from the centre of national life? Without
deceiving himself he became casuistic. Was it not a form of
selfishness to live thus at Norwich? Thus to choose the easier
way? And sometimes he could not help thinking: Would
Doll be any worse off without him? If he decided that his
life was his own and that he *would* go to London, let her
stay behind if she had no mind to stand at his shoulder.
She was comfortably placed, would never lack for anything;

apart from the fortune he was always promising her, she would have the boy Kit, and as he had told her so often, she had mighty little use for her husband since Kit came.

Mind, if she did not come with him, he would be home to see her and Kit every so often. He thought: There are Alice and her husband in Bucklersbury would be delighted to have us lodge with them. Momentarily he saw Copson's face as the suggestion was made. Kit and John would be playmates; Alice and Doll might have been made for each other; he and Copson—at least they need not get on each other's nerves.

He knew his mother intended him never to leave home again. This dreadful possessiveness usually annoyed and rarely frightened him. And his father had taken it for granted he would stay part of the business; so what with his wife and child, what could he do but sigh and blow and puff and pant, and occasionally reproach the world for being against him?

Without a crisis he could never leave Norwich. He knew it. And the crisis came.

Its herald was the unlikely Adam Bolton. Idleness was eating Adam's brain like a rodent ulcer. He could talk about horses and dogs and women and drink, about bear-baitings and bull-baitings, about a ride to hounds, about fairs and players, and that was all. He had become as dull as other country gentlemen with the same interests and pursuits, but he had an unmistakable affection for Greene. He had sent him and his wife a splendid wedding gift, he had hinted strongly he would like to stand god-father to the child, but Greene's father had forbidden this absolutely.

"You are a lucky fellow, Robert," he would complain; "lovely little wife, lovely little boy. Ay, ay! Now look at me, practically alone in the world as you might say. No father, no mother, no brothers and sisters, not a chick nor child to call my own. Dear, dear, dear!"

Greene, who was sometimes bored with him, sometimes downright angry, nevertheless had to like the good-natured fellow. "You ought to get married, Adam. There's not a girl within twenty miles whose father would not jump at your head, and you know it."

Adam was pleased to think so. "In a way you are right. Only I've got fixed in my habits, Robert. I don't know what it would be like with a woman of my own about the place. I like to go to bed with my boots on when I've had a good night and don't want the trouble of taking them off."

"Your wife might take them off for you."

"I doubt it, Robert. And if I had curtain lectures I don't know what I should do. I know men a-plenty who'd just up with their fists, but you and me, Robert, we are alike in this. We've both got soft hearts. I should just have to suffer under it, Robert." Robert felt there was an unflattering deduction somewhere here, but let it pass. "And there is this too, Robert. I don't know that I could be faithful to one woman. I'm a bit of a rover. I'm just bursting with strength and manliness, that's the truth about me. Why, I've only got to see a pretty woman—so long as she is nothing to do with anyone I know, naturally, Robert—and you'd never believe the way——" He made interesting explanations. "And I'm always thinking this way, Robert: if Liz is fat and forty, little Jess is dark and slight, and just eighteen; and Belle has such dancing eyes, and Nell——"

Greene gave him a couple of minutes. "Yes," he commented, "Ovid said something of the kind."

"Did he? I have forgotten my book learning, Robert. But I'm glad to think Ovid and I thought the same. I used to like those Mattermorses of his. He's a good writer, that Ovid." Greene wondered at the title, but Adam was clapping his hand to his head. "Just like a sieve, that's my head, Robert. I got news for you. Just the news for a lad like you. The players are coming."

"The players! No!"

Yes, yes, they were. Coming to the Red Lion in a week's time. Adam had it from Mistress Petherill. The Queen's Men. To stay four days. Oh glory!

This news threw Greene into a frenzy of expectation. Four whole days! Let his father say what he would, the accounts should have a rest each day while he attended. This would be contact with London once more. The playing and the talking in the Red Lion afterwards—if he spent a guinea or more it would be worth it. The news he would hear! Oh London Town! Oh glory!

He told Doll the actors were coming. "Are they?" she said. She had never seen a play. He tried to explain what they did. "Oh," she said, but her mind was on pastry.

He told his mother. "Are they doing *Barnaby?*" she asked. "You were always fond of *Barnaby*, Robin."

His father found out for himself. "Godless crew! Why do they come to Norwich? Why not stay in London, with thieves, bawds, beggars, outside the walls?"

And so he must wait consumed with impatience, longing to talk about plays and players, but meeting at home ignorance or hostility. By these standards even Adam Bolton was a quick wit.

"I should like you to arrange for me to have the next four afternoons free, father," he announced on the Monday. "I am going to the plays. You'll not be coming, hm?"

"I shall not. Nor your mother. And I hope you have more sense than to take your wife amongst such surroundings, Robert."

"No one there will eat her, father."

"I know that. Players! There is something feverish about this age, Robert, that you did not find twenty, thirty years ago. We were calmer, we worked harder, we had rather less of education and luxury, we made a quieter show to the world. We had standards that are being imperilled to-day." It became a short sermon. "Where will England stand to-morrow? We older men grow afraid. Bustle, hurry, a striving for what will be ashes in the mouth, no better. Admit now, Robert, you are a happier man here at home, with a steady job, holding your head up as you go about the town, a married man starting a family—aren't you happier now than you were when you scurried from Cambridge to

Italy, from Italy to London, from London to wherever-it-was?"

The answer he wanted to make he could not. "Happy in a different way," he admitted tactfully. "But you can manage with Vose and Gurley?"

His father smiled. "You can take your holiday. Till Friday, is it?"

Tuesday afternoon Greene went to the play like other Christian men, paid threepence for his seat, applauded William Johnson as Ozymandias, and went straight back home. It had been a superb performance, he told them. "Would you like to come to-morrow, Doll?" he asked her that night in bed. No, she did not think so. "Aren't you interested in anything except that brat of yours?"

She fired up. "Don't you call him a brat, Robert Greene!"

"He's as much mine as yours, isn't he? I shall call him what I like."

"Will you?" she challenged venomously.

"God above us and all his moulting angels! Where's your sense of fun, Doll? Can't a man even——" Suddenly he recalled how Alice had slapped his face behind the shop in Bucklersbury. Spitfires, ye gods! But if Doll ever dared to slap his face—well, married men needed a sense of humour! He started to laugh.

"What are you laughing at?"

"Oh, just you and me and the world in general. You have to laugh sometimes, Doll, when you think about things."

"You'll wake Kit, you stupid!"

But he went on chuckling till she jabbed him in the ribs, when his good temper vanished. "Oh to the devil with Kit!" he said angrily.

"What did you say?"

"I said, Can't we forget about Kit for a single minute? I come to bed, I ask you to see the play with me, I laugh a bit, and what do I get? 'What about Kit? Don't wake Kit! Kit this, Kit that!' You ought not to be allowed to bring up a child. You and my mother, the pair of you, you are making a fool of the boy. If ever I'd thought——"

"Well, go on!"

"Nothing," he snapped; "go to sleep." He made a violent turn in the bed away from her, dragged the sheet up under his chin, and lay still as a stone. Let her cry! Why should she always have the last word just because she cried? "Go to sleep," he ordered, and then—"You'll be waking Kit." Thus turning the tables on her gave him a mean satisfaction that he detested, and he lay awake for hours.

In the morning there was no reconciliation. He, like a man, swung from under the bedclothes prepared to kiss, forgive and forget; she, like some women, answered him with frigid politeness. All right, he thought, have it your own way, my dear! He began to whistle to amuse his son and dandle him up and down because he knew he shouldn't do this so early in the morning. Then she snatched the child out of his arms. "I've never known——" he said in the most outraged tones, and left the bedroom with the dignity of outrage.

He went in the afternoon to see Edwardes' *Palamon and Arcite*. It was an old play, originally given at Oxford before Her Majesty twenty years ago, but good enough to take on tour. William Johnson was acting again, as Palamon, and Robert Wilson as Arcite. This time Greene did not pay for admission. Entering the house early with Adam Bolton that they might drink a glass of wine, or even two, they found themselves in the best room with the famous Richard Tarleton, and were allowed to treat him too. He had no part in that afternoon's performance and was slightly drunk. Bolton admired the red livery he wore with all the respect due to Her Majesty's own choice, and although he had never seen them, gave it as his opinion that Lord Strange's Men, and the Admiral's, and my Earl of Leicester's, and Lord Oxford's, were nothing to the Queen's. Tarleton measured his man and burst out laughing. How could the others be good? Hadn't Wilson and Johnson come from Leicester's? And Adams from Sussex's? And Dutton from

Oxford's? Add Bentley and Tarleton, the incomparable gagging Tarleton, and what other actors were there? Richard Jones, thought Greene, and the Alleyns and Burbage—there were other actors. Did Tarleton set them down as loobies? Still, he deferred silently to Adam's enthusiasm. Mistress Petherill entering, the talk grew more general. It drew near to three o'clock. Would Masters Greene and Bolton make two of a Party on the balcony? Their eyebrows lifted. Would they? Tarleton bustled off to help behind stage, so those favoured followed the hostess to the best seats. Wagons had been drawn out in front of the stables where Nat worked, and these, covered with boards, formed the stage. A painted cloth hung from stage to ground in front, hiding Limbo, whence would spring the monster that confounds the pride of Arcite and ensures, through providence eterne, that Palamon shall wed the fresh Emily. At the back of the stage hung other cloths, both decorative and useful, for they shut off from the spectators the tiring house established inside the stables and allowed impressive entrances and exits. "The best inn yard in the county," said the complaisant Adam, "and the best appointed for a play." He smoothed his leg, clad in blue silk, and nodded to some of the company: Sir William Paston, Master Wynsdon, Master Knight, Master Carfax. Sir William sat on one side of Mistress Petherill, Greene on the other. The audience enjoyed itself famously, and the players, assured of profit by fine weather and a full yard, enjoyed themselves as well. "When I was up in London," said Adam, seeking comparisons; "When I was in Venice," said Greene; "When I was in Denmark," said Sir William. Stay-at-homes very properly shrank snail-like into their shells as these connoisseurs commented on the action, on the diction, on the groupings. Inevitably Greene began to dominate the talk: his words were better and readier found than the others'. He disproved again his father's conviction that no man can do two things well at once, for he talked and listened well. Sir William Paston, who knew little of Greene, was impressed enough to ask him and his friend to honour him at a supper he was giving that evening to certain of the principal players. In the Red Lion, of course.

The play ended with a betrothal, a dance, and a fanfare of trumpets. The crowd broke up. With Sir William, who wished to compliment the players, Greene and Adam went behind stage. Greene was charmed and excited, by the properties as much as the men there. As he went pottering around, examining paints and masks and costumes, he came upon an old acquaintance, the Fabian Penton with whom he had ridden to London before his Italian journey. Penton recognised him too, though he had forgotten his name. Half-a-dozen words and "Of course! Master Robert Greene, I remember you!" He laughed. "You saw the women actors in Venice?" He wagged his head. "Well, well. You remember how Candler and Shanbrooke would not believe what I told them? Men actors, women actors, boy actors—what next, Master Greene, eh?" Candler was doing well in London, he thought, but he had no news of Shanbrooke. That lively lad Totnell? His voice had gone, but he had the talent. As for himself, he had been up and down the country, town and province, now this theatre shut on account of the plague, now that burnt down, out of work some months, scores and scores of parts; no, he had no reason to grumble. Life was too interesting for a man to find fault with any part of it. Greene agreed, earnestly, and with a strange empty feeling in his stomach. What a lovely world it was, so huge, so strange, so sweet—and he as good as out of it. He'd swop all his security, all his advantages, for the earth on this man Penton's shoes.

Till seven o'clock then. They parted, Adam Bolton to his orphan's home, Greene to Tombland. At home he was miserable, felt himself more cramped than ever, likened himself to a hen with the croup, a one-legged pheasant compared with Penton. Doll was still the madam. "What is the matter with you?" he asked surlily. "Nothing," was her indifferent reply. So—— "As you like!" he ended. He changed his clothes without telling her where he was going, and she did not ask. "I'll be home late," he said defiantly to the household, and off he went.

He saw Adam ahead of him in the fields and shouted for him to wait. "That's a fine suit of clothes, Robert. Where d'you see those slashes in the sleeves? New, aren't they?" Adam spread his feet ahead of him so that his long-toed shoes might be admired. "Pity we don't wear those big cod-pieces, like the Switzers," he suggested. "These slops, sometimes I think they don't set off a man of my figure as much as I should like, Robert." He did not allow this to weigh on him, however, and was soon hoping Sir William would have pork pies and herrings. He had never quite made up his mind whether he preferred herrings with soft or hard roes, stuffed, pickled, grilled, or fried. On the way to the Red Lion he expounded to Greene his theories about boning them, so that the flesh fell away white and plump and tender, like a young pullet's. Sometimes he relied on pepper, sometimes one squeeze of a lemon, sometimes with a real good fat herring no flavouring was best. He increased Greene's melancholy. Was this the life he too must lead—an epicure of herrings?

They had the upstairs room in which he and Adam had discussed the courtesans of Venice. Sir William was there, and dashing Mr. Carfax; Richard Tarleton, complete with squint and flat nose; tall, graceful Robert Wilson, and Johnson with his adopted brow of gloom; Adams, not unlike a hobgoblin, and much-travelled, much-grinning Penton. Mr. Wynsdon arrived ten minutes after the two newcomers, and then they began the feast. Not for the first time Greene realised how blessed he was in travel. He would have appeared the veriest furze-bottom amongst these men otherwise. While Adam had to fall back on his method of opening herrings, he went recklessly over England and Europe. And where were the Queen's Men going after Norwich? Back to London, back to the players' home, back to the hub of the wheel of the universe, back to Court for New Year's Day and Twelfth Night, back among lords and ladies, wits and witlings, fops and flutterers, back to the one and only, the *A per se* of cities. Thought Greene: If only I—— Sir William was returning to town for the winter too. He would see them give their Court performances. Thought Greene: If only I—— And Carfax was visiting relations there. All the world would be in London. Oh, London Town, London Town, his heart ached for it. He began to swear that whether Doll came to London or stayed in Norwich, for his part he'd be off. It wasn't fair to expect him to eat his heart out among doddipoles and clodheads. She *must* go. There were pork pies and herrings, beef though not of the best, game and cheese and fruits; there were sack and burgundy, rhenish and moselle, there were punch and spirits neat, and beer for the illiterate. How they talked, and eventually laughed and shouted! Adams did his Clown from *The Famous Victories*, Fabian Penton a lachrimosity of his own composition, *The Mourning Turtle ;* the great Tarleton stood on the table with tabor and pipe, his face alone enough to make men burst their guts a-laughing, and did the most comical hornpipe and improvisation the inn had ever known. Carfax would have emulated the professionals, but he slipped senseless between the trestles, and Adam Bolton went on discussing herrings, his audience one bottle empty and one bottle half-empty. Greene was called on after Tarleton, and repeated with shaky voice for the first few stanzas and then in a rant the most carnal of his eclogues. "There'sh nothing in Edmund Shpensher," said William Johnson, "an' there'sh nothing in Shir Philip Shidney, an' there'sh nothing in the Earl of Shurrey to compare with that." Adam recurred to ancient praise: "Thish man Robert Greene writes better than Virgil, shee—better'n the Head-mashter of Eton, shee—I *know*, 'cos I was there, shee!" "Why don't you go to London again, Master Greene?" Sir William asked him. Sir William was only moderately drunk. "A man of your attainments could go a long way there."

"I am a married man, Sir William," Greene confessed, as though admitting he was a highwayman.

"Thash right. He's married, Shir William. Now, I ought to get married, Shir William, but why don't I? 'Cos I like my life my own, shee? I got a shervan' at home, Shir William, an' she shays to my dog in the morning—when ish raining, Shir William—'Gerroutshide!' she shays. And when I shay, 'Lerradog alone, can' you?' she shays, 'He's bone-lazy, thash warrer marrer w'im. He 'abn' been out all the morning. He mush be burshting.'" Adam nodded at them before he revealed what a clever fellow he was. "And what do I shay? I shays: 'Lerrimbursht if he wantsh to. Lerradog deshide f'r'imshelf. That dog,' I shays, 'he been gib'n brainsh. He *knowsh*.' Now the point is thish. If I marry, Shir William, do I gerrawoman to shay 'Gerroutshide!' like that to me?"

They all agreed it was certainly a point of view. A single man could not be too careful. "You ought to come with us to town," Wilson declared. "You can write verse. We could do with a man to alter parts. Eh, Tarleton?" They discussed the idea with the pertinacity of drunken men. The very thing! That Edgar Cranston who'd been doing such work for them—he was a better fiddler than a rhymester, a better linguist than a fiddler, and everyone knew he was half ignorant of his own language. He was mentally costive, his brain needed figs. But this Greene now! Had he any more of his verse in his head? Had he indeed! Flattered, intoxicated, he recited *Ah, what is love?* The applause went to his head worse than wine. If he went to London with the Queen's Men, if he distinguished himself by some witty strokes—they would be at Court in three months' time—who knew what a heaven of bliss might lie ahead? Nor need he be tied to so menial an occupation. He was none of your knuckle-suckers, without a penny to scratch his backside with. He had a father with money, he had money himself, he had——

By God, he'd go!

"But I'm married," he said plaintively.

"Ah, what is marriage?" parodied Penton, and Robert Wilson declaimed:

"Ah, what is marriage? It's not a pretty thing;
    As tiresome to a shepherd as a king,
        More tiresome too."

—which struck even Greene as apposite and witty.

"You wouldn't be the first married man to go to London,
would you?" Sir William put it to him. Everyone seemed
to take it for granted his wife would not be travelling with
him.

"I shall have to think it over," he concluded.

He did not go home that night. "Come with me," said
Adam sapiently. "You know that father of yours." It was
to be an endless source of contrition to Greene that that
night he had no one to take proper care of him. He had
grown obstreperous and tried to embrace Mistress Petherill
before he left the Red Lion, reciting from his eclogue the
while, but that practised lady shoved him into Adam's
arms, and then kissed her fingers to him. It had been a
profitable night. Good eaters, good drinkers, good breakers
of everything breakable—and no fear of bilking. No wonder
she kissed her fingers. "Oi, come here!" cried Greene, but
Sir William and Adam Bolton were steering him across the
yard. They sobered up a little crossing the dry fields, but
once inside Adam's house nothing would do but further
hospitality. The talk inevitably turned to women, and as
inevitably to the two new girls at Mother Dowse's. Greene
argued aloud with himself, convinced himself he ought to
go home, but instead went with Adam behind the Market
Place. It was late, but Mother Dowse was obliging. Inside
they went, panting, to the two half-dressed whores, there
was more liquor to dull the edge of conscience, they won
what pitiful satisfaction they could, and had their pockets
picked during the stupor that followed.

Greene woke before Adam in the morning. Woke
frightened and ill and loathing himself. They had been
dragged to bed in a room of their own. As dazedly at first,
then with the shock of a thunderbolt, he recalled the evening

before, he had to sit on the edge of the bed or fall down for sheer agony of mind. Christ! Christ! Christ! that he had to do this! He clenched his fists then. He'd murder that bastard of a Bolton! The whole blasted houseful of them—he'd—he sat down again groaning. He must get out without being seen. That was the thing. They must say he had been at Adam Bolton's all night. They must——

The door opened and Mother Dowse came in. "You awake?" she asked affably. Should he strike her? Should he kill her where she stood? "Did you like the girls, Master Greene?" He waved her away, but she was used to the morning remorse of married customers. She tried to cheer him. "A married man's safe here, Master Greene. None of your kennel-crawlers here with Mother Dowse, none of your rotten goods here. I've got my gentlemen to consider. As I tell my girls——"

"Will you get out?" he shouted.

"There, there, you'll feel different soon. I don't wonder you feel the way you do. From what Mistress Catherine was telling me—— Of course, you owe me some money, Master Greene, but we'll let that stand over till after breakfast, shall we?"

"Fetch me some cold water," was all he would answer.

Catherine came in with a pitcherful and a basin. He ignored her greeting, the great blowsy, bloated, blub-faced bitch that she was; she went off with a smile and the unspoken but heartfelt wish that he might kiss her backside; and then he washed his face and poured water over his head. With a sudden spurt of ill-nature he flung the dirty water that was not spilt on the floor over Bolton, and so roused him. "Wake up for God's sake!" he snarled. "You look like a flayed bullock there." Adam made himself a martyr, said nothing, but bestirred himself.

They went out the discreet back way, Greene on tenterhooks till they entered Adam's house, by the back way too. Adam kicked the dog that came so often near bursting, and the servants took their cue from that. His pocket had been picked, Mother Dowse had a further bill for him, and as for poor Robert—— "Adam," Robert was saying, his voice unsteady, "I am as near hating you as I shall ever be to hating anyone. You couldn't even——" There were a dozen retorts Adam could have made, and every one of them just, but he only shrugged his shoulders. He would have his say later.

They tried to eat a little food, in silence. "A common adulterer!" said Greene all at once. "A filthy fornicating husband! My God, that this should come upon me."

Adam drank a little water. "You must go home and say you were here with me for the night. Say you drank a drop too much, if you like. They will know that, anyway. Forget the other, that's my advice."

"As though I could!"

"I'll call round in a couple of hours and see how you got on. We must tell the same story, you can see that."

"Hell and all its furies, don't you realise——"

Adam thanked his stars he was still a bachelor. He meditated. And Greene had called himself such a stallion too. Well, he wasn't the first to mess in his own bed, not even his wife the wiser, and he certainly would not be the last. He stood up. "After the cheese comes nothing, Robert. If we have finished, you had better go. No one could have seen us, so put a good face on it. As for me—mum's the word, Robert. Never fear!"

It wasn't Adam he did fear. He walked gloomily over to Tombland. Gurley met him as he came level with the shop. "Your father would like to talk with you, Master Robert, in behind there."

Was anything so bad as a guilty conscience? He had never felt like this even as a small boy with a beating waiting for him.

"Well, father, I hear you wish to speak to me?"

He watched him open the door into the shop. "Gurley, and you, Vose, take that piece of work out to the bench. Don't come back till I call for you." Letting even the servants know there was a row ahead. "I am ashamed to call you son," said Greene senior.

"I cannot see that I have done anything so terrible."

"You cannot? You have the impudence to stand there and tell me to my face you see nothing wrong in what you have done?"

"I said nothing of the kind. I'm not going to deny——"

"Be silent till I finish!"

"Indeed I'll not," said Greene, white-faced. "Speak more civilly to me. I'm not a child any longer. What d'you expect me to do—take my breeches down and bend over? Speak more civilly or not at all!"

"So," said his father heavily. "So."

"I'll not stand your treating me as you do! I'm no longer the child you used to whip whenever it suited you. You seem to forget that!"

"Perhaps if I had whipped you harder you might have spared me and your mother and your wife and child the shame you bring on us."

"And maybe not! Can't a man get drunk once in twelve months without you and your kind looking down your noses at him?"

"Drunk? My boy, my boy, if you had but got drunk!" This was it. He drew a tremendous breath into his lungs, for he felt airless. "Well?" he said.

"I don't need to ask you, Robert. Your offence is written in your face. You went to that wicked house behind the Market Place last night. As God is in heaven and hears me, I'll not let the week go by but I see them carted! Lashed at the cart end, lashed to the city's edge!"

"A job after your own heart, I doubt not. You've been good at lashing all your life, and my poor back can tell the story."

"Very well, Robert—that is as good an answer as you can make. What will you do now?"

"What should I do? Am I a leper? Must I have my dish and clapper? Am I unclean?"

"You may be," his father said.

"Pah!"

"Are you going back to your wife?"

"I am as fit to go to her as you to yours."

He did not flinch from the tremendous blow he saw coming. He stood half-stunned while his father seemed to rear over him. "Get out of this house!"

He put up his hand and looked dumbly at the blood that had gushed from his nose over the close mesh of thin red hairs between the knuckles. Then—"I'll not go!" he said fiercely. "I have a wife and child here. I'll stay."

"You will not! Never again in house of mine!"

"You think I want to? You think it's not on sufferance I've always lived here? You think I ever cared a tinker's damn for you? Then think the truth now for a change!"

"I tell you, and I swear it by my hopes of salvation, you shall not stay in my house, Robert."

He knew his father meant that. "Very well, I'll go." He wiped away blood. "I'll go back to Lincolnshire. I'll take Doll and Kit there."

His father checked himself. "Will you listen to me?"

"If you are brief."

"Judge whether I wish to say such things to my own son!" A spasm of intolerable pain crossed his face. "I must think of you, despite your deeds, that you have some natural feeling left for your wife and babe. Think, Robert, think— think of those in whose bones must tyrannize the horrid scourge of lust, who rot as they live—will you expose your wife and son to even the chance of that?"

Fear for himself tore at Greene, anger that his righteous father should be in the right, and pity too for the others. "I'll leave them here," he said. Through his head ran Go to London, Go to London, Go to London! He watched his father clasp his hands, close his eyes, move his lips in prayer. Go to London, Go to London, Go to London! More excitedly now.

But to go like this! Again he wiped away blood.

But to go at all!

"I shall need money," he said sulkily.

"You have money, surely?"

"My pocket was picked last night." His father grimaced. "The rest I'll leave with Doll. And I shall need a horse." "You shall have what you need. When will you go?"

That day. His belongings—he'd have to call at the house for those. That afternoon then, when Jane and Doll would be out marketing, would be the time. He would miss the play, but he thought elatedly there would be plenty of plays where he was going.

He went back to Adam Bolton's. Adam was about to leave the house, but he made no bones about putting off his affairs. This looked serious.

"Can you keep your mouth shut, Adam?"

"Well now, Robert, as though you need ask that! I may not be the brightest fellow, but true as steel, that's Adam Bolton. True as blade to sheath, boy. What happened? Was there a row? Ah, I was afraid so."

"I am going to London, Adam."

He whistled. Cooey! "When, Robert?"

"At once. I've had a quarrel with my father. I am to get my things this afternoon. Can I stay here with you to-day, till this evening?"

Adam patted him on the shoulder. "A day, a week, a month—as long as you like, Robert. But don't fret yourself—this will blow over. You have no idea how my poor old mother used to quarrel with me when I'd been up to some trick or other, but it always blew over." Greene told him curtly this would do nothing of the kind. "I hope you don't think it my fault, Robert. I'd be the last man in the world to get a friend into trouble. That's why they threw me out of school, Robert—because I wouldn't blab."

At half-past two he was outside his home. He knocked at the door, astonished that he must. His father opened it. "I've come," he said. He went up to his and Doll's bedroom, his father standing at the head of the stairs, and packed into a large portmanteau the things he would be taking with him. Skilfully he prized up one of the floor boards and pulled into the light a canvas bag containing most of the purchase money of Doll's house and goods at

Hartop. He fully intended to leave this in view for his wife, but suddenly he thought: It is my father who is driving me away. Let him look after them. He stuffed it into the portmanteau. "I am ready," he announced. He went with his father almost to the door, when he stopped to look around him. The old chairs, the one his mother had rocked him in, the cloth for cleaning dishes, the dry sandy floor, the fire, the lovely smell of home. "I shall come back soon," he said harshly to his father, but he just held out a purse. "Here are four nobles. They should see you to some useful employment. There is nothing Doll ought to know?"

"Only that you are driving me from home," he replied, with deliberate misunderstanding.

"Her money?"

"Is her own, not yours."

He rode away, and they did not say good-bye.

CHAPTER XXVI

HE ARRIVED IN London about the middle of the month and took lodgings with a couple named Desouter just below Strand Bridge. They were dearer than he need pay for, but he had a good deal of money in his pocket and was confident of more. For he had business to attend to.

Those were stirring days, in late September. On the 20th and 21st of the month Babington and his accomplices were executed at Lincoln's Inn Fields before a crowd which at first roared they be cut down and disembowelled while life was yet in them, but grew quieter, almost ashamed, as the young men met their deaths so nobly. Greene was there on the second day. Great God, what men will do to men! He could not shout. And at the same time the statute whereby the Council of Twenty-Four should seek out all who would make rebellion or invade the kingdom or hurt the Queen's person; for or by whomsoever employed that might lay claim to the crown of England; and that the person for whom they should attempt the same should be utterly incapable of the crown, and prosecuted to death by all faithful subjects. None other intended than that wretched Scottish Mary now at Fotheringhay, marked down to die, the means only in dispute. After this came news of Sidney's wound at Zutphen, incurred with fool-hardy chivalry, scolded and deplored by the Queen, and slower still the true report, the wonder of the age:—"Being thirsty with excess of bleeding, he called for drink which was presently brought him; but as he was putting the bottle to his mouth, he saw a soldier carried along, who had eaten his last at the same feast, ghastly casting up his eyes at the bottle, which Sir Philip perceiving, took it from his head before he drank, and delivered it to the poor man, with these words: 'Thy necessity is greater than mine.'" Greene,

hearing it, could not forbear tears. If Sidney went, could
the nation be the same again? And go he did, in October,
for his death to cast all London into gloom. But Leicester,
his uncle, would soon be home, the same vain, obstinate,
giddy, trifling favourite, not worth his nephew's shoelace.
Much power for him and Whitgift, still flinging into city
gaols dissenters from the Articles, though all around were
rumours of those prepared against him.

These were national concerns. Greene had his own. What
was Doll thinking of his flight? And his mother? What could
he tell Alice and her husband? The taste of Mother Dowse's
hospitality was foul in his mouth, and he feared it would
prove strong enough to pollute even his lies. Yet he knew
he could tell them anything, and they'd be none the wiser.
Or indeed, tell them nothing. A month had passed since
his arrival but he had not visited them. Nor had he seen
Coppinger, now in a small clerical post at Court. He shook
his head over Coppinger. What had he in mind? Why this
service with Mammon? Not for gain, that was certain.
There could be no good end to it.

But with it all—shame, doubt, remorse—he was glad to
be in London, to feel about him again the tide of human
existence. He told himself he felt twenty times brisker than
in Norwich, copying bills in sleepy Tombland. He drew
vitality from the crowds about the streets: the sharp young
men in coloured silks, hands on sword hilts, or carrying
caps that their glossed and curled hair might be admired;
the soldiers hurrying to duty or loitering on hot pleasure,
their breastplates agleam in rain or sun, sometimes long pikes
in their hands; the sailors at the river edge or docks, smelling
of tar and fish and distant waters, in their bearded mouths
a wild jargon of their own, fierce-quarrelling; men of law
like sleek black cats, merchant venturers in furs to show their
substance; churchmen; the ragged boys; the beggars, the
sellers of ballads, of sweetmeats, toys, of little pictures of
the Queen, of Spanish coins; loiterers around Paul's,
tradesmen of Cheapside, booksellers on the Strand, butchers,
bakers, and candlestick-makers; the ever-changing pageants

of the playhouses, the gaiety and viciousness of the South Bank, the rainbow pomp of spectacles and processions, the perilous tramp of armed guards, the headstrong clatter of royal messengers over broken cobbles—all these he loved; and the swirling talk of taverns, the quick encounters, the rapid interchange of news and views, the friendly pot of beer. The womenfolk of the city too: resplendent ladies bound for Court, escorted by their dandiprat lords; goodwives haggling at the markets, squeezing cabbages, turning over the new potato, rejecting turnips as maggoty; shrill fishwives, vendors of smalls, eel fry; young wives proudly bashful in the fields of an afternoon with husbands; young girls like lilies, like lilac, like apple-blossom in March, like snap-dragons too; the vinegar retorts of maidservants—no flowers, some of these; the drab and glittering hierarchies of prostitutes. For good or bad this was London; and from these crowds he felt strength and inspiration beat wavelike on his swelling heart. The old magic of names had not deserted him: Broken Wharf was finer than Genoa port, and London Bridge bore it over the Ponte Vecchio. What a world of instruction and delight in Lombard Street, in Allhallows-in-the-Wall, in Blackfriars or Ludgate or St. Mary Rouncival! Oh London Town! Dear London Town!

At last he did call on the Copsons. Two questions put and answered—Had he been to Norwich, Yes; Had he told about them, No—Alice was genuinely pleased to see him, overwhelming him with wishes and implorations, but Copson could do no more than accept him with the calm acquiescence of one who knows a bad halfpenny will turn up sooner or later. A thousand things to tell of home. "Why don't you go and see them, Alice? Leave the boy with Geoffrey. He is old enough." He suggested this, hoping she would not think of it, and then before he knew it— "But you don't know yet," he had announced. "I'm a married man, Alice!" They goggled at him. "Well, can't I marry the same as everyone else?" As for why he had not brought her to London—it would be a long story if he told all, so he told instead that he was in London to prepare the way for her coming. He had good expectations, he was fairly certain of a good but unspecified position, and soon he would be sending for her. And a boy too? His ears grew red at their congratulations. "To tell you the truth, Alice," he admitted, "I grew tired of it at home, with father and all the rest of it. I felt too much under his thumb. You did right when you came here. A married man ought to have his own home. He ought to live in London too—if he can."

He turned to his brother-in-law as expansively as though he meant to buy up all his stock. "Geoffrey, I owe you some money from when I stayed here before. How much?" They protested. They'd take no money of his. Besides, had he not given John three nobles, which they were saving for him? But he insisted. He never owed, if he could pay. "Buy Alice something," Copson advised him, resolute but pleased all the same. Greene was a big eater: it was good to know he needed no charity. They asked him what he was doing for a living, except digesting the future good. With pride Greene explained that he was then completing arrangements with Burdie and Danter, the booksellers, for entering and as soon as possible printing no fewer than three books. Copson shook his head. There was no money in writing. You had only to look at those hungry ink-splashers around Paul's to know that. Thought Greene, momentarily disgruntled: Does he expect me to sell ground-ginger?

He did not see John that visit. He was out playing with the children from next door, Alice explained. So they said all over again what they had said when they met, and he took himself off.

And now to see Coppinger. He decided on a new rig-out before venturing near the Court, for it was well known a man stood no chance of favour in Her Majesty's eye unless he dressed the part. He had plenty of money, so why shouldn't he lay some of it out like a merchant say, hoping for golden returns? There was the story of Raleigh and the cloak—look at what followed! He dreamed day dreams of how the Queen's eye would light on him, she would be impressed with his gallant bearing, the taste and distinction of his apparel, the unmistakable look of the poet about him, would make inquiries, he would be presented to her, would have the happiest reply to her question, and would be a made man for life. Just such another as Sir Walter or the late Sir Philip, in fact. If he dreamed much more he would be a rival for young Essex. He had a shock when he discovered how much the tailor wanted to make him the man of his desire, but after a minute's doubt went through with the deal. He had a fine peascod-bellied doublet of green satin with a small gold fleck in it, the sleeves of a slightly lighter shade, edged at the wrists with gold thread; round breeches of a cream colour, worked in front with a spiral design, and silk knit stockings of an exact match. After consideration he dispensed with garters, lest they mar the smooth shape of his leg. His shoes were of soft green leather, with slits on the instep, and tiny red rosettes on the toes. Under the doublet was a shirt of pale yellow cambrick, stitched with an open seam, and around his neck he wore a cart-wheel ruff, starched to such a degree that an onlooker might expect him to cut his throat on it any moment. For best wear he ordered, to go with this, a cape of black velvet worked with such gold thread as was about his wrists, and for an over-mantle a huge cloak descending almost to the ground. He admired himself before the tailor's mirror and his own, from all angles, and performing all kinds of gestures. His hair and mustachios, luckily, needed little treatment, for they were luxuriant and curled naturally and had a brave sheen. His cap of black velvet swinging in his hand, he felt he would not pass unnoticed in the crowd.

He could not resist calling on Alice for her to see him in his finery. He had bought her, with his wife's money, two kerchiefs for the bosom, and presented them with the ceremony that accompanies fine clothes. Next he went out past St. Botolph's to see Coppinger's parents and discover how to get hold of their son, and the same afternoon made his splendid progress to Court. As specks of dirt began to mar his green shoes and the ankles of his silk stockings he suffered more mortification than a lover, and was glad to get past Charing Cross to the more even approach beyond. He was stopped at the first gates and his business demanded, but the quick transfer of a coin won him his trick and a vague direction. The animation and bustle here were entirely after his own heart. He wanted nothing more than always to be part of it. Finally, at Westminster Hall he had more exact instructions, and pressed through a lot of sightseers to the offices behind the Star Chamber. Here he inquired for Coppinger, sending in his name with a boy whom he did not forget to reward—bribe, rather. He had to wait fifteen gazing minutes before Coppinger came out to him.

"Edmund!"

"Robert!"

It seemed unbelievable they were not still at Cambridge. Edmund was so unchanged. He even had a scrivener's gown on his back. "It really is you then, Robert?" he was asking.

He led him back inside to a bench. "No need to ask whether the world treats you well," he commented.

"These clothes, you mean? They might be worse. I am not complaining, Edmund."

"You look as though you have no reason to. You are living here in London again?"

Greene began his explanations. It was more or less what he had told Alice and Copson of his marriage and his new-found reasons for leaving home.

"So you are married? And to that poor child you met on the road to Cambridge? Well, well!" Coppinger wagged his head with wonder and offered sincere congratulations and good wishes. There was a son too? What new marvel——? "What does it feel like to be a father, Robert?"

Words could not describe it, so he went on to discuss his London and Court hopes. He was disappointed to see Edmund shaking his head. He looked as discouraging as Sir John used to be. "You'll not get what you want, Robert." "But why not?" "Because for every place at Court there are ten contenders, and eight of them with more backing than you. Unless you are content with some such job as mine—and would you be?" He described it—the copying of Star Chamber proceedings, long hours each day, dull work, poorly paid work, with no chance of advancement. "Then why do you do it, Edmund? You could get something better for the asking, surely?" Coppinger laughed at him. "Cambridge and the Court are two different places, Robert. Besides, I like it, dull as it would seem to you. I am far from discontented." Questions sprang to Greene's mind but went no further. If Edmund had no wish to talk, he would not force him. But Coppinger of all men scribbling for the Star Chamber! Helping the oppressors of his faith. "Watch your head, Edmund," he said despondently. "I don't ask what you are doing, but I can guess it is dangerous."

"Will you take my advice, Robert?"

"Probably not, but I'll listen to it. You are going to tell me to go back to Norwich and stick to saddlery, eh?"

"I was going to, yes. It will be better for you in the long run. Will you do it?"

"No."

"Ah well! When is your wife joining you, did you say?"

"Soon."

"Good. Let it be soon, Robert. A man is better off amongst all this"—he gestured—"if he has his wife with him."

"Why, Edmund, you do not suggest——"

"Nothing. But so much is common sense, Robert. You can see that?"

Greene grimaced. "Don't you grow like my father, Edmund, or I shall not like you so well. I am here to work hard to prepare a place for my wife and Kit. This gaiety, these people—I am not interested in them."

Coppinger hardly looked at the gay clothes. "Of course, Robert. Let us not talk about it." They began to discuss the immediate future. Coppinger was strong against application to Burghley: he'd not give a beggar a cup much less put a penny in it afterwards. Walsingham? Did Greene fancy secret service, delving, burrowing, up this warren, down that hole, hunting out the facts that hanged men and beheaded women? There was Hatton, there was Dudley, though his sun was setting; there were Sir Walter, Essex, George Clifford among the men; among the women Sidney's widow and the Duchess of Richmond. Greene explained more fully that he wanted to live by his pen, but Coppinger shook his head more determinedly than ever.

"You cannot succeed, Robert. Believe it now or you'll be forced to believe it later. I told Thomas Nashe the same at Cambridge, but he'll not believe me either. There is no place in London for writers, Robert."

"I don't understand you. Surely there must always be a place for the poet, Edmund. Think of the reverence with which the most barbarous peoples have always treated him. Is there a time so distant or a boundary so far-flung that in them you'll not find the almost divine art? And now when the Queen herself translates and caps distiches, when the late and universally lamented Sir Philip gave all his suffrage to poets and so publicly rebuked the low-spirited Gosson, when more than half the Areopagites are still alive and writing, when the fame of learning increases day by day, when this whole land is like a nest of singing birds—surely this is not a time when poets will starve?"

Coppinger was patient with him. The Queen was more lavish of her tongue than her purse; as well try to get blood from solid stone as money from her ministers; the soldiers needed every penny they had for soldiering, the sailors for their sailing; the Areopagites were wealthy to a man; Sir Philip was dead; singing birds were not always happy birds. There was a chance for the tutor, the clerk, the letter-writer, the translator of foreign dispatches, for news messengers paid by those for whom swift information might mean a throne or a bloody head in sawdust; but for the professional man of letters there was no chance at all. This only—"You can become part of that motley gang beyond the city walls, Robert; scramble at the players' table for a player's share, and so become an outcast, a rogue in the eyes of the law, liable to a whipping but for some great man's writ; or you can peddle ballads up and down the town like the sorry fellows you've passed to-day, doubtless; or you can "—he leaned forward—"you can write against the bishops and get no money for it, and maybe one day when you least expect it there'll be the hand on your shoulder and it's good-bye sun and trees and laughter. That is all, Robert."

They argued for twenty minutes but Greene would not be convinced. There was Lyly, there was Peele, and why forget Edmund Spenser? He could conquer. "Why, only last week, Edmund, I settled with Burdie to bring out my *Morando*, and Danter will pay me well for my *Planetomachia*. It can be done, I tell you!"

"You place so much reliance on George Peele? Come with me, Robert."

Puzzled, he followed Coppinger away from the Star Chamber, past Westminster Hall, and so to the Court itself. Coppinger seemed sufficiently well-known by countenance or dress to make his way to the great waiting room. It was crowded with people, either sight-seeing or waiting. He pointed out to Greene a tall thin man near one of the doors. "That is George Peele, Robert. Do you go and talk with him. Offer him a dinner and he's your man. It may do more than my words can to convince you." He held out his hand. "I must get back to my work. You will come to see me again?"

When he had gone, Greene walked slowly around, keeping what discreet watch he could on Peele. His clothes, like Greene's, were bright, but unlike Greene's they were far from new. They were of tawdry material too, and brushing immediately behind him Greene saw many and not too skilful darns in his doublet and stockings. But what were clothes? Was not this George Peele, the author of that sweet pastoral *The Arraignment of Paris*, whose honeyed lines had charmed without cloying the palate of every lover of poetry in England? Fresh from his conversation with Coppinger, Greene could feel this darned gentleman superior to all others in the room. He wondered how best he might make his acquaintance, and after one or two uneasy doublings thought there could be no harm in it if he went boldly up to him and announced himself. Was he not a writer himself? One of the fellowship?

"I beg your pardon, sir."

Peele turned eagerly.

"You are Master George Peele?"

"I am, sir."

"My name is Robert Greene, of Norwich and St. John's, Cambridge. Will you forgive me? I wished to make your acquaintance."

"You are very welcome to it, Master Greene." He studied Greene's clothes. "It should not come so barely if I could grace it otherwise."

"You know Edmund Coppinger?"

"Coppinger? Not I. Ought I too?"

Greene smiled. "It was he suggested I should speak with you. I took it for granted you had some friendship together."

"It need not worry you," Peele assured him, his longish nose scenting a meal. "You have a suit at Court perhaps, Master Greene?"

"I have." He felt important saying this.

"Hm. Perhaps you want guidance. I have wasted more time here than I care to remember. Let me grant you the benefit of it, shall I?"

Greene knew the other was going to get a meal out of him if he could, borrow money too—if he could—yet this made no difference. This was George Peele, *primus verborum artifex*. You did not meet a George Peele everyday. "Your business here is pressing?" he asked.

Peele laughed. "It has waited ten days and may wait as many more. You were about to invite me to eat with you, were you not, Master Greene?"

It would be hard in any case to say no now. They laughed together. "Yes, I was."

"I accepted ten minutes ago. I accepted as you censured the darns in my stockings. I should make that a quarrel for my wife's sake, the scorned darner. No, no, I meant that only in jest! Don't be confused, I beg of you. Where shall it be?"

This was dispatch, with a vengeance. "The Five Black Feathers?"

"Where better?" said Peele. "Shall we go?"

As they walked along, Peele, who, Greene noticed, had no outer cloak despite the cold, talked with the greatest liveliness. "And why did your friend Coppinger want you to speak with me?" he asked, suddenly interrupting his sharp observations on scenes and persons they passed.

Greene was still telling him as they waited for their food to be served. He was there in London to become just such another as George Peele. "God forbid!" said that gentleman, both merry and wary of eye. "You know, Master Greene, you are giving me my first bite to-day? And I assure you this is no rare experience for me. Pray, do not wish to become such another as George Peele."

"But your play? Your reputation? Your production of *Dido* before Alasco at Christ Church. Surely, Master Peele——"

"Go back home to Norwich, sir. That will be wisdom in you."

But Greene was past discouragement. He was set on showing men what he was made of. It must be that Peele was lazy, that he lacked application. "I tell you, Master Peele, I am determined to conquer London."

The other leaned forward to touch his sleeve. "You are Greene and should keep green," he punned; "I am Peele and peel white." He pulled back the join of his doublet and Greene saw his bare chest underneath. "Sometimes goodwill makes me abase myself, Master Greene—as now. Better moments I regret later. I wish you well. Go back to Norwich." He proceeded with a long and entertaining account of hardships to be met by the writer, leading to much the same conclusion as Coppinger's and Sir John's before him. "You see how honest I am with you, Master Greene? I could so easily have persuaded you into the course you yourself wish, and kept you here in London till I had helped you spend your money and you were as beggarly as myself. Consider yourself fortunate," he went on, and was still eating, "that you found me in my cousinly not cozening mood; that my pity not my rapacity was excited by your unattainable ambitions."

He was in daily attendance at Court, clinging desperately and with a thousand humiliations to the favour of men like Sackford and Tilney and Blagrave, that he might supply the New Year's pageant, some masque or revelry. Meantime his wife stayed in her one room at Holborn and hoped for good news. "She eats oftener than I," said Peele casually. He confided that if Lyly had been given the Mastership of the Revels or even the promise of its reversion, things would not be so bad with him. Unless Lyly would want to write all himself, for he confessed that if he ever had the chance to decide the authorship of masques it would be George Peele first, second, and always. "Maybe not even you, Master Greene, would get the wherewithal to line your belly." It struck Greene hard that he echoed other of Coppinger's words, though with added brutality. "Are you married, Master Greene?" He listened. "Then fetch them to town. These women you meet here, they will suck you dry of wealth and health. Heed the gipsy's warning!"

Greene now thought fit to tell this fed man that he had two books as good as printed. From this it was a short step to the first part of *Mamillia*, and when Peele showed signs of interest he was glad he had a copy in the lining of his outer cloak. Would Master Peele accept it? "I accept everything given me," said Peele graciously. "I am the best accepter in London, perhaps in the world. I accept kicks and I accept ha'pence; friendship and enmity; compliments and insults; the world, the flesh, and the devil. A neat little volume, Master Greene. A handy size. At the lowest estimate it will not go unappreciated in my little household."

Greene grinned uneasily. "The last refuge of authors," he agreed, but half-heartedly.

"I assure you," said Peele, "I have not a page much less a copy of anything I ever wrote. What with my wife's curls, my own beard, and the fundamental needs of both of us, their mortality has been high, Master Greene."

Within an hour they were bound for Peele's lodging in Holborn. "Next to the Unicorn," said Peele, "and, counting heaven, one floor from the top." It was in a squalid side-street, the stairs they climbed were filthy, each landing had its peculiar stench. Greene felt the air would tarnish his gold lace. Yet Peele knocked ceremoniously at his own door, and in answer to a question called out, "George and a friend." A bolt was drawn and they went inside, into a room smelling more of the mounting effluvia of the floors below than any particular mess of its own, and Greene was introduced with flourishes as the new Whittington. Peele was Greene's own age but looked older, his wife was three or four years younger than he, with the bedraggled prettiness of an ill-kept flower plot. She was wearing too fine a dress for her surroundings, and Greene was curious to know whether it had been bestowed in charity or was the result of some reckless prodigality of her husband's. "Cherish him, sweetheart," said Peele, "for he has fed me well." He seemed shameless enough about his needs. "The family bed, Master Greene," he pointed out; "the family laundry, without shirt or shift; the family larder, of which I say with the scholiast *ex nihilo nihil.* Do you still want to be an author?"

Greene was still looking for the right answer when Peele offered him part of the bed to sit on. He was to take care not to wake the baby sleeping in it. If Greene was embarrassed, neither George nor his wife was. He had a brazen cheerfulness in the face of his poverty, she a matter-of-fact acquiescence. He began to explain to her, with much facetious comment, Greene's ideas of literary earnings, and Greene watched her face with interest, for her expression changed five times a minute in sympathy with her husband's. Finally he set Greene holding his stomach as he told of some of his subterfuges to get the price of a meal. "You'll not believe this, but ask my Arabella. There have been times, magister, when I've taken children a mile from their homes in order to take them home lost and reap a reward; I've collected dog-droppings for a tannery—followed them about the streets, squeezed them, magister, treasuring their leavings as though pure gold; I've tied fat men's shoestrings; I've pushed a woman into Thames and waded in to save her; I've wheedled a pipe and tobacco and sold them back to the man who gave them me. I have done everything but be a player, magister, and one day I may come to that."

The harangue was ended by a knocking at the door. Would Master Peele not talk so loud, please; it disturbed the children in the room below. But Peele grabbed the objector by the arm and fetched him into the room. Pointing to his own little girl fast asleep behind Greene, he asked heatedly whether other folk had need to grumble. Was he the Bull of Bashan? Spoke he with Gargantua's mouth? Did they reckon him Stentor? "You see this gentleman?" —indicating the glories of Greene's costume rather than his person. He warned his interrupter that Greene stood not far from the Lord Mayor, and that he wanted no more incursions on pain of complaint in that high quarter. He then packed him out, and burst out laughing like a horse. Almost at once there was another knocking. "If it is the same rascal——" said Peele, and went to the door like a dancer. But this was a welcome visitor.

"I had just told a rascal who called here that Master Robert Greene stood near the Lord Mayor. Well, Rhadamanthus credit me with one lie less, for here comes a former Lord Mayor's son—Master Thomas Lodge!"

Lodge had a big basket with him, with bottle necks sticking out of it. Peele sniffed. "Ah!" he said, "Arabella?" Greene felt somewhat out of it as the others used Christian names, and was pleased when Peele all at once began to call him Robert. There was to be a feast, and he must stay. No good to say he was not hungry. "In this commonwealth of four, Robert," Peele assured him, "you must eat whether you are hungry or not."

There was a knocking again. It was the first interrupter. Peele eyed him in silence, then went to examine the labels on the bottles, chose the smallest, clapped a string of sausages up against it, and handed them to the man on the doorstep. "One word, and we'll come in to fetch it all back!" He disappeared like a rabbit into its hole.

Greene was delighted with everything. His nose had grown used to the smell, his lungs to the air. True, Peele's daughter woke up and cried for her mother to feed her, which Arabella did with a sausage in her hand and a glass of red wine at her side, but she suffered a drowsy satiety immediately she finished sucking, and after a change of napkins back to bed she went. So there was Peele, begirt with the glories of the *Arraignment, Iphigenia,* and the *Dixie Pageant,* Greene with his *Mamillia,* his *Gwydonius* and *Arbasto,* and Lodge with tales to tell of the Gosson controversy, his share therein, and his pastoral *Forbonius and Prisceria.* Now that their work was their topic, Peele was not allowed more than his third of the talk. Indeed, by the time the wine was almost finished, each would have liked to address the company in a set speech on the subject of himself and all he'd done. Lodge—by this time Tom— had been a lawyer; Peele—now George—had produced plays at Oxford; Greene—happy to be Robert—had been no home-stayer. They had manifold virtues and a willing audience. And through it all Arabella in her gorgeous gown ate to bursting and washed it down with glassfuls of wine. She impressed Greene as a really sensible woman, not a bit like Doll. She was no great talker, neither about herself nor others, but that only made her a better listener, and that was what they wanted. He thought George, like Jephthah, had a treasure.

It was a shame they had ever to go. Greene thought cunningly, hitching his cloak around him, that George and his wife had overeaten themselves in the expectation of empty morrows. This seemed pitiful, and he wondered whether he ought to offer George money. Perhaps to-morrow. The stairs seemed more awkward going down, but the smells not noticeable.

He and Lodge set off gaily for the city centre, sometimes singing, and sometimes saying "Sh-sh-sh, Robert! Sh-sh-sh, Tom!"

CHAPTER XXVII

THROUGHOUT 1587 GREENE was every month promising himself he would return to Norwich for his wife and child, or that at least he would take steps to find out how they were. But there was always something to prevent him. Now it was the consciousness of his guilt in robbing them when he left; now a fear of what his father might have told them; now a distaste for the journey; and as the months rolled by he found himself ever poorer in pocket and no richer in prospects, so that he could argue it would be better to leave it for a time again. He never quite understood where the money went—but go it did. He seemed always to be in need of something; whether it was a new pair of stockings for attendance on young Essex, or new gloves to make a fine show at the water-pageant Peele was responsible for at Tilbury; or perhaps it might be a loan to Peele or Richard Vennar or Will Monox, or his share of an entertainment after the play, or the purchase of writing materials—there was always something. But the others never worried—apparently—and why should he? Again, Peele was married, and Lodge too. But you didn't find them creeping from pillar to post as a result, and no doubt Doll was a sight better off than Arabella or Tom's wife. Once he really settled down to work, then he would show them!

But it was so devilish hard to get the right work done. There were so many fascinating things to fill your time. This pageant of Peele's—he might as well have taken lodgings at Tilbury for it. He lived with it, was entangled with it, poked his nose into every detail of it. He was almost as proud as its maker that day the Queen came down, and the English ship attacked the pirate with a Spanish rig, took her, and sent her heavenwards in a burst of fireworks, while the sailors thrown into the sea became fishes, and

amongst them, on the backs of dolphins, were Alleyn and
Richard Jones, reciting the bravest verses to Her Majesty.
He sat in a good seat, with Arabella on one side of him,
complete with baby, and an insufferable fool called Jaster
on the other. Arabella received a hundred compliments
from one or another—she was Venus with the infant Cupid,
or Juno with young Hercules, or Ceres with Bacchus—
but she let it all go in one ear and out the other, not even
bothering to explain it was a girl and not a boy at all.
Greene admired her and was puzzled by her, calm as she
was, and ruminant, and yet no fool. She was to startle
him that day, for as they gazed like owls at the presentation
of author and producer to Her Majesty, she whispered in
his ear: "She's a cruel bitch yon, Robert, and not a happy
one." He wriggled his finger inside his ruff—it felt like the
axe-edge—fearful lest she say more and louder. He saw the
Queen smile, showing her ugly blackened teeth, and Peele
louting to the ground. If only he were in Peele's place
now! Not for the money alone, for if he knew anything of
George he'd soon be rid of that, but for recognition and
favour. Perhaps writing for the revels or the stage would
be the thing, not those romances. *Penelope's Web*, just entered
in the Register, *Euphues, His Censure*, taking careless shape
in his mind—neither might prove the key of gold. He
was melancholy for an hour before Peele carried him off
to get determinedly drunk.

These were strange men he had for friends. Since his
return from Italy he had known none remotely like them.
He saw at least this much truth in Coppinger's and Peele's
own warnings that there seemed no proper place for them
in the society of the day. The very circumstance that they
wrote for money effectively barred them from respectable
households, and on the other hand they felt themselves
too good frankly to go over to the South Bank and live
among players, bear-keepers, wrestlers, and all the riff-raff
gathered there. Lodge and Peele despised the men they
wrote for, and advised Greene strongly against renewing
his acquaintance with those of the Queen's Men he had

met at Norwich. A player was a common rogue, a proscribed man, but they, Peele, Lodge, and Greene, were
gentlemen from the Universities, they had wit and learning
and good breeding. Greene was not likely to quarrel with
this distinction, and so kept away from Tarleton, Wilson,
and the others when they were in town. Suspended thus
between the world that wanted them not and that they
wanted not, these writers were an outcast band of their
own. Nor were they ruly men. Lodge had been before the
Privy Council for his excesses after the Gosson controversy,
and it was all his influential family could do to keep him
out of the Clink; Vennar had been gaoled for debt and
theft; Garrimond had nearly died of the pox; Peele himself,
as he had said, was the best "accepter" in London, his
wife, unjustly, was held no better than a whore, and his
daughter condemned from birth; Monox had killed a man
in a brawl and been reprieved at the last moment at the
suit of Oxford for whom he had performed the most dubious
services. Their lives were spent in continual squalor, hardly
relieved by ill-spent spells of brief prosperity. They were
unbalanced men, men with few ties, with little conception
of rights and duties. Their influence upon Greene was almost
entirely bad. He was drinking too much, in part because
his companions drank too much, in part because he liked
it, in part because he thought it the proper thing to do
to drink and swagger and talk like a rake and brag
and drink again and generally distinguish himself from
the puritans on the one hand and dull citizens on the
other. Was he not Robert Greene? Had he not written
books? Was he not a sight cleverer than you and you and
you?

The graver fault of sexual immorality he had so far
avoided. He was appreciating that part of Coppinger's
advice, though he could make no use of it. These women
disturbed him greatly, but he had not forgotten the extreme
disgust of that morning at Mother Dowse's and kept away
from them. Thinking of this he would say: I must go home
at once! But he did not go. Tenuously he remained faithful

to Doll, and the women of his romances were studies in idealism.

Not unconnected with this he heard an odd story from Lodge one evening when they were drinking together at the Nakerer. Lodge had heard it from the woman herself and swore it was true. She was a woman of twenty-three, of the game these five years, dwelling at a trugging-house behind St. Andrew's, with as much welcome for the oldest lecher as the youngest lover so long as he brought meat in his mouth. About three months ago a quiet handsome man called at the house, which sold wines and ales, and asked for drink. He looked unwell, but the whore served him and sat with him and talked lightly at first and then earnestly that he should make use of her. This he refused, but without insult, and said it was a sad thing so strumpetlike a behaviour should mar so fair a woman. He left in a quarter of an hour, but the woman did not forget him, being greatly taken with his handsome person—so much so that she wished to lie with him for her own pleasure and without gain. A fort-night later he returned, and fortunately she was at a window looking into the street, and saw him, and ran downstairs to meet him at the door, and asked him if he would drink. He told her he had come for no other purpose, so she led him into the common room of the house. Here he sat again, as though in the greatest doubt, and soon she was urging him with a deal of lascivious talk that he should take his pleasure with her. He shook his head now, recurring to his former talk that it was a shameful thing for a woman to live in such a house and sell herself for gold at the peril of eternal damnation, and suddenly offering to place her in a good household, if she were willing. This she inter-preted as an invitation to become his mistress, and without choosing her terms very carefully she agreed; but he reproved her now for the nakedness of her lust and made to leave. But now, throwing the last of her caution to the devil, the whore flung her arms around his neck and begged him to gratify her, if only this one time. "In this common chamber?" he asked sternly. Hurriedly she pulled him by the arm into a room on the floor above, but he told her it was too light and that for nothing in the world could he possess a woman in a lighted room. But her impetuosity was such that she immediately led him to her own receiving room, drew the blinds and the curtains of the bed, and asked whether that would be close enough. "By no means," he objected; "the blind is of thin stuff, and not wide enough for the window; and the bed curtains are ill fitting. Maybe some watching eye shall spy in at us." And then he spoke of his credit being as dear to him as his life, and continued so till at last she took him to a tiny back loft, so dark that at noonday it was impossible for any man to see his own hands there, and reserved for those frightened sinners who dreaded even their own shadows at the act of darkness. "Well, sir," she asked, "is this dark enough?" He sat down on the bed, fetched a deep sigh, and said doubtfully: "So-so, but there is a glimpse of light in at the tiles. Someone may yet see us." "No one," she told him. "Only God himself could see you here!" "God?" cried he. "Why can God see us here?" At this she cried out on his simplicity, for surely the eyes of God could pierce walls of brass much less into a loft. He must be a heathen or a papist! "Alas, poor woman," he replied, "if God so sees us, shall we not be more ashamed to do such a filthy act before him than before men? I am sure you are not so shameless you would not blush and be afraid to have the meanest commoner in London see you in the action of your lust, and are you not the more ashamed to have God, the maker of all lovely things, see you—he who avenges sin with death, whose eyes are clearer than the sun, who is the never-deceived searcher of hearts?" Embarked now, he gave her the most powerful sermon in the world, exhorting her to put away that mode of life and embrace one more virtuous, and that if she did he would look after her like his own sister, and the affair ended that she left the house with him straightway, and he found her lodgings with respectable people at the other end of the town.

"And is that the end?" Greene asked.

"Not quite. Make your guess at the upshot."

"He married her," said Greene.

Lodge shook his head. "This is not a fairy tale."

"She lived with him as she suggested, as his mistress."

"How much more like the world! No."

"Go on then. Tell me."

"She is back in the trugging house."

Greene thought it likely enough.

"Her tail was too hot, Robert. Virtue had no chance. She tells the story to her intimates. The man's name was Copover or Copping or something like that."

He reached for the bottle and helped himself. Poor, poor Edmund! Greene was thinking; poor, poor, dear fellow! Just the thing he would do—impracticable, unwise, yet noble. He had left Edmund too long without a visit.

He met him at his home not a week later. He looked ill, Greene thought, as though overworked and worried. He had craved a week's leave of absence from reporting the transactions of the Star Chamber, but in answer to Greene's request that they spend a day or two together in quiet and rest he said that he must undertake a short journey into the country. No, he could not put it off, and it was impossible for Greene to accompany him. Despite his long neglect of Coppinger, Greene was mortified by this and convinced that his friend was upon some dangerous undertaking. There was the now familiar dialogue, Greene begging him to take care of himself, Coppinger making calm answers. It was in the last minutes before he left that he appeared to make up his mind about something troubling him, and asked Greene if he would do him a kindness. Greene vowed he would, but was shocked by the request none the less. He was to go to the Fleet Prison, and see Roger Flamstead, and give him as a message the words, *Where their worm dieth not, and the fire is not quenched*. That was all—no explanation was needed. Greene pulled at his beard. He felt he was about to meddle where he should not. He asked who this Roger Flamstead might be, and Coppinger, holding his head in his hands as though it ached and bled, told him Flamstead was the Rector of Edginton in Hertford-shire and that he was now awaiting his third examination before the High Commission. What was his crime? That he was a man of judgment and irreproachable character, beloved by all who knew him, but that he omitted the sign of the cross in baptism, that he did not insist that those receiving the eucharist should kneel, that he did not wear a surplice, although ordered by Aylmer to do so, that he had preached against pluralism and non-residency. The usual charges. "Oh God, God, these unhappy times!" cried Coppinger, "when to be true to Thy faith is to be persecuted!" He controlled himself, adding, "But you need not do this, Robert, if it is against your conscience or your wish." Watching the deeper lines that marked his friend's face, "I'll go," said Greene resolutely. "He will under-stand," said Coppinger, and sighed. "Why are we made so that we grow tired, Robert, when there is most to do?"

It was the first time for Greene to enter a prison. He hoped it would prove the last. Prisoners were conveyed to the Fleet from Westminster by water, through the Water Gate, but such visitors as cared to go there entered from the market side. It was now used almost exclusively for the detention of those marked down by the High Commission, such as had been convicted and ruined by enormous fines being held in the Beggars' Ward, those in somewhat better state, perhaps still awaiting their first examination or even the formulation of a charge, lying in the Common Ward, and those least fortunate, the *close* prisoners, imprisoned solitary in cells without light, air, or the possibility of exercise. When Coppinger last heard of Flamstead, some weeks before, he was still in the Common Ward, along with fellow sufferers for conscience' sake and some of the un-fortunates and rogues who spent more of their lives within prison walls than outside them. Greene's first request at the gates to see one of the prisoners gained not even the spare courtesy of a reply till he passed over money, and then he was admitted. Possibly he was considered a profitable visitor; at any rate he was now conducted before the Warden, the infamous Alexander Parrett, who raised a number of difficulties about his seeing this particular man, and had in his turn to be placated with a gift—to be applied, said Parrett, to the alleviation of the poorest inmates' lot. He was now conducted into the prison itself, where the most unbearable stench rose to disgust his nostrils. Above and beyond the smells of decayed bedding, sweat, excreta, the grey-black accumulations of nameless filth on the walls and floors, rose the fetid horror of decaying humanity. To Greene it seemed God's fresh air had not played here for a thousand years, that the frenetic reek of every corpse that had lain within its walls had blended with the stale choking miasma of its spiritual rottenness, till the smell was like a liquid to be pushed from the face as one moved through it, flooding the heaving lungs. At the threshold of the ward he motioned to the gaoler and rested his hand against the wall, as though to brace himself; but this posture he could not keep long because of the sliminess that made his skin crawl. There was little light inside this hell-pit, and in a way that little was too much. Around the walls, their backs or shoulders supported by them, were the hopeless figures of the decent prisoners, their miseries increased by the depravity of their other companions. There were small groups with dice and cards, gambling for what wretched pence their friends had brought them, gambling to incur debts that would be settled after their release, gambling even for a turn with each other's wives, gambling merely for oblivion. Roaming where they pleased were the foulest women of the city, those beaten from the light of day by their monstrous looks and their diseases, too grotesque to be pitiful, too horrible one would have thought for the lusts of the most desperate. Yet here they did custom, coupling in filth and vermin. There were no arrangements for sanitation; the floor was the common sewer, and in its mess these stood or sat or lay. In the winter it must be freezing cold, despite the mass of lice-eaten flesh that should sweat to warm it; now it was close enough to make even the turnkeys of a morning vomit and turn giddy.

Flamstead was not there, but Greene's guide, though bribed already, would take him no further. Kicking his way over some prostrate bodies, which might hold life or not, he led him back to the ward door, and then suggested Greene try the Beggars' Ward. In a way, things were even worse here. There were none of the oaths, the gambling, the quarrelling, the ugly viciousness of the other ward; but instead the same filth, the same overpowering stench, and a deadly hopelessness. To be here was in most cases to be past salvation. Sentenced to pay fines that never could be paid, their few possessions sequestrated, without the recognised claim of a pauper or criminal to the barest necessities of life, they must depend entirely on the charity of friends unless they were to starve to death. The death-rate amongst these men was very high. The money supplied by friends went almost all into the pockets of the Warden and gaolers, their only beds were rolls of mouldy, urine-soaked straw, there was no means of avoiding contagion when goal fever did break out, no means of attending to any form of hurt or indisposition. In the sacred name of religion they lay in such extremity as the bishops would not keep a dog that bit them in. Greene marvelled at the faith that could support them, at the resolution with which they met their fate. Stepping carefully to avoid besmattering his shoes, he uttered the heartfelt wish that Edmund Coppinger might never be put to this test. As though conforming to Three Hundred and Ninety much less Thirty-Nine Articles was not a thousand times preferable! Greene, he told himself grimly, you'll never make a martyr.

He found Flamstead in a corner. He seemed a decent old man, this Flamstead, fatherly, mild, the sort it would be good to see at eventime with his seat at the fireside, his friends around him, his family too.

"Who are you?" he asked urgently.

"I come from a friend."

"With a friend's message, I hope?"

"I know nothing of that. But hear it." He repeated Coppinger's words, and Flamstead nodded his head slowly. "I was told you would understand."

"I do understand."

Greene, watching him closely, could not tell whether it represented good news or bad.

"You will see your friend again?"

"Not for a week or more. He has gone into the country. I shall see him when he returns."

"Then tell him I am prepared."

"You are prepared. That is all?"

"It is enough, and it is all."

Greene shuffled his feet. "I will tell him. I am sorry, Master Flamstead, to see you in this distress."

"Never fear for me. It may be that for all of us here in Beggar's Ward the day of our reckoning is near. I know you not, I ask not your name, but judge, good sir, where you had rather be a hundred years from now—with these afflicted men you see around you or with Whitgift and Aylmer and Lancelot Andrews. And that will be not for a day, nor for a month, nor even a year, but for all eternity."

Such talk alarmed Greene. "I will deliver your message, Master Flamstead. Maybe in some happier time we shall meet again."

Flamstead did not try to keep him, and he made his way back to the ward entrance, where the turnkey was waiting to escort him once more before the Warden.

"You saw your man Flamstead?" Parrett asked him.

"I did."

"I wish we could put him more comfortable here," said Parrett; "but you know the way of it—the national economy affects us worse than any. Not a penny piece am I allowed for these unfortunate men, Master Greene, not a penny piece. I say _unfortunate_ not because I excuse their recalcitrance, their stiff-necked opposition to Her Majesty's most excellent Commission, but because the vials of a good man's tears are unloosed even for the unworthy. But what can I do? For so small a sum it would be possible to give him new bedding, a measure of food each day——" He watched Greene like a cat, waiting for his offer, but Greene merely nodded and switched his cap through his nervous fingers. "As it is," Parrett began again, "unless such help is forthcoming within a day or two, I have no choice but to put the poor man in *little ease*, Master Greene."

"You could not!" He had heard of these cells of *little ease*, so constructed that as in the cages of old the prisoner could neither stand, sit, nor lie at length, but must constrain himself to a squatting posture for days on end, and oftentimes till death came to release him.

Parrett was already fingering his fee, he knew. "What choice have I, Master Greene? I get my orders. I must obey them. Sometimes, it is true, one can do one's poor best to soften the enjoined rigour, but as a rule——"

Greene parted with four shillings with the fearful conviction that it would do nothing to save Flamstead. That old man would need all his faith now.

It was a month before he saw Coppinger again, well on into August. He gave him Flamstead's message. *I am prepared.* "Thank you, Robert," said Coppinger. "The man is dead."

Another month and he had met an interesting youngster down from the University—one Christopher Marlowe, a man of humble birth though great talents, according to Peele, and now thrown on the town like the rest of them. He had a tragedy, *Tamburlaine the Great*, of which rumour said it was like no other play that had ever been penned, and there were hopes the Admiral's Men would bring it out before Christmas. At the same time Greene, now very low in pocket, received payment for his tale in the manner of Lyly, *Euphues, His Censure*. On the strength of the money and the prospect of an early publication he felt inclined to patronise this Marlowe when he met him. Young fellows down from the University, without a month's experience of the world, they might well set up as reformers of the drama. But when he did meet Marlowe, he found him an awkward man to patronise. He was of quick spirit, ready with retorts that you might consider lively or impudent according to the state of your liver, shrewd in affairs, and independent of judgment. He was no blind respecter of persons or authority, and Greene could pretend to no great liking for him. And he was certainly as dissolute as Monox and shameless as Peele. Perhaps his play would be a failure, and the reverse would do him good. He believed Peele too hoped so after that fierce argument in Lodge's house when they debated the future of the drama and Marlowe showed so clearly his contempt for its past.

"Nothing done?" Peele cried indignantly. "Nothing done by College loobies, you mean!"

"College looby yourself!" retorted Marlowe, working his eyebrows. "Will you tell me *Gorboduc* is fit for anything but wiping bottoms?"

"Well, of all the puppydom!"

"And your own play, Peele, since we are on the subject —what more is it than pretty? If you wrote twenty such the stage would be the same."

"What have you done half as good?" Greene challenged him.

"Go to the Bel Savage when they give it, and see for yourself."

"About my play——" This was Peele. "You have still more impudence than a tinker, Marlowe. Didn't I show the way to write blank verse? Didn't I clear its joints of stiffness? Didn't I make it supple, flexible, with give and bend? Didn't I?"

"You should have rhymed the stuff, I tell you. You never mastered the principles, I tell you. With you blank verse is still in binders, Peele. Poetically speaking, you are still yellowing napkins. And without blank verse—and a new kind of blank verse—there is no hope for the drama of this country."

"You are going to show us how, are you?"

"I think I am."

"And what sort of blank verse do you think the drama needs?"

Marlowe struck the table. "Verse that pants and glows, verse that leaps and rushes, verse that thunders. That is what is wrong with you, Peele—and with those poems in your romances, Greene—that is what is wrong with the whole crew of you. You are like pipes when you should be trumpets—or thin baby voices when a strong man should declaim and roar. You are afraid to rant lest you be ridiculous like Kyd, but the poet without rant will likely be without inspiration—the dramatic poet almost certainly so. You must risk much to gain much. You want verse in buckram or baby-linen, but I want verse like a scarlet cloak, like a forest fire, like a river that bursts its banks and dashes down to do battle with the sea. God, if only I could say what I want!"

"Christ!" said Lodge, and spat on the floor; "can't the fellow talk?"

"And your subjects are all wrong," said Marlowe.

"To hell with the subjects! Let's settle the medium first. You are shouting pretty loud, but be more informative. Where does George here fall so short? Never mind about scarlet cloaks and forest fires—and I dismiss with contempt your praise of bombast. Now, I'll read you a dozen lines from the *Arraignment*—get it from over there, Robert, will you? Thank you. Listen, Marlowe!" He read.

"If they were another man's I'd call them good, those verses," vowed Peele; "and since they are mine, I call them exquisite." He stuck out his long nose like a vulture smelling Marlowe's blood.

"Well?" asked Greene.

Marlowe shook his head. "I never said you were not a poet, Peele. I said you were not a dramatic poet, not a blank verse poet. I maintain it still. You are not without skill in lyric."

"Thank you," said Peele, too humbly. "The world agrees with you."

"It will agree with me in more than that before I have done with it."

"Not in your estimate of your own modesty, I imagine."

"What is modesty? The refuge of mediocrity!" He glared at Greene. "The saving grace of fools!"

"Then you can acquit yourself of mediocrity and folly. Or of being without a refuge, perhaps."

"What about some verse from you too?" Greene asked him, angry at his stare.

"I am no player. Go to the Bel Savage at the right time and you'll hear all you want. And you will be converted."

"To what?"

"To the new verse." He swelled his chest. "To the model of futurity."

They wrangled for a long time that night, and only one of them, and he was Marlowe, could think other than that the new author was a braggart and probably a fraud.

They were at the Bel Savage for the first performance. There would be a bigger crowd there on Ludgate Hill now that the weather was cold than at the theatres outside the boundaries. It was the first play for Greene to see in that setting. The place was magnificently suited to its purpose, the whole yard easy of access by a number of archways leading under the inn buildings; of huge size, and surrounded by three galleries running the whole round, each communicating with the upper floors. The players had their place prepared at the eastern end, with musicians in the gallery above them. Marlowe had found them free places, but the faithful Arabella was not with her husband. She was unwell almost all the time now. "Something or other," Peele said vaguely. The result was that the handsomely garbed Greene was much importuned by the ladies to come and sit with them, and one persistent creature, in a mask as though she had been trained at Venice, and dressed in red and gold, insisted not only on removing two pairs of gloves for his benefit and showing him her rings, but bought him an orange, at the same time making it clear there would be better entertainment than the players' in one of the darkened rooms opening off the gallery. Lodge and Peele strongly advised him to board the lady, but he was content to be virtuous, and eventually she shifted her seat and made advances to a fat man in light blue. By the end of the second act he was sitting with her, and not even the triumph that followed kept him in his seat after the third. Paradoxically Greene spared time to envy him. She was a handsome woman.

They grinned at each other during the prologue. Here was Marlowe carrying his brag on to the public stage. They jeered a little at the long list of kings and emperors and found scope enough for witticisms throughout the first scene. With the coming of Alleyn as Tamburlaine there was a difference. It was a part that suited his strength of delivery; never before had he been given so marvellous a gush of lines; he grew drunk with his own mimetic splendour. The long set speeches when he advanced to tower over the groundlings came from him molten, as the author himself would wish. The less critical section of the audience was stunned with sheer and sustained rhetoric, the more know-ledgeable overwhelmed by this undreamt-of virile lyricism, which beat and pounded over their hearts. Even the bombast, as Alleyn delivered it in that mighty baritone of his, was superb. And the range—there were passages like the cyclops' hammer clanging on a brazen anvil; others where the words soared on wings to heaven; others again where strength wed sweetness to produce celestial beauty; lines the colour of blood, lines like silver and sable, lines that blazed like meteors, lines that rang like trumpets. At the end of the fourth act Peele leaned forward to say to Greene: "The fellow is mad, but he's poetically mad. Thank God he is ridiculous often or there'd be no living with him after this." Lodge scowled, he had been so transported. In the fifth act came the most magnificent poetry of the play, the most magnificent poetry the drama in England had known till that day, putting into words the inexpressible. Those three poets listening were impressed with a sense of such perfect fitness of words and music and thought that envy temporarily had no place in them. The divine incantation had the effect of bringing to Greene's mind half-forgotten memories of sweet and lovely things, moonlight at Hartop on Doll's white upturned face, candlelight on tall green cellar-cold bottles, the soft hum of parents' voices heard from upstairs, the timid, delicate girl of the Ponte Vecchio, the too-quick vanishing of moments fragile and fair. He felt he would never write again.

And then to save him and make the groundlings roar came the imbecility of Bajazeth dashing his brains out against the cage, and the unparalleled fustian of Zabina's grief. He was grateful for this chance to escape from the spell cast over him, and laughed that he might not cry. When she too ran against the cage and brained herself he set up a great hand-clapping that was taken up all over the yard, and Zenocrate's next speech was hardly heard for chatter and general disturbance. He watched Alleyn and listened to him as he dealt with the glorious rant that remained rather as he had watched a tight-rope walker, quite frightened for him lest he make the one false step that ruins all. But there was no need to worry. The great actor did justice to his material, and the play closed to the most deafening applause the inn yard had ever known.

They went round to the tiring room at the end. Marlowe was there, as white as a sheet, and Alleyn, as red as a turkey-cock. Robert Browne, Richard Jones and James Tunstall, and Alleyn's brother John—Greene knew none of them, and taking his cue from his fellow writers he ignored them now. But for Marlowe they had congratulations and good wishes. They would all be glad to eat from his dish after this. Good old Marlowe! Peele forgave him all and hurried home to tell his wife that Marlowe was the man; Greene told him he was fit to rank with Sophocles, whom he had never read; and Lodge shook his hand till it flapped loose from the wrist.

Within a week Greene was deep into his first play, *Alphonsus, King of Aragon;* and Lodge as deep into his *Wounds of Civil War.* They wrote with Marlowe's left foot rather than his right hand, but felt they were as good as their master.

CHAPTER XXVIII

THEN, AFTER MARLOWE, came Nashe, up to London for a season before taking his examination and master's degree, and finding the other University men like a ball of quicksilver its fellows. They would be a colony if this went on much longer.

Many things had happened before his arrival in August. First for all Englishmen there was the long-drawn anxiety of the Spanish war, the certainty over many months that invasion would be attempted, that Drake's raid on Cadiz and along the coast to the Tagus had but delayed the enterprise. They hung on the fitting out of ships, the raising of land levies, the building of land fortifications. Then came knowledge that the Great Armada was on its way, disquietude from disputes between the stingy queen and her admiral, fearful expectation after Fleming put into Plymouth with news of the Armada's approach, joy that hardly dared be joy as the first reports of Spanish losses came through, relief and fear mixed when men heard that English sailors had no gunpowder to fight with, then increasing jubilation from the scattering of the Spaniards before Calais to the harassed flight northwards. But the alarm was kept up for a month and more yet, and it was not until mid-August and the breaking up of the camp at Tilbury that the nation knew danger had finally passed it by. So, for those inclined, thanksgiving by prayer or wild debauchery—and Greene did not pray. Men and women rushing through the streets of London, shouting, kissing, dancing, drinking, like the pagan festivals of old, and erecting great bonfires in the fields around which they danced like maenads and satyrs, in dionysiac frenzy. Not for Greene and Peele the grave words of far-seeing men, or humble address to the God of Elizabeth's medal, who, watchful of the imperial destinies of his second chosen people, blew and dispersed the enemy; not for them the conventicle, the quiet chamber, or even the national churches steaming with incense and praise. There was the occasion for rejoicing and times were good with them. Marlowe had followed his *Tamburlaine* with a second part, in which that blood-drunk conqueror must himself fall to Death's black blade; he was between whiles in mysterious employ with Walsingham; and Greene had refreshed his pocket with good sums from his *Alphonsus* and that second play, *A Looking Glass for London*, which he and Lodge had hurriedly thrown together before Lodge left with Captain John Clarke on a voyage to Terceras and the Canaries—a restless fellow, Lodge; his romances, *Perymedes* and *Pandosto*, had not been unprofitable as such things go and had greatly advanced his reputation. Peele, true, had no major strokes to his credit, but just in time for the period of rejoicing he had been commissioned for the device of a pageant to be borne before Lord Mayor Calthrop at the end of October, and the prospect was well worth a loan at usurers' interest. Arabella was still ailing and growing thinner, and Greene saw less of her, but that was no disadvantage, as her husband confessed, in the promiscuities of rejoicing. Greene had before this ceased to be faithful to Doll. Almost two years' abstinence was too much to ask of human nature. He now shamelessly hung up his hat to any woman, married or single, who seemed both fair and kind. Occasionally, he did not demand that they be fair.

He thought of Doll often enough, sometimes with contrition, never with longing. He could see so clearly now that she had not been the wife for him. Perhaps no woman was the wife for him, if he was to live his life the way he wanted. Marlowe might well be right—that women were inspirations to work, but that a man was always in need of new inspiration. And as dull Adam Bolton had said, more or less with Ovid and Chaucer's Pandarus before him, if this one's tresses are long and yellow, that one is neat and roguish; if this one's bosom juts high and firm, that one's waist slides smoother under the hand; for this one's light, that one's dark; for the red of this one's mouth, the shadows of that one's promising eyes. And so in poems of this period he hymned the fleshly beauty of women, following to perfection and at times to his own disturbance those anatomical catalogues of his predecessors. Who now a better ogler at the play than Robert Greene? Who now cast more sheep's eyes at the passing wives of prosperous citizens than he? Who quicker to compliment, to find the missing glove, to help with cloak or shoe, to squeeze the hand or press the foot, to make pregnant contact of knee and thigh? To glance and purse the breath, to apostrophise, to mimic adoration? And whose judgments were better on the harlots passing Paul's, the fucus'd traffickers of the Strand, the light-stepping demure misses of the Exchange, the painted watchers of Deadman Place? His eye lighted hotly on all, and he sinned in heart and tongue with more than his purse or good fortune could win him. As Peele told him, if breeding followed his eye, as it did the sun, there'd be more born to women than to herrings.

As for his son Kit—he would not admit it even to himself, but he cared little whether he saw him again or not. He was not a family man—by this time he knew it. He had made a mistake, and Doll had made a mistake, and it had been best for him to go the way he did. Doll and Kit, they could never be so happy elsewhere as at Tombland. How easy to recognise the hardship and want they must experience if they came to him in London. And yet never a word to them. Never a word from them. He might be dead for all they knew. And by God, he thought, they might be dead for all he knew! Doll and Kit and the cold grave! Thinking thus, he swore he would write the very next day; but the next day he felt differently. Who was he to take the first step? It was all his father's fault. He had driven him away just as he had driven Alice, and just as Alice was too proud to go creeping back, so he would be. No, let them stay at Tombland, and let his father look after them, that would be best. There was the hostess of the Red Lattice in Tormoyle Street—he told himself she meant more to him than Doll and Kit and home and Norwich and boredom in Tombland.

He moved in to the Red Lattice immediately after the celebrations that followed the dismantling of the camp at Tilbury. He had been going there for drink for six weeks past. The hostess was a big woman, with hair redder than his own, and he lusted for her exceedingly. Mistress Sue Porter, that was her name, and one well-known—too well-known. In Peele's opinion she was for the cart one day, and that not so far ahead. But she dominated Greene for a time, though he pretended to his cronies that his court-ship was a cold-blooded one. "Well," said Peele, alluding to her size, "if ever you do go to bed with her, watch out she doesn't overlie you." While Marlowe guffawed, he compared what would result with a flatfish, a cow-splash, an untossed pancake. But her very amplitude was the attraction to Greene—that and the chance of free board and lodging for as long as he could manage it.

Although a frequent companion of Marlowe, he had little liking for him. At bottom he was jealous of him, and angered because the two parts of *Tamburlaine* so easily triumphed over his own two plays. And Marlowe was not a modest man. He knew himself a greater poet than his friends, and it was debatable whether he was the more offensive drunk or sober when he let them know it. He despised pastoral, and Greene's romances and his best verse were pastoral; he thought writers of masques and revels mere threads on the sleeve of the Muse, and that annoyed Peele; and most infuriating of all was for him to rate his imitators for their fustian stuff. This from the author of *Tamburlaine*, where emperors served as footstools, where kings not horses dragged a conqueror's chariot, where brains were dashed out against cages, where the extravagance of language was beyond anything in *Cambyses*!

"You think, Greene," he had the impudence to tell him, "that once you sing soprano you are in the way of heroic verse. It is beyond you, man."

Greene scowled in reply. "And you think, Marlowe, because you bawl louder than the bulls at mating time, you are the only tragedian this world has seen."

Try as he would to keep his temper, he'd be quarrelling with him before long. "He is a mere mouthful of noise," he would tell Peele; "and as for his morals—— Is he any better than an atheist, d'you think?"

"I shouldn't preach if I were you," Peele reminded him. "How is fat Susie of Tormoyle Street?"

Fat Susie was very well, and Greene well enough with her. He had spent many an afternoon lounging on the Red Lattice bowling green, puffing gingerly at a pipe (for he was learning to smoke), and many an evening at one of her tables with a pint, before making up his mind boldness was best. And then one day he approached her almost as frankly as Panurge the haughty lady of Paris, with much the same baconian argument, and with better success, for she was willing and able both. She was witty at bed time about her dimensions, but gave and expected good service. He was pleased to think himself a new Villon, and better off than that rapscallion in his Grosse Margot. Where was Doll now, for whose sake he had sworn purity and knightly devotion? Where the sweet child of the Ponte Vecchio? With much else that was good they were away in the past.

He no longer called on his sister and brother-in-law. Alice was angry with him for leaving his wife and child, and with her it seemed as though to be angry was to up-braid. He wasn't going there to be shouted at and scolded. Let her keep her tongue for Sidley's bastard. And that weak-kneed husband of hers. One afternoon at the Red Bull, half watching the interlude, half jesting with Monox about the herd of stinking groundlings, he kept silent after a joke about shop-keepers and their wives that he knew he should resent. Thenceforth he knew it would never do for these companions of his to guess he had a brother-in-law who sold spices. They would never forgive him a thing like that. Your father might be a saddler, like Greene's, or even a cobbler, like Marlowe's, but after all no man could choose his parents. The present generation was different. Citizens were fools, their wives were cows; they were good to laugh at, to throw things at when they attended public places, and they were best of all to owe money to. But these brisk-witted lads with Latin at their finger ends, with their romances and plays, their bursts of poetry, their confused realisation that what they left behind them would be one of England's greatest glories, could not be expected to truck friendly with them. For that reason as well as his poor welcome, Greene avoided the shop in Bucklersbury.

During this time too things were happening that gravely affected Coppinger. The conflict between the bishops and the puritans had taken a more serious turn. From April on the country was enlivened or made despondent by the book warfare launched some years ago by that *Brief and Plain Declaration* in which Greene was convinced Coppinger had a hand. Month by month, surreptitiously printed by Waldgrave and the Welshman Penry, appeared the attacks of the one party, from *Diotrephes* to the *Defence* of August, and the far less able replies for Whitgift. Was Coppinger mixed up in this too? Greene had now decided what his role was: the perilous one of working in Star Chamber employ that he might know something of its plans. Thinking further, he guessed it impossible that the keen Archbishop and his keen men should not know all about Coppinger's sympathies, and was forced to think them spying on the spy. For a long time his way of life made him ashamed to speak to his friend, but one day he did seek him out at his home and suggest his doubts and fears. Coppinger's conduct puzzled him. He seemed indifferent to what Greene had to say, hardly thanking him for his warning, and then, as Greene thought, in order to change the subject, asked quite natural and yet highly embarrassing questions about Greene's family. Giving clumsy, unprepared answers, Greene knew he was not believed and began to lose his temper.

"In Tormoyle Street?" said Coppinger. Everyone knew
the reputation of the Red Lattice. "You are staying
there?"

What if he was? Greene asked angrily. But Coppinger
only shook his head. Now, for the first time, Greene looked
on him as a fool for imagining his brains could carry it
over the High Commission party. He was more stupid
in other ways too. He was growing into an old man, without
ever having been a young one. He had never gone kissing
under the white hawthorn trees, never played hot cockles
in laughing parlours, never warmed his chill brain with
the fumes of spirits, never felt fat and full and spread his
belly to the fire. Unless he was careful, if he lived he would
be the usual tight-brain, old narrow-lips. If he lived—
for he seemed careless of the perilous task he was committed
to.

"I know what you are thinking of me," he said bluster-
ingly, to cover his shamefacedness.

"You do, Robert?"

"Everything that is bad. You are contrasting me with
yourself, are you?"

"No, Robert, I am not doing that."

"But I can't live your way, Edmund—and I would not
want to if I could. I couldn't stay—half-dead."

Coppinger smiled at that, but sadly. "You think me half
dead then? Because I don't do the things you do?"

"It's not natural to live the life you do, Edmund, without
pleasure of any kind. Without laughter and wine and poetry
and—why shouldn't I say it?—without women."

"You have a right to speak. You are a married man."

Greene felt his cheeks grow hot. "It is easy for you
to talk! It's different in the world out there. A cloistered
virtue—what will God himself think it worth?"

"You talk of cloistered virtue? Robert, you don't know
what you are saying. Have I ever pretended to be anything
I am not? Have I ever set up as saint? Have you thought
of me as without passions, without the feelings of other
men?" Coppinger was deeply moved. "If so, you do me

wrong. Great God in heaven, Robert, to hear you speak, I have had no lusts to subdue, no temptations to fight against! I tell you—I have said as much to no other man —I have fought—yes, I have fought harder than most. I have wanted to do the things you have done. I have wanted to forget the whole world at the mouth of a bottle. Christ who hears me, have I not wanted? And to seek oblivion in women's arms and forget that ever I was born for the work my Creator would have me do. Do you think I have never been sick of my drudgery? That there have never been days and dreadful nights when I could curse myself for my—my dullness, you would call it—and fling out on to the streets and into the first stew I came to? God, God, God, as though easy lechers like you know anything of the torments of the flesh! As though you who slake your appetites with less compunction than dogs in heat know what it is to want these things! I tell you, you know nothing! You and all your cursed kind!" He hid his face in his hands and began to sob. "And you would judge me! You who debauched yourself at the University, and in Italy practised all the abominations man may lay his tongue to. And now you come home and marry a woman too good for you, desert her and your infant son, and here you are in London, the friend of penny-pamphlet scrawlers, and living with a whore in Tormoyle Street—and you have the impudence to sit in judgment over me!"

Greene swallowed hard. He was wounded and embarrassed at the same time. "I did not mean to judge you, Edmund. That would be impudence, as you say. I might retort it was you who did the judging."

He watched Coppinger's head and shoulders as he fought for self-control. "Robert," he said, raising his face; "let us forget all we have said, shall we? There are times when I am not myself. But—it hurt me, that was the way of it, I suppose. I thought I had learned to command myself better."

Greene wondered why he could not be more affectionate towards Coppinger. Perhaps the hurtful things he had said.

He would not forget to-day in a hurry. So that was what his friend thought of him? "It is easier to say too much than too little," he replied coolly. "As you say, we'll forget it. In any case, I must be going. I think I told you, I am meeting young Nashe within the hour."

"Very well, Robert—go if you must."

"Will you take some advice from me?"

"Usually I offer it. Well, Robert?"

"For two reasons you should leave all work and go to the country. You are in danger of breaking your mind and body, and I think you are in danger of your life. That is all."

"It sounds enough."

"You'll go?"

"I cannot. I have work to do that must not be delayed."

Greene showed his disgust, and took a colder leave than ever before. Edmund had gone too far this time. He was like the rest of the puritans, a bigot and a spoilsport. Well, he'd not be able to say no one had warned him. He snapped his fingers. It wasn't worth trying to stop a barrel rolling downhill.

Then he thought: How ill he looked! I should have been kinder. I'll go back now and say I am sorry. I must never quarrel with Edmund.

But he walked on, all the same.

Coppinger, left alone, sat for a long time sorrowful. He regretted his outburst twofold: because he had told Greene truths that would only part them and do no good, and because he had shown something of his own heart—and for longer than he now cared to remember he had been trying not to show that to anyone. He was so hopelessly tired that he could wish the very world to stand still while he slept and slept and slept. Not the sleep of one night, but years of it, while his crawling brain might forget its troubles. And forget, forget his duties. No word, surely, so lovely as that *forget!* Even now, the persistent buzzings came back to haunt him: Henry Barrow examined in court by the Council, Udall and Chatfield at Kingston, how to get news through to Penry at East Molesey, Penry at East Molesey, Penry at East Molesey, Udall and Chatfield, Chatfield, Chatfield, Chatfield, the names billowing like clouds inside his swelling head. If there were only some-one else! But he thought of all the brave men fighting for their faith, all the men who had died or were dying for it, all those yet to be called—there was no one else, he must keep on. So Greene could see that far, could he? That as he, Coppinger, spied on the Commissioners, so they spied on him. He rubbed the side of his face. That he of all men should be cast for such a part! To play this desperate game with two-edged weapons, and all the time to wait for the hand on his shoulder, the brief official voice, the march for ever from the light of God's sun. This game at three removes. How soon before the High Commission grew tired and he was taken up for a traitor? Only from God could he expect faith and strength. To the world he was lost already. And yet he knew it sweet. Sweet the sound of men's deep voices and the laughter of women and the singing of children, the very barking of the dogs. When you looked back on happiness, remembered the snoring of the gleeman's strings, the quaint harmonies of pipes and fluting minstrelsy, saw again the swing of garments, the colours and textures of stuffs, the dingy pages of old books —it was hard sometimes not to cry for it. Mellow evenings in a room at Cambridge, the beauty of the College Backs, hard walks when frost was in the air, the comfort of blankets, the putting on the master's gown—these were all dear to him, and they were gone. His father and his mother too— how could he leave them with a maimed name? But he had won that battle and would not fight it again. And the old College dreams of a wife and son—well, they must be only dreams. One could but trust to the hidden purposes of heaven, for this fool Greene had both and must run from them to an empty life in London.

Poor Greene, he thought the next moment. Poor Robert! I pity him and he pities me, so we should both be pleased

with ourselves. He had seen in Greene that day the
youngster so completely under Sidley's influence while
at Cambridge. Like the chameleon taking his colour
from wherever he found himself. Deceiving himself with
fine thoughts that he was more the man for being a bigger
rascal. And consorting with men like George Peele, the
jest of London, like Christopher Marlowe, an atheist it
was rumoured, and now with young spider-brain Thomas
Nashe. Married men too, Lodge and Peele and Monox,
he believed. Was it to moralize too severely that he thought
them worse than beasts? He remembered so well that
girl-wife of Greene's, as they had seen her in the day of
her great distress. Who knew what her distress was now?
Had he more time he should go to Norwich and find out
—he shook his head. No, he could not do that. And Greene's
sister? He had seen her just that one night at Cambridge.
How was it with her? A pleasant girl then. A lovely woman
she would be. A great happiness to some lucky man.

Other people married. His own life—he saw why to
Greene it appeared wasted. Even in small things. He
thought unhappily of the woman he had tried to rescue
from the brothel behind St. Andrew's. Back there not a
month after he had found her shelter elsewhere, the whole
thing a tap-room jest. How often since had he thought of
her arms around his neck, pulling him to soft surrender,
the will-weakening warmth and beauty and eagerness of
her. Would Greene, if he knew the story, think there had
been no temptation then? Surely he would not laugh,
degraded though he might be this last year and more.
And now again, memory grew stronger, quickening that
old desire. Why not forget for a time, there with that
woman who would love him, show him the ways of love
unknown, bring him peace and rest if only for a night?
The thought of her was torture to him for several minutes.
She was as a warm sea in which he could drown himself.
Be lost to the world and all its insistence. Udall and
Chatfield at Kingston, Henry Barrow examined, news
to Penry at East Molesey: these and phrases like them,

some relating to matters settled twelve months before, came to beat upon his brain, already overwrought with his struggle to forget the relief that might be bought at the house behind St. Andrew's. A dark cloak to cover him from head to foot—no one would know. He could be there in so short a time, a sentence or two, the transfer of a miserable coin—no one would know. Even hired kindness, some break from this endless strain and worry. Sink down his head to her white shoulders, sleep there, murmur, soon forget, hands through his hair, his tired head caressed—no one would know. NO ONE WOULD KNOW. He rose from his seat, that devilish sentence too strong for him. The cloak! Where was the cloak? It was in his hands, ready for the swing around him, when he threw it to the ground. Great God who ruled the world, why should men be so weak? Why, oh God! It seemed to him then that man's weakness must frighten God, sitting in changeless splendour in heaven. These poor feeble creatures he had made—what could he think of them? Except that he must pity them on the day of judgment for that very weakness. Pity saint and sinner alike, pity poor Flamstead who had died for his name in the Fleet and pity the Primate who now on his stool prepared death for other martyrs. And saint and sinner would be alike in need of mercy, for what was the goodness of the best of men compared with the goodness of God? He himself, who had spoken such bitter words to Robert Greene, was he not as great a whoremaster in his heart? And in love with infamy because it was hidden from all eyes save those all-regarding eyes of God who made him. Poor woman he had tried to save—her case was no worse than his. It was the heart that counted, for how should there be good deeds without a good heart.

How calm he felt now. That tearing at the heart, those shifting visions searing his eyes, that thick, dull pulse of cloggy blood—what of them now? If a man called, he should find help. He began to pray, on his knees there, thanking God that he had strengthened him in his time of need, and not without whispering that when the greater need came he might not face his enemies alone. He prayed for all mankind, that cruelty might vanish from the earth, and the spirit of persecution rest from its intended victims. He prayed that men might cease from wickedness and practise only charity and compassion. For Robert Greene he offered up a special prayer, for his wife and son, his sister and her family. He prayed for the woman the thought of whom had come so near undoing him. When at last he rose he was clear-headed, as though purged of all that had weighted and tired him.

He went into the living room, where his father and mother were waiting for him to eat with them.

"You look less tired than when you came home, Edmund."

"I am less tired, mother, thank you."

"Your mother and I have been talking about you this evening, Edmund."

"Yes?"

"We thought: Why not go back to Cambridge again? You were better in health there. It is the life that suits you, the scholar's life."

"I love no other so well, father. But I'll not go, with your permission."

"I cannot force you, and you know that I would not if I could. But it would be better, we think that."

He expressed in words that came from his heart his love for them, his appreciation of their thought for him, but he told them it was impossible. His mother later went out upon some errand, and his father said to him: "I think I know something of what you are about, my son. Do as seems right to you, but—oh, Edmund, remember your mother's grief if you come to ill." His son turned to him, his face irradiated. "I have thought of it, father. All things are in God's hand. We must trust to him, for we may."

So he went back to his work. A strange and tortuous work it was. Transcribing the proceedings of the High

Commissioners, keeping his eyes and ears open for anything that might help the nonconforming party, and knowing all the time that his employers knew him a spy and were supplying him with pieces of information to lead him astray and betray the movements of those suspected to lie behind the present controversy. Always the need to scrutinise and rescrutinise each scrap of news, to weigh probabilities and possibilities, to determine methods of getting in touch with those messengers he could trust, to send Penry and Waldgrave such warnings as from week to week proved necessary, to keep in contact with other puritan leaders such as John Udall, Giles Wigginton, Francis Merbury, John Field, Eusebius Paget and Job Throkmorton, and to forward the work of the unknown who would shortly be before the public as Martin Marprelate. Like the other puritans he spoke to, he was ignorant of this Martin's identity. Their great protagonist would work alone and trust no name of his to the printers. His first tract appeared in October from East Molesey, the second in November from Fawsley, for Coppinger was able to send Waldgrave news that the first hiding place of their secret press had been discovered. It was his great joy to do such essential service, for without the press they were dumb men. He could not save Wigginton from his fourth spell in gaol, when that usually sharp-witted divine came in all innocence to preach in London and found himself before Whitgift, accused of being Martin himself, but he had the pleasure of being present at the examination, himself closely observed, he knew, when Wigginton resolutely refused to take the oath till he knew his accusers, and then proceeded to chop passages of scripture against Whitgift and Bishop Cooper. It was with difficulty he kept his face straight when, Wigginton having alleged that those apocryphal books appointed to be read by the Archbishop included errors in doctrine and practice, the Archbishop demanded what errors, and Wigginton replied that the devil was said to have loved Sara, *Tobit*, vi. 16, which was fabulous. "Is it strange to you," asked Whitgift, "that the devil should love men and women?" He made some enlargement on the matter, after which Bishop Cooper added: "If you had read either divinity or philosophy, friend, it would not be strange to you that the devil should love women." Said Wigginton, looking into the court where sat Bishop Clarges, famous for his concubinage: "I know well, as do all men, that the devil's servants love women most devouringly, but I am read in no such divinity of the devil. Shall I admit I am wrong?" Coppinger would like to have written as marginalia, *erubuit archiepiscopus*. Yet, despite no proper charge and an entire absence of witnesses, it ended so that Wigginton lay five weeks in the White Lion Prison, Southwark, close confined and loaded with irons, with no more food than served to keep him alive, before he was released by representations made to the Queen herself by certain eminent men concerned that the principles of national justice should not be destroyed as well as flouted by the Commission. Coppinger dared not visit him in person, but he so managed it that after his release Wigginton was able to send indirect word to Penry that the press should be again shifted as suspicion was turning towards the knight of Fawsley.

He did not see Greene again till the year's end, but was not without news of him. December was a famous month for that diligent writer of imitations. First came his romance *Alcida*, but this was almost lost sight of in the glories of December '26, when the second of Greene's plays (not to count his collaboration with Lodge), *Orlando Furioso*, was given at Court by the Queen's Men. He imagined the stir into which this must throw its author, the need for new finery, the palpitations.

His imaginings fell short of the truth. The day he knew his play taken Greene was off to John Tilney, Her Majesty's Master of the Revels, for an advance on payment. This would be the crisis of his life. If Fortune smiled he was a made man for ever. And they said Her Majesty liked a shapely and well-appointed man. So off to the tailor,

and work to do for Shan Cuttelero. He could not improve on the cream silk stockings, ungartered, but drew
them tight to bursting over his model calves; his breeches
were of gold cloth, decorated with in-worked devices of
butterflies, his doublet the red that he thought matched
his hair, his ruff and laces the same colour as his stockings.
His cloak was red outside and gold within, his hat a sober
black velvet picked out with red, his shoes red with cork
soles. His profits were thus swallowed up before the night
itself, but Mistress Porter of the Red Lattice, who had
previously shown signs of tiring of him, was now willing
to stuff a pound into his hand, and entertain him like an
ambassador before he set off for Court. She believed his
own tales of his prospects, and when you kept none too
respectable a house it was as well to have a friend at Court.
She would have liked nothing better than Burghley and
Hunsdon for customers, and to oblige the whole bench
of bishops on the quiet.

She was capable of it, Greene knew.

It took half-a-pint of the sweetest hippocras to conquer
the bad taste in his mouth, but Mistress Porter could deny
him nothing this day. Arrived at the Palace, he was treated
with a proper deference, and at last led into the private
room where Orlando should grow furious before the
selectest audience in the kingdom. None of the great
ones wasted time on him, but two or three there, strugglers
like himself, hung on him enviously, gave him good
wishes, and tried to interest him in matters of their own:
a play on the subject of Thisbe, a masque of the Ten
Thousand Virgins ("You will never find them," said
Greene. "Haw-Haw-Haw!"), a romance in the vein of
Master Lyly ("He is out of fashion; the booksellers will
never take it."), a satirical poem of the Fox and the Goose.
He stood with the rest when Majesty appeared, then fell
on his knees, and remained so till she was seated. Elizabeth
was now in her fifty-sixth year, her face long and fair and
wrinkled more than it need be, with thin lips that revealed blackened teeth when she smiled, her nose slightly

hooked and the more regal for that, her eyes black and
sharp, her hair almost as red as his own, but, so he suspected, not so firmly attached to her scalp. Her appearance
was most queenly, for she carried herself well, as though
the earth belonged to her, and her array was worth her
own ransom. Her dress was of pale green silk, heavy to set
well, embroidered with crowns of various colours and
pearls the size of beans. Three rows of pearls hung around
her neck and to below her waist, and from a collar of
emeralds depended on her bare breast a small coat of
arms worked in rubies and emeralds. Her ruff was closed,
not to cover the neck, of the most delicate bone lace with
purl edging of fine gold; and there were pearls in her hair.
Each stick of her small fan was tipped with a diamond,
and the rosettes on her shoes were of rubies. When he dared
raise his eyes to this splendour, it was to think that a word
from her could set him up for life, but that she was reported meaner than the Treasurer himself. He sighed
privily, for so few hours would show all.

His play went well, and he thought the Queen's Men
not unworthy of it, but he was increasingly upset by the
conduct of the distinguished audience. Her Majesty was
talkative and disposed to be witty; she was continually
jesting with the curled and puffed Essex behind her fan;
and he at least pretended to be sufficiently amused to
laugh loudly and disconcertingly at maddeningly frequent
intervals. They seemed to pay no attention to the play
itself, except that now and again, after one of Essex's
tributes to her fertile mirthfulness, she would make a short
wave of the fan that the checked actors should continue
with their parts. Johnson, Wilson, and Dutton were evidently used to such conduct and went dexterously on with
their business, but it became more and more evident to
the author that there was only the most perfunctory attention for his play from anyone. The tenderest passages,
the neatest strokes, the finest declamations, meant nothing
to them compared with the part Elizabeth played. It was
a lesson in the disappointment that, as he had always heard,

attended on hopes at Court. Smiling constrainedly, he thought gloomily of what might have been: an audience rapt during the performance, deafening with applause after it, the gracious words of Majesty, a collar of gold around his neck, instructions to the Secretary, fame and fortune overnight. Essex laughed again, right in the middle of that glorious speech of Orlando's that had cost him so much trouble, the Queen tapped his arm reprovingly; they were like lovers together, the handsome boy and withered woman. It was indecent, Greene thought. He knew now he would get nothing from her. She had always been a bitch to everybody. He thought of Davison, thrown into the Tower and fined ten thousand pounds only for doing her will. Put not your trust in princes! A painted old hag and that young pimp of an Essex, with nothing better to do then guffaw through his play. A fine Virgin Queen she was too. Seymour would have something to say there, and Leicester, and Alençon, and Simier, and God knows how many more who'd visited her abed and helped her shift a nightgown. She yawned behind the jewelled fan. The old harridan! Of all the shameless old whores, sitting there with that lusty youngster, rubbing her withered shank alongside his, her dry hand seeking his moist one, grinning like a death's head, and yawning at his play. Yawning! That had damned it. There was no hope now. He wished he had stayed at Norwich.

But she had a word for him when it was all over. He was conducted between kneeling sycophants to where she sat. Playing the expected part, he sank as though his knees had no strength before her beauty and puissance.

"So you are Master Robert Greene?"

His forehead almost touched the ground. "If it please Your Majesty."

"It pleases me very well, and your play pleases me very well, Master Greene." She smiled across at Essex before showing her learning. "But you took some naughty liberties with our poet, did you not?" She enumerated

them, amazing Greene, who could not believe she had
heard ten lines altogether. Angelica's change of father,
the embassy of suitors, the part of Sacripant, the death of
Brandimart, the unaccountable changing of the king's
titles, these she checked off on her blazing fingers while
Greene, mortified, wondered who had told her as much,
and the others present raised mooncalf faces at such royal
scholarship. Still, this put her in a good humour, and
she accepted without reproof Greene's excuses and pleas
for originality.

"Your age, Master Greene?"

"I am thirty years old, Your Majesty. I was born the
year Your Gracious Majesty succeeded to the throne of
this thrice blessed kingdom."

"Who would have thought it! We might be your——"

"Sister," said the dexterous Essex.

"You think so?" Faugh! thought Greene, watching her
roll her eyes. "Well, all flattering lords aside, as the poet
says, the times bear change and we must change with
them. Do you, in your short life, Master Greene, find
the truth of that?"

Greene prostrated himself again. "In Fairyland is no
passing of time, Your Majesty."

She turned to Essex. "Was that a pretty answer, my
lord?"

"A good player's answer," he commended, to Greene's
annoyance.

"And I like my players. You will have seen to Master
Greene's needs, Master Tilney?" She patted her mouth
delicately with the fan. "My lord, your arm."

He dared not leave his knees till she had left the room.
So that was all!

"Her Majesty was pleased?" he asked Tilney, following him to the Accounts Room.

"I think so. But I have learned, Master Greene, that
plays are made for Her Majesty, not Her Majesty for
plays." He counted over the money. "You will sign
here."

It was the bare balance, not a penny more. He would still owe the tailor half the price of his cloak. And Fat Susie would be expecting a handful of gold, no doubt. Well, he thought grimly, the fat sow will always need another feed. Let Fat Susie want as much too.

CHAPTER XXIX

DURING THE FIRST half of the next year Greene found himself in all kinds of difficulties. Yet money would have solved them all. Some of this he got, for he sold his *Orlando* to the Queen's Men for twenty nobles, but by the time his hostess of the Red Lattice got her claws into this and Peele had come a-borrowing and Monox with his pitiful tale of need, it was gone. Undoubtedly he was well known now, but no one seemed willing to advance him a loan, just the same. He contrasted his arrival in London from Norwich, with the sale money of his wife's house at Hartop in his pocket, when he was wealthy and unheard of, with his present plight of fame and famine. Peele would be delighted to lend, but he never had any money, and these last months there was another daughter with a stomach that needed filling, and Arabella was ill; Lodge, home again from the Canaries, had outgrown his cronies and had no other offer for Greene than that he might keep all his share of the price of the *Looking Glass*. For his part he was through with writing for the stage; he would never again tie his pen to penny-knaves' delight; it was an occupation unworthy of a serious man of letters. Besides, during the voyage he had written a new romance, somewhat in Greene's style, only better, and he thought that romances should be his only form of recreation from his new study, physic. No, he would lend no money. Frankness was best, Greene would agree. He had been a sailor, and would keep his affairs shipshape and Bristol fashion henceforth. Greene then thought of asking Monox for a loan but when he called on him found Monox had just been taken to gaol for debt; and he knew Vennar's affairs too well to ask him. There remained Marlowe, from whom he met with a blunt refusal.

"Not a groat, Greene!"

"But you have the money! I tell you, Marlowe, I am in great need."

"All the better," Marlowe assured him. "You will get nothing from me."

"All the better! I thought you were a friend of mine. I see I was wrong."

"Better late than never, Greene." They wrangled like school children over a juicy apple. "Very well, I'll tell you why. You thought I would pay no attention to what you wrote of me in *Perymedes* last year? Shall I quote to you: 'I keep my old course to palter up something in prose, using my old poesie still, although lately two gentlemen poets had it in derision that I could not make my verses jet upon the stage in tragical buskins, every word filling the mouth like the burden of Bow Bell, daring God out of heaven with that atheist Tamburlaine——'"

"You can shut your mouth," Greene told him rudely. "I am glad you paid me enough attention to memorise me. It is more than anyone has ever done for you."

"I'll shut my mouth, and I'll shut my purse at the same time! You are a poor jealous fool, Greene, that's the trouble with you. Your *Alphonsus*—God help it! And the kill-cow ranting of *Orlando*—I tell you I laughed the whole way through."

"A fair exchange, for I slept through the second *Tamburlaine*. I won't forget this, Marlowe. That a self-styled poet, a tragedian, should be such a money-grub he'd deny his master in verse the price of a night's lodging! You ought to announce the phenomenon from the stage."

"Master, is it! I borrow from no one, money or poetry or ideas, and don't you forget it! I call no man master but myself, Greene. But if ever you were a master, then all I can say is: God help the taught!"

On this note they parted, Greene telling Marlowe where

he might profitably stuff his silver pieces, and Marlowe retorting a little tamely that he would rather do that than let Greene get hold of them.

On top of this came his expulsion from the Red Lattice. Neither he nor Fat Susie lost their tempers. She was tired of him, and he was tired of her; she had lost her profit and he his pleasure; so he tied up his few belongings one morning in April, and humped them on his back down Tormoyle Street, and so through the town to his old lodgings in the Strand. He was there three days before his bill came up for settlement, and two more days before he left after threats. Things were getting serious. He had not a farthing to bless himself with. In this need, it occurred to him he might pawn some of his wardrobe with the Admiral's Men, then playing at the Boar's Head, beyond Aldgate. The doublet and cloak he had bought for that disappointing night at Court last December were still in perfect condition, though the breeches were spotty. It was a pity the Queen's Men had gone on tour. He would have done better with them. Still, he was too much the beggar to choose too precisely, so he brushed down the cloak and doublet and, having won an unwilling promise from his disgusted landlord not to throw the rest of his stuff into the street, off he went.

He had a reception that surprised him. The garments? Well, it might be arranged. But before they came to terms—had Greene a play on the stocks? They had need of something new and striking to help fill the gap till Marlowe had finished his *Faustus*. Something with the author's name guaranteed to please. That struck Greene as a pleasant thing to say, and still more pleasant to hear. He asked questions about *Faustus*. Hm, rather far-fetched, didn't they think? Robert Browne was inclined to agree, but Edward Alleyn, scenting the part of a lifetime, thought it would prove a greater success than his *Tamburlaine*. "Of course," Greene said amiably. "*Tamburlaine* gives the uncritical plenty to laugh at." But back to the question of this doublet and cloak—hm, Alleyn thought they might come to terms, but about a play now? He was sure he had nothing? What about *Orlando?* Who held the copyright? The lie was out of Greene's mouth before he had made up his mind to tell it. Greene's, eh? But what about the cloak and doublet? In a moment, Master Greene, in one moment. Had he thought of selling *Orlando?* Well, perhaps—but in the meantime—— There need be no meantime, if he would consider selling *Orlando.* They were working out the price within a minute. Greene pointed out that the play had been given before Her Majesty, Richard Jones countered with the time of year; Greene urged the value in publicity for any other performance, Alleyn doubted whether it would be more successful than *Alphonsus.*

"Well, gentlemen," Greene bluffed, "if it is worth twenty nobles to you, you are welcome. If not, I know a market, should I need one."

They talked for five minutes. Ten nobles?

They talked for another five. Fifteen?

Settled. Twenty nobles for Master Robert Greene.

He walked back to the Strand, complete with cloak and doublet, the money already in his possession, but worried over what would happen when the imposture became known, as soon it must. Anyhow, he could not be expected to starve in the meantime. But when a man remembered the Fleet, by Jupiter it gave him something to think of. He must get some writing done, earn another twenty nobles, and so settle his debt with either the Queen's Men or the Admiral's. This latest romance of his—that would do the trick. It ought to, anyway.

But his luck was out. The Queen's Men were back in town three weeks before their proper time. He had spent most of the money then, and his romance would not be finished for a month at least, so after some hesitation he decided he had better go along to Wilson and Johnson

and make the best of a bad job. They were staggered
at first by such an unheard of thing, that a dramatist
should sell his play twice over, but like sensible men
avoided making a quarrel of it until they had got their
money back or their copyright. To get the second was
easy, but it meant gaol for Greene, and his wits were
the sharper for that knowledge. Why not, instead, allow
the Admiral's Men to keep the play—it was none too
good when you thought it over—and in its place he would
give them free of charge—unless they chose to offer a noble
or two, say—his new comedy *Friar Bacon and Friar Bungay?*
The men of business looked at Greene, at each other, and
at the tips of their noses, and thought it might be as well
to put the question to the entire company. After three
days, during which Greene could meditate on the slime,
the stench, the death-rate of Her Majesty's unbreakable
prisons, they announced that they would accept his
offer. Unless the Admiral's Men raised objections he
was safe; and, mercifully, they saw no gain in going
to law. The only other embarrassment for Greene was
that he had to pay the legal fees for a new agreement
between the two companies. In a fortnight he was
penniless once more. This time it was to the Queen's
Men he carried his doublet and cloak, and received
four pounds for them, with the uncomfortable knowledge
that he was saying good-bye to them for ever. He
might even see them worn by the personages of his new
play.

In another month *Menaphon* was finished, and he thought
it the best of his romances, with the possible exception of
Pandosto. He had incorporated in it a number of poems
composed years before—indeed, this was his practice in
most of the romances—and a couple of charming songs
composed almost in a breath, like Doron's description
of Samela and Sephestia's song to her child, with its only
half sincere reference to his own desertion of his wife and
child:

Weep not my wanton, smile upon my knee,
When thou art old there's grief enough for thee.
The wanton smiled, father wept;
Mother cried, baby leapt:
Nature could not sorrow hide.
He must go, he must kiss
Child and mother, baby bliss;
For he left his pretty boy,
Father's sorrow, father's joy;
Weep not my wanton, smile upon my knee,
When thou art old there's grief enough for thee.

This out of the way, though not yet sent to the printer, he turned at once to his new comedy. Never before had he experienced such joy in his work. The idea of it came from his conversation with the Admiral's Men about Marlowe's next play. As that was to be tragedy unrelieved, this should be comedy. And since in his heart he deferred to Marlowe as the greatest tragedian the English stage had seen, he felt he could only enter into direct albeit contrasted competition with him if he produced the greatest English comedy. As *Alphonsus* had been designed to rival *Tamburlaine*, but had failed to do so, now *Friar Bacon and Friar Bungay* should take the wind out of *Faustus's* sails at the best and equal it in merit if not in kind at the worst. Let the atheist do what he would with the Faustbuch; he'd get all he wanted from the late romance of the conjuring friar; and in addition he would have the sweetest countryside comedy wherein a prince should woo a milkmaid by proxy, but all should come right in the end because milkmaid and proxy fall most delightfully in love. Despite the past and present squalor of his life, he put into the character of Margaret, the country maid of Fressing-field, all the idealism of his best moments. In his portrayal of her he gathered up all that had been loveliest in the heroines of his romances, added that conception of his wife's perfection so precious during his first stay at Hartop, added also something of the girl's face on the Ponte Vecchio. He never thought of her without thinking too of the dog-roses in country hedgerows, the clean cream-bowls of his mother's kitchen, the freshness of new-washed aprons drying in a spring wind, the little balls of mirror-mist pearled on the heads of grasses after rain. She was so real to him, he was jealous of the men who wooed her. She should be his title to fame, whatever became of the rest of his work. As he wrote he fell in love with Margaret. He had as soon hear ill of his mother.

Midway through this, he was interrupted by the arrival of Nashe, safely through his answers, and just such a Master of Arts as Greene himself. He was in town for good now, finished with the dullards at College, looking for heads on which to bang his cudgel. Perhaps because of their stay in the same room at Cambridge, he paid more attention to Greene's advice than anyone else's, so Greene, knowing the vigour of the youngster's pen from his pamphlet published last year, suggested he would do himself good if he again put his name before the public with a preface to his *Menaphon*. It could be in print within eight weeks. Nashe agreed, glad to distinguish himself.

"What shall I write against, Robert?"

"Anything and everything, except you and me. Why not have a whack at Marlowe? He is in the news of late. And a general attack on the players? After all, why should such parrots make profits over your head and mine? We are the men, Tom, you and me, not these geese who gabble our lines."

Nashe went at his task like a hurricane, reciting aloud most of what he was setting on paper, till Greene could have kicked him over the street to other lodgings. Yet he mouthed good phrases: "Alchemists of eloquence who think to out-brave better pens with the swelling bombast of a bragging blank verse"—that would be Marlowe; "the spacious volubility of a drumming decasyllabon"—an excellent

description of his ranting; and sucking over his own gibe
at the "cobbler's eldest son," he felt Marlowe would not
enjoy what was coming to him.

Naturally, they did not work all the time. Young Tom
was no puritan. He had nothing against bull-baitings, a
throw of the dice, something pleasant in a glass. And he had
an unrivalled store of energy that he simply must use up one
way or another. After hours of table-shaking—he was the
fiercest in action of any penman Greene had known—he
would be up and into his cloak in a wink, and then:
"Come on, Longchops," he'd be calling, "let's be going!"
"Going where?" "To where the wine is cheapest."
He would sit and watch Greene's slower manœuvres.
"You would be last in a snail's marathon, Robert. All
you need is a bag of nuts and you'd be asleep for the
winter."

"D'you want some good advice, Robert?" he asked from
the other side of the table one afternoon.

"I don't know that I do, thank you."

"Good. Here it is. You know this Marprelate fellow?"

"I have heard of him."

"That and read him is all anyone has done. I'm going
in against him, Robert."

"No doubt he is trembling in his shoes. What do you
expect by way of thanks?"

"I'll tell you. I and Lyly——"

"Ego et Rex."

"Lyly and I are offering our services to the Archbishop.
Martin has been one too many for the pens against him so
far. Think of Sutcliffe and Some and Cooper! Pap-ladles,
Robert, nothing more. But the satirist must have humour,
wit, and vitality; he must work in tragedy, comedy, farce,
and melodrama; and deal not in abstractions. Hard,
cracking words will suit him best, jag-edged compounds,
a swelling and boisterous rush of stabbing epithets. He
must have tang and savour more than a quince. He
must be illuminative, hurried, cataract-like. He must lap
his adversary in derision as the devil will lap him in

pitch. His onslaught must be like a Turk's, with club and knife, gun and dagger, and a chorus screeching all the time." He paused. "I have been explaining as much to Cooper's secretary, and in short, Robert, the job is mine."

"You have kept it quiet enough, haven't you?"

"Least said soonest mended. Time to shout when you have landed your salmon, not before."

Greene admitted the truth of this. Thinking of Coppinger again, "What is Martin at these days?" he asked.

Had he asked Coppinger he would be asking one better fitted to tell him. He could have told of the secret press always one move ahead of the Archbishop's pursuivants: from East Molesey to Fawsley in Northamptonshire, thence to Norton-by-Daventry, and then early in February to John Hales's house at Coventry. Then days of desperation when it was known that Sir Richard Knightley's man had blabbered too loud in a London tavern, Waldgrave leaving Martin's service, but Penry finding John Hodgkins to take his place as printer. Before the end of July four more Marprelate tracts, unanswerable by the slower wits on the Bishop's side, then the press shifted from Coventry, the pursuers hot on the trail now, by way of Adderbury, to Woolston, to Warrington, to Manchester. And there at Manchester, only a week before Greene's *Menaphon* and Nashe's preface came out to delight the Gentlemen Readers, the Earl of Derby's men broke in on the printers as they were setting up *More Work for the Cooper*. Half a day before fast riders brought news of the seizure of Hodgkins, Simms, and Thomlyn to Whitgift, Coppinger had from an unknown man a message that the press was lost and he must flee. He had his arrangements for such an accident, said a brief farewell to his parents, and had vanished before the hue and cry began. In the north of the kingdom, at the same time, Penry had gone to ground, to make slow and secret progress to Scotland; both of them lucky to escape the torture and death Whitgift intended for them.

"You will be out of work before you get half started," Greene told Nashe, when most of this was known.

"Not I. Why, man, that Welshman Penry will throw you out a pamphlet like last year's shoe—no more trouble to him. You don't think one of those they have caught and racked is Martin, do you? They can pull old Hodgkins' bones till he is star-shaped, but he will tell nothing because he knows nothing. I'm not worrying."

He was right. Marprelate's *Protestation* appeared about the middle of next month, and Nashe and Lyly settled themselves to the task, not of rebuttal, but of abuse. After the publication of his first squib in October, Nashe left the lodgings he had shared with Greene, and entered rooms paid for by Whitgift at Croydon. The two met occasionally throughout the winter, when Nashe would sneak away from holiness for a bout of manly dissipation, and do most of the paying, for he knew and insisted on his value to his cause. The arrangement suited Greene very well, and he now gave most of his time to his new play. No trouble was too great for him. He re-wrote some passages half-a-dozen times before reverting to his first and freshest version. He would confess as much to no one, but sometimes he did think that all he had done so far was to imitate. Always he looked about him for a model, partly to save himself trouble, partly, since the model was always the rage of the day—*Euphues*, the *Arcadia*, *Tamburlaine*—for his greater profit. But this new venture was to be Robert Greene— not Lyly, Sidney, nor Marlowe. Here at least he was inno- vator. And as for Margaret—he knew her shape, her feature, the tones of her voice, her little gestures, the way she held her head on one side as she listened to Lacy, even the way she dressed from day to day. Now, when the sun shone outside his window, she was in petticoat of red stammel, with a white straw hat; now, when it rained or froze, she was muffled in a warm red cloak. Margaret, the country maid of Fressingfield. She was fresher than Chaucer's Emily; there was no one in literature to compare with her. Sometimes he thought: If only I had met a girl like Margaret, I might have loved her, married her, and now be living in the light of her dear presence—for he never thought that he had met a hundred Margarets, that Mistress Petherill was such, and Benita in Genoa, and Doll, and all the others until he had spoiled it for himself. Nashe, who knew him in love with his own creation, laughed at him as the new Pygmalion, but said to him one day: "I cannot understand you, Robert. In all your writings, romances and plays and fables, the women are sweet and chaste. Yet your life—I'll say nothing of its sweetness, but I'll vouch it has not for a long year been chaste. You are the antipodes of the Roman poet, Robert, of life jocose and writings verecund. Why?" Greene found it hard to answer, and he resented the question. How could he explain it? The distaste he felt for portraying a lewd or graceless woman—no, he could not talk about it.

"You'll be the Homer of women, Robert," Nashe said. He thought it a good phrase and stored it up for future use.

At the end of the year Marlowe's play and his were put on by their companies, *Doctor Faustus* by the Admiral's Men at the Rose, Alleyn in the title part, *Friar Bacon and Friar Bungay* by the Queen's Men at the Bull in Bishopsgate Street. Both were successes, *Doctor Faustus* perhaps the greater, because of Alleyn's inspired rendering of the knowledge-drunk doctor. The connoisseurs had their choice: the tragic intensity of the one, the delicacy and verve of the other. Dross was burnt out of mind by the fire with which Marlowe portrayed the scholar's lust for immeasurable knowledge, his delving into mysteries of heaven and hell, his signing the irrevocable bond, and later his desperate shifts to drug remembrance and harden himself in spirit till that dreadful day when hell must gape for him and there is no escape. What a play! The fierce agonies of Faustus, the grim admonitions of Mephistophilis, the

candour and sinister sincerity of the Fiend, the unique
triumphant lyricism of a hundred speeches, and the magnificent, image-laden exordium to the ghost of Helen whom
Faustus calls from the shades not for physical desire but
for the satisfaction of his thirst after the heavenly quin-
tessence of perfect beauty which he had hymned in
Tamburlaine—Apollo and the Nine, what a play! On the
other hand, Greene gave them the clear air of Suffolk
countrysides, the drift of early summer wind, something
of an eager innocence of love; the neat device of the
wooing, the fun and tumble of the necromancing friars
and the numskull Miles, the rare stab of tragedy and
the smashing of the glass; he gave them too the elegant
Edward, the gallant Lacy; he gave them Margaret. So
within two days men might hear for sixpence the best
tragedy and comedy that had yet graced the English
stage.

On the whole then Greene had every cause for satisfaction. He had met the master-tragedian and fought
him to a draw—with different weapons, admittedly.
Hearing too that the Queen's Men would assure him a
gratuity after the fifth performance, he was in the mood
to let bygones be bygones when he called to see Marlowe
behind stage the afternoon he saw his play at the
Rose.

He found Marlowe furiously angry. "I've been waiting
to see you," he shouted at Greene, who was holding out
his hand. He struck it down, but Peele was holding tightly
to Greene's dagger. "You dirty thief!"

"Shut your mouth, Marlowe," Peele told him.

"I'll not shut my mouth! Am I always to have these
blasted sneak-thieves hanging round my neck? I know
what you tried to do, Greene, you bastard you—you wanted
to make a jest of my *Faustus*, did you? With your cursed
conjurors on the stage, prancing about like monkeys, with
no more feeling for the subject than—— By Christ, I'd
like to strangle you!"

By this time Edward Alleyn was pinning one of his arms

and his brother John the other. Greene stood free, smiling at him as offensively as he could. "You are drunk with your own vanity, man. Nor is that an excuse for your making a fool of yourself in public."

"All right, Alleyn," said Marlowe. "You can let me go. I won't hurt the poor addle-brained little cheat."

"Cheat!"

"Quiet now, Robert!"

The players crowded round to hear the authors of the two. best pieces of the age curse each other. Marlowe went on swearing that Greene had not one idea in his head and that his blank verse suffered from glanders; but Greene countered with Marlowe's complete absence of humour and the glaring truth that he had not the slightest conception of how to portray a woman on the stage. Each childishly appealed to the suffrage of the onlookers.

"Women!" cried Marlowe. "There's none of yours I'd look twice at, Greene."

Greene held his nose. "Can you smell him from where you are, George?"

"You and your——Margaret of Fartingfield!"

Mad with temper at this, Greene yet went on smiling. "Pah!" he exclaimed, with a false refinement. "Has he messed himself, d'you think? Gentlemen," he said to the players, "I give you warning. Keep clear of Master Marlowe if you'd not grow itchy with bugs or the—— Ah!"

They were fighting like cats on the floor, tooth and nail and fist and shoe. Dragged off, they still panted to get back at each other.

"I'll kill you for this, Greene!"

"We shall see. Where is my cap?"

Peele offered it to him, he spat at Marlowe's feet, and they left. On the way to his lodgings Peel tried to talk him into a better frame of mind, but it was useless. He was vainglorious, and bragged bigger than Friar John. It was later, when the excitement had ebbed from his

veins, that he saw the shamefulness of such a quarrel
before such garrulous and mimicking listeners. It could
do neither of them any good. They would not be allowed
to forget it, either. As for Marlowe's threats—poof, that for
them!

CHAPTER XXX

IN MAY GREENE received the most unexpected message
by the mouth of Peter Bredon, a lad attached to the Queen's
Players. He was now lodging in Hoyser Lane, sharing a
dark and smelly room with a mysterious fellow named Gadd,
who spent much of the day in bed and much of the night
in a way Greene never tried to find out. He was certainly
a thief of some kind, so Greene consoled himself for his lack
of means and temptation. He would hate to have his
throat cut while he slept and only wake up when it was
too late. Bredon sniffed as he entered the room, but Greene,
hopeful, did not clout him over the head. Would he proceed
to the Bell Inn at Charing Cross, to see Sir Ralph Sidley?
On Monday or Wednesday at three o'clock in the afternoon. It was then four o'clock on Monday, so he scolded
the boy for his delay, had a cheeky answer, and drove him
out unrewarded. "These brats," said Gadd, from the bed,
"they need kicking, Master Greene." "If my shoes were
heavier——" Greene concurred.

So old Gutless wanted to see him, did he? Old Toadstool
from Braiding. For what then? A twelvemonth of speculation
would not help him. He tried to go on writing, but his
attention wandered too often to his last visit to Lincolnshire, his meeting with Sidley the son, his beating the father
over the pate, his acquaintance with the Braiding dunghill,
his walk in the rain to Hartop. Five years ago, it could be
no less. Amazing! Times had changed since then, and men
and women with them. And not for the better, he knew.
This last winter he had not lived as he should. Gambling
again, too much drink, the company of loose women—
the common weaknesses of men. There were those still
worse than he, that was one comfort. Marlowe and Monox
and George Peele—and George a married man living home
with a dying wife. Surely he was the worst of them. Arabella

had sagged and shrunk till it hurt your heart to see her. Her calmness was patience now. Down on the South Bank where George now lived, in bed, the only kindness she knew from strange men and women whose lives had turned out wrong for them. He frowned, hearing Sidley's voice: Not a woman's world this, Robert.

But this would not pay the landlord at the end of the week. He went on writing.

Wednesday he dressed himself in his poor best, for other items had followed the cloak and doublet to the Queen's Men's wardrobe. His clothes were worn but there was no lack of bright colours, and he'd not be overlooked in a crowd. Had he new shoes, you would not find him complaining.

"Meeting the Queen's Majesty?" asked Gadd, from the bed.

"I saw her only yesterday. There will be talk if I see her again to-day. We must be wary."

Gadd laughed. "Give her my love next time, Master Greene. We kept house together once, did you know? Ay— only she had the state rooms and I had the Black Hole."

Well, it was no news to hear that friend Gadd had seen the inside of a gaol. Indeed, the Sheriff would merit instant dismissal had he not. You had only to look at friend Gadd. Greene left the room, whistling.

"Sir Ralph Sidley?" he asked, at the Bell.

Sir Ralph was expecting a gentleman named Greene. Would he follow the boy? He did, two steps behind, studiously. It was the first time for him to go upstairs at the Bell. He was announced, and entered.

Sir Ralph was seated at a table set between door and window, so that at first it was hard to see his face. Something oddly familiar about the——

"Robertus!"

Greene's face went slack with astonishment. "Why, Sidley——"

It was the son, not the father. Greene felt indescribably stupid. He felt, too, strangely free from emotion. Sidley!

Then he stood up, and Greene saw that he had only one arm—the left one.

"You are surprised to see me again?"

"I thought it was your father had sent. The boy said Sir Ralph."

"I am Sir Ralph. My father is dead these two years, Robertus."

It was now Greene saw Sidley's face. It had changed greatly. "Why did you send for me, Sidley? You above all?"

"It is a long story, Robertus."

Greene pondered. "I never expected to see you again without hate."

"That was your right, but I hope you won't maintain it. Will you sit down? Will you listen to me for a time?"

Greene sat down. "Why I am doing this I don't know. Because I am a fool, I expect. What do you want?"

"I want to know where your sister is, and the boy."

Greene shook his head. "I'll not tell you, Sidley."

"That is your right again. But think that this time I sought you out—doesn't that make any difference? For the moment I don't ask you to tell me where they are. But will you say you know?"

"Yes. I know."

Sidley sat for a time silent. "You will think me a hypocrite, and possibly a liar. I want to do something for them, Robertus."

Greene did not make the easy retort. Different circumstances, perhaps a different man. He was unlike those Italian heroes of some of his own tales, a poor hater over long years. When it was so far behind you—he shrugged his shoulders.

"I am making arrangements to settle money on your sister, Robertus, and on my son."

"This is a strange turn-about, isn't it?"

"You must believe it sincere. Oh I know how you are thinking of me! Look here, Robertus—you see I have only one arm now?"

"I had noticed."

"I left the other in America. With the Indians. Shall I tell you something of my story, Robertus? You'll find it not unconnected with this visit."

Greene threw up his hands, prepared for anything, and listened. He watched the lines and wrinkles of the narrator's face. No doubt of it, this man had been through the mill. He heard how. Sidley had gone out to America with Raleigh's expedition to Virginia in 1585, and arrived home last year to find himself head of his house. America was a hell, with all hell's fiends there. There was never a week's truce with the Indians, never a minute free from anxiety, peril, fear. A race of butchers, white and red alike, polluting the superb land. Each year waiting for reinforcements in the autumn, each year they never came. Each year waiting for new faces, but they never came. And with the passing of each long month hating those around you ever the more. The men, and the few women—hating them to desperation. The cramped life of stockade and camp, the sharp terrors of sorties and expeditions, the dull ache for home, while all around them crept bitter death and torture. "A great green forest hell, Robertus, that was America. We came back, some of us. The rest are with my arm. I lost it in a night attack on the camp. A little axe came down on it— chop-chop-chop!" Sidley screwed his face and shivered. He laughed disconcertingly as he described the horrors of camp surgery, the brutality of those he cursed and could not call friend. "We were all devils. We were worse than the Indians, if anything. We had something to teach them, Robertus. In a way I admired the relentless fight they put up for their homes and lands. I doubt if white men will ever make a settlement there. Their plan was a simple one: to wipe us out, burn us out, cut us to shreds and make ashes of us. For the present they have succeeded. America will be the death of Raleigh, unless I am much mistaken. The death of countless thousands—and so horrible a death, Robertus!" His eyes had their old glitter now. "We used to hear them at it." He sat staring past Greene, till a cold flood swept down his listener's spine. "Not to be taken alive, the pitiful summit of the white man's ambition. Kill and be killed. Anyhow, they got my arm."

Greene stayed silent. Beginning to see reason for change in Sidley.

"They got more than that, Robertus." He whipped off his—his hair, the startled Greene thought for one fraction of a second. The whole of his scalp was a bluey-red, except for ragged rims of hair. "They got my scalp, Robertus." He laughed savagely. "I'm a fine figure of a man, don't you think?"

"Good God, Sidley!"

"Did it frighten you? By God, it frightened me, I know!" He crossed to where a mirror was standing in the light of the window and fitted the tight cap of his wig over the skinned scalp. "I must be the only man in England in such need of other men's hair."

"It seems little enough to say, I know, but I'm sorry, Sidley. I am sorry beyond words."

"I was knocked down in a skirmish—that is how I came by this monstrosity. Or own men carried me off for decent. burial, but I cheated St. Peter, damn him! I grew better of it in time. But I had plenty of time to think in, and towards the end I was thinking hard." He half-scowled at Greene. "Are you waiting for a repentance tract? If so, you will be disappointed. I mapped out the rest of my life those weeks I was lying there with this cursed thing and the sickness that came with it. Thinking of the future, and all the time the copper death creeping through the trees. When the future might be that same little axe splintering your forehead. But that is over and done with. I have come back alive, and plenty of the other swine are dead and rotten. I am going to travel, Robertus, but I am going to see to one or two things first."

He went on to explain that he had heard of his father's death only at his return from America the previous autumn. He had been at Braiding over the winter. His mother was still there, and was well and looked happy. Elizabeth had married Gilbert Hurrish—he was Sir Gilbert now that his father too was dead. Greene thought he remembered him, but Sidley knew they had never met. It must be what his sister had told him. They were living at Lincoln, and there was a daughter, Cecilia. His mother had helped him make up his mind; she had always been fond of Alice, Sidley thought; and now he had seen the lawyers and worked out with them the details of a settlement whereby the sum of one thousand pounds should be held in trust for the boy, to provide for his education and set him up in worthy fashion when he must enter the world, and the sum of two hundred pounds be settled on Alice, with no possibility of its alienation to any other person. "It is nothing but robbing Cecilia," said Sidley wrily, waiting for Greene to make some comment.

Greene asked where he was of use in such a scheme.

"Because someone must approach her and her husband. It cannot be I, it ought not to be the lawyers. But you can do it for me, Robertus."

"There may be trouble, Sidley."

"I guess as much."

Greene deliberated the sums mentioned. Hm, hm! "I think Alice would accept after a time, but Copson— he is a managing sort of man, Sidley."

"Too good for his business, I know. If I could put him at Braiding or Leesome—but he would never accept it. Still, it has nothing to do with him, has it?"

"No? It is easy to see that you have never been married, Sidley."

"The oracle pronounces! Why, by the back teeth of the martyrs, Robertus, you don't tell me *you* are married?"

No question could have embarrassed Greene more. He could have bitten his indiscreet tongue. Yes, he was married. A girl he had met on the way to Braiding. "So I have brought you some luck after all!" Sidley reminded him. Luck? Oh yes. Yes, he was a father, yes, most certainly a father. Three years old, thereabouts. In Norwich for the present. He could tell lies now without a blush. He was having rather a struggle of it in London; he sent them what little he could, but the companies were bad payers. Sidley knew all about his plays. Yes, he had seen *Friar Bacon* a fortnight before, and thought it the finest comedy in the English tongue. No, did he then? Come to think of it, yes, he was thirsty. For old times' sake then—a bottle of red wine. "Your boy and mine!" Could there have been a more unexpected toast.

"Tell me something about him, Robertus."

Greene skated dexterously down a long glittering lie. Just fancy that the two of them were fathers!

They had a pleasant hour, talking over the more suitable portions of old times and their hopes for the future. They were older and wiser now, and better. Greene grimaced his agreement. Older, anyway.

Where would he go? Sidley took in the horizon with his left hand. He would undertake the greatest journey yet attempted by mortal man. He would start with Africa, following the route of Pharaoh Necho's men, doubling the mighty southern cape, and climbing back to the meridian and so to Egypt. Thence he would march through Arabia to Persia, from there undertake the sea journey to India, go by foot across that continent, and so continue by land into Cathay.

"And from there?" cried Greene, aflame.

He did not know. "Except that I'll not retrace a single footstep! I'll press on, Robertus, let ship, beast, man, or bird take me. I'll see the rising sun each morning, and for the rising sun I'll make. I'll make the world contract to my fist, oceans to raindrops, mountains to warts. Deserts will be grains of sand before my ambition, forests blades of grass. By God, I'll not stop!"

"How long?" cried Greene.

"Five, six, seven—nine, ten years. What if it takes fifteen or twenty? What is time to me? And then I'll come back, white-bearded, to Bristol in the West, my own language rock-chips on my tongue, instead sweet sliding sounds of

Nippon, the gurgle of Cathay, hoarse rumblings of Muscovy, the Aztec chuck and clutter. And I'll wear not this doublet and hose, but yellow robes of silk, and in my chests I'll have furs for raiment when the nights are cold, and jewels with their unlidded eyes, and carpets forested with colours lovelier than this Occident can show."

"And if you never come back?"

"It will be because I found a saffron girl to live with me under a cherry tree, or because in dim lands chasm-shielded I reign like Prester John; or maybe I am old and hermited and the brow of my cave is better than the courts of princes. Who knows this world? Its magnitude, its marvels, its infinity of creatures? I'll not drone out my life at Braiding, grow old and drool and shrink my hams to the fire when space and time are waiting to enfold me. Men are ugly but life is beautiful, befoul it how we will. I saw that lying on my boughs in America. And I'll be famous, Robertus and fame now seems to me a lovely thing. Maybe I'll not come back. Maybe the seas will take me, slid from a brown man's dhow, melting into blue with the crackling flash of whip-spray, churned madly with green and black of tempests; maybe it will be the yellow sands. They say that on that endless route Venetian merchants know each step is whitened by the bones of men, and that in eastern wastes, so preservative is the sun and dry air, you may follow still the routes of Genghis Khan and Tamburlaine by the unsepulchred slaughter they left behind them. I'll discover for myself. And if I freeze or if I roast, if I die of plague or knife or weariness, of thirst or hunger——"

"Well, Sidley?"

"So much the better for the inheritors!"

Greene shook his head at the jeering conclusion. "I never heard you talk so well, Sidley. You have the makings of a poet, I do believe."

Sidley poured out the last drops of wine into Greene's glass. "Every man these days has the makings of a poet, Robertus. There is a surplusage of poetry. You will need to be good to get above the ruck."

I am good, Greene thought, and waited in vain for Sidley to tell him so. He coughed, thinking. Finally he said he would call on Alice before the night was over.

"You make me your debtor, Robertus. I cannot thank you enough."

"Yes." He coughed again. "Oh—er—Sidley, if you have five or six shillings you could spare——" His voice died on a discreet mumble about some money to come next Tuesday afternoon and the expenses of something or other. "Thank you, Sidley. Or ought I to be calling you Sir Ralph?" This was a new way of borrowing he had discovered—borrowing with no intention of ever paying back. Yes, he would be there at the same hour next day.

He walked the whole of the way to Bucklersbury, pondering three things: Sidley's story, his avowed intentions, and his own chances of profit. Strange though it struck him after the nursed-up angers he had expected to gush forth, he did not doubt Sidley's sincerity. It was not an unparalleled reformation. And it was not as though Sidley was denying himself anything. He had looked and spoken like a changed man. Not a saint, though—just a man with his eyes opened, and opened wide. Suddenly grinning, Greene thought America sounded almost as bad as Europe.

His arrival at Bucklersbury brought him so poor a welcome that any other time he would have walked out, offended. The boy John, now twelve years old and the image of his father, except that his colouring was less vivid, was teaching a puppy tricks in one corner of the room; Alice and her husband were checking over a list of figures and not getting the same answer, and so checking it again. The boy greeted him from the floor but continued his instruction; Alice said "Oh, it's you, Robin," and went on counting with her husband, who said nothing at all. He bent to scratch the puppy's head, but the animal twisted impatiently from him, engrossed and important.

"Can I sit down?" he asked.

"As though you need ask!"

He grunted.

He watched Copson's bent back. God, he had come to look a proper little scratch-purse these last few years. Dead and he didn't know it, that was the trouble with Copson. Living like a barnacle, not a man. What could Alice see in him? He shook his head, baffled. What did women see in ninety-nine husbands out of every hundred? And the other way about, too. Some truth in it, marriages must be made in heaven. The country mouse, that was Copson. Never a dream of the great and glorious, no conception of the beautiful, no ideals, no longings, passions, exaltations, despairs. Greene thanked God he was no cabbage himself. He looked at Alice. Still putting on weight. She wasn't the handsome woman he had expected her to become. A bit shrewish too, easy to see that. Lead you a dance she would, when she wanted a thing badly enough. Odd to sit here in Bucklersbury and think back to that time she had dropped her tired horse-shoulders into the garden path, or the time at Wroxham when they sat by the pool and flies, brisk navigators, put in at the ports of their ears and mouths to know what they thought of the future. Fame, charity, the undimmed splendour of life— he scowled.

"If you are not too busy, I have some news for you," he said, putting oil in his voice.

"We have almost finished."

Of all the impudence! "Well, I can't wait. I've taken the trouble to come right across town, and I'll not sit here like a schoolboy in a corner till you finish."

The dog gave one shattering bark, making them all jump.

"You don't have to stay," Copson muttered.

"Don't say that, Geoffrey. What is it, Robin?"

"Send the boy out," said Greene importantly.

There were whys and wherefores before he went in to the neighbour's. "I have seen Sidley," he announced bluntly.

Alice put her hand to her heart. Copson scowled. "If that is all your news, it's a pity you took the trouble, as you call it, to come and tell us."

Greene felt rightly his revenge for this rudeness would
come when he disclosed Sidley's proposals. He turned to
Alice. "Would you like two hundred pounds?"

"Not of his blasted money!" shouted Copson, banging
his fist on the table.

"Hold your breath, man. You will be in need of it before
you die. Would you, Alice?"

She wanted more information. Was this a prank of his?

"Prank! And would you like a thousand pounds settled
on John?"

"I tell you, Greene——"

"For God's sake keep quiet, man! You'll stop yourself
thinking if you bawl so loud. Because if you do, Alice, it
is yours."

"Are you giving it away?" Alice asked him, laughing.

"It's not a laughing matter, Alice. I won't have this
brother of yours coming here——"

"Was there ever such a roarer? Can I hear my own voice
for a minute while I explain? Can't you tell him to keep
quiet, Alice?"

That was hardly calculated to keep the peace, but Copson
sat sulkily on the edge of the table when Alice met his eye.
"Go on, Robin," she said.

He enjoyed himself as Sidley's emissary. He gave something of the man's story—— "And a damned good job!"
said Copson, which even his wife thought unnecessarily
vindictive. He then told them what Sidley proposed to do.
"Remember," he said incautiously, "he will never have a
son of his own."

"And what about me? Is he the only one? Shall I ever
have a son of my own?" Copson looked as though he would
weep. "Don't talk to me of that beast. Go back and tell
him—by God, I'll tell him if ever I set eyes on him!"

"I don't think you ought to say that, Geoffrey."

"Don't say you believe this pack of lies! The fellow is
laughing at us, Alice. Can't you see that? This blasted
brother of yours——"

"Geoffrey!"

"Well, haven't you said the same? Isn't he worse than a carrion crow? Unnatural as a cuckoo? He left his wife and son; he is up here in London whoring and drinking and gambling; now he has fallen in with this pot-fellow of his; they want to get the boy, but they shan't. D'you hear that, you? The boy is mine more than his. I've worked for him. I've ruined my life for him. He is mine, d'you hear!"

"He doesn't want the boy. He only wants to look after him better than you can."

"Then he can't have him! And the sooner he is in hell with his money, the better I shall like it. Tell him that. Eh, Alice?"

"You think it over, Alice, will you?"

"I think we ought to, Geoffrey."

But Copson grew quite unmanageable. Soon it became a hot quarrel between husband and wife, Greene looking on helplessly while their tempers burned them up. Alice, he could see, was thinking ahead. The boy was more to her than to her husband. The two hundred for herself she cared nothing for, but that John should become a gentleman was a bribe too strong for her. At last she turned to her brother. "You had better go, Robin." She took him to the door. "Call back and see me to-morrow. I'll try to talk sense with him. You think he means it?"

She went back in to her husband. How to manage this man of hers? This would be harder than the time of her marriage even. But if there was a thousand pounds to be obtained for her John she'd not see it lost because her husband was against receiving it. "We must talk sensibly, Geoffrey. We both lost our tempers. Let us talk it over, shall we?"

"No!"

She sighed. The folly of men! She told him she would never accept a penny for herself, but the other was different. It was money Sidley owed his son. It was a return he owed Copson himself. "I'll manage without it, as I have done so far," he replied, though more calmly now. But surely he would not stand in the boy's light? He stayed stubborn.

He would not touch a penny of that infernal Sidley's if
he had to beg his bread through the streets of London.
"But you have done so," she pointed out. "We bought this
shop with the money we brought from Braiding." He went
red as fire. So she would taunt him with that! He would
count up his money, he'd have enough, he'd send it back
to Sidley the very next day, and the devil give him good
of it.

"Now you are just being silly," she told him.

She'd see whether he was silly or not. Next day, she'd
see! She felt a little frightened he might really be so hare-
brained. She set herself to calm him down before they
called John in to his supper. Once on their own in bed she
would be at him again. She would give him no rest till he
came round to her way of thinking. "Not one penny piece,"
said Copson, gloomily satisfied to have the last word.
Well, they would see.

He did not even give Greene good-day when he came into
the shop next morning, but went on with what he was
doing. Poor fool, thought his brother-in-law, going his way
to the living-room upstairs.

"Well, Alice?"

"It is difficult, Robin. I'll take nothing in any case."

"Two hundred pounds?" He whistled. "I should like
the chance of it myself."

"Yes, you might see about your family then. Don't you
ride the high horse with me, Robin. I know you too well."
Her willingness to scold him thus gently showed she had
gratitude of a kind for his messengership. "But I'll talk him
round, never fear. It may take a week though. You really
think he means it, Robin?"

This was the report he had to take Sidley, genuinely
anxious for once in his life to do someone good. He asked
a lot of questions about his son, wondered whether it would
prove possible to see him, if only from a distance, before
he set off on his world journey. "Why not?" said Greene,
as though it depended on him.

It was settled they should do nothing to hurry Alice in

her conversion of Copson. They would wait the full week, and who knew what changes would have taken place by then?

Certainly not they, for within a week the first cases of plague were reported in the city.

It was on June 6th that the sheriff's officers put their red cross on the door of a house in the parish of Trinity in the Minories, outside the walls. The family's name was Barracombe, come to London in the service of a Devonshire knight. On the 7th day of June doors were marked in St. Saviour in Southwark, St. Sepulchre's, and St. Giles's by Cripplegate, all without the walls; on the 8th in the parish of St. Olave and St. John in Southwark, outside the walls, and St. Mildred in the Poultry within. The first deaths were on the 9th, three in the family of Barracombe, and one in St. Sepulchre's. Thereafter there were cases in most parts of the city, appearing each day, as though one should throw a handful of gravel over a pool and set up a hundred tiny ripples, each swelling out to meet those nearest, until the whole surface is a-wrinkle. Man-borne, rag-borne, rat-borne, louse-borne, it crept rapidly from parish to parish, ward to ward, street to street, house to house, husband to wife, wife to husband, mother to child, child to parent, Death growing fat to sweating in the hot weather. To have a face flushed from drinking was to be avoided like the devil himself, for the disease came on with a rise of temperature, with great pains through the back and loins and severe headaches. Then came weakness and chills, and then the eruption of lentil-shaped pink spots on shoulders and trunk, these deepening in colour through purple to reddish brown, extending to the extremities and, if the afflicted man lived long enough, to the palms of the hands or even the face. Chance of recovery there was almost none, chance of survival once it entered a household small; for as the pest raged and more and more were stricken and died, houses were barred at doors and windows so that the wretched inhabitants might not wander the streets in despair or frenzy, and so spread their sickness to a score of others. Soon play-acting was prohibited, the houses for bull and bear baiting closed down, men forbidden to congregate at any place of amusement. At street corners stood preachers with no better message than resignation to the grave, crying aloud that God would destroy the new Gomorrah and all those not washed in the blood would find the plague sweet to their lot on the far brink of annihilation. Business came almost to a standstill, for no man wished to have dealings with another, movements of soldiers from the capital were countermanded, the taverns kept open with little or no custom, the streets were empty save for those who must be out of doors—officers, soldiers, doctors, scavengers of bodies. Alchemists, apothecaries, physicians pored over old books of Zosimus, Diodorus, Galen and Hippocrates, the newer studies of Cardan, De Toro and Fracastorius, filling their heads with subtle distinctions of the *morbus pulicaris*, the *febris putrida et maligna*, the *febris petechialis vera*, and the *typhus carcerorum*, and carrying with them in the musty sleeves of their gowns death for themselves and their patients. By day an unnatural midsummer silence hung over the city, by night the silence was broken by the howling of those in pain and terror, by the shuffle and tramp of armed men enforcing the curfew, by the rattle and rumble of the dead-carts taking their burdens to the corpse-holes at the city cemeteries. Broken too by the shouting of those who sought in revelry to forget their fears, and not rarely by the outrage and rapine of those to whom a time of plague was a time to rob and kill. Every gallows in the city bore its twisted dead, and at many cross-roads, especially near the known haunts of rogues, men swung in chains as a warning to their fellows.

Among those hanged was Greene's room-mate Gadd. Greene had been horrified and not a little frightened by his reactions to this time of dread. He came in one morning, just as dawn was breaking, with doom in his furtive step, and carrying a small sack. Carelessly he spilled gold from his pocket, then turned like a viper. Greene pretended to be asleep, but it was all he could do not to scream out when he heard Gadd cross the room to stand over him. It was when Gadd, apparently satisfied, went back to his own bed that Greene, peeping, saw the dark blood on his hands and sleeves. Two nights later he went out and did not return, but after twenty-four hours his body was decorating the corner of Hoyser Lane. He had been killed out of hand for attempted robbery, and a written message pinned to the flesh of his chest warned his like to mend their ways. Greene was not present when his room was searched, but received an order to attend a sheriff's court for Holborn. Here he was examined with offensive thoroughness by an officer unsympathetic to writers of plays, but his references to Sir Ralph Sidley at the Bell and John Tilney at Court led to his dismissal at last.

He did not call at Bucklersbury till the unforgettable evening of June 28, when he arrived there to find Copson in the first stage of his illness. He had never seen such terror in a man's eyes as in Copson's when Alice had suddenly pointed at him and screamed. Perhaps he had felt it coming on for some hours, for he had no need to ask what she screamed at. They had been sitting at supper—a very early supper so that Greene might get back to Hoyser Lane before curfew—glad to hear Greene's news, though none of it was good. There was no mention of Sidley's intended benefaction, for he hoped to ask Alice on her own how her pleading had been rewarded. And then, as though dead tired, Copson rested his head on his hand, looking from one to another. It was then Alice screamed. Greene jumped up and went towards her, but she thrust him off. "Get outside, Robin," she gasped. He asked no question, gave one glance at Copson, at Alice, gone deathly white, at the boy John, more puzzled than frightened and still on his chair at table; then he was running down the stairs. He knew that the nearest doctor was over Cheapside, in Old Jewry, and he ran there as he had never run before. With frantic blows of both fists on the door he roused him, gave his message, and hurried back with him to Bucklersbury. "My first sleep for thirty

hours," said the doctor. "He looked hot, you thought?"
Greene had only five minutes to wait in the street outside.
It was the plague.

He was not greatly frightened for himself. He must have
been in contact with the disease fifty times since it came to
town. But if Copson died, what was to happen? He thought
him certain to die. He must see Sidley the very next
day.

He was still in London. Greene could only guess why he
had not fled to the country straightway. The old selfish
Sidley would not have lost colour as he did now to learn
that the plague was in the same house as his son.

"I'll take him away, Robertus. I'll take him away now,
this day. I have found it a new experience to be in this
plague-struck city. It will be something to tell of."

"You can't take him, Sidley. It is not allowed. You
will be killed if you try it."

"I will, if I want to. Who is to stop me? He is my own
son, isn't he?"

"I know he is. But that is not——"

"And Alice is your sister. Will you help?"

There seemed to be no choice. He would help.

"We'll get horses and food and wine. They must not
touch the city water. We'll get them away to the country.
You are not afraid?"

"Why should I be? Are you?"

"More afraid than I am of hell fire!" He scratched at
his wig as though it had a message of fantastic courage.
"We had better do it now."

"And Copson?"

"What of him?" Sidley asked coolly.

"Well, surely——"

Sidley was gathering up some things he would need.
"I am sorry for Copson, but there is nothing we can do
for him. Look after the living—it's a good motto, Robertus."

Greene thought he could discern some unaccountable
joy in Sidley—perhaps the joy of almost hopeless daring.

"She will never leave him, Sidley."

"She will have to. He is as good as dead, is he not?"

"Perhaps we all are," Greene said sombrely.

"Perhaps we are, Robertus. We keep struggling, though. Are you ready?"

They left the room and Sidley paid his score. They had their choice of horses at the mews where Sidley stabled his Prince, and rode straight to Bucklersbury. The shop was shut, and on its door was the red-painted cross. Sidley hammered on it with a riding crop, but he waited in the street while Greene went inside to begin the matter. He thought horses' hoofs had never before beat so loud a measure on an earth floor, their bits and harness never so challenging a jingle. Perhaps they should have come after dark, noiseless without horses, risking an encounter with the watch or armed bands. "Damn your eyes, Prince!" he swore at his horse; "can't you keep your feet still five seconds on end?" Meantime, up there—what was happening? This Copson fellow—He made the sign of the cross for himself and Copson. Habit he told himself; it meant nothing. He watched Prince's ears. Why not ride away? Christ! why not? But he braced himself. When you had lost all he had you must show the world you'd kept your courage. He noticed the flies swarming up from the third horse's dung. What did Alice look like now? He would never be able to look her in the face, he'd not find one word to say to her. For at least half a minute! He must get ready to look ashamed. How?

Why didn't Robertus come down again? You'd think they would be only too glad to get away to safety. If it was safety. He shuddered, despite the warmth of the day. Perhaps this very minute from this house of death the air came to his lungs loaded with destruction. Perhaps Alice and the boy would bring death with them. Well, he'd not run. Maybe from Greene's handshake, from the exchange of money with his inn-keeper, from the backs of these horses, from the very sheep killed for his dinner, maybe he had it himself already. This might be the last hour before the pains and wastings took him, before his body was a tetter of corruption. He wavered. Should he spur horse and away up the street? Why such a fool as to stay? He blasphemed horribly, comforted himself with a spawning obscenity. He would stay.

Why didn't Robertus——

The door opened. Greene came out to speak to him. "She'll not come."

"But the boy? For Christ's sake, the boy!" He was frightened. He must get away soon. Where was the boy?

"They are afraid to trust him to you, Sidley."

"But to save his life! How is Copson?"

"Worse."

"Go back, Robertus, I beg of you. Promise anything! Say I'll stay with Copson myself if only they'll let the boy go with you! Tell Alice that, will you?"

Greene went back inside. Three minutes later he came out again, not alone. He had the boy with him. Sidley covered his face.

They got on horseback, Prince pawing under Sidley. The boy turned to wave to the upstairs window, and Sidley knew Alice must be there, looking down at them. Something happened then he had thought lost to him for ever. A great choking took him in the throat and the tears ran down his face, but he dared not look up to see her. They called no greetings but spurred quickly down the street.

They rode in single file, Sidley ahead, the boy next, and Greene bringing up the rear. Greene left the choice of direction entirely to Sidley, who, as he soon saw, was making for the Cripplegate. In Wood Street they met one of the preachers who always followed the plague, addressing himself with the comfort of Jeremiah to a small audience. "Not one shall escape," he was shouting as they slowed down to a walking pace in the narrow way; "Flee not from the Wrath of God, for death shall take you where He pleases. Alas! Alas for the city! This is the time told of by the prophets, when God shall avenge himself on this wicked generation of men. The time is at hand. Ye have but a short hour to pray!" He saw the three mounted men.

"Descend, fools, and pray! Whither would ye flee? Is not the pestilence in your blood already? Is it better to perish in the fields like brutes, or here with your voices raised to the Almighty? Descend, I say!"

"Out of the way, clown!" snarled Sidley, his old self, as the preacher laid hand on his bridle.

"Descend, I say! The Day of Judgment is at hand!"

"Damn you for a fool!" Loosening his foot from the stirrup, Sidley kicked him full in the throat. "Come, Greene," he called, and put his horse to the gallop among the frightened crowd. Greene felt his horse's hoofs pad down on something soft and lumpy, and then he was through, though a huge stone whanged past him before they rounded the corner and bore away for Little Wood Street and the Gate. A company of soldiers was on guard there, but made no difficulty of letting them pass, whereupon Sidley turned left to pass the western end of Barbican and join the St. Albans Road. Here they caught up with others fleeing the city, on foot many of them, weighed down with bundles, and armed to protect their goods and purses. Sidley went past them as hurriedly as the road allowed, sometimes sending up clouds of white dust to call forth the curses of those left to breathe it, sometimes thundering down the grass verges. Here too justice had been hard at work, and every so often they would hasten past men strung up on temporary gallows, always with their crimes written up for men to see. In two hours they were half way to Chipping Barnet, and it was then Sidley led them into a coppice and said they would eat and rest the horses.

He had not yet said a word to his son, nor had John had a proper look at his face. Now, if he guessed the relationship between them, he said nothing of it, but ate obediently and washed his meal down with a harsh dry wine.

"Where are we making for?"

"The house of some folk called Gray, the other side of St. Albans. They know me, and will shelter me."

"You think it far enough?"

"If not, we can go farther. Are you tired of the saddle, John?"

He was aching, he admitted it. He had never ridden so hard before.

"Never mind that. Can you keep going?"

He could.

"That's my brave boy! Well then, are we ready?"

Joining the road again, they saw the boy look back the way they had come. "That's a fine horse of yours, John," Greene told him. "He'll not need spurring." They rode on.

They put up for the night at the Wait for the Wagon, eight miles further on. Greene and Sidley shared a room, the boy sleeping with the landlord's children.

"I don't know what to say to him, Robertus. I can't think—— Isn't he a fine lad, though?"

"I think he suspects, Sidley."

"I know he does. Poor little devil, how unhappy he must be!"

They talked for a while of Copson and Alice back in London. They dare not express the thoughts that grieved them both, and instead relied on vague hopes and encouragements. Greene would ride back as soon as they reached the Grays'.

In the morning John confessed himself a mass of aches and bruises, but was all the more determined to show his manliness by getting first into the saddle. Greene too had a raw seat and tired back, but they were off at a steady pace, Sidley again leading, and with no opportunity and little desire for complaints. The Grays' house proved nearer Luton than St. Albans, and Greene suspected Sidley of deliberate understatement the day before. Still they were there by the late afternoon, delighted to hear there were no cases of plague known within fifteen miles, and those but few. The Grays had been servants at Braiding for some years and were content the new knight should be master of their house, but he was wise enough to spend freely at the beginning, insisting that they take a gold piece for the things they wanted. The boy was put to bed early, in a room of his own, and Sidley and Greene, after a smoke together, once more shared. The only thing Greene did not care for was Sidley taking off his wig.

It was after midnight when he was roused by someone shaking him. He sat up, striking out, a cry on his lips, for he had been dreaming of Gadd in London. Then he saw Sidley holding a taper before his face, and his face was enough to get Greene out of bed. "Come," said Sidley.

They went to John's room. From outside Greene heard a faint moaning. Oh Christ! Christ! Christ have mercy! "Inside," whispered Sidley, and Greene saw the light from his trembling hand throw monsters along the wall. He held the taper over the boy. He was flushed and tousled, and moaning in his sleep. "God have mercy on us all!" said Greene.

He led Sidley back to their own room. "It is the plague," he whispered. Sidley nodded. He set down the taper on the small table and covered his face with his hand. "Don't give way, Sidley. What are we to do?" Sidley shook his head. "We must rouse the people of the house." "No!" said Sidley; "No! They'll not keep him here." "Wait then," Greene told him, and freed himself from Sidley's grasp.

He knocked at the Grays' door, and when the man answered told him what was the matter. "I know," he said angrily, cutting across the other's despairing oaths. "Where is the nearest doctor?"

Directed, he went back to Sidley. "You stay here with the boy. I shall be back with help soon."

He did not reach the house with a surgeon till towards seven o'clock in the morning. He examined the boy. Would he live? He shrugged his shoulders. Was he God that he might decide it? "Look," said Sidley, grabbing his arm; "I'll give you fifty pounds for a cure." "And who are you?" asked the man of science. Greene hurriedly explained. "I'll come back this evening," he told them.

They waited through an eternity of hours till his return. The boy was far worse, they needed no doctor to tell them that. They had bowls of vinegar in the room and chewed

tobacco till they were near vomiting to safeguard themselves.
It was a longer examination this time. Evidently the doctor
had the Grays' word for it that Sir Ralph was what he
declared himself. But he could only shake his head.

"He'll not get better?"

"He will die to-morrow. Maybe to-night."

"But there is no rash," Greene cried. "If there is no
rash——"

They listened dully to a disquisition on *petechiæ* and *peticuli*,
the whole science of eruptions. Perhaps his physicianship
expected a larger fee for explanations. He had hardly left
the house when Gray came to see them, asking, as Sidley
had feared, that the boy should be moved. Right was on
his side, not even mercy could plead against him. The boy
must die—why then pollute the house? Why risk spreading
the plague? What of his own wife? Sidley listened unmoved.
It was doubtful whether he even heard him after the first
useless sentence. Greene had to repeat Gray's question.
He shook his head. "The boy stays here."

Gray's wife now added her tears to her husband's appeal,
but Sidley ordered them out of the room, and when Gray
disputed his right to do so frightened them by drawing
his pistols from a case by the bedside. "But what will you
do?" Greene asked him, for twenty minutes later the unfortunate Grays had left the house, fleeing infection.

"I'll stay here, Robertus. And you?"

"What can I do? I know it, Sidley—we'll die. God help
us, we shall all die!"

"The boy will die," said Sidley slowly. "Who ever would
have thought we should come to this, Robertus?" He picked
up the pistols he had laid down. "But he shall not die like
a dog in the fields." Greene looked up at his tone. "You
must leave us, Robertus."

Greene began to sob. "Where can I go? Oh, where can
I go? What can I do? What can I do?"

"You can hope, Robertus. At a time like this no one
can do more. Go back to London, if you like. Or into the
country away from here."

"But the plague is in London!"

"The plague is here too. Here, take this money. Take it all. I shall not need it again. Go where you like, only go soon." He moved towards the door. "This is good-bye, Robertus."

Greene ran after him. He could not bear the thought of being left alone. "Don't stay, Sidley! Don't stay! For God's· sake come with me! Don't leave me on my own. I'd go mad, I tell you, I'd go mad!"

His nerve was gone. He was convinced he too had the plague and that he would die horribly under some hedge, with no one near him. He even clung to Sidley, begging him to change his mind and come with him. "I may as well stay," said Sidley at last. "I know it has me, Robertus."

"No, no, no! You must save yourself, Sidley. You must not die here!" He went on pleading till Sidley agreed to leave John there and take him on to Braiding. Elated now, tears of relief streaming from his eyes, he hurried downstairs with Sidley to get out the horses. He was leaving the house when Sidley, from behind, struck him a heavy blow on the back of the head with the butt of his pistol. He sank down, groaning, and Sidley with difficulty dragged him a yard or two away from the doorway, locked and barred the door and quickly fastened the shutters on the ground floor. He was upstairs with all secured before Greene came to himself again. Watching from the small window of John's room, he saw him finally bestir himself and stand up.

"Robertus!"

Greene understood. With a wave of the hand he set off for the stable, saddled Prince, and led him round in front of the window. "We shall meet again," he called, and even made a jest of it. "When we do, I'll not forget my broken head."

"You had best be off before anyone comes. Good-bye!"

"Good-bye."

"And good luck, Robertus!"

"God bless you, Sidley!"

That was all. I stand in need of blessing, thought Sidley, closing the window. He heard hoof strokes down the path, then their quickening, fading thud as Greene galloped off. It was better so. He turned to his son, who was crying with a smother of unrecognisable words, and gave him a drink of wine thinned with water. He touched the boy's forehead. It glowed, and he saw the gleam of sweat on his fingers. So here he was, he thought with that, and he might have got away to the country, a hundred miles from London, and it would have made no difference, for the boy would die, and Alice would die, and Copson must already be dead. So he had acted in vain, and thrown away the journey to Cathay. How like him the boy was. Like all the Sidleys. How unlike him in experience! Standing there, the hot wet hand of death sweeping from the boy's brow to his own, he came near thinking it was best to die young, without that great burden of sin he must drag from his ugly grave before the Throne where but for God's mercy his judgment would be to the pit. The old jest came up: It would be little hotter than where he was now. The boy began to call on his mother, so Sidley sat by the bedside, smoothing with his one hand the throbbing forehead and wet hair. What a thing for him to be doing! He felt a kind of guilt that these last weeks had so overthrown a lifetime's cold philosophy. It crossed his mind that his deed in staying with his son might stand to his account at the judgment near, but he contemptuously denied the thought as bribery. He was staying for the old animal reason: he would not see his son die without shelter. He wanted no one's favour —not even God's. As the boy cried out more shrilly with his agony, he rose and began fingering his pistols. So small a thing, a bullet, to bring a man from pain. He felt the blood flush into his head, and a sudden giddiness made him stagger. Well, it had him, as he had told Robertus. He had treated Robertus badly, and hoped he would win through wherever he was going. He hoped Alice would live, if she wanted to. He was glad he had arranged about the money without waiting for Greene's news. What a brute he had been to her! Suddenly he flinched away from the tomahawk that was hacking at his arm, struck at the copper face glaring into his. By God! He'd be seeing Caranella next, feel the knife again. He poured wine from a bottle over his head, fought for self-mastery. John— what was he saying? The room was full of faces. "Father —father——" He cocked his pistol. There was one kindness he could do him. Pointlessly, on the point of freeing him from his torment, he gave the boy another drink, and then, as he half rose in bed with the throb of pain that followed, he shot him through the heart. The noise was like a cannon- ade in the small room. It filled his ears, filled his head, seemed to volley through his chest and stomach. Staggering, he flung the bedclothes over the boy, straightening them clumsily. Then, his arm steady, he set the cold iron barrel of the other pistol between his teeth.

After he had left the house Greene felt a queer light- heartedness. Merely to be in the air, with the swiftness of the horse lending him wings, dispersed his gloom. With no other change of circumstance, a tremendous faith in his own survival buoyed him up. Copson dead—why not? Alice maybe—why not? The boy certain to die—what strange about that? And if Sidley went, well, men must die sometime. But Robert Greene, he, Robert Greene, for him to die was absurd. Some distant time no doubt, but now? Impossible! It couldn't be. He pinched his arm, he rejoiced in the bumping of his seat against the saddle, he wriggled his toes, he talked aloud to hear his voice—no, nothing could happen to him. The whole world seemed spun from his own consciousness; he might be forgetful of parts of it, which then ceased to exist; but that he himself should cease—he felt the air on his face, saw the sun westering fast, heard the beat of hoofs under him—he would never die. Rebelling against the strain he had laboured under he wanted to laugh and sing, and even remembrance of Sidley's peculiar tone brought but a light- headed horror soon forgotten. "We are immortal," he shouted to the horse, and smacked him affectionately with his bare hand, grateful for the sensation of living blood and muscle in steady rhythm. "Giddy up there!" Ha-ha-ha! He waved his hand like a lunatic at passers-by, delighted that they should think him a fool. Ha-ha-ha! Life, life, life! At St. Albans he rode straight to the Hard Canter and within an hour was in bed. Nightmares rode him for hours, thunderous hoofs trampled his brain to pash. He woke a dozen times to drink water which his trembling hands splashed on floor and bed. Dark night never-ceasing, oh where was day? Where was light under the rim of the world? What strange paths had Phoebus gone? Scraps of his reading jostled a half-created mythology of his own. Slay us, Zeus, but slay us in the light! Ha-ha-ha!

At daybreak he was off again, soberer now, ashamed of himself, feeling the effects of his night even more than the preceding days. Sidley's Prince was a magnificent stayer, and carried him hour after hour towards London. It was when he was still four miles from the city that he felt so hopelessly jaded he could have fallen to the ground and never risen again. At the same time the ache in the small of his back and his thighs grew well nigh intolerable. He put this down to hard riding and sleeplessness, and nerved himself to continue, but now he began to feel too warm, which was strange, for the hottest hours of the day were past. In a flash his fright was greater than his exhaustion. The plague! He had the plague! A sudden network of pain around his temples gave him no room for doubt. He could hear himself panting. He would die! Oh God, he would die, and all this world be hidden from him! Then, No, he'd never die. All the others might die, but not he, not Robert Greene. Die and Not Die thumped their way through his brain at every stride of his horse. What could he do? Where could he go? Who would take him in? Opposite the Charterhouse he changed his route, setting the lathered horse towards Moorgate. Would the guard allow him inside the wall? But he found no guard there, and went straight down Colman Street to Bucklersbury.

Sweating, lolling in the saddle, his head as though axes were splitting it second by second, he yet could see passers-by draw back at the sight of him. He had the plague! Pray God Alice was at home. Pray God Alice wasn't dead. Pray God she'd be there to see to him. He shook one foot free of the stirrup and fell headlong to the ground. Half-stunned, he crept to the door on his hands and knees, groped for a loose stone, and began hammering on the bottom of the door. The people in the street ran away when they saw him. God in his high heaven—he was praying, gasping, trying to drag himself up by the door post. This was Death. This was the great grinning skull of Death. He saw the red plague cross before him and tried to cling to it, calling with horrible throaty noises on God the father, Christ the son, the Holy Ghost.

The door opened. It was Alice. "Alice! Alice!" He stretched out his hands towards her, and fell senseless over the threshold.

CHAPTER XXXI

As from the assassin's knife at Genoa, he recovered from this again. He was as lucky as one in ten smitten, luckier than the nine who died. Yet no one could have come nearer death than he. For the rest of his life he was to remember the intolerable agonies that consumed him while the fever ran its course—the beating of his molten brain as an egg is whisked in a basin, the cavern of fire that was his breast wherein fiends from hell smashed with iron hammers on the anvil of his heart, the turning of sword blades over his eyes, the poniard stabs through his loins, the infernal cudgelling that battered strength from his limbs—remember, too, the frightful lassitudes that marked his recovery, when he felt all force and health gone from him for ever. He was much tormented by dreams all the while, from the frantic phantasmagorias of his deliriums, when shapes unknown to nature swirled out of darkness to devour him, to the nightmares later in which he dreamed of hell and the devil and himself the wretched dish-clout flung madly on their three-pronged forks. The blazing hell of his father's faith, this, the hell of corner illuminations of old manuscripts, the painted monster mouths of the miracle plays and moralities. Not an episode of his life but rose to accuse him through the mouths of its personages; men and women singly and in chorus, friends and enemies, rose to shout him down; and he experienced night after night that clogging horror of dreams when the tongue will not speak, the feet will not run from pursuit, the hands will not clutch at salvation. Even Flamstead denounced him from the Fleet, Benita from the Gifts of God, Wotton Secundus from the hayloft of the Red Lion at Norwich. All were accusers, not a voice among them pleaded for him. Then one night, when the fever had spent itself, he was confused by stupid memories of Marlowe's *Faustus*, at times thinking himself the necromancer, his soul bought by the devil, at times more sensibly seeing a parallel. Sometimes he acted, sometimes he lived that last scene where Faustus waits for the bond's redemption, the swift tick-out of his last hour on earth, where he curses himself, his parents, Lucifer. Surely that scene was written for him, Greene? Not that he remembered Marlowe's last lines, but in his own confusion he wrote the scene again, superbly, with an incredible majesty and beauty, making Marlowe's version a student exercise in comparison, so that he cried weakly when he woke because he could not recall it. But he did remember the old man calling on Faustus to look up to heaven and know God's mercies were infinite, and with it from his childhood came Augustine's golden sentence: *There was one thief saved and no more, therefore presume not: and there was one saved, and therefore despair not.* If he lived through this there would be a great change.

He and Alice talked together now for as long as Greene could endure the exertion. She knew from his ravings earlier that John was dead, and it was only for her brother's sake she had not given up the struggle to live. Death was all around one. It was easy to die. Still, she nursed him doggedly, with more kindness than skill, for there was nothing to do but hope and pray and carry out such tasks as common sense dictated. Now that he was better she told him how her husband had died the day before his return. She spoke of him with a jealous pride, lest her brother should not admire him enough. "He was—I can't tell you, Robin, how good he always was to me and John. It never made any difference to the way he looked on him that he was not his own son. He wasn't as happy as he deserved to be."

"He was a brooder, Alice. He thought too long about things."

"He did brood, Robin—you are right. He wanted children of his own body, I know, and that made him miserable when he knew I couldn't bear another for him

after the one who died. Can you believe this, Robin—
in all the years we were married, through all our quarrels
—and we did quarrel, God help me—all the time he never
said a word against me for what happened at Braiding?"
She began to tuck the clothes in at the bottom of his bed.
"When I think how in the early years I just made use of
him for my own ends, thinking only of John, and the
bitter things I said—but he never said the things he might
have. I don't think any other man would have done that,
Robin."

"I know I could not have done it. He was a good man,
Alice."

She cried bitterly then, remembering only his virtues,
his gentleness, his steadiness, his devotion to her unmarred
by all their differences. Remembering too those endearing
ways he had, the boyishness that still kept with him in
certain moods to the end, the lighting up of his solemn
face when he was happy, when he was weighing out spices,
when the boy called him father and made much of him.
A hundred tendernesses made her weep, his anxiety at
the birth of her children, his thought only for her when
his own child died at three months. If only she had been
kinder to him! If only she could look back on those years
together and know that there had never been a cross word
from her side, never a sulk, never a cruel rejoinder. To
have him back again, only for a year, a month, a week,
a day, only one hour so that she could tell him as never
before how she loved him and admired him. If only he
could know!

Greene too thought of Copson, as Alice cried beside
him. Not a showy man, his brother-in-law, by some
standards a dull man, a plodder, a mere tradesman.
But judge him by true standards—what then? While he,
Robert Greene, had abandoned his wife and son and
eaten husks, this man had given up his life for the woman
he loved and who he was not certain loved him. To save
her he had worked for another man's child, and held
his tongue, and become a grubber in Bucklersbury, and

now the plague had carried him off and let Greene live,
as though Job indeed was right and there was no justice
under the heavens. His former ungenerous estimate of
Copson grieved him now. He had passed shallow judgment
on a man far better than himself. His eyes opened, he saw
that Copson had lived a none too happy life without
over-much complaint. He had in him the elements of
greatness.

"What will you do now, Alice?"

She could not make up her mind. The shop would be
hateful to her now Geoffrey was gone, the house behind
it only a receptacle of memories. She'd not stay in Bucklersbury, but what she would do she knew not. "And you,
Robin?"

"I am going back to Norwich to my wife and son. Come
with me, Alice, will you?"

She shook her head. Not that. No running home now
that her world had crumbled. "Think, Robin, we don't
even know they are alive there."

"I am going home again, Alice. You must come with
me. I'll not stay in London. I told you, Alice—Sidley
was a changed man after what he went through in America.
And now I'm changed too. Suffering is what changes
us, Alice. Sidley said that too, I believe, and if he did
he was right. It is not what we see and do that moulds
us, it is what we feel and endure. I have thought myself
a wonderful fellow before this, but this summer has shown
me what I really am. I'll go home to Doll and Kit, I'll
make amends somehow. I'll work there with father, do anything I can, give up writing. It never brought me any
luck, I can see that."

Alice remembered the conversion of his boyhood, which
had not lasted long, but perhaps this, as it was more
terrible in its causes, would be more lasting in its effects.
"When will you go?"

"Before the winter. I shall be strong again before then,
won't I?"

Once or twice he tried to thank her for looking after

him, but she would hear nothing of it. She had escaped
miraculously, so why should she not nurse her own brother?
"But if half you talked about those first days was true,
Robin, you have plenty on your conscience."

"Too much, I know it, Alice," he replied gloomily.

The plague had now slackened, and the city was taking
up its business again. The autumn was wet and cool, which
helped to cleanse the air of infection, and strong breezes
towards the end of August blew health back to London.
Greene came to move about freely, yet was conscious he
would never be so strong again. His gratitude for his
escape was complete. He had set wickedness behind him
for ever. That painted red cross towards which he had
crawled and climbed should be a symbol ever before him.
He deliberately avoided his usual haunts when again he
got about the streets, caring not at all who among his
acquaintance might be dead, and taking great care of
the money Sidley had given him. He knew nothing yet
of Sidley. Had he escaped? He knew it impossible. What
a strange end for Sidley, though. There in the empty house,
with his son dying of the plague, sitting, waiting for the
hectic in his own blood, perishing quickly once it set in,
dying dreadfully alone. The pistols though—maybe he
had not waited. Once he had thought him a god, and
once a player's Vice—how think of him now? Strangest
of all that he and Copson should be struck down the
same way. How unwilling Copson had been for the
boy to go, and then he had yielded to Alice's pleading,
and the boy had gone with the plague in him from
the man he called father to kill his real father. There
was a working of providence in that. Well, God be good
to them both.

A week before they were to set off for Norwich Greene
found a buyer for the shop. The very next day a clerk
waited on Alice and asked her to call at the house of
Mulliner, the lawyer, in Mitforth Lane by the Temple,
on a matter of the greatest importance to her. Lawyers
were frightening people, and it took all Greene could say

to persuade her to go, and then only on condition he went with her. Mulliner was a famous man, his dealings were with the noblest of the land, and Greene made a good guess in advance what he wanted with her. Mulliner was not informative. He seemed to think it enough to say that he was empowered by the late Sir Ralph Sidley to pay her the sum of two hundred pounds, but Greene pressed him with questions. What of the thousand pounds to be settled on the boy? Mulliner supposed they knew the boy John Copson was dead—did they?—and explained that the terms of the settlement were such that the sum or any part of the sum remaining should be paid back into the Sidley estate if the boy John Copson should die before the age of twenty-one. He had no information to give them on the subject of Sir Ralph's death, and he was a busy man—good morning! His clerk would see to the details. "There was nothing for me?" Greene could not help asking. Mulliner stared at him, not hiding his distaste for the question.

"So there you are, Alice," he told her, back at Bucklersbury. "You are a rich woman. What with Sidley's money and that for the shop you'll never want, that is certain. And now let us go home, shall we?"

"I wonder where they buried John, Robin?"

"Don't think of it!" For it did not bear thinking on. Like Copson, he would be tumbled into a hole in the earth, without name or record to mark the place.

"Can we go that way home?"

He was against it but had to give way, so in five more days, having arranged for bonds with a London friend of Sir Roger Portington's, to be redeemed within a fortnight at Norwich, they set out by way of St. Albans for the Grays' cottage. He told something of their flight as they went: the place in Wood Street where Sidley rode down the preacher, the copse where they halted for a meal, the inn they stayed at, where he and Alice stayed too. He was relieved to find her so calm that evening, but in the morning knew how sad she had been when once alone with the ghost of her son. He did not quite know what he expected to find at the Grays' house, and approached it with dread, but nothing seemed changed. Gray was not too pleased to see him again, explained curtly that he and his wife had burned everything in the room where the boy and his father were found dead, and that there had been no plague locally despite the tragedy. It was now Greene heard that Sidley had shot the boy and then himself, but he begged the Grays not to let Alice hear of it. Yet she should have been pleased to know John was spared a deal of useless pain, and surely she cared nothing for Sidley's end? He asked where they were buried, and had the unpleasant task of telling Alice that the two bodies had been burned to ashes to prevent infection. Strange final mingling of father and son. So there was no grave for her to deck, no place of pilgrimage towards which she might periodically turn for the solace of her heart. Was it better so? he wondered.

He saw her shiver as she looked up to the window. He touched her rein. "Come on, Alice." He was glad when the house was hidden by trees.

They rode on to Bedford, and from there to Cambridge, and then took the way Greene had so often travelled in College days. They talked much about what their welcome would be, and settled how much of Alice's story they would make known. He had to check back to find what lies he had told his mother about Alice before he set out for Italy. There was no Sidley in it, anyhow, so it would be enough to say that she had lost husband and son in the plague, and that long-lost son and daughter were returning home again. "Are we prodigals, Robin?" He swore he was, straight from the husks and swine, but reckoned she had nothing to be ashamed of. The nearer he came to Norwich the less eager he was to reach it, but Alice's presence and the circumstance that she was only following his advice kept his nose forward. His mother —no doubt about whether she would take him in. Though he were crippled, a leper, a murderer fleeing justice, she'd not shut her door to him. But his wife? His father? His son? At least he would make no excuses. They must do as God directed them. He could only guess at Alice's thoughts, going home in such a fashion after a twelve years' absence. His mother would be thinking of her as the same girl who left for service at Braiding, not a day older, not a hair changed. Christ! he thought, some of his godliness leaving him—there was something ridiculous about it, really there was. Riding along, the pair of them, two black sheep together. One at a time was as many as the story would stand. "Look!" he said, as they turned down the long slope: "Home, Alice."

His last interview with his father grew more prominent in his mind. It might be better had he not been so hasty. London was not a bad home for the outcast. If he and Alice had kept on the house at Bucklersbury—oh well, it was too late now. They must go on.

"Are you nervous, Alice?"

"And sick, Robin, dreadfully sick."

"Judge how I feel then! You don't think it might be better if we—say, if we stopped at the Ramping Lion there and thought it over again?"

"Certainly not. We have come so far: we'll go on. Don't you want to see your wife and child again?"

Did he? "My feelings have not altered, Alice," he assured her, to assure himself. "Do we go in together or one of us first?"

"Which one?"

"Oh, either of us. It doesn't matter much."

"Very well. You go, Robin."

He thought of arguments to convince her they had better go in together after all. Here was the Blue Boar, and there the lovely castle, here were the lowing beasts at market on their right. His eyes were fast on the Cathedral. When he got as far as the Erpingham Gate——

This was Tombland, not a cobble different, the same old house, the very knots in the timber the same. He threw a boy a penny to mind the horses, and without knocking led the way inside.

His mother screamed, looking up from darning a tiny pair of stockings. "Robin! Oh, Robin, Robin, Robin!"

"There, there, mother, never worry. It's all right, mother."

As she clung to him, the door from the kitchen opened and Doll came hurrying in. "Don't you know me, Doll?" he cried. "Look, mother, here's Alice!" He went to embrace his wife, but she drew back ever so slightly, so he stopped without even kissing her. Behind him, mother and daughter were in each other's arms, but he was not listening to them.

"You—you haven't forgotten me, Doll?" She shook her head slowly, amazement, alarm, disbelief, in her eyes, but no pleasure. "I've come home—if you will have me. Where is Kit?"

"In the saddlery, with your father."

"I know you must think badly of me, Doll. There is nothing I can say. Is he well—the boy?"

"He is well. He is always well."

"Shan't I kiss you, Doll?"

She let him kiss her, and then started to cry, so that they were all crying, except him. Let them! He must see his father. He left the three women and went into the saddlery. His father was setting Kit on a saddle, and the child was using a tiny whip on an imaginary horse.

"Father!"

Robert Greene the elder turned round and went very white.

"Father! oh father, can you ever forgive me?"

"My boy, my boy!"

Greene wept too, seeing tears in the eyes of that stern man, his father. It was now the doubts of the journey vanished, filling him with a happiness and relief without blemish but for Doll's cold welcome, and that must be because of the shock. He picked up his son, kissed him till he too cried, and with no small accompaniment of roars. He did not even feel concerned that it was his father who had to soothe him. Why, the boy could have no idea who he was.

"Alice is inside the house, father."

"Alice? What Alice?"

"Alice, your daughter. Alice, my sister. You have not seen her these years, father." She had lost her husband and her son with the plague this year. She was in great need of her home. Her father would never be other than kind to her?

The transports that heralded their arrival were quickly over for all except Jane. It was to prove a melancholy winter. His first natural reactions past, Greene the elder became critical, remembering why both son and daughter had left his house before. After his vow ought he to receive Robert again? He could not help worrying lest he had taken God's name in vain. And he became curious to pry into those portions of their lives they were clearly unwilling to talk about. He could not reconcile himself, as could his wife, to this curtaining off of the past as though it had never been. Could one be sure there was full repentance for old sins? There were many questions he wanted to ask, and as the weeks went by he was emboldened to ask them one at a time, and nothing irritated him more than to find them evaded or answered with lies. Added to that, he had no real work for Robert to do. What with Tobias and himself and Gurley and Vose no more hands were wanted, yet he must find him some, add another charge to his business, and get little but muddle in return. What wages should he pay him? And ought he to deduct from those wages sufficient to make up in time the money he had so wickedly stolen at his flight to London? Greene senior believed implicitly that every farthing between himself and his wife belonged to him, but would not accept this as so in the case of his son. He must make restitution. His son's demeanour when he suggested as much convinced him he was not yet as chastened as Jane tried to make him believe. Alice assured them she had money enough, but why was she not franker? Why not state the sum and allow him to make the best arrangement for her? Why so much secrecy if there was nothing bad to conceal? The neighbours gossiped, he knew, and he disliked gossip about his home. His temper was short when he thought of these things. And what was still wrong between Robert and his wife? If there were a quarrel, he told Jane, he would support Doll, who had had more than enough to put up with from that husband of hers already.

Greene, indeed, had never been more miserable. Before the end of the year he was telling himself he had been fifty fools ever to come home to be treated so outrageously. His father was bad enough, still harassing him with schoolboy treatment, talking like a pulpit on every possible occasion, but as for Doll—Good God, you'd think when a husband came home after long years, came home repentant too, wanting nothing but to make amends, you'd think she would be willing to forget the past and make the best they could of life, if only for the boy's sake. But no! He might be a stranger. Treating him as though she could not endure him to touch her? That first night all tears, and all because, as even the most regenerate man would, he had wished to embrace her; beating away his caress, crying: "Oh leave me alone! Leave me alone!" "Why, Doll——" He had started to explain, but she would go on crying, shivering away from him in the bed, till with a vile unspoken oath he had risen and prepared a place for himself to sleep on the floor. Had any man been treated worse? A stranger to his own bed! Humiliation, shame, anger—were these to be his lot in Norwich? Then better London, better anywhere. A week later he tried again, creeping into bed when she must be asleep, waking her gently, but she cried out with fright and outrage, struck at him in panic, and this time he came near striking her back. There could be no greater abasement than this, and it soured his whole mind. He hated her intensely, standing beside her bed, and then, groping his way back to his pallet on the floor, he swore he would never again want anything to do with her as long as he lived. Let her live and die without him! If only he had not come home!

It was a small thing, maybe, but there were few bed-clothes for him, lest his parents know the way of it. He was cold and slept badly every night, and had too much time for embittered thought. If only he had not come home!

How long the days were here in Norwich! No happiness inside the house, nothing to do outside it. Doll would not even allow him to see more of his own son than she must. If it were not for his mother and Alice, he thought time and time again.

"Aren't you happy, Robin?" Jane asked him one day when they were alone.

"I am happy enough, mother."

"I don't think you are, Robin. What is the matter?"

As though he could tell her. Everything, everything was the matter! "Nothing is the matter, mother. I get a bit low-spirited now and again, that is all. The plague it must be, mother. It took away something I shall never get back, I fear. I think of it sometimes, and of the people I knew who died, but that is not to say I am unhappy home, is it?"

"Is it Doll?"

Why must the blood redden his cheeks? "Certainly not, mother. I can't imagine why——"

"She is not happy, either. Since you came home she has been different. Tell your mother, Robin. You know you can."

"There is nothing to tell—nothing. If she is not glad to see me—well, I can't very well complain, can I?"

"Indeed, you can't, Robin. You must remember—but

you do remember without need for me to tell you. None
of us really expected to see you again. You know how we
used to talk about Alice, you and I? That is how we had
come to think of you. You made us all very unhappy,
son."

His eyes filled with tears. "And haven't I been unhappy?
Haven't I had my share? Mother, you don't know all
I've been through." He shook his head with vexation.
"And when I come home again, to be treated like an
outcast! By my own wife!"

"I'll speak to her, Robin, shall I?"

But he insisted she should not. It was humiliating enough
now, but that anyone else should go pleading for him—
he'd not have it! Let her keep her widow's bed. He wasn't
the kind who could not find someone kinder. And it would
not be his fault this time, either. Everyone in the house
could see the way he was being treated. He would not
put up with it.

One day he called on Adam Bolton. "If it's not Robert!
I knew you'd call, see, Robert, that's why I bided my
time. Tell you the truth, Robert, I didn't know how things
were with you at home, and your father—I like your
father, Robert, he's a fine man, far better than me, but
when he looks at me it properly takes the starch out of
my neckband. So I waited for you to call. Ay, ay! You are
thinner, Robert. You were getting quite a paunch on you.
Tell me, what happened?" They drank while he listened.
His amazement was equal to the news he received. "I
can imagine how you felt, Robert. Last spring that dog
of Joshua Handcross's bit me, and I thought I might
get my death of it. I was in an absolute tremble for days,
Robert, till the danger passed. The plague, eh?" They talked
for an hour. "Mother Dowse isn't there now, Robert. Only a
week or two after you went they carted her and Catherine
and Rose. I tell you, Robert, when they went past here,
with the blood running down their poor backs, and that
old devil of a beadle laying on the cat, I thought to myself,
Robert: It's not right. That's what I thought, Robert."

He became even more confidential. It wasn't everybody knew of it, but there was a place four doors from where Charles Hamer used to live—make no doubt about it, Robert, it was the place for the man who wanted all the comforts of marriage with none of its inconveniences. Greene shook his head firmly, but when at last he went home he had enjoyed himself more than for months, and he told the gratified Adam that he was the most human thing he had yet met in Norwich. After that he paid him frequent visits.

These helped him over the winter, till the time when in early April, the ground being dry with light frosts, he borrowed a horse, put on his best clothes, and informed the family he was visiting Coppinger at Cambridge. They accepted the lie, perhaps not without reflecting that his departure was more certain than his return, and Alice, in response to an urgent request, lent him five shillings. "You are coming back, Robin?" she asked him outright. He grinned: "Are you afraid for your five shillings? Don't worry, Alice. I'll be back within a week—within ten days at the most." Ostentatiously he took the Thetford road for a couple of miles, and then struck away across fields and footpaths to the road for Dereham and followed it. He was bound for Braiding. Months before, the fear of God stronger in him, he had vowed to pay such a visit to Sidley's mother, for he was the last to see her son alive; and now the journey would relieve the tedium of life at home and help satisfy the restlessness that was always sending him on his travels. Besides, who knew what might come of it? He was an optimist by nature, and the future always looked better than the present. He had found a wife on his last trip to Braiding: what would he find this time?

He avoided the inn associated with some harsh memories, and rode straight to the Hall. Master Robert Greene of Norwich to see the Lady Sidley. Was that the dunghill he smelled? He smiled at the pictures on the wall as he waited. The Lady Sidley would see him.

She was in black, a broken woman. Yet her ravaged face had been painted, her lips reddened, her hair elaborately piled. She welcomed him as though glad to see anyone and escape her own company, and as they talked they avoided the many matters of dispute between the two families. He would stay the night? She told him, unemotionally, of changes in the household and the neighbourhood. Ferrers was still there, and Mistress Mako. Did he remember them? He wanted to ask:—And what about the fellow who set the dogs on me, and the girls who—— Are they still here? He heard from her, but at greater length, what he had heard from Sidley about Elizabeth's marriage. They kept house at Lincoln, she and her husband; Lady Sidley saw them frequently. His own people, were they well? She asked questions about his wife and son, and told him how lucky he was to have them. They laughed together at the mention of the charm Lady Sidley had sent to Jane when her child was born.

Alice was at home, he told her. She nodded, not answering. He went on to tell her of Copson's death. Her tears were waiting. "Poor lad," she said, and burst out weeping. Then for hours they talked of her son, and the boy John, and all the unhappinesses of the past. She could not hear enough of those last few weeks. Mulliner had discovered much, but Greene was the eye-witness and companion. He was inspired to a fine lie. "When he knew he was going to die he thought of you. He asked me to tell you that." What had he said? How had he looked? What had he done? He was changed, changed, changed. She heard the whole story of the Copsons, as Greene knew it, everything he could tell about her grandson. She asked a lot of questions about Alice before they went to bed.

He slept that night in the room that had been his when he visited there while still a lad at Cambridge. How long ago that seemed! If a man tried to cover those intervening years he would never sleep a minute of the night. It was here Sidley wronged his sister, here young John was born, here she had taken fright and fled, here he himself had been deceived and beaten. He stared thoughtfully at the faint glimmer of the window, for the wronged were still alive, if not exactly flourishing, the wrongers dead, dead, dead.

He had a few words with old Ferrers the next morning, eager for news of young Copson. Why did they still think of Copson as young? He was no younger than Greene surely? As though people out of sight grew petrified, slept an ageless sleep, were not subject to Time the ravisher. The steward was crabbier still as he grew more rickety: plagues, wars, he knew not what; was the world run mad? he asked Greene. "Tell your sister, Master Greene, old Ferrers hasn't forgotten her. She was a fine bit, your sister was. If I had been twenty years younger I don't say I wouldn't be your brother-in-law." He had grown absurd over part of the past, shaping it to fancies of his own. "Some of these young bitches about the Hall to-day —huh, I'd take the horsewhip to 'em, if I had my way. Saucy, flighty, all eyes for the men—bitches, Master Greene, bitches!" If they were the same who had mocked him on the dunghill——"Quite right," he agreed; "bitches they are, Master Ferrers, and the horsewhip is what they need."

He left on the second day with a strong invitation to his sister to go and visit Lady Sidley. This was the whirli-gig of time, was it not? At home he waited until Alice and he had gone for a walk on to the Heath, and then told her the news. How like her to blame him first of all for telling lies about going to Cambridge! "You'll go?" She did not know what to say. "Go, Alice. She is a lonely sort of woman, I think. It will please her. She was always kind to you, wasn't she?" Almost always, she admitted. Yes, she would go.

He accompanied her a month later. A dull month, relieved only by a couple of good evenings at Adam Bolton's, a visit to the Red Lion where he had a long chat with Mistress

Petherill, and a great row at home on the subject of his
deceit. He shouted that he had changed his mind at the
last moment and that he would please himself where he
went, and waved his hand contemptuously at his father
when he went on with his reproof. Treating him like a
child in long clothes! They'd drive him away again, that's
what they would do.

There was a certain shyness behind Lady Sidley's stately
reception of Alice. Shyness behind Alice's ceremonious
behaviour too. Some things from her previous stay they
recalled, some they thought best when most left alone.
Greene went back to Norwich straight away, but Alice
would not return for more than a week, and then he
would fetch her, glad to have something to do. At
home Doll still treated him with unnatural coldness, he
felt the edge of his father's temper near to cutting, so
he got the better of them by spending much of his
time with the willing Adam. He'd show them! Then
he fetched Alice at the appointed time. They had a
conversation on the way back that marked a turning for
both of them.

She kept her counsel for three or four miles and then
came out with it plump. "She wants me to go and live
with her, Robin."

He was not surprised. "You will go?"

"What do you think?"

The question showed him she had made up her
mind. "You will regret it for the rest of your days if
you don't, Alice. I knew when I went there first——
She is a lonely woman, she wants some link with her
son. I know one thing too—she was too good for
that old lecher who married her. All Sidley's wickedness
came from him, not from her. You go, Alice. I shall
never give you advice I more want you to take. You
will?"

There were the people in Norwich, of course. What
about them? He put merciless questions. Was she happy
there? Was she any more fond of her father than in the old

days? Had she any real love for anybody there except her mother? "You are like me, Alice. You were never made to stay home by the fireside. There is something about us—you and me—you don't find it in Tobias for example. He is content to plod like father, but you and I fell in love with life and have never fallen out again. Let's admit it. Old Grancher Beetham, he knew it. He used to tell me." He went on to explain how he felt at home, half justifying the resolve in his mind. Didn't she agree?

"But Doll is your wife, Robin."

"Alice, listen to this. I've not been in her bed since I came home. Is that right? You must have seen how she avoids me! Will she even let me see more of Kit than she must? A wife in name only! There can be no sanctity in such a bond."

"Whose fault is it?"

"Say that it is mine. What if I admit it? Alice, you've been married, and you may get married again—it's no good pulling faces, you may very well—you know what it means to a man of my nature to sleep on the floor of his wife's bedroom. You had no idea of that before, had you?"

She met him shrewdly. "Well, don't you think because you are advising me to leave home that I'm bound to advise you to do the same. You must stay and do your duty by the boy however Doll treats you."

"I was only telling you. You need not jump to conclusions. Anyhow, you will go to Braiding, Alice?"

Yes, she would.

"What about father and mother?"

Father would be easy to dispose of. What he did not like he was welcome to dislike; but she was worried about her mother. "If you went too, Robin, I don't know what she would do."

He thought this an attempt to push responsibility on to his shoulders. He grunted. "When are you telling them?"

"At once. Why not?"

He grunted again. "And when are you going?"

"By the end of summer. Will you be taking me?"

"Hm," he said; "there'll be fireworks."

As it happened, there were none. Everyone took the news quietly. "You will be able to come over sometimes," Jane declared, making the best of it. It was he who supplied the next fireworks.

He decided in July to settle one point with Doll for ever. She could live with him or he would leave her, and he would not care to tell her which way he hoped she would decide. It was settled within five minutes in their bedroom. "Doll," he said firmly, standing by her bedside, "can I come to bed with you?" She was afraid of him. "No," she gasped. He tightened his lips. "You know you have lived a virgin for me since I came home. I'm only flesh and blood, Doll—God only knows what you are! There's got to be a change." "No, no!" He gestured as though he had an audience. "You need not be afraid I shall want you against your will. That was never my way. Are you going to let me love you, ever?" No, no, she couldn't, she couldn't explain, he must understand, she wanted nothing to do with him that way, ever again. "Very well," he returned, relieved; "don't say I haven't been patient." He had not yet undressed, and now he turned towards the bedroom door. "Where are you going?" she asked. He stopped like an actor, his hand on the latch. "I don't see that it concerns you, Doll. You had better go to sleep." He gave her no chance to say more, but slipped outside, went downstairs, and having hesitated for just a moment by the door went into the street. Imagining that she might be looking after him from the window, he set off jauntily in the moonlight, as though his destination was quite settled.

No doubt she would be thinking he was going to some other woman. Well, let her. Walking about in the moonlight, schemes, even hare-brained schemes, come easily, and he

now determined that before the week was out he would
leave for London. There must be no end of money waiting
for him there, and suddenly the best idea of his literary
life came to him. Why, he would be the talk of the town!
Why not give up writing romances? Surely they had had
their day? Instead, tales of low life, moral tales too, in
which the unhappy, unfortunate, sinning and sinned
against hero should serve as a warning to all young men
foot-free in London. He need only draw on his own
experiences to make books that would sweep the country.
Innovator with *Friar Bacon*, he would be innovator again
with these. These were great days for English literature,
and the corridors of the centuries to come would echo
with the names of those who were now giving England
as much claim to fame as Greece and Rome among the
antique nations, as Italy, mother of the arts, and France
among those modern. Sackville, Wyatt, Lyly, Peele,
Spenser, Sydney, Nashe, Marlowe, Greene—it was only
modesty made him put his own name at the end of the
list—they should never be forgotten. Imps of fame, scions
of immortality, graftings on the everlasting tree. To
London then, and let Doll have her own way of life, and
let her bring up the boy the way she liked, till at last he
would be old enough to know how great a man his father
was.

Thinking this way, a man could walk a hundred miles
and not tire. What was young Nashe doing all this year
apart from writing against the silent Marprelate? Had
Marlowe another play on the boards? And Peele? And his
Arabella? Who were the men of the hour? What of
Coppinger? God, it would send a man mad to stay here
like a stone in Norwich when London was waiting over
there!

"Someone left the house late," said his father next
morning.

"I did," he replied briefly.

"And why?" Those eyebrows.

"Because I wanted to."

"But, Robin——"

"Surely, mother, I can go out walking in the moonlight. I'll not be moonstruck, you know."

"We are not afraid of that," said his father. "But the night is no time for honest men to be abroad."

"Sometimes, father," he replied smoothly, "the company of rogues is more to a man's taste than that of too honest men."

That led to another outburst, as he knew it would, but he rudely paid no attention to the disturbance round him and when his father began to question him pointblank, he left the room.

He went to see Adam Bolton. "Why don't you go to London for a winter, Adam? You'd not know yourself when you came back. It broadens a man, like foreign travel. Remember how you used to tell me about London when I was a youngster and you almost as big a ruffian as you are now?"

Soon he convinced Adam that he was serious. "I am going there myself, Adam. I thought we might go along together and see the sights together, eh? I know my way about, and I'll wager you do, Adam, too."

Adam scratched his chin. "Taking your wife, Robert?"

"Not this time again."

"Hm. Ay, I think I might come, Robert. My word though, I'll find it changed. I'll hardly know the good old streets I trod so proudly. Of course, I shall have to put things right here first. When were you thinking to go, Robert?"

They settled to leave Norwich a fortnight that very day. "And mum's the word, Adam."

"As sheath to blade, boy! Never fear me. I remember how in—what year would it be, Robert?—I was in London with my father—no, that wasn't the time. It was when I met Mistress Beatrice Constant—no, my father wouldn't have been with me, hardly. You wrote a letter to her for me—that was when we began to grow friendly. Ah, Robert, she was a lovely woman! You don't find women like her under every bush, Robert. I wonder if she would still be a widow in Exeter Street. Ever know Exeter Street, Robert?"

CHAPTER XXXII

THROUGHOUT THE WINTER of 1590–1591 Greene and Adam Bolton kept the same lodgings in London, off the Strand. Greene told his friend frankly they were dearer than he wished to take, but Adam, the soul of a certain kind of good nature, told him they would be as comfortable as they could for as long as they could, and if the time came when Greene was unable to pay, then he would be pleased to pay for both of them. It was a pleasure to take Greene about town, he was so appreciative, so willing to be charmed with everything he saw. Sentimentally, he insisted their first outing should take them through Exeter Street, and as they passed the house of the widow Constant he punned several times on her name, told himself he had been a proper devil in his day, and in general gave his companion a deal of amusement. He recounted exploits in the main harmless to all except himself as though in his late 'teens he had been a devourer, a graceless, a gutter-spout sparrow. He showed Greene where he and Johnny Tomkins had been set upon by thieves, the place where he had laughed in the great ladies' faces as they went to the ball, the point on the river where the wherry had overturned and almost drowned him.

"Don't tell me, Robert," he would beg, leading him by the sleeve into the Partridge or the Three Pilgrims; "I know where you'll get the sweetest cup of wine in London. No, I'm none of your blockheads, thank God. None of your country lads. How now, mistress, dost remember me?" The tactful mistress did, gradually winning his name from him, letting him do the reminding of earlier visits. "There you are, Robert—they don't find it easy to forget Mad Adam. The Old Adam, eh? More wine, mistress! I can remember, Robert, in those old days a man coming in here and sitting not a hand's breadth from where you are now,

and then he had the impudence——" At the end of the
story Greene would commend him for his cunning, his
valour, his wit, or whatever quality Adam brought forth
for inspection. They went to the theatres twice a week,
and to Greene's satisfaction saw the Queen's Men at the
Bull act *Friar Bacon and Friar Bungay*. On this occasion
Adam was everything a friend could be: "Wonderful,"
he muttered, "beyond praise, astounding, I never saw such
a thing in all my born days." Where he had to laugh he
laughed like a camel; where he should be moved he was
moved past purging; when amazement was the cue his
eyes grew round as chamber pots. He told Greene the
play was evidence of the genius he had always known
him to possess, and flattered himself that he had been the
first to call it forth. Behind stage he was affability itself,
with no notions of a gentleman's superiority to players.
And as Richard Wilson said, smiling, even Master Robert
Greene did not carry over into uncomfortable practice
the opinion he and Tom Nashe so fiercely set forth in
print. Would Master Bolton like to look inside the monster's
head? Or examine more closely the painted cloths? He
explained simple mechanisms to the grateful Adam:
how the devil sprang from hell, how Jupiter was wafted
from the clouds; but explaining how in an outdoor scene
they had just made the innovation of placing a shovelful
of horse dung on the stage for verisimilitude, he was forced
to admit the justice of Adam's challenge that on his own
words they left the dung there till the end of the play,
incongruous though it was during the banqueting scenes
that followed. Naturally this success made Adam more
confident in offering advice later, when he had invited
the whole company to drink inside the Bull. Wilson, convinced of kindliness if not of intellect, promised to consider
all he had said, and it remained one of the happiest days of
Adam's life.

He met Peele too. For some time Greene could not get
hold of George, but found him at last by reason of his
commission to write the verses for the Tilt Yard Enter-

tainment of November 17, when Sir Henry Lea would
resign his honour as Master of the Tilt and make it over to
the Earl of Cumberland. "And I needed it," said George.
"My first job worth having this year." Greene inquired
after Arabella and was startled by the anger in George's
usually happy-go-lucky face. "I thought the whole blasted
world knew. She is dead." He had a second shock for him.
"I shall be married again before the end of next month."
Arabella had died eleven months ago, Peele could not live
alone, there was the question of the children and their
upbringing; he thought Mary Yates would be the answer
to all his problems. Remembering Arabella, Greene
thought him callous and unnatural. Said Peele: "You and
I, Robert, we'll not make too good a showing in the eyes
of posterity. But I can't reproach myself. In her way
Arabella was happy enough. As happy as I have been,
anyway. It would have been different had I been born
without this itch in my right hand."

He had already drawn his money from Tilney and spent
most of it, but, his depression gone in a breath, he was
jubilant at the thought of the presents he must get from the
knight and earl, from the Queen's Majesty, and, with luck,
from the more distinguished taking part in the Entertainment. "I tell you, Robert—and you, good sir—there'll be
no breathing for the gentry. Not a dog but will lift his
leg against a dukedom, not a palace cat but will mess for
a baron's foot to find it; the man who faints will find props
in arms with four quarterings, he who falls will be trodden
under with elegance unsurpassed in this kingdom; it will
be the bravest reek of the reign."

Adam dangled out a hope, and Peele caught the words
out of his mouth. Yes, for a friend or two of the author's,
no doubt, at great expense it would be possible to obtain
from the Master of the Revels a place, not among the highest,
mind, but from which nothing would be missed. "Judge
the difficulty," he put it to Adam, winking first at Greene,
"not even my wife-to-be can be present, such is the un-
reasoning rapacity of the Revels Office. For my part I'd

not pay, I tell you so frankly." Before they left, Adam had
parted with six shillings and Greene had significantly
promised to pay for his place later. Peele did not argue,
he was six shillings to the good; he could get room for the
two of them for nothing.

The Entertainment was all Peele had said it would be.
It took place in the Yard at Westminster, beneath the
gallery-window at which the Queen was seated with
Turenne, the French ambassador, the tilting being on foot
across an open barrier, and no one coming off much the
worse for it. Each tilter attended with a retinue of his men,
most gorgeously attired, each one trying to out-do the others
in splendour. Each had his device, that of Lee a withered
running vine, that of Blount the sun, of Carey a burning
heart, the Knowles brothers' golden boughs; all were
attired in armour gilded and engraved, announced by their
own trumpeters and waited on by their own pages. Greene
had never seen such splendour as this, but unlike Adam he
would not admit it. The Yard was ablaze with colour, for
the spectators were robed almost as dazzlingly as the com-
batants, and every fashion known to the age was represented.
Here were ruffs like cartwheels, like organ pipes, like wind-
mills; doublets of the French, Spanish, Italian styles, peascod,
winged and welted, lined and slashed and puffed and
gashed; breeches of Venice, of Parma, of the Low Countries,
squat as napkins, blown to the middle thigh, draped
to the knee or below it, plain, worked, inset, with raised
seams, multi-hued gussets, gartered to the hose; stockings
of silk, shoes that matched the limits of invention, of leather
light or stout, of velvets raised or smooth, laced, ribboned
or with rosettes, straight to the ankle or with a turned-
down cuff, single or double soled, with cork heels or without.
And on the ladies still greater ruffs, still rarer laces, still
finer jewels, still daintier shoes; the incredible falfaldrum
of bodices and skirts, ruffling out like peacocks' tails,
swelling over tun-belly hoops and bolsters, farthingales
of a celestial pregnancy, petticoats, ten at a time, ringed
like rainbows; silks, taffetas, velvets, satins and brocades,

arched to bosoms, shaped to shoulders, jimped to waists, bracketed with hips. Cloth of gold on scarlet, yellow on sapphire blue, cream on emerald green, pinks, whites, orange-tawny, silvers and blacks—the eye swept over a spilt casket of bright treasures. And she, the greatest of them all, long-faced, black-toothed, wire-haired, looked down on all and found it good. The running at tilt over, from the ground rose a fair pavilion, like the Temple of the Vestals, within it an altar strewn with gifts, before the door a pillar crowned and wreathed with eglantine, and as Hales the singer raised his voice with "My golden locks time hath to silver turned," the Vestals brought the Queen a veil and cloak and safeguard, its buttons bearing the emprezes of Lee's friends fixed to an embroidered pillar. The pageant now drew to its end. Lee put off his armour, presented his successor to the Queen, armed and horsed him, and himself gave up office in a side-coat of black velvet and a buttoned cap of country fashion.

"Well, Adam?"

"I never saw such a sight, Robert. That Master Peele of yours, he's very nearly as good as you are." He watched Fulke Grevill go past like a sunbeam. "And yet you might say, Robert, it's not the apparel that makes the man. Now I don't say it to flatter, but by way of a leg, Robert, where will you see a better than your own?"

Having attended Peele's pageant, they had to attend his wedding. Greene luckily had some money owing him from the Queen's Men and was able to buy a handsome though useless present. Adam's was handsomer and still more useless, but Peele, true to his old description of himself, was too good an "accepter" to look even a spavined gift horse in the mouth. It would have been discourteous not to get drunk, and they all, bridegroom too, had a grand old time. Thought Greene: If Arabella were here, she would be happy as a queen with one of these sausages and a glass of wine. The reflection was eloquent of his state.

Will Monox was another of Greene's friends to whom he introduced Adam, but their acquaintance was brief.

Will made no pretence of his plans to get all he could out of him, but this Greene, to his indignation, would not allow. "He's a thin man," said Adam thoughtfully. Greene agreed. "He's the last rasher on the side of bacon. He's a pig's-apron among men, Adam. If you value my advice at all, never lend him the tenth of a groat. Eh?" Nor would he rest till Adam had promised.

Meanwhile Greene was writing busily. He would come in from a jaunt with Adam, throw off his cap and cloak, and in ten minutes be deep into his story of Sophonos and Philador, or when that was out of the way, deep into the fortunes of Francesco and Isabel. He was not above borrowing from his earlier work to get this done the quicker, and in November and December had the satisfaction of seeing his novelle printed. Chuckling, he wondered whether brains in the future would be wasted over the question of how much of Philador's and Francesco's stories should be reckoned his own. Chuckling too, he smacked his hand against the money in his purse. It was a profitable vein, he'd not see it close. He thought it a master stroke to change the old title page motto of his romances, *Omne tulit punctum qui miscuit utile dulci*, He bears away the bell who gives lessons with fun, into the concise *Sero sed Serio*, Come to my senses at last.

Of Coppinger he knew nothing all this while. Nashe could tell him, maybe, for he was still beating the air at Whitgift's command, but he had not seen brisk Tom since his return to town. What sent him out to Croydon at last was the startling fact that in March he actually saw Coppinger and knew that Coppinger saw him too but hurried around a corner and disappeared before he could catch up with him. He puzzled greatly over this. They had grown less friendly, true, and Coppinger was possibly still a proscribed man, but he must know Greene would never betray him. Why then flee from him? Had it been the angle of his face, the rapidity of his glance, or had Coppinger looked ill and thin? Strange, indeed.

Nashe was none too pleased to see him at Croydon. It would do him no good with his employer to have players and playwrights calling on him there. He thought Greene understood— "Oh, shut your mouth, Tom! What d'you think Whitgift will make you—a blasted bishop for your pains? If he does, by God I'll denounce you! What d'you know about Coppinger?"

"I know that he is mad."

"Mad? Come now, just because he doesn't see eye to eye with honest Tom? You'll be as bad as Marlowe at this rate."

Nashe began to laugh. "Mad, Robert—I mean it. Cracked as a bell, mad as a March hare, more lunatic than Herod. Have you seen Marlowe since you came back?"

"Never mind about Marlowe. Tell me what you know about Coppinger."

"Here it is. You know he fled the town after the seizure of Martin's press? They caught him last year at Northampton. On principle my noble master's men gave him the rack to see what he had to tell them——"

"Oh, Great God, no, Tom—that's not true, for pity's sake!"

"I am talking now, not writing. Why shouldn't I speak the truth? They racked him three times, so I hear, so he must be appreciably taller by this time. Oh very well! Very well! Though why you waste sympathy on an old compass-legs like him, I don't know. They would have racked him to death, I fancy, had not the governor of the gaol there refused to permit it. Not a word from him, of course. I will say that for Coppinger—he'd not talk for a trifle like racking. So they left him in Northampton gaol, Robert, for six months, and then—I don't quite know why, unless it was some of his Cambridge friends—they let him go. He spent some time in Kent, and now he is here in London, though I believe the watchdogs of the common weal lost sight of him a week or two back."

"Why do you serve such a devil, Tom?"

Nashe leaned forward though there was no one near. "I'll tell you this much, Robert: I had rather kick him than kiss him; but I happen to have a belly, Robert, and I have to fill it, and I have to cover my back from the wind and my head from the rain. These may appear unimportant matters to you, but they engross me, I confess it. Now my exalted master, whom God preserve, needs sharp pens against his enemies, whom God preserve too, and he finds mine the sharpest he can buy. I hope this puritan squabble lasts another fifty years, Robert, and may I never lack a a curse for Martin and a kick for his followers."

"But Coppinger? You said he was mad—what did you mean?"

"What I said. Have you ever heard of William Hacket?"

"Not I."

"You will, and that shortly. He is more knave than mad though. And Henry Arthington?"

"No, nor him."

"Coppinger met Hacket in Northampton gaol. It is just possible he had met him once before through Wigginton—you'll remember him? There Hacket most hopelessly corrupted him, so we learn since. Hacket had previously been whipped from York for calling himself St. John the Baptist, and promising to perform miracles. According to Coppinger he performed a number at Northampton, so we deduce he turned the poor fool's brain, weakened by his racking. That is as much as I dare tell you, Robert, and unless you keep it to yourself the pair of us may suffer. But remember the name—William Hacket!"

This was painful news to take back to London with him. Coppinger on the rack! Surely the finest man he had ever met, the noblest hearted though far from the wisest, that they should treat him like a hardened criminal was too dreadful for belief. It shook a man's faith in providence to hear it. Hacket, Hacket, Hacket? As St. John the Baptist? And Coppinger was in with him? Then his brain must be gone, as Nashe had said. Arthington was the other?

He had heard nothing of him. What was to come? If he
could see Edmund again, he might be able to do something for him. He determined to call on his parents, and
see if they knew anything of him. They did not, however,
or would say nothing, and Greene had to believe he had
deliberately allowed his parents to know nothing of his
whereabouts lest they be troubled by Whitgift's men. They
knew about Northampton though, and the rack, and he
thought it best to take his leave quickly.

The next event of importance, and the last before Adam's
return to Norwich, was the Spring Fair in Finsbury Fields.
This was held in the second week of May and differed little
from those fairs at Norwich and Wroxham Adam was even
more accustomed to than he, save that it would be bigger
and patronised by more rascals. Greene would not have
admitted that his own toothache meant more to him
than Coppinger's racking, and intended nothing should
spoil his enjoyment there. The money would be tighter
once Adam went, so they would have a last fine fling together
first. The fair was set out in the usual long rows of booths,
tents, carts, light wooden structures, where you could wander
about all day as the fancy took you and spend little or much
money for about the same enjoyment. This fair was notorious
for its thieves, for half the kennels of London were emptied
for the new business, but Greene thought himself too fly
to worry, and Adam was too thoughtless. They had a
couple of meals together, one of faggots made of liver and
bread and spices, the other of Adam's favourite herrings,
hot from the grid; and staring around him Greene meditated
whether a play could be made out of a fair. Characters
started up, ready for his need—that sharp-faced fellow
yonder, looking for dupes, the fly-blown woman by the
second wagon, the grave old gentleman who gave legal
advice for almost nothing and was dear at the price, the
clown they had just seen tumbling, and the man who
walked the wire blind-folded—there was enough here for
a dozen plays much less one if only a man could get it
down on paper. The eager woman admiring the strong

man's muscles, which stuck out over his back like cables, her husband more interested in the fat lady—they could go in; and even faithful Adam, why not he? They threw their last scraps to the fighting dogs, drained their pots, and were off once more, this time to Spanish Row.

Here the pair of them were much attracted by a handsome woman at a ribbon stall, wearing a splendid and yet draggly dress. There was evidently neither charge for, nor objection to, admiration; so they stood there quite a while choosing gew-gaws which they might not carry away after all, and at last were talking cheerfully and none too politely with her. She was no wit, but she made them feel witty, and that was better still. Oftentimes there were other buyers, and Greene noticed in particular that a good-looking man of her own fair colouring was more than once pressing past them. A most unobtrusive way he had with him, too. Still, he went on fondling his beard, twiddling with his rings, and wondering how to get rid of Adam so that he might make his suggestion to this Venus of the fair. Adam was equally wondering how to get rid of him, so it must have appeared a pretty comedy to any interested onlooker. The woman knew what they were at, and might have her preference, which might be for neither of them, but they held their ground a ridiculously long time until Greene, determined to settle matters one way or the other, walked boldly round the stall to whisper in her ear. This flabbergasted Adam, whose face when she laughed aloud was a joy to Greene. Whatever her reply, he came back to the front of the stall beaming, and immediately led the sheepish Adam away. Ten minutes later, having annoyed his friend by refusing to tell him anything, he turned back towards the Row so that they might watch the golden woman from a distance. There were men at her stall like wasps around a honey-pot, and she was talking with the unobtrusive yet handsome fellow he had noticed about her before.

"Come on, Adam," he ordered. "It is time to find you a partner for this evening."

"But aren't you——?"

"I have a meeting arranged with the lady who sold you those ribbons in your hand."

"You rogue, Robert! I have a good mind to finish with you for this." He looked as though he more than half meant it, so—"You can have her to-morrow," Greene offered magnanimously. They were half way to where they would eat more herrings or eels when he clapt his hand to his side and found his purse gone.

"I've been robbed, Adam!" He scowled. "What the devil are you laughing at?"

Adam slapped his thigh he was so delighted. "What will you do now about your beauty with the golden hair, Robert?"

As though humouring him, Greene laughed with him. "It's a love match, Adam. There'll be no passing of coin. You will have to lend me some money, though."

"Not a penny, Robert—not one penny."

He quickly came to see that Adam meant it. "I'll lend you sixpence to see you home, and I'll pay for all you can eat and drink, Robert, but I'll not lend you anything more."

"You could never be such a bad friend, Adam. You are joking."

"We'll see!" Adam chuckled. "You thought yourself clever a shade too soon, Robert. I tell you what we'll do— we'll go back to the stall and give her her choice: you as you stand, breeks and beard thrown in, myself with gold in my purse. Shall we?"

"We shall not!" Greene said angrily. He did not want to lose his temper; he had lost too much already; but if Adam persisted—but there, he was a good-natured fool, he would have his sport, and then who more generous? He walked moodily along, surprised himself at the strength of his desire to see again this woman he might now lose, afraid to appear ridiculous by taking seriously threats Adam could never mean to keep, and yet worried more by this aspect of the loss of his money than any other.

"Let's eat," Adam advised him. "You'll need a full stomach to keep up your spirits." His evident enjoyment of his embarrassment became a greater trial to Greene each minute, but he sought for a joke, found and uttered it, and ate what he could. The only thing that comforted him was that Adam did not know the time he had said he'd be back at the stall before his lady packed up for the night, and he now kept Adam busy looking at one thing or another and paying for both till it was only ten minutes short of the hour. It was now unlikely Adam would know his exact bearings, and Greene asked him seriously for a loan for the night. Adam shook his head decidedly. No, he swore he would lend him nothing, but held out a shilling. "I am not jesting about this," Greene told him. "I'll make a quarrel of it, Adam." Adam shook his head again, and his face was not quite so good-natured. "I'll not lend, Robert. You were sharp, getting round to talk with her, but it's my turn now." Another sentence each and they were ready to fight. "Then keep your money," Greene said bitterly, "and may what you buy with it give you the scours! Good-bye." He was around a booth before Adam could move, dodging away towards Spanish Row. Courage was needed, more than money. Frankness would win the day, he knew it by her face. He was at the stall as she was folding up her goods into two huge but not heavy packages.

"I'm here," he announced himself, unnecessarily. "Shall I carry these for you?" He grimaced and dropped his hand to his dagger at a man in a grey cloak who looked eager for the same errand. Then: "You look only that much less charming a lady than you did this afternoon in that your cloak permits less of you to be seen."

"I may believe a man one day," she told him.

He took her by the hand, feeling like the hero of one of his unwritten plays. "I am risking that you think me a rascal. I have no money, and I have a friend coming here with a well-lined pocket who will be only too happy to buy you fairings."

He thought she was laughing at him. "Do you usually come to fair without money?"

"I have had my pocket picked."

She pulled free her hand and caught at one of her bundles. "Is that any reason why a woman should break her back with these?"

Mentally he was thumbing his nose at Adam Bolton. There was nothing he would like better now than for that dolt to arrive in time to see them off. Nothing he would like more than to see his gander's eyes on this. "Away for where?" he asked jubilantly.

Through Moorgate to Budge Row was their route. "My name," he said, "is Robert." "And mine is Katerina." "Those I love best call me Robin." "Those I love best call me Kate." "Then I'll call you Kate, shall I, Kate?" "Do, Robin!"

He was play-acting and he knew it. But if she were willing, why not? There were methods less pleasant. "Can you understand this, Kate—I cannot believe I am here walking with you. Why have I never seen you before?"

"Perhaps because you never looked. You live in London?"

"Where else? Why do you ask?"

She grinned at him. "Your friend—had he something of a country turn to his toes?"

"My friend Adam? And where do you live?"

"London, all my life. Where else, as you said?"

"That was your brother at the stall—the man your colouring, and much your size?"

"Ask no questions, Robin Good-Fellow, and you will be told no lies."

He hoicked his bundle higher. "You must find a bundle like that heavy, Kate."

"I can bear."

He looked sideways at her, meditating her meaning, but made no comment. "Are we going back out, Kate, once we put these in safety?"

"Where?"

"You may leave that to me," he said grandly.

"And what will you use for money, Robin? The trimmings of your beard?"

"Surely we'll not say good-bye?" he asked anxiously.

"It will be all the same to-morrow, Robin. Robin What are you?"

"My name, you mean?" He did not want to give it, but was afraid to offend her. "Robin Greene."

She mimicked him. "*My name, you mean—Robin Greene!* Are you a writer of ballads?"

"Do you ever go to the play, Kate?"

"Not often."

"Will you come there with me?"

"I might."

"Say you will!"

"And pay for us?" She began to sing under her breath as they turned St. Pancras. She must be a strong woman as well as a beautiful.

"Kate, you'll not believe me, but I have been at Court in my time and I never saw there with all their damasks and diamonds the woman I'd prefer to you in drugget."

"Chance would be a fine thing, Robin Good-Fellow. Do you talk like this to every woman you meet? Are you a desperate fellow with the ladies, Robin Good-Fellow?"

He wagged his head as well as his bundle would permit. Who was she? What was she? At the stall he'd have said she was of the game, now he was not so sure. What he did know was that he felt ten years younger than yesterday, sprightly as a boy, eager for adventure. In Budge Row she stopped before one of the smallest houses, took a key from inside her cloak, and set it in the door. "Well?" she asked.

"Well?" he said huskily.

"I'm home."

He swung his bundle to the ground. "You'll not leave me now, Kate?"

"Why not?"

"Because I want to stay with you. Because you are beautiful as a star. Because if you go there'll be no moon for the night, no sun for the day, no light." He put his hand on her sleeve. "Because I am a poet and I worship beauty."

"A mere play-making poet, Robin, is it? The heel of the players' shoe. I know." She looked at him closely. "Had you a purse to lose, I wonder."

"Don't say that, Kate!"

She snapped her fingers, strongly, like a man. "What does it matter? Come inside, Robin."

Of the game then? He was both glad and sorry. Glad that she'd spread her beauty for him like a bed, sorry that some poor remnant of his ideals was already dwindling. Margaret, the lovely maid of Fressingfield—she would look like this—could he without his everlasting loss lie at a first encounter with his Margaret? Suddenly he was thinking: Consummation is nothing. To live with Pallas not the Cyprian. Ah well—he picked up his bundle and went haltingly after her into the house.

She lit a couple of tapers in a small and not very clean room. "Sit down, Robin." He was clearing a few odd-ments from the chair when she asked: "Are you easily frightened?"

"Good heavens, no!" He placed the chair so that he could see both doors. "Why should you ask?"

"Curiosity, that's all."

As though something in his dress irked him he dropped his hand to his dagger and made certain it was ready for withdrawal. "You know, Kate, you remind me of a girl I wrote about in one of my plays." Yet Margaret was cleaner than the thrice-scrubbed cream-bowl, and Kate looked careless. "Will you come to see it with me?"

Yes, she would. "Tell me about her," she invited.

There he sat, on the safe side of the table, a queer tingle of danger giving zest to every moment. She still wore her cloak, as when out of doors. He talked well of Margaret because of her he could talk almost without thinking: the freshest maid in literature, her eyes like flowers in the dew-spattered mornings, her lips the arch of Cupid's bow. "When I saw you this afternoon, Kate, I thought of her."

He knew she was listening hard. "You did, Robin?"

"What's your other name, Kate? Or ought I not to ask?"

She shrugged her shoulders. "Ball. Kate Ball."

"Are you married?"

"You ask too many questions, Robin Greene. Tell me about yourself. How do you live?"

Something of this he did tell her. Writing, writing, writing, nothing else really.

"Hm. Fame and a bald head at forty, is it? How old are you now? Thirty-six?"

"Thirty-two. No, thirty-three. Do I look older then?"

"No. Have you a watch?"

"Somewhere here." He dragged it out. "It is near ten o'clock, Kate."

She began to tap her foot on the floor. Whom could she be expecting? Secretly he felt for his dagger, eased the blade slightly.

"You would like to stay here, would you, Robin?"

"Yes." He laid his hand on the table, the palm upward. "Who are you expecting?"

"You'll see."

He breathed hard. Yet he was not afraid. He was about to open his mouth again when he heard footsteps approach the street door, voices, and the fumble of key in lock. He jumped up, drawing his dagger, as in came the handsome young fellow he had seen at the stall that afternoon, and with him a thick-set, ugly, middle-aged man.

"Good evening," said Greene politely.

"Watch the door, Burd!"

"You can save your breath, Harry," the woman said.

"You fool!" he snapped at her. "Who is this fellow?"

"I'll tell you when you all put your daggers up," she replied coolly. "Sit down again, Robin. Sit down, Harry, and send Burd about his business."

Harry looked uncertainly from one to the other. He was not prepared for his part. "Why did you do it, Kate?"

"Will you sit down! I'll not have you standing there ready to cut each other's throats. And tell Burd to go for to-night."

"Why the devil should I?" Then he changed his mind. "Go on, then. Till the morning, Burd." Out went the third man, and Harry, scowling at his sister, sat down.

"This is my brother Harry, Robin. This is Master Robert Greene, the writer of plays."

"We have met before," Greene said.

"I have forgotten it."

"Yes, when you took my purse this afternoon."

Harry touched his dagger, but took his hand away and grinned. "I lose my touch, do I?" He turned to his sister. "Is he a friend?"

"Are you a friend, Robin?"

"I am. But I'll have my purse back, if that's not presuming too much too early."

Harry went into some mysterious pocket of his, to pull out a handful of money. "I keep no purses. Was yours the red one? Be more careful next time. I suggest a stout chain and a mesh bag inside leather—and maybe a half-ton anchor." He counted out coins. "That was it? What's to eat, Kate?"

She brought a plateful of chitterlings from a cupboard, a loaf of bread and wine. "You'll join us, friend?" asked Harry.

Eating, Greene wondered. So Ball was a pickpocket and his sister—what? Her part in his schemes must be defined, must be ugly. She must play decoy—a hateful idea. Was she loose? Was she wary? He narrowed his eyes, Harry watching him.

"Don't you think too hard, Robin," she advised him, so she too must have been watching. "Maybe it is like much else—it'll not bear thinking on."

Harry showed himself a philosopher. "Take life as it comes, Master Greene. Life is a succession of purses, eh? Budge Row to-day, and who knows where or what to-morrow?" He drank. "I expected your friend here, not you. Is he a play-writer, too?"

"He is a wealthy man."

"Kate, Kate! Can I ever forgive you? I take the first purse and you miss the second man—there's no thriving that way, Kate."

"I could have had him, Harry, but I preferred Robin. You'll stay here to-night, Robin?" He hesitated. "He can, can't he, Harry?"

"I tell you what, friend," said Harry. "Are you in need of money? Quite so—like the rest of us. All you players——"

"I am no player!"

"Whatever you are then. We can still go through with our scheme. Will you give us your friend's address?"

"Why should you want it?"

"To rob him," said Harry bluntly.

Greene looked at Kate. What a glorious woman she was! And Adam would be going back to Norwich in less than a week, and had he not refused to help him that very day? "How?" he asked.

"You know the cross-biting law?"

"Yes, I heave heard of it, but you don't think——"

"I certainly do. We may be leaving this house in two or three days, so why shouldn't we try?"

So that was Kate's lay. The old cross-biting law! To entice a man with money to the house, and then, as they cooed or bedded, in bursts the pretended husband with his witness, threatening first blood and damnation to a naked man and then the process of the law unless the poor devil buys him off with all he carries. Oh, Margaret,

Margaret, oh country maid of Fressingfield! "I'll not do it!" he said abruptly, and stood up.

"Quiet, friend," said Harry, who could laugh easily and look nasty just as easily. "There's always time for thought."

"Great God!" cried Greene. "What sort of man are you who'd prostitute your own sister for gain? I'd die in the gutter first and so would any decent man!"

"Oh no, you don't!" Harry had his dagger out, and Greene his. "So you're a canter, are you? A square toes? A preacher? Get out of the room, Kate."

"I'll not. Will you put your daggers up, you fools!"

"I'll put it up nine inches under his shoulders," said Harry unamiably.

"And hang for your pains? You silly, silly fool, Harry!" She ran in between them, to prevent a blow. "Let him go. It was my fault he came here." Greene, cold as ice, was watching the quiet weaving of Harry's arm. "You'll not betray us, Robin?"

"I betray nobody."

"You'll not have the chance," said Harry.

Suddenly he struck down his sister's arm and was at Greene. A short jab tore the shoulder of Greene's doublet as he whirled to avoid him, Harry was momentarily off his balance, and with that Greene struck him hard under the chin with the handle of his dagger. He fell like a stone, his dagger rattling away from him. "Well?" said Greene.

"You had better go," she told him.

"I'll go. Christ in heaven, Kate, I thought better of you than this! When we were walking here together I thought——"

"You thought me a whore," she retorted. "Well, I am one. Now get out of the house, will you, before he comes to himself. I'll look well here with a corpse on my hands, won't I?" As he picked up his cap she said: "And if you want to see me in Bridewell you know what to do."

There seemed nothing else to say, so he turned his back on her and went without a good-bye. He walked silently through the black streets, saying to himself: If only you had been different, Kate; if only you had been different!

The whole day was like the first act of a play.

CHAPTER XXXIII

WILLIAM HACKET, Edmund Coppinger, Henry Arthington, the names Nashe had coupled together—he began to hear of them in late June and early July. From Nashe again, from Arthur Browne of Knightrider Street, from Will Monox, who had a close friend in the Archbishop's service. "He's a-watching them," said Will, "he's a cat with a mouse, that Archbishop of ours, Robert. He treats them like a pimple on the country's face—he'll let them ripen, come to a head, and then——" he pressed his fingers together—"the core is out, Robert." There were rumours about town of a rebellion next month, of an attempt to throw down the bishops, to establish such a regime as did the Anabaptists in Munster, even, men whispered, to depose the Queen. If the Magistrates did not govern well, so the story ran, the people might draw together and seek a Reformation. Nothing, however, could be more certain than that the citizens of London had no wish to seek a Reformation. These mysterious plotters, whoever they were—and the names of Hacket, Coppinger, and Arthington were not generally whispered— what could they hope to do? It was a worse madness than the jesuit Parsons', than Babington's. Yet no precautions were being taken, no special bands called out, no reading of proclamations—perhaps it was the midsummer madness over London, and no truth behind it.

It was with an unexpected suddenness Greene found himself knowing more than most. He was on a mission to Danter, the bookseller, then living on Garlick Hill, Queenhythe, and as he walked through Carter Lane below Paul's he recognised the figure of a man in front of him as Coppinger's. Resisting the first impulse to run after him, he followed him down Sermon Lane, and thought him making for Broken Wharf. He was walking with a

distinct hobble, and Greene noticed how from time to time
he jerked his arms, drawing the attention of passers-by,
and Nashe's description of him as mad came strongly to
his mind. He walked more briskly as he turned from the
Lane to the waterside, but Greene closed up on him,
waiting to see what he would do. Then, as he stopped at
an overleaning house on the Wharf and it looked as though
he might loose him, he called out: "Edmund Coppinger!"
Coppinger did not turn. He stood as though enrooted,
but made a short jerk of his arms once more. "It's Robert!"
Greene cried, almost at his shoulder. Coppinger half
way round to face him, his heart was struck to see that
he was almost white-haired, and his marked face was
pitiful. "It is only me, Edmund—only Robert Greene.
You have not forgotten me?" "No," said Coppinger.
"No."

Greene held out his hand. "Say you are pleased to see
me, Edmund."

"Yes, I am pleased to see you." He took him by
the sleeve. "Come with me, will you?" They moved
away fifty yards before Coppinger halted by some moor-
ing piles, lying useless on the river bank. "Are you
alone?"

"Of course I am alone, Edmund."

"I am glad of it."

He stood looking out to where the bull-baiting theatre
could be seen across the water, Greene waiting for him to
speak. He gave his unnatural jerk again.

"What are you thinking of, Edmund?"

"Thinking?" He came back to reality. "I was thinking,
Robert, as I looked south how Christ's tears must flow
for the New Jerusalem." He pointed to the South Bank
and then swung his arm back to include the city and
Westminster, and sighed.

"No doubt," Greene said placidly. "But, Edmund——"
He hesitated a moment. "Are you safe in London?"

"We are under God's eye in one place as in another,
Robert."

"I know all about that. But in London you may be under the Primate's eye too. I have heard your name of late, Edmund."

"Not for ill, I hope." He was still staring out across the river. "I wish you had not found me, Robert. It may do you harm. Go away now, will you?"

"Not just yet. I heard about Northampton, Edmund."

"And you pitied me? Yet we parted with coldness, you remember, Robert? That was good of you. And yet —is it not God's way, that?—at Northampton I——" For a time he fell silent. "I saw a great light at Northampton, Robert, whose brightness and glory will grow before me till I die."

"You saw William Hacket there."

"I saw our Lord Jesus Christ there!"

"You have seen him at all times and in all things, Edmund."

"I tell you," said Coppinger, turning to him, gripping at his shoulder, "I tell you I saw him in the flesh! The Son of Man! Again descended!" He began to mutter as though it were a schoolboy lesson: "The time is near, but it is not yet. The Son of Man, the Son of God, but the time is not yet. Not yet."

"Edmund, you are ill!" This was the madness Nashe had spoken of. "Why not leave London again for the country, for Kent, for rest and peace? You are in great need of them."

Coppinger smiled. "Because I have seen my Saviour? I am therefore in less need of them. Were the disciples without the peace that passeth all this world's under-standing? Were the prophets in need of rest? I tell you, Robert, that as certainly as this river runs downward to the sea, I have seen Him."

Greene shook his head, despondently. "Where are you lodging now, Edmund?"

"No matter where. So short a time, Robert, and the world will know of us."

"Us?"

be dashed to the wall, the white hairs of age muddied with the blood that nourished them. When the Four Horsemen shall thunder from the heavens, and the hoofs of their steeds dash to nothing the roofs of hovels and palaces. Repent, England, repent against the day of reckoning!"

"If you love life, Edmund, talk quieter!" They were doubling around the basin at Queenhythe, but he had forgotten his mission to Danter. "Where are you going now?"

"To Broken Wharf, to the Most High."

"I'll come with you, to the door at least." He led him to the bottom of Trinity Lane and so to the back of the houses facing the Wharf, Coppinger meanwhile discoursing like one rapt of miracles and revelations. If he could do nothing else with him it would be a gain to get him indoors. "Is this the house?"

"I'll not go in the back way. Am I a criminal or a slave that I should hide my goings and comings?"

Greene, afraid of the front of the house, was inspired to reprove him again for his presumption, and Coppinger contritely agreed and pushed at the door. "I'll come inside," said Greene, greatly daring. Coppinger was a child to him. Whatever calmness he had at the beginning of their talk had left him; he was excited, confused—Greene confessed it with grief—almost idiotic. He had not even a dignity of madness.

"Come then," said Coppinger.

They went through the first room and then up a narrow stairs to a landing. Coppinger knocked at a door there, and in answer to a question Greene could not hear distinctly, answered: "The Prophet of God's Mercy." "Enter then," replied a voice, he opened the door, and Greene found himself on the threshold of a bedroom. Coppinger's arm was across him, and he soon understood why, for he had to follow his example and remove his shoes. He had opportunity to see how ugly and deformed Coppinger's feet were, and how the joints of his knees were swollen.

Then he saw the curtains of the bed pulled back and a man gazing out at him. Coppinger went to the bedside, where he fell on his knees as though in worship, his hands raised, his head bent. "Who is with you?" Hacket asked, and Coppinger replied: "A poor man in spirit, O my Master, but one who at the touch of your hands will be a faithful servant." With that Hacket swung his legs out of bed, and Greene saw that he was a tremendously strong looking man of middle age, with a bull's head set on a short, thick neck. It was easy to believe what Nashe had said of him, that in his youth he had been a notorious fighter, a terror to quiet people wherever he went. He had keen little button eyes well protected by cheekbones that looked as though they had first bulged and then been flattened and heavy brows shagged with hair, and by the opening of his nightshirt, for he was still wearing this, Greene saw that his chest was like a forest. His bare feet were splayed and knobbly, his toes appearing to grip at the ground. A smell of sweat came from him.

"Who is with you?" he asked again, in a bass voice.

"A friend of my young manhood," answered Coppinger. "Robert Greene, Master of Arts." Neither of them saw anything ridiculous in the academic title, but Greene did.

"I have no friends," said Hacket heavily. "I have subjects, and there are those that rebel against me. He who is not with me is against me."

In his nightshirt he kneeled by the bed alongside Coppinger, and Greene thought it wisest to do the same. With a strong desire to laugh struggling with a kind of horror, he heard Hacket praying to God as his father that the heart of Robert Greene might be opened in time to his message. That he might find grace not tribulation, that God's spirit might direct them in all things, and they from greatest to humblest obey that spirit to the glory of God only. He prayed that he, Christ-Hacket, might prove worthy of his task, and that his prophets, Coppinger and Arthington, should stand near him in grace on earth

and in heaven. Thereupon they rose all three, and Hacket,
who seemed to combine earthly with heavenly interests,
asked Greene what was the news in the city. Greene imagined he must already be accepted as a convert and
disciple. This seemed the chance he wanted, and he spoke
vividly of Whitgift's knowledge of their movements, of
rumours among the people, of the certainty of destruction
if they persisted in their present ways. All this while
Coppinger hardly dared to raise his eyes to Hacket's face,
and Hacket was frowning or smiling. "How now, Edmund?" he asked, when Greene ran out of breath and
advice together; "Is not your friend, as you say, a poor
man in spirit? I tell you, my brother—for brother you
are in God even to me—I tell you there is that at hand
before which the Archbishop who has neglected my
office on earth shall be lower than the snake that tempted
Eve. He and his kind, shall I not cast them out utterly?
For know—and all men know!—that I come not now as
a lamb before the shearers, but with the vials of my father's
wrath in my hands. Be strengthened, I say, for no hurt
shall come to those who have faith in me, though for the
race of the ungodly there shall be three great plagues.
Shall they not perish by the sword? Shall not the spear be
raised against them? Shall not the pestilence come in brown
clouds from the East, with purples and reds of corruption?
And I will give the land over to famine, so that from the
four corners of it there shall be no sound but the wailing
of those that starve and the whimper of the dying." The
button-eyes fell on Greene. "Judge then, my son, between
the Archbishop and your Saviour Christ—for as surely
as this flesh was once William Hacket, yeoman of Oundle,
so now doth it clothe and compass about the spirit of the
only son of God. Do you believe?"

"He believes," said Coppinger, gratefully.

Greene was beginning to think it easier to get into the
lions' den than out of it. That Coppinger was mad but
sincere he did not doubt, but of Hacket he was not so sure.
He had a peculiar way of looking sharply at you, even in

the midst of his ranting, that suggested he was searching your head more than your heart. "You have armed forces?" he asked, like a man almost free from doubt but with a mortal's weakness.

"I have myself!" said Hacket.

Greene thought that might be comfort to those equally demented, but that it would be still greater comfort to the Archbishop. He bowed his head, puzzling how he might get outside. A knocking at the front door solved his problem, for it was clearly impossible for Hacket to answer doors, and Coppinger's tortured feet gave Greene the excuse for service. His shoes were still in his hands, and carrying them he went to let in Arthington, for so Coppinger declared it must be. On the stairs he pulled them on to his feet, and as he opened the door and a dark young man entered past him without a word, he slipped outside and hurried away as fast as he could. His brain went quicker than his feet, thinking over the extraordinary events of the last couple of hours. That Coppinger should be a bedlam! He who had always been so calm, so balanced, so ready to battle against himself—to be worshipping a smelly knave like this Hacket, a maltster, a cudgel player, a fist fighter and wrestler, a rogue whipped out of half the towns of Northern and Midland England. That sweet and radiant Cambridge scholar, that noblest of puritans, now sunk to the foulest blasphemy in company with wretches and madmen. How could God permit it? But he thought later of that harassed man who cried out against him and wept, the older, death-weary, overburdened Coppinger, perpetually astrain, month after month adding its tale of worry and trouble, his brain never a moment relaxed in service of a cause meeting slow but certain defeat, his exceeding loneliness and peril. Add to that his body on the rack, the incredible agony that must have been his for weeks, perhaps months on end, the never-to-be-healed laceration of his spirit that must follow the shame of his body's torture—was it so strange after all? He had gone near the edge for a long time, and at last had come the push to send him over. That face rich in grace and beauty, the strong, fine, manly shape of him—instead of them now the distorted limbs, the hair white before its time, the deep channellings cut by experiences worse than anything Greene knew of. He walked sadly over to Garlick Street, telling himself there was nothing he could do.

He wondered on what Hacket based his hopes. Perhaps on the puritans, but they would never stir for such a blasphemous pageant. Perhaps the papists, who would be willing to burn him. And who were the discontents, when you came to look over them? Mad, mad, mad they must be. God help them, for none other could.

He went out to Croydon on a fool's errand, for Nashe was not there, and no one knew what had become of him. As he went back to London he realised that Nashe could tell him nothing, should he find him.

He did not see Coppinger again till Friday the sixteenth of July. Yet he woke not a morning without wondering what the day would bring forth. He found it impossible to work, his money was gone, and what he got from the players for part of his wardrobe would not last him long. These three things together put him into a low state of spirits which normally would have been the prelude to a burst of drunkenness, but now he felt that even if he could find a friend to pay for it he wanted it not. From thinking of the grief in store for Coppinger's parents his thoughts turned to his own family at Norwich, for this too was a symptom of depression. His wife and son, how were they? His mother? What of Alice at Braiding? He lacked even the resolution to promise himself he would find something out. Perhaps before the winter—— He mooned about the streets, tired of his own company, yet eager for no one else's. Once or twice he passed the Red Lattice in Tormoyle Street, but did not enter and saw nothing of Fat Susie; several times he lounged his way towards the Court but no one there had any use for him; but usually he was to be found on a bench in Paul's Yard, among cut-purses and sneak-thieves, down-at-heel poets and out-of-work players, letter-writers with their bottoms through their breeches, old soldiers from the Low Countries with more lies to the minute than there were ounces to the pound, and the usual beggars. The regulars never asked him for anything now. Despite his occasional windfalls he was of Paul's brotherhood. He was on pleasant terms with many of the sisterhood, too, usually because of the windfalls. One face he thought many times he would like to see would be that of Mistress Ball. What a handsome woman she had been. And more than handsome, some appeal, what should he call it? But brother Harry—easy with a smile, easy with a knife-glide under the fourth rib, and far too easy with another man's purse—he wasn't so sure he wanted to see Harry.

He did though, the day he saw Coppinger again. He was at Paul's that Friday morning, sunning himself free of charge, breathing free too, with not a farthing in his pockets, when a lean fellow in amber and blue came rushing from the south end of Old Change with news of a disturbance in Watling Street. Many of those near him were on their feet and scurrying in a moment, for street disturbances were much in their line of business. In a scuffle if you liked profit you could nip a purse, steal a gold lace, tear away a watch, or if you liked doing damage hurl stones and sticks, kick at shins, lam out at jaws, or if you liked sensation just let the tide of it rise and flood you. Greene waited not a minute before he was off too. The scurriers before the crowd were now entering Old Change, so he threaded his way between them till he had to fight forward to where the crowd was thickest, and then went viciously through the last dense ranks with play of his feet and elbows. He lost his hat, and the sleeve was torn almost off his arm, and once a savage tug at his hair made him yell and turn to dash his fist into a woman's face. He could hear Coppinger's voice now, raised in declamation, and that of another man he guessed would be Arthington. "Repent, England, repent! For He has come before whom all sovereigns bow down. Jesus Christ has come with his fan in his hand to judge the world." As he fought his way clear to the front row the whole mass was being pressed by those behind into Cheapside, and so up towards the Cross. "And if any man ask me," Coppinger cried, "where Christ is, I tell him he lies now at Walker's house by Broken Wharf; and if you will not believe this then go to kill him, for as truly as Jesus Christ hath been in heaven, so truly is he come to judge the world. Repent, England, Repent!" His eyes passed over Greene a dozen times but appeared not to see him. At the Cross they came to an empty cart standing in front of the Falcon, and seeing this Coppinger and Arthington climbed on to it, the better to give their message. Greene was so near Coppinger he could touch him; he plucked at him in vain, for Coppinger, shouting to be heard, was now telling his audience that Christ walked the earth again in Hacket's glorious body, and that he was in London to separate the sheep from the goats, and that he would establish the Holy Gospel in Europe and bring in discipline and reformation and the Holy Cause. They were two prophets, Arthington of God's Judgment to call the world to its dreadful account, Coppinger of God's Mercy, whereby those who repented might be saved. The uproar was now considerable, and many there, terrified by the blasphemy, were for stoning the preachers to death. They waited on the first blow. After again announcing Christ's coming, Coppinger now went on to talk of the Queen, how she must mend her ways or be deposed, at which the crowd set up a great howling, and of the Archbishops of Canterbury and York, that they should be trodden into the dust, and of Hatton, that he was a traitor before God and should perish and leave no name. The lunacy grew worse as Hacket and the Queen's officers arrived at much the same time. It was a coincidence that as these latter cleared a way towards the cart Hacket could follow undisturbed in their wake. "See," cried Arthington, reading it as a miracle, "see where cometh the King of the Earth." He fell on his knees to worship him as Hacket jumped up on to the cart too. Arthington was now dragged down, and Coppinger, but Hacket had time to shout in his deep and tremendous voice that they beheld the coming of the Lamb before one of the officers struck him in the mouth. Enormously strong as he was, Hacket made no move except to put the back of his hand to his mouth and draw it away to look at the blood. "Behold," he thundered, "the Blood of the Lamb! Shall ye not writhe forever in Hell fire for this?" Several men laid hold of him, but he still stood firm. "Oh wicked generation, shall ye not rue it that this day the Lord's Annointed——" He took a heavier blow in the face and could not continue, and the three men were now led off towards the City Sheriff's. Greene followed with the shouting crowd as far as the house, but the door was there banged to and a file of men to guard it outside.

It was then he saw Harry Ball a dozen paces off to his right. Stirred though he was by what happened, he could not resist pushing over towards him. He stood behind him, half a pace, and said quietly: "We want you, Master Ball." Harry whirled like a cat, his hand under his cloak. "If it's not my old friend, Master Harry!" Greene said then, holding out his hand.

Harry grew less white. "Red-nob, is it? Brother Green-shanks of Budge Row." Cautiously he shook hands.

"Business good, Harry?"

Harry's eyes danced like gnats of an evening. "It might be worse. And you?"

"I have been poorer." Why he told the lie he could not say. "You find those crowds more evidence of God's providence than his self-styled apostles?"

Harry screwed up his face. "If there are nine fools among every ten men, how many here at the moment?"

"I have forgotten whatever I learned of mathematics. Is your sister still with you?"

"Let's go back to the Falcon," said Harry.

On the way they discussed the day's wonder. Harry, he found, was past admiration at the foolishness of his kind. He merely accepted it as a means to a livelihood. Inside the Falcon he called for a bottle of white wine, and Greene wondering at his affability, helped him drink it.

"Your sister?" he asked again.

"So you asked earlier. What did you think of her, Greene?"

"I never saw a handsomer woman," said Greene.

"So you'd bed with her, eh?"

Greene scowled at this fine brother. "I thought higher of her than that."

"Did you now? You would do little enough to oblige her when you had your chance. Are you any more willing now?"

"No," said Greene. "I could never bring myself to——"

"Never is a long day," Harry reminded him. "You have no money."

"I certainly have!"

"On your person?"

"Of course I have."

Harry smiled and poured out a drop more wine for both of them. "You are a liar, whatever else you may be, Greene. I tried you as we walked down together. You are as bare as a bottle." He took Greene's disbelief as a tribute to his art. "I'll make you an offer. Why not throw your hand in with us for a time?"

Greene shook his head. "I don't know why you should ask me."

"For a number of reasons. One of them that I'm working out a new law of cozenage and I need a writer for it; another that Kate took a fancy to you and I'm not against obliging her once in a way. Think of it, man, money in your purse again, and all of us happy as pigs in the sty!"

His simile seemed ill-chosen to Greene. He frowned, was uncertain of himself. Money in his purse—that lovely golden woman—it must be thought over carefully.

Harry finished his glass. "Why not come out and have a look at us? Not far—just below Knightrider Street. We can be there in ten or fifteen minutes. Kate is at home now. She'll be glad to see you."

The temptation was strong and Greene yielded. Walking back to Old Change and on to the house, his mind was equally divided between Coppinger and Kate and the prospect of making money with Harry Ball. After all, if it was just a question of writing a few letters, say, or copying something Harry put in front of him—he need ask no questions, it was no concern of his, a mere exercise with the pen. He grew very excited when they came to the Balls' door. Inside they went and up the stairs. He tapped at a door. "Harry," he announced.

"Here you are, Kate," he said, as it opened. "I've brought you better than a purse."

"If it's not Robin Good-Fellow!"

"Himself, Kate, and no other!"

She was as beautiful as ever, though at the moment none too clean. She seemed very pleased to see him, he thought, and thought too that if Harry had spoken truth there was nothing to prevent him being her man. Or did that mean her bawd? She made them both welcome, offering them food over which they told her the morning's happenings, which amused her greatly. "I can't laugh," Greene admitted. "Coppinger—remember, Harry, the one who jerked?—was my best friend at Cambridge—he and Sir Ralph Sidley."

"He will soon have done jerking," Harry said unfeelingly. "If you were at Cambridge you'll know Latin, eh? Good."

He was quiet, thinking, while Greene and Kate asked each other questions. "You'll be staying the night?" she asked all at once. He remembered the question from their last meeting. How many times? How many men? "Shall I?" he asked in return, looking at Harry rather than at her. Harry waved his hand as though he couldn't be bothered. "I will then, Kate."

"You can write Latin?" Harry asked. He chewed over Greene's affirmation. To Greene he looked like the man who picks up something good from the gutter. He felt himself almost trembling with excitement. "I have no money again, Kate."

She snapped her fingers like a man again. "We can't have everything, Robin. Bless the weather, curse the dog. We'll take you in for charity."

Later he said to Harry, imagining a man of his profession an adept at legal processes. "What will they do with those three men, do you think?"

Harry looked disinterested. "Examine them and put them into gaol, I should say."

"Which gaol?"

"The Fleet is handy. Undoubtedly the Fleet."

CHAPTER XXXIV

HARRY WAS WRONG. It was not the Fleet but Bridewell into which Hacket and his prophets were cast. News of their fantasy was in every man's mouth, with horror at their blasphemy, pity for their madness, and anger against their sedition. From the Friday they were examined daily till a week the following Monday, but without torture, for nothing could exceed the frankness with which they reiterated their claims. Once more Greene knew more than most, for on his second visit to Bridewell, though there was no hope of seeing Coppinger, he found that Hunter, the soldier he and Sidley had clashed with at Cambridge, and who had bred in him a four hours' ambition to become a soldiers' general a year after his return from Italy, was now the Warden there. With money given him by Kate he was able to take Hunter out to Fleet Street, treat him to wine, and ask him questions, some of which the wary old warrior would not answer. All three, he heard, were obdurate in their villainy, and other, even graver, matters had come to light. Hacket had openly declared Her Majesty worthy to be deposed, and had in the house of one Roger Keyes, in Knightrider Street (Greene knew the house well), defaced the royal arms by pricking out the eyes of the lions and dragons, and, worst of all, had driven a knife through that part of a picture of Her Majesty which might be held to represent the heart, to the great offence and derogation of the person and royalty of the Queen's Majesty and to the subversion of the state of this realm of England, contrary to the form of a statute in this case made and provided. Hunter was positive that what he had heard of the examinations ensured that Hacket would die the death reserved for traitors. About the others he was not so certain. Their madness was apparent, they had been led by Hacket, and though they had uttered sedition it was not clear they had any share in the razing of the coat of arms, and certain they had nothing to do with the mutilation of the Queen's picture. Hunter, who justified Sir John Harrison's long-past compliment that he had more sagacity than most suspected, still remembered Sidley, and was interested to hear of his death in the plague. The mortality in the prisons, he told Greene, had been such as almost to empty them. He concluded with the friendly wish that he might never have Master Greene as one of his charges.

Late on Sunday night he was told that Hacket alone would be put to trial the next day at the Sessions House, near Newgate, but he could not enter despite his bribe to the doorkeeper. The result was soon known—Hacket must meet his end by that Cross in Cheapside where his prophets had with him present uttered their grossest treason—but what most intrigued the gossips was his conduct before the High Council. To the first indictment, that he had offered treason on the twenty-fifth day of July, he answered calmly enough: "All must be as you will"; but to the second, relating to his actions on the first and sixteenth days, he answered more perversely, first saying to the Bench: "You have wit enough to judge for me and yourselves too," and later: "Few words are best; it is good to know much and say little." It was now shown him that not to plead could not serve his turn, for thereby he stood to be condemned of treason, but when once more he was asked to plead guilty or not guilty he said "Ambo. Both." Still the Council persisted, and at last he pleaded not guilty; but now being asked by whom he wished to be tried he would not answer *By God and the Country*, but only *By the Country*. With that he burst out into such hellish blasphemies as might induce the Court to declare him mad, but they chose to interpret this as impatience against God because he found himself in such peril, and shut their ears to his cries to God his father to revenge, and it so ended that he was committed to Newgate till Wednesday, the day of execution, that he might be brought to repentance and provide for his soul's health. Only two matters in this trial concerned Coppinger: the one that he was Hacket's Prophet of Mercy, the other that Master Attorney had a letter which he read before the Council, from Coppinger to Udall, praying him and the rest in prison not to faint, for he and others were taking a course for their speedy deliverance. This was bad news to Greene, for it seemed to establish his guilt almost as great as that of Hacket.

The Wednesday Hacket was to die Greene was at Newgate early. Again with money given him by Kate he covenanted with two soldiers of the escort to walk immediately behind them as they made towards the Cross. Harry was making arrangements of his own. As he told Greene, the moment of turning him off would make purse-cutting the merest child's play. Kate, from some superstitious scruples connected with her brother, never went to see executions, so they left her at home to prepare dinner against their return. Hacket was brought out from Newgate at ten o'clock, and with the greatest difficulty dragged to his hurdle. The streets were wedged tight with people. Men, women, and children, they leaned from every window, thronged every door, some had even clambered on to the roofs to watch him go by. It was only by constant shoving and blows the officers could make way for the hurdle, and it was here that Greene benefited from his foresight. Close to the elbows of his two soldiers, who were among those bringing up the rear, he trudged forward slowly and exhaustingly. Watching Hacket closely he had still that doubt of his madness he had known at Broken Wharf. Most of the way he was shouting at the top of his voice: "Jehovah Messias, Jehovah Messias! Now is the time to save!" or, as though he addressed the bawling multitudes: "Look, look how the heavens open wide, and the Son of God cometh down to deliver me!" But there were intervals when he fell silent, and then his face was that of a man frightened past all telling. At last they fought their way to the gibbet at the Cross, on the right hand of the street coming from St. Paul's, and there, the noise of the crowd having been stilled, he was exhorted to ask God and the Queen forgiveness and fall to his prayers. Greene was immediately in front of him now, still with his two soldiers, and heard how monstrously he fell to cursing the Queen. Again admonished, he fell to such prayers as terrified the populace. "O God of Heaven, Alpha and Omega, Lord of Lords and King of Kings, O God Everlasting, that knowest me to be the true Jehovah whom thou hast sent, send some miracle out of a cloud to convert these infidels and deliver me from these mine enemies! If not, I will fire the heavens and tear ye from thy throne with my hands!" Around Greene men cowered at these words, thinking indeed some dreadful punishment must split the skies and confound them, but Hacket had turned to the executioner, crying: "Ah, thou bastard's child, wilt thou hang William Hacket, thy King?" At this the magistrates called out that his mouth should be stopped, and the people roared for him to be turned off, but the only way six men could get him up the ladder was by pinioning him and hauling him up like a sack of coals, and he all the while cursing God. But once on the platform, his arms now secured, he struggled with his head to and fro, that the noose might not be put over him. For a moment his frenzy left him, and he cried out in a broken voice: "What do you do? Oh, what do you do?" But the noose about him, the knot hard under his ear, he left off this humanity and, his mouth a-dribble, screamed at the assembly: "Have I this for my Kingdom bestowed upon ye? I come to revenge and plague ye! O thou God, my Father in Heaven——" Here he choked on the rope and was turned off, but the people yelled that no mercy should be shown him, and so instantly he was cut down alive and quartered before them, his bowels coming out under his glazing eyes, and then his dripping heart torn from him and held up by the blood-soaked executioner. So perish all traitors! God save the Queen!

God would have the more time for that, thought Greene, in that Hacket was off his hands.

He was back at Knightrider Street about one o'clock, but there was then no sign of Harry, so he and Kate went on with their food together, Greene meantime drawing a still more highly-coloured picture of the sufficiently highly-coloured occurrence. He even snatched up half a loaf of bread to show how Hacket's heart came out of him.

"That is what you get in this world for godliness," commented Kate, as though his explanations had never been made. "There's this Hacket without an inside to call his own, and your friend in Bridewell likely to hang too, everybody against him, his poor bones never a moment's rest from the tugging they had—he can't be very happy, can he? And look at you and me— very calm and comfortable, filling our tripes with good food, money to spend, someone to warm our backs when we go to bed at night—I don't trust godliness, Robin lad."

He had a drink. "It does seem as though it doesn't pay, Kate. Still, till he went mad there was something fine about Edmund." He told her about Coppinger's attempt to convert to a new way of life the harlot behind St. Andrew's, and was angered by her amusement. "Don't laugh, Kate!"

"Women of pleasure convert for two reasons only, Robin: for profit or because they grow old and ugly. Your friend was a fool or he would have known as much."

He blinked at her, the woman of pleasure who on her own showing would never convert. Ignobly, he thought of his own marching orders. "You ought to get married one of these days, Kate. A woman like you could have her pick."

She crumbled a piece of bread. "Me? Marry a penny poet and then get the chance of a fatbags? Not in a hurry, Robin Good-Fellow!"

He resented the penny poet, thinking this the rejection of an offer he had not made. "But if the fatbags offered now?"

She grinned. "I should probably want a title."

"And if a titled fatbags?"

"I should want him young and handsome and strong. Perhaps with red hair and a long pointed beard till it's like sleeping with a nettle, eh, Robin?"

This made him smile and pull at his own long pointed beard. "You are a wicked one, Kate. I don't know what will become of you."

"I do. I'll grow old like the rest of the world, and that's why I'll take my pleasure while I'm still young enough. Come on, Robin Thinbags, kiss me!"

She ran around the table from him, mocking him with her eyes and tongue, and he, forgetting Hacket and Coppinger and Harry, ran after her. He was kissing her when they heard a noise at the door.

It was her brother. He glanced at their flushed faces without comment. "Pretty little hanging, Robin," he said, and drew some food towards him at table.

"Have you brought anything home with you?" Kate asked him.

"Not much. I am sorry for poor Londoners. I wish them long life and wealth."

They discussed the hanging again, and Greene noticed how indifferent Harry seemed to be to the prospect of a similar though less ceremonious end for himself. For nerve he thought purse-cutting under a gibbet took some beating.

"Remember your Norwich friend—the one who should have come to Budge Row?" Harry asked abruptly. Greene said he did, very well. "Does he ever deal in bills?" Not that Greene knew of. "Hm," said Harry, "then it is high time he started. Where are you going this afternoon?" Greene did not quite know. "Then you had better walk as far as Bridewell. I heard this morning he'll not live another day or two, this Coppinger friend of yours. If you are still interested in him." "Of course I am still interested in him!" He pushed back his chair. "If I could do anything to help him, I'd do it." Harry told him unhurriedly that his information was that Coppinger had eaten nothing for six days and was like to kill himself. He stuck his thumb in Kate's direction. "Did you ever think we should sink so low, Kate—consorting with this friend of lunatics and traitors?"

This amused the two of them greatly, but Greene was now in no mood for laughter. "I shall need some money," he said hesitantly. "Do you think——"

"Willingly," said Harry, "on condition." He looked from Greene to his sister. "You'll help me with a piece of penmanship, or maybe two, and the money is already in your pocket. Eh?"

"Of course he will," said Kate.

Harry dropped a gold piece on the table. "I'm not Mayor Whittington, nor yet his cat. You'll help?"

Coppinger's need, the gold in front of him, Kate's bright promising eyes—"I will. Thank you, Harry. Good-bye, Kate."

He went scurrying down the street into Blackfriars, and so to the gaol. There he asked for Hunter, and of him requested he might be allowed to see Coppinger, and when Hunter frowned, waiting for his perquisite, was inspired to swear he hadn't a penny but would not forget his kindness once things were better with him. With that Hunter, with a show of good nature triumphing over the stern voice of duty, led him into the Inner Ward and appointed a warder to escort him to where Master Coppinger lay. Conditions here were little better than that Common Ward where Greene had visited Roger Flamstead on Coppinger's behalf: the same filth, the same sullen silence or thick uproar, the same stench of humanity and its emissions, the same gamblers, the same harpies about their loathsome trades. Coppinger was lying on a clean bed, though, and some earlier visitor had brushed away the mess from the floor about him. His father, so the warder told him, who had left not long since. He had shifted his son's clothes too. Saying so, the fellow held his nose between finger and thumb, assuring Greene with oaths that the stink of a morning was ten times worse than the Fleet brook, and that until he had a dram inside him he was more a monkey than a man. Then, his hint unheeded, he swore none the less and moved away.

Coppinger's eyes were closed, and Greene stood by him for a while wondering whether he should speak. Despite the sunken cheeks, the hollows of his eyes, the whitened hair and beard stubble, he thought his friend's face had now again something of the serenity that had distinguished it at Cambridge. His breathing was light, his chest hardly lifting with it. His eyes filled with tears as he watched him, remembering the hundred kindnesses Coppinger had shown him, his care and watchfulness at Cambridge, his devotion to what he thought right. Why, why, why? The insoluble problem of the good man's deserts came to vex him, and Kate's words—"Stuffing our tripes with good food, money to spend, someone to warm our backs in bed." No trust in godliness. Well, it had brought Edmund to a pitiful pass. Death on a pallet, with thieves and murderers and loose women about him. Yet he thought, as oftentimes before, this man had some quality of happiness denied men like himself. Why then weep for him?

"Edmund?" he whispered, bending down beside him. "Edmund?"

His eyes opened at once. "Who is it?" he asked, in a whisper lower than Greene's. "You, Robert?"

"I came to see you. I heard you were ill, Edmund. Are you better?"

The trite, ridiculous question! He knew it.

"I shall soon be well, I think."

A quarrel at cards cut off the end of his sentence. Greene sat on a corner of his bed, inclined forward to hear him. "They hanged *him?*" Coppinger asked. "You were there?"

"I was there, Edmund."

"Tell me."

It was a different account, this, from that he had given Kate.

Coppinger stirred. "I have sometimes thought, lying here, Robert, that we were indeed mad. So much of it I cannot remember. So much of it——"

Greene patted his shoulder. "No matter about that. You must get better, leave Bridewell here, go back to your mother and father. You have done your share, suffered too much. There is a fine life ahead of you, Edmund, once you get better. Cambridge again, St. John's, books and disputations. I'll come there with you. Never fear."

"You are a dear fellow, Robert, to say these things." He smiled at Greene, the old lovely smile. "But I'll not go back. I am going forward, Robert, into that great unknown future where only the mercy of God can avail us anything." He appeared to summon up strength from some recess of mind and body. "I think what we have done will matter little, for he is a good Father. If we were demented, He will not misjudge." He caught his breath for a half minute. "You believe in hell fire, Robert?"

"I must, God help me from it!"

"Don't believe, Robert. For though it burns beneath our feet, there is none our Father will leave there." He smiled again. "That is heresy, Robert, isn't it? Maybe I should burn in this world for that, for men are less merciful than God. I have been lying here as though a thousand years— I have looked back over all my days, and I see that my life has been ugly in His sight. But I am not afraid to face Him. Maybe He will think the rack was enough." They sat quiet for a time, and then the dying man started to speak again. "For one thing I would stay, Robert. One regret I have, that I may not live for a new mission, to call the earth to compassion and pity. We are in need of them more than laws and faiths and judgments. Christ

excelled us most in that, that his compassion for mankind was such that he shed his blood for us. To make
that a text to rouse the world—but I'll not live to do
it."

"Of course you'll live, Edmund. In here I know it is
easy to be despondent, but once we get you outside all will
be different."

Coppinger had closed his eyes. "Yes," he said,
"yes."

"You are tired. I must go. I'll come back to-morrow.
Your father has been here?" He thought Coppinger
nodded slightly. "I'll say good-bye, Edmund." But his
tears fell fast from him, some on Coppinger's forehead as
he bent to kiss him. He opened his eyes again. "You are
crying? Don't cry for me, Robert. I am very happy. I
have found something here I never knew life held. Good-
bye. You'll not forget me?"

"Oh, Edmund! Edmund!"

"And never forget my words, Robert. Be compassionate
beyond desert. The world is in need of that. Some day
we'll laugh together, Robert." His head sank tiredly back.
"Good-bye."

Greene stumbled away, frantic with misery. To be away!
To be alone! To weep and weep and ease his stuffed-up
heart! God help Edmund and all men and take them in
his keeping for ever. Past the indignant turnkey he wiped
his eyes before entering Hunter's room, whom he found
playing at cards with some of his inferiors. Seeing Greene,
he looked up from his hand. "Arthington has recanted,"
he said briefly. Greene nodded, unwilling to speak, and
went through the gates into the fresh air. He cursed Arthington with savage oaths, to relieve his grief for Coppinger.
Two men come to their reason, Coppinger dying and this
cur Arthington must recant! Was Coppinger's compassion
for such as he? It was an hour before he saw how wasted
his indignation was. He could not return to Knightrider
Street till late into the evening. He was too upset, and he
knew how indifferent brother and sister would be to his

sorrow. Why go back at all? he asked himself half-heartedly; for go he would and he knew it. Something drew him powerfully to Kate. Bad as she was, cold towards other people's troubles, she had established sway over him in so short a time like that of the sprite of Helen over Faustus, in Marlowe's play. He could not see himself leaving her.

That night in bed, he asked her: "What is the finest thing in the world, Kate?" Turning like an eel, she gave him a lewd answer, and though he had intended to give her something very like a sermon she would not cease till he had entered into her mood and loved her with a brutal intensity that shocked him even at the flood-tide of his passion. Later he could lie awake and think: Poor Edmund! How little the world would care for your doctrine and mission though you should be spared to carry it out. What compassion in lust? In selfish love? What compassion in ambition, in the amassing of wealth, in the struggle for reputation, in the bare fight for daily bread? The finest thing in the world! Now, his whole being tuned to purity and pity, he could not resist the urge of his own desire, could not beat off this slut, this siren with a throat of oil, but must call her his darling, his golden woman, his Kate. Clearly and with loathing he saw himself the swine into which Circe turned those who denied themselves nothing of greed. His life was beastly. He thought: All that is good in it is my work. And who am I to pronounce on that?

The next morning he was again a visitor to Bridewell. For twenty minutes he talked with Hunter, for Coppinger's father was with him and Greene shrank from intrusion. Hunter thought he would not see the day out, so at last Greene made his way to where his friend lay. The old man was busy about his son, who had just died. He had straightened his limbs and closed his eyes, and on Coppinger's face was that wonderful unworldly peace of those who die easily and happy. Greene did not stay. He said not a word, but walked slowly back from the Ward and away from the prison. His thoughts turned to his own mother far off in Tombland, how she would feel if he died, and ashamedly he muttered a short prayer for Charity Coppinger, waiting for news beyond the Bars.

He hated Kate and Harry.

CHAPTER XXXV

Edmund's death would have affected Greene harder had it not been for his immediate dealings with Kate and Harry. Somehow his grief for him, real, even poignant though it was, was swept away by the press of Harry's dangerous business and his infatuation for Kate. And he had little chance to talk of it. There was a visit to Edmund's parents and nothing more of tenderness. Nashe refused to be bothered with it more than brother and sister. "Ah well, he is out of all his troubles," was more or less what they told him. "Dead men are best forgotten. Time enough to worry when it comes to our own turn." They even thought Coppinger lucky to miss the gallows, with full rites.

There was the question of a living for Greene. They had a talk around the table one afternoon. "This writing," Harry asked bluntly; "it brings you in—what?"

Greene calculated, caressed his beard, looked at Kate. "My new play should bring me twenty nobles, maybe more."

Harry looked at Kate too. "How long before you finish it?"

"Once I get started, a week. I shall have to make a copy of parts of it, though."

"Then the sooner you get started the better."

He tried to explain that poets did not write to order. At least—it was not easy to put it into words they would not blow away contemptuously—not their best work, work for immortality.

"Has immortality a belly to fill?" Harry asked bluntly. "You have, don't forget."

Greene tried to silence him with a superior smile.

"And you'll have to fill it for yourself from now on, Robert." He tapped on the table. "Well?" Greene sitting silent, he brought Kate in to clinch it. "That is, if you want to stay with Kate and me."

Greene pondered. "I have an idea," he announced slowly.

"Have you a gold piece or the prospect of one—that is more to the purpose?"

"This is worth a lot of gold pieces." He winked at Kate. "Listen, Harry!"

It was a development of his determination that night he walked out of Doll's bedroom the last time, that he would exploit the tale of low life, put through a dozen changes the story of the Prodigal Son, and with a sufficiency of invention put his own life into fiction. *Never Too Late* and *Francesco's Fortunes*—hadn't they sold well? There was money in it, plain to see! And now, what of an exposure of rascalities, as Harman had done it, only better? Harry to supply the raw material from his undoubtedly plentiful store and he work it up into literary form. Talking to convince them, he convinced himself still more. The book-sellers would fight for the stuff. Once they saw the first pamphlet they'd be like tomcats after it. And easy—pooh, it would be the merest snap of the fingers to him! The Barnard Law, the Trugging Law, the Cross-Biting Law, the Vincent's Law—how many more? And if you told lies, so much the better. What a variety of wit-living gentry! What gradations of crimes and their practitioners! It was bound to pay.

Harry shook his head. That Greene was a writer was to the good—it proved him a rogue like himself—but a man must have more than one string to his bow if he would thrive. "I was thinking of something quite different, Robert." He smiled as though he were Greene's best friend. "A matter of a bill drawn on the right person, Robert."

Greene too shook his head. "I couldn't do that, Harry."

"So you said before. I think you could. I like your handwriting. It looks to me the kind the unwary pay out on."

Greene looked worriedly towards Kate. "Don't you think my idea the better one, Kate?" He had the feeling that he was slowly but surely being driven to the awkwardest corner of the field. "And it keeps us on the right side of the law too."

"You, maybe, Robin. Not Harry and me."

Later he begged them to let him finish his play first, anyhow. It was *James the Fourth*. He was already at the end of Act Four, and he thought it the best history yet produced. If the Queen's Men did justice to it at the representation, it might well put Marlowe's nose out of joint as badly as *Friar Bacon* had done. He had not seen Marlowe for a long time, did not even know whether he was still in London, only those rumours that he and some fellow up from the country were patching up the old chronicle play of *Henry the Sixth*. Shakespeare or some such name. Marlowe must be going off, perhaps those first triumphs had sucked the marrow from his bones, and now he must seek collaboration with the veriest clod-hopper to make any showing at all.

"What of it, Harry?"

Watching Harry weigh the question, he was thinking with a touch of shame that were it not for Kate he'd throw brother Harry over the house and off to go. Hanging on another man's word like this! He narrowed his eyes with dislike, and Harry did not overlook the fact.

"We'll give you a fortnight to produce your twenty nobles," he agreed at last.

"And I'll pay you everything I owe you," Greene promised. "And, Kate, you and I'll need for nothing that day, I can tell you."

So *James the Fourth* it was. He worked hard and with a conviction that what he was doing took on a life of its own. Cinthio had given him the plot and most of the characters; he had but to transpose his action, time and scene, for a moderate success; but with this he was not content. Ida and the chaste Dorothea grew like daughters of his own, nothing in them of Kate. All part of them was father save their middle; purity and dignity were natural to his pen as he set down their words. It seemed to him his verse had never shown such flexibility, such range and mastery; that now he attained perfect fusion of form and material. Marlowe indeed! Shakespeare! George Pyeboard! By God and by Jesus, he'd show them the way to write histories. More thought, more honourable emotion, more tribute to the good things—something of Edmund in this play, he thought. The company would leap at work like this. It was half a regret that it must go to the Queen's Men. No doubt of it, since the death of Tarleton they were in less repute. Fewer performances at Court, more time in the country. Still—to an extent he was a beggar, and the proverb held good. But not for one penny less than six pounds—not one penny! He could always play the Admiral's Men off against them, if they tried to rob him.

But the Queen's Men haggled only for form's sake before paying him his price. He reminded them: Alleyn had his hands on the two parts of *Henry the Sixth*, reworked by Marlowe and Shakespeare; they must have their counterblast. Wilson, biting his fingernail, nodded his head and suggested that nothing could make it surer the Admiral's Men would not look at another history; but they were old friends and understood each other, the manuscript and gold changed hands, there were careful signatures at the bottom of the agreement, no tactless reference to the twofold sale of *Orlando*, and Greene was hurrying back to Kate, hoping Harry would be elsewhere.

"Where's Harry?" he asked.

"Out."

"Thank the angels for that! Look, Kate—look at the money!" He flipped a coin up against the ceiling and dived desperately after it as it was deflected from the beam and rolled into the corner of the room.

"Oh, Good God, be careful, Good-Fellow!" She put her hand to her heart and pretended to pant with alarm.

"I want you to come out with me, Kate. Now. Yes,

this very minute! Put your cloak on—go on. We'll spend some of it, eh?"

She laughed. "You make me laugh, Robin, you do. Why the hurry?"

"Because it's the first time since we met that I've had money to spend on you, and I'll not wait for my pleasure longer than it takes you to get into this cloak. Here!" He ran to get it and began bundling it over her shoulders as though tying up linen.

"What about washing my face first?"

Margaret had faded. "Never mind that! You look magnificent. Come on."

"There's companionship in your own dirt," she admitted. "I once knew a man, Robin, used to wash all over every month, except in the winter of course."

"He should have been born a fish. Come on."

He took her to a mercer's in Cheapside and watched her choose stuffs for a dress and a cloak and fumble with a dozen changes of mind among piles of kerchiefs and bands for the hair. She was Hebe, she was Venus or Ceres, none other than Syrian Astarte! She was—he narrowed his eyes —need she be quite so familiar with that mercer fellow? Was it fancy or did her eye turn his way invitingly? Of course it was fancy. He was elated carrying her bundle back to their lodging.

"Give me a kiss for these, Kate!"

"And another to-morrow for more!"

He wouldn't promise. "Do you love me more when I have money, Kate?"

"Of course I do."

"When I have things to give you?" He wanted her to answer No. Whether she meant it or not, to say the fine, right, splendid things.

"Wouldn't anybody?"

He took her hand. "I wouldn't, Kate. What you had or had not would make no difference to me. No, Kate —don't laugh. I mean it. If I could take you in your shift I'd be satisfied."

And he would. But she answered with the obvious witticism, and he had to shake his head sorrowfully at her. "You are past hope, Kate, God help you."

Then she asked: "When will you grow tired of me, Good-Fellow, now you have money in your purse?"

"Never, Kate. I wish to God you wouldn't say things like that! If you knew how angry they make me!"

She smiled at him so affably he would never suspect her capable of such a question. "You'd not make a cross-biter, I can see."

He began to tremble. She saw the twisting of his face. "Kate, if that brother of yours—— You can tell him, I mean it—I'd kill him, Kate, as God is my judge, if he tries that again!"

"You would?" She was contemptuous of him, and he knew it.

"Why do you make me unhappy?" he asked her. "When I came home wanting only to please you, and now you say things so terrible!"

She knew she had gone too far. "Why worry, Robin? You take everything I say for gospel. Where's the fun in you?"

"Fun! I'd kill him, Kate. I mean it. Don't tempt me too far! Say you'll never say such things again, Kate!"

To pacify him she promised, promised him everything he went on to ask. She would have promised him the stars from heaven. She knew all poets were mad, but he must be the maddest. Life to him must be a player's dream. And she his Margaret, maid of Fressingfield.

"When shall I see your new play?" she asked, and smiled as he cheered up and began to talk, hesitantly at first and then with his customary flow, of the treat in store. He was a child and a fool. But she must tell Harry how he had reacted to her suggestion. She would be willing to share any man: why shouldn't he share a woman? Well, Harry would know what to do.

They went together to the first performance of *James the Fourth*. Wilson and Johnson, Adams and Dutton, the

old hands were in the cast; and the boys Richard Palmer
and George Grimes delicately suitable for Ida and Dorothea.
Droussen the hack had written in a comic scene or two,
and as they unfolded, Greene had to admit they were
not so bad as they might be. Harry he could not persuade
to attend, but for Kate and himself there were seats in
the first gallery, and he was less embarrassed than proud
to be greeted by Tom Nashe and Monox. There were
introductions, and he thought Tom made himself more
ridiculous than impressive by the string of highfaluting
compliments he delivered, hand on heart. Behind her
back, resplendent in the dress and cloak made from Greene's
present, both Tom and Monox jerked up their thumbs in
approval, and grimaced their envy. He was partly gratified,
partly annoyed, his attention divided betwixt their antics,
Kate's appearance, and the glories of his play. The audience
took to it like wine. He could have blown kisses to the
honest louts standing in the yard who clapped their heavy
hands together, thumping applause. "You like it?" he
asked Kate, between acts. She thought it not so good as
Friar Bacon, championing Margaret because she knew this
would please him; but his friends were emphatic he had
done nothing better. "I don't say, mind," Nashe began,
but Wilson strutted forward, and his reservations remained
his own property. It was near the end of the play that
Monox plucked silently at Greene's sleeve, and then pointed
down to the corner near the right hand cheap entrance.
"Behind the fat man in brown," he whispered. Greene
craned forward, then leaned back and winked at Will.
He could see Marlowe distinctly, standing behind the fat
man, and as he watched he saw him talking to a man much
his own age at his side. "Shakespeare," Monox whispered
again. Greene nodded, grinning now. They would have
something to talk about, he doubted not. What were they
thinking of their own play now? The Admiral's Men would
soon know they were riding the wrong horse. Play-cobblers,
nothing better. Creeping in among the groundlings to pick
up an idea or two, were they? At the idea he glowed with

good temper. He'd not begrudge them a lesson in their trade. Marlowe like an old pear tree, gone past bearing: this Shakespeare fellow looking for hints. He saw Nashe staring too, and grinned across at him, "Promising lads come to school," he whispered.

He decided to have a word with Marlowe before he went. Leaning past Kate, he suggested to Nashe that he keep them talking in the street for a few minutes till he could come down. "Who is it?" Kate asked sharply. He squeezed her hand. "Mouther Marlowe. The man with the loudest stage voice in London." She shrugged her shoulders. "Well, don't spoil your own play by whispering." He sat back, huffed. Who had a better right to spoil it than he? The thought was so absurd he had to smile again.

The play ended and now, not keeping to his original plan, he made a hurried excuse to Kate and left her with Monox, while Nashe and he ran down to the street. Sure enough, they were in time to see Marlowe and his companion turning towards the Horse and Hounds. "Remember how you parted," Nashe warned him, but he only waved his hand. "He will be glad to see me."

"Hullo, Marlowe," he said mildly, pushing up behind the pair of them. Marlowe stopped dead. His hand dropped, but Greene was holding up both of his. "No need," he laughed. "Let the years bring their changes, Marlowe."

Marlowe looked rapidly at all his companions. "Very well," he said finally. "Why not?" He too laughed. "I'll be dead soon enough, without your dagger through my eye." He shook Greene by the hand.

"You have been seeing my play?"

"Why not?"

"No reason at all. I hope you learned something, eh?" He tried to sound inoffensive as he said it. "I wish you had had a seat. If I had known you and your friend——"

"Ah yes. Will, this is Robert Greene, of Cambridge. Master William Shakespeare, of Stratford-on-Avon."

"And Nashe—don't forget honest Tom!"

"Honest? Will, after Greene here he's the biggest bastard this side Ireland. Never trust one of them!"

"As for Marlowe—hell flames!"

They began to laugh together with a forced good fellow-ship, edging friendly insults with venom. "Well," said Marlowe, "we were going to drink in the Horse and Hounds. The successful author, his pockets loaded with moidores——" He looked across at the tavern.

"And I will! Gentlemen, the reckoning must be mine. But we have other friends. If you will permit me——" He made such explanations as Nashe could amplify and hurried back to the theatre. He could not forget his respects to the players. They must be invited to the Horse and Hounds. And there was Kate. Though it would certainly be easier if she were not——

Nor was she. Of Monox and her not a sign. The blood ran from his cheeks, flushed hotly back again, he went rushing from one place to another. What could possess that imbecile Monox to lose him like this? Behind stage he had quick promises to meet him at the tavern, but where in the name of hell and all its fiends was Kate? The sus-picion that she might have gone off with Monox could not be kept at bay. He could not harbour it without sickness. He'd cut the bastard's throat, he'd split his guts like a dead pig's, he'd—— Where, where, where could the infernal fools be?

He hurried off to see old Jeffryson, who collected tup-pences at the Sausage Street door. Had he seen the lady and gentleman who had sat with him earlier? Jeffryson had. The lady that was with Master Monox? They had gone off together up the street. Looking very pleased with him-self, was Master Monox. Greene stood glaring, hearing this. Gone off up the street. He had always known she was a whore. You bitch! he called her. You sow! You common-pasture, bull-bearing——"

And Monox! For a moment he could not see, then he threw the keeper a coin, turned away.

Do what? He walked slowly over to the tavern, mastering

himself. He must be calm. No one must know. He'd not be all men's fool, bare his heart for an unwashed whore, let them and her laugh at him. But afterwards! Though it meant the end, he'd settle.

Drink though. That was it. Forget her, forget she was with Monox, stifle thought and imagination. Drink! Drink! Drink!

The company was assembled, save for the more dilatory players. Nashe had begun ordering on his, Greene's, account. He greeted them almost furiously, called the drawers, gave bigger orders. He had sent her home, he replied grandly to a question from Nashe; he put down a pot of ale, and before Nashe could express his surprise was asking Marlowe where he had been hiding himself so long. He had non-committal answers, and as though to shield himself Marlowe kept pushing Shakespeare forward. Greene unnecessarily asked him which College he had graced or disgraced at Oxford. None? Nor Cambridge? Greene made a show of ill-concealed amazement, and then, as though he had routed an enemy, put down another pot. "Well, Master Shakespeare," he admitted, "but for good fortune and good wits I might have had nothing more than a grammar school education myself." "You surprise me," said Shakespeare gently. He watched Greene drink deeply the third time.

They broke up an hour and a half later, leaving Greene with a huge bill. He thought of flinging his tankard in Marlowe's face, for it suddenly seemed to him that Marlowe was delighted to have taken money out of his pocket, but somehow he controlled himself. Instead he spoke vain-gloriously about hail-fellow-well-met and Robin Good-fellow not begrudging any lousy rascal a cup of wine so long as he had the price of it. Not like some. He looked straight at Marlowe and repeated his words: NOT LIKE SOME. Excitement had gone to his head, and what he drank that much quicker to his legs. "I'll see you home," said Nashe, but he refused his offer. See him home indeed! "He thinks I'm drunk," he told Shakespeare.

"Foolish fellow!" said Shakespeare enigmatically. He went off with Marlowe.

It was mid-evening when Greene returned home. At first he had decided never to return, go off with some of his friends, and let the Balls go hellwards on their own. Yet not even the way his friends had praised his play could drive Kate from his mind. He hated Nashe almost as much as Monox, remembering the thumbs up of the theatre. See him home indeed! He began by hurrying, but soon slowed down, uncertainty tried him greatly, and he made and unmade resolutions every fifty yards of his journey. He'd not see her, he'd kill Monox, maybe it was all a mistake, he'd tear the clothes he had bought her from her back and march away, he'd find her home, he'd not find her home. Was he not eating the prodigal's husks? To give your heart into a giglot's keeping, the sister of a snatch-purse, a shameless—— Christ, how she was shameless! If only he had never seen her! Without in the least deceiving himself he even thought: If only I had stayed at Norwich!

Well, here was the street. It was enter or stay out, no third option. He wished he were drunker, so that brutality would come easy. He pushed open the door.

She was sitting calmly by the table, exactly as he had left her at the Bull except that she was without her cloak. Possibly to pass the time away she was unpicking the seam of a grubby gown.

"Well?" he said.

"If it's not Robin Good-Fellow!" She went on with what she was doing.

"I said—Where have you been?"

"Where have you for that matter?"

"You impudent bitch!"

She threw down the work she was at and stood up. It seemed to him the wind whistled up her nostrils, she breathed in so fiercely. He stood momentarily helpless watching the strong sweet pillar of her throat. "What did you say?"

"I said you were an impudent bitch. And I'll say so again. You are an impudent bitch."

"And what are you?" She evidently thought he would strike her and was prepared for battle. "What are you so fine?"

"Never mind what I am. None the better for meeting you, I dare say! Where did you go? What have you been doing? Tell me that!"

Her temper was suddenly calmer. She sat down again. "I might, when you trouble to ask me properly." She took up the gown, and he lost what had been very nearly his fear of her.

"Why did you go, Kate?" he asked, less roughly.

"Who went first?"

"But I only went——"

"And I only went! What did you expect me to do? Sit till I got corns or you were pleased to come and find me? All because you saw some three-halfpenny friends of yours and wanted their company more than mine?" She shook the gown. "And what next, Robin?"

"Where did you go then?" he asked. "If that devil's dung Monox——"

"What, Robin?"

He was not too earnest to suspect she was now laughing at him. "Kate," he cried, "don't make me unhappy. I can't quarrel with you. It's desolation to me. Tell me it's all right. Tell me you didn't."

"Sometimes you are such a fool. Of course I didn't. But I wasn't going to stay upstairs there waiting your pleasure or anyone else's. You took me out for the afternoon, and when you do that—if you find somebody else, so will I. Isn't that fair enough?"

His relief was such that he could have danced. "I've been as miserable as hell, Kate. I never knew anyone in the world could make me so miserable. Let's forget about it, shall we?"

They did so, before Harry's return. She could not finish her story before he was reproaching himself extravagantly for leaving her even for a minute, taking all the blame upon himself, making her laugh at the threats he had uttered against Will Monox—some of them—promising a hundred things he thought would delight her, asking her fifty times to say she loved him. Yet, strangely, he could never feel certain that she did. Some sourness was always in his cup. One day this would end, ignominiously he feared. Women of pleasure never convert. He had her own word for it.

"You ought," she said all at once, "to help Harry as he asks." And when he shook his head: "Help us all at the same time. Why not, Robin? Harry has been a good friend to you. And you promised, remember?"

Clumsily he tried to explain that when he made that promise—well, couldn't she see for herself that they could never expect—— No, she retorted, she could see nothing of the kind. "Did they never tell you in school, Robin: honour among thieves, Robin?" At first he wanted indignantly to deny he was a thief, but second thoughts were best. "To please me, Robin, even if you won't do it for Harry. I should think the more of it then, Robin." He wriggled. "I'd do anything for you, Kate, you know it. But I can't do this." She raised her eyebrows and started to unpick the same old seam. For a minute or two he watched her, and then placed his hand on her arm. She shook it off, wordless.

"What exactly does he want?" he asked dubiously.

By the end of the year Harry and he were in partnership. In two ways they worked together. First, Harry agreed to supply him with the raw material of the conny-catching pamphlets; secondly, he put his penmanship at his—well, why not?—his brother-in-law's command. The results were profitable. In December John Wolfe printed for a good price his *Notable Discovery*, with a new motto for the title page, *Nascimur pro patria*, We are born for our country's good. Into this he had worked a loose account of that Barnard's Law or art of card-sharping he himself had suffered from on his first visit to London, and the Cross-Biting Law or your-money-for-the-use-of-my-wife lay which he did his best to forget Harry and Kate knew at first hand. As a makeweight he threw in some of the tricks practised by colliers in London, most of them feeble stuff, but covering the page blackly enough. Harry was immensely taken with his pose of reforming the town by such exposures, and rejoiced in the high moral tone of Greene's prefatory letter. Within a fortnight he had been approached by William Wright for another book of the same kind, at an enhanced price, and this time he did tongue-in-his-cheek justice to the mysteries of the Prigging or Horse-Stealing Law, the Lifting Law, and the Black Art or picking of locks. To justify his motto, he set before this a lurid account of how the conny-catchers and cross-biters, frightened by his exposure of their methods, had sworn either to break his bones or hack off that right hand which so confounded them, but he, Greene, born for his country's good, defied them, and though his reward should be death or such mutilation as the Roman Scevola's, would continue to work for justice and innocence against wickedness and guile. He would be the first to admit to friends intimate enough that there was some poorish stuff here too, but he had a crowd waiting to be fed, and who was he, the first professional man of letters England had known, to let them and himself in their different ways go hungry? The other booksellers were pricking up their ears, they'd be wanting their share of the profits, there would be imitators, but none of them as good as the originator. He could work this vein half a dozen times at least. The three of them had now moved their lodgings and were staying with a shoemaker and his wife, Isam by name, in Dowgate; and here, one night in early January, snug in a chair by a good coal fire, he saw that the next move after pretended threats against himself was a well-written reply pretending to pour scorn on Robert Greene. And who could supply it better than himself? Hm, hm? He outlined his plan to Harry and Kate, who thought it a good one and entered eagerly into its spirit, and before they went to bed they had their course planned. There should be a third part of conny-catching in a month's time, preferably printed by Scarlet for Burdie, and after that a *Defence*, ostensibly by one Cuthbert Conny-Catcher, attacking Greene bitterly and at the same time slily exploiting further rogues' laws, and ending with savage threats. To this Greene should reply in his own name with yet a fourth pamphlet, not more than a fortnight later, and rapidly follow this up with a fifth and promises of a sixth and seventh. It would be a help to sales and therefore to prices if he should give out that the enraged conny-catchers had attacked him in force, wounded him even; there would be no harm in printed names that he invented, or in escorting imaginary scoundrels to Tyburn. "And when we have run through all the laws you know, Harry," he vowed, "we'll start inventing them. What of it?"

They seemed often to be asking each other just that question. What of it this? What of it that? He told himself he'd be picking pockets soon if Harry had his way.

His first gift of penmanship to Harry was the copying of a bill drawn by Sir Walter Thorne on Egbert Flood, the city merchant. The clerk's hand of the agreement was child's play. It was the signature that demanded the artist; but after twenty or more attempts he had the way of it, and Harry, who was not afraid to risk his neck, presented it and successfully cleared the money. Taking his share, Greene yet detested the business. Frankly, he was frightened. If anything went wrong, it was the Fleet or Bridewell, and he had seen them in all their glory; and after that the Tree, and by all the gods of hell he had seen that too in all its glory. When a man couldn't call his neck his own—brrr!

Harry meditated the drafting of other bills. He had never forgotten Adam Bolton and swore he would bleed him before he finished. Meanwhile he put forward a safe and easy plan for a quick gain. Greene knew that Peele was ill with an inflammation which would keep him to his bed for another fortnight, so Harry, hearing this, suggested he forge a note from Peele to the Admiral's Men and to Nashe out at Croydon, and send it by a girl he knew the age of Peele's daughter by his first marriage, asking for money. This seemed to Greene despicable and he flatly refused to have anything to do with it. Harry looked unbelieving at first, and then unpleasant.

"You think yourself too good for it?"

Greene declared emphatically that he did.

"Listen to him, Kate. Did you ever hear such a stretch-conscience? He spends five nights a week hatching out frauds with us and then finds a little egg like this too big to fit under his feathers."

"But hell beneath you, man," Greene cried; "there is all the difference in the world between the two things. The one may not be honest but at least it is not foul to heaven. When it's a question of your own good friends there is no more in it than proper decency."

"Is it? I thought you gave up decency a long time ago, Greene."

"When I met you, you must mean! Anyhow, you are wrong."

"A man with your past to have the cold impudence to pick and choose what he will do!"

"Never mind my past! It is better than yours."

"Listen to this fellow of yours, Kate! Just listen to your fine white boy!"

The gibe hurt by its truth. "By God, Harry Ball——"

"Oh, stop quarrelling," she interrupted. "A pair of fools, nothing better, the pair of you. What's the good of fighting when we are all alive and comfortable? Can't you think of something else, Harry?"

"Yes," he said baitingly; "you and Rednob here can try the old cross-biting game again." She frowned and Greene went white. "Why not?" He smacked the table impatiently. "For Christ's sake, Greene, either call yourself honest and get out of doors or stay with us, black or white, and make a good job of it!"

"There will be no more work of that kind for Kate again," Greene said savagely.

"You are not the one to decide!"

"I warn you, Harry—I'll put a knife through you if you try it!"

Harry made a rude noise. "That for you and your knife! And don't act the player here. We took you in for charity and for my part I'll have no regrets when we see the last of you."

"We?"

"Yes. We. Kate stays with me. Eh, Kate?"

"So long as it suits me. I'll stay with no one I don't want to."

"Then let him do his share," said Harry.

Kate got up to put the supper for them. "Let the talk rest overnight. We are far from starving." She turned to them from the cupboard. "And there will be no cross-biting just yet." Greene rose to his feet with gratitude. "I shall know within a week whether I'm with child by Good-Fellow."

The two men stared at her. "Hell take your soul," cried Harry, "for a fiftyfold fool! You'd have to carry a bitch-drop for this fool Greene.!"

"Hold your tongue!" shouted Greene.

"Hold my tongue! Hold my——" He jerked his head with unspeakable disgust. For a long fraught moment brother and lover seemed ready for each other's throat. Then Harry walked away, grabbed for his hat and cloak, and with one foul word for his sister had gone, slamming the door behind him.

Greene stood there, plucking at his breeches. "Is it true, Kate?"

"You think I'm as big a fool as yourself? As I said, we shall soon know. Then we can decide what to do."

"No," he said hoarsely. "No, you mustn't, Kate. If it is—then it's got to be born, Kate. I could never again hold up my head——" He stood staring at her. "I can't believe it, Kate."

"I fail to see why not," she jested. "You think very poorly of yourself, Good-Fellow."

In the first week of February, that dreadful month of cold and snow, they knew for certain she was with child by Greene. By that time they had had every chance to think the matter out severally. Harry had the clearest ideas of all of them, he expressed them once and once only, and then kept his mouth shut as the way of least harm. He despised his sister for being such a fool, was at first mad against Greene for springing the trap, but he never cried after spilt milk. He would not risk Kate's life, but maybe once the child came—he would nod his head, thinking of the possibilities. A bribed midwife, clumsy handling, a finger and thumb momentarily across the tiny nostrils—yes, there were possibilities. Kate seemed neither glad nor sorry at her condition. A hint now and again— Greene was afraid to ask whether she had been pregnant before. For his part what could he think? Would he choose to have a child by her? He thought not. And yet, now that in her womb was the burgeoning of life that was part of his life too, his seed coming to crinkly, fleshy flower, he felt a great tenderness for mother and babe to be. Mingled with this was renewed remorse for his desertion of Doll and Kit back there at Norwich. He heaped on himself a thousand gloomy curses for his heartlessness and selfishness, made resolves impossible of execution to find out how they were at home, plans for a visit to Braiding even, where Alice could tell him everything. Would he be as bad a father to this mite as to Kit? He vowed not, and yet could place no faith in his own self-promises. Had he not vowed before?

But this time he had the perfect excuse for making no move. The weather would not permit it. The snow had started on the third day of the month, and with intervals of frost and sleet continued till the ninth, so that in the memory of living men there had been no such drifts and snowbanks. Reports coming in from the villages around

London told of lanes filled, gates and hedges, even houses, submerged; and on the morning of the eleventh Greene, fighting his way through a salt-like snow to the wharf at Steel-Yard was able to confirm rumours of the previous evening that the river was freezing over. The snow-spray was too dense for him to see the far side of the river. On such days men took the world on trust. It was blanketed out of sight and knowledge. One would as soon seek Scotland as Chelsea. As he went the beaten, muffled way towards the Bridge he could see the ice ever thicker. The smaller boats had been lifted from the water many days before, but below the Bridge there were motionless sailing ships, as it were huddled together with their canvas furled, and no sign of life on board. Struck with a kind of desolation, he left the river by way of New Fish Street, and so through the east end of Thames Street back home. The wind was in his face now, the snow scalded his skin like red-hot needles, and he was exhausted when at last he came indoors. Reality was paled by his description of the scene to Kate and Harry. They sat over the fire an hour or two. "The strangest thing about it is the quiet!" Kate exclaimed. The snow in the most-travelled roads had been trampled to a stone, but not a footstep sounded on it, not a wagon wheel bit through it, the coaches that usually rumbled and rattled and bumped and clattered now went smoothly and noiselessly forward. For days together they had not heard the familiar trap-trap of horses. And each day the cold was growing more intense, keeping travellers off the road not even the snow had daunted, and by holding up all dealings at the wharves intensifying the silence. They wondered how it would end.

"Are you warm enough, sweetheart?" he asked Kate, and wanted to fetch a blanket from the bed to put over her shoulders.

It was to grow still colder, though more cheerful. From the twelfth till the seventeenth there was no more snow, but appalling temperatures by night and no sun by day. The sky was a dull and near thing. The river was now frozen so thickly that it was preferred as a highway to the snow-clogged streets. Coaches fitted with drags, the horses with their feet tied up in cloths, ran smartly up and down between the Court and the great houses; as though English-men could turn an honest penny under any conditions booths were set up in rows; there was more chaffering and cheapening there than on land; the Queen's Majesty, with a rare start of generosity, supplied a little money for fireworks for her faithful subjects, and, as she expected, sycophants supplied much more, and Lord Charters an ox for roasting. For more than a week there was an enforced public holiday, and the lucky ones made the most of it. The unlucky ones —they found some of them as the snow cleared later. Plenty of hot food, plenty of hot drink, warm clothes and heavy —those were the things. Greene remembered Sidley's cloak of black and white fur—that would be the thing. Sidley, eh? And here he was, stuffing his tripes with good food, money to spend, and someone to warm his back in bed. If only Kate had a cloak like that, though! If he saw one lying about where a snatch and a saunter would do the business, he'd not be uncomfortably honest. It was not the same as stealing for yourself. Think of Robin Hood.

They were on the ice for the fireworks. He could not wrap Kate up enough. "I shall look like a plum pudding," she complained, but he went on tucking a scarf around her neck. "You'll look divine—and you know it, Kate." Harry would not keep them company. While fools gaped at fire splashes, hot fingers took their chances. He looked a muscovite, save for his shoes.

The ox was roasted a whole afternoon on the ice opposite the Three Cranes. Such was the thickness there, the fire itself burned on ice, and the enormous tripod which sup-ported the carcase was spiked down to a depth of almost two feet. On a day colder than charity, darkness setting in by half-past four, there could be no braver sight in the whole cold world than the char and glow of the huge logs and the constantly dripping carcase of the monster; no braver smell than the richness of prime beef in chill nostrils;

no braver prospect than a full belly and fireworks to come. The fireworks should go off from the Lambeth side opposite the Savoy; Her Majesty was expected to watch them. It was likely the day would end with great cheers and shoutings for her.

"You thought the silence the strangest part of this frost, Kate. You could hardly think that to-day, could you? You know what I find strangest?" She shook her head, holding on to his arm. "That, look where you will, there are no horse-droppings throughout London."

Nor were there. The birds, some native, some drawn to the towns like men before them for want, some winging it from the river and sea flats further down, set the city officers a new standard of scavenging. Not the tiniest particle of animal rubbish they did not spy out and devour. Even so, they died in thousands, their little bodies in turn devoured by the flesh-eaters among them. Now, despite darkness, there was a flurry of gulls over the roasting, their hunger sending them down and down again in hopeless raids, and balked, with short raucous screams of despair back into the night. Eat or die, he thought; the same for birds and men. Sauntering like a lord, his golden woman on his arm, he was in the mood when men discourse at large.

They had their slice of beef among the first, spent more than an hour with hot punch in a wooden inn erected off Broken Wharf, so rich in memories of Coppinger and Hacket, some of which he told her over their drink. Then they set off in time to get a good position at the display of fireworks. They had seen nothing of the shrouded Harry, and Greene was glad of it.

Almost there, who should they meet but Nashe and Marlowe's friend Shakespeare. Yes, they were bound for the fireworks too, so they went all four together. Nashe was full of forced gallantry and classical allusions, Shakespeare pleasant and, with Greene's approval, modest when he asked him what work he had in hand. The third part of *Henry the Sixth* was out of the way, and he was working at a play on the life of Richard the Third. He was so different from Marlowe in his diffident account of his work that Greene could not imagine how they had kept company so long. Where was Marlowe? Shakespeare did not know. He came and went, he did not encourage questions, Shakespeare was content to take him on his own terms. Greene came near dropping a hint about Marlowe's atheism and bad habits, but let the moment pass. This Shakespeare fellow was out of napkins; he must look after himself. While Nashe and Kate got on famously together, he and Shakespeare went on talking. Where had he been since he left Stratford? About a good deal, he admitted. More experience than fortune. So he was a married man? Children? Good heavens! Greene said nothing of his own state, but fancied Shakespeare already knew. Quite the fashion this progression, wifeless, to London. He decided to respect the other's silence, lest his own be challenged. No doubt wandering up and down with the players, maybe an usher for a year, *abecedarius* for alphabet-ignorant witlings—and hadn't there been some talk about holding horses outside the theatres? Never mind. What an odd thing it was though, he from Norwich, this fresh lad from Stratford, both leaving their wives and children, both here in London for fame and fortune, both writing histories, both this same night walking down the Thames to the Savoy. He thought: Only dullards stay at home. He felt kindly towards Shakespeare. He encouraged him with praise of his collaborative work, asked whether he had written verse besides, and eventually came to his own much-discussed pamphlets. Had Shakespeare read them? Only the first one? He must see that he got copies of the others.

Jobling of St. Clements had been venturer enough to transport benches from nearby taverns to the ice, and the four paid for seats. Greene, some years older than Nashe and Shakespeare, lovingly conscious from their free admiration both of Kate's beauty and the child within her, felt quite the old married man among the lads. And now again, not in the least guilty-minded, he grew spacious, impressive, he might have been responsible for the river's freezing. He chaffed Nashe about Marprelate, and hardly waited for an answer; he insisted on treating Shakespeare as almost a stranger to the city. He was like a blackbird in spring, the hen-bird on the hedge watching him.

The fireworks were superb. Two things only prevented them from being the best display Greene had seen—so he explained. There was no water in which they might be reflected, and no clear depth of sky behind them.

When a man came past selling hot punch they had some, at Greene's expense. When a second man came past they had some more, Nashe paying; and within the hour Shakespeare had shown the colour of his money too. Greene was glad Monox was not there.

Before they parted they had made vague arrangements to go to a bear-baiting in Paris Gardens, as soon as the weather permitted such sport. The two younger men escorted them to their door, lest thieves be abroad. "Some of those conny-catchers you mentioned, Robin," Nashe amplified. "Though it's a cold night for dragon-breathing, eh?" Greene agreed, wondering whether Nashe was amusing himself.

Harry had not returned, and they sat by the fire for more than an hour discussing their evening. Greene was warm with punch and love, and longed to write again. Not the prose of the pamphlets to-night, but the old amorous songs, the sweet catalogues. At last—"Let's go to bed, Kate," he said, taking her arm.

"And Harry's supper?"

He condemned Harry's supper to the unplumbed depths of hell, impatiently watching her set out food and dishes. She knew this and rejoiced in her power over him, her strong sexual dominion, tantalising him, playing him till her lust was roused too, and she allowed him to embrace her fiercely. "You love me?" she asked him. He groaned that he did. She gripped him till he could have cried. "And this child of mine—you'll love him too?" "I will!

I will! I will!" Suddenly, unaccountably, she began to curse at him, telling him he had better; that he'd not leave her as he had left that other in Norwich; she would do the ordering of affairs, not he. And then as he, frightened, half-disgusted, seeing in her now nothing but a vampire draining him of blood and seed, tried to pull himself from her arms she forced him down to her wet mouth and shameless kisses, her strong and vicious will. Dreadful surrender, he knew. But soon he was content to lie there and let all the black waves of sleep and night flood him to forgetfulness. It seemed years later that he woke to hear Harry in the next room.

CHAPTER XXXVI

THEY WERE NOT very happy, the months that followed. There were times when he was reminded of those last helpless weeks of dependence on an insolent Sidley in Italy, when self-respect and poverty fought their battle hourly. He had come to see that Harry was more to Kate than he was. She might change lovers, but always she would follow her brother. This angered and humiliated him; at the very time when she should be most grateful for his love and care, most bound to him by the child within her, she was cooling unmistakably, losing all interest in him, making plans for the future which referred not at all to him. She·was a strange animal, this Kate. She had never been so delightful as those first hours when he saw in her that dear Margaret of his own creation, hardly a trace of whom was left now. Always mocking, she was now cruel if the whim took her, willing to make him look a fool, cynical if he ventured on transport, ruthless to the thwarted idealism that he had never lost however badly his conduct had tried it. Indeed, there was something about her that repelled him as her brother had done, a peculiar confusion of moral values, an assumption that good was in no way better than bad. During the worst moments of his life he had never believed such a thing. Following the worse, he had yet regard for what was better than himself. And these last months his conscience was rawer than ever. Remorse and compunction never long absent. He knew himself in the worst of all servitudes, his life pledged to an evil woman, but he had no consistent purpose to break free. For a time his life had been as it were sunk in Kate's, and now it was too late. The child had altered everything. When miserably he thought of Kit back in Norwich, he always swore he would not repeat that desertion. He would rear this child with affection. Kate should have nothing of it.

That deep-set yearning of his for devotion to something good and lovely was now pitched forward in time. That it had always failed him—or he it—he forgot. He thought of Kate's child as a girl, and checked over a hundred times what her upbringing should be. If Harry had the say— he saw it too clearly—there would be a dreadful life for her: thieving, promiscuity, the brothels in her 'teens, the swift progression to rottenness of mind and body, no end of grief and suffering. His own daughter like many of those his vicious eye had judged. By Christ! he swore, gritting his teeth, forced to rise from his chair by the strength of his emotion: there'd be none of that! He would take the child by violence if need be, he'd find some decent woman as nurse, he'd write till his fingers dropped off, he would even become a player, wear his heart out to gain patronage, no task too base for him. Like the pelican he would feed the child with his own blood. Guard her from all wicked-ness. And maybe, if all went well and he became famous and rich——He had to bring his wandering thoughts back from dreams of unattainable things.

He sighed, thinking of Kate. If only she were different! How happy they could be. Harry given marching orders, some quiet, respectable home of their own where those old influences should never be recalled. "Kate," he asked her frankly one day, "why can't you and I set up house together?" "We have, surely!" "No," he said, "I mean you and I alone. For the child's sake make something of our lives. It can't be too late. Shall we?" She laughed at him, told him jeeringly he was always looking round the next corner, and spoke sharply when he put his question too insistently. Though not in words quite so blunt she let him know he must take what she was prepared to give, and be thankful.

In a way pride kept him with the Balls. He had not hidden from his friends his attachment to Kate or that she was with child by him. How could he now make an end? Would they not think she had thrown him over? Would there not be whispers behind his back, jeers, gestures?

He had laughed too often at other fools to expose himself in turn.

It was an unexpected turn that he grew dissatisfied with his conny-catching pamphlets just as they became most profitable. According to plan and under the name of Cuthbert Conny-Catcher he had written a counterblast to his first three exposures; and then, in the first week of May, he produced his masterpiece in this kind, his *Disputation*, wherein a thief and a whore debated which of them was the more hurtful to a commonwealth. This was not the mere retailing of laws and stories he had so far practised, but a grim bit of original humour. Do as he would, Harry and Kate were present to mind when he wrote the ghastly and yet comical dialogue between thieving Lawrence and whoring Nan. The prize went to Nan, for while Lawrence made good his claim to supply work for the gallows, she took credit for keeping busy gallows, devil, and surgeon. Here again he dropped hints of bravoes pledged to murder him, of Nan herself with a long Hamborough knife under her skirts with which to give him the wristy quietus, of fourteen or fifteen ruffians setting upon him within Ludgate, and his escaping only with the help of courteous citizens and apprentices; one poor devil sorely hurt, three rogues spreadeagled to the Compter. And as a nightcap to the *Disputation* he had given that tale told him by Lodge of Coppinger's attempted conversion of the strumpet behind St. Andrew's. He felt a little guilty using it, and though he consoled himself with the usual tag: If he would live to write, he must write to live— nevertheless, he felt it would be the grossest treason to his friend's memory not to give the episode a happy ending, and he allowed the converted woman of pleasure (Oh, Kate!) to marry her saviour. But possibly because this last pamphlet contained all best he had to say on the subject, he found no pleasure in preparing his sixth item, *The Black Book's Messenger*, and viewed with actual distaste the prospect of the promised seventh. Yet the booksellers were after him one and all; he knew no other pamphleteer

in London obtained his prices; given industry enough, he could look forward to a comfortable living. Industry and health might be truer, for he was not feeling too well in April and May. Of course, he had his imitators and despised them, forgetful of his own debt to Harman. The truth was, he knew, that he wanted a change. This realistic description of low life should be a side dish, not the whole meal. He could not survey the pamphlets with as much pride as the romances, the plays, and the poetry. Those had been an escape from squalor, these but reflected it. He told himself the artist was not confined to life as every jacksnap could see and measure it, but with the inner reality of things; and the pamphlets offered no scope that way. He had travelled a long way since *Mamillia*. Was it all forward movement? As a writer he now had all the tricks at his finger ends; some of the early work had stiffnesses, gaucheries, he could do ten times better to-day if he went back to the romances. Something in the manner neither of Lyly nor Sidney—a blending of romance and realism—a new kind of writing that should establish itself as the classic form of prose composition for narrative, and hundreds of years hence men would look at a broad stream and know that if they traced it to its source they'd find it welling from his own bright brain.

Later then, when the child was born, he would do it. What a name he would leave! Not the mere mangled record of his life. Say that with the coming of his daughter never again a crudity in his writing. What had Nashe called him? —The Homer of Women! There were worse titles.

Fittingly enough, it was Nashe who was responsible for his striking out not in a new but in a for many years forgotten style. He came to Dowgate one afternoon in mid May, bringing with him a copy of the *Discourse* of Richard Harvey. Why had no one written a proper reply to that ungenerous attack on the gentlemen-poets? Greene professed he neither knew nor cared. It was old stuff, twelve months old at least; yes, he had a copy once but he gave it to the barber for wiping his razors. There was only one

office he thought it fitter for. Why not forget such contemptible scribbling?

"I expected you to be keener, Robert," Nashe confessed.
"After all, in a way——" He appeared to grope for the
right words. "There is an obligation of a sort."

"That I should answer Richard Harvey? Not at all!"

"I was talking to Peele last week—d'you ever see George
these days? That new wife of his—— I thought not. With
Peele and Marlowe too, and Tom Lodge. Then there is
Lyly. They all think my way. There should be a reply."

"Then why not write it yourself, young Juvenal? You
throw your brains about enough in matters that don't
concern you. Now's your chance."

"I'm very busy, Robert. Day in, day out, never a
moment!"

"You are not the only one."

"No. But all those I mentioned think as I do—that you,
as a leader, might do it best of all." He went on to say
the most flattering things. Yes, even Marlowe had said
as much: Greene was the man. The reproof would come
with most weight from him. Who more representative of
the University men, the wits? "Hm," said Greene, "the
University wits, eh?" It struck him as a magnificent title,
distinguishing the group from all other men—from playwrights like Shakespeare as much as from mere balladists
like Deloney. Writing was a job for educated men. There
ought to be a licensing system, and University residence
compulsory. It was the only way to preserve the standards
of literature. "A good title, Tom. A very good title." He
stroked his beard lovingly. "We ought to hold together,
we University men. Why should every beggarly extem-
porizer who can afford a pennyworth of ink and pens invite
himself into our company? It's to make a bad poet and
spoil a good ploughman, Tom. Don't you think so?"

Nashe certainly thought they should hold together. "And
let the voice that speaks for us be a representative one,
Robert. That is what I've been telling you. It is a reflection
on all when there is an attack on one." He smiled, with

equal guile and affability. "We need a leader. This reply to Harvey now—there's the first chance. You'll do it?"

"I might think it over for a day or two." He asked a couple of questions about Nashe's own pamphleteering, and demurred none too strongly when Nashe esteemed it lightly alongside his own. "Then it occurs to me, Tom —I know nothing about this Richard Harvey."

Nashe dismissed that as of no account. He knew nothing either. "Truth is not essential to satire, Robert. It is what you have wit enough to make people think that counts."

Greene wagged his head. "Truth will prevail one day, Tom."

"But by that time the other fellow is dead and you are dead too, so what does it matter? I tell you what, Robert. This Richard is a parson, I know that much. What about him kissing his parishioners' wives? Can you imagine a man appearing a more solemn kind of fool than when he takes oath he never cuddled a girl? Hm, hm?" He smacked his knee. "That's your line. Under-sheet confessor, eh?"

Greene nodded and laughed. "I never did like his brother Gabriel at Cambridge. He thought he knew more about verse than Edmund Spenser. I'll do it, Tom, and by God I'll lay about me with a vengeance."

"I like to hear you say so. Toast the whole damned family of Harveys as black as you like. No one will dislike it except themselves."

In this he was not correct. Greene rushed his libel through at a frantic pace, Nashe arranged for a speedy publication, and it made its sensation before the end of June. But by that time Greene had far greater things to trouble him than the Harveys' threats. Two days before his *Quip* was published. Harry was taken red-handed with a purse belonging to no less a man than John Tilney, Master of the Revels, and was straightway thrown into Bridewell.

Greene and Kate heard of his misfortune in a particularly shocking way. They were in Dowgate, quarrelling together, when three of the sheriff's men pushed open the door

and came hastily in. "Harry Ball lives here?" Greene had more sense than to draw his dagger. "He does. Why?"

Their leader made no reply, but pushed past Greene to confront Kate. "You know him?" He grinned at her frightened nod, and made a crude speculation.

"Keep a civil tongue in your head!" cried Greene.

"Civil tongue, eh? And who are you?"

"By what right do you ask?"

"In the name of the Queen's Majesty, fellow."

"Then why do you ask about Harry Ball?"

"Because he has just been taken to Bridewell for picking purses. Get out of the way!"

Kate cried out at that, and Greene went over to her and put his arm about her shoulders.

"Who are you?" the fellow asked again.

"My name is Robert Greene—you may have heard of me. This is Harry Ball's sister. You have nothing to do with her. I—we'll come to Bridewell with you to see him."

This amused the sheriff's man. He turned to his companions, sharing the joke. "He says he'll come to Bridewell!" They guffawed, and one of them said it was rich. "You live here, Greene?"

"I do. Why not?"

He jerked his head to his followers. "We'll take them both."

"But you can't take this lady to Bridewell. You can see —she is with child. You can't force a woman against whom there is no charge——"

"If you resist it will be at your peril. Get ready, the pair of you."

He saw Kate desperate and frightened, for Harry's sake more than her own, he thought. Indeed, what they had just heard was equal to Harry's death warrant. There was nothing he could say, and they prepared themselves in silence for their unpleasant journey, watching without protest the sheriff's men turning their goods upside down and rummaging everywhere. Though Harry was a careful

man, they made a small haul that would not help him—
the most damning item a richly worked purse from which
Kate had delayed to unpick the gold wire. "Don't be
afraid," he whispered, touching her hand. For himself he
had no fears. He had friends in plenty, he had some money,
he expected to find Hunter not unreasonable even if he
were not instantly released on bail. Harry would hang,
that was certain. He could not maintain even a pretence of
hope before Kate. His greatest worry, a selfish but natural
one, was lest the news of his detention become generally
known and make him a butt for ever. He asked the sheriff's
man which direction they would take, at the same moment
opening his palm to show the silver there. As the dexterous
transfer took place, the other said with greater gentleness
than he had used so far that he was far from wishing to add
to a gentleman's difficulties, and at Greene's suggestion
they took the quieter streets past Queenhythe, Broken Wharf,
and Baynard's Castle. Broken Wharf brought back, as
ever, memories of Edmund and his plight in gaol, and he
had to square his shoulders or be overcome. If he found
himself in Bridewell too—if they would not believe him—
if his friends did not come forward—— He mastered his
fears, grew less selfish, and wondered what Kate must be
thinking as they neared the great, ugly prison. He would
get her out though. The sheriff could never hold them,
with no case brought or provable. However great the bail,
he could muster it. He grew quite frightened thinking she
might spend even an hour among the horrors of the Common
Ward. Where was the humanity of the law to put a woman
to such trials? If only he told them——

They were taken before an impersonal and busy sheriff,
who cared not a farthing for anything Greene had to tell
him. A poet, eh? A playwright? He realised he could
expect little sympathy on those grounds. What were poets
better than caterpillars, playwrights than weeds, fat-
sprouting over the fair garden of the commonwealth?
If Robert Greene could find two men of standing to speak
for him and offer bail, he might for the present go free;

yes, he could write his letters there and then; as for the woman, the sister of the arrested Ball, she must be detained. Almost sick now, Greene protested and prayed, she silent all the while, but he in authority waved his hands impatiently and they were taken away. So soon to lose her, seconds only now, his love for her grew strong as ever. He could hardly speak, there were tears in his eyes. "I'll get you out, Kate," he muttered, kissing her before the impatient guards. "And Harry. I'll get him out too." She looked at him stupidly, he thought, surrendered to disaster and hopelessness, and before he could say more she was gone, and he being led to a small room near that of the Warden, where he might write his appeals to his friends. If anything went wrong with her, if the child suffered, he would do terrible things that he put no name to. He would see the Queen herself for justice, Burleigh, Walsingham, Essex.

To whom should he write? Checking over the list he realised vividly how graceless was his acquaintance. Finally he decided on Tom Lodge, though he had not seen him for years, and Nashe out at Croydon. Not as poets and make-plays—that would not do. But Lodge as the son of a one-time Lord Mayor, and Nashe as a member of the Arch-bishop's household. Lest either be absent from home or indisposed to meddle, he added a letter to Portington's father, on whom he had several times drawn bills in those old days when his home was still Norwich, when he was single and unencumbered—those incredible days.

He paid for a messenger and then offered a small bribe to be taken before the Warden. Hunter evidently knew everything and pretty certainly was expecting him. He was sorry to see an old friend under a cloud, was Hunter. Any-thing he could do, consistent with duty, Greene could be sure he would do. Until the question of bail was settled one way or the other he would not hear of Greene being other-wise than comfortable, and in exchange for his word of honour would allow him the use of his own quarters. Relieved, Greene did not wait to hear the conditions, but

passed over money to be shared, so he said, among Hunter's subordinates. The position was perfectly understood; there was no awkwardness between them. Greene even sat on the corner of the table as he asked Hunter what he could do to make Kate's position more bearable, and here again he found that money could work wonders. Hunter, once he confessed that the child Kate was big with was of his fathering, agreed that she deserved better quarters, at least until they knew something about her immediate future. To spare each other's feelings, they wrapped up the financial side of Hunter's humanity in a soft blanket of words, so that not one sharp corner of ugly reality might be felt sticking through. No, Hunter was very sorry it would not be possible just yet for Greene to see either brother or sister. Somehow Greene had tact enough to realise that this was not the occasion for yet another bribe, and that Hunter for the good of his conscience must be allowed to refuse some of his requests. Nor would Hunter discuss Harry's crime; his prospects no more. He preferred to hark back to matters Greene rather expected him to have forgotten, old stuff about Sir John Harrison and Sidley and exploits of his own they put him in mind of.

He stayed in Bridewell that night, but in a fairly comfortable bed of Hunter's. He had cheap wine to drink even, thrown in as part of the bargain. He was very unhappy about Kate, but took surprisingly little interest in Harry. He was past hoping for. Early next morning he was visited by Lodge, who went straight from him to the sheriff and spoke so strongly for his old companion that Greene's battle was almost won. Before noon he and Portington's father had offered to go bail for him, he waited to hear nothing of Nashe before paying up his own small share, and then sought out Hunter to see what could be done for Harry and Kate. He thought he could read the superficially cunning processes of Hunter's brain when once more he refused him access to Kate. He would not incur suspicion of being too obliging. But he allowed him to see Harry in the Common Ward.

His previous nosefuls of it had not rendered gaol-stench less shocking to Greene, nor was Harry as grateful as he might be. "You have taken your time over it!" he said angrily, when Greene stood in front of him.

His explained that he had not been permitted to see him earlier, that——"

"Where is Kate?"

"In the women's ward."

"You worthless bastard, Robert! You couldn't keep her from that!"

Greene kept his temper and went over most of what had happened since they were taken up. But if he expected a better opinion from Harry he was mistaken.

"You had to put your cursed carcase into a good bed, had you, and leave her with those sows in there!" He cursed Greene with a cold, angry relish, till the other interrupted him impatiently with: "Shut your filthy mouth! I came here to help you. Do you want help?"

Harry kicked the wall with rage. "Help? The infernal fiends themselves couldn't help me now! Christ! Christ! Christ! That I should be taken over an old sheep-head!"

Greene listened impatiently to his oaths and damnations. "But there must be something I can do?"

"You can save your own skin," Harry sneered.

"My skin? I don't understand you."

"Have you forgotten the bill we drew on Egbert Flood?"

Greene went quite faint. "For God's sake, Harry——"

"For whose sake?"

"You'd never want to drag me into that, Harry!"

Harry jerked his head. "Wouldn't I? Why should my neck stretch for the pair of us? You will do as I tell you or I'll tell right enough."

"What do you want me to do?"

"Get Kate out of prison."

"Don't I want to? Haven't I done everything humanly possible?"

"You found yourself a comfortable bed, I do know that. Now you go and think it over. You get her out of gaol

before the morning they make an end of me or when I'm on the road to Tyburn I'll make sure you follow me. Well?"

They talked for another couple of minutes, Greene expostulating with all the sharpness of a frightened man, Harry sullen one moment, incensed the next, but unshakable. Then he left him.

He had never been so frightened in his life—and there were occasions when he had been very frightened indeed. When, brooding over the problem, he came to the unbearable conclusion that even if he freed Kate, Harry bore him such ill-will as to ensure his arrest and execution, he was physically sick, leaning against a wall, to the amusement of passers-by who thought him drunk. O Horror! Horror! Horror! To hang, to choke on the rope, to hear the howling of the mob, to see the last frantic, out-blotted swing of a sea of faces, to die horribly, dreadfully, gasping for air like the cock with the knife down his throat! He wiped the sour threads of mess from his lips and beard, shuddered in the sun, and dragged himself on lump-feet back to Dowgate. The emptiness there he feared would send him crazy but he must have quiet to think, he must beat down fear, conquer himself. God, how he must think! For hours he sat there, undisturbed, his brain sometimes so dead that he was like a man in a nightmare, struggling with an enveloping horror for one clear piercing thought, sometimes fecund as frog-spawn with fantastic schemes which he rejected with growing agony of despair. He did not notice the darkening of the room, it was the gnawing of his empty stomach that told him of the morning become afternoon, the afternoon become early evening. He went to the door and called to Isam's wife to fetch him food and drink, one moment thinking he could not possibly eat a mouthful, the next that he could tear meat and bread like a wolf, sickened though he was by the hard, round, hollow ball he imagined under the trough of his breastbone. Mistress Isam brought him something from her own table, and asked what had happened. Watching her kind, shrewd face change at his tidings, he felt overwhelmed

by a new fear, this time of loneliness, and made excuses
to get her to sit down, and when that must be at an end
begged that he might come and sit with her and her husband.
In their tiny room, smelling of Isam's craft, stocked with
honest awls and knives and lasts and hammers, he felt
better; the race slackened in his veins and head; he could
hardly believe the thing had taken place. He was to amaze
himself by laughing before it drew on to bedtime, and he
must go back to his own company and fright and misery
again.

It was the third day of July, not three weeks before
Kate expected her confinement, that Harry was tried and
sentenced to hang. With a kind of perverse logic it had
been decided that no proceedings should be taken against
his sister till she had been delivered and the innocent
child so freed from future reproach. There was now no
question of action against Greene. He was a free man, not
even on bail. He saw Harry several times, and Kate still
more often, and his stock of money was almost at an end
to provide them with the comforts they needed. For a
wicked sum each week Hunter would allow Kate a place
with only two other women prisoners, where she had a
fairly comfortable bed and good food. Greene met her
companions, both cloth-stealers in a good way of business.
He was pleased to find them far from brutalized, interested
in Kate's condition, and willing to put themselves about
for her convenience. They did not go unrewarded. He
had not expected Kate to give way so abjectly. She appeared not to hear his pleas that she could best help her
brother by making a brave show to the world, that she owed
too much to the life inside her to ruin her health by apathy
or despair. The strength of the tie between the apparently
heartless Harry and the far from sentimental Kate, though
he had always known it strong, now amazed him. Harry
was certainly thinking more of his sister's future than of
the very short one left to himself, and she, he felt sure, could
not imagine a world without Harry. But with all this,

his own troubles were greatest to him, his own peril the most dire. He had a plan too by this time, which he discussed at length with Harry, who gave it doubtful approval, telling him he could never get enough money to carry it through. What it was he revealed to Hunter, cautiously.

He had a private interview with him the day after Harry was sentenced, a harassing now-or-never kind of interview, Hunter more potent for life or death than the Almighty himself. He first turned their conversation adroitly to the subject of gaol-fever. Hunter was ready to talk, for it was only a month back that sixty-two persons, not all of them prisoners, perished in the outbreak at the Compter. Drawing as he did the moral that it was dangers such as these that made a warden's life so hard and precarious, he supplied Greene with an opportunity for the decisive insinuation.

"A very hard life indeed, Master Hunter," he agreed. "I doubt whether the world at large recognises how great your responsibilities and worries, how small your recompense." He let Hunter elaborate the point for a minute or so, and then repeated in a graveyard sort of voice: "How small the recompense!"

Something in his tone and manner struck Hunter as significant. He looked sharply at Greene, whom he had milched mercilessly these last weeks, to see whether he intended to mock him. He knew a trick worth two of any Greene could play. He held all the high cards, and he knew it. But Greene's eyes were shining, he was leaning forward, there was no mistaking that rubbing the face for an itch. "So it must be expected," he was saying, "that there are occasions when a humane gaoler, mindful of the mortal danger in which some of his charges find themselves, will satisfy his longing for kindliness with a proper regard for his own needs in the matter." This was a triumph of vagueness, but he knew he must avoid quick offence. "Would you agree, Master Hunter?"

Hunter too leaned forward. "I don't fully understand you, Master Greene."

"For a sum of money—a sum of money to be agreed on, Master Hunter—it might or might it not be possible to arrange a gaol-delivery somewhat outside the ordinary process of the law?"

He felt his heart beating and gushing as though its terror would be known to Hunter. Would he never answer? Answer, man! Can't you say something?

Hunter was shaking his head. "I have not begun to understand you, Master Greene. I could say, though, that if you were putting the case of—Harry Ball, shall we say?—and I know you are not—I could say at once it would be impossible."

"Not Harry Ball, Master Hunter, not Harry Ball. No one condemned!"

"Then who?"

"His sister Kate."

Hunter sat back in his chair. "She'll get gaol-delivery, never fear, Master Greene." He began to laugh, had to throw back his head he was so amused, but Greene watched his eyes and did not despair.

"For a large sum of money, perhaps?"

Hunter was laughing and wagging his head.

"Listen, Master Hunter! Women die in Bridewell sometimes?"

They did so, very often. And if they did?

"There is no great ceremony before burial?"

Hunter had stopped laughing. He was beginning to see. "Well?"

Greene felt a madness bubbling up inside his breast. This was it!

"Perhaps a visit from the Warden is sufficient, and the body is then—shall we say it vanishes? No one cares, I should imagine." He paused. "Coffins are dear, I know. The dead need no luxuries, Master Hunter."

Hunter nodded. "Go on."

"If Mistress Ball died——"

"If she did?"

"A quick burial——"

"Well?"

"Of an empty coffin, if coffin there be!"

It was out. They sat staring at each other.

"A pretty tale," said Hunter slowly.

"With a happy ending still prettier. Shall it be done?"

Hunter stood up, walked briskly to the cupboard, took down a bottle and glasses. Pouring out wine, "How much?" he asked bluntly.

"Every penny I have."

He shook his head. "I doubt whether that is enough, Master Greene. You know what you are asking?" He offered him a glass. "You know my risk?"

They settled down to argue, keen as hawks, and, the price fixed, to settle ways and means.

"You realise," Hunter told him "that, if I do this, she must leave London for ever?"

He had not thought so, but nodded his head in complete agreement. "She shall. For ever," he promised quickly.

CHAPTER XXXVII

HE HAD LITTLE more than a fortnight in which to raise the sum of twenty-five pounds. Could he do it? He told himself there was no room for "could he?"—he must do it, and in so short a time, for Harry was to hang on the twenty-fourth of the month, and Hunter was insistent Kate must be out of Bridewell before she had her child. He little imagined how much more compelling the first date was to Greene than the second. But twenty-five pounds! He had never possessed such an amount not even in the palmy days of his out-fitting for Italy. There was the price of his reply to the Harveys, true, but that was already pledged to Hunter for the prisoners' keep. He called on Lodge, Nashe, Peele, Marlowe, Will Monox, Tilney himself, and came back with a few paltry nobles. Some of them, he knew, would not lend if they could; most were as poor as himself. By the time he had called on Portington's father and been given another ten nobles, three days were gone. The elder Portington, in receipt of frequent messages from his Norwich estate, had heard too much about Greene's mutilated reputation to do much for him. Bail for the son of an honest and sorely-tried fellow townsman, for the one-time friend of his own son Roger at Cambridge, that he had not denied, but to keep a beggarly writer of bawdry and insolence in comfort—ten nobles was being generous, not another penny! Thought Greene, near panic: If only Sidley were alive! From that to thoughts of Braiding was a short step. It was his one hope. He must go there and see Alice and get what money he could from her, from Lady Sidley, from anybody, and if the devil drove him further he must go to Norwich and throw himself on their mercies there. Think what he would, his father would not let him hang.

He left London at once, delaying only to tell Harry of

his plans. He was now at Newgate, where all the condemned felons were taken before execution. "I wish you luck," Harry told him, "because as sure as heaven is above and hell beneath your neck depends on it." With this admonition to mumble in his ears, he borrowed pistols from Hunter, did not wait for a slow company, and rode from the city by the Cripplegate, following as far as Chipping Barnet the road he, Sidley, and John had taken when they fled from the plague, the road too he had ridden with Alice when they returned so contritely to Norwich. Maybe, he thought, wishing the miles behind, his destiny was bound up with this road. Then, forking right, he was on the little-travelled way to St. Neot's. He had never ridden it before, but it kept him clear of the Cambridge road and the possibility of encounters there. His own troubles and the quarrel with the Harveys made him desirous to avoid the University, so he kept steadily ahead through Hatfield, Baldock, Biggleswade, to St. Neot's, where he put up overnight at the Market Inn, and then on the next stretch to Yaxley and Peterborough, bearing right for Crowland, and then he was asking directions every mile or two as he followed paths and field tracks across country to Braiding. He was there at the end of the second perfect summer's day, completely exhausted, fretted in mind, and with a light-headed fear that his trouble might all be for nothing.

His welcome was warm enough, and Lady Sidley expressed only conventional surprise at his visit. She looked none the worse for Alice's company, he thought as he ate supper with the two of them, forcing his attention to their chit-chatter of country trifles, himself discoursing of everything except what was nearest his heart. Perhaps his manner was not as free from strain as he thought, for Lady Sidley made an obvious excuse to leave brother and sister together immediately afterwards, and Alice asked at once what had brought him.

"Alice," he said, "I'm in dreadful trouble."

Her face fell, though she might have expected it. She had a plump, comfortable look about her, had Alice now,

as though the unhappiness of old days had seeped from memory. Country breeding, country feeding, he had thought at table, noticing the increased fleshiness of her neck, the way in which the wrist bones were burying themselves in a kind of baby-fatness, the pudginess of her cheeks. She grieved no longer then? He would have moralised had he not remembered how easily he had forgotten wife and son—and had he not been trembling with excitement and fear.

"What sort of trouble, Robin?"

How could he tell her? "I must get hold of some money, Alice. At once."

"So you come to me? It was kind of you to think of me, Robin!"

He looked ashamed and felt it. "I know, Alice—you must think badly of me. I deserve it. But, Alice, you must lend me money!"

She shook her head. "I don't see that I must, or ought. What about all the money you make by writing?"

"It's not as much as you think. In any case it has gone, Alice. I haven't a penny. And if I don't get it——"

She saw the sweat break out on his face and was frightened. "What have you done?" she asked quietly. "You must tell me first, before I can think of it."

He swallowed and mopped his face with the sleeve of his doublet. How explain? How possibly explain? Haltingly he began to tell her about Kate, about her brother, hardening his heart to her look of contempt. Then he told of Kate in Bridewell and Harry now at Newgate waiting to die. He could not let his child be born in Bridewell, he told her again and again. The scorn and disgust in her face gave way to fear and alarm as he pleaded his own danger. He had intended to say nothing of that, but once started there was no holding back. His meeting with Kate at Finsbury Fair, Harry's invitation after the meeting in Cheapside, the forged bill, he told everything; and Harry's threat, and the probability of his carrying it out even if he did get the money. Yet she listened with resolution not to lend.

"I've been in hell since then, Alice!"

The words seemed to envelop her. Her brother in all his self-concern was startled by the sudden whiteness of her face. For it was her husband's voice she heard, that night so long ago when she walked with him under the tall Braiding trees, the long silence between them, that dear, dear voice of his. "Alice, I've been in hell since then," he too had said. It was good to shut your heart to the past, for out of it came nothing but pain. "Alice, I've been in hell since then." And now this one saying it again, and begging help. Against his vileness there stood Geoffrey's nobility, against his treachery the devotion and self-sacrifice so generously given her. She must help him for Geoffrey's sake. No rights and wrongs in the matter. Some way of repaying always came. To be willing to recognise it was everything.

"How much do you want?" she asked stonily.

"Will you, Alice? God bless you, Alice! God bless you!"

"How much!" she repeated.

"Twenty-five pounds," he answered, as dumbfounded by the amount as if he heard it for the first time.

"Oh, but I could never——"

"Alice, for Christ's sake, Alice! Don't you realise? They'll hang me, Alice! Hang me!" He buried his face in his hands, sobbing aloud. "They'll hang me!"

She stood up uncertainly. Twenty-five pounds! Such a sum of money! The things a woman could do with twenty-five pounds, the security it gave her, the strength and assurance. To be thrown away on a dishonest gaoler. And maybe in vain. For a moment she was angry. Let him get out of his own scrapes. Or if not, let him rid the earth—— But twenty-five pounds! It was the price of a good house, fine living for a couple of years, a splendid dowry, you could stock a farm with twenty-five pounds. It was also the price of a brother's life. She thought now, as she used to think when she heard Robin boasting of what he had done and intended to do, how life flowed to you without your

seeking it, bringing you its trials and triumphs, its joys and tribulations. But twenty-five pounds! "You shall have your twenty-five pounds, Robin." She sat down again, hating the thought of gratitude. Let it be over and done with, the whole wretched business. "But I'll never help you again, Robin, as long as you live. You understand?" He began a shamefaced mutter of thanks, but: "No," she said firmly, "you must not talk about it. I'm going to bed." He hated the idea of being alone, he was the little boy again who used to clutch at his sister's skirts as she went upstairs to bed in front of him, immeasurably protected. But in his bedroom, after a civil good-night from his attendant, all he could say was: "I've got the money, I've got the money, I've got the money!"

He was at Braiding two days. The draft with which he returned to London was drawn in his name by Lady Sidley on Mulliner the lawyer. He was too ashamed to meet her eye, for though Alice had told her nothing of the facts, she had been forced to plead that he was in great trouble and that something like disaster lay ahead if he returned moneyless. She helped without argument, because there was now between the two women a most deep and tender affection, and in the case of the older woman a considerable degree of reliance upon the other. Each had taken blows enough to appreciate the peace and ease they found in each other. Lady Sidley did little entertaining, they lived very much for themselves at Braiding, and in that small self-contained world of theirs change was not a welcome thing. Once a year they were visited by Sir Gilbert and Lady Hurrish, but Alice found no discomfort in this. Elizabeth and she were easy with each other, kept their positions with graciousness on the one side and tact on the other. Maybe one day Elizabeth's son (she had two children now) would be the disposer of Braiding. She gave little thought to it. While the Lady Sidley lived her course was plain and easy; after her time——
"I have seen to your comfort, child. Never think about it."

Become housekeeper if she wished, there at Braiding; go back to Norwich; or who knew? "You might marry again, child." She had flushed up at this, declaring she could never think—— "Maybe not. But you are not an old woman, are you? The years make their own differences. It does not do to struggle against them." There would be chance enough, she knew. Meantime, quiet life of women there, welcome after buffets; to check accounts, tally goods, number sheets and household linen; know dairy matters; stitch, unpick, embroider, work gently at frames; oversee, instruct the few newcomers, gossip, plan mild pleasures. And old well-wishing friends were there, like Ferrers and Mistress Mako, ancients with kind hearts, kind voices. Reading aloud to her one night from Master Edmund Spenser's new poem, the episode where the Red Cross Knight would rescue Sir Trevisan from Despair but himself falls into his power, Lady Sidley repeated thoughtfully certain words which sank into Alice's memory, so that she never again forgot them. "Sleep after toil, port after stormy seas; Ease after War, doth greatly please." Words indeed to echo.

Lady Sidley offered Alice no advice for the present, and in no way changed her attitude towards her brother, yet everyone was glad when he was gone. He had promised to send word to Alice the day Harry was hanged, and now, easier in mind, he begged her not to worry about him. He heard news of the folk at Norwich too. Everyone was well there, except his mother. She was breaking this last year. "I'll go there again once this is over," he promised Alice. "Whatever comes of it, I'll see her again." Doll, he heard, was happy enough, and was a great help now that Jane's powers were declining. The boy—he was a lovely boy, the image of his father. Seven years old now— he had not seen him for more than two years. "If I were to tell you, Alice, how ashamed I am——"

She would not let him make promises about the return of the money. She knew how vain they would be. The twenty-five pounds was gone as surely as if she had flung

it into the sea. They said another good-bye as he set his foot to the stirrup. "If anything goes wrong, Alice," he told her, "I shall be safe, never fear. I'll leave the country instantly, but I'll send you word. Don't let them know at home, will you?" She watched him this time till he came to the curve in the avenue of elms; he turned, checking his horse, to wave and kiss his hand to her; she kissed hers back, and he was gone. Death, exile, a mere hiding the head—which lay before him? Would she ever see him again? She turned back indoors despondently, knowing that if he were anyone but her own brother she would not think him worth twenty-five pence of her money.

"Menfolk are a great worry to us women," Lady Sidley said gently, noticing her poor appetite at table.

He was in London not an hour before he was presenting his bill at Mulliner's. The lawyer never forgot a face, and surprised Greene by asking about his sister. He wanted the whole amount in coin? That would be unwise, surely? He shrugged his shoulders, had a strong box brought before him, and counted out the gold coins twice over and with the greatest deliberation. He must ask for a receipt.

Now for Hunter. At Mitforth Lane he was handy to Bridewell, and hurried straight across. Hunter was eager to see him, and they shut themselves away from eaves-dropping or interruption. Had he the money? Greene struck the bag concealed under his cloak. All of it? The twenty-five pounds.

When could the exchange take place? As an after-thought Greene asked whether Kate was well.

"Well enough. What should be wrong with her?" It was then Friday. Harry was to hang the following Thursday. "We'll get her out Monday or Tuesday. And you pay me half the money now."

Greene counted it out. Hunter swept it away in a piece of cloth, which he stuffed under his waistband. "You know the risk I'm running," he said.

Greedy, heartless devil! thought Greene, agreeing whole-heartedly nevertheless. They went on talking for half-an-hour, and then he must hurry away on his third call, this time upon Harry at Newgate. He found him not in the condemned cells, alone, but enjoying the company of three gamblers, and swearing as desperately at a small loss as though he were facing bankruptcy not death. Seeing Greene, however, he got rid of these others with a kind of authority and waited for the news. His voice was thickened with drink, but Greene saw no trace of irresolution or despair about him. Repentance he had never expected. He forced Greene to drink with him as they spoke together, and evidently enjoyed his unexpressed fear that he might talk in his cups. Was he comfortable? Greene asked. He smiled. He was not complaining. He had company by day, as Greene could see, good enough fellows too; he had plenty to eat and drink; his money reached to a woman every night. He would make the best of what time was left to him. He appeared to Greene the sordid reality of Marlowe's Faust, who drugged his agony at death and damnation with all sensual delight the devil could provide for him. But Faustus on a couch of down and silk, clasping the white body of Greek Helen, made a better showing than Harry Ball in Newgate filth coupling with a punk under the shadow of a gallows. No beauty of eternal sin here; its rankness instead.

He bit his lips, his life in Harry's hands. He gave him all the small money he had, and Harry asked for none of the coins that were to free his sister. Greene must come back each day.

He was now without the price of a meal or a bed. He already owed the Isams for a couple of weeks' lodging, he owed small sums to Nashe, Peele, and Monox, he knew not a soul who would lend him a penny. The Queen's Men were out of town, there was nothing to be gained by seeing Tilney again; what hope lay in the Admiral's Men now at the Rose? He was very tired and hungry, but forlornly he trudged the whole way to London Bridge, crossed the

river, and turned west towards Paris Gardens. He found
the crowd pouring away from a performance of Shakespeare's
Comedy of Errors. Christ! if that wasn't enough to make a
man bitter. A mere bumpkin, the mud still on his shoes,
and already this year they had played his *Richard*, and
now this comedy. While he dragged his aching feet all over
London because the Queen's Men were driven to the
country—what he had told Nashe about the University
men, the University Wits, by God there was truth in it!
If every runaway hostler, maltster, tapster was to take the
bread out of their mouths, because they were willing to
sell their farthing dip souls to that blasted Henslowe——

Henslowe! Could he get a loan from him for a promise
to write a new play? He must try.

The doorkeeper knew him and let him pass through to
where the players were still busy replacing their wardrobes.
Henslowe was there watching every item go on the pegs or
into chests, ticking them off on his long list, the biggest
old jew in Christendom. Shakespeare was there too, talking
with Marlowe of all men. Greene cursed. If there was one
man he did not want to meet it was Marlowe. The swine
would be only too glad to know he was short of money
again. He was tempted to back out, but the great trouble
he had been to, his merciless need, would not permit this,
and he went forward giving greetings to many there of
his acquaintance.

"Robert Greene, of all men!"

This was Marlowe. From his tone Greene was prepared
for mortification. "Well, Marlowe?" He turned to congratulate Shakespeare on his play. "You saw it, then?" No, he
admitted he had just arrived, but from the obvious pleasure
of the large crowd he judged it a success. Shakespeare
thanked him, modestly enough. Despite his lack of education,
he seemed not devoid of breeding. He saw Marlowe about
to open his mouth, but rudely turned his back on him and
went over to where Henslowe was scanning his completed
list. It was his turn to be rebuffed. "I cannot be bothered
now, Master Greene," Henslowe declared flatly. "But

about my *Orlando?*" Greene persisted. "I want to know whether there is any chance——" "Not this season!" Greene pocketed his pride, furious with Marlowe for hanging on his shoulder to hear what he was saying. "I was wondering whether you could let me have a loan against my next play, Master Henslowe?" "Against—— Come now, Master Greene, no joking! No, no, you must see Wilson and the Queen's Men. Let me see now, one robe de chambre trimmed with imitation lynx——" He poked into a heap of costumes, leaving Greene to feel and look ridiculous.

"Short of money?"

Marlowe again. "Yes, I am."

"Hm! Pity." He called over to Shakespeare. "Greene's short of money, Will."

Shakespeare seemed embarrassed, the players frankly interested. Greene knew his face must be as red as his hair. "There is no need for you to pretend you want to help me, Marlowe. I'll trouble you to mind your own business."

"So I do. I think you far from grateful, Greene. You have taken plenty from me in your time."

"You are a liar!"

"What with ideas and imitations. Watch out for him, Will—he's a bloodsucker. The biggest, blackest bat in London."

Greene felt himself ringed in by a suddenly hostile band. Why was Marlowe baiting him? What a memory for a quarrel the fellow had! "I'll not quarrel with you, Marlowe," he said. "You are not worth it."

He started to push through the expectant players, but Marlowe's voice stopped him dead. "Is your brother-in-law to hang on Thursday next, Greene?"

"By God, you go too far, Marlowe!"

"Let me explain, gentlemen. This Robert Greene of ours, who pretends to despise mere players, not content with running away from his wife and child, has now taken up with a cutpurse and his sister. The old cross-biting law, eh, Greene? The gentle broker!"

"Will you fight?" said Greene.

"Any time. Anywhere."

"Then now!"

But Henslowe interrupted like the Thunderer that there would be no fighting in his theatre or after his play. Did they want the place closed down? At the reminder the players, willing though they were to see bloodshed, changed their minds about an immediate contest. There was a movement to bundle Greene outside, he found himself more or less shoved across the floor of the house, he was at the door before he knew it. "Then you wait, Marlowe," he screamed back at him; "Wait till we meet next. I'll cut your blasted throat for you!"

But he was outside, enraged and humiliated, and only old William Toole, who played the parts of ancient men, to say a word for him. "Come on, Master Greene," he was urging, and took him by the elbow; "you'll get naught here." He raised his hands at Greene's threats. "No, no, be a good lad and come away. The walls are too thick: they'll not hear you."

"Swine!" cried Greene; "Bastard! Jakescraping that he is! I'll wait for him to come out. I'll stay here till I meet him, and then I'll murder him!"

"No, no." The old player led him back in the direction of St. Mary's, talking earnestly the while, giving good counsel more to keep Greene quiet than because he thought him likely to act upon it. They were almost at the Bridge when Toole stopped, saying he had no time to come further. "But go home, Master Greene——"

"Home!"

"Or go find your friends——"

"My friends!"

"They can be a great comfort. Trust an old man's word in this. And one final word—Give over quarrelling with Kit Marlowe. To know him well is to know him dangerous." He lowered his voice. "He has employment that you and I do best to know nothing about. Employment of state with Walsingham, now in England, now in France. Nor would

Walsingham care to lose his agent. Be careful, Master Greene, or it may go ill with you. Good-bye."

"Good-bye." For a moment or two he watched Toole returning, thinking he had accompanied him merely from policy, to prevent a fight outside the Rose. A glib old man, Toole, with his advice and his warnings. Though Marlowe were the Earl of Essex he'd not let him escape. He rammed his dagger harder into its sheath. Next time!

God, he was hungry and leg-weary. It didn't bear thinking on how hungry he was. Not a bite since morning, and him walking about with twelve pounds in gold under his cloak. You'd laugh at it in a comedy, think it a fine invention of the poet's; in reality it was hell. He walked under the gate, without a glance for its crop of heads, poor grinning devils past hunger and tiredness, and crossed the Bridge, stopping once beyond the first buildings to stare moodily at the water sluicing between the piers. A small boat passed through, helped by the skilful shoving of the waterman, dipped, rose, dipped, and was out of sight. To be humble, unknown, a stranger to the world's gauds, like this waterman, care-free, dull as the beans he stuffed his guts with—to be born obscure, live unknown, die the death-in-bed of the unmarked man—why not, Robert Greene? What a question! You never put that sort of question save when the answer must be wrong. He spat carefully into the flecked channel, cursed at his dabbled lip, swabbed it with his cloak, and went on his way.

He would go back to Dowgate and trust to the Isams' charity. He had paid well in his time, and the little he owed them—they'd not let that stand between him and a meal when they knew he was starving. The old fellow, just such another as that boatman, golden-slumbered on a bed of straw; his wife a kindheart, she'd not see him turned away. He felt somewhat lightheaded as he neared the house, faint and giddyish. If they did not take him in— what?

It was the woman who answered the door. She invited him inside, asking him questions before he was properly

over the threshold. She took him into the room where
Isam was working quietly at his craft. Certainly he could
have food. They had known him too long to let him go
hungry from their door. He felt a different man when at
last he finished eating. He explained that he had no money
but was expecting some within a week or two. Would they
let him stay on? There was the reckoning against his name,
he knew, but until these last weeks and all their trials and
expenses had he ever failed them? Husband and wife looked
over his head, he saw Isam nod gravely, and could have
wished for a thousand pounds to give the kindly couple.
And thank God ten thousand times for food and shelter
this next terrible week!

He did not see Kate before Monday. Hunter had so far
insisted she should know nothing of the arrangements made
to free her, but on Monday morning he gave Greene exact
instructions for his share in the matter. He should be waiting
at twelve o'clock that night at the river end of Water Lane.
He should have a large cloak in readiness. Hunter would
bring Kate to him along the black river walk from Bridewell,
the rest of the money should change hands, and they must
get away to the country the very next day. They knew now
that the child would not be born for ten days, and before
then they must put fifty miles between them and London.
They agreed it would be best for Greene to see her this
morning and let her into the secret, but with no mention
of Hunter by name. Otherwise she might be afraid to venture
with him. He found she was now in a small cell of her own,
with a stone slab at one end to serve as bed and table,
but she was keeping it moderately clean, and he thought
that a good sign. There were no tears at their meeting,
not even when she asked about Harry and heard the half-
hearted hopes and consolations that were all he could
offer. She could not sit still while he told her of the plans
made for her escape, and asked nervous questions about
points he had not made clear. Yes, she felt well enough.
No, the child would not be born yet. He asked her whether

she knew of a safe house to which he could take her overnight, whose inmates were rather against the law than for
it, and she told him to go to the house of Clarence Appleby
at the Buttery in Little Britain. That very afternoon, he
promised. "Tell him I sent you," she said, "and the word
is *founder*." He guessed that Harry had not told him everything. Perhaps not anything of importance.

"You'll not be worrying, Kate?" he begged her at
parting. "We'll get you out first, and then it will be Harry's
turn." But he dared not say for what.

Clarence Appleby proved to be a short and thin man,
about fifty years of age, completely bald under an ill-fitting
wig. Greene made the mistake of saying hurriedly that Kate
Ball had sent him, and it was only after Appleby had
politely told him that he had never heard such a name that
he remembered to add the password *founder*. "Come
inside," said Appleby at that. Greene discovered he knew
everything about Harry's hopeless case, and that he knew
a good deal about Robert Greene. "Your child," he said,
interrupting him once. That night? He left Greene alone
for a few minutes. Very well, it could be arranged. He
would himself be at the corner of Water Lane and Fleet
Street that night at twelve o'clock and would fetch them
safely to the Buttery. He explained that he knew the exact
movements of the watch, and besides, you needed a hand
on your arm from Shoe Lane to Smithfield after dark.
"You'll not come too near?" The words were hardly out
of Greene's mouth when he realised their foolishness, and
Appleby did not bother to reply to him.

The hours passed very slowly after that till the time of
his meeting with Hunter. He dare not drink, could not
write, was not disposed to walk about. He did not tell
the Isams he would be out all night, and even made a
pretence of going to bed. There he lay, sick with impatience,
now drawing a covering over him because he was cold,
soon casting it off because he was too hot. At last his watch
told him it was eleven o'clock and he prepared to leave,
carrying his shoes in his hand till he was at the door.

Everything these days reminded him of something done before—carrying his shoes now of that time in Broken Wharf when he made his escape from Hacket and Edmund. If only this were so easy! He took down the bars from inside the street door, went outside, and drew it to after him. Isam would be up with the light, so there was no danger of anyone breaking in, he hoped. He went by way of St. Thomas Apostle to St. Paul's Church, and so down Ludgate Hill through the broken wall into Fleet Street. He was too early, but all the same he turned down Water Lane to sit on the grass at the river edge. Then this struck him as dangerous. What if Hunter did not keep faith? What if he were waiting for him to bring the money, and then whisk a knife through him, strip him, and tumble a corpse into obliging Thames? It had been done before. Brrr! no, he'd not sit there. He went back into the pitchy shadows of the nearest houses, stood for a time a-strain, and then sat down on the cloak he had brought for Kate. He checked his panting breath. You would expect the night to be a quiet time, anteroom to the black grave, but this one—the river alone had a hundred voices to ripple and gurgle and lap, *gug-guggle*, *slap-slap-slap*, *putchuk-putchuk*, *gug-guggle-gug*—you'd think you heard talking and quiet laughter all around you—and somewhere over in Paris Gardens a dog whoof-whoofed at intervals. The stuff of his cloak grated like sandpaper on the wall behind him. Surely that was someone standing——
He felt sweat on his forehead, and fought back recollections of old tales of fat-lipped vampires, of cobweb-fingers round the breathless throat, of vague, dripping shapes prowling the river verges before dawn. Was it twelve o'clock yet? The hour when God and day put off dominion. He loosened his dagger, brought it ready to hand, one snatch and phut!—it would be home. Cold iron, prophylactic, ghost-layer, ghost-liberator—it was joy to hold its friendly hand in yours. That rustle from the right—what? Was that a cough, there, behind? A tiny wave fell over as though hands had clapped together, then murmured an apology for frightening him. He'd be believing anything soon. Why

had Hunter not come? What was the time? Had all the city clocks lost their voices?

He heard footsteps coming from the left, from Bridewell. He got to his feet, made ready. This would be Hunter and Kate. Himself in darkness, he saw two blurred figures approaching. A dozen fears coursed through his brain. Hunter and a fellow assassin? But he nerved himself and stepped forward, baring his head. At the same time one of those approaching drew back the cloak around her head. It was Kate. Hunter, he saw, was carrying a drawn sword. They halted six or seven feet away from him, Hunter keeping hold of Kate's arm, Greene pulling out the bag of money. Then he threw it to the gaoler, who untied the neck and counted the gold and silver. He nodded, and without a word turned cautiously and moved off, keeping Greene in view all the time. Silent too, Greene and Kate went up Water Lane.

"I saw Appleby," he whispered. "He is at the top of the Lane."

A shadow himself, Appleby was waiting among shadows. "Follow me." Despite the darkness and broken surface of the streets he went confidently ahead, holding Kate's arm. A quick turn put them into Shoe Lane, and soon they were crossing Holborn Bridge and passing Greene's old lodgings in Hoyser Lane. Twice Greene thought men stood back into darkness at their coming, but there was no challenge. Another ten minutes and they were at Appleby's house in Little Britain. Here their guide gave a distinctive triple knock. "The word is *mome*," said Kate then, the first words she had spoken throughout their journey. Appleby nodded. He was listening with his ear against the door. "The word. is *mome*," he repeated, and the door opened. Greene in darkness heard the heavy bars go smoothly home, and then a woman held up the lantern she had been shrouding with her skirts. "Welcome, Mistress Kate," she said. "And you, Master Greene." It was quite ceremonious. They went into the room Greene had seen before, where they took off their outer clothes and were invited to share the food and drink

set out on the table. Kate's face was a dirty grey colour, but the wine seemed to strengthen her somewhat, and she asked Appleby whether there was any hope for her brother. "While there is life there is hope," he replied, and shrugged his shoulders as deftly as Mulliner. "If you could get me out," she then said to Greene, "you can get him out, can't you?" He too rested on a shrug. "But you must! You must! He mustn't die! Are you afraid?" "You must go to bed," Appleby's wife told her: "Let me take you upstairs." Greene expected defiance, but she went out with her quietly enough.

"Even brothers must die," Appleby told Greene soberly. "You will sleep here. On this mattress."

Why not upstairs too? he wanted to ask.

"Kate will share my daughters' room," said Appleby, as though he were a thought-reader.

He was awake for hours, thinking over the ugly fantasy of his existence.

The days went round till Thursday with no remission of anxiety for Greene. He visited Harry on Tuesday, was listened to intently and angrily, and then asked how Harry was to know he was not just telling lies. The question was so unexpected that at first he had no answer for it. So detailed a story, the names of Clarence Appleby and his wife, the passwords, the obvious truth of it all—what else could he be expected to say? "You try to trick me, Greene, and by God above me I'll see you hang at my side! Give me proof, I say! Not words, damn you! Proof!" Walking the short distance between Newgate and Little Britain he cursed and cursed again the infatuation that had made him listen to Kate in this matter of the forged bill. And now after all his pains she cared not a button for him! He spoke with Appleby, suggesting he might accompany him to Newgate and support his story, but he, rubbing his hand over his bald head, made it plain neither he nor any of his would show their faces inside Newgate for more gold than it took to get Kate out of Bridewell. This was a desperate fix of

Greene's. Kate must stay in hiding, and no one else could help. Would Appleby give him something in writing to take to Harry? He rubbed his head again. Not he. He was not concerned with the fate of individuals. Whatever he did he did for his law's sake. "He will hang the day after to-morrow whether he believes you or not. It is nothing to fret over."

Isn't it? thought Greene. Hell upon earth! Isn't it?

He saw Harry again on Wednesday. He had to wait till the parson came out from Harry's cell, shaking his head, and for the first minutes after he had entered had to listen to a string of curses and blasphemies. He could only imagine that Harry's trade had shown him a violent death was all he could expect. In Harry's place he should expect to die with fright before the dreadful morning dawned. In Harry's place! The words struck him like hammers. "What is your news?" he was asked at last. He panted, talking. "You must believe me, Harry! You must!" Hadn't he found that almost impossible sum of money? Hadn't he risked his life for Kate's? Hadn't he done all Harry had asked? "I don't know whether you have or not," Harry reminded him, grinning. Almost frantic, Greene recognised this much of the truth, that Harry was playing with him, amusing himself with his tortures, and that God alone knew what he would do before he died. "Get me into trouble," he pleaded, "and what will happen to Kate? Only I can help her."

"So you say," said Harry.

That night he would be put in the same cell as the three others who were to suffer with him. Greene would never see him alone after this. "For Christ's sake, Harry! Have pity! Say you believe me." He began to swear to the truth of what he was saying, to swear by his hopes of salvation, by his mother's soul, by everything he had ever prized, while Harry grinned and then jeered at him. "There's only till to-morrow to wait now," he told him, and slapped him on the back. "But, Harry, as you hope for mercy——" "I hope for nothing!" "For pity's sake, Harry——" Harry

pushed him roughly towards the door. "Get outside with your whining. I've told you you will know to-morrow. You'll do well to see me off, Robert."

If only there were some drug he could take! he thought, back at the Buttery. Something to kill his power of thought till to-morrow. He counted all the hours that remained— twenty vast and endless hours, twelve hundred vast and endless minutes. And once there had been days blown before the wind like thistledown, weeks gone by while he called out on sweet time to stand still. Those first months with Doll—if he betrayed her, how he had paid! Paid for everything these last weeks, not a fraction of the price stinted. Oh misery! For him the seconds slowly beating forth with the thick, dulled beating of his heart, and for Harry in Newgate the hours trampling out to the hoof-strokes of Hyperion's hurrying horses. Oh misery! The long night——

He went down to the river again. Comfort in the sight of running water. Comfort and peace.

—By God, he had it!

He turned, trembling, and made for Little Britain.

"Kate," he said, at Appleby's house, "you'll be there to-morrow?"

"I'll not! Of course I'll not. However could you ask!"

"He would like to see you again, Kate."

She shook her head. "I could never go."

"Not though he wanted you to?"

"I couldn't go as I am." She passed her hands over her swollen figure. "Another two days, Mistress Appleby says. And I should be known. I should be taken back to Bride-well."

He despised himself for the part he was playing. "When I saw him this afternoon, Kate, there was nothing on his tongue but you." In the midst of his deceit, some compunction moved him to say: "Not at the Tree itself, Kate. He wouldn't ask that. But if he could see your face at the window of one of the houses on the way, for a moment though it might be—— Could you do that for him, Kate?"

She needed little persuasion. He would that evening arrange a place for her in a house on Holborn Bridge. He himself must see Harry in the morning, but Appleby or his wife would certainly go with her. It was near and convenient, she could muffle herself in the great cloak, there was not the slightest danger of detection, though Hunter himself should be of the procession—and nothing was surer than that he would not be. Agreed on this, they consulted Mistress Appleby, who agreed with relish to do her part.

All that remained was to borrow a few shillings to pay for their places. Since the previous Friday Greene had not handled a coin, and Kate was as destitute as he. For their keep they were indebted to their host, but everyone understood that some time or other the reckoning must be paid. He now approached Appleby for a loan, if only of a few shillings, telling him what he knew already, that Kate's freedom had cost not only his own money but all he had been able to borrow; and Appleby advanced him two shillings and eightpence. With so much encouragement to action he set off for Holborn Bridge, and eventually arranged at a cost of sixpence each for two places for the duration of an hour and a half the next morning. All the gravity of his situation could not take away his pleasure at still having one and eightpence in his pocket. After stark poverty for a week you knew just how much could be done with one and eightpence. And the very fact that he was doing something eased his mind.

Kate went up to bed that night, but whether she slept he did not know. By fits and starts he slept far better than he had hoped. The carts were to leave Newgate at half-past nine in the morning, but Greene, after a few words with Kate from the bottom of the stairs, was at the prison by eight o'clock. He had an hour to wait before he was admitted to see Harry. He could only hope no one would notice how his hands were trembling. Harry seemed entirely insensitive still. He managed to whisper to him that he would see his sister at the first floor window of the second house on Holborn Bridge. "And if we don't go by way of

the Bridge?" Harry asked him. He would not listen to the myriad fears whispering in his ears. "You'll see her. No one can do anything for her except me, Harry. Think of that." Harry waved him away, and asked for drink.

The offenders were too humble to attract a big crowd. All four were thieves: an elderly man stunned with terror, Harry himself, a dark man a little younger than he and equally hardened and defiant, and a boy literally dribbling from the mouth as they got him on the cart. What onlookers there were lacked enthusiasm; they booed and flung a few lumps of dirt, but this small fry could not hold their attention for long. Greene found no difficulty in moving along a little behind and to the right of the second cart. If only Harry had been hanged yesterday! How glorious the world would be! He did not deceive himself: when his own neck was at stake he had neither time nor inclination for fine sentiments. He was waiting for one thing only—the moment when Harry would die and take his secret with him. Several times he saw Harry's eye upon him. Soon they were at the Bridge. He held his breath when Harry looked up to the window. He saw Kate bare her face momentarily, give a little wave of the hand, and Harry bent his head and made a movement that would be greeting and farewell to Kate but of no significance to other onlookers. He did not look up again or backwards once they were past. What was he thinking? Greene would have given ten years of his life to know. Now he *must* believe. Now he would leave his sister to Greene's care. Now he was safe. He stepped out a little faster as the carts rattled more. Safe!—Or soon would be.

Now they were at Broad St. Giles's, now in the open country of the Oxford Road. There was no special crowd to see them. Small fry, not worth putting yourself about for. Some children played around them for a time till a couple of soldiers were ordered to put a whip to their shoulders; Harry and the dark man could even laugh when their cart nipped a dog's paw and sent him yelping into the field. It had begun to rain. Greene walked as in a dream, hearing the tramp of the soldiers' feet, the rumble of the

wheels and thudding of horses, the exhortations of the
preachers, the high-pitched weeping of the condemned boy.
He had no cloak and felt the rain come through to his
shoulders. Plod, plod, plod, like the walk to Hartop. Plod,
plod, plod. He found that he had covered a hundred yards
while he thought over that walk of his to Hartop. He shook
his head, licked up at the rain on his moustache. Perhaps
he *was* walking to Hartop, and this procession of death
mind-begotten. Chimæras all. Nothing real since they
threw him out of Braiding. Plod, plod, plod, the rumble of
carts, the boy weeping. He knew he must fight against the
strange dizziness that was invading his head. Nothing real.
All this world around one some queer projection of oneself.
Nightmare. The steady drone of unexpectant preachers,
the soldiers' tramping, the faint threshing of rain in the
hedgerows. He knitted his forehead, wishing there be
thunder and lightning, vexed he could not create them for
this world of his. He was troubled whether this was the
Hartop Road and Doll at the end of it.

Then ahead of him he saw the gibbets. Two of them against
the sky. The boy still wept, high and thin like the child he
was, and now the oldest of the four began to cry out on
God, till they were both silenced by the kettledrums—at
first a purring, then a noise like the sudden flack of hail-
stones on thin boards, then a persistent hellish rattle that
set every nerve a-shudder. *Rurra-rum, rurra-rum, rurrara-
rurrara-rurra-rum*, till Greene's stomach was like a churn.

So small a crowd to see them go. The elderly man and
the dark one first. *Rurra-rum, rurra-rum, rurra-rrrum!* How
easy men died! Then Harry and the boy. Green, bewitched
out of fear for himself, saw Harry say something to the
boy as the nooses went over their heads. He'd never betray
him now. Never, Never, NEVER! He gripped at his
trembling stomach. *Rurra-rum, rurra-rum, rurra-rrrum!*

He looked down to the earth which seemed to be turning
under his feet. Die! Die! Die! To shriek, to shriek with
laughter! Then a cry of horror from those near him made
him lift his head. The boy was hanging, kicking feebly;

Greene saw the hangman leap for his knees; but the rope that bore Harry had snapped a yard from the beam. With the other spectators he tried to rush forward, but they were driven back by a barricade of pikes. "Let him go!" men were shouting, as the executioners were seen settling a new rope into position. "Let the man go!" They went on with their work, almost stealthily. "Let the man go!" They made another rush for the gibbet but were again forced back. They saw the wretched Harry dragged upright and the rope placed over his head a second time. A fury possessed them, they tore up stones from the ground and flung them madly at the executioners. The boy was quiet now. Greene saw the whole world heave up towards his face, and then he was staggering to the side of the road, holding his head. Let him die, God! Oh let him die! A howl of wrath told him that Harry was on the rope, and then he was knocked headlong by someone fleeing from the soldiers. They came on, striking out with the shafts of their pikes, some with the butts of their fire-arms, made vicious by the stone-throwing, themselves enraged by the hideous thing they must uphold. Greene dragged himself to his knees, stumbled once more, and was again knocked flat by one in flight. This time his head struck the ground with a thud, but as he was losing consciousness he had one piercing moment of realisation that Harry had said nothing and he need no longer fear for his life. He could never be unhappy again.

CHAPTER XXXVIII

KATE'S CHILD WAS born two days later at the Applebys' house in Little Britain, Mistress Appleby the midwife. It was not the girl he had made so many plans for, but a boy, and not a healthy boy at that. It was one more trial for him to endure. And how strongly he felt he should get the child away from these surroundings. What hope for any child born so? Hardly a moment's ease of mind now, never happiness an hour together.

At the beginning of August he went out to Croydon to find Nashe. He walked the whole distance, his shoes half off his feet, and did not find him after all. Nashe had gone to town. The serving man he spoke with noticed his exhaustion and worry and invited him into the servants' quarters for rest and food, and while there he thought it best to leave a message that Nashe should come to see him at the Buttery. He could never manage this walk again. Luckily, two of the Archbishop's men were riding to Westminster late that afternoon, so he had a lift back behind them, changing horses at their direction. The next day he spent on a useless round of visits, returning penniless and dispirited at night. He had not the heart to talk with Kate or even to look at his son, and slept downstairs, dreaming confusedly of Harry and Doll and things likely and unlikely.

One thing remained to do. He must write. He could raise money on a manuscript, though only half finished. Write what then? What quick enough to the pen?

His own story? He stood looking out from the doorway in Little Britain, not wishing to walk again till he found shoes for his feet. A *Life and Death*, perhaps, wear his heart on his sleeve to please the motley, start with the innocence of youth, show the pranker's path to husks and ignominy. With all his sins come home to roost—lay on with heavy, wet brush—for his contempt of God, contemned of men;

for his swearing and forswearing, believed of no man; for his gluttony suffering hunger; for his drunkenness thirst; for his adultery ulcerous sores. He went indoors, took Appleby's pen and paper from the cupboard, sat moodily to table. *In the City of Norwich where I was bred and born . . .* he had started to write, and for a long time he wrote no more, but sat there at his table tracing with an inkless pen time and time again the outline of those words, with capital letters disproportionately large and decorative, twists and curls embellishing them. The garden in Tombland in Norwich—when you thought back there, there were too many things to forget. Kate and the boy, Doll and Alice and Sidley and Edmund and Hacket and a world of others, and Harry. The heart had gone out of him. He brooded. Would he ever see the home in Norwich again, or Alice, or his son Kit?

He went upstairs to Kate. His golden woman looked none too golden now. "How is the boy?"

She was in a bad temper. "Have you any money yet?"

"How in the devil's name can I get money? Didn't I borrow from everyone I knew to get you out of Bridewell? Do you think my friends are made of money?"

"Perhaps you wish you never had borrowed it? Perhaps you would like me where my brother is?"

He turned from her. He must not lose his temper. "It's no good quarrelling, Kate. I tell you I am doing all I can. I am going to write a book for Danter. I can do it in a week—in less."

"Well, once I'm on my feet again——"

"I'll get money inside a week, I tell you!" Once more he checked his temper. "What will you call the boy?"

"What should we call him but Harry?"

"That's the last name in the world for him, Kate!" He was quick to find the one argument to convince her. "It is unlucky to give names—names—of people who meet Harry's end, Kate. Everyone knows that."

"Maybe. You think of something better then."

"I will. A lucky name, Kate! We'll call him Fortunatus—
the Lucky One."

"Fortunatus Greene—or Fortunatus Ball?"

"If I give him one name I'll give him two. Fortunatus
Greene!"

This put him in a better humour, and when he went back
downstairs he thought he might well write for the rest of
the day. The same words were there in front of him, and
for a time he sat staring at them. The trouble was, when
you started to think back like this, your sense of reality
weakened, you wanted to sit dreaming, like an old man
living in the past. Like Grancher Beetham, say. Make a
start then. Impulsively he dipped his pen in ink, scratched
out the dozen or so words on his paper, and began again.
*I need not make long discourse of my parents, who for their gravity
and honest life are well known and esteemed among their neighbours ;
namely, in the City of Norwich where I was bred and born.* He
checked here, reflecting that he was no further ahead
than when he began. *But as out of one self-same clod of clay there
sprout both stinking weeds and delightful flowers. . . .* He was
launched, and hours later when Appleby came into the
room he did no more than look up vacantly, grunt, and
sink his head to work again.

The very next day he broke off his *Repentance* at the point
where he discussed his conny-catching pamphlets, and
instead plunged into the rather less realistic tale of *Roberto*.
He had become a little frightened by the nakedness of his
first confession, and swung back to his old style of fictitious
embroidery. It was one thing to use your life as literary
material, quite another to offer yourself as a mark for every
pointing finger. Three days of this and the tale was nearly
done. He went off at once to William Wright's shop to show
it him, and came back with a new pair of shoes and eight
shillings on account. He had not been so lighthearted since
that time, only a month distant but yet seeming years,
when Harry was arrested and nightmare followed. He
wanted to stop people on the streets and show them he

had money. It was incredible the difference money made to you. It converted a hangdog into a free-stepping gentleman, a fugitive into a poet once more. The only person he did not want to see any of it was Appleby. Once Kate was strong enough he would need money to get her and Fortunatus away from London. Appleby must wait. He told Kate that Peele had given him the shoes and said nothing of his visit to Wright.

On the twentieth of the month, as he sat writing, he was told that a gentleman wished to see him at the door. It was Nashe, with an invitation to join him, Peele and Monox, at supper that night. "I couldn't get here before this, Robert. I've been a slave to my work. You will come?"

It would be like heaven to meet these friends again and be a man among men. Get back to living on the old terms, with talk about poetry and plays and masques and pageants, about hardships that Greene would think pleasure henceforth, and tittle-tattle of the Court, the stage, the taverns, and the council chamber.

"I shall be out until late," he told Kate. "Don't be alarmed if I am not back until to-morrow."

"Where are you going?"

"To supper with some friends. Why?"

"Nothing. I thought you might be taking me, that is all."

"But, Kate—be reasonable!"

"Be reasonable indeed! D'you think you are in greater need of an outing than I am? D'you think I'm not sick and tired of being cooped up here with nothing to do but think? When thinking is the last thing I want to do!"

They quarrelled bitterly before he set off. "You understand," she warned him, "if you'll not get the money into this house, I will!"

"Don't talk like a fool, Kate."

"Like a fool! You think I can't? Because I have borne a brat for you, you think no one else will look at me? We'll soon see, Master Robert Greene!"

"You——"

"Well? Go on! Say it!" The child began to cry, adding its dismal caterwauling to her shrill outburst. "Tell me I'm a whore, go on."

He tried to keep his dignity by a show of contempt. "I think I'll say good-bye."

"Good-bye, is it? Perhaps it is! What are you waiting for me to do? Go on the streets to keep you?"

He raised his hand to smack her face. No, he could not. He let it fall heavily to his side. And this was his Kate? This his sweet Margaret, the country maid of Fressingfield? This foul-mouthed, cursing drab. "We are given the gods we deserve," he said sadly. "I'll not stay, Kate."

Hysterically she shouted him out of the house. She was vicious—how had he ever been deceived? What caul had hung over his face when he met her? And yet so beautiful that day at the fair, so charming a companion those first months—and he must not forget that she was the mother of his son. He made excuses for her on his way to the Strand: Harry's evil influence, her heavy trials in the past month, surely everything was against her too. They must do better than tooth-and-nail it. They ought to help each other. When he got back he would seek a reconciliation, take the fault on himself. He thought such impossible things as that they would both leave London, take Fortunatus into the country, settle down, be married folk to their neighbours. But first he must get his hands on money.

He looked thankfully at his shoes. The rest of his outfit was good. He'd not have the company staring at him, thank God.

The other three were waiting for him, and he felt his cares slough from him as he took their hands and sat to table. Nashe was the provider, so evidently he flourished like the green bay tree, Will Monox was his own rather harsh-looking self, Peele was the shabbiest of them, but unconcerned.

It was Peele who told him what they jokingly called his bad news. It related to the Harveys. "There is talk, Robin lad, that Gabriel will take you to law for slandering his father and brothers. It's the Fleet for you, no mistake!"

"And as though that is not enough, he has a pamphlet on the way, to flay, cauterise, and then salt and pepper you, Robin!"

Greene snapped his fingers. "Do I look worried? If he comes into the field, I'll batter his hide for him. I'll mash him like bran, I'll bash him to pig-swill, I'll carbonado him, I'll drag him fifteen miles by his snout, I'll kick his breech from here to Scotland."

"And I'll help you," Nashe promised. "You can read it in the stars—the natural conjunction of my foot and Gabriel's tail."

"Ay," said Greene, "so you ought. You brought me into it, remember? I shall fall back on you if there are any fines, Tom."

They talked for a time of the work they had on hand, Nashe making them roar with a couple of valentines he was putting out anonymously. Peele confessed his brain for the present drier than ship's biscuit at the remainder end of a voyage.

"And you, Robin?"

He gave some account of the history of Roberto. "Roberto? You are near home now, Robert," Peele criticised.

"I shall be nearer before I have done."

"God knows, Robin, you've been baring that honest heart of yours these last three years. I don't see the world much reformed."

"I do it for money, Tom. Wouldn't you?"

"Think of my valentines! If sir reverence the Archbishop knew of them, would I march, eh? March? I should run, lads! What won't we do for money! Did I ever tell you the Nashe coat of arms?" They waited. "A motto, *Money at All Times is Money*, the device a hand extendant and grippant. What is yours, George?"

"*Semper et ubique*, and two hands, not one."

"These country lads," said Greene; "Shakespeare from Stratford, Harvey from Saffron Walden—shall I make it my life's work to kick them back to their ploughs?"

"What's that? Better not, Robin. This Shakespeare may be the coming man. I should let him be. It takes more than a course of lectures to make a dramatist. We must judge by results—that is the only fair way."

"Results? What results? Has anyone done better than the University Wits? Why, St. John's itself could furnish out the stage had we not set ourselves in pawn for the lining of our bellies! It gets worse, Tom—George—worse! Every frothblow from Mudshire thinks Jack as good as his master, and writes of kings and popes and emperors to the manner born." Greene let his tongue run for sheer delight at sharing such talk again. "It was bad enough in the old days when it was Marlowe with his bombast and bellowing, and Kyd piling the horrors of Ossa on the terrors of Pelion, hangings, ravings, rapes and throat-cuttings, scene after scene, as though the world's a madhouse. But now, when Kit Cabbage writes tragedy and it's Tom Turnip for wit—we'll starve, you and I, unless we get together and do something. You can't sweep morality out of a gutter, drain rhetoric from the rinsings of a clod's peasoup. Why don't we act?"

"Because we should make ourselves fools to no purpose, Robin, that is why. I'll not stick my head in front of an avalanche. I'll not stop a rolling boulder with my bare hand. I am not in love with crushing, and that's the truth. I'm seated with the reapers at harvest home, and I'm very comfortable, thank you."

They upbraided each other good-naturedly, for were they not the salt of the earth? Their reproaches were almost compliments. Greene knew he had not been so happy for years. He did not leave till after eleven o'clock, and then Nashe brought him out to the dark street.

"I think I ought to tell you, Robin—because of that *Repentance* you said you were at work on. Go no further with it. Try the old stuff again instead—you can do it. You know the mixture: exciting, plausible, edifying, and yet low-life; vinegar and milk, blood and red-currant jelly, Ned Brown being turned off with a sermon on his lips—

I needn't remind you. You can do it better than any man alive. But not the *Repentance*."

"And why not, Tom?"

"Because Marlowe has been spreading the story abroad that you and Kate Ball—to put it bluntly, Robin, and I speak as a friend—that you and she have played the cross-biting game. Harvey will get hold of the story—he is looking around, believe me—and that is why I'd have you be careful before you paint iniquity in your own person."

"Hm. Thank you, Tom. I always promised myself the pleasure of cutting Marlowe's neck through. I shall see you get a front seat when the time comes."

Nashe laughed, relieved he had taken it so quietly. "We'll say good night then, Robin."

"Yes. You couldn't lend me a shilling or two, could you? I know I still owe you all that other, but I'm hellishly pressed, Tom. I've got two books practically ready—the ones I was telling you about—but meantime——"

"But, Robin, when I saw you come in dressed better than any of us, like a lord in goose-turd green, I thought it was I who'd be the borrower!"

Greene laughed as at a pleasantry. "Old clothes well looked after, Tom. But can you? However little."

"There's my reckoning indoors——" He fingered coins in his hand. "If two shillings won't insult you, Robin——"

"Insult me, Tom? They will save my life. Good old Tom! I'll see you within a fortnight and square accounts and to spare. Good night."

Nashe wagged his head, entering the tavern, and Greene picked his way into Fleet Street. He was afraid to take the shorter but less even way behind St. Clement's. What an evening! Company, food and drink, and money in his pocket as he left for home. The tide of his misfortune must be on the ebb. Despondency was a black devil: you could always conjure him away if you had the proper golden spell. If it were daylight he would be stepping like a roe.

His attention was attracted by a dark shape crouched on a doorstep ahead to the right. He stopped dead, swinging

his cloak loosely forward and drawing his dagger. He looked
behind him but saw and heard no one. Swiftly he stepped
into the darkest shadow he could find, and stood waiting.
Nothing happened, and after a while he decided to go
forward. It might be a drunkard, a corpse, some poor
wreckage of the night. Why not look and find out? He
thought: Why not rob him?

He stopped dead again. Why not? Maybe fortune ready
in a silk-tied purse. Words of his own came to his ears, that
if he had not feared the judges of Her Majesty's bench more
than he dreaded the judgments of God, long since he
would have been a diver for shells on other men's sand-
bars. Keeping his dagger bared, he went stealthily to the
doorway. Harry should be proud of his pupil away in his
thieves' paradise. Why, he thought, is it a woman? Time
for withdrawal. Yet—was she alive or dead? He tried to
rouse her by shaking, uncertain of her shoulder in the
huddle. She moaned and stirred, shook the cloak back from
her head, he heard a frightened gasp as she caught her
breath at sight of his weapon. But not a woman who called
on the watch. "No, no," he said quietly, "I'll not hurt you.
Who are you?"

She came docilely into the roadway with him, a woman
used to obeying men. Greene looked into her face. It was
heavily bruised under the eyes, her lips were swollen and
cut. Dull, stupid, animal face; she herself ugly, shapeless,
the old instrument of lust. "You've been beaten?" he
whispered.

His nails drove into the palms of his hands with rage.
He looked on truth and found it horrible. White lily paps,
nipples of rose, the sweet amorous songs of thoughtless
lovers—Christ! Christ! Christ! That men could be so foul!
And in a second while he stood with her, down the corridors
of memory marched all the girls he had taken casually,
the women he had used and paid for using, those on whose
faces he had set his heel, thrusting them down till all was
mildew where once there had been freshness, till they too
were ugly and shapeless and old before their time, turned

out from the stews where their death's-heads frightened off custom, their faces bruised as the breasts of this world's sad virginity.

"Can I help you?" he asked. "I should like to help you."

She had nothing to say to him. If he wanted her, he must have her. It was only when he began questioning her about her troubles that she slowly realised he was kind, not just another brute. Listening, Greene could not feel proud of his sex. What would she do now? She rubbed her hands. There was nothing she could do. She dare not go back. She must manage about the streets as long as she could, and then——

He remembered when a boy at Norwich, walking through a coppice and finding a gull that had thrust itself into the hollow bole of a tree to die. To die without ceremony. To die unnoticed.

He reached for the two shillings Nashe had given him. She should have them. "I don't know," he said irresolutely; "We don't realise, that must be it. It is all a dreadful tangle. Will you take this?" He would not listen to her thanks. It was Edmund's voice he could hear, not hers. A new religion of compassion, needed more than faiths and judgments. In what unlikely ways words came to fruition.

He was tempted to be quixotic and empty his pockets, but thought of Kate and Fortunatus. They had first claim. "Good night then," he said to her. "God look after you!"

He had plenty to think of the rest of his way to Little Britain. Had he acted like a fool? Or should he have given more? No doubt she would make bad use of it. He sighed. Who was he to moralise?

The door was locked in the Buttery and a quiet knocking brought no one to open it. He grew worried. Uproar would not serve his turn. If they didn't answer—— He rapped again. He had to admit it was no hour to be returning. On the whole then—— He remembered the alley between the baker's and the house with the flag further up the road. He

would try it. The wall of the bakery would guard him from chills. So there he went, settled himself as comfortably as the cobbles allowed, and was soon fast asleep.

It was a new experience, this sleeping out, and he did not care to think it might become his habit. When he arrived at Appleby's house first thing in the morning it was to hear that Kate had left not long after him the day before, taking the child with her. She had not returned. Appleby first made light of his fears, telling him a woman as fly as Kate Ball would know plenty of places for shelter, and then suggested it was time for him to settle what he owed for board, lodging, and the expenses of Kate's confinement. To this Greene replied that he had no money, and it ended that he got marching orders. He now told Appleby he would see him to the devil before he paid him one penny, and walked away with the threat pursuing him that he would end up in gaol himself if he tried any of those tricks.

He had rather less than eight shillings, a couple of unfinished manuscripts, and the clothes he stood up in. The first thing was to find cheap lodgings and finish Roberto's history; the second to look for Kate. The first he knew himself capable of without trouble; the second might prove impossible. Search for a runaway woman in London! If it were not for Fortunatus he would say Go and good riddance. This was the revenge of fortune surely, when you thought how he had left Doll and Kit in his turn, and they not looking for him. Fortuna minor in the evening sky, favour was what he needed.

He found a lodging near the Wardrop, and within an hour was writing. The greater necessity first. He was annoyed that two or three times a griping in his stomach drove him from his work. He had felt clutchings there all the morning and afternoon. He wondered what could have upset him, and put it down to the rhenish and pickled herrings he had eaten so greedily last night. Later in the day he became faint, the room closed around him, and he

had to get outside for fresh air. He had not walked a hundred yards when he was driven into a back alley and kept there a long time. He must get home and to bed. Cold or hot—which was he? He did not know. Both, surely. He was actually undressing when he discovered that his purse was missing. Ill though he was, he must drag on his clothes once more, go hunting frantically through the passage and all down the street to the alley way. If it were gone—but it couldn't be gone! He found nothing there, and had not time to return before the griping came again to double him up. Two passers-by lifted him and at his direction carried him to his lodging. God! This pain was dreadful. Was he poisoned? He was on his hands and knees, searching everywhere for his purse, then was violently sick over the foot of his bed, and groaning so loudly that his landlord burst in without knocking. Should he fetch a surgeon? Anything, anything! He would need money first though. Could he hand Master Greene his purse? Lost it? Lost it, eh! Had he any other goods or valuables? The landlord went outside to speak with his wife, his intention clear. They would turn him out. Great God, they'd turn him out!

The chimes were striking eight o'clock when he stood with his thin bundle of manuscript outside that too-brief lodging. To stand seemed all he could hope for. Where could he go? Peele, Monox, Appleby, his former lodgings, he thought of them all, leaning against a water conduit. No hope in them. The Isams? He owed them too much money—how much he did not know exactly. They would never take him in, his score unsettled. But something he must do. Maybe his best chance lay there. He set off painfully. If he failed there, he could go no further. He must look for a doorway or some sheltered alley like that in the Buttery.

It was well over half-a-mile to Dowgate, and many times he thought he would not complete the journey. But the devil driving is a compelling fellow, and he kept to his task. The nearer he got to the Isams' the more certain he felt that they would have nothing to do with him. Yet he kept on. He would try.

This was the street at last. He knocked at the door, hung like a rag to the post. Did he speak? Appeal? He did not know, but they were helping him inside. He made senseless explanations, knew they were undressing him, washing his filthy body, putting something into his mouth, lowering him to a bed on the floor, after the last spasm wiping his face over. It was dark there in the familiar old room, and it comforted him to know that all around him were things he had known so long. He could sleep here. No strength to think further than that. Sleep took him.

He felt very weak and ashamed in the morning, dreading the moment when he must meet his host's eye. He had no weapon against kindness. It made him feel pure scoundrel. He had not spared the Isams a thought except when he wanted to make use of them, and now they of all the world took him in and tended him. They could not think he would do other than desert them again once he was well enough. Shame, deep shame, so to treat worthy, kindly folk.

Not long after daylight Mistress Isam brought him a bowl of gruel, but he could not keep this down more than a few minutes. Patiently she cleaned him again, chiding him when he cried to realise his weakness. Afterwards he lay there listening to noises from the rest of the house where she and her husband were about their work. It was laugh he did then, weakly to himself. This was a fine state of affairs! Soon he would be without a guts to call his own. He'd have thrown it all away. Nashe and his pickled herrings! He wondered whether any of the others were ill too. Well, there was nothing for it but wait till he rid himself of the poison. Some strong purgative? At the thought of it he felt an incredible emptiness throughout his bowels. He could never stand it. "I don't know why you are so kind to me, Mistress Isam," he told her when next she came to see him. "I did not treat you and your husband very well."

That afternoon they fetched a surgeon to him, who gave him an ill-smelling concoction that in an hour almost tore his stomach walls asunder. The surgeon came again hurriedly, but did him more harm than good, and for the

first time Greene feared he would not come easily off with his life. This threw him into the greatest agony of mind. He must not die. He had too much to do. He must find Kate, he must make provision for Fortunatus, there were all the folk at Norwich to make his peace with, there was his writing. And the world with all its hardships was sweet. He'd not leave it. He would fight—if he had strength to fight. But this emptiness, this falling away of his middle—that was the frightening thing. He was awake almost the whole of the second night in Dowgate.

The next day, the twenty-fourth, he felt rather better. He was at once more cheerful and making plans for what he'd be doing in a couple of days' time. Before all things he swore to himself he would settle the Isams' debt. Yet he increased it slightly by sending Mistress Isam out for ink, and afterwards when she had somewhat propped him up he added a page and a half to his *Roberto*.

The next day he was not so well again, and instantly pessimistic. Did they think he was going to die? Of course they did not. Did the doctor say he would live? There was no question of it. He stirred at that. "Sometimes, Mistress Isam, I am afraid I shall not get over this." Pah, he must not talk so foolishly. "If you knew, Mistress Isam, how I feel—here." But she sat and talked with him for more than an hour till he grew quite cheerful. When she left him he was again preparing to write, and she was horrified at her return towards the end of the afternoon to find him sitting at the table, some of the bedclothes around his shoulders writing for dear life. He refused to go back to bed. Writing, he said, was all that was left to him. He was putting himself on paper for posterity to judge him, reporting himself unfavourably too, revealing himself a true devil's gobbet, the parbreak of hell, and taking a sombre pleasure in the fierceness of his self-denunciations. He was thinking as he wrote how in his time he had made the price of many a meal out of repentance, until now he hardly knew how much of it was true, how much pap for fools. It gave a man a habit of protestation, almost despite himself, this attempt to

square the Almighty and the landlord by the same show of grace. Nor could he help himself. Once more his writing had taken possession of him. That its path should be dark who could wonder? Yet there was healing for the spirit with it. His work was greater than his life. Like Horace, he would not wholly die. Some part of him should escape Libitina. Like Horace too, not uncrowned with the Delphic laurel. Too much he had been driven by need of money, some of his work had fallen below the level he would by choice have set himself, for a man must come to terms with the world or starve, and only fools who had never gone hungry talked of starving. Starve! With the word his mind swung to the poor woman of Fleet Street—where was she now, God help her? Surely not nearer decision than he.

His work would be himself to posterity when his body was not even a dust puff and his soul ragged on the skirts of infinity. He thought back to the pure idyllic fancy of his burgeoning, the sky-clear prose set with bright lyrics as the heavens with stars, romances like flower chalices bubbled with raindrops; the smoother grace and fairer pattern of the novels of his maturity, rich yet chaste, brimming with beauties descriptive and moral, every phrase a cadence, soft as lovers' flutes or harsh as drums of conquest. Why, he could thread titles as a girl does beads. And so far nothing of the plays. Let those who decried *Alphonsus* do so, and the *Orlando*—they were welcome to their fault-finding—but with his countryside comedy he had shown the world something new, fresh as the country maid of Fressingfield, potent as the necromancer. And he could leave to fair-judging posterity whether his *James the Fourth* was or was not the best history of the age. Greene by name and green by nature, a fine tree of literature. As for the pamphlets and the repentance books—had he not brought real life into the courts of literature? He would not be forgotten.

He must stop now. He must get back to bed. He had been working too hard. He had been a fool to sit there fighting against the conqueror. Bed then.

He was drowsing when the Isams entered the room. He did not trouble to open his eyes. "Poor lad," said Isam, and he, Greene, a man with a red beard these ten years and more; "You think he'll make an end?" There was no reply, but Greene seemed more alone than ever in his life before.

Strangely he was not frightened. For one thing he could not really believe he would die. He was weak, true. He could not eat. A strange hollowness had taken the place of his belly and the small of his back. He thought he was laughing loudly, but his face was not moving nor could anyone else hear him. It was impossible not to laugh at the notion that you were now in two parts, divided at the waist by a wide band of nothingness. He must put it down in his next play. He could hear the audience laughing with him, here at the Bull.

It was the last day of the month. Puzzling. The days in between must be like the nothingness dividing him. Where were the days? Give me back my lost days! He and Varro a pair, crying for the spoils of annihilation.

They told him he was very ill indeed. He had not been in his right mind, they told him, and had been uttering strange things they had no wish to repeat. With that something of the veil was lifted: those unspeakable frights of his— Harry, the rope breaking, such nightmares. Though all men should stay frightened to the end of time, there would never again be fright like his.

No one had called to see him? Yes, Kate Ball had called there, asking if he had any money. She had gone when she saw how ill he was. Fortunatus had not been with her. He tried to struggle from his bed—he must find Fortunatus. He wanted to strike at Isam but had no strength. And Mistress Appleby had called to recover her debt. She too had looked on him and gone away.

Nashe had not called? Not Nashe? Not spider-brain Tom? No one but the two who sought money? They told him not a soul. He might be dead for all the world knew of him.

Dead. What a strange word it was! Dead! If a man had time he could write a book to shake the world around that one dead word. Dead! Gone into nothingness, not a handshake again, not a laugh from friendly men, not a thought to fill the empty brain. If a man had but time enough to write!

When he opened his eyes next he could see his beard stretching a furlong in front of him. He had been a long way down. Down where, he did not know; but down so far, so long, it was a question whether it was worth coming back again. Toiling up from those black lethe-waters below.

The Isams, standing by his bedside, heard him say the queerest things. He lived in countries unknown to them, cried names unknown: Sidley, Edmund, Doll. Once he burst out very clearly with "O Lord, forgive me my manifold offences. O Lord, have mercy upon me. O Lord, forgive me my secret sins, and in thy mercy, Lord, pardon them." Some mother-taught lessons they judged these phrases must be.

Mistress Isam was with him alone when he opened his eyes and said very clearly: "When I am dead, crown me with a garland of bays, Mistress Isam."

Last piece of vanity for Greene.

On the morning of September the third they found him dead in bed. He had been writing. They picked up the scrap of paper and kept it till the late morning, when two gentlemen arrived and asked for Robert Greene. One of them, a Master Gabriel Harvey, read the writing in silence and then remarked that the dead man had saved himself a deal of trouble. He hurried from the house, but Master Nashe went into the room where Greene was lying.

"I should like it had his life been more virtuous," said Isam, shaking his head.

Said Nashe: "He was a true poet. Maybe that will go to his account. Besides, Master Isam—debt and deadly sin, who is not subject to? I am a poor pot to call a kettle black. The paper, you ask? I'll read it to you."

He read:

Sweet Wife,

As ever there was any good will or friendship between you and me, see this bearer, my host, satisfied of his debt. I owe him ten pounds, and but for him I had perished in the streets. Forget and forgive my wrongs done unto you, and Almighty God have mercy on my soul. Farewell till we meet in heaven, for on earth you shall never see me more.

This second of September.

1592.

Written by your dying husband,

Robert Greene.

He handed the letter to Isam. "You had better present this soon. I never saw his wife." He thought for a moment. "It might have been better had he never seen her, too." He looked at the dead man, felt cold, and with a muttered excuse went out into the sunshine.

THE END